Herbert Kastle was born a
been an English teacher, an
he now devotes his time to
many successful novels in
Country, *Hit Squad*, *Dirty*
War.

HERBERT KASTLE

The Movie Maker

GRAFTON BOOKS
A Division of the Collins Publishing Group

LONDON GLASGOW
TORONTO SYDNEY AUCKLAND

Grafton Books
A Division of the Collins Publishing Group
8 Grafton Street, London W1X 3LA

Published by Grafton Books 1970
Reprinted 1971 (twice), 1972, 1973, 1976, 1979,
1983, 1986

First published in Great Britain by
W. H. Allen & Co Ltd 1969

Copyright © Herbert Kastle 1968

ISBN 0-583-11692-2

Printed and bound in Great Britain by
Collins, Glasgow

Set in Linotype Times

I wish I hadn't broke that dish
  I wish I was a movie star
I wish a lot of things, I wish
  That life was like the movies are.

Sir Alan Patrick Herbert

It May Be Life,
But Ain't It Slow?

OF the two men in the back seat of the Maserati
Quatro Porte, one was very large and strikingly handsome.
The other was older and bald and fat, expensively dressed
and so relaxed as to suggest boredom. He was watched with
awe by the boy in blue cap and ill-fitting blue jacket who
jockeyed the car through some of the worst traffic in all the
world. *Signore* Markal was someone to watch. A cold man. A
deep man. And so *rich*. Even for an *Americano*.

'I'd like to try for Lollobrigida,' the handsome man said,
worried by Emperor Nat's attitude.

Nat Markal made a noncommittal sound.

'Why not?' the handsome man asked, arguing with himself. 'What's she done lately? If we open the budget a little
why shouldn't she accept? So *Trials of Romulus* isn't art.
It's money.'

'You can try her,' Markal said.

'You think she'll laugh? She's not young enough to laugh.'
He waited for Markal to speak. Markal didn't speak. 'What
the hell, I prefer Monterri anyway. I can sign her tomorrow.
Should I?'

Markal nodded. The chauffeur's eyes watched in the rear-
view mirror, then snapped to the road as a Fiat 500 squirted
across the intersection from the left. The chauffeur slammed
his horn and raised explosive fingers in the *cornuto*, the sign of
the cuckold. Markal looked at him. The chauffeur smiled into
the mirror. *'Perdone, eccellenza.'*

'What about sets?' the handsome man asked. 'Should we
build a Temple of the Virgins or keep it all in that mountain
shrine? Cinecittà isn't the bargain basement it once was. If
we want a little class—'

'You're in charge, Wallace.'

'I might have to go over budget.'

'You won't.'

'But if I *have* to?'

'Then you'll have to,' Markal said wearily. They were on
their way to Leonardo da Vinci International Airport. He
was sick of Wallace, sick of Rome, sick of movies.

7

No, not sick of *movies*! What else was there?

He sighed and took out a cigar; then didn't want it. A bad day. A lousy, gray-faced day.

Or was it the day?

Nat Markal hadn't doubted himself since he was nineteen years old. Now he was the single biggest entrepreneur in motion pictures. And yet, lately, he had been filled with vague doubt, vague disquiet, not so vague boredom.

'DeFracora wants to revise half the script. I think it's all right the way it is. Will you make the decision, Nat?'

'I can't. I haven't read it.'

Wallace Severin was shocked. 'Listen, Nat, if you don't mind my saying so, you haven't been giving me the correct time of day lately. Not even a hint. This is our last chance to talk before—'

Markal turned on him, eyes and voice cold. 'I said you were in charge. If you don't *want* to be in charge, just tell me.'

Severin laughed and tried to think of a graceful retreat, and was saved when Markal's attention was diverted. The chauffeur swerved and screamed curses. Italian obscenities spewed back from a Vespa. Behind them a horn blasted and a hoarse voice shouted, '*Ecco!*' Let's go!

'This city,' Markal muttered. 'Four days seem like four years. The Eternal City. Every day an eternity.'

Wallace chuckled. 'That's very good, Nat.'

The van behind them passed and the driver leaned out and shouted at the chauffeur, who was listening to Markal.

'This loud-mouth city,' Markal said with deep disgust. 'And to think they make fun of Hollywood.'

The chauffeur grew angry. Who could say such things about *Roma*? He drove even more violently.

Markal fixed him with his eyes in the mirror. The chauffeur held to his anger a moment, then slowed and said placatingly, 'Soon, International.'

Markal looked out the window. 'This pizza-palace city.'

The chauffeur decided to hell with the *nobile* and to hell with the job. He floored the gas pedal and derived considerable satisfaction from *Signore* Severin's grabbing the seat. But Markal continued to look out the window, leaning casually into the corner to brace himself. *Freddo*, the chauffeur thought. A cold one.

At the airport, Severin shook his chief's hand and said,

'Regards to Adele and Elaine. Lovely girl, Elaine. Talented,' Then hoped it didn't sound too much like kissing ass.

Markal stepped to the front of the car and nodded in at the driver. 'Very good, very good,' he said, smiling, and walked to the plane, amused at the man's surprised, almost disappointed look. Never do the expected; that's how you stayed on top.

Except that staying on top seemed senseless today. On top of what? A ton of celluloid exactly like the tons that had been piling up since movies began?

Of course, there *were* a few movies that stood away from the pile. Mostly the great silents. Like D. W. Griffith's *Birth of a Nation*.

So American, even in its mistakes ... and Nat Markal felt *very* American as he boarded the plane and was ushered to his seat by the stewardess.

Back home to Adele and Lainie and Avalon Pictures. Good to get home. Hell yes, good to get back to a country that wasn't rotten with age; that knew how to do things *successfully!*

But Adele and Lainie and Avalon Pictures? Back to the same day-in-day-out work and talk and golf? Back to the same day-in-day-out life?

He shook himself, looked around, tried to identify the other passengers by nationality. Americans, Italians, English, Germans, maybe French that couple behind him. He wondered if foreigners could *really* prefer their countries to America.

God, the whole of Europe stank!

The plane was taking off. He looked across the empty window seat at the blur of countryside. Voices spoke behind him. French. A word that sounded like *'Amaireecan'*. And laughter.

He didn't understand French, but it was fashionable to make fun of America. Even Americans did it.

There had been times he had done it himself. He remembered, and it upset him. Times he had heard criticism, hatred, mockery of America's ways, and had agreed because some of those ways were irritating, hateful, foolish ...

Something happened. He no longer heard the voices or saw outside the window. He sat very still and thought surged and changed and jelled. He began to understand his feelings of the past few hours; of the past four days; perhaps of the

9

past months or even year. He began to understand that he was moving toward a means of ending the boredom, the sameness of his life.

The plane climbed deep into the sky, and still he sat and stared at nothing. His thoughts came to the surface and there he read them and formed an opinion, an idea – one of Emperor Nat Markal's 'hunches,' famous in the industry.

He would produce a movie. A movie so important it would make all the world know what America was, and America know itself! Not a blare of trumpets and Fourth of July crap. Nothing so simple. But a true thing, a complex thing, a thing so enormous . . .

He called the stewardess and asked for paper, lots of it, and began to work. He spread sheet after sheet on the empty window seat (he always reserved two, to sit alone) and referred to them and covered other sheets with his heavy scrawl. Later, he boiled it all down to one tightly written sheet. He would have done the same with *War and Peace,* and felt he had something much bigger than that.

Book One

TUESDAY SEPTEMBER 14
TO WEDNESDAY SEPTEMBER 15

CHARLEY HALPERT

SUNSHINE lay over everything, including Charles Zacharias Halpert, a tall man made slightly less tall by a middle-aged thickening of chest and shoulders. The stomach, despite situps and sidebends and squats, was thickening too, because fear and indecision led to eating and nine months of the cold sweats preceded this day of days.

He walked from the parking lot and glanced left at two palm trees, but the studio was directly ahead and this was the movies, the end of fear and indecision, the Big Chance. Palm trees couldn't compete. The startlingly beautiful blonde driving the yellow Triumph couldn't compete. Not today. Tomorrow maybe but not today.

He crossed the street, enjoying the warmth, the brilliance of Hollywood's September sun. Back home the leaves were turning toward fiesta-colored death. Here, if there was any turning, it was toward a shorter summer day.

Two men and a woman went through the studio gate without glancing at the guard, talking vociferously; birds of bright plumage who would cause heads to turn and eyebrows to rise on Madison or Fifth, who would bring a whispered, 'Now *there's* a group for your collection of strange characters,' from Collin and a thin, contemptuous smile from Celia.

To hell with Manhattan snobbery! To hell with the *New Yorker* and *Esquire* and *Time* movie reviews and sly literary laughter. He had laughed himself, been contemptuous himself, been upset and repelled himself, but no more. *Naïve!* Enthusiasm! Action! Year-round sunshine and suntans and swimming and flat bellies and money and more he would learn about and was certain he would love. He loved it already. Especially the money ... and go and knock that, penniless intellectuals of the cold, cold East.

Bobby would grow taller, tanner, stronger here. Celia would

13

bring herself and the child as soon as he sent her enough money and she could settle the major bills and sell the house. She might still be a little upset at his abrupt departure ...

But this wasn't the time to think of Celia. He would call her tonight.

He approached the studio's western gate. To his right, a two-story wall of brownstone office buildings ran three long streets east, then gave way to high wire fencing which ran another street before turning north. The wire allowed passersby to see storage houses, workshops and the backs of on-the-lot buildings. Wire changed to brick and brick to blank walls of enormous stages, and this variety of barriers continued all around Avalon Pictures, a jealously guarded film-story factory. Outsiders were kept out.

He was an insider now (at least that's what Carl Baiglen's letter had stated), but he didn't really believe they would let him in. His fear of being turned away as just another tourist became certainty, and he prepared assured statements, arguments and finally abject pleas to be allowed to speak to Baiglen's secretary. But she would have forgotten his name and Baiglen would be unavailable and the deal would have fallen through. (Benton & Bowles and the 'sure' position as senior copywriter and the rejected knowledge that he couldn't write copy anymore, couldn't think ads anymore, couldn't put off the need to be a writer of stories anymore, couldn't do time in offices the million hours of his life. He'd tipped them off somehow and on the day of the final interview the secretary had forgotten his name and the creative director had been 'in conference' and the personnel director had taken him to lunch and without saying so had let him know the deal had fallen through.)

The cold sweats hit him. He had to get inside! This was the answer. This was the way to be a writer and live the good life. The only way for a novelist whose three books hadn't earned their meager advances.

The guard sat in a gray wooden booth to the left of open iron gates. He was heavy, big-handed, ruddy-faced and wore a blue uniform. A typical cop, and what could you expect but trouble from a cop? Inside the gate an old man, also in uniform, waved a red flag at things unseen.

'Charles Halpert to see Mr. Baiglen.' His voice, a croak, embarrassed him.

14

The guard checked a clipboard of sheets, flipped the top sheet back, spoke with a mild Southwestern burr. 'This here for casting, Mr. Halpert?'

It took a second to sink in, and suddenly he liked this man who obviously wasn't a cop. 'No, I'm a writer. I start working today.'

The guard flipped a second sheet and stabbed a name with his pencil. 'Ten-thirty it says, Mr. Halpert.'

Relief came, and was followed by chagrin. He had wanted to walk around the studio. Now he would have to kill an hour. He nodded and began to turn away. The guard said, 'Gives you time to go to Security for your pass, your parking permit, maybe look around.'

He listened to directions and smiled his thanks and walked through the gates. He came toward the old man with the red flag, and saw what the flag was for. A warning to cars and people not to infringe their sight and sound, their modern presence, on a re-creation of the past. Off to the left was a dirt street and a Western town. Perhaps fifty people and horses were working there. Cameras were moving. Two men with guns were running into a saloon.

A movie. Or one of the eight television shows filmed at Avalon.

He passed a hangarlike stage and saw the section of airplane fuselage sliced open and mounted on springs and wooden blocks. Workmen were shaking that fuselage and actors were inside it. Cameras weren't manned, so it was a rehearsal.

Wasn't that Frank Sinatra at the waistgun?

My God! And what difference did it make that Halpert, Charles Z., 12178980, had piloted a B-17 over Germany when he was nineteen? It was so unreal compared to this.

He stood watching until he felt foolish. He walked on, reaching for the cool professional approach.

A beautiful Eurasian girl in tight, flowered Mandarin dress with a slit up the side hurried around a corner toward him. He nodded. She smiled and passed him. He wondered what, if anything, she was wearing under that costume, but didn't turn to look at the movement of her buttocks. A lovely sight, he was sure, and one he dearly wanted to see ... but a professional wouldn't turn and stare, would he?

He paused to light a cigarette, remembering stories of starlets and wild parties. Publicity, probably or jealous gossip. He was certain no *In* person believed them.

15

But then again, there'd been *Confidential* and the notorious lack of libel suits.

The normal sex-play of a community put under an abnormal spotlight because of its eminence. Besides, that was the *old* Hollywood.

He threw the cigarette away after three puffs. He was going off cigarettes soon. More exercise and organic foods and a healthy life in the sun. That guard had mistaken him for an actor.

NAT MARKAL

Nat lighted one of his thin Havana cigars, a gift from Umberto Degardez, the Mexican producer who was on speaking terms with Castro. The buzzer sounded and he picked up his phone. 'Miss Yee is here,' Bertha said. Nat felt excitement, and told himself he felt nothing. The Eurasian was early. 'Have her wait,' he said.

He puffed, looked at the cigar, sighed and jabbed it out in a deep blue bowl made of shards found in a Syrian tell; shards perhaps two thousand years old. A gift from Sir John Dembry, who handled distribution for Avalon throughout the Commonwealth. He had to find out if there were any Romeo & Juliettas hidden away in the humidor rooms of the better New York tobacconists. There was little pleasure in smoking since R&J's and Uppmans had disappeared.

He sat behind his desk, which was actually a table; perhaps the most expensive table in Los Angeles. It was marble with curved, clawed legs. The purchase had been arranged by De-Fracora, who directed Markal's breastaculars at Cinecittà – Roman Empire historicals starring a muscle man and a big-breasted woman. Three a year. Gross budget well under a million dollars. Gross take two to three million. Which, along with the 'art' imports that had first stunned Hollywood with their solid net and then brought imitators in every distributing corporation, had financed Markal's entry into Avalon thirteen years ago as an independent producer. This in turn had led to his gaining enough shares of stock to dominate, along with Dave Sankin, the entire Avalon operation. They'd had trouble with Odel Dort's widow, Olive, but fifty-two percent was fifty-two percent and she could scream all she

16

wanted to about cheapening her dear departed's memory with gauche ventures.

Olive thought throwing French around made her something special. Instead, she should have been thanking him in English. Her dividends hadn't been this high since TV arrived. And what the hell had Odel done besides Westerns and musicals? What had any of them done since the great silents? Wasn't *that* the reason so much action was leaving for Italy's Cinecittà and other European studios? They blamed TV and steep production costs, but it was lack of fire and meaning and excitement, lack of inspired production.

He touched his breast pocket. He had the answer there, on one folded sheet of paper.

He thought of Isa Yee, and signed some letters. He picked up the top volume of a stack of eight novels. Each had a green comment slip attached to the dust jacket. The comments were by independent producers, producer-directors, directors and stars who wanted to buy or option the properties. Until recently Markal had read each and every novel under consideration by Avalon. At one time he had worked at this desk, or his Manhattan desk, or his Rome desk fourteen to sixteen hours a day. Adele would call from their home, where ever it was, and ask if he could be expected for dinner and he would say no, too much work. She always understood, and approved. They wanted the same thing: the biggest slice of the pie. Make them all – the entire damned upper crust of the world – know who Mr. and Mrs. Nat Markal were.

So DeFracora, who was a count and wrote poetry, directed his B-pictures, shopped for him and wanted to pimp for him too, except that he quickly learned Nat Markal never debased himself. Absolutely *never*.

He put down the novel, fingered the next one, pushed the stack to the front of the desk for Bertha to remove. He would allow his men their own decisions now, as Wallace Severin had learned. They knew his standards. Let Fellini and Bergman make the art films. They were good at it. Avalon would make *money*, because Nat Markal was good at it. And he could always *buy* Fellini and Bergman, in the can, in completed features . . . if the stuff would pull at the box office.

Box office. He'd had his hits. *Net* hits. A dozen heavy money earners a year for almost ten years. No one, absolutely no one could match that today. But it was no longer enough . . .

This was one decision that couldn't be made in the usual

Markal manner – snap of fingers, just like that. This was one decision Dave Sankin would have to be gentled, perhaps tricked, into accepting; one decision Dave would have to approve in advance because it was certain to run head-on into Olive Dort and her little cadre of patient watchers ... men like Soloway and Besser; ambitious men stalking Nat Markal and each other for that coveted presidency of Avalon.

The girl was waiting. He had nothing else to do. But he stood up and walked to the center of the vast office. He hadn't built it this big, and had mocked it to associates on first moving in, yet he secretly liked it. Especially after he had thrown out Odel's ton of wood and leather. Now it was truly impressive. An office thirty by thirty feet, paneled in age-darkened mahogany, with a thin marble table four hundred years old; with three high-backed antique chairs and a clean-lined antique bench. And a center circle of cracked and faded tile flooring, blue and green, as old as the ruins of Pompeii, which should rightfully have been in a museum but which DeFracora had given him last April for his fiftieth birthday. A tremendous gift; one which demanded a reward. DeFracora would direct Gordon Hewlett in *Hadrian's Litter*, a widescreen historical, three to five million budget.

He looked around. He hadn't given much thought to his office lately. Now he wondered if it would impress Isa Yee.

He went to the phone and asked Bertha to send her in.

The Eurasian sat in the high-backed Italian chair to the right of the desk. Looking at her, he knew what he'd been thinking of when he wrote on his sheet of paper, 'One member of Jones slave staff, beautiful mulatto girl, sleeps with master, gets Negro blood into family . . .' They would have to make her part Arab, or whatever the writers could pull out of research. They would darken her skin for the slave sequences. then lighten it through the generations until the present, when it could be its natural color.

'They have chairs something like this in Lawry's Prime Rib,' the girl said, and smiled nervously.

He nodded. It wouldn't mean anything to her that she sat on antiquity. A *nineteen-year-old ass pressed to a five-hundred-year-old chair. Warm, pliant flesh pressed to cool, dead wood. His lips pressed to warm, pliant flesh. Kneeling, worshiping her flesh with his lips . . .*

He cleared his throat, fighting to clear his mind of the unbidden images, the humiliating images. He leaned back,

18

pressing his hands flat together, the pose *Time* had run on its cover, the attitude in which he had made the most important decisions of his career. He could see she recognized it. He could see how nervous and excited she was.

'You have a beautiful office, Mr. Markal.'

He nodded. 'I asked you to drop by because I've heard good things about you.'

Her lovely ivory face was suddenly attentive. Small features and pale lips and black hair falling straight to her shoulders. Long black eyes, beautifully shaped. She sat with legs crossed, exposed to midthigh by her slit skirt. Her breasts rose and fell quickly. They weren't large, but they jutted sharply against the thin flowered material of her Mandarin dress. She was not wearing a brassiere. He had told her agent she was to wear the costume she wore for her part in *Waikiki Nights*, the rock'n'roll musical now in production. '*Just* the costume, Jerry. You know I don't ask women to undress for me and I've got to have some way of judging the girl's physical properties if I'm to consider her for a feature role, especially anything like Pony Girl.' Jerry had been surprised. Nat had known it by the pause, the hurried, 'Of course ... I understand.' He had grown angry and wanted to tell the agent to forget the whole thing. But Jerry had said, 'She's really the most beautiful client I have. Nat, and that includes Sybil and Martha and even our magnificent Mona. And talented ... sings, dances, but her first love is straight drama. Perhaps most important she's ambitious.' Here he had cleared his throat. 'She's your greatest fan, Nat. Honestly. Real case of hero worship. Would do anything for you.' A quick goodbye before Nat could decide whether that deserved a remonstrance, a chilling laugh, or what.

He said, 'Would you mind walking across the room?'

She rose smoothly, turned and walked toward the bench. What she lacked in breast she more than made up in rear. The girl was very full in the buttocks. If she ever began gaining weight she would have a problem. But at the present, only nineteen and slim as a reed, it was her most exciting feature.

She reached the bench and turned, hand on hip, right foot forward in model fashion.

'Walk back to me, dear.' That 'dear' was inadvertent. Unlike most people in the business, he used terms of endearment only with members of his family. Still, what difference did it make? He would examine her as he had examined hundreds

19

of actors and actresses over the years. He would allow his instincts to determine whether or not she could make money for Avalon, whether or not she could fit into his masterwork. And that was all.

What was he, some two-bit lecher in the business to make the cheap little broads and a lousy forty, fifty grand a year? He was Nat Markal, worth in the neighborhood of fifty million dollars, and that didn't include what he controlled through Avalon. He was Emperor Nat, the biggest name since Louis B. Mayer, and he would close out his career bigger and better than Mayer, retiring from his job instead of being forced out; retiring undefeated with the greatest single credit of all time: *The Eternal Joneses.*

Isa Yee walked back toward him, doing something with her shoulders so her breasts bounced tautly. He had seen the trick before. He had seen every trick before. But he was pleased with this girl. She would photograph larger than life and she was a good size for several male leads he had in mind. Most important, she was light-skinned without being white. That was really why she was here. He had seen her in the commissary two weeks ago and a thought had come to him, a thought that had been growing for some time. An Oriental or Eurasian beauty was a good bet now. American men had always liked a dark-skinned sexpot, a woman they could think of as 'colored', and while they weren't ready to accept a Negro girl, in public that is, Isa would give them their kicks without stepping on their prejudices.

He nodded to himself, his decision beginning to jell; another 'hunch' in the making.

'Once again, please,' he murmured, and she smiled at him, a sweet and touching smile, and walked away. She gave her hips more roll this time, making those long, full cheeks slide up and down against the thin silk. When she reached the bench she murmured, 'Such interesting carvings,' and bent, turning her knees to the left, pushing her bottom out at him, the dark line of division emerging clearly.

Nat Markal told himself he was amused. He knew the games these girls played. Each thought *she* would be the one to end his strict adherence to a personal code of conduct that allowed for no nonsense. But his lips were dry.

Changes. Doubt and disquiet and changes taking place.

She bent lower and said, 'Lions! Little lions carved in the seat.' She looked back at him without straightening, and he

20

jerked his eyes to her face. She smiled again.

'All right, Isa.'

She returned to her chair. She was less nervous and uncertain now. A typical reaction, after catching his eyes on her rear. She was beginning to hope for a pass now. She was beginning to think that of all the desirable women Nat Markal had known, perhaps she was going to crack him.

'You're very lovely, Isa.'

'Thank you.' She crossed her legs and that slit opened up. Her thigh was ivory, like her face. Her smile was part of her expression now, faint and soft and endearing.

'Jerry tells me this is your fifth feature.'

She nodded. 'I also did television and summer stock.'

'A lot of experience for one so young.'

'I started young, Mr. Markal.'

He liked that Mr. Markal. Some of them tried for Nat after he looked them over. And she didn't give her words a leer, a double meaning the way so many of them did. Of course, bending that way ... but she had to pitch, didn't she? That was why she was here, to show him she could interest and excite men.

'I want you to see Carl Baiglen. I'll arrange for an appointment.'

'Mr. Baiglen does those scary features, doesn't he?'

Baiglen would do the special effects on *Joneses* – the floods and earthquakes and fires; the great crashes, sinkings, explosions; all sorts of disaster scenes – though he didn't know it and might very well resist being downgraded from producer-director. His own production would have to be shelved and financial compensation substituted. Alan Devon would be perfect as assistant producer ... actually producer, with Markal as executive producer. Devon was his own man now, and unless the project excited him highly might fight joining it. Cole Staley and Terry Hanford would head up publicity. And other people, the best in the business. An office would have to be set up ...

He would call Dave Sankin *today*!

He said, 'Mr. Baiglen does horror, science fiction, suspense. A very successful producer.'

Her smile weakened, though she nodded. He said, 'Jerry may have mentioned the role of Pony Girl in *The Squaws*.'

She didn't beat around the bush. 'I was hoping for it. A chance to work under Tyrone Chalze.'

21

'It's not even scheduled. Chalze is still editing *Lonely Day*. Meanwhile, you might want some work at Avalon. Featured work.' He paused. She waited. He said, 'In the way of a continuing audition for bigger things.' (What he wanted was for Baiglen and Devon and others to comment on Isa Yee, to support his growing certainty that she could become box office.)

Her smile was again convincing. She spoke quickly. 'Yes, thank you, I didn't understand. And it was foolish of me ... even without Pony Girl ... *anyone* would be grateful for your interest.'

'My interest is very selfish, as you'll soon find out.'

She grew quiet, watchful. But she wasn't apprehensive, as some were when they thought they finally had hooked him. They used their sex tricks and then he seemed about to make a move and their vestigial morality flickered into life.

'I expect to make a great deal of money on you, Isa.'

'I hope you're right, Mr. Markal.'

They smiled at each other, and he glanced at his watch, wondering if he should ask her to return in two hours for lunch. She misunderstood the gesture and rose. 'I've taken too much of your time.'

He rose with her, murmuring, 'Not at all.'

She walked to the door. He stood watching her, and again his lips felt dry. 'Isa.'

She turned.

But he didn't ask her to lunch, didn't give in to the sudden feeling to keep her with him. 'Have Jerry send me your complete portfolio.'

She nodded.

He sat down, picked up a letter, murmured offhandedly, 'You'll be hearing from me.'

She said, 'I hope so, Mr. Markal,' and her voice was warm and he felt she was smiling, waiting for him to look up.

He didn't look up, not until the door closed. It opened again almost immediately and Bertha came in, a tall angular woman who had been with him seven years.

'Anyone in the outer office?' Markal asked.

'Eli Charabond. And Howard Nesman with a client.'

'I won't see Nesman. He should know better than that. Who's the client?'

'Pier Andrei.'

Nat Markal sighed. He had given Pier her big chance in

22

American films thirteen years ago. She had done well for half those years, despite four divorces; then her drinking and sex life had gotten out of hand, had become public knowledge, and he'd had to cut her off via the morals clause. A few independent films, a feature or two in Italy and France, more public drinking and sexing, a year of oblivion and now she was here to beg.

'Send her in, alone.'

He came around his desk as the door opened. Pier was made up, dressed up, strapped up, and she'd had another face lift or skin tightening. But she still looked like hell. He was shocked, even though he had expected it. She was a red-head now, and her big face was skull-thin. He came forward, hand outstretched. 'Pier. Good to see you.'

She threw an arm around him and broke into tears. He could smell the whiskey. She couldn't stop drinking, even for an important interview. 'Now, now,' he comforted, and led her to a chair, the same chair Isa had sat in. The comparison was chilling. She pulled tissues from her bag and sniffled.

'Old friends always affect me so,' she said, and launched into a nonstop exposition of her trials and tribulations, all caused by 'lies, slander and those terrible *paparazzi* with their filthy cameras making things look like something when they're not.' He remembered the telescopic shots of Pier and a seventeen-year-old bellhop on the deck of a sailboat in the Mediter-ranean. She went on. He barely listened.

How old was she anyway? Forty. Forty-two. But old. Especially in the face. Aged by booze and boys. An old woman with young boys. Disgusting.

'. . . Hollywood is finished,' Pier was saying. 'Nothing but the ugly little television and bad, bad pictures. Except, of course, some *you* do, darling Nat. But you and I *together*, ah! We can do something *great*! You remember *Adelia*? I could do it again, only with mature wisdom, slow fire instead of childish passion.' She stood up and came to him in a rush, pressing those bloated breasts into his chest, those unnatural breasts that stayed firm from silicone injection to silicone in-jection. 'If you want to do something fine, I have ideas. Oh, and properties! There's a story by Ignazio Silone . . .'

He finally buzzed for Bertha. Between them they man-euvered Pier out, and he nodded as she begged him to keep her in mind for a part.

She'd gotten to him. He felt pity as well as revulsion. There

23

was bound to be something, a featured bit, that she could handle in *Joneses*. If she stayed sober.

He would have her see Baiglen and Devon, the same as Isa. Her name still had some box office, if only because of notoriety.

He spoke to Bertha about Isa and Pier, telling her to set up appointments. Then he saw Eli Charabond, who was in charge of allocating studio space. Eli wanted to discuss an emergency on the *Desert Marauders* television series. It seemed they needed the special facilities of Stage 15 for retakes, but Moe Sholub was still—

'As you see fit, Eli,' Nat interrupted.

Eli blinked behind thick glasses. 'It's a matter of some delicacy. I thought you might have an opinion.'

'No, Eli. My opinions are reserved for other things from now on.'

Eli blinked again, and Markal was annoyed with himself. Eli had received a hint of something.

Alone again, Markal used the phone to tell Bertha he was unavailable until after lunch. Then he took the sheet of paper from his breast pocket and unfolded it on the desk. He read it once, quickly, trying to see it with a fresh, objective eye, telling himself to be cautious; looking to find fault with the concept, as Olive and her group of patient watchers certainly would.

But his face grew flushed and he thought, *Screw caution and screw the watchers!* This is what he wanted to do and he would do it. In Hollywood, where it *should* be done. And D. W. Griffith would be topped at last!

He would produce the world's greatest single feature film, an epic that would stand as a landmark of film making, and money making, for all time; that would perpetuate his name, his standing for all time. And not just because of its size. It must have something that had died with Griffith; that DeMille hadn't had and no one else had; something that no one expected of a *Ten Commandments,* a *Cleopatra,* a *Bible*. It would have what every domestic Markal film avoided and what most Markal art imports contained in great degree. *Reality*. Not the surface reality of post-Griffith Hollywood films – the sex and violence and slick formula shocks – but the reality of history, reality seen not just through the eyes of the majority . . .

That was the key! Not just through the eyes of the Ameri-

24

can people as they wanted to see it, or had been led to believe they wanted to see it. He would make this feature so full of power and imagery, so strong in stars and story, so grand in scope; that the public would line up to have its lies destroyed!

Once again he read the sheet of paper, slowly this time, using his pencil as he went along. Printed in block capitals on the top was: 'THE ETERNAL JONESES.' He read on.

'The story of an American family from Virginia Colony to present ... each star will continue from start to finish of picture, playing various members of family throughout history. (Eight to ten *top* names!) Wars, big. Disasters, big. Patriotism, big. Contradictions and prejudice and cruelty also big. Ending with Vietnam and the question of whether this is a just war left to public to answer. *Open budget*. (Set some sort of figure for Sankin.) Slavery and killing Indians (genocide?) and Chinese labor and kicking Mexico around and everything we don't talk about yet clear to see in history. Anti-Semitism too, and how we treated Irish and Italians at first. But through it all America growing, becoming great. Have some character compare us with Roman Empire, but message of our pic is Romans grew worse and we will grow better. And Carl Jones (Gordon Hewlett, with Mona Dearn opposite) marching off to Vietnam, not sure about justice of this war, but obeying orders in tradition of American forefathers – sad, with doubt, etc. Two hundred years of American history in one movie! *Birth of a Nation* but bigger, better, more honest in overall message. *Message!* This will be the big difference! An epic with *meaning*! Reviewers will flip and public will flock! (Use this phrase in trade?) *Negroes*. Must have Negroes. One member of Jones slave staff, beautiful mulatto girl, sleeps with master, gets Negro blood into family. These become the Big City Joneses, some passing for white, and in this way we can cover Negro history and get to problems of our times. Pic must cover *all* great problems! Pic must be America! Pic must be *all* of us!'

He made another notation, about building a set before the script was written. The world's greatest set to go along with the world's greatest movie; which would be more in the area of publicity and promotion than production. Then he folded the sheet of paper and put it back in his pocket. Writers would take it from here. Maybe use someone new for the treatment? Someone clear of Hollywood and studio taboos?

25

Because this picture was going to be a great big taboo in itself!

That novelist Baiglen had brought from New York? Make a note to have Bertha dig up his war novel. Very good reviews. Stark realism and faultless ear for the way people actually talk, the *Times* said. Can get him cheap and put him to work immediately. Larson Wyllit for screenplay. A third writer? Abby Mann?

He would have to present Sankin with a projected budget. Ten million? He'd never believe it. Fifteen was better ... but that was just to keep him from balking. Twenty-five or thirty million was a more realistic sum. Should run four or five hours, tightly edited.

Sankin wouldn't be happy. Or Olive Dort. Or the stockholders. Until they were made to see what an enormous triumph it could be.

Whatever the opposition, whatever the budget, whatever the length, it would be done.

He asked Bertha to get him Dave Sankin in New York. He talked for half an hour, brooking no interruptions, concluding with, 'I'm going to get started immediately, Dave. That includes a set, a big one, to focus attention on us and pull publicity.'

'What kind of set?' Sankin muttered, and Nat knew he was unhappy.

'I haven't decided.' (And even when he did, he would *ease* Sankin into awareness of its size, and its cost. No use pushing the accountant too far.)

Sankin was silent. Nat said, 'Now, about Lou Grayson and *Killjoy*—'

Sankin laughed, a high, unnatural sound. 'Fifteen million? You really think you can do a feature like that for fifteen million?'

'It's a point of departure, Dave.'

'Departure for the moon!'

'You know my track record. I'd as soon make anything that doesn't earn money as throw away my Avalon, RCA and Polaroid stock.'

'You want to do a big feature? All right. Take eight, ten million and that bestseller about the Mormons—'

'And make another lousy Western.'

'Nat, this Jones picture worries me. I never interfered before—'

26

'We're going to make a fortune, Dave! Can't you see it? A fortune!'

'You really think so?'

'It'll run a year, two years at special prices, reserved seats. We'll make our investment back right there. And then the neighborhood houses, lines of people . . .'

'You think *Cleopatra* made back its investment like Twentieth says?'

'*Cleopatra* wasn't produced by Nat Markal.'

'It had Taylor, Burton—'

'It had troubles. There aren't any troubles on a Nat Markal production.'

'I know you can handle things better than anyone, Nat . . . but *such* a picture! The whole American history . . . and wait, they'll call us Communists!'

'They'll call us geniuses. They're sick of empty spectaculars.'

'You know the old saying: "Don't sell your soul for a pot of message".'

'David, stop being a scared rabbit.'

'Me? Didn't I go all the way on the art imports?'

'Be strong enough, confident enough, to make fifty, sixty million for Avalon.'

Sankin was silent again. Nat talked about *Killjoy*. Sankin said, 'I've been thinking of coming out to the studio . . . a vacation . . .'

'Fine. I'll need you when Olive starts screaming.'

Sankin sighed. 'You're *sure* now, Nat? You've thought it all out?'

'I have. Good-bye.'

'Wait. Instead of my coming to Hollywood, maybe you'd better come to New York.'

'I was going to anyway. A press conference at the Forum to announce *The Eternal Joneses*—'

'I'll want an outline, and you should talk to the board.'

'All right. But you and I *are* the board. You keep forgetting, David. No one counts but us.'

'A dangerous way to think. Other people's opinions—'

'Are worth nothing. My opinion, David, and yours—'

'Mine isn't so certain.'

'It will be. Good-bye.'

He was hungry. He was, strangely exhausted. But everything was going as he wanted it to and he was no longer bored.

27

No longer plagued by the vague doubt, the vague disquiet?

He sat at his desk a moment, trying to read and understand himself. Always before he had been able to dig out every last vestige of what was bothering him, and turn it to his own advantage. But this time . . .

He said, 'Foolishness!' and stood up. And thought of Isa Yee. Yes, a pretty girl, and from all indications a hell of a talent. If she worked out, it would be good for Avalon, and good for *The Joneses*.

He left his office. He used the chauffeur-driven limousine. He had much to consider, much to plan, much to set in motion.

CARL BAIGLEN

The phone had been ringing all morning. Agents, mostly, but a few actors and actresses who thought a personal word might advance their cause. And friends who directed and friends who wanted to direct. And TV people wanted to break into features, and out-of-work writers, and friends of friends.

Nat Markal's secretary had called to say lunch wasn't possible and to mention two actresses. 'Mr. Markal would consider it a personal favor if you gave them serious consideration, Mr. Baiglen.' Which meant that he would do his damnedest to use them in *Terror Town*. You didn't pass up a chance to do Emperor Nat a personal favor!

The phone rang again. Carl Baiglen waited for Cheryl's buzz, then picked it up, lean face ready to smile in pleasure at another friend's enthusiasm, at another talented person's eagerness to work for him. Next to the actual shooting of a feature, he enjoyed this buildup of excitement, this prelude to action, this time of promise when no problems had yet arisen and hope was high and the big time beckoned.

'Yes, Cheryl.'

'A Mr. John McNaughton on the phone.'

'John McNaughton? Do I know him?'

'From Devereux, he said.'

Someone from his pre-Hollywood days. Someone who would want to reminisce about the suburban township north of St. Louis and the old bunch and Myra.

His first impulse was to give him the brush. But then he wondered if there hadn't been a McNaughton in Myra's family, and he didn't want to seem unwilling to talk to his first wife's relatives. Not that any had called him in years.

He took a cigarette from the box on his desk and stuck it between his lips. It was probably the usual: someone who had two week's vacation and a list of names and wanted to see the studio.

'What does he do? Who recommended him? Who do we know in common?'

Cheryl clicked off and Carl lit his cigarette and inhaled deeply. Goddam tourists.

Cheryl said, 'He's a police officer. He said Myra recommended him.'

Carl Baiglen sat absolutely still for a moment; then put down his cigarette. 'All right.' When the smooth male voice said, 'Mr. Baiglen?' he spoke quickly, coldly: 'Whoever you are, there's something you should know. My wife has been dead since 1954.'

'Oh, I know it.'

'Then your sense of humor is disgusting!'

'Not really. I could explain at lunch. Could we get together today?'

'No, we could not.'

'You name it then.'

'Never. And don't bother me again, Mr. McNaughton, or I'll contact your superiors.'

The man laughed. 'I guess I mishandled this, Mr. Baiglen, but you'll have to see me. We've important business.'

'I don't know what you're talking about and I don't care.' But he did, he did, except that there was nothing anyone could do to him. They hadn't been able to at the time and they wouldn't be able to now and it made no difference what this man or any other man thought or said or did.

McNaughton began to speak. Carl hung up. He took his cigarette from the ashtray and smoked and thought of Devereux and the big old house amidst the raw new ones and the long steep staircase and Myra toppling down it, the scream breaking as her neck broke. It was an accident, her own fault, though neighbors had heard them quarreling and Myra's mother wouldn't go near him and others wondered. An accident, and the coroner's jury concurred, and the matter had been closed for almost twelve years.

29

Was McNaughton really a police officer? It wasn't likely. A police officer with official business would state it.

Whoever he was, if he bothered Carl Baiglen again he would regret it!

With that, Carl pushed the matter from his mind. He had more important things to think of. His writer was coming in today. The action commenced today.

The phone rang. He waited for Cheryl's buzz, tensing in case it was McNaughton.

Cheryl said, 'Mr. McNaughton again.' He took a deep breath.

'I'm not in. I won't *be* in.' He hung up. No one would make a mark of Carl Baiglen. The anxious young photographer who cut prices to shoot television commercials for local St. Louis channels was no more. He was a man of growing substance, growing importance now, despite what the envious wise guys called him. (That stupid name. That degrading, idiot name!)

He had his plans. Avalon wouldn't allow him top money for established screenwriters? All right, he would bring in writers who would work for credit. Writers who could out-think and out-write hacks getting fifty thousand and more. He had read back issues of *The New York Times Book Review* and *The Saturday Review* and contacted publishers and through them agents and novelists. He didn't know if anyone had ever worked that way before, but he was going to get a hundred grand worth of writing for five! And he wouldn't be exploiting the writer, either, because this credit was going to *make* Charles Z. Halpert — was going to bring him other feature offers.

He turned his swivel chair left and looked at the wall six feet from his desk; the wall with the large corkboard covered by stills from his eight feature films. *Produced and Directed by Carl Baiglen, with Original Story by Carl Baiglen, and Special Effects by Carl Baiglen*. Not a bomb among them, and he had made the first two on a shoestring. It was after the second release that Markal Associates had contacted him and he'd moved onto the Avalon lot. Markal knew it was net, not reviews (those egghead Eastern fags!) that made a producer. That was why Carl Baiglen didn't pay a nickel in rent for his Avalon facilities and Zig Eisler, who called him Two-Cent Bagel, paid the first of every month. Baiglen made features and showed profits, so he was a member of the Markal team. Eisler talked about turning Tennessee Williams one-acters into 'meaningful' films, talked about releasing his 'take-off' Western (shot two years ago and still in the can), talked about doing a series of modern-dress Shakespearean films, talked and talked ... and paid rent, as any producer had to who wasn't on a shared expense-and-profit deal with Avalon.

Carl's next five films had been budgeted between a hundred and a hundred-fifty thousand, and with the Avalon organization behind them had all earned fat profits. His sixth was shot but not yet edited. Now Nat Markal was upping his maximum. Not half a million, as the publicity releases stated, but a solid quarter of a million on a straight fifty-fifty deal. Markal had promised that if *Terror Town* really scored, the half-million would become reality.

There was a light knock at the door and Cheryl came in: a heavy brunette with a pretty face, the best typist and all-around secretary he'd ever had, and she had given up on the acting bit, which was a blessing. She closed the door behind her and murmured, 'Mr. Halpert is here.' This was their procedure on arrival of appointments. In here he could tell her anything – when to interrupt with a reminder of a previous appointment, for example, in case he wanted to cut the thing short.

'Fine!' He rubbed his hands together. 'No interruptions, including calls ... except by Ruth or the brass, of course.'

Cheryl nodded and went out. Carl's eyes touched briefly on her backside, and he felt slight irritation, recurrent irritation. He wondered when she would realize she required a girdle and was ludicrous otherwise and certainly wasn't good for office prestige.

Cheryl returned, ushering in the man in the dark suit. 'Mr. Baiglen, Mr. Halpert.' She stepped back and closed the door. Carl came forward quickly, hand outstretched. Halpert was about six feet tall and big on top with a big head. He hadn't sounded big on the phone.

'Mr. Halpert. How was the flight from New York?'

Halpert's hand enfolded his, but gently. 'I drove,' he said, and the voice was the voice on the phone, soft and rather uncertain. The mild smile fit too. Yes, Charles Halpert as Carl had envisioned him, and the size now fit the picture.

'Drove, did you?' He took Halpert's elbow, guided him across the office to the couch and waited while he seated

31

himself; then dropped into the facing armchair, crossing his legs briskly. 'That's not too common anymore. Five hours from coast to coast has us all a little spoiled.' He chuckled. Halpert smiled.

'I wanted to see something of the country. Haven't been out of New York since my Air Corps days. Felt it would . . . be of benefit.'

'Broader horizons. A writer's intellect. Of course.'

'And it saves rental on a car.'

Carl nodded; then laughed as he saw Halpert was smiling in anticipation of a laugh. Writers. Had to handle them delicately. Turn them off and they could screw up a beautiful concept.

'Look, Charles . . . do they call you Charles?'

'Chuck.'

'And I'm Carl. You and I have a job to do. Together. A most difficult and important job. Half a million dollars and the efforts of roughly a hundred people are involved. And it all lives or dies on what you and I, especially you, do with the script. Your agent explained the deal before you signed the contract?'

'Yes. And I read well.'

Another smile requiring a response. Carl chuckled briefly. 'You're satisfied? No resentments over Guild minimum? Because we can still call it quits without damage to either of us. Hidden resentments over money often lead to bad writing.'

'No resentments, Carl. Besides, I need that first movie credit more than I need—' He stopped quite suddenly, looked unhappy.

'Ben told me you had no previous feature experience and your TV was minimal and quite some time ago . . . Armstrong Circle Theatre and other New York live stuff. But that's all right with me. Your second novel – *The Stranger* – showed me you were expert at dialogue. And story sense . . . superb.'

Halpert muttered, 'Thank you. *The Vital Strangers*.'

'I sometimes forget titles, Chuck, but never the quality of a man's work. That war novel of yours . . . the best air-combat scenes I ever read. I sent it to Nat Markal. He okayed you shortly afterward. And your third novel, about the apartment house, very fine, though too downbeat for my tastes. Three novels, is that right?'

Halpert nodded.

'Every one a testimonial to your talent. We need writers like you in Hollywood, Chuck. Too many self-satisfied hacks

32

out here. You're mature, yet full of excitement and surprises.'

Halpert mumbled, 'Again, thanks.'

'All right. Let me say right now you have the ability to do the biggest features. Even classics like *Psycho* and *Baby Jane* are well within your range.' He rose, went to his desk and picked up a stapled sheaf of Xeroxed papers. 'This is a ten-page story, my original story, *Terror Town*. I'm a writer – did the scripts for my first three features – but as a producer-director I've outgrown my poor writer's talents.' He chuckled, and Halpert smiled. 'I'm only a craftsman. Now I need inspiration, true creative talent, genius.'

Halpert flushed and began to murmur protests, but Carl shook his head impatiently. 'That's my evaluation, Chuck, and you're stuck with it. I want you to read this story, think a while and let me know your opinion. The basic premise is already sold to management, but everything else . . , well, you're the writer. It's how you spark, what chemistry takes place, that will determine whether these ten pages become an acceptable movie, a good movie or a major motion picture.'

He looked hard at Halpert, searching for hidden cynicism, embarrassment, even stifled laughter – signs that would show him he had a New York egghead on his hands. Which would mean a week or two of futile labor and a quick cutoff of contract.

But Halpert was leaning forward, face intense and full of interest.

Carl walked to the couch and handed over the story. 'Ask my secretary to show you to your office. I'll expect you in just about every day. Writing a feature is different from writing a novel or a teleplay. I have to check with you step by step, almost day by day, so as to prevent any rushing off in wrong directions.'

Halpert rose. He hesitated, and then said, 'I think I'm going to enjoy it, Carl.'

Carl smiled. 'Good luck, Chuck.'

Halpert left. Carl went to his desk, reached for the buzzer, then remembered that Cheryl would be showing Halpert his office.

The phone rang. 'Yes?'

'Mr. Baiglen, this is John McNaughton. I'll see you at your home tonight.'

'Fine. Several members of the Beverly Hills Police Department will be there too.'

'If you want them to see Myra's letter, that's all right with me.'

Carl knew he shouldn't bite, but what the hell ... he had to wait until Cheryl came back anyway. 'Myra wrote you a letter?'

'Not me, Mr. Baiglen. It was addressed to "Whoever Finds This." It was in a crack behind the medicine chest in the upstairs bathroom. It's dated the day she died.'

'McNaughton, you're going to end up in jail. No such letter was ever found. Chief Kilmer knows my address and he'd have informed me?'

'Chief Kilmer is retired, but you're right about the Department knowing your address. They don't know about this letter because I found it myself, just a week ago yesterday.'

'Sure.' He smiled angrily. 'Typed, isn't it? And you just *happene*d to be searching a house where an accident took place twelve years ago.'

'Handwritten. It matches letters her sister gave us, remember? Letters saying you were asking for a divorce. And I didn't just *happen* to be searching your old house. I've lived in it for three years. Last week I decided to install a new medicine chest. When I took off the old one I found this letter, written in pencil on the back of a cardboard toothpaste box which had been torn open to make a flat writing surface. Want to hear what it says?'

Carl Baiglen didn't answer. His hand holding the phone was slippery wet. McNaughton said:

'My husband is trying to break down the door. He says he will kill me. He says I won't live out this day. I won't give him a divorce. He's going away now, but he is going to kill me when I come out. He's crazy mad. If I die today you'll know he killed me. No matter what he says, he killed me. Please give this to the police and tell them my husband Carl Baiglen killed me. God save my soul.'

Carl got a cigarette in his mouth and lit it. 'Ridiculous.'

McNaughton was silent.

'What did your superiors say?'

'I told you. They don't know about it yet.'

Carl forced a laugh. 'You're protecting me.'

'I want you to help me.'

'Let me guess how. My bank account. My home. My life's blood.'

'If we could sit down and talk—'

34

'You're a blackmailer. If I turned you in, you'd end up in jail, not me.'

'I'm investigating a lead on my own, Mr. Baiglen. Trying to check it out before bringing it to the attention of Chief O'Neil. And don't be too sure about your not ending up in jail. There's no statute of limitations on homicide. A case can always be reopened, as long as the suspect hasn't been tried on the same charge.'

'I'd never be convicted.'

'Maybe. But you *would* be tried. Your mother-in-law and sister-in-law would see to that. And some people who still talk about how you got away with murder. You'd be tried, Mr. Baiglen, and wouldn't that be fun? A producer of spook movies tried for murder?' He laughed briefly. 'Either I see you today or I go back to Devereux.'

Carl told himself to hang up and call the police. Once you started paying blackmail it never ended.

'I'll talk to you,' he said, 'but I'll take my chances in court before I let you enslave me. Understand that.'

'I have no such ideas, Mr. Baiglen. I'm just sick of being a cop. You won't have to do much more for me than for any young actor.'

'Actor?'

'I've dreamed of it all my life. I've no training except the Devereux Little Theatre Group, but there are such things as naturals, aren't there?'

'Yes,' Carl said, and dragged on his cigarette and switched the phone to his left hand. He wiped the sweaty palm on his trousers. 'Do you know Sawyer's Devil Bar off the Strip?'

'I can find it.'

Carl give him directions. 'Be there at eleven-thirty tonight. Wait for me. I've got a preview and can't be sure exactly when I'll get away. Bring the letter.'

'Thanks, Mr. Baiglen!'

Carl almost smiled. Gratitude and enthusiasm, as if he had extended a helping hand to a struggling actor. 'Think nothing of it,' he said, and hung up.

He smoked his cigarette down to the filter and lit another. If the man asked for too much, he would tell him to do his damnedest.

He wouldn't be convicted. He might not even be tried, no matter what McNaughton said. But it would get into the newspapers.

35

How would that affect Ruth? And Andy, who had been only five at the time? He had told them both the truth, in terms of basic fact. Myra had fallen down a flight of stairs and died. He hadn't told them of wanting a divorce, of the inquest, of the ugly suspicions. So far as they were concerned, he had loved his wife, lost her and left Devereux grief-stricken and shattered to find a new life. Which was as far from the truth as you could get.

He had never loved Myra. He had felt a definite sense of release at her death. He had wanted to come to Hollywood since touring the studios as a sailor on leave in 1944.

And what about his position here at Avalon? There was a morals and bad-publicity clause in every contract, including his own. With Nat Markal being such a stickler for the letter of the clause . . .

He stood up. He'd handle it. Time now to get to work. He had a session scheduled with the sound team on his soon-to-be-released film, *Microbe Monsters*, and a meeting later this afternoon with Eli Charabond on stage allocations for *Terror Town*. He wanted to speak to Nat Markal . . . plant some early seeds of enthusiasm for an increase in budget. And there was the all-important first story conference with Halpert.

Worry about a petty blackmailer? The hell he would!

CHERYL CARNY

'There's no buzzer connecting our offices,' Cheryl said, 'but I'm right down the hall. Drop in anytime if you have a question or need some supplies. Just fill out the Personnel papers and leave them on your desk. And check that the phone is operating, will you, Mr. Halpert?'

He sat down behind the desk, put the phone to his ear, nodded. He looked around the office and smiled. 'Thank you.'

She liked his smile. He was a big man and she was a big woman and on that basis she liked him. He wasn't an actor, director, producer or Hollywood writer, and on those bases she liked him.

'This is very nice,' he said. 'I'm being spoiled.'

'Not at all. All the offices are more or less alike. Nice, but nothing special.'

He glanced around again, and then his eyes flickered over her and he quickly picked up Carl's story. She liked that too.

36

Some men couldn't care less about Cheryl Carny, and others began pitching the minute they met her. Charles Halpert would have liked to pitch, she was sure of it.

When she came into the hall, she glanced left toward Devon Productions. The door was open, as usual, and Sandy waved from behind her desk; then pantomined drinking. Cheryl smiled and walked toward her.

Mr. Devon appeared at the desk with a folder in his hand. He glanced up, saw Cheryl, and that stupid smirk crossed his face. He wasn't a bad-looking man until he smirked. He didn't smirk at Sandy, who was a cute twenty-year-old, or at most of the actresses he interviewed, from what Sandy reported, but as he had once said, Cheryl reminded him of a young Mae West and Mae had been his passion as a boy.

Or was it knowing about Jim and thinking she was hungry all the time that turned him on?

He straightened as she approached, giving her what he thought was a youthful wave. He was sixty, a widower, and had his good days and bad days. Who didn't? But most of the time she found it difficult to think of him as an old man, what with his carefully tailored slacks and sweaters, his thinning but meticulously combed and tinted dark hair, his tanned face, and lean, exercised, massaged, taken-care-of body. Sixty, and so much more alive than Jim.

What right did he have to be so alive? Where was the justice of it?

He watched her every step of the way. She walked with her normal swing, a big girl of twenty-five with big breasts, big rear and big, beautiful face. A fat, plump or *zaftig* girl, according to your tastes.

'Hi, darling,' he said with that faint trace of foreign accent, straightening and tugging at his red, button-fronted sweater. *Joe College*, she thought, and murmured, 'Hi,' and entered the office. 'I came to steal a Coke.'

Sandy said, 'Wait'll I get Mr. Devon's instructions.'

'Let me serve you,' Devon said, hamming it up but tense as always, hurrying from the desk toward the waist-high refrigerator tucked into the corner behind the door. He passed her and one speckled, veiny hand – no matter what they did they couldn't hide age in the hands – stroked her arm. She looked at Sandy and winked. Sandy shook her head slightly. Devon handed Cheryl a Coke and spoke to Sandy. 'Retype the three letters with my additions.'

37

Sandy nodded. Cheryl looked at the Coke. 'My teeth aren't *that* strong, Mr. Devon.'

'Oh, must have left the opener on my desk.' He turned, as casual as a tiger about to spring, and went through the door. 'C'mere, darling. I'll open it for you.'

She hadn't entered his den in months, nor had she intended to, ever again, after his last little display of affection, but now she did.

She knew where he would be even before she saw him. She squeezed between the desk and wall, out of sight of the waiting room, to where Devon stood pressed into the corner, taking the opener from his pocket. She came toward him and he watched her with wild eyes, trying to smile. She thought, *You pawing, sickening old bastard, why do you need me when you've got the little make-out actresses fighting for parts in your features, your TV shows?* She reached for the opener. He took the Coke from her hand and put bottle and opener on the desk and put both his hands on her upper arms and stroked them, looking at her with those wild eyes, expecting her to pull away as she always did, at which time he would grab at her, whispering and pleading and touching wherever he could. She didn't pull away. 'You like fat arms?' she asked.

'Beautiful arms,' he said, his voice shaking. His hands moved to her back and drew her toward him. She could easily have broken his hold, sent the old idiot flying, but she allowed herself to be drawn close, looking into those frightened, jumpy, wild eyes, hating him for standing on his own feet and reaching for goodies and dressing so well and living so well. At sixty. When Jim was twenty-six and kaput. Because she had backed a car from a garage and his shout had come too late and turned to a scream. And he'd come home in a wheelchair, slapping his dead thighs and looking at her, looking at her. And the Cupid Carnys (had they really called them that at U.C.L.A.?) were dead, kaput, finished.

She moved tight against Devon, to stop the thoughts ... and to teach him a lesson, him and his dirty games.

His eyes half closed. 'Cheryl,' he whispered, 'let me take you out, sweetheart.'

'Impossible, Dev. You know about my husband.'

'I'll pay for a sitter.'

The word 'sitter' infuriated her, galvanized her into action. She rubbed against him and was startled at the strength of his response. His arms crushed her. She felt his manhood. His lips slid over her neck and cheek and found her mouth. She really gave herself, hoping Sandy wouldn't look in. A kiss or feel was SOP, but not what they were doing now. His hands were obscene. She enveloped him, flowed about him, almost took him into her body through her clothing. He was shaking, sweating, and she gathered up her coldness, her contempt, and prepared to break away and leave him with the fire burning in his guts.

But *he* did the breaking away. He pushed her back and shook his head. 'Tonight,' he whispered hoarsely. 'Listen, darling, you'll say you have rush typing and I'll send someone to sit with him and we'll go to Frascati's for dinner.'

She turned her back, bending to pick up the Coke and opener. Those hands of his couldn't resist the target. *Obscene, obscene!* And yet, she stood still for it, because it was another flame to add to his pyre.

'He'll ask how much I got paid,' she said, still bending over the desk, still allowing those hands of his to perform their nasty tricks. How she despised the man!

'Oh, I'll pay ten dollars. But you agree?'

'Ten dollars?'

'I don't mean ... whatever you think would be a realistic sum.'

She bent all the way forward, coming to rest on her left forearm, sipping the Coke held in her right hand. 'I can't do it.'

'But why?' His hands stopped, and she moved her bottom slightly to spur him on, to taunt him, to keep him burning. As soon as she did, he lost all control. His fingers entered her — two, three, he was pushing his whole hand inside — and his weight pressed down on her back and his lips sucked at her neck and his breath raged in her ear. Now was the time to straighten and walk out. Now was the time to pay him back.

Pay him back for what?

Like that, the hate was gone and she was left with those frantic fingers digging inside her, setting *her* insides afire. All the planned insults and rejections were gone and she wanted him, wanted a man's organ, wanted the pounding toward satisfaction, wanted to be served, wanted the partnership of service instead of the degradation she suffered each evening, wanted *Devon*.

He knew it. 'Cheryl dearest, where?'

'Here.'

'But sweetheart—'

'Close the door.'

'But Sandra will suspect something.'

She put down her head. 'Now or never.'

He hesitated only an instant; then went to the door, shoved it closed and came back to her. His fly was distended, and for one sick moment Cheryl forgot where she was and almost fell to her knees to service him. Two years of that and only that had trained her well. Two years of Jim's twisting her hair and the revulsion growing, growing, as she understood it could never be good again, not even a little, not with his lust being part hate and his satisfaction being part revenge and the nausea tickling her throat and the prayers turning to murder in her heart because two years of this was an eternity and no one should spend eternity in hell, not before dying. Not for a mistake regretted so bitterly that there were no words, not even thoughts, to express it. And how could love-true, love-sweet, love that had swept them both away from their pasts and into what was briefly a paradise turn to something like that?

'Dev!' she said, her voice a cry; and he read that cry as passion and went behind her; and she lay on the desk, her cheek pressing cool, polished wood.

He had always been so wild, so frantically grasping, she expected he would take her the same way. But there was nothing wild or frantic about him now. Her dress was tucked up around her back, her pants drawn down, his penis first rubbed between her buttocks then passed under them into her sheath, and all gently, methodically. His hands, when they stroked her hips, thighs and belly, were no longer trembling. He was a man, a whole man, in charge now, possessing her, and he did it with tenderness as well as passion.

How good it felt! She had almost forgotten what lovemaking was without hate and nausea. She had begun using Jim's methods – sex for revenge – but something inside had remembered and turned the tables. She moaned and put back her left hand. 'Dev.' He took her hand, held it as he drove deep up and into her. He went on that way until she began to gasp and rotate wildly, and he began snapping his loins. He did it all so well, with so much finesse, so much control. A sign of his years, she thought, and then stopped thinking. *'Faster!'* she gasped, and shook in ecstasy and slumped forward. But Dev was still moving, and she resumed her proper stance and worked for him. His thighs trembled against her buttocks.

His breath grew harsh, ragged. And suddenly he was out of her. She turned to look. He was facing away, trousers and shorts down around his ankles, ejaculating into his handkerchief.

Poor Dev. *Coitus interruptus* at his age.

She arranged her clothing and waited until he had finished and made himself presentable. He looked older now, his face pale under its tan. She expected him to begin worrying about Sandy and moving her toward the door and thinking of how to protect himself against any demands she might make. She was, herself, calm and without emotion other than warmth for him. 'You're very good,' she murmured, and smiled at his proud shrug. A boy, really. The years made no difference that way. She kissed his face, said, 'Mr. Baiglen will fire me for sure,' and turned to the door.

'When can I take you out?'

She looked back, realizing he wanted more, he wanted a relationship. At first she was surprised and touched because her thoughts were still suspended in warmth.

'Tomorrow night?' he asked, voice growing anxious.

'Tomorrow night?' she echoed, and something began to change.

'Tomorrow night's no good? Then Thursday. I'll get a real nurse for him. He'll be fine. We'll drive down La Cienega and you'll pick whatever restaurant you want.'

'My liking to eat shows that much, does it?' She smiled slightly, but affection was gone; and what did he want with her anyway when he had his actresses? Was it some special kick, knowing about Jim? Would he expect revelations, confessions, intimate details the next time?

'No, no,' he protested. 'You're beautiful. Perfect. It has nothing to do with eating.'

'A restaurant has nothing to do with eating?'

He made a motion toward her. She shook her head sharply. He said, 'When then, Cheryl? You name it.'

She picked up the Coke and gulped it. It was warm but still full of fizz. She stifled a burp and turned to go.

He grabbed her arm. 'But *when*, sweetheart?'

'When what?'

He stared at her, moved his lips, tested her with an uncertain smile. She returned his look soberly. She'd needed a screwing and that was all there was to it. But if he thought he could use her regularly . . .

41

'Bye,' she said, sweetly, and her feelings had come full circle. Once again she wanted to hurt him, wanted to humiliate him.

'I don't understand,' he whispered, releasing her arm. 'I swear I don't.'

'You didn't make me an offer.'

'An offer?'

'A part. If I'm so perfect, so beautiful, offer me a part,'

'You? But . . . a part?'

She had to control laughter. He was shell-shocked. 'I'm a secretary only because I couldn't succeed as an actress. I had several roles on television four years ago. I was in stock in Santa Monica. Have you a part for me?'

'Cheryl baby, be realistic. You'd have to play characters. You good enough for characters?'

'Characters? You said I was beautiful. I want to play beautiful girls.'

He didn't answer. She began to turn away. He stepped in close and grabbed her shoulders and looked into her face. 'You *are* beautiful. I tell you and I know. More beautiful than any of the greedy little sticks that come in here. More beautiful and more exciting with more in your head—'

'You're going to give me a part?'

'But beautiful on camera is something else. What a national audience considers beautiful—'

'You're *not* going to give me a part?'

He got it then. His face changed and he stepped back from her. 'You're making fun of me.'

She walked out. Sandy was on the phone and gave her a curious stare and signaled her to wait. Cheryl shook her head and went into the hall. Devon wouldn't ever figure it out. She liked that.

But she didn't like herself.

She walked past the closed door near the midhall staircase, the door to the office that Charles Halpert was now using. She had just ordered his nameplate from Personnel Printing Division.

She wished she could order Charles himself from some division. Charles free and clear for Cheryl free and clear.

God, she was sick of Hollywood and Hollywood people! Sick of herself too and that frightened her. Because she might be able to get away from Jim (it was possible; she had dreamed of ways) and away from Hollywood (go back home to Albuquerque for a few weeks, or a few years), but where could

42

she go to get away from the fat girl, the mean girl, the sometimes nympho sometimes frigid always crazy girl?

She concentrated on Albuquerque. This time of the year
the days were mostly bright and warm, the evenings cold
enough for coats and fires. And that air; that sharp, clean,
thin air that filled your lungs with champagne bubbles. She
could lose weight and men would look at her and want her
and one, a mature man, would ask her to marry him and she
would say yes. She would have Jim in her past and he would
have his wife in his past and they would be wise and kind with
each other, more capable of love because they both had
suffered in their first marriages. She would love only him,
never really seeing other men, as it had been with Jim ...

That smashed the fantasy.

What was he doing now? Was he sleeping? Watching TV?
Reading? He read a great deal lately. He did it, he explained
carefully, to keep himself sane ... as he watched television
and listened to music and sat beside her at drive-in movies
and drank and had her make oral love to him. Sanity was the
day-by-day objective, he said.

He said it a dozen times a week. He smiled as he said it,
looking at her with hollow eyes, eyes which seemed different
even in color from the warm gray eyes of the boy she had
married.

She hurried to the office. Carl Baiglen was pacing near her
desk. 'I said *show* him his office, dear, not settle down in it
with him.'

He asked her to get him Nat Markal. He turned to the office
and then stopped. 'What do you think of our new writer?'

'Seems nice.' She sat down and reached for the phone.

'He's never done a screenplay, you know. Novelist, and a
very good one too. Highly praised by the best reviewers. *New
York Times* said he was reminiscent of the young Hemingway.
Things like that.'

She realized he needed reassurance. 'He's quite serious
about the project. Got right to work.'

'Yes, and he's competent. I can spot a competent writer
every time.'

'Then you're going to get a superior job. You might have
a fight on your hands, a fight to keep him from writing a *Best
Years of Our Lives*, but that's all to the good, isn't it?'

He smiled. 'Exactly why I hired him. I have hopes for this
feature. Hopes that would surprise Markal and Sankin.'

'Bigger budget?'

'You're a bright girl, Cheryl. A very bright girl. Time you did a few things around here besides secretarial work. I'm going to have you read for me. And give your opinion on *Terror Town* as it develops.'

'Sounds interesting.'

He nodded. 'I'm very pleased.' He went into his office.

She dialed. *Cheryl Makes Good at Last. Or, How to Succeed in Hollywood on a Hundred-fifteen Dollars a Week. And think how pleased he'd be if I hid my fat behind in a girdle.*

She got Markal's office, buzzed and hung up. She lit a cigarette and inhaled deeply. They either flipped over Mrs. Carny or were nauseated. Carl was nauseated, but only a little. The football player turned actor in Carl's last movie had been nauseated a lot. Most actors, in fact. She'd had better response from the female of the species – that old dyke Marla Troy, for example. Still dropped in every so often. Still threw out baited lines.

Sick of it. Sick of it.

She took her paperback copy of Waugh's *The Loved One* from the drawer. She had read it twice before, but when the black spell was on her she wanted something that razed Hollywood to the ground.

Carl came out and said he would be with Eli Charabond. 'We'll be shooting in three months, mark my words.'

She marked his words, and returned to reading Waugh.

Charles Halpert came in, holding Carl's story. 'He's gone,' she said, and wished it had been him and not Devon. The first experience outside the marriage vows should have been planned, should have meant something. 'He probably won't be back until after lunch. How did you like it?'

'Well, a discernible basic idea, but it needs ... character development, plot, suspense, humor, excitement and a denouement. Also, credibility.'

She laughed. 'Outside of that it has everything.'

He pushed a smile. 'I hope Mr. Baiglen doesn't expect ...' His voice ran out and so did his smile and he stood there, staring down at the story.

'Mr. Halpert,' she said, 'Carl expects exactly what you're doing – tearing his story apart. He'll be delighted, if you can put it together again, your own way, the right way.'

'How do I find a writer around here?'

44

'His name?'

'Lars Wyllit.'

'Avalon's Dalton Trumbo? You just ask. But I'll get the number for you.' She dialed once, said, 'Could I have Larson Wyllit's extension, please?' and wrote on a pad.

He came to the desk and took the slip of paper. 'I'm in your debt.'

'Let's think of a payoff.'

'I'm rich in everything but cash.'

'We'll keep that in mind.'

He finally smiled, and walked out. She returned to *The Loved One*, but Waugh's humor seemed too cruel and she put the book away. She went to the water cooler and the storage compartment where she kept her lunch – a scrambled egg sandwich on roll, a large portion of camembert and a banana. She decided to skip the cheese and banana.

She was eating when the phone rang. She checked her watch, and steeled herself. 'Mr. Baiglen's office.'

'Come home for lunch, Cheryl. I've got something good and hot for you.'

'I'm in the middle of dictation,' she said, and hung up on his laughter, his soft, raspy laughter, his laughter that had nothing to do with things that were funny or even sane.

She ate the camembert and banana.

LARS WYLLIT

Lars had smoked twenty-six cigarettes, down to the filters, since nine this morning. Twenty-six cigarettes in two and a half hours, breaking his own record. He could almost feel the cancer cells multiplying in his lungs. He could almost feel his heart beginning to spasm under the deadly overload of stimulation ... but this last was too real, too close to the truth for him to consider for more than a split second, even though he had been flouting its reality in every phase of his life.

'Only big men die of heart attacks,' he said to his typewriter. 'Big dumb bastards with big dumb faces.'

He poised his fingers over the keys and said, 'Here we go, Lars baby, think!'

He thought ... of half a dozen girls, putting each one through his sexual fantasy machine until even he, the greatest

45

sex maniac (self-proclaimed) since Jack the Ripper, was repelled. He then turned to exploratory visions of plump boys
and Krafft-Ebing chickens, but failed to achieve loss of tension.

He was on page two of what must eventually become a hun-
dred-fifty- to two-hundred-page script. He had been on page
two for six and a half working days and one weekend. He felt
he would be on page two until the new ice age arrived and a
glacier moved across Southern California, driving him (relieved and grateful) from his typewriter into what would certainly be a far less hopeless situation. Or until Moe Sholub
informed him that he had bombed out, the honeymoon was
over, Avalon Pictures in general and Sholub-Byrne Productions in particular no longer had need of his services and his
option wasn't being renewed and he could pack his inspira-
tional wall art, office exercise kit and carton of throat lozenges
and clear out. Back to television, and after a while he would
dry up there too; then back to New York and the cold-water
flats and two cents a word for articles in *Hardwood Furniture
Monthly* and *Soft Goods Review*.

The phone rang. He said, 'Thank you, Odin,' and picked it
up. He listened, and his hard ferret-face changed. 'Chuck
Halpert? You're kidding. Chuck Halpert wouldn't leave his
acre of weeds and tumbledown shack in Hendrick Hudson
country, not for love or . . . well, if the money ran out. It did?
Good. I always hated you for being able to survive in that
monster print-shop. Where are you? On the lot? *This* lot?
You sonofabitch. Just because I owe you ten bucks. Must've
cost you at least fifteen in shoe leather walking cross country.
Let's lunch. How does five minutes grab you? Sure they're
open. Open at eleven-thirty and run out of tables by eleven-
thirty-two. If you were making a grand a week like me you'd
know that. Hang up already and let's go. I've worked so hard
this morning I'm hip-deep in paper. Of course, I'm standing
in the wastebasket.'

He paused for breath and smiled tightly. 'That's right, you
perceptive hulk. I'm suffering at the typewriter. Get going.'

He stood up, reached for his cigarettes, then muttered,
'No, not another butt until tomorrow after lunch.' He threw
the pack over his shoulder, went to a closet near the desk,
opened it and looked at himself in the long mirror he'd hung
on the door. Carefully, he combed back his heavy blond hair,
then just as carefully mussed it from the top, causing the hair

to fall to both sides and over his forehead. He stepped further back to take in his tight, oft-laundered green chinos and rich green velour shirt. 'Lars *bébé*, you're *très au courant*,' he said, and laughed at himself, a little bantam rooster of a man, five-two and whipcord-lean. A man old beyond his twenty-six years in experience, in toughness, in self-awareness .;. none of which did him any good when the wildness came and he was launched into what was known as his 'speciality act.'

He took a final look around, gave the Italian screw-you gesture to his typewriter and ran. As soon as he saw Chuck Halpert outside the commissary, he said, 'You got a cigarette?'

They sat in the large dining room at a two-place table, sipping coffee Lars had ordered the moment they'd walked in, smoking, talking about New York. Lars dominated the conversation, recognizing that he was enjoying playing the Hollywood Success for his old friend. (Or could he ever feel real friendship for a man as *big* as Halpert; gut friendship, not what went on in the head?) He tried to lower his volume, remembering Chuck as a decent guy, but the man bulked so large in his chair and Lars went on about his contract and his agent and the dough pouring in and really gave it to Halpert, dug his knife into the poor broke bastard.

Seven years ago, Lars had four stories published in high school and two in college magazines, and felt ready to make the New York literary scene. Collin Warner, who was Chuck's agent, had agreed to represent Lars on the basis of a single short story submitted by mail. He expected the relationship would continue that way – through the mails – for some time, but he didn't know Lars. Needing no further proof that he was on his way to fortune and the Pulitzer Prize, and desperately anxious to become *big*, Lars left a father, three older brothers and his unfinished college education and materialized, suitcase in hand, in Collin's Manhattan office. Collin had been surprised but not immediately daunted by the arrival. Lars quickly changed all that, daunting even the most hopeful and helpful of souls with a positive genius for failure.

'You were the object of my deepest envy,' he told Charley quietly, and turned to find the waitress. She was leaning against a partition wall that separated the dining room from the kitchen. 'Coffee, coffee, *coffee*!' he shrieked. She jerked away from the wall, startled, as were two other waitresses, the woman at the register and Halpert. Lars smiled sweetly.

The waitress stared at him, then went to get the Pyrex off the warmer.

'Wealth hasn't dimmed that bright gleam of insanity.'

'Wealth? Not yet, baby, though I'm surviving nicely.'

'That's exactly what I want to do, learn how to survive in darkest Hollywood.'

'Anyone who can write can survive in Hollywood. Almost all television is produced here. And most features are *written* here, even if a good many are being shot elsewhere.'

'Is that a problem? You hear that Hollywood is dying and the Europeans taking over.'

'It's no problem for me. The studios are busy doing what they're supposed to be doing, filming stories. The public still pays the bills, and nicely. I think it's like the so-called death of the novel. Whatever it is the novelists are writing – non-novels or fact novels – the stands are still full of them and the public still buys them. The same goes for Hollywood. So we're filming more hour television and less hour-and-a-half features. The writers still write, the actors act, the directors direct, the producers produce. We swing, baby, and you don't swing when you're dead.'

'But the Europeans—'

'Compete – in film festival circles. But Hollywood still rakes in the sugar, one way or another. Especially Avalon. Nat Markal is the man with the magic touch. The reviewers and intellectuals can predict doom, but only when the country rises up *en masse* and says we stink, will we be in trouble. How long do you think before that happens?'

Halpert smiled a little. 'Okay, I've stopped worrying.'

'You should. You can write reams around anyone I know. But I don't have to tell you that. You read your own reviews.'

'I couldn't find a publisher for my last book.'

Lars found it hard to believe. 'That bad?'

'I guess so. Collin didn't even want to send it out, but I was desperate.'

The waitress came and filled their cups. 'You're in good voice,' she said to Lars. 'You gonna call that way when the place fills up and Mr. Markal is at his table?'

'Haven't I before, when you were in love with another customer?'

She laughed and turned away. Lars patted her rump. She squealed like a teen-ager, though she was at least fifty, and the other waitresses looked and the woman on the register

48

looked and Chuck shook his head. 'Same old Lars.'

'No, not really. I make a profession of it here. The wild man. The eccentric writer. It's good for my image and my price.' He sipped coffee. 'How could you not know if your book was that bad?'

'I wrote it because I needed money, not because I had a story. I wrote it in a panic, and when I finished, I thought I had a novel about an advertising executive who lost his job, discovered he was unemployable and died over a period of six tragic months. What I actually had was my own fear, endlessly repeated; my own growing insanity, endlessly examined.'

Lars was chilled and looked away. Chuck said, 'Except for those three workmen, we're the only customers here. I thought you said it filled up quickly?'

'I wanted out of my office. It'll fill up about twelve-thirty. Then you'll see actors, directors – the whole spectrum.' He looked at the three men in work clothes. 'And they're called grips, not workmen.' He pointed to his right, at a wide archway leading to a smaller dining room. 'Some of the producers and stars have permanent tables in the executive section. Others wouldn't seclude themselves from the action if you paid them. But you'll see for yourself. You'll see it all in the next few months.'

'If I get past the outline.'

'The treatment. A feature outline is called a treatment. Get the patois. It'll help on your next assignment.'

'If there'll be a next assignment.'

Lars leaned back. 'That's the one sure way to commit suicide out here – cry insecurity. In Hollywood, everyone comes on strong. Not many people can do anything well, but all come on strong.'

Chuck nodded. 'I actually feel I can write scripts. Or did until I read Carl Baiglen's original story.'

'Baiglen? I didn't realize he'd gone into straight feature – non-teen-age or horror stuff.' The minute the words were out he realized he'd goofed.

'He hasn't, as far as I know. I'm on a horror story.'

'A snap. And with that first feature credit you'll get something better. Who's your agent?'

'Ben Kalik.'

'Good man. Very strong in television. You'll be making big money inside of a year.' He was going to dish out more

49

encouragement when Terry Hanford came in. Instead of Mona Dearn, she was escorting a little Eurasian number, who swung by without benefit of undies and had the three grips twisting around like pretzels. Lars enjoyed the show, but his eyes were mostly for the auburn-haired publicist. She seemed to grow lovelier, cooler and more desirable by the day. She didn't say hello, but that might have been because she didn't see him.

He let her get clear across the room, enjoying the way her neat figure moved alongside the undulating sexpot's. Terry knew how to dress, knew how to walk, knew everything a lady should know, and she wasn't more than an inch or two taller than he in her high heels. As she reached for a chair, he jumped up. 'Oh Miss Terry, ma'am,' he called, his high, sharp voice snapping her head around. Other heads turned too; there were now a dozen or more people scattered around the restaurant. 'You reached the age of consent yet, or do I have to wait another few years?'

She smiled a little, flickering her pale eyes over his small, tight frame, up and down, up and down. 'Any day now for me, son. When do *you* make it?'

He felt himself beginning to flush, heard the titter move across the room, said, 'Whenever I can, Red. Whenever I can.'

A grip guffawed. Terry colored deeply and turned her back. Lars seated himself, pleased that he'd put her down. But he wasn't pleased about anything else, felt real edgy in fact, and when the heavyset guy with the crewcut walked past, glaring at him, he reacted swiftly. 'See something you don't like?'

Crewcut went on, face dour and haughty. Lars felt the twin pulses begin to pound in his temples. Halpert was saying something, but he didn't hear and he didn't care and he was coiled in his chair, ready to go for that big prick and rip his guts out and change that *look* on his face to fearful respect for Larson Wyllit.

Crewcut went to Terry Hanford's table and took a chair. He had a fullback's build, though he wasn't too tall – five-eight or nine. He leaned toward Terry, who sat with her back to Lars, and smiled and spoke. Terry's head moved and Crewcut turned toward the Eurasian sexpot and said something. The three began to chat cozily. Lars was still burning, but Crewcut never glanced his way and Chuck was tugging at his sleeve.

'All clear?' Chuck murmured.

Lars didn't like that ... but realized there was little he would like at the moment. He nodded.

'What're you working on, besides the young lady?'

There was something *elderly* about that question, something elderly about Chuck himself – heavier than five years ago and his eyes so uncertain looking. Weakness. Lars had no patience with weakness.

'I'm doing *The Streets at Night*.' He saw the brown eyes flicker, the head tilt slightly in involuntary homage. *Streets* had been last year's biggest novel, on the *Times* list over forty weeks. 'Before that I did *Twice Around the Cell*. My first for Avalon was *Moribund*.'

'You must've sacrificed much young flesh to Odin for receipt of *those* kudos.'

Lars smiled, pleased that Halpert remembered the old gag about his worshiping the Norse god. 'No, the sacrifices were made in Frigga's name.'

For the first time Halpert really laughed. 'You'll forgive this infidel—'

'You're forgiven. And while you're here ... By the way, the family with you?'

'No.'

'Expect them soon?'

Halpert took a moment before answering. 'Not too soon.'

'Then do a little frigging yourself. This is *the* town for it.'

'So I've always heard. But I thought it was publicity, or sour grapes.'

'What you've always heard is movie stars at wild orgies. What I'm talking about is girls, beautiful young girls. The town is loaded with them. And with minor exceptions they function according to an advanced sexual morality. Dig?'

'I dig. How did you break into features?'

Lars accepted the abrupt change of subject. If Halpert was a sexual repressive, as so many New York Jews were, tough for him. But he couldn't resist pointing to the basket of assorted crackers on the table. 'We have matzos for the fanatics.'

Halpert broke off a piece and nibbled. 'What's the occasion. Or do they always serve them?'

'Always. The minority status is reversed at Avalon. I've done everything but have myself circumcised to assimilate.'

'In your case,' Halpert murmured, 'circumcision isn't necessary. Abnormal wear and tear—'

51

It broke Lars up ... but he was still aware of Terry Hanford sitting there with her back to him and that crewcut bastard yokking it up with her. He didn't hear Halpert's question, and looked at him inquiringly.

'I'm still waiting for the details of your success story. Did you go directly from New York to Avalon?'

Lars shook his head. 'Before Avalon I had two years in television. Before that, eight months in a little room off LaBrea – no car and no work and New York all over again.' He smiled, but inside he remembered and there was no smiling. 'A sunny little hell—'

The stocky, suntanned man came up from behind, stuck his face in front of Lars's and grinned. 'When am I going to get that first fifty pages of script?'

Lars introduced Moe Sholub to Halpert, annoyed at Sholub's approach. 'As for your script, you'll get it when I can scale my talents down to a level low enough for your particular audience.'

Sholub laughed and patted Lars's shoulder. 'My angry young writer.' To Halpert: 'But he's good. The best.'

'We've known that a long time in New York.'

And then, before Lars could see it coming, Sholub said, 'You ever read his *Whistling on Third Avenue*?'

It was too late to talk fast now. He just had to sit it out; look natural, turn to Chuck, wait for his answer. Chuck shook his head.

'In his prize-winning anthology. Beautiful. Just like Lars himself.' He walked away.

Lars waited for questions. They didn't come. Chuck Halpert was looking around the commissary.

'I had it printed privately soon after I began making money in television. I added the name of a publisher. Alfred Knopf struck my fancy. And to ice the cake, I awarded myself the Pomery Ascot Prize for Short Stories in a banner across the dust jacket.'

'You must've had your reasons,' Halpert muttered, unable to hide his embarrassment. It infuriated Lars.

'You're damn right I did. Fifteen thousand reasons. That's how many more U.S. dollars I got for my first feature than I would have gotten if I hadn't been the one, the only recipient of the nonexistent Pomery Ascot Prize.'

Halpert nodded, eyes elsewhere. Which infuriated Lars the more.

'And don't think that anyone ever guessed the truth. Even my own agent doesn't know. Because basically no one cares. Out here books are crap – words to be boiled down to a plot skeleton and then refleshed for screen. No one really reads novels for the movies. They read *story*, skimming along and noting interesting twists and turns. Bestsellers are bought for their titles more than for anything else.'

Halpert nodded again, very briefly. 'I'm starving,' he said.

Lars was sweating with rage now. What did this man mean to him anyway? What the hell did the whole New York publishing *shmear* mean to Lars Wyllit, screenwriter? Two-bit littérateurs working at other jobs of starving. The pros were *here*, in the seventy towns that made up greater L.A., among the two thousand some-odd members of the Writers Guild of America West.

'They were better stories than the trash that gets published,' he said ... and then hated the line – the lousy, sour-grapes line.

Halpert said nothing. Lars twisted around, waving angrily at the waitress. He wanted to get back to his typewriter. He had things to prove.

They ate quickly, quietly. When the checks came, he grabbed both and walked away from Halpert's protests. He paid the cashier with a fifty and pocketed all but ten of the change. Outside the commissary, he shoved the bill into Halpert's handkerchief pocket. 'The ten I've owed you for five years. We're all square now. See you around.'

He knew his voice was sharp, his manner edgy, his entire personality aggressive and unpleasant. But that was the way he felt and he didn't have to hide it from Halpert or any one else. The world was his oyster – his big, tough, stubborn oyster – and he was prying it open with his own teeth, nails, and claws, and no thanks to anyone, no debts to anyone.

'Thanks for the lunch,' Halpert said.

'Sure.' He turned and went right back into the commissary. It had grown crowded, people lining up near the door for tables. He pushed his way past them, saying hi to those who said hi to him, and went across the noisy room to Terry. He bent over her from the back. 'Honey,' he said, listening to his heart banging away, 'can we get together later to discuss personal matters? My office?'

She was startled. 'Personal matters?'

53

He nodded, and raised his eyes to the Eurasian, who smiled prettily, and slid them flatly to Crewcut, who looked disapproving.

'Aren't you going to introduce us to your friend?' Crewcut asked.

Terry laughed a little. 'I don't know his name.'

Lars said, 'That's right. We've never been introduced. I'm Lars Wyllit. Now about that personal—'

Crewcut interrupted in decidedly unfriendly fashion. 'Picking-up is a fine old sport, but do it somewhere else. We're talking business.'

Lars stepped quickly to his side, looked down into his face, smiled, but not pretty-for-the-camera. 'Thus spake the big man.'

Crewcut's face turned red. 'And the little man should listen.'

Lars was glad he had said that. It made everything so much simpler. It pressed the button for the countdown. Oh, he would go off with a beautiful explosion!

'Why don't you follow me out into the sunlight where I can see the color of your blood?'

Crewcut began to rise. Terry said, 'Bob, please sit down!' Crewcut said, 'He was the one—' Lars said, 'Ten, nine, eight, seven ... I'll belt you right here, if I have to.' Crewcut got up fast, looming over him. Terry said, 'Mr. Wyllit, if you'll just leave us now, I'll be in your office at five-thirty.' Lars never took his eyes off the target. Crewcut said, 'Don't be blackmailed—' Lars said, 'Six, five, four, three—' Terry stood up. 'People are looking at us! Aren't you ashamed, Mr. Wyllit!' Lars said, 'More than I can bear,' and went into his 'speciality', He kicked Crewcut's left shin with his leather heel. As the man cried out and bent over, Lars whipped his fists left and right, with every ounce of will and rage and strength, up and into the square, massive jaw. Crewcut dropped like a stone. If he got up, Lars was ready with a judo jab to the short ribs and a chop to the neck. If *that* wasn't the end, it would get messy, with hari goshi and osoto gari and ground work. However, Crewcut was on his side, groggy, unable to rise. Lars bent quickly, helped him up and put him in his chair. His heart was thundering now, and he remembered the slogan his mother had authorized: 'Rheumatic fever at ten means no excitement ever again.' Perhaps if her meter had been better he might have paid it some attention.

He looked at Terry. Her face was so white he was able to

54

see a scattering of previously invisible freckles. He wondered if they appeared elsewhere on her person, say her saucy little breasts. 'Five-thirty then,' he said, and nodded at the Eurasian. She smiled, as calmly as she had before, and despite everything thundering around inside him he had the thought that this was a tough one, tough enough to make it.

He turned to go, keeping his eyes straight ahead, trying not to see anyone as he began walking past the tables, because now that it was over he was horrified. He had pissed on his own doorstep, as the boys back home used to say. Always before he had kept his 'speciality' for bars or the beach or occasional parties – and only when he had been certain no studio personnel were present.

He saw Moe Sholub in the doorway of the executive dining room, staring at him, shocked. Was Nat Markal somewhere behind him – Emperor Nat who had kicked people off the lot for far less than this?

The commissary had never been so quiet before. He walked through the silence, the almost palpable stares, a hard little man with a hard little smile on his face, telling them all to go to hell. He walked, it seemed, several miles before he reached the door.

He was entering his office when he felt the first stab of pain, dead center of his chest. He immediately turned around, thinking to go to the infirmary. The second stab was so strong, however, he stumbled back inside, and lowered himself to the couch. And waited, the fear of death on him. He lay there for half an hour, eyes closed. There were two more stabs of lesser intensity, and then he got up and belched and wondered if the pain hadn't been due to gas and an overactive imagination.

He went to his desk and made a note to visit the doctor tonight, then threw it away. What was the point? He knew what Feidler would say, what they all said. It amounted to his mother's slogan.

He started to work. He got right into the opening scene that had stumped him all week: a series of close-up cuts, Madge and Robin. He pounded out brief, brittle dialogue, the characters attempting to mask, yet subtly revealing animosity, curiosity, growing romantic involvement. He hunched over the typewriter and his fingers flew and his mind was deep in the characters, racing ahead to the next turn of plot. He worked frantically, brilliantly, because it was the only way

55

he could stave off the blazing memory of that scene in the commissary.

ISA YEE

Isa sat on a low stool in a dark corner of Stage 3, leaning back against the softness of exposed insulation that lined the walls of the enormous, hangarlike building. This was one of the oldest stages on the lot, in existence during the days of silent films, she'd heard, and the insulation was its soundproofing. Of course, some of the newer stages used exposed insulation, so she didn't know whether that silent-film bit was true or just Hollywood bull.

So much in Hollywood was bull. A good half of what you heard and read was phony. Half of what you saw too.

Take what was going on right now, about fifty feet away, past a tangle of cameras and cables and technicians and grips and floor-spots and chairs and actors and actresses. And Zig Shroeder, the director, and his assistant and script director, and others she didn't know and some who might be visitors, even though Lobo Stretch insisted on a closed set. For good reason too. Hollywood bull. He didn't want the outside world to know just how phony *he* was.

Waikiki Nights was in color, so the rafters high above the shooting area blazed with spots, perhaps a hundred of them, all sizes and all kinds. The scene, a Hawaiian nightclub, hurt the eyes, it was so wild with costumes and props of red, yellow, blue, green and dozens of in-between shades. Lobo wore a ballooning pink-satin shirt and tight yellow-brown pants and stood on a bandstand in front of his two sidekicks who wore black pants and yellow shirts with the name 'Lobo' stitched across the chest. The extras – those waiting to begin dancing and those sitting at prop tables – were only slightly less colorful. Nina Pearl, the female lead, was in her place at the table nearest the bandstand, sewed into a cocktail dress of silver sequins cut low enough to prove she had finally graduated from kid parts. And those blazing spots, millions of watts of light, hitting it all up. Heating it up, too, so that those under the lights were sweating, even with the air-conditioning.

Shroeder said, 'All right, everyone,' and jabbed a finger at his chief cameraman. 'Roll 'em!' The assistant put the little slate with scene and take number in front of the dolly camera. Shroeder turned to Lobo. 'Action!'

Isa leaned forward. Phony or not, this was the part that excited her, the moment when you fished or cut bait, the moment that could make you a star or bomb you out of pictures. Rock-'n'-roll musical or ten-million-dollar production or half-hour TV show, when the cameras began to roll you were on, you were alone with those glass eyes, you had your chance. Every second on camera was a payoff for the running around and shaking your can in producers' faces and smiling pretty when they handled the merchandise and waiting, waiting, always waiting for parts. Every second on camera, no matter how many other people were with you, was a personal introduction to ten or twenty or fifty million people. And if you didn't know this, if you didn't work toward it and make it your peak, then you'd never become Greta Garbo, Kim Novak, Monda Dearn.

The Lobo Trio began to play, the dancers to dance, Nina Pearl stood up and moved toward the bandstand. When Lobo and Nina looked into each other's eyes and Lobo opened his mouth to sing, Isa leaned back, the excitement dipping. They were such second-raters.

She fingered the thick mimeographed script in her lap, but didn't bother opening it. She knew her lines, what few she had. She was Kowali, 'a native girl who loves Lobo madly but knows she hasn't a chance'. She had two dance numbers, one a solo, two scenes with Lobo and Nina, and one meaty-scene in which she stood hidden behind a garden wall, listening to Lobo sing to Nina, and acted out the fantasy that he was singing to her, making love to her. About twenty minutes total on camera, and she was sure to lose part of it during editing, but she had known from the moment she read the script that the fantasy scene was a standout, that she could steal the picture if it came off right. And now there was the contact with Emperor Nat Markal.

She smiled to herself. What would they think – Shroeder and Lobo and that top-heavy cow Nina – if they knew Markal was sponsoring Isa Yee? Oh my, wouldn't she have a passel of 'friends' eating their hearts out?

But that wasn't the half of it. They wouldn't believe the most important part. Even Jerry Storm, her agent, didn't believe that the great Markal could get interested in her *personally*. Only little Isa knew the score. Only little Isa had caught that look in his eyes and known, clear down to her bones, what it meant. Whether Emperor Nat himself knew or not. Whether Emperor Nat planned to do anything about it or not.

She wondered if he had read the biography Jerry sent out on her. If not, he certainly would when he received her portfolio.

Markal was the biggest, the sharpest in the business. He knew how hoked up actors' bios were. How much of hers would he believe? Where would he begin to smile? And when would he sic his 'research' boys on her?

Born in the Galápagos Islands, sometimes called the Colón archipelago, Isa Yee was given a classical Castilian upbringing by her mother's patrician family, tempered by the warmth and wit of her father, Chang Yee, a wealthy Chinese merchant trader. On the tragic death of both parents aboard a racing sloop during a hurricane, the ten-year-old Isa was brought to San Francisco by her maternal grandmother. The regal matriarch died shortly afterward, leaving Isa in the care of the headmistress of an exclusive girls' boarding school. Isa excelled at her studies, which included voice, dance and dramatics, and absorbed American culture, language and tradition at such a rate that as graduation approached she received no less than three full scholarship awards to major American universities. Then sixteen years old, thoroughly Americanized, and already showing the exotic delicacy of form and feature, the extreme sensitivity of temperament that are currently bringing her acclaim, Isa took a week away from the halls of learning to think things out. It was at this time, while strolling along the beach at Malibu shortly after dawn, that she was seen by producer Gale Gardet, then associated with the popular *Tortured* television series. Struck by her ethereal beauty, he offered Miss Yee a role on the show. She accepted, and charmed everyone with her looks, her penetrating characterization of a Polynesian princess, and most of all the pervasive warmth of her personality. For having known loneliness, nineteen-year-old Isa Yee values human relationships above and beyond ...

She laughed. A young electrician turned and peered into her corner. The laughter still on her lips, she returned his look. 'The pervasive warmth of her personality' made him smile. In fact, he began inching his way purposefully through the maze of people and equipment toward her, so the next time he smiled she gave him a taste of the real Isa, a malevolent glare which froze his horny white balls and brought him to a full stop. Then she stared right through him at the set.

There were two Negroes working here today, the first she had seen on this job except for Emma, the make-up assistant, and an elderly man who had dispensed coffee before last Wednesday's six A.M. departure for location at Anacapa. They were extras, a couple, good and black so as to stand out. Every crowd scene these days was integrated, but nothing much had changed. Negroes still starved trying to break into movies. In fact, what with Freedom Now and Black Power and the new sensitivity there were fewer parts available. The servant roles were all going to Chinese and Japanese. Which didn't make little Isa one bit unhappy.

The Negro couple danced the jerk, along with the other extras. The boy was tall, well-muscled in his short-sleeved sport shirt, bullet-headed and broad-featured. He had strong hip movement, and Isa found herself wondering what he would be like in bed. Would he be bigger than a white or Asiatic? Would he go longer, stronger?

Not that she had much basis for comparison. It had happened just once, and then only because she wanted Jerry Storm for her agent. He'd been honored at being the first and was easily turned off afterwards.

But sex for kicks? Not little Isa. She had seen too much of that sort of kicks in her young life, and what it generally brought was bitterness and bastards. Sometimes even death. That brawl in the commissary today had shocked Terry Hanford, the publicist who had taken her to lunch, but it hadn't fazed little Isa. Men fighting over women? It happened all the time. Maybe even in the Galápagos Islands, sometimes called the Colón archipelago.

She sighed, fidgeted, wished they would finish shooting this scene so she could get before the cameras. That was the answer. That was the true path, the true kick. And today she was going to be right in the groove. Emperor Nat had to be reassured. Emperor Nat had to know his pleasure was good business.

Zig Shroeder called an abrupt halt to the action. He didn't look happy. But who could be happy listening to Lobo Stretch, *live*?

They began again. Lobo's guitar picked out the melody, the

electric and drums pounded out rhythm, the crowd danced. Nina walked to the stand and Lobo went into his vocal of *Hey, the Islands Swing!* He was awful, like most rock-'n'-rollers. No voice. No acting ability. Just a hoody kid with ten pounds of hair. Yet he thought he was Frank Sinatra. As if anyone was fooled by his recording live here on the set. That was where the Hollywood bull showed to worst advantage. Tonight Lobo would be in a sound studio, recording the same number fifteen to twenty times. The engineers would take over and begin working to build a single decent tape. They would pipe sections through an echo chamber, speed up spots for bounce, cut and splice sections from different tapes, hot up the accompaniment or dim it out. They would play around for a week until they got a tape that Lobo's mother wouldn't recognize. Then they would lip-synch it into the filmed sequence, release it as a record, and Lobo's loyal fans would pay off in squeals and cash.

But Isa didn't envy him. Lobo would fade, just as all the no-talent creeps faded.

She wouldn't fade. Just let her get up there and she would last until they planted her in Forest Lawn. Because she *did* have talent. Because performing was the one thing she did well.

It was getting the first break that was murder. 'The nineteen-year-old Isa' was actually twenty-two, and had been pushing hard for five years – a millennium of longing, and part of that longing was to wipe away the agonizing memory of Louella Walters from Dovenville, Kentucky.

She stood up, stretching her lithe muscles. She wouldn't think of Dovenville. She wouldn't lose her cool. No need for it, ever again. Nat Markal would see to that. She would *make* him see to that. Then there would be an apartment in Century City; and not too long afterward a house in Coldwater Canyon and a pool and servants, all blond, and reporters eating up the bull Terry Hanford turned out and two big features a year with directors like Wyler, Chalze, Lean . . .

'Isa Yee, let's go!'

Teddy Base, the assistant director, was paging her. She stepped forward and felt the adrenalin begin to flow and began to change, to grow toward that necessary peak of excitement. She moved past the tangle of people and cameras and lights and cables, and the young electrician looked at her and she saw him catch his breath because she was coming on strong now, her body flowing inside the Mandarin sheath, more exciting than she had been any time today even though she now wore a tight brassiere and panties for the dance number – more exciting because she was more *excited*. She came onto the shooting stage and looked up at Lobo and his sidekicks and Lobo gave her that special leer he thought so damn cute and said, 'Hey, baby.' She smiled at him with the feeling building, building, the feeling for the cameras and the millions of people sitting in the darkened theaters, the people watching her and wanting her, yes the women too, because she gave for them too, for all of them, and they would hunger for Isa in some way, want Isa in some way, love Isa in some way, every one of them. Emma came over and dabbed at her face with powder and then took her to the lighted table behind the stage and worked quickly, freshening eye shadow and lip paint. The lean colored woman looked her over and murmured, 'Just lovely, Miss Yee.' She went back to the stage, and Mike Fandem, the choreographer, gave his little talk.

'This is the first time you see Lobo, Isa. You begin to fall, and even though you've done your dance a hundred times before for Islanders and tourists, it becomes something special now. After the first few seconds, you forget the people at the tables and dance just for him. Lobo, you look at her and play for her, but you're thinking of Nina and how to get the money to help her brother. When Isa turns to you after her number, you really don't see her. And that murders you, Isa.'

He went to the table area and was joined by Zig Shroeder and they talked and moved people around and she saw the colored couple, the girl watching Fandem and Shroeder the way most of the extras were, the boy looking right at Isa, his eyes glinting, reflecting one of the standing spots that hadn't been killed. She turned away from him and looked into the center camera. She waited, her pulses pounding and her heart pounding and the blood pounding up through her veins, waited and turned to the left camera and the high camera.

Teddy Base called out and all the spots went on and she could no longer see beyond the cameras. The chief cameraman came forward and looked around and went back. There were still some murmuring voices as she walked left to the blind area where she would make her entrance and Teddy Base shouted, 'Quiet and roll it!' The prop man held up his slate and withdrew. It grew dead and still and everything waited. Isa closed her eyes against the terrible glare and

61

heard Shroeder say, 'Action!' and the music began – rock-'n'-roll Hawaiian with a strong drumbeat. She didn't care about the music. All she needed was the drum. Lobo said, 'Now a girl all you regulars of the Club Mangrove know and admire, the lovely *Kowali*!' The music grew louder and she counted to three and slid forward, opening her eyes.

She was Kowali, looking up and seeing her dream of love in Lobo. The coarse kid with the insinuating grin and the cheap line of chatter disappeared and he was a man above all men, a desire beyond all desires. She danced for the club audience, but all the time she knew Lobo was behind her and she took advantage of the movements of her dance to snatch glimpses of him. The tempo of the part hula, part jerk, part musical-comedy-modern decreased and she came to a virtual standstill under the bandstand, her hips and belly undulating slightly. The guitars cut out and the drum alone sounded, muted and anticipatory. Slowly, its beat and volume began building, and slowly her hip and pelvic movement built along with it. Now the central and high cameras were moving in on her, the first on its dolly, the other on its skeletal metal boom. She put back her head, exulting as she felt her command of the medium, her control of the scene. She looked up into that camera hanging in air, looked into its milky glass eye, which was the eyes of all the millions who would watch her, lust after her, love her. Her pelvic movement grew stronger, more abandoned, though always within limits. These limits were like bones under her skin – she didn't have to think of them to operate according to their structural rules. She knew just how far she could push those rules, and when the drum reached the height of its volume and wildness she pushed to the very edge of acceptability.

Now there was a dampness between her legs. Now the pulsing and passion were barely within control. She lowered her head and looked into the central camera. Her arms rose and her body writhed and she begged to be taken, the asking directed at Lobo, and at Nat Markal who would view the rushes and be gripped again by what had gripped him in his office.

The guitars entered, jangling harshly, brutally. Which she felt was right for the act of love. Which helped her reach the summit. Which finally wiped from her mind Lobo and Nat Markal and actors and technicians and everything except that thick glass eye of the central camera, moving in for its close-up. Which finally brought her to the biggest kick in the world, the moment in which she received the sexual attack of every man and woman who would view her.

The music ceased. She turned to Lobo and the left camera, and as she did she wiped away passion and substituted, subtly and swiftly, naïve longing. His coarse face looked down at her; his feeble talent formed preoccupation; he nasalized, 'One more time for the pretty lady.' Kowali turned back to the central camera, defeated, and her final ten seconds of dance was a retreat from joy and passion. She left the stage to the applause of the audience.

Isa walked directly to the dressing table and leaned forward and looked at herself in the bulb-lined mirror. Shroeder called, 'Cut! That's it. Print it! A *fine* take, Miss Yee!' Someone else said, 'Wild!' and there was a general hubbub as they prepared for another nightclub scene. She didn't care very much *what* they thought because she had known how good it was all along.

She was suddenly very tired and wanted to sit down at the mirror a moment. But she remained standing, bending over the chair as she wiped cosmetics and sweat from her face with cleansing cream and a square of cotton. Unless Emma brought her to the chair for an important bit of preshooting makeup, it was taboo, reserved for Lobo and Nina.

At that very moment Nina walked up and murmured, 'Excuse me,' and slid into the chair. Isa turned away, and Emma was there. The makeup assistant looked nervous. Isa said, 'Sorry about the dressing table.' Emma said, 'Oh, that,' and glanced toward the set. She spoke quickly, the words tumbling out, her eyes blinking and darting. 'My nephew, he's almost like a son, or he was . . . what I mean, Miss Yee, I promised him I'd speak to you, but only 'cause he's got this wild streak—' She faltered, tried to smile, looked miserable.

Isa said, 'I don't understand,' but remembered the Negro extra staring at her and turned to the set and there he was, sitting casually at a table, still staring. She snapped her eyes back to Emma, and the makeup assistant quickly said, 'He's a college man and he'll be a lawyer someday but now he's got these wild friends and wild ideas—'

Isa said, 'I'm really beat, Emma,' and, 'We'll talk some other time,' and began to move away.

Emma's voice was so tight, so unhappy, Isa just had to stop. 'I'm *sorry*, Miss Yee! I told him you wouldn't want to meet

63

him, but he said he'd come over anyway and I only wanted to stop trouble. You understand, don't you?'

Isa said, 'Sure, I was young once myself.' Emma laughed, grateful for the joke, and added in a rush, 'If he *does* talk to you, just you laugh 'cause underneath he's a gentleman.'

Isa nodded and headed back toward the chair in the far corner where she'd left her things. She was burning a little because where did that fool get his nerve!

She was putting the script into her large straw bag when she felt someone behind her. It was the colored extra.

He said, 'That was a marvelous dance, Isa.' He remained very close, and the chair and wall were behind her, and she put out her hand and smiled thinly. 'Please.' He stepped back. He smelled of aftershave lotion and clean skin and looked very tall, very strong, very black this close. 'I'm Paul Morse, Emma's nephew. I was wondering—'

'Didn't you speak to your aunt?' Isa interrupted, busying herself with the bag.

'No ... and you have to understand about that.' His voice was different, and she looked up at him. He was having trouble smiling. 'I asked her about you, and her plantation instincts panicked, and since she was once very close to me I couldn't say the hard things necessary to stop her.' He shrugged, and his smile grew easy again. 'I wonder if we could have a drink one evening?'

'I don't think so,' she said, as coldly as she could.

'I'm sorry about that.' But he didn't look sorry. He looked wise and knowing and sure of himself.

She slipped the bag over her arm and began to move by him; then felt a quick, light pat on her backside and whirled, shocked speechless.

He took out cigarettes. 'Smoke?'

'I could have you thrown off the lot for that!'

'Maybe beaten up too?' he murmured, unsmiling but managing to look amused.

'Maybe.'

'Maybe lynched?' He lighted his cigarette.

She turned away. 'You're no credit to your race.'

'But I *am* a credit to U.S.C. We were taught to be democratic there. Eurasian girls are every bit as good as colored girls, we were taught.'

She walked off, heart pounding more wildly than it had when she'd danced. She reached the heavy inner door and tugged at it, and Morse's hand closed over hers, very black against her pale, pale brown. Before she could pull free, they had opened the door together. She stalked ahead of him, but waited this time while he opened the outer door. They came into brilliant daylight. He put on a pair of wraparound sunglasses, which made him look harder, older.' 'Mind if I walk along?' he asked.

'Yes, I do.'

'Don't like Negroes, huh?'

'Don't like fresh guys.'

'That's positively archaic. And psychologically dishonest. Every girl likes a fresh guy.'

She walked more quickly. 'Emma would be ashamed of you!'

'That's all right, I'm ashamed of Emma.'

She decided she was handling it all wrong. She had lost her cool, but good. So he'd patted her ass. She'd had it patted in just about every studio in Los Angeles.

What made this different was Morse's being colored. And it shouldn't make *that* much difference. (But it did, it did, and rage and fear and hatred and shame and feelings she couldn't even identify surged inside her and she tried to laugh them down and they wouldn't be laughed down.)

They were approaching the gate, Morse walking silently beside her, when she felt under sufficient control to handle him properly. 'What's the point of all this? I'm not going to have anything to do with you.'

'I was hoping you would.'

'And now you know it's hopeless.'

He didn't answer, and she finally trusted herself to look at him. His bullet head was turned to her. His broad-featured face smiled and he said, 'Nothing is hopeless between man and woman. Not until they've been married a few years.'

She almost answered his smile, then realized he was still working on her. The rage returned and she changed it to ice. 'I won't date a Negro.'

'Don't date me. See me in private.'

They passed by the guard, who nodded briefly at Isa and didn't seem to see Morse. Which was the way *she* should react, Isa thought, and at the same time despised the damned cracker with his red face and thick hands and flat blue eyes.

They paused at the curb for two cars to go by, and Morse took her elbow. She sighed. 'You live dangerously, don't you?'

'Not really. I never try for a girl who isn't blood.'

It hit her like a fist. She ran the last few steps to the opposite curb and part of the way into the commercial parking lot. He caught up as she reached her Corvair sedan.

'When you turned away from me on the shooting stage, I was sure—'

She got inside and slammed the door.

He bent to the window. 'You're really Eurasian?'

She put the key in the ignition and started the engine. She gave it a moment's warmup, looking straight ahead. He was a nothing – a college kid and an extra and a Negro. A nothing couldn't hurt her.

She backed out toward the clear aisle. He walked alongside. 'Paul Morse,' he said. 'I'm registered with Central Casting. You can reach me for lynchings or dates.'

She turned the wheel and roared backward, then forward so that he had to jump out of the way. Tires screeching, she shot toward the street and, barely pausing to look for traffic, off the parking lot. She drove up Gower to Sunset, and then west toward the Strip.

Her apartment was in a hi-riser south of the Strip, the twelfth floor of sixteen. It was expensive by L.A. standards (excepting the unique Century City area), but she had wanted something cosmopolitan and new, something better than the two-story places everyone else lived in. Even so, she didn't expect to live here very long. Century Towers was waiting. Coldwater Canyon was waiting.

She showered and dressed in a Japanese kimono and curled up on the couch with a cigarette and her copy of *The Squaws*, the novel on which Markal's production would be based, but after a few pages found herself looking around, vaguely unhappy. Oriental designs and gimcracks. Pagoda lamps and Chinese figurines and other junk. This place was about as real as Isa Yee of the Galápagos.

She tried to read again, then went to the closet and stood on a chair and got down the worn cardboard portfolio. She took it to the couch and unwound the string and her stomach contracted in the old bittersweet feeling. She didn't want to reach inside, but after a while she did and took out the high school program. She didn't have to read it, she knew it by heart. '*Spring Follies*, a musical comedy (copyright Yolo Productions) starring Louella Walters, John Lewin and Stanley Prevone.' She opened it to the cast of characters, and credits

66

to teacher producer, teacher director, teacher musical arranger. She fingered the yellowing paper and it was legitimate and real and brought memories. High school days in Chicago and Sue-Ellen and the beginnings of Isa Yee. Not the *very* beginnings. That had taken place in a library in Dovenville, Kentucky.

But there she was again. Memories of Dovenville weren't bitter-sweet, just bitter, and she didn't want to remember ... and in a perverse and human way she did.

She held the program and her face took on a drawn, solemn expression her Hollywood friends wouldn't have recognized. *She could remember as far back as infancy. Yes, no matter what they said. Smells and foggy colors ...*

The phone rang. She turned her head and looked across the room. It continued ringing, and her expression changed and she stood up and ran to it. She was rescued from memory.

It was Leonard Fry. She asked how things were at C.B.S. Television. He said hectic, and she well believed it. He was script consultant on a Western premiering in two weeks. 'Listen, honey, I was wondering if you wouldn't reconsider about dinner tonight.' She said, 'All right, you've convinced me.' He said, 'That's the spirit! I wish I could convince you in a few other matters.' She laughed softly. 'Keep plugging. One never knows.' Which was his reward for rescuing her from memory. Which would keep him happy – at least until after dinner tonight, when he would take her in his arms and kiss her and want her to feel more than she felt.

She returned to the couch and put the program back in the portfolio and the portfolio back in the closet. She read *The Squaws*, her dreams in command again.

Once she looked up at the phone and smiled in anticipation of another call that would rescue her ... from the *present* this time. A call she expected within the week, from Emperor Nat Markal.

TERRY HANFORD

As a junior at Bennington, Terry had dated a local boy who was waiting to be called up for Army service. He was a graduate of Brown, sociology major; a tall, Lincolnesque youth with dark hair, shy smile and rumbling, hesitant voice. Every time

67

he kissed her she thought of Gregory Peck – which was very pleasant and led her to wonder if she wasn't, perhaps, in love with him. After five weeks and much mutual caressing of erogenous zones, they went to a tavern and did considerable drinking and close dancing. When they left, the die was cast. They would spend the night together at a motel. A few minutes later, the boy lost control of his car on a turn and they careened off the road and into a telephone pole. Terry was thrown forward, but managed to brace herself and didn't go through the windshield. She did, however, shatter it with her head. When she regained consciousness, she tasted her own blood and had a blinding headache. Moaning, she turned to the boy, then struggled out of the wreck and began walking up the dark road. She squeezed her eyes shut every few minutes, but it did no good. She could still see him, head twisted grotesquely toward her, mouth frozen open in a shriek, blood and viscera puddled in his lap ... impaled upon the steering column.

After three days' hospitalization, Terry returned to classes. She was rather subdued for a while, but then began dating again and soon seemed her natural self. Not until graduation day did her roommate, Marge Landreux, a psychology buff, question Terry about her feelings in regard to the accident. Terry postured broadly and orated: 'In the midst of life we are in death. Vanity of vanities, all is vanity. Gather ye rosebuds while ye may.' Marge felt it rather gruesome, certainly in questionable taste being that funny about it, but then again she didn't intend to see Terry except at reunions.

Marge could have used further training in psychology, especially the analytic end. Terry wasn't being funny. While the accident wasn't the sole or even dominant factor in the decisions she made during the next year and a half, it helped her reject a marriage proposal, break free of a mother who honestly believed Terry was all she lived for, and leave White Plains for Hollywood where a male cousin at Fox Western had offered to get her into the publicity department. Which in turn led to a three-year career at Avalon, triumphs with Mona Dearn and (or so she was convinced) staying single and living a life far superior to that of a Westchester *hausfrau*.

It was also partly responsible for the rage in her heart at the exhibition that little maniac Wyllit had put on in the commissary.

Bob had insisted on finishing lunch, pressing a handkerchief to his lips every few bites, but he had failed to hide either his blood or humiliation. Which was the sole reason, she assured herself, that she was leaving her desk in the Central Building and walking through the connecting corridor to the South Building, where Lars Wyllit was located. She would tell him exactly what she thought of him!

She had previously been amused by the oddball who grinned at her whenever they happened to pass, who looked her over as if he were planning to have her for dinner, who tried to stop her several times. But she wouldn't be stopped. She considered him too young, not more than twenty-four or -five, while she was only weeks from twenty-seven. And he was a pipsqueak — cute but kid-brother size.

She held that last thought as she approached Wyllit's office, examined it and wondered if perhaps the same kind of thought hadn't been in Bob's mind. Now that she looked back at the incident, at the moments immediately preceding Wyllit's eruption, she recalled Bob's speaking rather sharply, almost contemptuously to the writer. But she hadn't worried about it because Wyllit was so young, so small . . .

She slowed, uncertain as to how much of her anger was justified. Besides, she had to get over to Mona Dearn's. Two calls in the last half-hour, including complaints about an article in an exposè-type book, meant that Mona was entering a downsweep stage and needed handholding and reassurance. Not that *everyone* didn't, at one time or another, but being a movie queen was a larger-than-life occupation, and pain as well as pleasure, defeat as well as triumph, were outsize. She really should leave right now.

She suspected herself of chickening out, and went on to Wyllit's office.

His door was open and she walked in. He was slumped back in his chair, facing the typewriter. She was shocked at the change since noon. The pugnacious brawler was gone. This was a pale, sweaty, weary little man with dull eyes.

'Five-thirty already?' he murmured.

That ended the sympathy. He had actually expected her to come for a social visit!'

'It's only *four*-thirty,' she said coldly. 'Shall I leave before you punch me for disobeying your instructions?'

He rubbed his face and stood up and stretched; and while he still looked sick he smiled. His eyes gained life and did their

69

little man-trick, moving over her with relish. 'What a beautiful girl you are!'

'I want you to know why I'm here,' Mr. Wyllit.'

He came around the desk and fell rather than sat on the couch. He patted the cushion beside him. 'I know why you're here.'

'I don't think so.'

'To see me. To give in to the obvious chemistry between us. To let yourself go.'

'I was right. You don't know why I'm here.'

He patted the cushion again. 'It's you who don't know. You told yourself I'm a brute, a wild man, and you're going to give me a tongue lashing and all the time—'

She felt herself flushing. 'Why don't you pick on someone your own age?'

He leaned back and closed his eyes. 'Dirty pool, baby. Your instincts are sharp enough to know it's not "age" but "size" I'll read into that.'

'I had no intention—'

He opened his eyes again. She knew her face was flaming, and turned to leave. He said, 'Terry, I'm twenty-six years old, five-feet-two inches tall, very tired right now and not able to pitch in my usual irresistible fashion. How old are you? How tall are you?'

'Twenty-seven,' she said. 'Five-two without heels.'

'If there's anything I like it's an old, short woman.'

She fought a smile.

'Will you sit down a moment?'

She went to the couch and sat down. His hand lay between them, almost touching her. It was a surprisingly large hand for so small a man; a strong hand, thick in the fingers and big in the knuckles. She was very aware of it.

He said, 'I'm not sorry about Crewcut. I'm constitutionally incapable of feeling sorry for big men and what I do to them, even if I push them into insulting me. But I *am* sorry if I did anything to hurt my chances with you. Believe that.'

She kept her eyes from him, not certain how she should feel, and was angry at herself for the uncertainty. This was a difficult little man ... Scratch that *little*, for the love of heaven! This was a difficult man to handle. 'Do you know who it was you attacked?'

'If he's Emperor Nat's brother-in-law, please don't tell me.'

He had a sharp, thin face, the eyes were much alive now. Those eyes were hovering around her lips; then, deliberately, he dropped them to her breasts, her stomach, her knees. She tugged at the short skirt. He reached out and took her hand and said, 'Forget it. You've got lovely knees. You've got lovely everything. I've thought so for a long time.'

'I'm with an operator,' she murmured, beginning to relax. 'That was Bob Chester, script consultant on *Desert Marauders*.'

'Lucky I'm not doing TV at the moment.'

'Let's hope he doesn't have close friends in other Avalon departments. But whether he does or not, it makes no sense for a writer to create enemies in the business.'

'I've never made sense.' He was leaning back again, his fingers tightening on her hand. He closed his eyes and said, 'It's been a lousy day. Do you mind if I stop operating? I've done eight pages of script, but it's been a lousy day until about two minutes ago.'

'Well, I'll have to leave—'

He had his arms around her and was kissing her. Just like that – and she was unable to move, unable to do anything without fighting hard. And this didn't seem to call for fighting hard. She let him kiss her, watching as his eyes closed, then closed her own as the kiss went deep into her, a long, sweet kiss surprisingly free of demand. The kiss went on until she felt the change in him, and in herself. She turned her head away, and his lips brushed her cheek. His arm tightened around her shoulders and the other arm went to her waist. 'I've waited for this,' he said. 'A very long time, I think.'

The sweetness was still on her – the surprising sweetness, the enervating sweetness. But he was a man and this was an office and Terry Hanford played the game of life a different way. She stood up. His eyes pleaded.

'How's my lipstick?'

'Delicious. And unsmudged.'

She smoothed down her skirt and patted her heavy red hair and walked to the door. He said, 'Why don't we have dinner?'

'Duty and Mona Dearn call.'

'You play much nursemaid after hours?'

'Publicity, like history, is made at night. Besides, Mona is a friend.'

'I've heard that's what you consider her. But the truth now. Can an actor be a friend?'

71

She knew what he meant. They were a breed apart and the bigger they got the more apart they grew. But she and Mona were different. They had *fun* together. 'Yes and I haven't the time to go into nuances.' She opened the door.

'When can I see you?'

She hesitated. The kiss had been sweet and she liked him and perhaps the liking could grow. But she hadn't forgotten that scene in the commissary. Why look for trouble? What did she need a male prima donna for when she had Mona? And then there was Stad Homer who took care of dinners and, dancing and biological needs very nicely and whom she might even be in love with, or fall in love with. And there was faithful old Bert back home who sent cards on all the holidays and flowers on her birthday and loyal, pained, forever-yours reminders and whom she suspected she would yet marry if he made good his threat (promise, damn it!) to come to Holly-wood and not return home without her. And there was an occasional evening with a beautiful glamour boy who needed a date on half-hour's notice for some public function or other.

Mr. Lars Wyllit just didn't fit in. Her card was filled.

'You've taking one hell of a long time answering,' he said. 'If you'd like the help of a calculating machine to figure out all the pros and cons and come up with a scientifically balanced answer—' He stopped short and muttered, 'C'mon, Red, give two nice people a break.'

'I'll call you.'

His head went back and he closed his eyes. 'Like I said, a lousy day.'

She walked out the door. He called, 'There's weeping and wailing in heaven right now, in the department where those perfect matings are made.'

'That's *marriages*,' she said, laughing, and headed for the South exit which would let her out near the parking area.

Mona Dearn lived in a pink Mediterranean villa up a long tortuous street in a part of town no longer high fashion: Hollywood Hills. But it had more of a view of Hollywood itself – its street and people – than the new posh spots of Bel Air and lower Sunset and Coldwater Canyon. Besides, Terry had strongly recommended the house after their three-month search *because* Mona would be the only major star in the area. It gave her exclusivity, and lent itself to news stories of her appreciation of age and tradition, common enough in the New England area, but a rarity in Southern California where

72

age and tradition were more often associated with poverty than stardom.

The exterior of the villa had been allowed to retain its original personality, but not the interior. Terry had hated to change those cool, lime-green rooms, despite Mona's couldn't-care-less attitude about anything not directly concerned with advancing her career. Once begun, however, it *had* been fun. Elliot Tresh, the decorator, had shuddered at the black kitchen, but it produced dozens of magazine articles and three pages in *Life* – 'Black Humor in the Black Kitchen of Mona Dearn'. They had made up a black dinner to go with it, and black drinks too! The polka-dot bedroom had been Mona's idea, based on memories of a cloth doll. It was too patently sentimental to do well anywhere but in the movie mags. (Mona's Polka-dot Dolly Still Rules Her Heart.)

Terry pulled her Mustang into the driveway, shifted into low and went up the twenty percent grade toward the three-car garage. Mona's MG, Continental and Rolls were inside, and on the large blacktop circle were two other cars – a blue Caddy and a black Chevy sedan with MD plates. The Caddy belonged to husband Number One, Peter O'Dunough, who the trade reported was on his way to location in Tahiti. What he was doing here Terry couldn't imagine, but this in conjunction with that unknown doctor's car gave her a sudden intimation of Vermont-type disaster.

She hurried to the flagstone path leading around front, and met Buddy, the colored chauffeur-handyman. He was standing there, moving his feet as if torn between going to the front door and to the cottage out back where he lived with his wife Lena, the cook and maid. 'What's going on?' Terry asked, smiling to take the curse off.

'I don't know. Miss Dearn shut herself up in her room a few hours ago. Lena let in Mr. O'Dunough and he went to Miss Dearn. A little later this doctor we don't know drives up and he's in there now.'

Terry ran to the door. It was locked, and she pressed the bull's-head knocker. The theme from the *Pathètique*, which she had chosen as Mona's favorite melody, chimed inside. When no one answered, she kept her hand on the knocker and gave the door a kick every few bars.

'Enough, dammit!' O'Dunough's he-man voice bellowed. The door flew open and his dissipated black-Irish face glared at her from Olympian heights. He was six-three and built,

73

He was also a sot, a boor, a cad. She came in and he said, 'What's this funeral music attached to the doorbell? Mona likes Irving Berlin.'

'Where is she?'

'Her bedroom.'

She ran toward the back of the house. When she opened the bedroom door, she didn't know whether to feel relieved or not. The beautiful blonde lay with eyes closed, blouse open, and her chest heaved rhythmically. So she was alive. And no blood. But the doctor was too busy to look up, pulling a hypodermic from her arm, then placing a portable oxygen unit (with tank that looked like a large can of shaving cream) on the bed. Mona tossed her head and moaned as he slipped the rubber inhaler over her nose and mouth. 'What is it?' Terry whispered when he finally glanced at her.

'Heart attack, I'm told.'

Terry was suddenly weak and dizzy. She went down the hall to the oval Roman bathroom and washed her face with cold water. Her own heart felt ready to burst.

Jerry Storm was in the living room when she came out. A neatly built man with graying blond hair and moustache, he looked as self-possessed as always, ready to discuss his client's contract now that she had entered what he would undoubtedly refer to as her 'terminal' stage. He gave Terry a somber nod and continued listening to O'Dunough.

'—having a heart attack. I didn't buy it. I said, So why bother me, baby? You told Hedda Hopper I was a degenerate. She said, Just to say good-bye to someone I lived with, someone who took the sacred vows with me, or some such crap. I told her she'd lived longer with Carrew, her second husband. When she said our years together were the good years, the simple years, I told her she'd lived longer with Carrew *those* years too and the only reason I didn't bring it up during the divorce was that I refused to wear the horns in public. Instead of blowing her stack she said, Oh, it hurts, and then I heard something fall. She didn't answer me after that so I came over.' He tossed down a Jack Daniel's and poured another. 'She was out cold and I called the doc and then you.' He glanced at Terry. 'I called you too, but you weren't in your office. I figured the people who owned her should be around if she cashed in.'

Terry made a sound of protest.

O'Dunough smiled and raised the bottle, offering her a

74

drink. She shook her head. He poured a drink for Storm, who took it and said, 'No one except we three knows about this, right?'

O'Dunough shrugged. 'Unless she called someone before me.'

Storm chewed his lip. 'I doubt that. Whoever she called would have arrived by now.'

Terry said, 'Did the doctor—'

Storm went on as if she hadn't spoken. 'I'm sure she'll be all right. The important thing is to keep it quiet.'

Terry looked at him. '*That's* the important thing?'

Storm returned her look. 'Even Markal couldn't have known what a gem he was getting in our Miss Hanford. Did you ever hear of a sex queen with a bad heart? Men don't fantasize about women who may die under them.'

Terry kept looking at him. '*That's* the important thing?'

'The doctor is concerned for his patient's life. I'm concerned for my client's career.'

'Bless your little ten-percenter soul,' O'Dunough murmured, wiping an imaginary tear from his eyes.

Storm smiled and held out his glass.

Terry said, 'Mr. Markal should be informed, and I know he would want a specialist—'

'The doctor is Carlos Fletcher,' O'Dunough said. 'I've known him for years. He's a top cardiac man, not a Hollywood handholder. But by all means call in whoever you want. I've done my Good Samaritan bit for the year.'

Storm rose. 'If you take it on yourself—'

The doctor interrupted from behind them. 'Miss Dearn is in no danger. Not from her heart at any rate.'

They turned to him.

'I'm not a psychiatrist, or qualified to make neurological diagnoses, but I'd say she shows very definite signs of stress.'

Storm said, 'Do you mean that all this—'

'She took three sleeping pills. Not enough to really harm her. Certainly not an attempt on her life. But imagining, or claiming, a heart seizure—' He paused. 'What she said about this house and her work and her relations with people leads me to believe a re-evalutaion of her way of life is in order.'

O'Dunough chuckled. 'An act. I was right in the first place. A grade-Z performance.'

The doctor turned away. Storm said, 'I'd like to see her,' his voice tight.

'No recriminations,' the doctor said. 'Not tonight. Give me five minutes, then you can look in.' He left.

Overwhelmed by relief, Terry fled to the kitchen ... and stopped dead. The black walls were striped with wild, irregular swaths of white. Two spray cans were on the counter. She stared a moment, paling; then returned to the living room.

'Mona Dearn,' O'Dunough said, speaking into his fist as though it were a microphone, 'insisted on a black kitchen, and despite all that interior decorators and studio advisers—'

Terry began to cry, sitting stiffly on the pink-and-brown couch, fighting hard but unable to stop. This place was a Disneyland, not a home. She had always known it, but it had seemed such *fun* ... and while Mona was a little square to appreciate the gag she had seemed to go along with the idea that it was good business. She certainly had never indicated she *hated* it, was suffering from living in it.

'Don't let it bug you,' O'Dunough said. 'Mona's had it made for years. She could have stopped the black kitchens and funeral-dirge doorbells—'

'It's Tchaikovsky,' Terry sobbed.

'She could have stopped being a promotion and become herself any time she wanted to.'

'But first,' Storm said, 'Terry would have had to tell her who she was.'

O'Dunough grinned a little. 'True. They would have had to work it out at board meetings, and then Mona—'

Terry felt like a fool, but she cried even harder. She couldn't help it. They were kidding her – probably out of the same sense of relief she had felt – and here she was, bawling her head off.

Storm patted her on the arm, muttered, 'Sorry,' and went to the back of the house. O'Dunough stood up and rubbed her shoulder and then her breast. She told him to get the hell away. He said, 'Sure,' and went back to his chair and the Jack Daniel's. 'The only civilized people in the world are actors. *Big* actors. I mean the men. Because we know life and death are shit, and only screwing and drinking make sense.'

Terry stopped crying. 'You can't believe that.'

'But I do. That's why I won't cut my wrists or take sleeping pills or play at heart attacks.' He paused to drink. 'It was an abortive suicide attempt, you know. A first step.'

She stared at him. 'Suicide?'

He took out cigarettes and used his lighter for both of them.

After inhaling, she said, 'How could it have anything to do with suicide? The doctor said three pills weren't enough to harm her.'

'Death wish, baby. Wanted to see how we'd act at her wake. Wish is father to the act. Suicide has to start somewhere.'

Storm came in. 'She's fine,' he said flatly.

O'Dunough stood up. 'Then I'm off. Have to take a plane out over the broad Pacific to the land of the wild wahines. Aloha, or whatever the hell they say in Tahiti.'

'Which reminds me,' Storm said to Terry. 'How did you like Isa Yee? Markal said you'd be able to devote some time—'

'Stop it!' Terry whispered, clenching her fists. 'Mona did something frightening today!'

'Not really. Dr. Fletcher said the faint was just a mild neurological reaction.'

'I don't care what he said.' She glanced at O'Dunough for support. 'She took three pills. She experimented with suicide. The next time—'

'There won't be a next time,' Storm said. O'Dunough was already moving toward the door, checking out of the discussion. 'She'll have someone with her day and night, at least until this period of depression passes. And a few sessions with a good analyst. *And* we'll change the color of that damned kitchen.' He paused. 'You've gotten all the play out of it anyway, haven't you?'

Terry walked toward the foyer.

'You coming?' O'Dunough asked Storm.

Storm said, 'Terry, why don't you move in with Mona awhile?'

Terry kept walking. She turned the corner and reached the master bedroom. The doctor was just closing an aluminium valise. He was thin and rumpled and sour-looking. Mona looked better than he did, though her hair was matted cornsilk, her broad Swedish face oily and sullen. 'How do you feel?' Terry asked.

Mona stared up at the ceiling. 'All right.'

Terry looked at the doctor. He pointed at a bottle on the night table. 'One tablet every four hours to relieve tension.' He picked up his case and moved past her into the hall. 'Be right back,' she said to Mona, and followed him.

'She won't be left alone?' the doctor asked.

'No. She has a maid. And I'll stay awhile.'

'This isn't for publicity, is it?'

Terry was shocked. The doctor shrugged and walked away. She saw him to the door, then returned to the bedroom. Mona was sitting up. 'Don't ask any questions,' she said. 'I thought I was dying. Or maybe that no one would care *if* I was dying. Did anyone care, Forget it. I was sitting in the kitchen and I suddenly thought how much I hated black and I got the paint cans ... You saw?' Terry nodded. 'I took a sleeping pill and called you and took another pill and called you again and took the third pill and called Pete. He really bugged me ... you know how he is ... and I felt the pains in my chest. They got worse and I fainted. I'm fine now.'

'We were terribly worried, Peter, Jerry and I.'

'I wish I was working. I can't wait four months for the next picture. I want Jerry to see Markal and insist—'

'After you have a long rest, and see a good doctor.'

'I just saw a doctor.'

'A psychiatrist.'

'Uh-uh, no headshrinkers.'

'Mr. Markal will insist.'

'Markal's not going to know.' Her voice was suddenly firm. 'I don't want Markal to know.'

'Jerry—'

'Is my agent and I'll handle him. Let's have a drink.'

'Alcohol and sleeping pills don't mix.'

'Always protecting the investment, aren't you?'

'That's not fair,' Terry whispered.

Mona took a deep breath. Maybe not with *you*, honey, but lately I get so damned tired—' She shrugged and slid to the edge of the bed. She was wearing a pale blue robe spotted with sputum or vomit. It parted and her long perfect legs emerged. She stood up and said, 'Ugh!' and tore off the robe. She walked to the attached bathroom, nude except for a cheap snake bracelet on her left arm. Terry recognized it as a gift from Lou Grayson, with whom Mona had appeared in a feature just after Grayson had cut loose from his vocalist partner, Mamie Lanns.

Funny business, Terry thought, Mona wearing that piece of junk. Grayson had handed them out by the gross that year, and everyone at Avalon knew how his female co-workers were pressured into earning his little gratuities. The Grayson touch in films and TV was childlike, but in real life he was about as childlike as a hand thrust under a dress, which was his usual opening gambit. Terry herself had been 'invited' into the large portable dressing room, then told it was either put out or get off the production. Grayson had been annoyed that he'd had to state what everyone was supposed to know before accepting a job on a Grayson feature, and that included nonacting personnel. So she'd gone to Markal's office to ask to be relieved of her assignment. Markal's secretary, Bertha, had been most helpful, keeping her from a confrontation with Emperor Nat, telling her to go on about her other duties and see what happened. Markal had never alluded to the incident (Grayson had already become an independent and one of the biggest money-makers on the lot), but it seemed to Terry that her career had begun to accelerate after that.

Mona turned. Terry found herself uncomfortably aware of Mona's nudity. 'That bracelet,' she said, to say something.

Mona raised her wrist. 'Lou Grayson.'

'I know. I was wondering—'

Mona gave a wan version of her famous crooked smile, a smile that made middle-aged men write fan letters. Terry wondered what those middle-aged men would write if they could see Mona now. Even *she* could feel a tingle of excitement at that big, bountiful body, that aggregate of fertility symbols. And thinking this she began to turn away. 'I'll get Lena.'

'No. I don't want her around yet. Make some coffee.'

Terry nodded and went to the door. Mona said, 'Honey.' Terry faced her. Mona said, 'You were wondering about this bracelet.' She smiled again. Terry's eyes fell and she wondered what was wrong with her. Not that she'd ever stood talking to a totally nude woman this way before. Embarrassing ... but still ...

Firmly, she returned the eyes to Mona.

Mona's voice became a whisper. 'I never tried it.'

Terry felt her face flame, felt her heart hammer. She kept her eyes and voice steady by an enormous effort of will. 'Tried what?'

Mona looked at her a long moment, then moved her shoulders in a tiny shrug. 'Lately, I feel that men ... in my *mind*, that is ... not that I really—'

Terry refused to bail her out with questions. She held herself still, held her vast embarrassment, and fear, in tight check. Mona was distraught. Mona wasn't herself. And even if she *was* herself, it had nothing to do with Terry Hanford who had never played girls'-school games even when she went to girls' school.

Mona looked away at last . . . at the bracelet. 'Part of what I was saying before. About being an investment. About being used. I was looking through my jewelry this morning and I saw this and I remembered what it was like with Grayson. Seemed to me it was the same with everyone.'

Terry relaxed. 'Come now. Grayson is the exception, not the rule. And you'll never have to deal with anyone like that again; not at your level.'

Mona's eyes were bleak. 'My level? They laugh at me.'

'Not the audience. Your last two pictures broke attendance records.'

'Why do they come to see me? Because I'm a great actress, or a great piece of tail?'

'Your charm, attractiveness—'

'Tits, ass and bedroom smile.'

Terry nodded, catching Mona by surprise. 'Yes. But sex is part of every woman's attraction. And every woman, when she's depressed, can say the same thing, and be right.'

Mona took off the bracelet and threw it across the room. 'I *am* depressed. Anyway, I was.' She turned to the bathroom. 'You're right. Every woman – Anyway, I've made them pay like they've never had to pay for a piece of tail before. That's something, isn't it?' She looked back, and her eyes asked for an answer, a serious answer.

Terry chose her words carefully. 'You've made a career of being desirable, yes. A great career.'

'Would you change places with me?'

It was Terry's turn to be caught by surprise. The answer was no, she wouldn't. There wasn't enough *pride* in being Mona Dearn, not for a certain type of woman. But she said, 'Of course. Almost a million dollars a year—'

But Mona must have read something in her face, her brief hesitation. She smiled that crooked smile and said, 'I'd change with *you*, honey. You're so solid. You know just what you want, what your life is about.' She went on into the bathroom and began to sing in her high, babyish voice.

Terry put up coffee. She found English biscuits and orange marmalade and set the table. She didn't look at the walls, and she didn't think of Mona standing nude and vulnerable, and she didn't think of her own confused reactions. She thought, firmly, of the truth Mona had stated 'You know just what you want, what your life is about.'

She *did*. And that was why Lars Wyllit and far-out sex and

80

other alarums and excursions would never be allowed to intrude on the even tenor of her existence.

NAT MARKAL

Nat hadn't lunched at home after all. On leaving the studio he had made a spur-of-the-moment decision, telling Bill to drive him to the Century Plaza Hotel. He did it in reaction to several things – one as nebulous as the feel and smell of sun on the black-leather interior of his custom Cadillac, another as specific as the speculative smile of a tall redhead walking towards C-gate. But the reason he gave himself was *The Eternal Joneses*. He needed quiet, needed uninterrupted time to think of his masterwork. He had to decide on a set and get it into production. There was room for almost anything at the back of the lot since the two old warehouses had come down and their space had been added to the sixteen acres of open ground. And that Spanish galleon could be dismantled an the huge canvas sky taken down.

Olive and Soloway had pushed for sale of the real estate to a development corporation, using Fox's sale of the Century City acres as a glowing example. Nat had resisted giving up any part of Avalon, though the chances of expansion of a major Hollywood studio were nil. Now he was happy the price hadn't been such that he'd have been convinced.

At the hotel he dismissed the chauffeur and lunched in the suite that he, as executive officer of Avalon, maintained on a yearly basis. While eating he glimpsed himself in the full-length mirror on the closed bathroom door across the room. His fine features and small hands and feet gave him a neat, almost delicate appearance. But his body . . .

He pushed away the dessert of strawberry shortcake and sipped his coffee black and unsweetened. He had always been big in the waist. From boyhood on. Not that it mattered. He was Emperor Nat and a portly, dignified mien wasn't out of keeping. Not at all out of keeping, he told himself.

But he turned from his reflection. The way he looked was something he preferred not to think of, something too close to the driving center of his existence.

He poured more coffee and lit a cigar, an affable man outside yet quite dour inside. A man who looked far shorter than his five-feet-eight because of his forty-inch waistline. A fat, cheerless man with a strong head that would have been nearly bald if it hadn't been shaved. A prideful, aggressive, compulsively active man who had driven himself all his life, worked twice as hard as most men all his life; who had recently begun feeling there was no longer any *reason* for him to work, and who had now realized that the answer to that lay in a capping monument of a movie, an undying memorial of a movie.

Three or four weeks ago, when he couldn't fall asleep, Adele had said, 'You've accomplished everything you set out to do, Nat. Maybe it's time you rested?'

The idea had given him one of his rare moments of panic. Do *nothing*? Why then had he worked so hard? Who would know him within six months?

Adele had mentioned the position offered him as head of a great Jewish charity. But it was a figurehead job. His name would be used to draw contributions. Besides, even occasional visits to that grim building with Kremel and Mrs. Beider and those sad-looking, refugee-type file clerks and typists would depress him. The set up reminded him of the old days when he had been an actuary for McDevit's Insurance, Lt. Downtown New York and the Automat and saving every nickel and dreaming every night. The terrible hungers. For respect and luxury and the friendship of important people, For beautiful women. (He wondered how much health he had wasted, tearing at himself to ease *that* hunger.)

Adele had been beautiful in her small, round way. She had reduced the hunger, and her father's money had bought Nat a piece of Zantaly, Inc., a theatrical promotion and publicity firm. Nat's drive and ability had done the rest. No better place to learn show biz than a promotion firm. No better way to grasp the essentials of box office than by publicizing films. Crap films at first, a few of which he had bought into because of their sex or derring-do, elements he had instinctively felt he could exploit; these followed by standard A and B releases from Avalon as Zantaly, Inc., became Nat Markal Associates. Then the first flyer: outright purchase of an Italian historical for peanuts. *Romulus and the Tyrants* had featured what was to become Nat Markal's trademark – a weight-lifter-actor tossing around villains against a background of heaving breasts. The heavy publicity and advertising, the massive investment in promoting what everyone thought of as material barely fit for Saturday morning television, the solid distribution and incredible net ... and he was on his way. Romulus had served him well. Romulus had led to some of the finest French and Italian imports reaching the American public, where before only small art houses had exhibited them. Romulus was still defeating villains and making money, in sequels.

He retained ownership of Nat Markal Associates, and Romulus ... but now it was only a small part of the Avalon complex. From start to finish, production to distribution, Avalon was self-sufficient. As self-sufficient as the giant studios of the old days, without control of exhibitors and theaters.

And he ran it all. Emperor Nat Markal, as the industry called him (with a little help from a publicity firm). Emperor Nat Markal, top man in Hollywood – in the *world*, when it came to movies.

He stood up and deliberately turned to the mirror. And turned away again. It wasn't his body, he told himself. It was his suit. It was wrong somehow. It made him look ... old.

Perhaps, he quickly amended, stodgy was closer to the truth. He was fifty, yes, but with his advantages fifty was barely middle age. A laborer was old at fifty, not Emperor Nat Markal. His father had been old at fifty and dead of a heart attack at fifty-two.

He didn't want to think of his father, and did anyway – Meyer Markal who had given his life for a few lousy dollars a week in New York's garment industry.

His father hadn't lived to see him in his full glory. His father couldn't even have dreamed of wealth and power such as he now had. Poor Pop ...

He went to the window and looked out at the incredible Century City view – a panorama of broad avenues and open spaces, dramatically interrupted by ultramodern hi-risers. To his left, twin office buildings and Beverly Hills. To his right, the huge Century Towers complex. And other buildings coming up day by day. Exciting evidence of the vitality, the promise of Hollywood and Los Angeles – or so he had thought on moving here from the Strip's best hotel. Now it left him cold. Now he turned from the view wanting something ... something else ... something different.

New York. He would be there soon. The change of seasons. Here there was always sunshine. He hadn't thought of it in a long time, but he missed the change of seasons.

He would drive up along the Hudson River and enjoy the show of autumn color, something people talked about that he had never done, that he had never had time to do.

And the great restaurants. Forum of the Twelve Caesars, his favorite, where he held his big press conferences, and where he would hold one for *Joneses* that would make the others look like nothing. (But not right away. Not this trip out. He wanted to be able to announce at least half the stars as well as director, writers, other name functionaries.) The Forum, where he ate sirloin in red wine, marrow and onions, and that fantastic dessert, crêpes of Venus with ginger and ice cream. The Four Seasons. Le Pavillon. The Colony with that rich, creamy pâté. '21' where the strawberry soufflé was a super production. San Marino, not show biz but with the best *langustine* and pasta in the world, including Rome. And thickcut corned beef and pastrami sent to his Americana suite from the Stage Delicatessen. And the Chauveron's gelatine of duckling . . .

He took out his notes on *Joneses*. He sat at the leather-topped desk and fiddled with his pen. That set: *Old Ironsides?* The *Monitor* and the *Merrimac?* Old hat.

The Empire State Building under construction? The San Francisco earthquake? No. Something never before done, at least than the public was aware of. Something that would automatically draw publicity.

Something Americans preferred *not* to remember?

He got up and turned on the television and found an afternoon movie. Big-name cast. Made in 1938. Producer won the Irving Thalberg Award some years later.

Rumor had it Nat Markal would get the Thalberg Award this year or not. A nice ribbon to tie up his career. The Pulitzer Prize of Hollywood producers. Five years ago it would have made him very happy. Now . . . he wanted something more.

He called for his car and returned to Avalon, where he worked steadily, further defining his ideas on *Joneses*, until shortly before six. Then he left his office. He drove the studio Imperial between stages and office buildings, drove at the prescribed fifteen miles an hour, stopping at all intersections, nodding at the occasional person high enough up the Avalon ladder to greet him. Finally, he came out onto a huge lot, a lot empty except for a portion of Spanish galleon and a curved canvas backdrop of sky. They could come down. So could the old workshop building currently being used as a maintenance warehouse. But even if the workshop stayed, this lot was big enough to hold any set, with proper planning for long vistas.

Johnstown and the flood? And authentic flood presented huge problems. Besides, the Pennsylvania disaster, despite its loss of two thousand lives, wasn't *historically* dramatic or important enough. Not for *The Eternal Joneses*.

It had to be something better. Something uniquely American as no flood or earthquake could be. Something . . . but what?

He left the lot and the studio with the question still unanswered.

CHARLEY HALPERT

Charley saw Carl Baiglen at four o'clock. They spent an hour talking, or rather he talked and Baiglen sat smoking and listening. He tore the ten-page story to shreds and didn't retreat an inch from his contention that, with the exception of the ghost-town setting and two characters, everything had to go.

Baiglen stubbed out his third cigarette. 'Everything?'

'Everything,' Charley muttered, frightened by Baiglen's grimness, but even more frightened of trying to do a script based on the cliché-ridden, comic-book story.

'You've got a plot to take its place?'

Charley was prepared for this. 'I think so. It's not really worked out yet—'

'Tell me anyway.'

Charley told him. It took only a minute, and when he finished Baiglen frowned down at his hands.

'That's only the barest outline, Carl. It would depend very heavily for effectiveness on a buildup of suspenseful scenes.'

'You have any idea of what those scenes will be?'

Charley stood up. 'I'll work them out now. A pretreatment—'

'No. Go home and relax. Don't think of it anymore. Come in early tomorrow and start fresh.'

Charley moved toward the door. Baiglen said, 'You feel you know what you're doing?'

Charley remembered what Lars had said about coming on strong. 'I know stories. I know character and action. I can make this an original and exciting script.'

Baiglen looked at him a moment, then nodded, 'I agree,

Your idea is unique.' He smiled. 'I like it, Chuck. I like it very much.'

Charley got his station wagon from the lot outside the studio, reminding himself that he had to put on the Avalon windshield sticker. Tomorrow he would drive right in through the gate. And begin to sweat out a horror story that made sense, that had reality, that he could work on without becoming someone other than himself.

He concentrated on finding the Hollywood Freeway. Once there, he followed the signs to North Hollywood, glancing around and in the rearview mirror at those incredible mountains – incredible because they were right in the city, amidst the streets and houses and people. Mountains all over this beautiful land. Along with the sunshine, they lightened his heart.

He had ideas for the treatment. Despite what Baiglen had said about starting fresh tomorrow, he would put them down tonight. Only then could he rest.

He drove east on Magnolia Boulevard, watching the right for the Bali-Ho Apartment Hotel. Six blocks from the freeway, he saw the sign rising above the street of one- and two-story buildings, the name in sea-blue letters, bracketed by idealized palm trees, far more lush and attractive than what he had seen of the real thing.

Last night when he had checked into the U-shaped, two-story brick building, the sign had been spotlighted in green and white. The twin entrances and open part of the U, which fronted the street, had also been spotlighted, and in at least six different colors. It had worried him. Where did one see a hotel or apartment house bathed in colored spots? A quick drive further down Magnolia, and a quick call to his agent's home to assure himself he wasn't in a cathouse district, answered his question: all over Southern California. And not only multiple dwellings. Private homes, banks, mortuaries, restaurants, cancer clinics and churches.

'Think of it as Christmas in July,' Ben Kalik had said, and Charley hadn't been sure enough of his man to laugh. 'A few weeks and you'll love it.'

Turning into the open end of the U, which was a driveway leading to the parking area and pool, Charley felt he already loved it. Once his family was safely transplanted, he would be a loyal Angeleno. And wouldn't Bobby enjoy the long swimming and fishing seasons, the warm weather ...

Thinking of Bobby was a mistake. His insides ached. He

86

hadn't seen his son in nine days. Previously, the longest they had been separated were the one-night abandonments due to office crises, or to vivid quarrels with Celia which required solitary healings. Once, a three-day abandonment, or lockout, when Celia had realized he wasn't going back to advertising after his two-week vacation; that he had quit and was going to try a fifth novel (the fourth being his unpublished adman book, *A Death in the City*). 'Leave,' she said, 'and either get a job or a divorce.' He was lucky. Collin was on vacation in Bermuda and had left the keys to his apartment with his secretary. On the third day, Bobby refused to go to school, so Charley was asked home that night. He and Celia sat at the kitchen counter and talked and talked. He insisted he had a great idea for a bestseller and she looked into his eyes and his eyes dropped. 'I have,' he said, 'but I think of all those books in the stores and libraries and I wonder how I ever had the gall to write novels and think anyone would give a damn.' Celia nodded. 'And they didn't give a damn,' she said. 'The unkindest cut of all,' he said, but she was right. She made sandwiches and Keemun tea and they didn't talk. Finally, after all the years of talk, they had nothing to say. The silence had lasted – except for the monosyllables necessary to existence – almost nine months. He wouldn't have minded, except that silence had set in at his typewriter too. He began sneaking magazines into his study, waiting for the silence to pass . . . but it didn't pass. He no longer wanted to write novels. Or short stories. Or anything else, it seemed. Three weeks of this and he began sipping bourbon to get through the days and taking sleeping pills to get through the nights. Another week and he began steeling himself for a return to Manhattan and advertising . . . 'a fate worse than death,' he kidded himself, without being able to summon up the faintest degree of humor. That Friday, Collin called and asked if he'd be interested in going to Hollywood on a small movie deal. Collin didn't recommend it. Five thousand dollars, if he completed all three sections of the contract without being cut off. No travel allowance and no living expenses.

Would he? His whoop was a whoop from the tomb. Call him Lazarus Halpert. A new chance to remain a writer. A new field offering new enthusiasms. And California!

Celia had agreed with Collin. She didn't recommend it. She wanted him back in advertising. He'd made twenty thousand a year as a copywriter. He could do it again. Traveling three thousand miles for five thousand dollars and not even being guaranteed the five thousand ... 'No, Charley, all it does is put off the day when you'll have to give up free-lance writing. Better give it up now.'

He hadn't grown angry. Celia had been talking of his giving up writing since the second year of their marriage. She didn't believe in writing, not for him. But he had grown stubborn ... if that was the word for the grasping a man does at the chance to live the one way he can live.

He parked against the tall concrete wall and walked to the ironwork gate and looked in at the pool and the sundeck behind it. He opened the gate, deciding to use the back entrance, and walked by two elderly women standing and smoking at the edge of the pool. One wore a two-piece bathing suit and had a fantastic body – a taut, young-woman's body with a shriveled old-lady's head atop it. She looked up as he passed and spoke in a whiskey baritone, 'Why hi stranger there.' He flushed and nodded and hurried on, feeling as if he'd had a sexy thought about his own grandmother, and almost tripped over a supine shape. He sidestepped just in time. A young Tarzan, perhaps eighteen years old, was sunning himself flat on his stomach. Charley noted the ridged back muscles, the powerful biceps and, surprisingly, the wispy black Van Dyke beard.

He would get some sun too. He would swim and tighten his muscles. Not tomorrow – all the tomorrows he'd been promising himself for years – but right now. He walked past the pool to the back door and up the flight of stairs to the second floor. He turned into the eastern arm of the U and walked along the clean, blue-carpeted corridor empty of smells and filled with piped-in music. His room was two doors away from the front staircase. He used his key and stepped inside, and music came from the little grille in the wall beside the door. He turned the knob under the grille and the music went down and off; satisfied, he turned it back up again. Just as long as he could control his own destiny.

He put his Avalon parking sticker on the counter separating the combination living room–bedroom and the tiny kitchen with refrigerator and two-burner hotplate. Everything new, everything compact, done in modern modern; very bright in blues and reds; very cool once he turned on the wall-set air-conditioner. He looked around his bachelor apartment with satisfaction and wonder: $87.50 a month with switchboard service and once-weekly cleaning, change of linens, change of towels. Old Ben Kalik was a wise old agent. (How old was he anyway? He sounded like a grandfather on the phone.) He had chosen this place for Charley. He had warned Charley against cheap rooms in private houses on the one hand and 'swing joints' on the other. 'Unless,' he had written, 'you want me to book you into a joint with ass?'

Charley had replied, airmail, that ass wasn't necessary. And so he had a quiet, respectable apartment with all conveniences ...

At that moment he realized there was no TV in the room. He checked around, and accepted the fact that Mr. Terrence hadn't delivered the twelve-dollar-a-month rental portable. He would have to drop into the office and remind his genial host. But first he would change into bathing trunks and put that windshield sticker on his car. And phone Ben Kalik. He wanted his agent's strong, grandfatherly voice to commend his actions today. He wanted support and advice.

He went down the front flight of stairs, out into the street, not embarrassed by bathrobe and zoris because this was sunland, funland. He went into the driveway and peeled the backing from the wet sticker and applied it to the inside of the windshield, lower right-hand corner, as per instructions. A squeegee by thumb and he stepped back to admire his work.

AVALON PICTURES
EMPLOYEE'S ON-LOT PARKING
PERMIT NO. 2224324

My God.

He returned to the street and went left, to the western arm of the U. Inside the double glass doors, against the left wall, was a row of three open pay phones. A thin girl in a knee-length towel robe, talking with a heavy Southern accent, was using the first phone. She stopped and looked right at him. He nodded. She continued to look at him, and through him, with eyes focused elsewhere. He went to the last phone and dialed Ben Kalik. A secretary said Kalik was tied up and would return the call. Charley said make that half an hour, then went to the office door across the small lobby. The card taped under the chime button read, 'Ring for Manager.' Before he rang, he wondered at the sound beyond the door. Like a stormy sea.

A woman's voice shouted, 'C'min!' He opened the door

and saw the color TV and Arabs on horseback attacking a troop of French Legionnaires. A re-run of the old half-hour *Desert Marauders* series, which was still holding down prime evening time in its hour format.

Yet he wondered why the television was on, and on so terribly loud, when the woman had her back to it – a big-faced, sullen woman with strange white hair who sat at a desk to the right of the door, a phone to her ear. Alongside the phone was a tilt-top panel of numbered buttons. She pressed a button with the rubber tip of her pencil, and he realized this was the switchboard service. She said, 'No answer from Mr. Amos. Yes, I'll tell him.' She wrote on a pink-slip pad and looked up at Charley, eyes gloomy. 'Yes?'

He began to speak. The *Desert Marauders* counterattacked. Charley raised his voice. 'Is Mr. Terrence in?'

'He won't be back until eight. I'm his wife. You got a repair?'

'A repair?'

Her mouth sagged hopelessly. 'Something broke in your apartment, Mr . . .?'

'Halpert. No, nothing broken.' He tried to smile, but she gloomed it out. 'Mr. Terrence said he would have a television set installed when I got back from work today. Of course, I got back rather early'

'All right. I'll see to it.'

'Apartment thirty-four.'

'I know.' Her chair swiveled and she was looking at the television. He said, 'Thank you,' but she didn't seem to hear. Good for her. She was buying *his* product.

He came into the hall. The thin girl was still on the phone, and turned so that she was looking at him again. He began to nod, then looked away, disturbed somehow. Mrs. Terrence and this fool girl, acting as if he wasn't really there. He needed someone to know he was there. A friend.

He laughed at himself. Two days in L.A. and he was lonely. Besides, Ben Kalik would call soon. Perhaps they would get together for a drink.

He swam the pool four times and was pleased with his performance, until the thin Southern girl from the lobby phone came out and dove in and began swimming effortlessly. She was joined by the bearded young Tarzan and he too seemed prepared to lap the pool the rest of his life. They were still stroking up and back, up and back, when Charley climbed out and lay down panting in a beach chair. His teeth chattered.

The sun had lost a good deal of its strength, and so had he. The return to a good life wasn't all that simple. Discouraged, he felt that he was pasty white and flaccid. Especially flaccid.

What if he tried to pick up a woman? A young woman. Someone under thirty. Like that Eurasian girl at the studio. Or Baiglen's secretary. Late twenties. *Zaftig*. Lovely face and hair. Big breasts. Big rear.

He felt a stirring and was assured that the flaccidity wasn't permanent. But what did she think of him? If she saw him now, saw him nude, would she like him?

It had been a long time since he'd worried about what he looked like in a woman's eyes. This new land, this new life, also seemed to demand new self-appraisals.

As he got up to leave, the thin girl emerged stooped and trembling from the pool 'Ah always overdo,' she gasped to Charley and shook her head in self-recrimination. 'Now ah got *craimps*!'

Charley felt sorry, but also somewhat reassured, and changed his mind about going upstairs. He did another three laps and emerged exhilarated. Back in the apartment, he changed and relaxed with a cigarette and a beer. And saw the twelve-inch television sitting on the dresser. Good Old Mrs. Terrence. He would watch the news and a few shows. But first he would get out his typewriter and put those ideas for *Terror Town* on paper.

CHERYL CARNY

It was as if she hadn't seen him in years, sitting there so lean, so handsome, with his strong arms and shoulders and long, dark face. She began to smile. So very handsome until he wheeled out of the shadow of the corner where he was pouring whiskey into a glass and said, 'Home is the bread-winner, home from the world of men who walk, home to the man of tomorrow, the man she created: *Wheelman!*' It was her Jim all right, and she had seen him this morning and yesterday and all the days before. And he wasn't handsome but ugly – made ugly from within, made ugly by her.

She put the package on the couch and went across the room and bent to kiss him. 'How are you?' she asked, and he turned his cheek and she kissed the stubble. He laughed in answer.

91

She made believe it was a fun laugh and went back to her package and into the kitchen. She took out the chuck steak – cheaper than other steaks and almost as good when you added meat tenderizer and garlic powder. She heard him in the doorway and turned with the steak in her hands. 'You hungry?' He drank and said, 'You bet.' She prepared the meat. She was starving. She took potatoes from the sack under the counter and washed them in the sink. 'Housewife and mother,' he said.

She didn't answer, praying he wouldn't start *that* routine again.

'Scratch the mother,' he said. 'Unless, of course, we decide on one of three possibilities: acrobatics, artificial insemination or adultery.' She went on preparing the meal. He wheeled away and she heard glass clinking in the living room. If he drank enough there would be no servicing him tonight, and he would be asleep early, and she might be able to get out for a walk. He came back to the doorway, the highball glass full, the liquid dark enough to be pure whiskey. She set the thermostat, turned from the stove and lighted two cigarettes. She put one between his lips, and he dragged deeply and jetted smoke. His eyes were growing bleary.

'I find acrobatics distasteful,' he said, 'even when they can be effected. Artificial insemination ... a cold business for a warm-blooded woman. Which leaves adultery the clear winner. It would provide you with the outlet every normal woman needs, as well as several important benefits. One, a chance to pick the general breed of child we prefer – say Nordic blond, Balkan dark or one of the more exotic varieties if we care to shop Semitic, Negro, Mexican, Oriental. And don't forget the possible financial advantages. You could command between twenty and fifty dollars a lay, more if you lost some weight.'

She set the table and took the half-gallon of California Burgandy from the cupboard. She poured herself a glass and drank gratefully. Cheap red with a lovely back-tongue bite that washed the bad taste from her mouth.

'But perhaps motherhood is not what you have in mind. Perhaps adultery for purely—' He mumbled, searching for the right word, and she said, 'Purely aesthetic reasons.'

'Yes, thank you – aesthetic reasons. Perhaps that's what you'd prefer? Perhaps that's what you've already accomplished?'

'Perhaps.' The smell of broiling meat filled the kitchen. She swallowed saliva and cut the long Italian bread into two- and three-inch-thick pieces so she could eat as much as she wanted without inviting his comment (as when she ate six or eight slices of white bread).

She heard the wheels and turned as he rolled up to her. He put his hand under her dress, and she was reminded of Devon. The memory didn't bother her. It was as if it had never happened. With Charles Halpert, on the other hand ...

It was a mistake thinking of him. She never knew what thought was going to be a mistake, but he was one and liquid steamed her eyes and pain choked her chest and she turned her head away. He dropped his hand, and wheeled out of the kitchen. Which meant he had drunk too much and she was spared this evening.

Not that servicing him was that terrible. After all, what was it? She had done as much of her own free will shortly after they married, led to it by a desire to love him, to experiment and enjoy him. If only he wouldn't twist her hair. If only he would say something human and loving.

The meat was done and she called him. He took his place at the head of the table and she served and sat down at the side. She hesitated, wanting to say grace, but he wasn't going to allow it tonight. 'Thank you, Lord,' he said, 'for all the wonders of this world. For the automobile and the wife who drives and the chair that wheels. Amen.' He cut into his meat. She cut too and tried to say a little prayer and found it wouldn't come. She ate. He had a few mouthfuls and crumbled a piece of bread and drank wine. He drank a lot of wine and his head sank low. She finished and reached over and got his plate. He didn't look up, so she quickly scraped his meat onto her plate and ate that too. After a while he looked up and waved his glass and she filled it with wine. 'The hospital sent someone,' he mumbled. 'Stuck needles and said be patient, change sometimes comes years—' He drank and his head sank again. She cleaned off the table and washed and dried the dishes and he sat there, asleep. She wheeled him to the bathroom and shook him awake. He had to go before she put him in bed. Otherwise he would have to go at night.

She helped him undress and when he was in his pajama top she helped him onto the toilet. 'My throne,' he said, rousing a bit. 'Get me another glass of something, would you?' She got him a glass of wine. He drank it sitting there and she waited outside until the toilet flushed and he called, 'Baby's ready, Mommy.'

In bed he sighed deeply and rolled over, his back to her. She began to leave. He said, 'My mother called today. I wasn't very nice. Would you write her and make some excuse? I couldn't stand it if she came here again. I really couldn't.'

'All right.'

'Cheryl, I won't go into the hospital. I don't care what happens, I won't go. You can't make me go.'

'I know that.'

'If it was for an operation or meaningful therapy, I would. But basketball in a wheelchair—' He rolled to face her. 'You'd give anything if I went, wouldn't you?'

He was right. 'Don't be silly.'

'Your life would become normal again. You would have friends, good times. But why should your life be normal when *my* life is the way it is? Why, when you made it the way it is?'

He was right again and they had been through this a dozen times. Any improvement in her life would have to take place within the current framework. 'Exactly,' she said. And then, off the top of her head, 'We're not making ends meet, you know.'

He grunted and rolled again.

'We need about twenty dollars more a week, and I can't get it from Baiglen, so I've decided on a weekend job.'

He was very still.

'I haven't begun looking as yet—'

'No,' he said.

'It's absolutely necessary.'

'No, I won't have it.'

'When we save a little money, I'll quit.'

'I don't believe you,' he said, voice muffled by the pillow. 'You want out. It's not money, it's me. You can't stand it here with me.'

Right for the third time. 'We'll talk tomorrow.'

'No,' he said. 'Not the weekends.' But his voice was shaky, uncertain, and she walked out, torn between joy at her victory and pain, guilt, pity. Not that victory was certain. He would return to the subject tomorrow, free of alcoholic fog. He would attack where she was most vulnerable – her guilt. He would work on her, and she would have to be strong to hold to the decision.

Weekends out of the apartment! She could tutor children, work in a department store, wait on tables – anything to be out in the world, away from pain and guilt.

Her very pleasure at the thought brought pain and guilt.

But they *did* need the money, though they were actually breaking even on her salary and the dwindling payments from the accident policy Jim had providentially taken out along with life insurance the day before their marriage. He had been a very thoughtful, a very loving man.

She checked him and he was fast asleep. She put on a sweater and left the apartment, closing the door softly. It was mild and pleasant and she walked toward the corner and the blue-white lights of the Esso station. She walked briskly to drive out the devils. Walking was her only exercise. Since she had put on weight, she no longer used the pool behind the L-shaped, two-story apartment house. Besides, Jim's remarks about finding herself a lover robbed it of pleasure. And there *had* been someone last year: Elliot Cissen, attractive and despicable and certain she would avail herself of his manhood. He had made one mistake, however. He had come to the apartment and sat and chatted, and Jim had seen through the man. The next time Cissen came he caught Cheryl alone in the kitchen and held her and kissed her while she struggled against him and her own appetites. Then he returned to the living room and Jim. Jim had listened to his talk of the electronics field, looking at him with hard, bright eyes, and asked him to get a box down from the closet. He had taken his .32 caliber Detective Special out and pointed the snub-nosed revolver at Cissen and said, 'I'll put six holes in your belly if you ever as much as say hello to her.' Cissen had left, declaiming shock and innocence, and moved at the end of the month.

Jim now kept the revolver in the night table beside his bed. She wanted to get rid of it but was afraid he would assume she was protecting another suitor.

She passed the service station, thinking it was early and she could go back and get her car and drive anywhere she pleased. When Jim drank heavily, he didn't wake for six to eight hours. She could drive to the freeway and out of Hollywood. She could drive to the coast and walk along the beach, looking at the water – to Santa Monica or Malibu or even further north where the land grew wild and the inlets were like fiords and surf lashed the rocks. Or to Glendale to look at the huge houses near the foothills – a section she loved despite the Birchers and Nazis and related nuts infesting the beautiful town. Or to North Hollywood and Magnolia Boulevard and the Bali-Ho Apartment Hotel.

She had copied Charles Halpert's address from his Personnel papers. She could be there in twenty minutes.

He was lonely. She was sure of it. A strange town and few friends and working on a cheap horror pic, which meant his career was in trouble and he was hard up for money and he needed comfort, needed companionship.

She kept walking. It would happen on its own. She wouldn't push it.

She walked to within six streets of the studio, then turned. Outside Tin-Tin's Café, two middle-aged men stood arguing in loud voices. They grew silent as she approached and one stepped forward and spoke with surprising dignity: 'Could I buy you a drink, miss?' She didn't answer. She went on as the other man laughed.

No more Devons. He had broken the ice, but from now on it had to mean something.

CHARLEY HALPERT

He was cleaning the counter after dinner when there was a strident buzz, like an electric alarm clock going off. He looked around. It came again, and he got up and went to the loud-speaker grille in the wall near the door. A third buzz and he knew. He had a phone call.

He stepped into the hall and saw the wall phone on his right. He ran over, picked it up, heard nothing, remembered Mr. Terrence's instructions and pressed the lighted member of a row of six clear plastic buttons.

'This is Ben Kalik, Chuck. Couldn't get back to you sooner. What can I do for you?'

'Wanted to let you know how it went with Baiglen. I tore his story apart, but he agreed—'

'He's a small-time nothing. Very weak in the head. You'll complete his spook show just as quickly as possible.'

'Well, I want to do a competent job—'

'Understood, Chuck. My point is you should be lining up television for the day you finish with Two-Cent Bagel.'

Charley felt a laugh was called for, and obliged briefly. 'Is that what they call him?'

'I think his mother made it up. You got a television set?'

'Yes, but first I'd like to talk about *Terror Town.*'

'Don't talk about it. Do it. Fast.'

Kalik was rushed and edgy. Charley began to feel unhappy. In his one letter and previous phone call, Kalik had seemed patient and understanding. But now that they'd come down to specifics, he sounded very much like other agents Charley had dealt with – in pre-Collin days, when he hadn't sold enough to convince an agent he was worth spending time on. A certain inner hardening began taking place.

'Perhaps I'd better call you tomorrow, Ben.'

'I'll be out most of the day. We'll get together for lunch soon.'

'All right. When?'

'I'll give you a call early next week. This is a rough time for me. Contract negotiations for several big clients.'

Charley said nothing.

'The new TV shows start this week and next. Watch them all. Not comedy or variety, unless you have a strong feeling for a particular situation comedy.'

'I have a strong feeling for all of them,' Charley said, the hardening process continuing. 'They sicken me.'

Kalik chuckled perfunctorily. 'Watch the Westerns. You've had a few Western shorts anthologized, haven't you?'

'Yes. E. P. Dutton, but that was ten, twelve years ago.'

'Watch the credits. Write to the producers. Tell them who you are. Say that of all the shows on television theirs are the best, spark a creative chord in you, so on. Ask for an interview.'

Charley cleared his throat, wanting to say he thought that was the agent's job, and mumbled, 'Well, yes, when my mind is a little clearer.'

'You've got to work for credits,' Kalik said. 'You've got to kick down the doors and be discovered. Look, I've got some people here. Let me know what happens. We'll get together.' He seemed about to hang up, then said, 'You haven't heard any rumors your first day at Avalon, have you?'

'Rumors?'

'About Nat Markal. Some new project. I handle Margo Lesseur. She did two big features last year.' He paused. 'Keep your ears open. You hear of anything, I'd appreciate a call.'

The line clicked. Charley hung up slowly. He felt abused

and told himself he was being overly sensitive. He had to go along with Kalik. He was a beginner, a new writer . . . in Hollywood. He couldn't expect Kalik to devote as much time to him as to top clients.

He turned away. Maybe he *should* hedge with an immediate campaign to interest TV producers . . .

But the idea upset him. He didn't want to complicate matters. He had to learn to write screenplays and to sell Carl Baiglen. He had to complete his current assignment and do it well – if not for Baiglen then for himself.

He washed the dinner dishes and went downstairs. It was growing dark. He got into his car and pulled around the circle. As he drove towards the street, he switched on his headlights and saw two figures off to the left. Thinking they wanted to pass, he stopped. But they just stood there, close to the building. He drove forward, turning his head left and right then left again, looking at them. They looked back at him, two girls in greens and browns and suedes and leathers and long hair and dark, dramatic eyes. He inched into the street, past a parked car on the left, and waited for a hole in traffic. The two girls turned and began walking slowly west, the direction in which he was turning. He looked at them again as he moved forward. They passed under a blue-white street lamp, moving along beautifully. Two pretty girls, tight pants outlining buttocks and pubic bulge. No lipstick. No bright colors. Sexy as hell. The new breed. Much too new, too young for Charley Halpert. But he could look, couldn't he? Still moving slowly, he shifted into second and nodded and smiled out his open window. The response was immediate, both smiling back at him, the one nearest the curb giving him a cute little-girl wave. He drove off, pleased. Nice kids. Didn't misunderstand. Older guy saluting their youthful beauty with a grin. Unafraid and unsalaciously they return the compliment with smiles and a wave.

He turned off Magnolia and cruised along a broad, dark avenue, looking for an isolated phone booth. He passed several, not isolated enough, then saw one standing by itself against the brick wall of a furniture store, an empty lot on the other side.

Placing his change on the little ledge, he dialed the operator and got Long Distance and gave his Peekskill number. He deposited a dollar-ten, the reduced evening rate, and gripped the handset tightly and wet his lips. He could hear the phone ringing and imaged Celia putting down her book or knitting. Or perhaps Bobby was running to answer. He hoped it was Bobby. 'Hello?' Celia said.

'It's Charley, honey.' And saying this he suddenly was afraid. She was one of a handful of people who knew his name. He was Charley to Celia, Bobby, Collin, a few old friends and himself. To everyone else he was Chuck.

'Where are you?'

'In Los Angeles, honey. I sent you a card from Kingman, only I guess I forgot to make it airmail and you know our good old rural delivery system.' He laughed. She was silent. 'I'm working at Avalon. Just started today. The weather is really wonderful here. How is it there?'

'Why did you leave that way? Taking the car and running off while I was at Dad's.'

'You know. I wanted to save us both a lot of arguing. But that's not important. Wait till you get out here!'

'It was discussion, not arguing. Don't you believe I have the right to discuss my own future?'

'Yes, of course I do.'

'I'm not joining you, Charley. I've got a job now. Dad is staying—'

'Of course you're not joining me. Not until I prove I can make it.'

'How long will that take? Another fourteen years?'

He laughed, beginning to sweat. 'I should complete this assignment in a month. With some television, I should earn between ten and twelve thousand in six months. Then we'll sell the house and you and Bobby—' He swallowed. 'Let me speak to him.'

'Are you joking? A nine-year-old child up at this hour?'

'But why—' Yes indeed, he was Charley and not Chuck. Good old Charley screw-up. He had forgotten the three-hour time difference. 'Maybe he could just say hello?'

'It's eleven-thirty.' How cold she sounded. 'He's upset enough by your sudden disappearance. He wouldn't go to school Friday, thinking it would bring you back. But he's getting used to the idea now. Talking to you would only disturb him.'

'He'll have to talk to me sooner or later.'

She didn't answer.

'You're right, Celia. It would be stupid to wake him. I'll call earlier next time.'

99

'Dad is staying with us. He said he'd give up his apartment if you didn't come home in the next few weeks. I'm working at the Motivational Research Clinic. Dr. Roergie's there, remember? It's wonderful working again. I'll say that for your cop-out. It put me back in the world.'

'What's the matter with you?' he whispered. 'I've got a film assignment. Five thousand—'

The operator cut in with, 'Three minutes are up, sir. Please signal when through,' and cut right out again. He had a dime in change, no more, but would go on talking. That was the reason for the isolated booth.

'I didn't hear you, Charley.'

'It wasn't important. Bobby's wrist all right? You feeling well?'

'Bobby's fine. And I haven't had a single headache since you left.' She laughed sharply.

How expert she was at making him feel lousy, at reducing him in some way. 'Well, look, I'll write you a long letter. I'll explain everything. This is a new deal, honey. A totally new deal. There's no longer any problem with my being able to write. All blocks are removed.'

'You know that on the first day, do you?'

'I said we'd have to give it several months. No hasty decisions.'

'Do you intend to remain celibate all that time? I don't.'

'Come on now. That isn't you talking.'

'Let me spell it out for you, Charley. I won't come to California. I won't give up my friends and the chance to use my degree in a job again. Because I don't believe that by changing coasts *you've* changed.'

'For heaven's sake, Celia,' he said, fighting the urge to shout. 'I've got a movie contract.'

'You had book contracts and what difference—'

'A new medium, that's the difference.'

Her voice rose shrilly. 'You'll *never* be able to support yourself and your family as a writer, Charley! Fourteen years of proof is all I need! Or am willing to take! I want you home, Charlie, in a *job*! I'm not a complete amateur when it comes to the human personality. I've watched you coming apart day by day. As a trained psychologist, I tell you you can't function as a writer.'

He couldn't talk to her. He had faith in this new chance and she didn't. Faith wasn't transferable. (But it was *vulnerable*, and her dagger words cut deep, brought back the feeling of failure and desperation he'd had at home.)

He ached to hear his son's voice, his wild little tender little man-child's voice. He wanted to beg her to wake him, but said, 'But if I *do* make it, what then?'

'It'll take years to prove.' She was calm again. 'I won't wait years.'

So there it was. But she was wrong. It wouldn't take years. Only months. No more than six months. Then she would come to him, if only for her child's sake, and they would be right again.

Had they ever been right, he and Celia?

Perhaps not. But it was no longer he and Celia. It was he and Celia and Bobby.

'I'll phone Sunday,' he said. 'At eight your time.'

'If you want to, Charley.' The line clicked.

The phone started ringing as he left. It was still ringing when he got in his car and drove away. He imagined the operator's shocked face (she had a sweet, gentle voice) and felt guilty as hell. But he was living on five hundred dollars that Kalik had advanced against his first payment from Baiglen, and could never ask Celia for money, and every dollar counted.

He went shopping in a bright new supermarket, then thought he would turn down Magnolia toward the Bali-Ho. But he didn't. The dagger words continued to wound him and he needed movement, pleasure of some sort.

He went on a voyage of exploration. He took one freeway into another and followed signs and finally drove to the Pacific and got out and walked along a railing at Santa Monica where the beach seemed much the same as Rockaway in New York. He didn't want it to be the same. It was different here — that was his thesis, his hope and his faith.

He turned and looked north and was gratified by the differences. In the moonlight the road was a twisted black ribbon hugging the sea. A sheer wall of rock rose up behind it, and houses were perched at the very top of that wall, at the edge of the cliff. One house in particular dominated: a condor of a house hanging out over the cliff, with angular concrete surfaces, buttressed and balanced, designed to allow the lords and ladies an unparalleled view of the Pacific. Inland loomed the shadow of mountains. Nothing so noble could be found in the Rockaways or Hamptons, in Cape Cod or Kennebunkport.

Nothing so indicative of the richness of modern life.

A light blinked out. The condor house grew dark. The lord of the manor slept, and it behooved all good men to do like-wise.

CARL BAIGLEN

It wasn't until he entered the shadowy, red-lighted bar that Carl realized he had forgotten to arrange some sort of mutual recognition procedure with John McNaughton. But Len Sawyer, the owner, clapped him on the shoulder and jerked his thumb at the last booth in back. 'Guy named McNaughton waiting for you. How're you doing, Carl? Scared any good people lately?' He laughed, his face falling into heavy creases.

'Careful,' Carl murmured, peering through the haze of smoke toward the booth,' 'or I'll give you a part in my next feature.'

Len, who had been an actor, a lousy one by his own admission, said, 'Then you'd really have a horror pic.'

Carl left him laughing as usual at his own joke.

McNaughton was seated, but Carl was immediately struck by his physical presence – his size and his looks. He was big, no doubt about that, and even in this land of beautiful people was strikingly handsome. He wasn't more than twenty-five, big-boned and big-muscled. His face was large, smooth, with a maturity that promised to last, unchanged, for a long time. When he smiled, as he did when Carl approached, he looked clean and boyish and charming. Carl couldn't help thinking how well he'd photograph.

McNaughton rose, showing himself *really* big – about six-four – though his solid build tended to reduce the impression of height. He stuck out his hand. 'Mr. Baiglen?' The convention, and the man, were too strong for Carl and he found himself shaking the hand. They sat down. 'I photograph even better than I look,' McNaughton said.

'The letter,' Carl said.

McNaughton took a folded sheet of paper from the pocket of his creased houndstooth jacket and placed it on the table. He raised his drink. 'Cheers.'

Carl unfolded the sheet, a photostat of an uneven piece of paper or cardboard covered with large-scrawled words. Myra's handwriting, or an excellent forgery. He read it and slid it back across the table. 'It's yours,' McNaughton said.

Carl tore it in half. McNaughton picked up the pieces and put them in his pocket. 'We don't want the waitress asking you for favors too, do we?'

As if on cue, Cleo appeared. 'The usual, Mr. Baiglen?' she asked, while ogling McNaughton.

He nodded. When she'd left, he said, 'For curiosity's sake, your credentials.'

McNaughton flipped a wallet open in front of Carl's eyes. He was an officer in the Devereux Police Department.

Cleo brought Carl's drink. He gulped half the Scotch and water. 'I don't think my wife wrote that.'

'Sure you do.'

'I don't know how much I can help you.'

'Sure you do.'

'Get an agent. Get a dramatics coach or enter a good school of acting. Then there's Central Casting and the Actors Guild and people to see—'

'Pick the agent, the coach, anyone else I need. Tell them what to do for me.'

Carl took out cigarettes.

'I don't have much money, Mr. Baiglen.'

Carl struck a match and inhaled deeply.

'I'll need a few dollars to set myself up. I'll have the bills sent to you, right?'

'And if I say no?'

'If you prefer to give me the cash—'

'And if I say I've thought it over and you can go to hell?'

'Then my career is down the drain and it's back to Devereux and a job I hate.' He finished his drink. 'But I might get a promotion for catching a murderer.'

Carl smoked and drank.

'Must we go through the whole thing again, Mr. Baiglen? I only want a start. If I can make my own way, you're done with me.'

'How can I believe that?'

'I'm not asking for money as such, am I?' He smiled briefly. 'My police training inhibits me in certain ways, protects you in certain ways.'

'From what I've heard of police shakedowns—'

'This kind of talk won't help either of us. I'll get an apartment, a small one, and some decent clothing, and keep the bills reasonable. I want a career, not money. Once I've proven my ability—'

Carl stubbed out his cigarette angrily. 'If that's all you want, why didn't you try Hollywood before this, on your own?'

'I did. I spent my vacation here two years ago. I didn't know what to do or who to see and no one was willing to help me. I had coffee every day in Schwab's and spoke to an agent and toured Universal Studios for three and a half dollars. And went home.'

'Which is what you should do now.'

McNaughton changed, became the hard-eyed, flat-voiced cop. 'You prefer a trial in Devereux, you can have it.'

Which was the crux of the matter. 'I'll humor you, but my wife never wrote that.'

'Do we have a deal or not?'

Carl took a five from his wallet and put it on the table. 'The bills are to be sent to my office and addressed *Personal* and *Private.*'

McNaughton leaned back, smiling charmingly again. 'What did you do, wait near the bathroom then throw her down the stairs? Or kill her before and use the fall as a cover?'

Carl rose and walked away, face white. Len called from the bar, 'You oughta have your next premiere in a mausoleum, Carl. Give it the proper—'

Carl went right on out the door, leaving his old friend surprised and hurt. He drove past the Strip, into Beverly Hills, the radio turned up high. He hoped Ruth hadn't gone to bed. He wanted a cup of coffee and some talk – talk to drive McNaughton and Devereux and Myra from his mind. Especially Myra.

Ruth was asleep. He stood beside the bed, looking down at her. Her face was composed: gentle and relaxed and beautiful.

Myra's face had been sullen in sleep. Myra had tossed fretfully in sleep, seething with a thousand slights and insults, a thousand plots against her security, her pride, her well-being. Myra had built a hell for herself, and for him, and the longing to be free of hell had mounted until it was a pressure threatening to burst him asunder.

He undressed quickly and got into bed and moved close to Ruth. She was a big, firm-fleshed woman. She was eleven years younger than Carl and filled with a quiet joy in life.

Myra had been small and curved and tense and full of bitterness,

He moved closer still, touching her side with his body. She smelled sweet. She was his sweetness in life. He put his hand under her nightgown and stroked her hip. She opened her eyes and turned her head to him. He kissed her face several times. She smiled and cleared her throat. He took her in his arms and burrowed into her neck, into the sweetness and warmth. 'What is it?' she murmured.

'Nothing, just missed you.' He kissed her lips. 'Go to sleep.'

She looked at him, puzzled. She returned his kiss. She placed little kisses all over his face and stroked his head. She showed him love. And it was here, not in temple, that he knew there was such a thing as the soul, felt their souls intermingle and wanted more than anything to make her happy, make her proud of him. Then she was asleep, and he remembered the emptiness, the loneliness of his life with Myra. And feared he would never be able to shake the remembrances of Myra.

JOHN McNAUGHTON

He had another drink on the fiver Baiglen had left and tipped the waitress lightly, making her like it with an intimate smile. She said, 'You come back again, here?' and he stood up and looked down at her and saw the way her lips parted and her eyes glazed. He walked past the bar, and a well-dressed brunette chattering to her well-dressed escort followed him with her eyes in the back mirror.

He smiled a little – a different smile this time, sly and acid. Devereux or Hollywood, some things didn't change. Which was why he was going to make it in movies – make it big.

He came out onto Sunset Boulevard. His car was just up the next side street, but he passed the corner, enjoying the mild, summery evening. Back home it was getting nippy. Soon it would be cold and night duty would be a real drag. And Loughlin and Carter talking football, and Sunday morning Mass, and checking shop doors, and those stupid lectures by O'Neil. And coming home to Mom and Dad and dear sister Angie with her big romances. And the dates with Tina and Mitsy, spaced out as far as possible but still abhorrent. Yet necessary, *vital* in terms of the mask.

The mask. The manly smile and clipped speech and rugged stance of a policeman. The mask of interest in things he not only cared nothing about but actually despised. The talk of women. Bergen's whore who paid protection in trade and Chenny's 'classy married piece of cunt' and Franklin's tender romance with a girl he had described as an angel who turned out to be a simpering, heavy-bottomed waitress who couldn't stop giving John the eye and said things like 'I'm proud to be associated with members of the law-enforcement program.'

Law-enforcement program! Men who could do nothing else. Who had no brains and no imagination. Who could earn their miserable five to eight thousand only by putting their lives on the line.

He walked toward the curve in the Strip, and a slender boy with a heavy shock of black hair approached and cast a challenging look at him. The mask was still firmly in place, and he passed him coldly. He stopped to light a cigarette, turning away from the direction of the breeze, and his eyes followed the boy. Then he continued along the street of bars and restaurants and sidewalk cafés and girlie shows and dance joints and shops and new office buildings.

Sunset Strip! Hollywood! Ripping off a medicine chest and finding a piece of cardboard and thinking it out . . . and he was here! From cop to criminal in one easy lesson – except that he didn't feel like a criminal. He felt like a dedicated businessman who had found his opening and was going on to make his fortune.

He would have to play Carl Baiglen carefully, sometimes giving him slack and other times jerking him up short. But always keeping that hook in his mouth. Because Mr. Baiglen was all-important. Mr. Baiglen would help him remove the mask.

LARS WYLLIT

He'd had only two decent hands all night – and lost on one of those when Mark Fellory filled an inside straight. Fellory, Wallace Cohen, Ben Fein and Lars made up the poker game in Fellory's apartment. They were all young men, all part of Avalon's creative staff. The stakes were the usual five-dollar limit, far from the table stakes that had cost Lars two thousand dollars one night last summer. But he still had managed to drop a bundle and was writing a check for a hundred. He handed it to Fellory, tanned and moustached, and received

106

ten red and five blue chips. Fellory said, 'I say, fellows, how about a rousing cheer for the man most responsible for our success at the gaming tables, the man whose good sportsmanship and ready cash has been an example, and profit, to us all. I give you Larson Wyllit. Hip, hip—' Cohen and Fein, two of a stocky, energetic, athletic kind, joined in a veddy British 'Hurrah!' They did it twice more while Lars dealt out the cards. Lars said, flatly, 'Funny. Very. Like your show.'

'Whoops,' Fein murmured. 'You may have played the overture to the specialty act, Mark.' He examined his cards. 'I can't open.'

'Nor I,' said Cohen.

'But I, Mark Fellory, born to danger, *can* open and *do* open, gloriously.' He slid a red chip forward, and glanced at Lars. 'Besides, my friend Lars rarely clobbers more than one per day.'

'Did I miss anything?' Cohen asked as they all anted up.

'In the commissary,' Fellory said. 'A sight to behold. Bob Chester was the victim.'

'In the *commissary*?' Fein asked, smiling in disbelief.

Lars discarded three cards. Fein and Cohen discarded three each. Fellory closed his fan and placed the cards face down on the table. He tapped them.

'Born to danger is right,' Cohen muttered.

'Born to bluff, you mean,' said Fein.

Lars dealt out the cards. He took one look at his own and tossed them in. Fein did the same. Cohen said, 'It's up to you, Mark Fellory, boy *nudnik*.'

Fellory bet a blue chip. Fein said, 'I'll raise you ten.' Fellory called him. Fein had three sixes. Fellory had three fours. Fein chuckled and raked in the pot. 'It is evident that the intellectual powers of a dialogue director on features, such as I, are far superior to those of an assistant director on half-hour television, such as you.'

Cohen said, 'What happened, Lars? In the commissary, I mean.'

'I know what you mean,' Lars said. He was feeling lousy. He really should have seen the doctor tonight. 'A man asked me what happened, so I hit him.'

There was an uncomfortable silence. Fein shuffled the cards and began dealing. Fellory said, 'Moe Sholub was there, Lars.'

'I know.' He picked up his cards. 'Did he say anything?'

'Not according to my informant. But he wasn't happy. I wouldn't make a habit of performing on the lot.'

Lars was tired of poker and of these three. They were bright enough guys, nice enough guys, not-too-big guys, but they weren't his friends, not really. He had no friends. He had never had friends.

He played out the hand and won, and asked to be excused. Fellory protested that it was still early, but Fein said he'd had enough for the night and Cohen, who was married, said it might postpone his divorce a month or two if he came home before three A.M.

'You ought to try it,' Cohen said to Lars. 'Marriage hath charms to soothe the savage beast.'

'All right. I'll try it tonight. The conjugal part, that is.'

He stopped his Triumph at a phone booth on Wilshire and called Lispeth Auron, his heavy action at the moment. She was grumpy and said he'd awakened her. He said a lot of things, complimentary and soothing and amorous, and after a while her mood changed and she said, 'You want to come over?'

She was an actress, just nineteen as he well knew after buying a hunk of good costume jewelry for her birthday, very leggy for a small girl. She was a wild, pretty kid who liked a good time, in bed and out. He knew he should get some sleep, but first there was in bed, and then there was out. They went to Cherico's, a small eat-and-dance spot and ate tacos, enchiladas and refried beans and danced the watusi and frug and fox-trot. The fox-trot thrilled Lispeth with its contact-sensuality, so they headed back home. On the way, they were buzzed by two motorcycle characters in German costume – decorated field jackets and jackboots, steel helmet and Rommel cap. 'Hell's Angels?' Lispeth asked as the cycles shot by, much too close for comfort. Lars was burning, but it had been a long, long day and all he did was shrug. 'Or another variety of trash.' He had once chased a bearded Angel along Santa Monica Boulevard, intent on busting him up after an exchange of insults at a traffic light. But the Angel had been alone and not inclined to play, especially on a well-lighted street where a piece of chain or a switchblade might be frowned upon by observers. 'Someday,' he said quietly, 'I'll meet my fate with those morons.'

She looked at him. 'What's that supposed to mean?'

He smiled and didn't answer, but it was simple. He was never more than a hairbreadth away from violence. So were the Angels. He despised their total lack of intellectuality and hated them for making him ashamed of his own violence. It was inevitable that someday they tangle.

Not tonight, however. Tonight he was committed to another sort of violence.

He had thought he would stay with Lispeth until morning, but dressed and slipped out shortly after four A.M. He went to his apartment off Cahuenga Boulevard and had a beer and a smoke and washed and set the alarm for eight and got into bed. He didn't need much sleep. Besides, he had to go on hot and heavy with the opening of the script. Pausing for breath this early could be disastrous. It was necessary to get what amounted to Act I on paper. Only then could he take time to see what he was doing and plan ahead.

He wondered what Terry Hanford's reaction would be if he picked up the phone and called her right this moment. How angry would she get if he asked her to breakfast? Very angry, probably.

He dialed information and then her number. He smiled to himself, and was worried and was relieved when she didn't answer – until he wondered whether she hadn't answered because of the hour, or because she wasn't there. And if she wasn't there, where was she?

He turned over on his face and wiped his mind clear of women and writing and fighting and Lars. He thought of nothing, and the nothing became Somerville, New Jersey, and the nice house on the street of nice houses and the 'perfect childhood' his father insisted he'd had. Well, some few moments had been perfect – moments with Mother when Richie, Herb and Tom weren't there and she took her youngest, her terribly sensitive youngest and smallest, and held him and read the stories that made him laugh or fight back tears. She died when he was eleven and there were no more perfect moments. And Terry Hanford was somewhere else at four in the morning and she wasn't interested in him anyway and he was writing stories to make himself laugh or fight back tears and he was alone and it had to change, all the fighting and gambling and running and emptiness, it had to change or his heart would burst and he would be alone in the darkness for all eternity and he was afraid. *Afraid, and please, please read me a story.*

She let Leonard see her to her door and kissed him again — it was after all little enough thanks for an evening on the town — and detached herself when he grew ardent. She watched him walk down the hall to the elevator and told herself she felt sorry for him, he was such a sweet guy. But at the same time she smiled as she entered the apartment, smiled and wondered what he would have thought of her in Dovenville.

The phone rang as she was undressing. Nude except for her brassiere, she ran to the foyer, thinking it could be Mr. Markal. He might have tried to get her earlier. He might want to see her tonight. 'Yes?'

'I didn't wake you, did I?'

The voice was familiar, though she couldn't place it. Cautiously, she said, 'No, I was just getting ready for bed.'

'This is Paul Morse. I—'

'I'm going to hang up now.'

'Please wait, I want to apologize.' He rushed on, trying to get it all in before she cut him off. And while she told herself to hang up, she didn't. 'I called several times tonight, but you weren't in. I kept thinking of the way I acted, and while I'm not apologizing from the standpoint of a black man approaching a woman of another race ... you know what I mean, don't you? I'm apologizing purely as a man for having pressed a pickup against the woman's wishes.'

She said nothing. His breathing was loud at the other end. She propped the phone between her cheek and shoulder and reached back and unhooked her brassiere.

'I really was ... quite taken,' he said, voice dropping. 'I'm not at all like what I led you to believe. I mean, I'm not a make-out artist. My friends actually think I'm backward ... with women, that is. My interests are more political than sexual.'

She shrugged out of the brassiere and put it on the table. She rubbed her breasts and stretched and was pleased that she hadn't allowed him to waste a second of her time. She had continued undressing, just as if he hadn't called.

'I certainly didn't mean to frighten you.'

'You didn't frighten me,' she said. 'You bothered me.'

'I wish I'd bothered you in a different way.' Wistful voice, soft and full of sadness. She leaned against the wall, rubbing her breasts and then her belly, thinking how good it felt to strip. 'I wish I'd remained in your thoughts as you've remained in mine.'

'You remained in my thoughts all right. I was angry enough to remember you for years.'

He seemed to read something in her statement that encouraged him. 'Then tell me off to my face. I'll come over. I'll keep my hands at my sides and my mouth shut and you can get it off your chest.' A pause and he whispered, 'Your beautiful chest.'

'Don't start that again.'

'See me,' he pleaded. 'I'm never been so hooked in all my life. Let me make myself known to you. Let me show you my world. It's an exciting world, a meaningful world. Whatever you are, you're not white. You'll be able to share my world.'

She heard a sound bouncing back from the mouthpiece, a heavy bellows-sound of breath. *Her* breath.

'You black bastards never learn,' she said, and hung up and waited near the phone, prepared with further insults in case he should be thick-skinned enough – or perceptive enough – to call again. He was neither, and she went to bed.

TERRY HANFORD

They were drinking coffee and playing rummy when Mona looked across the table and laughed. 'Jesus, what a damned fool Pete and Jerry must think me!' The tough words sounded strange delivered in Mona's silky voice and near-childish enunciation – something else that turned men on. 'And you.'

Terry said, 'No, of course not. You were terribly upset. You thought you were ill.'

Mona drew a card, discarded a card. 'I certainly feel better now.' She leaned back, sighing. 'Almost as if it never happened.'

Terry drew and discarded. 'I'm so glad.'

'One thing is sure, it'll never happen again.'

Terry looked at her. Mona was smiling. She was her old self again. Terry answered the smile and was suddenly out from under a pall of guilt. She looked up at the walls. 'I can have a painter in before the end of the week.'

'Why wait for a painter? We can do it ourselves, first thing

111

tomorrow.' She stopped. 'Listen, could you move in here for a week or two?'

Terry blinked, hesitated.

'I want to meet new men and see new places and it would be nice if you were here, giving me that strong right arm for support.' She leaned across the table, laughing, and squeezed Terry's arm, so delicate compared to her own round pillar of flesh.

'If you think it's necessary—'

'I do,' Mona answered with uncharacteristic firmness. She looked into Terry's eyes and rubbed her arm gently. 'I need a friend.'

Terry said, 'Well then, I'd love to,' and while smiling and nodding withdrew her arm.

'Great!' Mona jumped up and came around the table. 'We'll seal it with a kiss!' Before Terry could move, Mona covered her mouth with moist, open lips. One hand, as if by chance, pressed her upper thigh; the other rested lightly on the back of her neck. The kiss went on, and Terry didn't know how to end it without insulting Mona, without bringing this terrible thing out into the open where it would lie between them for all time.

It *was* a terrible thing. Her mind knew it ... but her body didn't seem to. There was no automatic resistance, no revulsion. Whatever feeling managed to get by her churning brain was ... pleasant. Not exciting, but warm and pleasant.

And then she panicked. It *would* be exciting. In another moment Mona would caress her more intimately and her own mouth would open and they would be embarked on something degenerate and ugly – something she wouldn't be able to live with.

Mona straightened and went back to her seat. She picked up her cards and looked at them and said, voice tremulous, 'You're my only real friend. I would do anything for you. Please ... understand how much I care.'

'I do,' Terry said, fighting to control her breathing.

Mona looked up. 'I don't want *anything* to spoil our friendship.'

Terry managed to smile. 'Your draw, Mona.'

Mona seemed to want to say something more. Terry said, 'We'll always be friends ... if things go on as they have up until now.' And added quickly, smiling, 'And why shouldn't they?'

112

Mona's hand shook as she drew a card. They played, and Mona relaxed, seemingly having gotten the message. Or was it, Terry wondered, that Mona didn't actually *know* what she'd been moving toward?

More coffee and more rummy. Mona began to talk and laugh again. She drew a card and squealed, 'Rummy! See? You're already changing my luck!'

Terry sighed. Mona didn't realize that her luck, her winning was Terry's lack of luck, Terry's losing. Nor did she consider that it might work out the same way in regard to the visit.

Mona said, 'Hey, don't be a sore loser.'

'What?'

'You look so darn mad.'

Terry laughed and dealt out a new hand. She thought of her comfortable apartment and privacy. And of the new assignment that was just shaping up. Isa Yee was slated for the full treatment, if she didn't bomb badly somewhere along the way. Isa Yee required much thought, much careful analysis, and that wouldn't be possible living here with Mona. Neither would visits from Stad Homer, and her program of serious reading, and unwinding by being absolutely alone.

Of course, there would be compensations: dancing at the top spots and dining at the best restaurants and meeting interesting new people and general late-hours whoopie. All on an expense account.

Two weeks. Three at the most. It represented change and change represented youth and she had been feeling a little less than youthful lately. And Mona would recover her natural appetite for fun-and-games and more than natural appetite for men. It would be a ball, a fling of the first order.

She picked up her cards, smiling at the thought that she was her own best client. She could talk herself into anything.

'Have you spoken to Mr. Markal lately?' she asked Mona.

'Last week.'

'Did he say anything about a new production?'

Mona concentrated on the cards, biting her lip. 'Uh-uh. The schedule is all set, isn't it? I mean for the next year.'

'I guess so.' She dropped the subject. Her imagination probably.

But Bertha *had* seemed strangely excited today. And she *had* put a sheaf of typewritten pages into the drawer when Terry approached her desk. And what was it she had said after

113

telling Terry that Markal wasn't in? 'Better get out your sneakers.' No, your *track shoes*.

What could it be? Terry knew she was going to work on *The Squaws*, Avalon's seven-million-dollar biggie. Maybe Markal had decided on an outsize promotion. That must be it. With Mona Dearn and Gordon Hewlett, that had to be it.

So she would work a little harder.

She needed one card for rummy, and drew it, and discarded it. She told herself she'd made a mistake, hadn't been concentrating. But she was pleased when Mona spread out her cards a moment later, laughing triumphantly.

The client, bless her soul, came first.

NAT MARKAL

Adele had waited dinner for him. He drank a good deal of Chambertin and kidded with Tess and sent his compliments to Dale on the lobster bisque. But he ate very little and fidgeted a good deal and lighted a cigar twice before coffee, which made Lainie wrinkle her nose and cough meaningfully. And he couldn't bring himself to tell them of *Joneses,* just didn't have the patience to go into it. But he told himself to relax, he was in the bosom of his family.

Dave Sankin called as Tess was serving dessert. Nat took it in his study.

'Listen, Nat. I talked it over with Julie. She brought up some questions – questions that were lying in back of my own mind.'

'About what?' Nat asked blandly.

'About *what*? About *The Eternal Joneses*, what else!'

'Well, I always said Julie was a marvelous wife and mother. And a great cook. Especially her roast duck in paper. But a movie producer?'

Sankin laughed unconvincingly. 'Nat, I beg you, reconsider. What do we need such a tremendous risk—'

'Investment.'

'All right. *Investment!* All those stars. All those locations. Four, five hours. It'll run *over* fifteen million and you know it. What do we need so much riding on one picture for? If it fails—'

'I've got the ball rolling, Dave.'

'That's not right! You were coming here—'

'I am. As soon as I can free myself.' He spoke very quietly.
'But I'm going ahead. I know this can be the biggest money-maker of all time. And the only way to stop me is by kicking me out of Avalon.'

'Now wait a minute. Who said anything about kicking you out of Avalon! I just want you to think this out very carefully before going ahead, before committing yourself irrevocably.'

'I'm already committed irrevocably. In my own mind. And you know what that means.'

Sankin sighed. 'Twenty million. It could be twenty-five before you're through. Maybe more.'

'Maybe. But the more I spend, the more we'll make.'

'One thing. It'll mean cutting back on other productions. I won't agree to an outlay of a dollar over fifty million this next fiscal year.'

'As far as I'm concerned you can cut *every* other production.'

'Yeah,' Sankin said. 'One big, blind spending spree. Tell me, Nat, what do you really think this monster will cost? If you have eight, ten stars like you plan—'

'I'll have a presentation ready for you and the board when I get to New York. A prospectus to warm every accountant's cold little heart.'

'This accountant's cold little heart can hardly wait.'

'Think big, Dave.'

'I guess I'll have to.'

Nat had his coffee in the study and worried about Sankin. Two calls today. And wait until he found out about the set.

Again he turned his mind to that empty lot and how to fill it. Not just one or more structures, but something that had a tremendously exciting event connected with it. Perhaps *the* most exciting, *the* most dramatic event in American history.

Bunker Hill? Pearl Harbor? Hiroshima?

He went to his bookshelves and ran his fingers over the leather bindings, most of them untouched since Adele had given them to him six years ago. He found a two-volume American history and began to skim.

He visited Adele's room late that night. She received him with eagerness, her plump body far more responsive than when she'd been young. She asked for obscenities, for pinches, for rough treatment, and dug her heels into his hips and bucked away, gasping out her pleasure, telling him she loved him, would love him until she died. He was gratified by the way she

115

was able to satisfy herself, by the way she had developed as a sexual being over the years. But his own satisfaction was mild, his love-making by rote, his orgasm a weak thing that left him depressed.

He told her about *Joneses*. She was sleepy and could think only of the work it would entail. She had hoped he would retire so there could be travel and more time together and much more time for nights like this. He stayed until she fell asleep, then went through the connecting foyer to his own room. He slipped into a robe and walked out on the terrace, looking down, far down the Palisades to the midnight sea, one of the most exciting, and expensive, views in the country.

Closer in toward the cliff, lights crawled along the Pacific Coast Highway. Cars. Men and women going places.

He shrugged, telling himself he could, as the New York expression went, buy and sell any of them. But after a while he leaned forward, staring straight down as if to see into those cars, his face bleak as it had never been on the cover of *Time* magazine. He wanted to be in one of those cars, going somewhere with someone exciting, experiencing joy. He wanted it intensely, and it seemed as far beyond his reach as youth was, as youth had always been, and there was no reasoning away the feeling.

The Eternal Joneses. That would be his excitement, his pleasure. *The Eternal Joneses*. That would bring him everything he wanted ... and he would spend no more time wondering just what it was he wanted, would waste no more time mooning about like a damned fool!

Later, in bed, he sat up and put on his lamp and wrote on a pad. He read it and underlined heavily and read it again.

'Build Washington, D.C., as it was before the War of 1812. *Then burn it, with a thousand extras as British and a thousand as Americans and a thousand reporters watching!*'

CHARLEY HALPERT

It was one A.M. when Charley returned to the apartment. He washed perfunctorily and stripped to his shorts and fell into the couch bed and almost asked Celia to put out the light. He got up and stumbled to the switch and only then noticed the

116

sheet of paper just inside the door. He picked it up, unfolded it, read the penciled writing:

Did anyone ever tell you your a doll? Just want you to know we do. Nice to see a New York guy again. We miss all the New York guys we know. Real swingers. Maybe you'd like to swing? Ha ha just joking. Or are we? If your not too busy with your movie work maybe you'd like a few laffs. Ha ha. Weer a couple of singers and dancers from out of town looking for frendly faces. New York hip faces. Don't call us weel call you. Your friends,

Lois Lane and Sugar Smart.

He read it again, unbelieving, and said, 'A gag,' and worried about it as he put out the lights. Lois Lane and Sugar Smart. My God. He got into bed and was asleep immediately.

Ten minutes later he was awakened by a knock at the door. 'Who's there?'

'Lois and Sugar,' a delicate voice replied. 'Can we talk? We been waiting and now we see your car's back.'

He got out of bed. 'Uh ... do I know you?'

'Sure. I waved. Remember? You were in the car and we were walking.'

The two girls on the street before he'd phoned Celia. The girls in greens and browns and leathers. The pretty girls in tight pants. Lois Lane and Sugar Smart.

'Well, unless it's important ... I'm undressed—'

She giggled. 'You New York guys. Open up, huh?'

He didn't want to. He walked slowly across the room and rubbed his face and tried to think and couldn't. There was a chain lock he hadn't used. He compromised by using it now, opening the door a crack. The young face framed in straight black hair smiled at him. There was a tiny pink mole at the right end of the smile and it comforted him, seemed to make the face human and trustworthy somehow. 'Hi, I'm Lois. This is Sugar.' Sugar pressed toward the crack, a young face framed in straight ash-blonde hair. No mole there, but a comic upsweep to the smile, a sappy-happy grin that worked the same as Lois's mole. So they were two human beings and what had he expected and what was he worried about anyway? 'Nice to meet you,' Sugar murmured. They looked like sisters, despite the hair. The hair was bottled. They were small, curvy girls of sixteen or seventeen, maybe eighteen, with pale, round cheeks and damp, pouty lips and close-set eyes.

117

'What can I do for you?' he asked.

Lois giggled again and pushed at the door. He darted behind it as it hit the chain. 'I don't want to be rude,' he said, speaking around the door, 'but this is no time for casual conversation.'

Lois was leaning forward into the three or four inches of opening. 'You better know it,' she said. 'People always talk, talk, talk.' He jumped as her hand found his thigh. Sugar said, 'Let's get inside. I think someone's peeking out down the hall.' Lois smiled into Charley's face and said, 'Any minute now, right, daddy?'

He stared at her, shocked, not believing what she was doing. 'Young girls shouldn't—'

'Oh, I'm twenty and my sister's eighteen and a half.'

The way she assumed he was questioning her legal status as a woman made him certain they were both jail bait. Statutory rape, that was all he needed. 'I meant young girls shouldn't come to a stranger's place at two in the morning.' His voice gave him away, shaky and uncertain. She smiled and worked her hand under his shorts. 'Yummy,' she said. 'Yummy yum yum. Open the door now and let's have fun.'

It was an erotic dream, the kind he'd had as a teen-ager. But he wasn't a teen-ager anymore, and they were. He was an adult and had to think as an adult and not get involved with minors. Yet he opened the chain lock, hurried to the bed and sat down. They came in and closed the door. The blonde, Sugar, felt around the wall. 'Where's the light?'

'Don't,' Charley said, suddenly afraid of how he would look to them.

'Who needs light?' Lois said, and came over to him and stroked his cheek. 'Sure is nice seeing a New York guy again.'

Charley cleared his throat. 'You're from New York?'

'No, but New York guys are In, everyone knows that.' She sat on his lap and kissed him. Sugar came towards them, unzipping her pants down the side. 'Kicky pad,' she said.

Charley lay down when Lois pushed him and helped her when she drew off his shorts and watched as she and Sugar undressed. He was desirous and afraid. 'I don't have much money,' he said. 'I can't spare more than a few dollars.'

'That's not nice,' Lois said, getting out of her tight brown pants and her panties and back into her high suede boots. She wore boots and a leather jerkin over a dark blouse. She was either hiding rubber padding or reaching for erotic effect.

118

Sugar stripped right down to buff and went to the other side of the bed and lay down and presented him with two taut, heavy-nippled breasts. He made one last effort to avoid what he felt was certain trouble. 'I'm married. I have a son. I'm over forty.'

'These hip New York guys,' Lois said to Sugar, shaking her head in admiration. 'You get it? You see the way they operate? All the lies those creeps told us. Remember?'

Sugar said, 'Man, do I ever,' and raised herself a little to feed Charley a breast. He sighed and capitulated. Her voice strained, she said, 'We've had *some* rough time, I'll tell you.'

'Man, haven't we,' Lois said, and squirmed in on Charley's other side. He lay sandwiched between them, coddled and caressed, hands and mouth full of girl, sinking rapidly into exotic mindlessness. Their scent was violet. They seemed to have bathed in it, but after a while he decided he liked it.

Five minutes of play, and they got to work. First Lois, the brunette, climbed on him, then Sugar. When he tried to reverse the posture they murmured he didn't have to, they wanted to make him comfy and happy, and so he lay back and let them. But he worried all the while about sounds in the hall and their ages and whether the door was locked and whether the people in the next apartment could hear. There was plenty to hear: chatter and grunts and sighs and protesting squeals from the bed. He felt exposed and threatened, and it held him back, made him a slow, effective, satisfying lover. He began to contribute his share to the sound – grunts and sighs. But not chatter. Even if he'd wanted to, he probably couldn't have gotten a word in. Sugar talked while Lois was on him, and Lois when Sugar took over. He missed a lot, but understood soon enough why he of all men had been so honored.

Sugar: 'Seven weeks and not one interview. Not even an agent. Hey, look at her face. She always does that when she's getting close. Funny.

'All we got was experience. And not singing or dancing. They all turned out to be factory workers or auto mechanics. It took time to find out.

'We been here three months. And we're running short of bread. And the manager's wife don't let him come for the rent anymore. Fun's fun, but what about our careers?'

(Here Charley voiced concern for their protection.)

'Don't worry about that, honey. One of the producers we

119

met worked in a drugstore. He fitted us up personally. You going bingo soon?

'So we decided we had to figure a way to find guys who *really* work in pictures. It was Lois figured it out. Look at her *now*. See? Like she's going to cry. *She's* going bingo soon.'

Lois whined and fell forward and kissed him feverishly. Sugar cried, 'Bingo!' and Charley was set back another few minutes by the carrying power of that shrill voice. Lois and Sugar changed places.

Lois: 'We were at Paramount last week ... no, two weeks ago. A Thursday, wasn't it, Sugar? Wednesday, right. She's not too sharp, but never forgets dates. She always passed history.

'Look at her face. Like she's praying. Maybe that you'll hold out. Just putting you on a little, baby.

'We were hanging around the gates at Paramount trying to meet Little Joe from *Bonanza* or another star. Even Hoss. He's not a swinger but he's all heart, so if we were orphans maybe he'd help us. We could try it. We were ready to try making the Creature from the Black Lagoon!

'Did Sugar tell you about CBS Television? We got into the lot all right. We just walked in while the guard was talking on the phone. He waved his hands but he couldn't get off the phone and we ran. We had a plan. Underneath we wore our teeny-weeny bikinis and we could go around looking like we were working on a show, see? So we found a john and changed and put our clothes behind a big wastebasket and went out – just high heels and bikinis. It wasn't too warm that morning, either. We went to the office buildings where they got the producers and directors and casting people. We were going to walk into offices and let them get a good look. Like we know what we got, man. Like you know it too, right? But that creepy guard just didn't let it drop. Not him, the fink. He was looking, and one of the secretaries was a bitch and she must've called him after she said her boss wasn't in. So there we were talking to some sweet guy who was an assistant to someone big and he was interested and wanted to take us into another office and talk a little. And the guard comes in. Real old square. Not old like you, doll. I mean from the dark ages! He was going to throw us out without letting us get our clothes after Sugar got mad and gave him some choice few words. You going bingo now, daddy?'

Sugar beat him to it by seconds. 'You're kicky,' she gasped. 'Oh, baby, *kicky*!' She lay on him a moment, then jumped off

120

and pushed back her blonde hair. 'Another day, another you-know-what,' she said, grinning. Charley smiled faintly and closed his eyes.

'You wash first,' Lois said.

'Okay. But tell him about Paramount, will you?'

'At Paramount I was watching the cars drive in when suddenly I saw it.'

The bathroom light went on, its glow reaching into the living room. Charley got under the covers. From the bathroom, Sugar called, 'She said, "Why didn't I see it before? They all got stickers." Parking stickers, right?'

'She can't let me tell a story,' Lois said. 'She's always got to interrupt.' She raised her voice. 'Did I interrupt when *you* were talking? Go wash your damned—'

Charley said, 'Please, it's two A.M.'

Sugar ran the water. Lois said, 'I figured it would be easier to meet movie people where they lived instead of at the studios. So we started looking for stickers wherever we went. Most of the studios use them, maybe all of them. Do they?'

Charley said he didn't know.

'You sure play it cool,' Lois said admiringly. 'We walked around all over. We saw one last Friday in a driveway in Pasadena, but it was a girl. There weren't any here at the Bali-Ho, but when we looked again today we saw yours. Avalon's a *great* studio. They got Mona Dearn. Gordon Hewlett too, right?

'We waited to see if it was a man and then we saw you and we checked with Ab after his wife went out like she always does about nine-thirty, ten, and we put the note under your door. Funny, you never expect to hit lucky where you live, but see how it turned out?'

Charley laughed a little, really worried now that it was over. 'Well, it turned out . . . to be fun. But just how lucky you hit it is debatable.'

'What you said about money,' Lois said, voice silky, hand caressing his arm. 'We wouldn't do this for *money*. What good's money? I mean, the little you get for a trick or two. So we're broke again in a week. We want to meet people, get some work, start our careers. We dance and sing.'

'Act,' Sugar called from the bathroom. 'We shared the leads in all our high school plays. Mr. Blessington always used us.'

Lois smiled. 'You better know it, baby.'

121

Sugar laughed. 'That kooky face, remember? And then crying. Was *he* ever chicken.'

Lois sobered. 'Well, he had a lot to lose.'

Charley sat up quickly. 'I gather you girls live here.'

'First floor,' Sugar said, coming toward them.

'Over near the pool,' Lois said, going past her sister to the bathroom.

Charley was sweating. 'Then the manager you mentioned must be Mr. Terrence.'

'Good old Ab,' Sugar said, yawning. 'I always get tired afterward. Lois gets hungry. How about you?'

'Tired,' Charley muttered, and thought about these two living here, and didn't know whether to laugh or cry. 'You have to understand something. I'm a writer, not a producer, director or casting—'

From the bathroom, Lois said, 'If you know anyone, introduce us.'

'I don't,' Charley said, thinking how obvious this would be to Baiglen. 'Not yet anyway. Perhaps in a month or two—'

'That's all right,' Sugar said, sinking to the edge of the bed. 'We'll hunt around on our own.'

Charley exhaled carefully.

'Just get us on the lot,' she said.

Charley stiffened. 'But you have no pass. I can't—'

Lois came out of the bathroom. 'Don't worry about the pass. We'll stop a block from the studio and get in the trunk.'

Charley grasped at straws. 'There's no trunk. I've got a station wagon.'

Lois came around the other side of the bed and sat down. They both looked at him. Lois said, 'So we'll get under a blanket or in a big box or something. Don't worry, we'll handle it.'

Charley wanted to say no, it was out of the question, but they sat there, one on each side, and he didn't want to hear about Mr. Blessington again and how he had used them in all the school plays and how he had cried. Lois put her hand under the blanket and rubbed his belly. 'Want us to stay the night, Mr. Halpert?'

He shook his head.

'Or one of us?'

'I have to be up early.'

'What time you leaving?'

'You mean tomorrow? You're coming along tomorrow?'

'That's right. But don't worry. We won't forget. We're not that kind. Even if we do real good we won't forget. Maybe we'll be tied up most of the day and night, but there's always the Two O'Clock Jump.' She giggled. 'My father collected Benny Goodman records. The Roaring Twenties. Imagine, man!'

Sugar said, 'The Gay Nineties. O-*do*-dee-do. Wicked, weren't they?'

Lois stood up. 'Well, if you're sure, Mr. Halpert.' She moved to the chair and her clothing. Sugar went to the door. 'Where's that fuckin' light?'

Lois said, 'There you go again. Excuse her, Mr. Halpert. Pop used to wash her mouth with soap.'

Sugar found the light. 'I'm sorry. I know it makes a bad impression.' She walked to the chair, all moving parts jiggling tautly. She was obviously the younger, also the more richly endowed. Lois had a lean, hard body, almost boyish, except in the saucy, jutting rear. They dressed.

'I don't know about tomorrow,' Charley muttered miserably, seeing himself exposed at the gate, dragged before the security chief with the two hoydens, ruined before he got started. At best, he'd become a laughing stock. No, they wouldn't laugh. They'd *snicker*. 'I think we'd better wait a few days. Say next Monday. Give me a chance to look around—'

'Forget it,' Lois said and ran a comb through her hair. Twice down and she was set. 'Leave that to Gert and me.'

'Gert?' Charley asked.

'We had pretty good names,' Sugar said. 'Gertrude and Billy-Mae Granson. That's not bad, is it? Not like those Hiffel-dinkers and Grabowskis and names you hear some of the stars had. But Lois figured we should get the best there is. Lois Lane and Sugar Smart. You got to admit that's in the nitty-gritty groove.'

Lois said, 'Now what time is it you're leaving?'

'Eight-thirty.'

'See you then, baby.' She smiled. 'Hey, you got it made, man, don't look like that. It's swingtime in little old Holly-wood *when* you want it and *how* you want it. No one's going to twist your arm, kicky poppa. We *like* you.'

Sugar nodded. 'Honest.'

He smiled a little, convinced in spite of himself. They were

123

at the door when he said, 'The truth now, how old *are* you two?'

Lois said, 'She's a year younger and I'm a year older,' and they walked out giggling.

He went to the bathroom and scrubbed, went to the sleeper couch and reversed the bedding, went back to the bathroom and showered and scrubbed some more. He remembered the sex information lectures and Mickey Mouse films from his Air Corps days – the oozing chancres and dripping penises and dramatizations of men dropping dead twenty years after a scene such as the one in which he'd just starred. Except that he wouldn't live twenty years the way he was going.

He wondered if Ben Kalik could recommend a good urologist, and reset his alarm for seven, thinking vaguely of leaving before the sisters arrived.

But at 7.30, as he was about to make a cup of instant coffee, they knocked at the door. They each carried a blanket ('for cover up, you know') and wore what Sugar called 'kicky crop tops and jams' – pajama-bright half-blouses and low-slung pants with frilly bellbottoms that left a solid expanse of sun-tanned belly, and belly button, exposed. Lois was in a blue and white print and Sugar in an explosive pink and brown on yellow. They insisted on making his coffee and frying a panful of eggs and ate and talked and joked and kissed him and washed the dishes and gave him a few close-body hugs and by the time each took an arm and led him out the door he had forgotten all about urologists and Mickey Mouse films. They were so animally, electrically *alive* that he would have truly enjoyed himself – if there hadn't been that fear of exposure at the Avalon gate.

The fear grew as they all got into the Rambler's front seat. Lois said, 'Here we go, baby. Operation Smuggle Stuff.' Sugar added, 'The *real* stuff,' and both giggled. He started the engine, and Abner Terrence appeared through the pool gate carrying a red plastic garbage can. Charley waved. Lois and Sugar called, 'Hey!' Terrence's fair, freckled, redhead face hovered briefly between automatic smile and sour disapproval – and settled on sour disapproval. He turned abruptly and went back through the gate.

Charley said, 'What's wrong with *him*?' but had a pretty good idea.

Sugar laughed. 'He's been sleeping with his wife.'

Lois said, 'The silver bombshell.'

124

'Silver *bomb,* you mean,'

'The white tornado.'

'Big wind, you mean,'

'Old faithful.'

'Old fartful!'

They broke up, clutching each other gleefully. Sugar said, 'Don't you think we could go nightclub with a kicky routine like that?' Lois said, 'It's all ad lib, you know.'

Charley pulled the Rambler around the circle. 'I'd have sworn it was written by G. B. Shaw.'

'No,' Sugar said, smiling proudly. 'Made up just then. Right off the top of our heads.'

'I mean,' Lois said, 'it's not like we were all body and no brain. There's *lots* like that, but we got it up here.'

They both tapped their temples to emphasize the point.

He had it up there too – a beaut of a newborn headache.

Three blocks from the studio he pulled to the curb and they got into the back – not the station wagon's loading bed, which they felt was too exposed, but the floor of the back seat. They covered themselves with their blankets (white-stitched 'Bali-Ho-Bali-Ho-Bali-Ho') and murmured to each other and stood up and made adjustments and, once, fell into a fit of giggling. He sat facing stiffly forward, certain that clusters of passersby would descend on him with pointed questions, but except for one elderly woman who paused, smiled vaguely and went on, no one even looked their way.

Lois finally said, voice muffled, 'Hey, check us.'

He leaned over the seat and moved the blanket to cover an exposed shoe. 'You're quite certain you want to take this chance?' he asked.

'What chance?' Lois said.

'It's a snap,' Sugar said. 'Go, man, go!'

He went, but not happily. By the time he reached C-gate he was ready to turn away and tell them it was impossible. But a delivery truck swung in close behind him and there was no turning away. He held out his pass. The guard barely glanced at it, already exchanging comments on the tight National League pennant race with his friend in the truck. Charley drove to the parking area. He found a spot as far removed from any other cars as he could get and slumped over the wheel. 'We're in,' he muttered.

There was a stirring in back, and he quickly added, 'Let me walk away first,' and jumped out and hurried toward the

125

Western Building. He was leaving the parking area when the heavily accented voice hailed him.

'Oh, Meestair Halpairt!'

He suspected, but tensed anyway as he turned. Sugar said, 'Eemagine meeting the famous Meestair Halpairt here!' Lois waved. They were posed prettily some distance from the Rambler and turned and swung away together, tight-pants fannies jiggling in unison. Two aging producer types looked at them and a young man on a studio bike looked at them and they looked back hopefully, smiling with great joy and great promise.

He had to smile too.

Book Two

FRIDAY OCTOBER 14
TO THURSDAY OCTOBER 20

CHARLEY HALPERT

CHERYL picked him up at the Bali-Ho and drove him to Avalon the second day in a row. They walked to the Western Building (named after a now defunct operation that had produced horse operas during the thirties and forties), and Charley thanked her again and passed on his mechanic's assurances that the clutch job would be completed this afternoon, which meant Cheryl wouldn't be inconvenienced again.

She assured him she didn't consider it an inconvenience. 'A pleasure, Chuck,' she murmured as they climbed the stairs to the second floor and their offices. Charley believed her and was flattered and tempted. But temptation was an academic point, since he was unable to function as a male beyond Lois and Sugar.

A problem, those two, and one he solved mornings by swearing to bar the door against them and surrendered to evenings when the summons to their *ménage à trois* came via Lois's soft knock and silky voice. They weren't doing well, despite parts as members of a harem in *Desert Marauders*. They now wanted to meet Carl Baiglen, a notion that gave Charley a graphic nightmare or two and made him decide to put them off indefinitely.

But today was Friday and he was getting away from it all. He was going to Sequoia National Park, his first real rest during the month he had spent in Los Angeles.

As he turned toward his office, Cheryl asked, 'Do you have an appointment for lunch?' He said no and she hesitated and he said, 'Let's eat at the commissary.' She nodded quickly and walked off. He put the key in his door, felt he was being watched and glanced up the hall at Devon Productions. Alan Devon was just turning away.

Charley read through his fifty-three-page treatment, made a few penciled changes, then went down the hall to Baiglen's

129

office. Cheryl said a Mr. McNaughton was with him but she'd buzz anyway. Baiglen said to have Charley come in.

The producer rose from behind his desk. He didn't look well to Charley. 'Yes, the completed treatment. Fine, Chuck, fine. We'll get together Monday.'

'I can start preliminary work on the script—'

'No,' Baiglen snapped, then muttered, 'We don't operate that way. I've neglected you, haven't checked your work in a couple-weeks. Got to see what you've done before—' He sat down. 'You don't have to stick around, Chuck. Have a nice weekend.'

Charley felt edgy. He hesitated, wanting to ask about the first payment. Baiglen seemed to read his thoughts. 'I'll have a check for you Monday morning.' Charley murmured, 'That's all right,' and turned to go. Eighteen hundred wasn't much, but how he needed it! And it was the first tangible proof of his new life.

Baiglen's visitor had been sitting quietly on the couch. Now he rose, hand extended. 'I'm John—' He stopped, chuckled, said, 'Brad Madison. The name is fresh from my agent's imagination.' They shook hands. 'Hope you have a strong role for me, Mr. Halpert.'

'John's new in Hollywood,' Baiglen said.

'Brad, Carl. If my friends don't use it, it'll never stick.'

'We're hoping to find a part for Brad,' Carl said. 'If not in features, then in one of the television—'

'I prefer features,' Madison interrupted, still smiling. 'Carl will end up using me in *Terror Town,* though modesty forbids my saying why.'

Charley glanced at Baiglen and wondered at the producer's expression. Some sort of conflict here.

'By the way,' Madison said, 'you hear about Nat Markal's new project?'

'Rumors,' Baiglen muttered.

'*Persistent* rumors,' Madison said. 'And what about that set being built on the back lot?'

Charley said he hadn't been getting around enough for shop talk.

Madison took a newspaper clipping from his pocket. 'Sheilah Graham is supposedly very hip on Markal projects. I quote: "Nat Markal of Avalon is out to prove he is indeed Emperor of Hollywood. His newest production, title unknown, will dwarf anything yet filmed here or abroad. A set in con-

130

struction has eyebrows rising and certain timid stockholders sweating, it's that *big*! Mona Dearn and Gordon Hewlett will be among ten, count 'em, *ten* top names to star. And word has it Mona will show more of herself in the super than she did in the famous *Playboy* shots." '

Since it hardly concerned him, Charley murmured, 'Sounds exciting,' and, 'Nice meeting you,' and went out the door. A sunny world was waiting, and he was a free man for three days! If he'd had his car, he would have left L.A. immediately. But then again, he'd wanted to explore Avalon – to walk around and see its stages and the old Western town and that new set everyone was talking about.

He told Cheryl he would meet her at the commissary, twelve sharp, and went downstairs. He felt marvelous!

Was it being away from Celia?

He was passing a phone booth when he suddenly realized she was working and Bobby got home from school at two-thirty. If he called at a quarter to three, he would get Bobby in. At a quarter to twelve California time, he could speak to his son!

His heart began to pound. Not that he wanted to antagonize Celia further. But it was the only way. He had called home twice since that first call, and both times she'd found excuses for not bringing Bobby to the phone. Also, he had received no answers to his letters, including those addressed directly to Bobby, which meant that the boy wasn't receiving them.

He walked through the old Western town, deserted as he had hoped, but only a little of the magic came through to him. He kept thinking of Bobby, the quiet little boy who could run hard all day, or sit watching things all day, or walk with his father through stores or woods all day. He kept seeing the lean, wry face and unkempt brown hair and startled-looking eyes.

He went to Stage 6 and a prison set and Stage 12 where a TV comedy was being filmed, and then it was eleven-thirty and he began looking for a phone booth.

He choked back a groan when his father-in-law's high-pitched voice answered. 'Hi, Pop, it's Charles.'

'Charles? Yeah?' The old man was getting hard of hearing. 'Where are you? When're you coming home?' The questions were shouted with unmistakable antagonism.

'Still in California,' Charley said. 'I'll speak to Bobby now.'

131

There was silence.

'Did you hear me, Pop? I'll speak to Bobby.'

'You'll forgive me for saying so, but your wife is having some tough time. You'll forgive me for butting in like I never did, you know, but you should come home today.'

'I've discussed it all with Celia. Listen, get Bobby—'

When the answer came he wasn't surprised. He should have realized he couldn't trick Celia. She would have extracted the promise from her father.

'He's not home.'

'How can you do it?'

'What? I told you. He's out. He's on Knollwood.'

Just then there was a sound in the background, not anything Charley could make out, but it threw the old man into a frenzy. 'I don't have to take that from you! Calling me a liar! Celia said – I don't have to talk to you!'

Charley knew it was not rage the old man was feeling, but pain. Charley's pain and Celia's pain and his grandson's pain. And while a vise squeezed his guts and he could almost *feel* his son a few feet from the phone, he said, 'Take it easy, Pop. It'll all work out.'

There was silence and then, wearily, 'Yeah, well, with God's help.'

Charley said, 'Couldn't you tell her he answered the phone himself? He answers the phone all the time.'

'No,' the broken voice said. 'She wants you home. If this is the only way—' The background sound interrupted, and Charley heard his son: 'Grandpa look—' The old man shouted, 'Good-bye, good-bye!' and the line clicked.

Charley took a few deep breaths and controlled the urge to say what he'd wanted to say to Bobby into a dead phone. He stepped outside. It was time to meet Cheryl.

He ate quickly, silently, more than he should have. He was aware of Cheryl's attempts to reach him, to establish meaningful contact, and he did his best to take a raincheck. But she was subdued when they left the commissary. Charley walked with her back to the office and found himself talking about his phone call, about all the phone calls. She murmured, 'It must be agonizing.'

He shrugged, embarrassed. 'You're just the one to bring troubles to, having so few of your own.'

'I'm glad you told me.' She slipped her hand into his.

His insides shook at the contact, the human contact, the

emotional contact he had missed since leaving home. They parted in a few moments and he returned to the old Western town and was able to experience fantasy and smiled in shock when an extra in cowboy costume materialized around a corner. He walked on, walked farther than he'd imagined he could walk within the confines of the studio; walked out of the area of stages and offices to huge shops where sets were manufactured, and to warehouses where the sets and costumes of fifty years were stored. He looked into open doors and all was dusty and silent.

The silence didn't last. He heard hammering and voices and suddenly came upon twenty-five or thirty workmen erecting half a dozen buildings. Not simple false-front sets like the old Western town. Not walls and doors propped up by planking. But buildings, going up much the way the real thing would.

It took a moment, since this wasn't the way any city on the face of the earth looked today. Then he recognized it.

There was the President's House, or Palace, as the White House had been called before its fire-blackened freestone walls had been painted. And there was the old Capitol, the two wings and connecting building, before the distinctive dome had been added. And workmen were lining a dirt road with poplars, full-grown Lombardy poplars like those Jefferson had planted to relieve the raw frontier ugliness.

Washington before the worst showing American arms had ever made, the most humiliating defeat the nation had ever suffered.

He walked up Pennsylvania Avenue, watching a plowlike machine rut the dirt road as the real avenue had been rutted. He approached the President's House and heard two well-dressed young men arguing about what town this was supposed to be. 'Whatever it is,' one said impatiently, 'why build it this way? Why spend a fortune on this kind of realism? You can't shoot real interiors half as good as you can interior *sets*.' Which was an obvious truth and only made this place more intriguing.

Passing behind the Capitol, the image of a real city weakened. A steam shovel was scooping a moat, or canal, in a straight line from the back of the Senate wing. And there had been no canal that Charley could remember . . .

But of course. This Washington couldn't go up exactly as the real one had. This Washington was for a movie. *Cameras* would create the sense of size and space. What was being built

133

were the important areas of action. The canal could become a waterfront. And that framework could become one of two warships the Americans had burned at the Naval Yard to prevent their falling into British hands. And that low building over there could be the tavern from which Americans had watched the President's House go up in flames.

He wandered around. He approached a stocky man with blue-prints. 'Washington, isn't it?'

The man shrugged and looked away. Surprised, Charley said it was obvious. The man hesitated, then said, 'Yeah, I guess so, if you know a little history. It wasn't obvious a few days ago. Going up fast now. Suppose to be hush-hush according to the brass.'

Charley wondered aloud how anything like those two famous buildings could be kept hush-hush, and the man laughed. 'That's show biz for you.'

They talked a while about the old capital. The man showed Charley his blueprints and said they were based on plans drawn up by Major L'Enfant. They walked around together and the man said Charley was right about the small building's being a tavern, the Indian Princess, and pointed out places where new buildings would rise: 'The Gallatin Home, first to be burned. The Post Office and Patent Building, which the fast-talking Chief of Patents saved. The Sewell House, burned. And Carroll's Row and the Treasury. St. John's church, which I've got marked for grazing cows—'

Charley thanked him and they shook hands and the man said, 'I don't know how far Mr. Markal intends to go, but even this way it's going to run into a fortune. I don't mean a small one either!' Charley had seen the truck unloading propane gas tanks and the men carrying lengths of pipe and fittings that looked like giant gas-range burners into the buildings. He pointed and said, 'And then to burn it all.' The man shook his head. 'No one's going to burn *this* set. Mr. Markal ordered that gas stuff for special lighting – authentic flames during filming *without* endangering the set.'

Charley said so long and hurried off. It was time to meet Cheryl.

At an intersection near the parking lot, he saw her approaching with Alan Devon. Devon was talking, gesticulating. Cheryl saw Charley, waved and walked more quickly. When Charley met them, Cheryl said, 'Well, have a nice weekend, Mr. Devon.' Devon nodded, curtly and strode off. Cheryl took cigarettes from her bag, and Charley held his lighter for her. They began to walk. Cheryl said, 'I've got some good-bad news for you. You're not going to Sequoia. That's the bad part. The good part isn't clear yet, but it might be *very* good.' She smiled at him. 'Carl got a call from Markal's office. You and Carl, others I imagine, are to leave your home numbers with his secretary. I already took care of that. You're to stay available today and tomorrow.'

'Sit around near the phone?'

'I'm afraid so.'

'What does it mean?'

She shrugged. 'The rumors, I suppose.'

He looked blank.

'Seems Emperor Nat is going to do something to make *Cleopatra* and all the other superdupers look like trailers.'

'But what does he want with *me*?'

'Who knows? Something you wrote. Something he heard about you. Something someone said. We sent your treatment over too.'

He didn't like that. Fresh opinion brought in to complicate matters – and a *level* of opinion he wasn't ready to face. His weekend aborted. And nothing would come of it anyway because what would Emperor Nat Markal want with Charley Halpert when he could command the biggest names in the business? A mistake. A damn fool mistake. Markal's secretary had gotten things wrong. He said so.

'You don't understand Hollywood, Chuck. This is the way things happen.'

He wasn't convinced.

'It must be something you wrote,' she said. 'I'm not saying you're going to be A-Number-One boy on the project, but perhaps you'll be used as an expert opinion. On World War II pilots or apartment houses or New York police procedure.'

He looked at her. 'You've read my novels?'

'Why not? The main branch Hollywood library has all three of them, and I wanted to know what sort of writer my boss was hiring.'

'Did you find out?'

'A very capable writer. A very honest writer. A very nega-tive writer who'll have to brighten up considerably for Holly-wood.' She snapped her fingers. 'Hey! Maybe Markal has a very capable, honest, negative writer in mind?'

He laughed. She said, 'It's worth losing your weekend just

135

to meet him. If you want a career here, Emperor Nat is the man to know.'

That at least made sense, and he nodded and said, 'We'll reschedule the trip for after the first draft.' She didn't answer, and he realized he'd used the word 'we', and my God was it a Freudian slip?

On the freeway she told him about her weekend job as a tutor. Then they were at the service station, and she waited until he was certain his car was ready. He wished her a pleasant weekend tutoring and added, 'As pleasant as work can be.'

'It can be very pleasant if the alternatives—' She smiled a little and shook her head. He reached in the window and touched her hand. She said, *'Ciao*, baby,' and drove off. He watched until the Plymouth sedan turned the corner.

ISA YEE

A few more days shooting and she would be through with *Waikiki Nights*. The garden-fantasy scene had gone well, though it had required four retakes because of Lobo and Nina. Isa felt she had actually done better on the second take than on the one they finally put in the can. If she had been a star she would have fought for the one that showed her to best advantage. But she wasn't a star and she was no longer sure she would become a star.

No word from Nat Markal. He hadn't called her, nor had he been in touch with Jerry Storm. Two weeks ago Isa had decided she would have to change her plans, drop the aloof waiting-game and contact Emperor Nat herself. She hadn't been able to get through to him. He was in New York, his secretary said.

She had seen Alan Devon, who had been cool, polite and toward the end of the interview, encouraging, though he said he would have to view the rushes on *Waikiki Nights* before he spoke to Markal. She felt he had taste and a real knowledge of the industry and would therefore be no problem. She had also seen Baiglen, who had seemed impressed with her credits and with the rushes he had already viewed, and had promised to consider her 'very seriously' for the ingenue role in his upcoming feature. It could pay as little as three thousand, less

136

than a lead TV role, but now that her confidence in swinging Markal was shaken and she would soon find herself in the position all actors dreaded, 'between engagements', *Terror Town* looked pretty good.

Isa was back on Stage 3, sitting in her shadowy corner. The nightclub set was again the center of activity – frenzied activity since Zig Shroeder was way behind schedule. *Waikiki Nights* was supposed to have been shot in thirty days, but would run more than forty the way things were going. Markal wasn't known for pampering directors who went so far over schedule and budget.

Lobo and the heavy, Wallace Brent, a longtime feature performer who had bombed out in a TV series of his own a few seasons back, were doing their big climax scene: a bit of dialogue, Brent pulling a gun, Lobo knocking him cold. Brent was a thick-set, world-weary lush now running to jowls and fat who liked boys as well as girls. He was always putting his hands on people. When he had tried it with Isa three weeks ago, she had ground her spike heel into his instep and murmured, 'Pardon', as he grunted in agony. He had looked at her hard and in his best heavy manner said, 'Be careful. I eat little girls like you for breakfast.' She had replied, 'No need to tell me *that*, Mr. Brent.' A few of the kids had snickered, and Brent had limped over to a blond dancer.

Now, no longer sure of Nat Markal, she was half-inclined to try Brent, who she knew had strong contacts in the gay network and could swing parts on five or six big television shows.

The blues. All week long the blues. And a weekend of playing in the sun wouldn't change anything. Only work or the promise of work did that.

Why hadn't Markal called? She *couldn't* have been wrong about the way he'd looked at her! Her instincts were always so sharp in that department.

She sighed and fidgeted on her stool and glanced at the group of extras taking their places at nightclub tables under Shroeder's direction. Paul Morse was there, since this scene was a retake and would follow her solo dance of a month ago in the chronology of the completed film. Morse hadn't tried to approach or greet her, hadn't even glanced her way that she had noticed. He was standing near his aunt, the make-up assistant.

She continued watching him. He wasn't good-looking, not

137

by Hollywood standards, being too Negroid, too kinky-haired, too black. But he was sharp enough, that much she was forced to admit. His instincts were every bit as good as her own – perhaps better in light of how she had misjudged Markal. He had sensed a sister under the ivory skin.

Could something like that have happened with Markal?

Paul Morse seated himself, then changed position as Teddy Base, Shroeder's assistant, redirected him, using a blowup still from the last shooting as blueprint. Now he was facing her, and before she could shift her gaze he looked up, right at her. She remembered the last thing she had said to him, on the phone that evening a month ago, and winced inside, but kept her gaze level. He did too, and then he smiled slowly and mouthed a word. Even as she told herself she couldn't possibly make it out, she seemed to hear him: 'Yassah.'

So what. So he was telling her he was Negro and proud of it.

Or that *she* was Negro and nothing could change it.

But he couldn't know. No one could know.

Nat Markal had millions of dollars and power and people who would do things for him. It was just possible he had found out about Louella Walters. It was just possible he knew what Paul Morse only suspected, and the knowledge had eliminated Isa Yee as both personal interest and star potential.

Why had she ever pitched Markal! She should have known he would be too much for her. Emperor Nat the Hollywood Giant, as *Variety* called him. Now word would get around and there would be laughter. And sneers too.

The music started, the cameras rolled, Shroeder called, 'Action!' Isa tried to immerse herself in the excitement of movie-making, but after a while she thought of Markal, of his reading her official biography and laughing and tossing it away. She thought of him constructing a true biography of Isa Yee, and the tidal wave of sneers and laughter rising and washing her clear out of Hollywood.

Born in the town of Dovenville, Kentucky, in the section of shanties sometimes called Coontown by white Southerners, Isa Yee – true name Louella Walters – was given a classical Negro upbringing by her mother's field-hand family (one old grandmother), an upbringing tempered by the warmth and wit of neighbors who helped her remember her father, 'that long-gone Chink.' Louella's mother, the

popular roadhouse waitress Sue-Ellen Walters, was herself
the result of miscegenation, *her* mother having been pressed
into service by a trio of white gentlemen who came upon
her as she walked from a field of famous Kentucky burley.
Sue-Ellen's experience was initially more pleasant, since she
welcomed the courtship of the Chinese air cadet she knew
only as Yee. But later, after failing to locate his field and
inform him of the impending arrival of an heir, pleasant
memories evaporated. So it was that Louella grew up the
third consecutive bastard daughter in the Walters clan (the
grandmother chuckled bitterly when asked if she had known
her father, stating she'd lost count after the seventh), but
she was destined for more exciting things than either mother
or grandmother. Affectionately nicknamed 'Slit Eyes,'
'Cheese Face' and 'Yellow Menace' by her schoolmates,
Louella firmly turned her back on all childhood fun and
applied herself to her studies. While spending summer after-
noons in the town library, she was surprised to be treated
with courtesy and consideration by elderly white ladies who
thought her Eurasian, an exotic species infinitely preferable
to them uppity Nigras. Despite her pride in and love of the
Negro people who had treated her with such warm good
spirits, Louella decided it was only right to recognize her
white and Asian blood. After all, those two races had given
her many advantages, such as straight hair, small features
and light pigmentation.

The death of the grandmother and the desire of the mother
to better her position presented Louella with the opportunity to go from rural to urban life, from small town to big
city with all attendant opportunities. Chicago was the city.
Fourteen years old and fast developing into a fair-skinned
beauty, Louella prevailed upon her mother to move to a
mixed neighborhood where she could attend a high school
with as many white as Negro students. The separate-but-
equal standards of Southern education stood her in good
stead, and after only one year of accelerated studies and
special assisance she was able to maintain a C— average. Always, she drew attention from the opposite sex, both white
and black, and in response acquired a manner which was,
to quote a male classmate, cold as a witch's tit. She did,
however, carefully select several friends, male and female,
of a better class, all of them white by some strange trick of
fate, and visited their homes occasionally. She did not feel

free to return the courtesy, because Sue-Ellen had entered upon an energetic social life with a series of 'uncles' who, one after the other, took up residence in the Walters' household.

At fifteen, Louella joined the Barrymore Society, a dramatic group. Afterward, she joined the school's dance and voice clubs. Regretfully, these extracurricular activities left her little time for home or social life, but she was already moving toward that dedication to career that was to mark her adult years.

At eighteen, Louella starred in the senior play, a musical that had three smash performances and was mentioned in the *Tribune*. A week later, only four days before graduation, the burgeoning beauty was orphaned when an enraged former uncle came upon Sue-Ellen and the ardent present uncle in a resort off the Loop. Two thousand dollars' insurance was no compensation for a mother's love, but it put Louella on a bus for Los Angeles. Somewhere along the way the idea that had first occurred to her in the Dovenville library became a full-fledged plan. Out of the mouths of old Southern ladies willing to accept a degree of color as long as it wasn't connected with Nigras came Isa Yee, Eurasian, half-Spanish-patrician, half-wealthy-Chinese. A rich mixture, but not too uppity, antagonizing neither the racist nor the liberal.

Miss Yee studied, worked in motion pictures and television, grew more beautiful and three years younger. Before her decision to leave the entertainment world for domestic service, she was an outstanding example of the heights to which an enterprising Negro girl can rise by not only denying her race but learning to hate it. . . .

Isa stared at the nightclub set, tasting the bitterness of her fantasy. The quiet male voice said, 'Black thoughts, huh, baby?'

She snapped her head to the left. It was Paul Morse. She glanced at the set again and saw they had finished reshooting and were setting up a new scene. She also saw Emma, the makeup assistant, watching, looking tense and unhappy. The aunt, at least, knew the score!

She began to rise. Morse put his hand on her shoulder. It was a big lean hand and very strong. He pushed her back down easily.

'Let me introduce myself.'

She looked at his hand.

He removed it – but slowly, his fingers lingering. 'Humphrey Barchester,' he said and ducked his head a little.

It had been a tough few weeks. She needed a laugh. She laughed.

'Can anyone with a name like that be a black bastard?' he asked.

She tried to turn away, but his eyes probed deep and held her. She murmured, 'I'm sorry about that.'

'You disappoint me. I'd expect that from fay, not mixed-blood.' She made her decision then. No more losing her cool with this man. She shrugged and said, 'What's the bit with the name?'

'No bit. It's my real name. Paul Morse is for Central Casting. Humphrey Barchester is the one on the birth certificate.'

'You poor thing.'

He smiled. 'I don't know. You'd be surprised how a name like that sticks in people's minds.'

'I'll bet.'

'And it's important that people, black people, remember my name. So they'll listen when I talk to them.'

'What are you when you're not acting, some sort of salesman?'

'You could say that. I sell black. Like in black bastard.'

She sighed. 'All right, Mr. Morse or Barchester or whatever. I've said I'm sorry, so if you don't mind—'

'The trouble is I do mind. I meant everything I said on the phone, even if you didn't.'

She looked at the set.

'I guess it's no use asking you out again?'

She shook her head.

'I thought not. So I'll have to call at your apartment some evening.'

She jerked her eyes to him. 'Don't you ever do that! We have a security system. You'd be very sorry!'

'Probably. But you're worth the risk.'

She stared. 'Why?'

He shrugged. 'Chemistry. Fate. Voodoo. Some old lady in Watts or Pacoima stuck a pin through my heart and I'm spelled.'

'A man with your education and nerve, you can get all the women you want.' She quickly added, 'Your own kind.'

141

He leaned close. She froze, not knowing what to expect. But it certainly wasn't what followed. 'You ever attend rallies?'

'What rallies?'

'C.O.R.E. S.N.C.C. Even that tired old N.A.A.C.P.'

She made a laughing sound 'I even turn them off when they talk on television'.

'The Eurasian backlash. We were afraid of that.'

She looked at the set. Emma was at the dressing table, try-ing to work on Nina and watch her nephew at the same time. The poor woman looked frantic.

Isa turned her head. Morse had bent lower, and their eyes and lips were suddenly very close. 'Mr. Morse—'

'Humphrey.'

'You *want* to be called that?'

'It's me. Like my Momma named me. Like my great-great-grandfather took his master's name. It's a big name, too big for a Negro to carry, people think. Funny for a Negro to carry, people think. Only it's not. Not for this Negro. I'm go-ing to have to add a middle initial before I'm through.' He grinned.

His teeth were slightly uneven, his eyes narrow and pene-trating. He had a real wicked look seen this close. An interest-ing look . . .

She stood up. 'Good-bye, Humphrey Barchester.' She shook her head a little, smiling.

He nodded, eyes reaching for hers. 'So long, Isa Yee. Which one of us is real, do you suppose, and which the put-on?'

Her smile weakened. 'All people are real.'

'That's so, *Isa Yee*?' And he went back to the set.

She glared after him, wanting to say something because he had angered her. And then took herself in hand and thought it through and realized there was only one man to whom she had anything to say, only one man who counted now.

It was ten-thirty. She wouldn't be on camera until late in the afternoon, the way Shroeder was going along. She had to make a move, had to take a chance.

She picked up her bag and walked toward the exit. She walked quickly, briskly, so as not to lose courage. A grip opened the heavy soundproofed door for her. She smiled and murmured, 'Thanks so much.' He nodded and hurried to get the outer door. She could feel him looking after her as she stepped into brilliant sunshine. She knew he was still looking

142

as she moved off, unhurriedly now, building her strength as a female, her excitement as a female, as she did when going on camera. *Exactly* as when going on camera.

She walked toward Nat Markal's office.

CARL BAIGLEN

Until last night, Carl had felt things were working out. Not that he was free of John McNaughton – or Brad Madison as he now called himself. But the heightened awareness of the past had receded as Madison busied himself with acting lessons and interviews and stayed away from the office. The bills had to be paid, of course, but they were reasonable, and besides, Carl had recently come into an unexpected bit of money from a TV deal. His natural ebullience, his physical well-being and drive and energy had reasserted themselves, and he was enthusiastic about the first half of the treatment Halpert had done and about several stories he had selected for future projects.

Home held Ruth, and she was an endless source of joy and comfort. Home also held Andy, and there the joy and comfort was flawed by disquieting changes, changes Carl attributed to Andy's time of life. No boy of sixteen was easy to handle, and Andy was at a stage where he had become rather caustic and withdrawn. Carl could understand, certainly, the sexual and social pressures on a boy that age. Andy was trying to decide what he would become, what profession he would aim at when he entered college next year. One thing was sure: he had no ambitions in the film industry. This didn't particularly bother Carl, but Andy's lack of respect for his father's work did.

It was a recent development; the change took place sometime around his fifteenth birthday. Until then he had been a joy to have along at previews, responding with excitement to plot twists and special photographic effects. When Carl had reminded him of this recently, Andy had said, 'Yes, a child's responses, and I'm no longer a child.' Which implied that only children could enjoy Carl Baiglen's work, that he made kiddie horror films.

Terror Town would show Andy, would show the entire industry what Carl Baiglen could do. Halpert had promised him

143

the completed treatment this week, and Carl had already let
Pen Guilfoyle, Avalon's head of casting, know what types he
was interested in seeing. (Guilfoyle's reaction had been disturbing, but then again he was one of those guys who jumped
at every rumor. 'Let's see what Markal *lets* us do, Carl,' the
slick little man had said. 'Let's see if any of us work on anything but that big deal of his.' As if Markal was going to stop
scheduled projects for some crazy trillion-dollar gamble! That
set could be for *any* good-sized historical.)

There were a few professional problems. There always
were. Like Pier Andrei. Carl had seen both of Markal's recommendations two weeks ago, and Isa Yee was fine – lovely and
with solid acting ability and fine credits. She should do very
well in the ingenue part. But the Italian was another matter.
Sure, she might help at the box office because of her name
and she might be right for the madwoman part. But she had
come to him stinking drunk, made a plain-out pitch for a sex
relationship 'so we can be as one in creating a smash hit for
Avalon' and had shaken her head and laughed when he described the madwoman part. 'No, no, that's not what my dear
friend Nat has in mind. A mature woman, yes, and possibly
a menace, but it would be ludicrous to make me out ancient
and a madwoman. I am not yet thirty-six. What we have to
do is consult with the author—'

He was lunching with Nat Markal today. He had tried to
contact him immediately after seeing Pier Andrei, but Markal
had left unexpectedly for New York and returned only Wednesday. They would talk and he would find out just how
strongly Markal was committed to the lush.

The week after next was his wedding anniversary. He was
thinking of taking Ruth to Las Vegas. She wasn't much for
gambling, but they both enjoyed the big floor shows and
change of pace.

So despite Brad Madison everything was more or less normal, the mixture as before that had made him a generally
happy man – up until last night, that is.

He had worked late with a film editor, cutting *Girl Giant of
Atlantis* down to prescribed length for television. He would
do the same to *Professor Roach* and a third feature still to be
selected, according to the deal Dave Sankin made with A.B.C.
It would mean upwards of fifty thousand dollars for him,
found money, and he drove home thinking he could exercise
his stock option and buy a few hundred shares of Avalon

common. He entered the house at nine, calling out, 'Ruth, honey?' eager to share his thoughts with her.

Violet came to the foyer. 'Company, Mr. Baiglen.'

He was surprised. 'Who?'

'A Mr. Madison. You want I should make you some dinner?'

He didn't answer. He was already hurrying to the living room.

Madison was sitting on the couch with Ruth. He held a brandy snifter and smiled ruefully when he saw Carl. 'Guess I picked the wrong day for a visit. At least to spend time with the master of the house.'

Carl managed a smile and went to Ruth. He kissed her and turned to Andy, who was seated in the armchair near the fireplace. 'How'd we do?'

'Ninety-two in math and eighty-five in history.'

Carl said, 'Fine,' and went to the sideboard and poured himself a Scotch. He drank it down quickly, his back to the others, and poured another before turning.

Madison chuckled. 'That looks like a hard day at the studio. I was giving Ruth my impressions of Los Angeles. We were wondering if they matched yours when you first came from Devereux. Andy says he was too young to remember.' He smiled at the boy.

Ruth said, 'As a native Southern Californian, my impressions don't count. I was twenty-one before I discovered that the entire world wasn't like L.A.'

She and Madison laughed. Carl went to the blue armchair beside the couch. He seated himself and drank and spoke carefully. 'What time did you get here, Brad?' It was now past nine.

'Four-thirty.'

'I never get home before five-thirty.'

'Actually closer to six most evenings,' Rush said. 'But Brad had the impression—'

'I'm sorry,' Madison interrupted. 'I thought you said you'd be home early tonight. Besides, didn't we have an appointment?'

'Tentative,' Carl said, and wanted another drink and lit a cigarette.

Madison stood up. 'I seem to have made a mess of it.'

'Come now,' Ruth said, glancing at Carl reprovingly. 'What difference does it make *when* you were supposed to come?

145

You're here and you've made Violet happier than she's been in years.' To Carl: 'He praised her meat loaf, and no one's done that in the three years she's worked for us!'

Carl managed the laugh, but it was an effort. Madison knew his hours well enough. Madison had never been invited here, never would be, and knew that too.

'I really have to be going,' Madison said. He stepped to Carl and patted his shoulder. 'We'll get together tomorrow morning.'

He turned to Ruth and thanked her for dinner and went to Andy and shook his hand. 'You're a very good-looking boy, though you don't favor your father too much.'

Carl tensed.

'Dad says I look like my mother,' Andy murmured, eyes down.

Madison turned blandly to Ruth. 'Oh?'

'Not me,' Ruth said. 'Didn't you know Carl's first wife?'

'No.'

She waited for an explanation. Madison smiled easily. Carl cleared his throat and said, 'We were ... business acquaintances. Just never got around to each other's homes.'

'And now we're changing that,' Madison said. 'You'll have to see my apartment. I'm just getting it furnished.' He waved and moved to the foyer. Carl began to rise. Madison said, 'Please don't bother. Good night.'

'I don't like him,' Andy announced as soon as the front door closed. 'He's pitching all the time.'

'What sort of thing is that to say about your father's friend?' Ruth asked. 'I found him mannerly and interesting. Incredibly handsome, of course.'

'Did he pitch *you*?' Carl asked sharply.

She laughed. 'Don't you trust your friend?'

Carl shrugged, seeing she was pleased by his reaction. 'He's not really a friend. An actor, trying to make out. He's using our common background as an entry point. So Andy isn't far wrong.'

Ruth sighed. 'That's show biz. You hungry?'

He said a sandwich in the kitchen would do, if she would join him. She got up and began to walk by. He took her hand. 'You're beautiful tonight.' She glanced at Andy, always a little reticent in her stepson's presence. 'Did you know your father was a mad lover?'

Andy slouched low in the armchair, eyes down, smiling

146

faintly. The smile was Myra's. His small, tight frame was also more Myra than Carl. He was shorter, slimmer, darker than his father. The similarities to Myra were many and, lately, disturbing. When Ruth went out, he said, 'Mr. Madison going to work for you, Dad?'

'He might.'

Andy examined his hands. 'Be careful how you cast him. He's a fag.'

Carl was shocked, and covered with a sophisticated shrug, 'Many actors are homosexuals. It doesn't stop them from doing good work. But not Madison. Just *look* at him.'

Andy smiled.

Carl said, 'Didn't he tell you he was a police officer?'

Andy's smile grew. 'Funny how little your generation knows about deviants.'

'Your generation will teach us,' Carl snapped.

'Well gee, don't get *mad*. I merely stated a fact.'

Carl put out his cigarette. 'What makes you think he's queer?'

'I have seen enough of them. Down at the beach last summer almost every other guy wasn't a guy.'

'Did Madison—' Carl began, upset and embarrassed.

Andy sighed in that superior way he'd been affecting lately, 'No, Dad. He didn't do or say a thing. It's just that he looks at Mom a certain way and at me a certain way and it should be reversed.'

'I think you're wrong.'

'Wouldn't be the first time.' He rose, stretched, started for the foyer. 'The Honda needs some work. Took me ten minutes to get started at school today.'

Carl said they'd bring it in to the dealer Saturday. He had another drink, a small one, and went to the kitchen. He ate his sandwich and talked and tried to relax, but Ruth finally asked what the matter was. He said he had a headache, and she massaged his temples. When she tried to discuss Brad Madison, he changed the subject.

He was in his office at eight-thirty Friday morning, tensely waiting for Madison to arrive. The ex-cop walked in at ten. Instantly Carl put himself on guard, careful not to let Madison see how anxious he'd been about this meeting. 'I can only spare a minute.'

'A minute,' Madison said softly. 'A president can die in a minute, a nation's destiny be altered. A life can be conceived

147

in a minute, or a world destroyed by atomic holocaust. You're too generous, my friend.'

Carl stared. Madison went to the couch and sat down. 'One of Bernard's little exercises. Take a commonplace remark and respond to it dramatically, melodramatically, or humorously. During the course of a normal day I get in more solid acting than a star in a full-length feature. Bernard was a very good choice as coach, Carl. I've been meaning to thank you.'

'How would you respond to this statement? Stay away from my home!'

Madison lit a cigarette. 'I've completed six performances at the Santa Ana Playhouse. My agent says I killed the ladies. Raskolnikov, no less. I donated a thousand dollars to the playhouse fund. You'll get the bill.'

'What was the idea?'

'To get a part. To prove to Lee that I'm as good as I know I am. It's vital that the agent believe wholly in—'

'I mean coming to my house!'

Madison leaned back and crossed his legs. He sat big and smug and smiling, and Carl suddenly hated him as he hadn't hated anyone in all his life, including Myra.

'The idea was to meet your wife and son. To let you know I had met your wife and son. To show you how simple it would be to let your wife and son know you killed Myra Baiglen.'

Carl moved his lips, trying to form the proper question. Madison spoke first.

'I'm going to recreate your thinking on the subject of Brad Madison, formerly John McNaughton. Here's what you've been saying to yourself. "A month has passed since Madison left the Devereux Police Department. I've paid the bills and have the canceled checks to prove it. In a short while he'll be working for me. Now what have I got to fear from him? How can he go to the police and say he has evidence against me? Won't it be obvious he's been blackmailing me? He has too great a stake in Hollywood now and he'll have more as time goes on. I don't think I have to wait for him to be earning his way. I think I can boot him in the ass soon." ' He dragged on his cigarette. 'That's right, isn't it, Bagel?'

Carl flushed. 'Watch your damned mouth.'

'See? You feel free to snap at me. You no longer fear me, Bagel. You think the ax I hold over your head has dulled. But you're wrong, and last night I determined just *how* wrong. Your son has fond memories of his mother. Your wife is a

148

lady, not a tough show-doll turned producer's wife, as I thought she might be. You'd lose them both, Carl. Never doubt that for a second. You'd lose them both, even if you beat the rap.'

They looked at each other. Carl said, 'I'll continue to pay the bills. Is that what you wanted to hear?'

Madison flicked ashes into a tray. 'Ruth told me you've been cutting a feature for A.B.C. television. And that two more are included in the deal. And that you're delighted with the exposure. She didn't discuss money, but I assume—'

Carl stood up.

Madison said, 'I need two thousand dollars. I can't bill you for everything. A social life requires cash in the pocket. Courting a beautiful woman requires cash in the pocket.'

Carl came around the desk, fists clenched. Madison put back his head and laughed. 'Come off it, Carl. I'm six-four, a hundred ninety pounds, and I was a cop.'

Carl stood there, trembling with rage and hatred. 'Social life,' he said, remembering Andy's comments. 'Courting a beautiful woman.' He laughed thickly.

Madison's expression changed, grew watchful.

'Who do you think you're kidding?' Carl said, giving his words all the sneer he could muster.

'You're very moral – for a murderer.'

The word struck Carl, drained him of strength. 'I'm no murderer,' he muttered, and retreated behind his desk.

'I think you are. I think you planned your wife's death and carried it out beautifully. Premeditated, as they say in my old profession. Murder in the first degree. A capital offense.'

Carl sank into his chair. Madison came across the room. 'My check, please.'

Carl wrote it out. Madison put it in his pocket without so much as glancing at it. He returned to the couch. 'Now that the unpleasantries are over, let's talk about my career. What have you been doing for me?'

Carl said it wasn't time for anything but training. Madison said he had been acting all his life, in one form or another, and had proved his ability in Santa Ana. 'Bernard says I'm ready for anything I can get, television or features. Call him, why don't you? And call Lee too. He said he would put his reputation on the line supporting me.' Carl began to answer, but Madison said, 'Don't discuss it with me, Carl. *Do* it. I want some work *next week*. The trouble with you, Carl, is

149

you don't really believe in my career. I'm an actor, a good one, and my looks will make me a star. Once I *am* a star, you're really off the hook. Because then and only then will I have as much – more, to my way of thinking – to lose as you do.' He walked to the door. 'By the way, don't be shocked at the bill for these.' He indicated his clothing with a sweeping gesture: blue cruise jacket, cream sport shirt, navy-blue trousers, black slipper shoes. 'They're the best.'

Carl said nothing.

'You don't think they're a little fruity, do you? The shop I patronize has a reputation ... well, people suspect it.'

Carl turned away in his swivel chair. Madison laughed. 'Think how tough it would be, baby, if I went ape over *you*!'

Carl's face flamed. Madison laughed himself out the door.

Carl phoned Lee Denkerson, the young agent to whom he had sent the then John McNaughton. Lee was either trying to be nice, thinking Madison a close friend of Carl's, or he actually believed Madison was a major prospect. 'With his looks, Carl, he doesn't need much else. And surprise, surprise, he can act!' Carl said to get Madison over to Myles Stone of *Winning the West* first thing Monday morning. Then he called Myles and gave ten minutes of hard sell, after which he sat slumped and still at his desk. His concept of not letting Madison go too far was revealed as nonsense. Madison would go as far as he wanted.

He checked his watch. An hour and a half before lunch with Markal.

'I think you planned your wife's death ... Premeditated ... Murder in the first degree. A capital offense.'

He felt a weakness, a trembling. No one had ever said that to him. He had never said it to himself.

Had he murdered her?

It was a cold day. He remembered that because Myra had bundled Andy up in far too much clothing and the boy had complained. But Myra never changed her mind, not about anything, and she slapped the boy and shouted, 'You *want* to get sick! You *want* me to slave over you like I slave over your father with his cramps and heartburn and saying I have to cook special for him.' Andy had run out, crying, and Myra turned on Carl. It was Saturday. Another happy weekend in the Baiglen household. 'Get me a fulltime cook and maid. I can't handle special diets and this house and all the work. I'm not well myself. My headaches—'

150

He had gone upstairs, his stomach cramping. He had never known cramps and heartburn before marrying Myra. Now his doctor said he had an incipient ulcer.

He went to the spare bedroom fitted out as a study and sat in the armchair and picked up the book he'd been reading: Bosley Crowther's *Lion's Share*, a history of M.G.M. He had some two hundred books on shelves along the walls, most concerned with the movie industry. There were histories, biographies, collections of articles, novels about Hollywood. There were ghost, horror and science-fiction stories to feed his dreams of producing special-effects films.

The door opened. Myra stood there. 'Reading that movie trash again?'

He didn't answer, waiting for her to go away.

'I know what you're thinking,' she said. 'Don't try it.'

'Don't try what?'

Her eyes bulged out at him, her face twisted. '*Filthy!* Hollywood with those filthy women and you think you can leave me and go there and live with those filthy women! I know you, Carl. Desertion. I'll get every penny you have. Everything here and everything you make there! But I'll never divorce you!'

He had heard it before. And always before he had told himself they would work it out – she would change and they would get along and he would get his chance in Hollywood.

But this dismal February day he suddenly knew she would never change, except to grow more hateful, more sick and suspicious. They hadn't made love in five months, by mutual consent. She was no wife to him any longer. She hated him, hated life. She would never let him go, and he would die with his dreams shriveled inside him.

He stood up. He didn't know what he was going to do. But he had lain awake nights thinking of ways out and had arrived, inevitably, at guilty fantasies of Myra's death. He had counted the ways in which she might die, and among them was the staircase.

She had often run down the long flight – twenty-three stairs by actual count – run wildly either to reach Andy when he upset her, or from Carl when he was goaded into raging at her, or from her own tormenting thoughts. He had once tried to phone a psychiatrist after a scene in which she mixed accusations of infidelity with charges of plots against her life. In sudden fear of being sent to an institution, she had rushed to escape to the street, had tripped and almost plunged down the stairs. He had told her how lucky she was.

Another time she had been ranting at him about everything she could think of and he had finally leaped up from his chair, insane himself for once, and raised his fist to strike her. This time her flight had been headlong, blind and gibbering. Had she tried the stairs, she would certainly have fallen, but she chose the bathroom instead, a favorite refuge when the bolt was thrown and the shower turned on to drown out all threatening sound.

When he finally did bring in a psychiatrist, she phoned her mother and sister, then got to the bathroom and locked the door. The two women arrived, and with them their lawyer. They contradicted everything Carl said and accused him of using extreme measures in a simple family quarrel. The psychiatrist was angry at Carl for involving him in 'a touchy legal question'. Carl then suggested Myra go home with her mother, but the resultant huddle with the lawyer brought a flat no. She would never give up her husband, her son, her home, her state of mind. The mother and sister left after assuring her they would see she was fully protected. They knew what Myra was and wanted her as far from their own homes as possible. It was Carl Baiglen who would carry the burden of Myra all his life.

But when he faced her in his study that February day, he was no longer willing to fulfill the martyr's role they had assigned to him. There was a burning impatience to be rid of his incipient ulcer. He raised his fist as he had that other time, and her voice choked off and he backed away. 'If you don't give me a divorce,' he said, 'I'm going to kill you!'

The terror burst across her face, the psychotic terror of a woman who lived in a world haunted by hatred and persecution, who suspected plots against her life all the time. She twisted and ran, a jumble of bathrobe and flying hair and flailing arms, careering into the hall and toward the staircase. A high, gibbering sound flowed in her wake, and her head turned, jerking, to look back at him. She was almost at the staircase. She was going to plunge down the staircase.

He watched, horrified, and at the last moment shouted, 'Myra, look out!' Her head jerked back around front and she ran on by the stairs and into the bathroom at the end of the hall. The door slammed shut, the bolt clicked. She was in her sanctuary. He went slowly down the hall and stopped

152

at the door. 'I'm sorry,' he said, because deep under his hatred and despair was pity for her tormented life.

'Tricks!' she screamed. 'You have a knife! I can hear you picking at the lock! Please don't kill me. Carl, don't, don't—' She beat at something, the wall perhaps, and wept hysterically. He tried to tell he meant her no harm. The shower came on, drowning out his voice. He went downstairs and had a drink. Andy came in. He went back upstairs and the bathroom door was still locked and the shower still ran.

He made Andy a sandwich and the child took it into the living room to eat while watching television. He went upstairs again. The shower had stopped and he heard Myra breathing just behind the door. He put his mouth to the crack and said, 'Myra, how can we live this way? It's wrong for both of us and for Andy too. A trial separation—'

She interrupted him. She spoke quietly, with an undercurrent of savage satisfaction. She told him that she had tricked him into marriage, five years before, purposely becoming pregnant while he thought she was using a diaphragm, that she didn't care for him – only for the security he represented.

Something happened in his mind. A protective barrier toppled, a door marked Danger opened. He removed his shoes. She called out, 'You're there, Carl. I know you're there.' He moved past the staircase to the master bedroom and inside and closed the door soundlessly and waited. Later, he heard the bathroom door open. He told himself all he was going to to do was grab her, make her see there was nothing to fear, bring her downstairs and give her a stiff drink and talk to her about changes they had to make in their lives.

She left the bathroom on hesitant, shuffling feet. He listened, then flung open the door and stepped out. She was about to start down the stairs. 'Myra,' he whispered. Her head jerked around. He reached for her and he was smiling. Of course he was smiling. What else would he be doing with his son downstairs watching television and the light only now fading from the windows and neighbors on both sides and kids' voices sounding from outside?

She leaned straight out over the stairs away from him and his smile. She fell without a sound until she hit face first, then cried out briefly as her neck broke. She rolled and tumbled all the way to the last three steps. He rushed down the stairs, shouting, 'Myra, my God! My God!'

153

The ambulance came and the police came and Carl spoke in a trembling voice, a man who admitted quarrels and problems. When the mother and sister came he said, 'Couldn't you see she needed help? When I sent for the analyst, when I wanted her to go to the hospital, you and your lawyer ... when she needed help, you and your lawyer—' No one said him nay and suspicions were not facts and the authorities had fewer suspicions than the others and that was what counted.

And all the time that letter had been upstairs, jammed behind the medicine chest – the letter that could destroy him.

The phone rang. He sat at his desk and looked at the corkboard wall of stills, at Halpert's treatment, at the double-frame photographs of Ruth and Andy, at the desk calendar where Cheryl had noted his luncheon appointment with Nat Markal. *This* was his life. *This,* not the past.

'God will punish you,' the sister had said at the coroner's inquest. 'Wait and see. God will punish you.'

He and Ruth hadn't been able to have children. And now, Brad Madison . . .

The buzzer sounded. Cheryl said Mr. Markal had canceled their lunch date.

Carl tried to read the treatment.

God will punish you.

It wasn't God but a blackmailer, a contemptible faggot blackmailer who was punishing him!

He sat hunched over his desk, thinking hard. There was always a twist, a turn of story to surprise the audience. There was always a way to trap the villain when he seemed to hold all the aces. He just had to search until he found it.

At four-thirty he was working with the cutter in the basement projection room, and Cheryl phoned. Nat Markal had okayed his edited version of *Microbe Monsters* and complimented him highly on the special effects. 'Just the special effects?' he mumbled.

'Mr. Markal wants you to keep yourself available tonight and tomorrow. And he wants to see whatever Charles Halpert has done on *Terror Town*. Shall I send over a carbon of the treatment?'

Carl said Nat Markal didn't read carbons. Send over the original.

He had intended to work until seven, but told the cutter he'd been called to an important meeting. He just couldn't

154

concentrate anymore. Too many things happening. Too many pressures building.

God will punish you.

NAT MARKAL

Bertha came into Nat Markal's office three times after informing him that Isa Yee was waiting, and each time he was going
to tell her to send the girl away. She didn't have an appointment, and he wouldn't have given her one had she asked. He
had already done as much for her as was necessary: contact-
ing Devon and Baiglen; asking Terry Hanford to give her preliminary consideration; and, something she couldn't know,
deciding she would test for a part in *Joneses*. So there was
simply no reason for him to see her. Besides, he was busier
than he'd been in years. Dave Sankin was flying in today.
Joneses was about to be brought into the open.

But he didn't send her away. He signed papers and saw Moe
Sholub and, without planning it, told Bertha to cancel his
luncheon with Carl Baiglen. 'And Miss Yee?' Bertha queried.
He waved his hand impatiently. 'Get me Sol Soloway.'

She nodded, surprised at the evasion, and went out. He had
surprised a lot of people these past few weeks, Adele included.
She couldn't believe he was going to work this hard when
'We've got everything and it will only go to taxes.' On the
flight back from New York she had reminded him of how they
had decided he would reduce his working hours, his duties at
Avalon, even if he didn't leave the industry. 'What happened
to change things, Nat?'

'I saw how bored I'd be.'

'But you were going to take time for *living*.'

'Living is working. Otherwise—' He had shrugged and
ordered drinks from the stewardess and not returned to the
subject, but his thought had been, 'Otherwise a man can go
rotten.'

The return to full activity had done him a world of good.
The days went quickly again. The nights were all right, though
he didn't sleep well unless he had considerable wine with
dinner, or took a tranquilizer.

Bertha buzzed him. He spoke to Sol Soloway, vice-presi-
dent in charge of all Avakon advertising, promotion and

publicity, about being firm with Lou Grayson. 'But he wants more trade ads on *Killjoy*, Nat. He's very insistent. He's talking about a better deal at Paramount or Metro again.'

Nat leaned back and closed his eyes. He would send Isa Yee away as soon as he hung up. 'All right, give him an extra ad or two.'

'He feels his promotion is minimal. Wants a campaign to make the columnists associate *Killjoy* with him *personally*. Feels we're not spreading around enough money.'

'*Killjoy* and Grayson? *Killjoy* is pure saint. Grayson is pure sex maniac. Does he want the columnists to print *that*?'

'He's not satisfied—'

'He's never satisfied. He's getting to be more trouble than he's worth.'

Soloway laughed. 'You're joking. He's bringing in more each year. Last year his production costs actually *dropped* while everyone else's rose, so his net is even higher than it looks.'

'You're in Accounting now, Sol?'

Soloway laughed again. Markal said, 'I'll take it up with Sankin,' but he wouldn't. He disliked Grayson. Anyone else who acted that way would have been thrown off the lot. In fact, he'd wanted to do just that several times, wanted to build up the new team of Wein & Cole in place of Grayson. But Sankin had been horrified, and Nat knew that Olive and the stockholders would have felt the same.

Soloway said, 'I meant to ask about Baiglen, Nat. Is he coming along briskly enough? He has a lot to do to meet his obligations, his six picture deal.'

Nat didn't bother commenting on this new excursion into non-Soloway areas. Sol was spreading out, trying to insinuate himself into overall management of feature production. He worked very hard – an ambitious man, a man to watch. Which, along with his closeness to Ron Besser and Olive Dort, was the reason he would *not* be included in the creative meetings on *Joneses*. Nat didn't mind someone wanting to be his heir, but Soloway wasn't willing to wait for his leader's retirement. Soloway's dagger was too much in evidence.

Nat said Baiglen was doing fine. Soloway paused. 'Olive was in to see me this morning.'

Nat smiled to himself. 'Wonder why she didn't drop by here?'

Soloway didn't allow himself to be sandbagged. 'She had a copy of Sheilah Graham's column.'

'Wonderful writer, Sheilah.'

'There was something about a big production.'

'Oh?'

'Any truth to it, Nat? We've all heard rumors. And that enormous set ... Olive feels that as third largest stockholder—'

'When I schedule a production, she'll know. Everyone will know.'

'But if this is a management decision—'

'Management will decide. Good-bye, Sol.'

They couldn't do a thing to stop him. They could steam and they could stew, but they couldn't do a thing. He and Sankin ran the show, and Dave would never turn against him.

Not that they should *want* to stop him. As stockholders, they were going to make plenty.

He had an instant of doubt. Could he possibly be wrong about *Joneses*? Could his desire to do something big and lasting have weakened his instinct for picking money-makers?

He buzzed Bertha and asked who was next. She said, 'Mr. Grayson just walked in. He would like a moment.'

'All right.'

The door opened, and the lean man burst in. Lou Grayson didn't simply enter a room, he *exploded* inside. It irritated Nat, but he rose and held out his hand. A star was a star.

'Lou, what can I do for you?'

Grayson gripped the hand briefly and looked around the office and shook his head and waved his long arms. 'Man, this crazy digs! You wanna sell it, Nat?'

Nat smiled and sat down.

Grayson jerked his head at the door. 'That little Chink out there. *Givald gishreigen!* Who is she?'

'That why you came?' Nat murmured.

'No, that's why I'll *come*!' He flung himself into a chair, grinning. Nat waited coldly. Grayson's grin faded. He was a tall, raw-boned man in a gray silk-and-something suit with tendons standing out on his neck, a man of forty-two with the face of an idiot child. His slips, slides and pratfalls looked natural, looked effortless on the screen, but they weren't. His staggers, sags, wild dances and famous 'fits' seemed to be the result of instant improvisation, but they weren't. He was an incredible athlete who worked incredible hours to perfect his routines, a man capable of startling feats of strength. Anyone but Nat Markal would have felt much discomfort when Lou Grayson

157

stopped smiling that abruptly. Nat Markal felt nothing but impatience to be rid of him.

'I'm not being treated right, Nat.'

'I spoke to Sol. We're increasing your advertising.'

'Not only that. I'm a producer as well as an actor, yet you don't bother informing me of anything that goes on. Your new production—'

'It's not a comedy, Lou. And I've always reserved the right to choose my casts. And there's nothing official yet.'

'I don't care about official. I want to be given some decent treatment around here. I've had feelers from Paramount, from MGM, from Fox. You think I can't go there?'

'Not while you're under contract to Avalon.'

'You think I can't make you break that contract?'

Markal looked at him. Grayson met his look, glaring, then jumped up and said, voice high, 'I'm not saying you haven't helped my career, Nat. I'm not saying you didn't pick me and Mamie out of the TV variety gutter and give us our chance. But I do things for you too. I bring in the *moola*!'

'Yes, you do.'

Grayson nodded hard, blinking his eyes, and Nat had the feeling he was close to tears. An enigma. A lecher, a genius, an imponderable.

'Tell me what you want,' Nat said, softening his voice and manner. 'Perhaps we can work it out.'

Grayson sat down again. 'Just a little respect,' he whispered thickly. 'Just to be treated like a *mensch*.'

Markal nodded and wondered at this man. Lou Grayson was worth ten, twelve million. Lou Grayson was adored by fully half the population of America. Lou Grayson did things, manipulated people, the way no one on the lot would dare. Yet here he was, a hurt little boy.

'The name of the picture is *The Eternal Joneses*. Would you like to hear about it?'

Grayson nodded eagerly.

Nat outlined the project, and as he talked developed it further for himself. When he finished, Grayson jumped up. 'My God, Nat! My God!'

Instantly, Nat forgave him everything. Grayson was exuding pure enthusiasm. 'It strikes you?'

'Strikes me! It's . . . it's fantastic, Nat! It's *genius*! My God!' He leaned over the desk, those neck tendons standing out like steel wires. 'I've gotta have a part in it!'

Nat began to answer. Grayson almost ran to the door. 'I don't care what. A walk-on. A little more than a walk-on. I don't care what. Funny or serious. Anything. Tyrone Chalze will direct, of course? You leave it to him. He knows what I can do. I don't care what.' He was halfway out when he stopped 'Full-page ads in the quality papers, Nat. On *Killjoy*, right? Full-page ads to kick it off. After that, so you'll squeeze me, so I'll scream. Okay?'

'We never squeeze you, Lou.'

Grayson closed the door behind him.

The man knew pictures. Whatever he was, he knew pictures and look how he'd responded! *Joneses* was going to make history!

He buzzed for Bertha to come in. He was going to tell her to send Miss Yee away. He said, 'Anyone else break in since we last talked?'

She didn't laugh. Her voice was strained. 'No, Mr. Markal.'

'What is it?'

'Uh . . . nothing. Mr. Grayson just left.'

He remembered Grayson's comment on Isa Yee. 'Did he . . . act up?'

'It's not for me to say, Mr. Markal.'

'Speak louder, please.' She was flushed, upset. He said 'Well?' She shook her head. 'Nothing. You know Mr. Grayson. The girl, Miss Yee, she . . . she struck him.'

He began to smile, and controlled it. 'Why?'

She dropped her eyes, embarrassed. 'I never saw Mr. Grayson in action before.'

That hand-under-the-dress bit? In Nat Markal's office? On the instant he was raging, reaching for the phone. Then he stopped. What was it to him? Everyone knew about Lou Grayson. Why should this be any different?

He lit a cigar. He had bought some decent Havanas in New York, secured via a contact at the UN. Steep at a hundred-fifty a box, but who could shop around these days? Yet he hated to be taken, by anyone, in any sort of deal, big or small.

Isa Yee thought to take him.

Again, his unconscious had served him well. Again his instincts had jelled and presented him with a 'hunch', a thought that crystallized his feelings and answered his questions.

Isa Yee thought to take him, and that was why he hadn't

called her. But now he would see her. He would make it clear that Nat Markal could not be taken.

'Send in Miss Yee,' he said. Bertha began to leave. 'Just a moment.' She glanced back. 'Wait for my buzz.' She went out.

He turned in his chair and stared at the wall behind his desk, then laughed at himself. But the thought that had caught him unawares persisted. He went to the wall, opened the compartment by pressing a nearly invisible knothole in the paneling and took out the teakwood chest. He placed it on the desk, opened it, examined himself in the lid mirror.

He chose a white china shake-bottle and applied cologne to his cheeks and scalp. Again he laughed at himself, but he opened a jar and dipped in his finger and carefully touched on a cosmetic ointment specifically blended for the skin tint under his eyes. He covered the dark circles, the web of wrinkles, then considered a blue vase that had embarrassed him when Bonné first described the powder it contained. 'To be applied to the genitals,' Bonné had murmured in his soft French accent. 'A *bénédiction* for the ladies. A *stimulant* for the gentleman. *Pour les tissus érectiles*.'

He slapped the teakwood lid closed and returned the box to the compartment. He sat down at his desk and raised the phone. 'Send in Miss Yee.' The fragrance of the cosmetics wafted about him. He puffed hard on his cigar. When the Eurasian entered, he was wreathed in billowing clouds of smoke. 'Miss Yee,' he mumbled around the cigar and lifted himself perfunctorily.

She walked across the room, past his desk, to the chair she had occupied a month ago. She was wearing another of those tight Mandarin outfits, and even with underwear her buttocks flowed freely. She sat down. 'You said you'd keep in touch, Mr. Markal.' She sat straight and rather stiffly, both feet planted on the floor. 'I phoned several times but was unable—'

'Out of town,' he interrupted, and smelled his cologne and wondered what the powder would feel like. Paul Bonné had given him the men's toiletries set about two years ago. Nat had considered throwing the damn stuff away the day he got it, but instead had put it in the wall compartment, thinking to give it in turn to one of his fruitier male stars. Now he had used it, and God only knew why.

'I left a message, Mr. Markal.'

He muttered, 'Unusually busy,' and looked away. She was

an exquisite thing, delicate and ripe at the same time. He was more convinced than ever she was going to make money for Avalon.

She was silent. He glanced at her. Only then did she continue.

'I was wondering if I'd offended you in any way.'

He was thrown off balance. 'Why would you think that?'

She crossed her legs. The slit opened and the ivory flesh emerged. She licked her lips. Her tongue was bright pink; narrow and fat and pointy. It made his own lips dry on the instant, and he grew impatient for her answer.

'This isn't easy for me, Mr. Markal.' Her voice was unsteady. Her eyes touched his and fell.

He was suddenly afraid. 'You're upset. My secretary told me. Lou Grayson—'

'It has nothing to do with Lou Grayson. He is what he is.'

'Yes, slightly unbalanced when it comes to pretty women.'

She shrugged. 'Women don't always think so. Some prefer his direct action to all the talk, all the dishonesty that passes for romance before bed.'

He was startled. 'You obviously aren't one of them.'

'I might be, if I hadn't met you.'

He laughed, too loud. 'Well, how have you been? Alan Devon and Carl Baiglen both approved of you, you know that? Devon thought your rushes in the Lobo Stretch feature were far above the general quality of the film.' He hadn't meant to buy her off with goodies, yet went on, afraid to let *her* continue. 'I have some plans for you and I think you'll like them. In fact, I'm sure of it. Want to hear about them?'

'You're not going to let me speak my mind, are you?'

'When would an actress rather speak her mind than hear of parts? Parts and contracts?' He was going much farther than he should, and yet it didn't change anything. She kept looking at him, solemnly, and he muttered, 'By all means, speak.'

'I'm a woman,' she said, voice faint, eyes falling away again. 'I have instincts. When we met, I felt ... we would meet again.'

He leaned back in his chair. This was marvelous! *Chutzpah*, Eurasian style! He hardened himself. 'I don't understand what you're getting at.'

Her eyes came back to him, violently, and he was shaken in spite of all his hardening and suspicion and refusal to be taken.

'Yes, you do. You wanted to see me. And since you're Nat Markal, I wanted to see you.'

No subterfuge there. No cheapness either, somehow.

'I've waited a month,' she said, 'and the waiting has become impossible and I want to know what I do now. Do I forget Nat Markal and go on with my life, or does my life change?'

'How would your life change?' he asked, smiling.

'Are you laughing at me?'

He shook his head. He *should* laugh at her and tell her to run along and do her acting in front of the cameras. He said, 'I wouldn't want your life to change. If I saw any woman it would only be . . . a temporary arrangement.' He smiled again, pleased with himself. But she held his eyes and nodded, and he suddenly saw her as he had the last time, her legs and lips end face and bottom, the youth and fire he needed.

'Yes,' she said, 'but I would belong to you. Temporarily. I understand that. But *completely*, for as long as it lasted. I wouldn't play at it, Mr. Markal. I would *work* at it, to make it mean something.'

He was held by those dark eyes, that somber face. Again her tongue flickered out to wet her lips. Again his own lips turned dry.

Why not?

Because he hated being taken, being used! Because he was too big a man, too busy a man! Because he had a reputation *not* to fall for this sort of thing! Because it was small-time, sordid, wrong to play these games!

'I told you I had plans for you,' he said sharply. 'You're going to get a chance at a featured role. Better than the ingenue in *Terror Town*, though Baiglen would use you for that. Better than Pony Girl in *The Squaws*, though Chalze would use you for that. A big opportunity, and it's already decided. You understand me? Nothing more will happen, nothing less will happen, whether or not we . . . meet.' He rose. 'Good-bye, Isa. Go on with your life. I prefer it that way.'

She also rose. 'I don't think you prefer it that way. I think you want me.'

'Oh?' He chuckled. Emperor Nat in benign amusement. Emperor Nat joking with a lovely child. Only it wasn't that way. Heat swept him, and he picked up his cigar and busied himself relighting it.

She walked to the door. He felt sharp disappointment. Poetry, dramatic lines, bits and pieces of popular songs came

162

to mind. *Stay, stay my love ... Press kisses to your hand ...*
arms ache to hold you ... feverish desire ... form divine ...
sweet breast ...

'May I lock the door, Mr. Markal?'

'What for?' His voice was a shocked, frightened whine, and
he laughed to cover it and sat down. 'Sure, go ahead.' His
hands shook and he spilled ashes on his lap and brushed
furiously at himself. She locked the door. He picked up the
phone. 'Bertha, I'm not to be disturbed.' She went to the windows. Light diminished as she drew one set of drapes. The
room grew dim and faintly golden as she drew the other, sunlight filtering through the heavy cloth. She went to the bench
and sat down. They faced each other across a luminous twilight,
and he could hear his breath and he wanted to say something
clever, something befitting Emperor Nat Markal, and was
afraid to utter a word.

'Have you any music in here?' she asked.

He went to the wall beside the glowing drape and pressed a
knothole. A panel opened. 'Classical? Popular? Rock 'n' roll?'

'I'm going to dance for you.'

He put on rock 'n' roll tape on the machine and threw a
switch. Music blared from four hidden speaker-combinations
around the room. He lowered the volume and turned to her,
aware of every pulse in his body. He had to say *something*.
'It plays for three hours without changing.' He felt silly.

'May I call you Nat?'

'Yes, of course.' He was afraid he sounded too eager and
added, 'Temporarily.'

She nodded. He muttered that he'd only been joking and
turned to his desk.

'You'll see better here, Nat.'

He went to the bench. She stood up. He wanted to touch her,
but he was shaking and she would feel it and think him a fool.

What the devil was wrong with him! He was Nat Markal,
Emperor Nat, and women were a commodity more available
to him than to perhaps any other man on earth. He was one
of the hundred richest men in the United States. He was known
and respected and envied throughout the world. What was one
little piece of ass anyway?

Changes. Changes deep inside of himself. Doubt and dis-
quiet and changes taking place.

He sat down and said, lightly, 'Action!'

'I could never dance this way for the cameras.' She bent and

163

drew her dress up over her head and dropped it on the bench beside him. She turned slowly, her buttocks bursting from tight blue panties. She began to rotate her hips to the music in a part belly dance, part swim. He shifted weight on the hard bench and tried to see himself as she would see him and crossed his legs casually. 'Lovely,' he said.

She reached behind her and unhooked the brassiere. '*Le strip-tease*,' he said and wished he had his cigar – something to hold and light and chew, something to do.

Her fragrance was delicate, composed of skin scent and perfume. She danced with her back to him, flinging her head about so her hair whipped back and forth. He told himself it wasn't very different from those bikini pictures Wally Sanford made and that he was perfectly at ease now and that no matter what she thought would happen *nothing* would happen. He would watch and enjoy himself and then pat her on the ass and send her along to Lou Grayson.

She had slapped Grayson. She didn't want Grayson. She wanted Nat Markal.

She glanced over her shoulder, hooked her thumbs in her panties and pulled down. Those long, perfect cheeks emerged. She stepped out of the panties, stepped backward so that her nudity was only a foot or so from him. She shrugged out of the brassiere, leaning forward to drop it atop the panties. She continued to dance and toed her underthings. 'Nat, please?'

He bent forward, reaching around her, and brushed her warm thigh. He got the panties and brassiere and began to straighten. Her arm dropped around him; her hand pressed his cheek to her hip and part of her buttock. Her scent was more complex now, delicacy of skin and perfume enriched by muskiness of glands and crevices. He leaned back, tossing her underthings on the bench. 'Let the dance continue,' he said, to show his composure.

She stood close, alternating sides and back to him, and did the hip-swiveling, belly-grinding, groin-snapping dances of her generation. The music changed – more drum, less guitar, a primitive chanting vocal. Slowly, she began to turn, coming about in an arm-high body-jolting jerk, and he saw her head-on for the first time. Her black hair fell straight to her shoulders. Her skin was dark in this dark room, her body fuller than he had thought it would be in breast, stomach and thigh. She danced even closer, just inches away, and smiled at him. One hand began to drop. The index finger crooked, beckoning. It dropped slowly, slowly, and he knew where it was going and he tried not to follow it and he had to.

She stood in front of him, still dancing. She leaned back, her breasts thrust up, her groin thrust out . . . out and at him. She rotated her hips and the pink slit emerged and the finger came down and traced the lips. 'Come here,' she said, voice harsh. 'Come here, you.'

He no longer worried about his image, his pride, or about being taken or used. He no longer thought of *The Eternal Joneses* and monuments to Emperor Nat Markal. He thought only of reaching for her, touching her.

And couldn't.

He watched and lusted for her and was unable to move. He didn't know how. He could only nod and smile. He couldn't break the rules of a lifetime. He was frozen to that bench.

She paused, surprised. He had to say something. 'You come here.'

She smiled and shook her head. She began to dance again, inching closer, closer, then turned abruptly about.

Now that her eyes weren't on him, he found he could move a little, his hands trembling as they touched her buttocks. She bent over thrusting her bottom almost in his face, murmuring, 'Is that your kick, baby? Come on then. Use it. Any way you want.'

He stood up. He fumbled at his clothing and his trousers dropped and he kicked them away. He rid himself of shorts and moved blindly into her. The first contact was electric. She bent further, hands on knees, and rotated her hips to the beat. She looked back at him and fit the motions of coitus to music.

He stroked her sides, her hips, her thighs. His body was alive now, free now, and he tried to enter her.

She straightened and turned. She laughed as he groaned and came at her. She backed across the room until the wall stopped her and stood spraddle-legged, laughing. He grabbed her roughly, kissed her breasts, said, 'Isa, please,' not recognizing the hoarse croak as his voice.

She moved her hips to the beat. She wouldn't stop. He said, 'Wait a minute!' but she gave him no minute. He fumbled, sweated, struggled, but she kept moving, kept laughing.

'Take off your jacket and stay a while,' she said. 'Loosen your tie and relax.' He looked at himself, fully dressed to the waist. He threw away the jacket and tore open his tie and

165

collar. He came at her again, and again she wouldn't allow him entry.

'Isa, enough games!'

'No game,' she sang to the music. 'No game, Emperor Nat, no game, for Isa, who wants you, to be loving, to do service, for his lady.'

He stepped back, enraged. She pointed to herself. He said no. She put her hands on his shoulders and pressed lightly. He sank to his knees. He did what she wanted — after a moment, gladly. She stroked his head and he listened for the explosion of gasps and sighs that would indicate his service was over. He didn't hear it, but it must have come because she sank down too.

They faced each other on the floor. She was smiling. 'That was nice, Emperor Nat. Do you know what I'm going to do for you in return?' She leaned forward and kissed him and fondled his organ. She put her lips to his ear and told him what she would do in a moment, in just another moment. She told him in detail, and her hand was too much and her sweet obscenities were too much and he couldn't help it. He gasped a warning and spent himself.

She looked around and saw the door beside the bench and asked if it was a bathroom. He nodded, too ashamed to meet her eyes. She went away and came back with a damp cloth and cleaned him. 'I'm going to wash,' she said. She gathered up her clothes and was gone a while and came back dressed. He too was dressed, sitting in the chair beside his desk. She kissed him, adjusted his tie a little, said, 'And so we begin.'

'I'm famished,' he muttered, still ashamed of his performance.

'That's to be expected. You know what they say about eating Chinese.'

He flushed, thinking how she had stroked his head and looked down at him.

He quickly stood up. It would be different from now on. In bed, with no more nonsense. In bed, with *her* doing everything to please *him*.

He felt a tingling, a reawakening at the thought. He stroked her hair, put his arms around her, kissed her.

'Sunday night,' she murmured. 'My place.'

'Why not tonight?'

'Dates. I'll begin changing things immediately. In a week, two at the most, you'll be the only man in my life.'

166

He ran his hands down her back to the dramatic swellings. The mindless heat returned. She shook her head. 'It's been a while. Your secretary—' He let her go. She went to the door. 'We'll lunch together,' he said, feeling on the threshold of the joy that had escaped him all his life.

They came into the outer office and Bertha rose. 'Mr. Sankin called. I said you would call back.'

When Bertha was told no interruptions, she would turn away the President of the United States. He asked Isa to excuse him and re-entered his office.

Sankin was at the Beverly Hills Hotel. He hated flying. He was going to have a leisurely lunch and then nap.

'And then come to my office.'

'It might be after hours.'

'I won't push you, but we should get together tonight.'

Someone spoke in the background. Sankin said, 'I'll try.'

'Do that,' Nat said. 'The sooner we move the sooner we'll be making movie history.'

'Have you talked to anyone else? I mean a professional opinion.'

'Lou Grayson. He raved. He wants a part – *any* part.'

'Grayson, huh? Really liked it, did he?'

'Make it tonight and he'll be there to tell you.'

'Well, we'll see. Lou Grayson, huh?'

Lunch with Isa lasted two hours, every minute of it a revelation. He felt he had never really talked before, never really listened before, never really laughed before. The restaurant was Pomeroy's on Cahuenga. It had opened only six or seven months ago and had not yet been discovered by the mob, which was a major attraction.

He had a small steak and cup of tea and was satisfied. She had soup and roast beef and potatoes and salad, and he wondered where she put it all. Toward the end, he began speaking of *Joneses*. She stopped eating and her eyes gleamed. 'Can I be at the meeting, Nat?'

'Sorry, no actors.'

'Why not?'

He thought a moment. Why not indeed? He could get Mona and Gordon, and that would take care of the talk that would start if Isa were the only actor present. But all he said was, 'We'll see. You'll have to be very nice to me.'

'You're lucky we're not alone now.'

167

'Always pay off, do you?'

She shook her head. 'No. I meant *you* would pay off, for that remark.'

He lit a cigar. 'I'm afraid that can't continue.'

'Can't it?'

'You said you'd belong to me.'

'The best way to belong to someone is to have them belong to you,' she said.

'I don't think I understand that.'

'You will.'

He laughed. 'My tough little girl. But let's be realistic. If I wanted to, I could impose payoffs. Five favors for being at the meeting. A dozen for a starring TV role. Fifty for a starring feature role. A hundred for a role in *Joneses*. And I could be specific. Do this and do that. I could, couldn't I? Admit it.'

'Perhaps.' She looked around the restaurant. 'But I don't think you will.'

He was excited by his thoughts and leaned toward her, smiling, breathing hard. 'Why shouldn't I? Why in the world not?'

'Because then you'd have a whore, like so many lesser men in Hollywood have whores. Then you'd reduce me and reduce yourself and we'd both lose.'

His smile died. It was as if she had seen into the soul of Nat Markal.

She turned her eyes back to him and read his expression. 'You'll have to work for your pleasure, not buy it. You'll have to belong to me as much, maybe more, than I belong to you.'

He didn't know if anyone was watching, but he reached across the table and took her hand.

Driving back to Avalon in the studio Imperial, he asked her to sit close. She slid right up against him and smiled out the window, a cool little secretive little smile.

He remembered looking down from his terrace at the Pacific Coast Highway and yearning to be in a car going somewhere with someone exciting, experiencing joy. And now he was, and it would get better, and it was all because of this girl who wasn't a whore, this strange, exciting girl who made him feel younger than he had ever been.

He suddenly hugged her, driving with one hand, and wanted to kiss the secretive little smile, and laughed aloud.

Isa and *The Eternal Joneses*. He had waited a lifetime to be this happy.

CHARLEY HALPERT

At a quarter to eight his buzzer sounded. He ran to the hall phone, telling himself it was Ben Kalik finally returning his calls. The woman's voice was crisp. 'Nat Markal's office, Mr. Halpert. Could you be here within the hour?'

'The studio?'

'The studio. Before nine, please.'

He dressed in his best suit, choosing his shirt and tie carefully. He examined himself and decided to change the tie.

There was a knock and Lois's voice called, 'Hey, man it's us!'

He opened the door. They sparkled in short dresses and subdued makeup and spike heels. 'I haven't much time,' he said.

'Same here,' Lois said.

They weren't coming in. They just wanted him to see how nice they looked. They were going to a week-end party in Palm Springs.

'Southern California's Atlantic City,' Charley said.

They didn't get it. 'It's not the beach,' Sugar said. 'But *kicky*, man!'

'An assistant director whose folks own a mansion,' Lois said. 'He's picking us up. We don't know who'll be there.'

'Maybe no one at all at all,' Sugar said, chewing gum vigorously. 'I got a feeling about that boy. But nothing ventured nothing gained.'

'As Mr. Blessington always said,' Charley murmured.

Lois grinned. 'Which reminds me. Monday you're going to introduce us to Carl Baiglen, right?'

'What good would that do? We don't even have approval on a treatment.'

Lois said, 'We'll talk Sunday when we get home.'

'*If* we get home,' Sugar said, touching Charley's arm and smiling up into his face.

He began to react. 'Good night. Have fun.'

'Don't we always?' Lois said.

Sugar stepped forward and kissed him lightly and murmured, 'I think the man would like us to take five.' The back of her hand pressed him. 'Mmmmm, yes.' The hand turned.

Charley pushed her away, muttering, 'Back, back, you devils,' and watched them run for the stairs, giggling and waving.

He didn't think of them for more than a minute longer. Nat Markal got in the way.

169

The name Markal was magic, like Goldwyn and Zanuck and Mayer. Like Levine. The name Markal was Movies with a capital M – the big time excitement that seemed to have left the rest of Hollywood.

He drove to the freeway and told himself to prepare for disappointment. But the name Markal stayed with him and the daydreams began, the excitement began.

BERTHA KRAUS

In all the years she had worked for Nat Markal, Bertha Kraus had never seen so many people in his office at one time. He had held creative meetings before, of course, but they had included no more than five or six people who had been handed the responsibility of carrying on from there. Mr. Markal was an *executive* producer, the town's biggest, working on a dozen or more films a year, not any one of them.

It was going to be different this time. She had known it from the moment he'd given her his first notes to type. And during the course of the past month she had become more and more aware of his excitement and of the immense size of the project. (What would Sankin and the others think if they knew that the Washington set alone was going to grow to a million-four or five!) Her one doubt had been whether Markal could actually kick it off, and that doubt had disappeared yesterday when he had told her to leak the news to Sheilah Graham. He would never con anyone who had treated him as well as Sheilah had.

Bertha had worked since seven-thirty with old Ben, setting up the office according to Markal's instructions. One of the three antique high-backed chairs had been placed behind the desk alongside Markal's, for Dave Sankin. The other two were at the left and close, for Mona Dearn and Gordon Hewlett. Then a few feet of space and a row of five conference chairs slanting in toward the wooden bench. On the other side of the bench, slanting out toward the door, was a second row of five chairs. In total, there was seating for seventeen or eighteen people, including three or four on the bench, all grouped about the circle of antique blue tile.

At a quarter to nine, Markal had her start the tape recorder, which operated from the same wall cabinet as his tape player, ran three continuous hours and picked up sound from the speaker units around the room. (No one would know of this, as Markal felt it might 'inhibit' the meeting, but he would later be able to review every word that had been said.) At ten to nine the young Eurasian actress arrived, followed immediately by Terry Hanford and Mona Dearn. Bertha showed Mona to her chair directly alongside the desk, and Markal chatted with her. Then Mr. Sankin walked in, and Markal rose and ushered him to his seat behind the desk. Mr. Sankin said, 'I can tell it's going to cost plenty,' and they both laughed. In the next fifteen minutes, everyone Bertha had been able to reach arrived.

She went to the folding chair near the recorder cabinet, checked the cardboard box on the floor and sat down. She looked around the room and felt pride and something akin to fulfillment at being part of this tremendous undertaking. A maiden lady living with her mother, she'd had few excitements in her life, and fewer fulfillments. Not that she hadn't had opportunities since becoming Markal's private secretary. There had been some very shocking offers from some very attractive and well-known men – *if* she would find out this, or suggest that, or do one thing or another to advance those men professionally. Bertha had been tempted once or twice, but a solid belief in the validity of her Catholic faith and a wry insistence on seeing the situation *exactly* for what it was had kept it from going further than one abortive rendezvous for which she never showed up.

Markal was speaking to Sankin, Mona Dearn and Gordon Hewlett. Lou Grayson sat fidgeting on the first of the conference chairs to the left of the desk, barely listening to Pen Guilfoyle, who was chattering away beside him. (Bertha felt Markal had made a mistake not giving Grayson equal billing with Mona and Hewlett. The comic didn't look happy.) The next three chairs were empty; then came the bench with Lars Wyllit, Terry Hanford and Isa Yee. On the other side, the row of five conference chairs slanting to the door held Cole Staley, Avalon's aging head of Publicity, Tyrone Chalze, as casual and relaxed as ever in boots and blue denims, Carl Baiglen, Alan Devon and, almost at the door, Baiglen's new writer, Charles Halpert.

'If I can have your attention,' Markal said and glanced at the three empty chairs. 'We haven't been able to reach several people who should be here, but those *most* concerned are present. To begin, we're all going to be working on a new motion picture, *The Eternal Joneses*. What makes this picture different

171

from others we've produced, from what *anyone* has produced, is its size, which is the biggest. Its cast, which is unparalleled. Its budget, which I am going to set at twenty-five million.' He paused at the soft gasp. 'And its approach, which is honest. We have two writers—'

The door opened; and Bertha's lips twitched, she was that surprised. Olive Dort came in, followed by stately Sol Soloway and his ally, Ron Besser, who was about half his size. Besser carried a conference chair, and they all moved over to Dave Sankin's side of the desk, where Besser set the chair down. Olive looked around, smiling faintly. She was at least sixty, but very well preserved, and wore a chic gray suit and enough jewelry to impress anyone who knew the real thing. Her aging baby face (she had been a perennial ingenue in B-films before Odel married her) was determinedly sweet, but her pale gray eyes were cold as dry ice. 'Good evening, David, Nathan.'

Sankin rose and they touched hands. Markal, who hated being called Nathan, lifted himself slowly and looked at her. Olive busied herself sitting down, touching her silver hair, smoothing her skirt. Bertha wondered what was going to happen. Would Markal order her out? Would Monday see the ax fall for Soloway and Besser? (Their tense smiles showed they were aware it was a distinct possibility, and that they hadn't been in favor of so obvious a move as crashing Markal's meeting.) But Markal nodded and said, 'Olive, glad you could come. Sol, Ron, would you please take your seats?' He waved at the three empty chairs across the room, giving the impression that these were the people he hadn't been able to reach.

Soloway and Besser walked across the blue tile and sat down, Soloway leaving a chair between himself and dark, ferretlike Pen Guilfoyle. Olive said, 'I hope we didn't miss anything, Nathan.'

'Just the name of the new feature Avalon is going to produce. *The Eternal Joneses*. And the fact that it's going to be budgeted at twenty-five million.'

She smiled. 'You're joking.'

'About the title or the budget?'

She spoke to Sankin. 'David, he's joking, of course.'

Sankin took out a pipe and pouch. He murmured, 'We'll find out soon enough.'

Markal turned to the others. 'I was saying . . . We have two writers here. Charles Halpert, who's been working with Carl

172

Baiglen. And Lars Wyllit, who as you all know is with Sholub-Byrne Productions. I'm going to want you, Lars, as soon as you complete *Streets at Night*.' He turned from the bench to the chair near the door. 'Mr. Halpert, you'll begin writing a treatment of *The Eternal Joneses* – assuming that your terms are reasonable.' He smiled. 'Just make sure you include the burning of Washington by the British.' Halpert seemed stunned. He nodded, and Bertha made a note to get his agent's name from Cheryl Carny. Mr. Markal would want to talk to him first thing Monday morning.

Carl Baiglen said, 'Should I get another writer for *Terror Town*, Nat?'

'*Terror Town* is suspended,' Markal said and nodded at Bertha. She took sheafs of Xerox paper from the cardboard box beside her chair and began to pass them out. Baiglen said. 'But if it's only a matter of a writer—'

Markal shook his head. 'I'll need you too, Carl. I'll need everyone here, full-time. We're going to set up a special office to conduct *Joneses* business only. Your office, Carl, with you in it. I'm sure you'll find it a rewarding experience.'

Bertha glanced at Baiglen as she handed him a copy of the six-page outline. He didn't look particularly rewarded. She finished with Sankin and returned to her seat.

'If you'll all take a minute to read this outline.'

Bertha glanced through a copy that she had helped phrase and had polished twice since Wednesday morning. It was a concise and illuminating bit of work, if she did say so herself. Mr. Markal had never been so expressive, so enthusiastic before. It was bound to convince all but the most prejudiced . . . and she glanced at Olive Dort. Olive was reading with wide eyes and parted lips, an expression of surprise and disbelief that, Bertha was certain, she was deliberately creating for effect.

Soloway and Besser read with resolutely bland faces. Most of the others looked . . . interested. Yes, that was the word, interested.

Olive laughed. Everyone looked at her. She turned to Dave Sankin. 'Now I know it's a joke.'

Markal said, 'Does anyone else think it's a joke?'

Olive turned to Soloway and Besser. 'Sol, what's your opinion?'

It was being put on the spot, and Soloway flushed angrily. 'I'd have to see a treatment before I could begin to form opinions. But it certainly looks . . . exciting.'

Besser followed suit. 'Exciting, very, with a few trouble spots, of course. That budget, and the emphasis on prejudice. Still, exciting.'

Olive smiled a little, but she had overplayed her hand. In fact, she had never held a hand. It was a mistake for her to have come here just to pick away at Markal. She needed Sankin on her side to accomplish anything. Or a complete lineup of all the others. She was here, therefore, to quibble bitterly, uselessly . . .

Bertha cut short that line of thought. Olive wasn't stupid. She disliked Markal, an emotional judgment, but she wasn't given to emotional displays at company meetings. In fact, she was a very clever woman who had all but run Avalon when her husband occupied this office. She had to have *some* hope of stopping *Joneses* or she wouldn't be here.

'What do *you* think, Alan?' Markal asked.

Devon looked at his outline. 'I've never considered a feature of such size. But that isn't what worries me. You can handle size—'

'*We* can handle it, Alan. I want you as producer.'

Olive said, 'Then you won't be producing it personally, Nathan?'

'I will, as executive producer. But very much involved this time. There'll be more than enough work for the two of us.'

'What worries you?' Olive asked Devon.

Devon was looking at Markal now. 'I'm not sure I can free myself, Nat.'

'We'll discuss it later. There'll be monetary compensation, of course.' And to Baiglen. 'The same goes for you, Carl. And for anyone else who has to leave a private production or pet project. We'll work it out.'

'Again,' Olive said, voice too sweet, 'what worries you, Alan?'

'Ron Besser mentioned it. The emphasis on prejudice. The stress on message – negative message. Frankly, Nat, I don't think you can be realistic about America's hatreds and still make the majority, who share those hatreds, come to see your picture.'

'Exactly,' Olive said. 'It would be much more sensible to concentrate on our growth as a nation, one portion of it; say the War of 1812, since we have to use that extravagant set. It would make an exciting feature, a major feature, at a reasonable budget. And without all that nonsense about prejudice and hate and Negroes, which isn't the business of a movie in the first place. They have books and plays about that.'

174

'It would certainly be safer,' Devon muttered, but he didn't seem pleased with what had been made of his criticism. Markal looked at him, waiting. Devon said, 'I don't want to castrate the project before it's had fair chance. I'd like to hear what a talented screenwriter like Lars Wyllit has to say.'

Wyllit shrugged. 'Anything can be done with the will, the skill and cash. This is no exception. If Mr. Markal wanted to make H. G. Wells's *Outline of History* or even Will Durant's *Story of Civilization*, he could.'

'What about butchering Indians?' Markal asked. 'Anti-Semitism? The other hatreds and prejudices? The hints that Vietnam might *not* be a just war? Think we can present such touchy subjects and still have a balanced picture of America?'

Lars thought a moment. 'I don't know. I don't think it's ever been done before. At least not on such a scale.'

Markal turned to Halpert. 'Mr. Halpert?'

Halpert wet his lips and hesitated. The hesitation stretched out for an uncomfortably long time, and Bertha began to suffer for him, for what she thought was an inability to answer. Finally he spoke.

'If you're asking whether it can be done in terms of profit, I'm not experienced enough to answer. If you're asking whether it can be made into a story, be presented in dramatic form, I believe it can. And if you're also asking whether your stars can play these parts and remain sympathetic characters, the answer is again, yes. After all, human beings are vital, creative, triumphant and at the same time weak and venal. Others are subjugated, mistreated, brutalized, poverty-stricken and at the same time vital and creative. Still others are cruel, criminal violent and at the same time understandable. So all we'll be doing in our picture is mirroring life instead of a lot of other movies.'

'Is that important?' Markal asked, and Bertha could tell from his expression how excited he was by this comment.

'If you'll forgive a pronouncement,' Halpert muttered; and then, firmly, 'Only as important as truth.'

'Is that important? And before you answer, consider the old Hollywood saying: "Don't sell your soul for a pot of message."'

'This picture, as I define your outline, *is* a pot of message. A beautiful pot with a beautiful message.'

'Then we'll have to watch it,' Markal said, but Bertha felt he was saying it for the others, not for Halpert and himself, 'Then we'll have to make sure entertainment comes first.'

175

Halpert smiled, and Bertha felt he should do it more often. 'With the story and action indicated, the sweep of history to be covered, how could it help but come first?'

Markal nodded. 'Lou Grayson is our finest comedian. *Hollywood's* finest. He wants a part in *Joneses*. Do you see humor in this picture?'

Charles Halpert knew who Lou Grayson was. He looked at him. 'I don't think we should *write* it in. The humor of history is incidental, not planned. Our humor should be the same. Mr. Grayson's role, whatever it is, wouldn't have to be *funny* – jokes and slapstick and such. He could give any role humor by *seeing* things as humorous, by directing his performance—' He stopped quite suddenly. 'But Mr. Grayson might not agree.'

Lou Grayson said, 'Who wants pratfalls? I agree a hundred per cent.' He looked around the room. 'And why are we hanging out the black crepe? *Joneses* is a great concept. We should be *celebrating*. At last something important is being done and we're part of it. I only wish I was Mona Dearn so I could dance naked from New Amsterdam tavern to Whiskey A Go-Go.'

There was a ripple of laughter, swiftly terminating in Mona's pained smile. Markal said, 'Sheilah Graham was using poetic license there, but it might not be a bad idea. It would certainly help draw.'

Mona remained silent.

Gordon Hewlett mock-flexed his muscles. 'I'm willing to take over for her, Nat, providing the old pectorals hold up.' He put back his head and laughed louder than anyone else.

Grayson said, 'When it comes to pectorals, I'll take Lassie's over yours. At least she's a girl.'

Hewlett was about to answer in kind when Olive said, 'is this anyway to conduct business? In Odel's day—!'

Sankin interrupted, 'We're not the board of AT&T, Olive. We're show business.'

Olive abruptly turned off the outrage, and again Bertha wondered what she was up to. She obviously felt she was scoring points, but in what game?

'A question, Nathan. When spending this kind of money, isn't it *de rigueur* to use a masterpiece of literature, or at least a bestseller?'

'*Cleopatra* was based on history.'

'And on one of the two best-known women of all time, the other being the Virgin Mary. *Your* major characters are all fictitious.'

176

'There just aren't any books, or established characters, real or otherwise, that fit what I have in mind.'

'Perhaps because what you have in mind is dramatically unsound.'

'Both my writers don't think so.'

'Writers have a vested interest in writing. How can they be objective when it could mean ending the project before it starts?'

'Let's take a vote.'

'And you'll abide by the outcome?'

'No, but I'll be interested in it.'

Olive met Markal's smile with one of her own. 'You're beginning to believe your own press notices, Nathan.'

Markal turned to Mona.

'I like it,' Mona said, 'but my agent will have something to say about what I'll wear.'

Gordon Hewlett said, 'It's fantastic. You'll get anyone you want for the major roles.'

Lou Grayson said, 'The minor roles too. I want a fat one.'

Sol Soloway looked at his hands. 'I'd like to see it brought into focus. Made tighter. A slightly smaller canvas.'

Ron Besser said, 'As head of the script department—' and paused.

Bertha added to herself, '*Nominal* head.' Besser had stock and that's why he worked at Avalon. His view of himself as a contender for Markal's position was ridiculous.

'—I'm interested in the concept,' he concluded lamely.

Lars leaned back on the bench. 'I'm delighted to be part of it.'

Terry Hanford smiled. 'It's a publicity agent's dream. Especially with that set. It'll place *itself* in newspapers and magazines.'

The Eurasian girl merely nodded.

Cole Staley, Terry's boss, said, 'Terry said it. This is something publicity people dream about.'

Tyrone Chalze seemed half-asleep, slouching low in his chair with legs outthrust. The directing genius who had won three Academy Awards and helped a dozen actors to do the same said, 'Fine, lovely, dandy.'

'That means you like it?' Markal asked.

'That means I'm hopeful I'll like it, after I rewrite the white script.'

Markal chuckled.

Carl Baiglen said, 'Of course, it's an honor to be associated

177

with a production of this quality—' He swallowed an unspoken 'but.' 'No matter what role we play in its creation.'

Alan Devon was peeling a stick of gum. 'I'd love to be part of it, if I can.'

'You can,' Markal said.

Charles Halpert said, 'A wonderful challenge.'

Olive Dort looked at Dave Sankin. 'Do you want to know what I think?'

'Certainly.'

'It's too big. It's too ambitious. The budget is enormous and it'll grow and grow until it reaches the point of no return, the point where we can't make back our investment, or can't make *enough* to justify the loss of other features and other income.' She looked at Markal. 'And finally, it has disaster built into it – that so-called *message*. Disaster for the entire Avalon operation.' She smiled quickly.

Sankin spoke around his pipe. 'It's a huge investment, no denying that, but I have confidence in Nat Markal and in the talent he employs. I think there's a need for caution in the message department ... but I know we're safe in deferring to Nat's judgment. After all, Avalon hasn't had one year in the red since he took over.'

'Famous last words,' Olive muttered, but loud enough for all to hear.

'All right, Olive,' Markal said, and he was no longer smiling and he was no longer soft-spoken. 'I'm going to talk business. If you have anything further to say, say it now. Because once I start I won't allow your brand of nonsense.'

She colored deeply. There was complete silence. Then she said, voice tight, 'I'll listen like a good little stockholder.'

Nat Markal turned from her. 'It's important that we start with as complete a picture of the project as possible. That's why I'm going to discuss what I expect of each of you with the others present.'

He began with Charles Halpert. Halpert was to do some general research in American history, but wasn't to worry about details. Markal would have experts for that. In about a week, Halpert was to begin writing a treatment running no less than a hundred-fifty pages, following the broad direction in the six-page outline. 'You can change anything except the Washington scene, if you first convince me it will help the story. I'll be available to you as any producer is available to his writer. You'll also have Alan Devon to answer questions and offer

178

help. But above all you must remember that the purpose of *Joneses* is first to earn money, second to earn money, third to earn money – and maybe then to earn its creators a little honor and prestige. So think of the message as leavening: about a grain to the pound of action, romance, sex, shock and spectacle.' He paused. 'But that grain can distinguish us. That grain can make *The Eternal Joneses* unique in motion-picture history.'

He asked Wyllit to look in on Halpert during his spare time, to offer advice and to acquaint himself with the developing treatment. 'There will probably be a third writer because of the enormous creative burden—'

He went on to Chalze, Devon, Terry, Staley, Baiglen and the rest, giving some a few words, speaking at length to others. He made Soloway responsible for budgetary matters, and Besser for setting up the research and expert-opinion unit jobs that neither could feel commensurate with his position and yet could not refuse. A subtle form of revenge, Bertha thought, smiling to herself at their sour nods and yesses.

It was twelve-fifteen when he finished. 'I've probably ruined a few week-ends and for that I apologize. But I think we're all going to remember this meeting as the start of our finest professional effort. Good-night.' As everyone began to rise, he asked Halpert to remain, and then he was standing alone behind his desk.

Bertha went up to him. 'I want to wish you luck, Mr. Markal. It's really a . . . a very *fine* undertaking.'

He took her hand, squeezed it, held it as he said, 'Thank you, Bertha.' He had never touched her before. He had always been polite, but never very . . . friendly. He wasn't what you could call an *affectionate* man, and his dealings with actresses proved it. There was simply no gossip about Emperor Nat Markal. None at all. And so that one touch, that squeeze of the hand, set her pulses to racing, and she went home to dream of a growing friendship, a tender relationship with the man she most admired in all the world.

SOL SOLOWAY

They stood beside Olive's Mercedes 300SE convertible in the dark parking area, Soloway's long face reflecting irritation. 'I warned you, Olive. I said there was nothing we could do at that meeting. The only place to stop Markal—'

'Is at the vital organs of the business,' she interrupted, giving a good imitation of his heavy, self-important delivery. 'The balance sheets. The profit-and-loss columns. The books, my dear, the books.'

He wasn't amused. 'All right. What did you accomplish besides making us look foolish?'

'You forget yourself, Sol. You want to be president of Avalon, don't you?'

'*You* want me to be president.'

'Yes, so that Avalon can return to a sensible pattern of production and profits.'

'You want me to be president because you hate Markal. You hate him because he insulted you by throwing out Odel's furniture, which you picked, and by throwing out Odel's policies, which you probably picked too.'

'Perhaps.'

The calm answer surprised him.

'But you're wrong about what we accomplished at the meeting. I started something. I set myself up as an opponent, a nucleus around which the opposition can form.'

'What opposition? There isn't any.'

'There will be. Did you ever know a production to go through from start to finish without someone – the director, the star, the assistant producer – *someone* wanting to change things?'

'That's the normal—'

'Yes. But in anything this size, normal irritations become abnormal. *Ten stars*, Sol! They'll be at each other's throats in no time. And Devon has his doubts. And there must be others.'

Soloway began to speak. Olive cut him short. 'Markal would be able to handle it if there was no top-level opposition. But there *is* top-level opposition. You and me and our faltering little friend Besser. I was an irritant at tonight's sweetness-and-light gathering, but later I'll be remembered as a voice of warning, the handwriting on the wall, the person to come and see with grievances.'

Soloway was looking at her, his expression changing.

'Then there's our ace, Lou Grayson. Once his nasty little ego is wounded, and it simply *has* to be in a situation he can't control, he'll want to strike out at someone. That someone can only be Nat Markal, the guiding light of *Joneses* and Avalon.' She crooked her finger. Soloway glanced around and moved

180

closer. She put her hand on his arm. 'Do you know that Grayson now holds almost six per cent of Avalon common? That he's quietly buying more? That he's willing to pay premiums? That Dave Sankin has little besides his Avalon stock? That the budget on *Joneses*, the enormous outlay of money, will cut Avalon dividends to nothing this year, putting the squeeze on Sankin? And ... that you haven't been to see me in almost a week? Is Estelle's chicken soup improving?'

Soloway flushed. 'I told you, Estelle and I have an agreement.'

'So do you and I.' She pressed up against him. He glanced around again, then took her in his arms and kissed her. 'Get in the car,' she said.

'Estelle—'

'And you have an agreement.'

He got in the car. She moved behind the wheel, her skirt sliding up. He looked at her legs, seemingly perfect in the dim light. But Olive was seven years older than he, and Olive was far from perfect with her stylish clothes off, and his secretary was nineteen and eager to break into movies.

They drove out the gate. Olive said, 'Who was that pretty little Oriental girl?' Soloway said, 'An up-and-comer, very highly thought of, probably going to break big in *Joneses*.' Olive murmured, 'And what was she doing at such a meeting?' Soloway shrugged. 'Markal always has his reasons.' Olive smiled. '*Yes*?' Soloway said, 'Now stop looking for *that* out.' You know Markal.' Olive said, 'He's a man, isn't he?' And then, thickly, 'So are you, sweetie, so are you.' She put her hand on him, pulling at the zipper, clutching, always clutching, looking at him with those arch eyes, that rotting baby face.

God, what he didn't do to get ahead!

TERRY HANFORD

Terry drove. Mona sat beside her, sunk in gloom. Terry finally said, 'It's going to be the highlight of your career. Your biggest role. Your biggest picture.'

'He wants me to do nude scenes. He never did before, not for the American market, but now—'

'Standards are changing. People accept nudity. They look on the female body as, well, an art form.'

181

'It's that new code,' Mona said. 'And Markal doesn't even have to pay attention to *that*. He does what he wants because the public buys it. Now he's trying to sell me like a . . . a two-buck whore.'

'Maybe you're wrong.'

'He doesn't kid Sheilah Graham. Some of the others, maybe, but not Graham.'

'Well, just a shot or two wouldn't be bad. To tantalize your fans. It'll create a sensation.'

'Yeah, let's go see Mona Dearn's snatch.'

'I hardly think—'

Mona suddenly laughed. 'You're blushing! Five or six years in this business and you can still blush?'

'I wasn't blushing,' Terry muttered. 'How could you see in this light anyway?'

Mona touched her cheek. 'Hot.' She laughed again and moved closer. 'Well, to hell with it. Screw 'em all. We'll form a committee of two against the world.'

Terry drove faster. Mona said, 'I'll call Jerry tomorrow. If he gives me any arguments, so help me I'll dump him.'

CARL BAIGLEN

Carl went straight home. Andy was spending the night at a friend's and Friday was Violet's day off, so he and Ruth had a bite to eat in the kitchen.

He told her about the meeting. 'An opportunity,' he said nodding emphatically. 'A real opportunity. To handle the special effects in one of the great motion pictures of all time. And when it's over, I'll not only go back to producing and directing, I'll go back with a *reputation*. That's something I've needed—'

Later, washing up, he looked in the mirror and allowed his bitterness to show. What the hell was he anyway, a hired technician to be shoved from one job to another? He was an independent producer, damn it, and Markal should recognize that! Taking over his offices. Making Alan Devon his superior. The least Markal could have done was allow him to get another writer and continue with *Terror Town* until actual production on *Joneses* began.

He didn't care about 'monetary compensation'. He would

182

tell Markal just how he felt. Why not? He was an independent, wasn't he?

He finished washing and got into his pajamas, and knew he wouldn't tell Markal anything. He was an independent, but there had been no nibbles, no offers or talk of deals from other studios. They had their quota of shock-pic producers. If anything, his kind of independent was a glut on the market. It was the big earners, those who broke through with major productions, who were sought after, and that wouldn't happen to him unless Markal came through with a major budget.

That would be one of the conditions he would set for his cooperation! Well, anyway, he would mention it.

Maybe.

Ruth was in the kitchen, cleaning up. He sat down and lit a cigarette. After a while she came over to him and stroked his hair. 'You'd prefer working on *Terror Town*, wouldn't you, Carl?'

'No, of course not. What makes you say that?'

'Whatever you work on, remember I ... I'm proud and happy.'

He was annoyed. 'What brought this on? Of course you're proud and happy? I'm on the biggest movie of all time and as my wife—'

'Yes.' She bent and kissed him. 'That's the important thing. I'm your wife. It *is* important, isn't it, Carl? Most important?'

He said certainly and let's go to bed and she left the kitchen. He sat and smoked. She returned a few minutes later, wearing the black lace apron he had bought her last year. *Just* the lace apron. His irritation mounted. She was solacing him, soothing her whipped and beaten husband. Well, that wasn't what he wanted from her! He wanted her respect and admiration as well as her love.

She walked slowly across the floor to him, and irritation weakened. Her big breasts bounced behind the thin lace. Her full body gleamed whitely. Her smile was shy and at the same time inviting. He stood up. 'Well, Fifi, come to serve the master?'

'*Oui, monsieur.*'

He put out his hand. 'What have we here?' She broke up and he shushed her and went on with the game, and took her on the floor in the apron with the laughter fading from her lips and the sweet pain of passion mounting, mounting ... If only the rest of his life could be as sweet.

183

He went to Cabrillo's bar and had a few drinks and played the bowling machine and talked baseball with Dominic the bartender. And still couldn't shake the lousy feeling, the feeling he told himself was anger. What the hell, a tyro like Halpert walking in and getting the most important assignment on Avalon's biggest production – maybe *Hollywood's* biggest production!

Not that he would be able to do the job. He'd flop. He was bound to. He just didn't understand enough about the art of the film. He couldn't. And his talk proved it.

'Only as important as truth.' New York intellectual crap! How could Markal have kept a straight face!

Not that Lars gave a damn. He would only have to rewrite the entire treatment once he was free of *Streets*, which now seemed a burden instead of a choice assignment.

Markal wanted him to help Halpert in his spare time. Well, he would drop in once in a while, but he'd be damned if he would make the guy look good.

He drove home. He considered calling Terry, but what was the use? She had practically ignored him at the meeting.

He wondered if Markal had read Halpert's novels, and what sort of job Halpert had done on Baiglen's spook show, and whether he would be competing with Halpert in the writing of the first draft.

Of course not. The man would do a little research and organization and then be dropped.

He remembered New York and his inability to publish and Halpert's strong reviews and how he had admired and envied his depth and how he didn't sit still long enough, didn't read and think long enough, to develop depth of his own. Not that depth was necessary here . . .

He had to accept it then. He wasn't angry. He was afraid. He didn't want to compete with Halpert. Any scriptwriter, okay. Any one of the dozen novelists working in Hollywood, okay. But not Halpert. Not that unknown quantity, that deep and hungry unknown quantity.

He had a final drink before going to bed. He disliked his feelings, called himself a prick for his feelings and couldn't stop his feelings.

The worst that could happen was that Halpert would make

it and work with him on the first draft. Work *together* with him.
If so, it would be all to the good if Halpert were on the ball. It
would make the script better, make the other writer look
better.

They would make each other look better. That was the goal
of collaborators.

He turned off the light and lay down. He resolutely closed
his eyes. How could he fear the man he'd lunched with a month
ago? The beaten, frightened, rather desperate man? The man
he'd thought of as poor old Chuck Halpert?

But didn't 'poor Chuck Halpert' look different lately?
That gut was going, the beaten look was going. He wasn't taking shit from anyone now.

Lars Wyllit was disappointed in himself, ashamed of himself. He wondered what Terry would think if she could read his
thoughts. And that helped him finally end his thoughts.

CHARLEY HALPERT

Charley sat beside the handsome marble-topped desk and
talked to Nat Markal. He talked a lot, led to it by Markal's
questions about his novels and his work on *Terror Town*.

He asked about the Washington set. Markal took papers
from his desk and talked about a crash research program and
the top architect who was overseeing the project. 'We're going
to use every available inch of space on that lot,' he said. 'We're
going to build as much as we can. Look at these sketches.' He
described how they would construct two rope walks and a
bridge over water representing the Potomac. How they would
recreate that section of the Arsenal at Greenleaf's that the
British had blown up along with over seventy of their own men.
'And the State, War and Navy buildings. And the George
Washington double house. And the rows of wooden shacks off
Pennsylvania Avenue—'

His enthusiasm was contagious, though Charley didn't need
any more enthusiasm than he already had. He asked how they
would fake the burning of the Capitol.

Markal gathered up his papers and put them back in the
drawer. 'Just write it as if we're burning the whole thing. Forget the word "fake". There's not going to be anything fake
about *The Eternal Joneses*.' He changed the subject back to

185

Charley's novels, discussing *Flight of the Drones* in a highly informed and complimentary manner, then abruptly said:

'I'd never have approved that treatment you wrote. It's not at all what Baiglen wants. Or what he's *supposed* to want. His specialty is monsters, freaks, horror, science fiction. What you wrote was an offbeat suspense story. Very offbeat and very subtle.'

Charley said he thought it a workable story.

'Sure, but not what the assignment called for.'

Charley muttered, 'Perhaps,' and waited.

'You bombed out there and helped yourself in here. Now, we could simply transfer your contract with Baiglen to me—'

Charley smiled. Markal also smiled and added, 'With some adjustment in money.' Charley kept smiling. Markal said, 'You're in no position to bargain and we both know it. I'm giving you your chance. Your big chance.'

Charley nodded. 'I won't bargain, Mr. Markal. I'll tell my agent what I think is minimal . . . in terms of *The Eternal Joneses*, not *Terror Town*. Minimal in terms of my being able to work with no end in mind other than a perfect treatment and the hope of being assigned with Lars Wyllit to the script.'

'And how much is minimal?'

'Too little to concern you.'

'I'm concerned with every dollar. Believe that, Charles. I might have to pay Mona Dearn a million to do what I want her to do. Gordon Hewlett seven hundred thousand. I might at some time pay a screenwriter as much as half a million . . . but not you.'

Again Charley nodded. 'I understand. My experience—'

'Not your experience. Your muscle. I won't pay much because you can't *command* much. If I don't hire you, you have to look for work elsewhere. No one is waiting to offer you features, though I may feel they should be. You see? I think you're worth as much as any screenwriter around, but no one else does. So I'll pay what I want.'

He waited. Charley knew this was an important moment and he had to make Markal know it. There were all sorts of subtleties involved . . . and he used something flat out and unsubtle, something Carl Baiglen had said.

'If a writer is unhappy about the terms of his employment, it can interfere with his writing – no matter how much he tries not to let it.'

'That sounds like a threat.'

186

'I'd like my agent to handle this, and not to talk about it anymore. I'm afraid I'll ruin things. It scares the hell out of me.'

Markal smiled a little. 'You're either a very shrewd dealer or a very honest man.'

'A little of both, I hope.'

Markal lit a cigar. Charley reached for his cigarettes. Markal shoved the cigar box forward. 'Try one. They're almost good.'

Charley accepted a light and tasted the smoke. 'Not almost. Not unless you're used to quality I can't conceive of.'

'I am,' Markal said blandly. 'But it's what *you're* used to that's important. You're used to being honest. That comes through in *Flight of the Drones*. It comes through in your conversation too. I want it to come through in *The Eternal Joneses*. Professional, of course, but honest.' He rolled the cigar around his mouth. 'What do you think of making prejudice an important part of our film?'

'It doesn't worry me, Mr. Markal. It's been done before. You know much more about movies than I do, but in the case of Indian genocide there was *Cheyenne Autumn*. In the case of anti-Semitism there was *Gentleman's Agreement*. There were several good films on the Negro problem, including *Home of the Brave* and *Pinky*. As for early mistreatment of the Irish and Italians, I know it's been part of many films. Mexicans too. Now whether any of them made money—'

'They did. Some of them big money, for their day. And so did *Crossfire* and *Snake Pit* and *Lost Weekend*, all of them bucking some kind of American prejudice and predictions that they would bomb through the floor. But you're talking about specialty pictures, movies *made* to present a particular message, movies *built* around that message, and costing beans compared to a feature like *Joneses*. Reasonable cost and strong message was their strength ... but we've got to draw like *Around the World in Eighty Days* to make it.'

Charley realized Markal was looking for some kind of reassurance; that no matter how enthusiastic he was he was also worried. 'I guess we'll be *more* of what made the message pictures and the spectacles successful. I guess we'll be the best of both possible worlds.'

Markal smiled. 'We'd better be. Plus a happy ending.'

Charley chuckled. Markal said he was serious. Charley said he didn't quite see how to end a movie about America considering what was going on now, with traditional Hollywood happiness.

187

'*Hope* is happiness, Charles. We've got to show that we're going to lick our problems, lick our prejudices, and once we do, become about the closest thing to a perfect society there is.'

'Hope, yes—'

'When a country as rich as ours stops hating, that's a happy ending, isn't it? I mean, what more can people want from life but plenty of food, leisure time and brotherhood?'

Charley murmured, 'Nothing, I guess.' Markal looked at him and said, 'So tell me.'

'There are other social diseases that grow as poverty, prejudice and violence decrease.'

'Like what?'

'Well.' Charley hesitated. 'The basic emptiness of life.'

Markal looked blank.

'In *Joneses,* a great deal of life will be taken up defeating nature on the expanding American frontier, in fighting wars, in planting crops and struggling for jobs and generally clawing tooth and nail for physical survival. But when one segment of the family achieves comfort then they're faced with an *absence* of engrossing activity and they start looking into themselves, into their lives, into what life itself is. And if there is an inability to find purpose, to find reason, to find anything but senseless repetition in food, sex, work and sleep, they become ill. Then they contract the most modern of diseases – hopelessness. I'm sure we've all had touches—'

'I never stop working long enough for such nonsense,' Markal snapped, and Charley felt he had hit a nerve. They were quiet a moment, then Markal shrugged. 'But if you can figure out how to work it into the story ... maybe one of the weaker-willed women characters— He leaned forward 'Would such a woman look for ways to fight the emptiness, the hopelessness? Would she, maybe, join some sort of rightest group, blame everything on Jews and Negroes? Could one member of the Jones family be working to put down another member, say the mulatto girl? Could we have some sort of confrontation, in a meeting hall or riot or what? Could the riot be Watts?'

Charley asked for a sheet of paper. Markal gave him a pad. They stayed there, smoking Markal's cigars and arguing and agreeing, until three-thirty. Then Markal checked his watch and said, 'Good God!' and made a call to his wife.

They walked to the parking lot together, and Markal got into a black Imperial. 'Good night, Charles. I'm very hopeful.'

He put his hand out the window. Charley shook it and walked to his wagon.

He phoned Ben Kalik's home as soon as he reached the Bali-Ho. Kalik mumbled a controlled yes and who is it, but let loose when Charley identified himself. 'It's four-fifteen, dammit! What sort of dumb—'

Charley said, 'Listen to me, Kalik, or I'll get another agent to listen.' He waited. Kalik said nothing. 'I've been to a meeting in Nat Markal's office. I'm going to do a treatment for him. I've figured out exactly what I want, and you're going to ask him for it.'

'Wait a minute. What treatment? Not that big deal? Not that rumoured—'

'*The Eternal Joneses*. A very big deal. I want you to ask for twenty-five thousand dollars.'

'If it's the zillion-dollar epic, you could get more. *If* he really wants you. If he's not just using you to paste a few ideas together until he finds the writer he really wants. In that case he won't pay you ten grand.'

'I don't know what's in his heart of hearts. I only know what he told me and what I want on the basis of what he told me.'

'I could ask for *more*. I could sound him out. We might not get the twenty-five and then again we might get thirty-five or forty. How do we know until we try?'

'No. You'll ask for twenty-five.'

'How did you get in on it? Why didn't you let me know?'

'By smoke signal perhaps? You haven't returned one of my calls in three weeks.'

'Real busy,' Kalik muttered. 'Called a few times and you weren't in. But I'm free for lunch Monday. The Avalon commissary, check?'

Charley said, 'Yes. Now do you understand what I want? Twenty-five thousand.'

'And if he says no?' An undercurrent of amusement entered Kalik's voice. 'I say you're not interested, right? If he says twenty, or fifteen, I say sorry, right?'

'Right.'

'Now wait a minute,' Kalik laughed. 'In this business—'

'Good night,' Charley said and hung up.

He went to bed. He didn't worry about Kalik or Markal or the money. He had made his decision and it seemed quite fair to him. The Writers' Guild used five percent of budget as a guideline for writers' fees. Five percent of $25,000,000 was

189

$1,250,000. Divide that by three to get his share for the treatment and you had $400,000. All right, it was patently impossible. But $100,000 wouldn't be impossible for a Dalton Trumbo or an Abby Mann. $50,000 wouldn't be impossible for a Lars Wyllit. And $25,000 wasn't impossible for a Charley Halpert.

That was the way he had figured it. That was the way he had decided it. That was the way it would stay.

He had to start controlling his own destiny *somewhere*,

TERRY HANFORD

Mona wore a silver gown with sequins, wasp-waisted and low-necked, so tight the lines of her gossamer-thin panties showed through, a glittering production that was almost a parody of what movie queens were supposed to wear on Big Saturday Nights Out. But on Mona it looked right, a proper accent for her flamboyant beauty. She turned in front of the couch where Terry sat, feeling rather small and dowdy in a pink cocktail gown, and the sequins flashed and her golden hair and pink face glowed and she said, 'Well, how do I look?'

'If I were a man—' Terry said, and then regretted the statement. Not that there had been any more kissing, any more obvious moves toward a closer 'friendship'. But the occasional weighted glance and inadvertently weighted remark were still there.

Mona flicked at her neckline with silver-tinted nails. Her bosom came up a full third out of the gown, and with a size 39-C that third was more than many women owned in entirety. 'What would you do?'

'I'm not that imaginative,' Terry said.

Mona maneuvered carefully and sat down beside her. She exuded what amounted to a hundred dollars' worth of delicate French scent.

'You look lovely too,' she said, examining Terry with obvious approval. Then she laughed. 'Aren't we two male destroyers tonight!' She stood up. 'Tell me about this gorgeous man I'm helping promote.'

'He'll help promote you too,' Terry replied. 'He's English. The new Liverpool type, but quite mature, not rock 'n' roll.'

'How mature? Size and age?'

'Big. And he looks older than thirty.'

'Thirty?' Mona murmured.

'You'll make a very handsome couple. Trust me.'

'I always do,' Mona said. 'You've been such a help, staying on with me. I know you must want to get home, but another week or two—' She paused. 'You don't mind, do you?'

Terry said no, of course not, though she couldn't become a permanent member of the household.

'Why not?' Mona laughed. 'No, of course not. You've a life of your own.'

Terry felt the month spent here had been the longest of her life. She had everything to make her comfortable, but she did not live by comfort alone. To be solitary again. To concentrate on her own friends, her own activities, her own thoughts. Yes, even her thoughts belonged to Mona Dearn here in the hilltop hacienda. Still, life here was pleasant, if not very illuminating.

Stad Homer, the single most important man in Terry's life, and Somerset Walpole Virgil (his general manager had catholic tastes in literature) arrived on the dot of eight, resplendent in formal attire. Terry felt both men looked beautiful, each in his way, but she had never completely adjusted to the Hollywood version of the tux. Stad, a broad five-feet-ten, all of it hardened by squash and tennis and sailing and swimming and anything else he could do to keep away from his desk at Revue's publicity department, wore a robin's-egg-blue ensemble with red cummerbund, red bow tie and pleated white shirt with thick damask cuffs held by massive silver cuff links made of antique coins. Sommy, as Virgil was called, was less conservative, both in dress and physique. He was about six-feet-two, heavy-shouldered and lean-hipped, with a long Greek-god face topped by a pale brown cap of hair. He wore a burgundy jacket, black trousers, plaid cummerbund with heavy silver buckler, plaid bow tie in loose droop, magnificent ruffled shirt and knuckle-length puffs of wrist lace. When he raised one hand and said, 'Hello-ello there, you gorgeous things!' he seemed born to Hollywood, though he was in fact a very recent import and had yet to complete his first American feature.

Mona looked him over and said, 'Introductions are in order, Terry,' in her best *haut style* manner. Terry did the honors. Stad said to Mona, 'What we wouldn't give to have you at Revue!' Sommy said, unexpectedly, 'I never thought the day would come,' and held Mona's hand and looked at Stad and Terry as if to confirm that this was actually happening.

Sommy finally tore his worshipful gaze from Mona and glanced around the living room. 'I've read about this house,' he said in hushed Liverpudlian accents. 'Could you take me through, Miss ... Mona?' Mona said of course. Sommy said, 'That black kitchen—' Mona said, 'We got as much publicity as we could and so we got rid of it.' They walked out, leaving Stad and Terry alone.

'*He'll* never be shown the bedroom,' Stad muttered.

'How have you been?' Terry asked primly.

'Bored. Bet you can't say the same.'

'Living with Mona isn't all *that* exciting.'

'I don't mean Mona. I mean *The Eternal Joneses*. It's making waves all over town.'

'We didn't know about it until last night.'

'Even so, working for Nat Markal—' He sighed.

'You have a pretty good setup, haven't you?'

'It's all right. But Avalon's got the only full-scale publicity department left in Hollywood. Avalon does star buildups and promotions the way the old-time studios did. The rest of us—' He shrugged. 'I'm thinking of going free-lance. More action that way.'

'I could speak to Cole Staley if you'd like. He's not only a boss, he's a friend.'

He came to the couch and sat down beside her. 'Am *I* still a friend?'

'I would say so.' He moved closer. 'Unless, of course, you found more exciting candidates in the past two weeks.'

'Candidates, shmandidates, let's swing.' He put his arm around her; his lips pressed hard; he murmured, 'Tonight you'll come to my place.'

'Because you want me, love me, can't live without me?'

He pulled back to look at her. 'What's your hang-up?'

She said, 'At least you want me,' and disengaged herself and stood up.

'I don't get it. We had something special. Then you move in with Mona—'

'I haven't moved in. And what—'

'A month. With vows of chastity. While Mona needs a new innerspring every week. Am I supposed to say I like it?'

'*What* special something that we had?'

'If you don't know—'

'I don't.' She had begun this in mild irritation, to chide him

192

for staying away two weeks, though she was aware that it was her behavior – her need for mood and privacy impossible in the hacienda – that had kept him away. Now she was thinking it out. 'Every man who sleeps with a woman has the same special something.'

He gave her the horrified look, the shocked look. It didn't impress her, it amused her.

'Are your intentions honorable, sir?'

'Are you *kidding,* madam?'

She heard Sommy exclaim, 'Smashing!'

'That's the Roman bathroom,' she murmured.

'Look, we're both mature, intelligent—'

'Hip, worldly-wise, sexually emancipated and so on.'

His face and voice hardened. 'I give as much as I get.'

'Then you haven't been getting much.' Which wasn't really fair because she had enjoyed Stad Homer . . .

Had enjoyed. Past tense. All finished.

'I'm sorry,' she said, and put her hand on his arm.

He nodded. They sat in uncomfortable silence. He lit a cigarette and looked at it and wet his lips . . . and muttered, 'I guess I should have told you how I felt. I *do* think seriously of you, but we always kept it so light—'

She interrupted by kissing his cheek. 'What's the itinerary?'

'Romanoff's. Go-Go. Party in Coldwater Canyon for Mijlas Halvich, the director who splashed big at Cannes.'

She glanced toward the foyer. 'Maybe you were wrong about Sommy and the bedroom. How long does a tour of nine rooms take?'

'Listen, Terry, let's play it cool a while. You made your point—'

'And I won't make it again. Peace, lover.'

'Amen,' he chanted, 'if it's spelled p-i-e-c-e.'

She laughed along with him, but the game was played out. She knew now she didn't want to marry Stad Homer; that she wouldn't have married him if he had asked six months ago. She just didn't care enough . . . which made *her* the villain of this scene.

Mona appeared, trailed by a flushed and smiling Sommy. Her lipstick was smudged, her gown almost imperceptibly disarranged on top. 'Be back in a sec,' Mona said, her voice the liquid thickness she used on camera. Fifteen minutes later they were on their way.

They didn't reach the Whiskey A Go-Go until midnight,

having spent almost three hours at dinner. Sommy used his size to clear a path through the teens-and-twenties mob jamming the street outside the Whiskey's entrance. He elbowed the kids aside with rather more élan than was necessary, and Terry figured he was playing hero for Mona.

They reached the door. The guard wore a blue serge suit and a flowered tie and was just as big as Sommy. He recognized Mona instantly and murmured, 'Right in, please,' which wasn't as easy as it sounded. The mob inside was backed clear up to the mob outside. But Sommy used his elbows again.

The guard called to a waitress in brief skirt and jabbed his finger repeatedly at Mona's back. The waitress looked blank, and the guard called, 'Mona Dearn!' The waitress hurried after Mona and Sommy. Terry and Stad, bringing up the rear, witnessed the word spreading among the dancers on the tight-packed floor and the generally older group of observers. By the time they were shown to a table (quickly and proudly vacated by two businessman types), more heads were turned to them than to the shell stand and close-packed Five Alive, just then beginning 'a trip down memory lane with that grand old favorite of years gone by, "Downtown".' Mona took off her silver mink. The close-packed mob howled. Mona smiled and sat down. Sommy bridled a bit, flexing his muscles as he slid Mona's chair in, but he was eating it up. Terry and Stad, hanging back until their charges were settled, took their seats. The crowd now divided its attention between Mona and the floor show, which was the dancers themselves, or rather the girls. Young girls, eighteen and up according to the house rules and the guard checking identity cards at the door, but who knew what switching of IDs went on. Young girls doing things with their hips, bellies, rear ends and groins their mothers hadn't done under the connubial blankets. Young girls who glowed with that special Saturday Night glow, who looked and felt highly desirable.

Mona stood up. 'I'd like to dance,' she said. Sommy said, 'Right,' and they moved around the table onto the dance floor. A space, small but still a precious space, cleared for them. The Five Alive ended a number in cacophony even more obvious than their usual sound. The leader, Wakefield Five, was waving his hand, and Terry realized he had cut the number short. 'From Mona Dearn's latest flick,' he said, keeping it cool by not acknowledging her presence, ' "Mash Mash Sweet Potato".' Mona kept it cool by not acknowledging the compliment, but it was still right out of the old musicals with the MC shouting Stop The Music! and introducing That Great Star Who Has Honored Us With Her Presence Tonight.

The waitress asked what they were drinking. The Whiskey A Go-Go had no cover, no minimum, no obvious system of making the individual pay for his presence. But the waitresses were a special breed who seemed to know just who had and who hadn't ordered a drink in the past half-hour. Terry ordered a double gin gimlet over tall ice for Mona, a rye and water, fifty-fifty, for herself. Stad ordered Scotch for Sommy and himself. 'Shall we?' he asked, jerking his head at the dance floor. Terry said, 'Not right now,' and thought, 'It frightens me tonight. It makes me think of orgies and loss of individuality and all sorts of public horrors involving private parts.'

'You mind if I do?' he asked, and walked away without waiting for her answer. He sensed the end of the affair. *The end of the affair. What an archaic expression here in the land of the watusi. What a lovely archaic sentiment ... and what the hell was eating at her?*

Was it Bert? Sentimental old Bert who would send her roses next week on her birthday? A call to Bert and she would be engaged. A four-hour jet flight home and she would be married. And all her troubles would be little ones and there would be a house in Westchester and country club dances and people who talked books and music and women who would, in the main, make her feel beautiful instead of a dowdy little Puritan as did the Monas and Isas and all the other glittering female productions ingathered from every state in the union, every country in the world.

She felt very much alone in this crowded, noisy room. When the drinks came she picked up her glass and said, 'Another of these, please,' and drank. The waitress said, 'That was rye and water, right?' and went away. She finished her drink. The voice behind her said, 'I knew you were the real thing. Rye and water.'

It was Lars Wyllit, boy maniac. He wore a black sweatshirt and suntan trousers and tennis shoes. 'You're beautiful,' she said, 'but the purple bruise doesn't match.'

She was glad to see him, and he read it and seated himself in Stad's chair. She glanced quickly at the dance floor. Stad had himself a small blonde with frenetic crotch movement. His own movement wasn't far behind.

'I got it defending your honor,' Lars said, which snapped her

195

eyes back to him. 'We were discussing Mona Dearn, and some-one said Mona was an underground Lesbian, a dyke with a sweetie who'd recently moved in with her. Since I hadn't been able to get you at your home and since I'm a *maven* at jumping to unsupported conclusions—' He waited.

She hoped her shock didn't show. 'I'm staying with Mona.'

'Then the bruise was in good cause, which is more than I can say for most of my bruises.'

She saw things in his face besides the bruise. 'You're not looking well.'

'I like rye and water too,' he said. 'Or rye and rye. It's not really rye, you know. It's bourbon and grain neutral spirits. It's American blended whiskey. No peat smoke or sherry casks. No crap. Just whiskey, as easy going down as whiskey can be.'

'You're still not looking well.'

'That's what I mean. Rye and water. No crap. I'm sick as a dog, and you're the only one to tell me. I need you to tell me things.'

She laughed, uncomfortable because she believed him and because she remembered his kiss going deep down into her, this funny little man with the sickness of violence. 'You're not going to make any trouble, are you? I'm with Mona.'

'I remember. Mona Dearn is your friend.'

'Please.'

'Sorry. I always want to strip you. I mean, well, that too, but I always want to see things that I know are just under—' He took cigarettes from an invisible pocket in the black sweatshirt and lit up. She realized he had been drinking – a lot. He said, 'I'll shut up if you'll dance with me.'

'Rye and water and no crap and you do those abominations?'

'I enjoy them. Better than the fox-trot and turkey-trot. Back to our savage heritage.'

'For you it's only a half-step back.'

His thin smile showed he didn't like it.

'You'll leave afterward?'

He liked that even less, but she couldn't help it. She was wor-ried about how he would act with Sommy and Stad. And how could she enjoy herself with a man who was *looking* to put that steering column in his chest?

'Now why did I—' she said aloud.

'Why did you what?' He leaned forward. 'Tell me, Terry. A thought to reveal something about the girl I dig.'

196

'I'll dance with you. Then good night.'

He didn't answer. She took it, hopefully, as an acceptance of her terms. They stepped around the table and onto the dance floor. He did a controlled jerk, but if his movement was moderate the total effect wasn't. He fixed her with his eyes and let go. She looked away. Dangerous. Sick and dangerous. She feared him. She wished she didn't know him, wished he didn't know where she lived. She located Mona and Sommy. Mona moved a lot and a lot of Mona moved. Still, she wasn't very good. People nodded and smiled because she was Mona Dearn, but she looked overripe against the backdrop of tender girls, and the kids danced better, with more effect and meaning. Sommy also moved a lot, and the Liverpudlian background was evident in his practiced shuffling, but he was faking, it wasn't important to him. Only Mona Dearn was important to him, Mona and his image as the man with Mona. Stad and his blonde were much better. Lars Wyllit was better still, the real thing, the violence and lust most of the kids only half-understood as they went through their motions. The violence and lust most people, young or old, only half-understood and half-tasted. A dangerous man.

The number ended. She said, 'So long,' and started for the table. He followed. 'Can I call you at Mona Dearn's place?'

'If you wish,' she said, and sat down at the table.

He stood beside her. 'That sounds suspiciously like a brush.'

Mona and Sommy approached, she flushed and smiling, he full in his pride. Mona stopped at the table, near Lars, who blocked her chair. She nodded and began to say hello. But Sommy came around the table and said, 'Excuse me,' and waited for Lars to step aside. Between the two big, beautiful creatures Lars looked pitifully fragile and shabby. As if aware of this, he drew himself up and said, 'Allow *me,*' sliding the chair out a bit. Mona said, 'Oh, thank you,' in her liquid whisper, and lowered her grand derriere as Lars slid the chair back in. Sommy's amused flick of the eyes and patronizing, 'Right,' made Terry speak quickly.

'Mona, this is a friend from Avalon whom you'll remember from the meeting last night. Lars Wyllit. And this is—'

Lars cut the introductions short. 'We met two years ago,' he said crisply to Mona. 'I revised a bomb of a script they palmed off on you.'

Mona looked surprised. Lars said, *'The Day Girls.'* Mona smiled brilliantly, 'I remember now.' The on-camera liquid whisper was gone, and she put out her hand. 'Larson W. Wyllit, additional dialogue. You saved my neck.'

Lars leaned down to take the hand. His eyes flickered to her bosom, and he smiled his tight little smile. 'In my memoirs, I'll claim I saved a lot more than that.'

Mona laughed. Sommy seated himself beside her. 'Somerset Walpole Virgil here,' he announced.

Lars's eyes widened. 'Where?'

Terry almost laughed, but it wouldn't be funny if Sommy took umbrage. This was one man the little maniac wouldn't be able to handle.

Sommy smiled graciously, showing perfect caps agleaming in a row. 'That's the way we say it in England. Jim here. Tom here. Y'know.'

'Ah,' Lars said, and nodded. 'Mr. Somerset Walpole Publius.'

'No, that's Virgil,' Sommy said, and shook his head and chuckled. 'I think we'll have to drink barrels to catch up, what?' He raised his glass and sipped. 'Ah! One thing you have to give us, we make the finest whiskey on earth.'

Lars looked at Terry. 'Rye and water and no crap and what is Virgil without Publius. I'm sending messages. Important messages. Is anybody listening?'

'Can't we continue this another time?' she murmured.

He turned to go. Mona said, 'You two have a code.' She pouted prettily. 'Can't I get in on it?'

Terry was surprised. Mona was reacting to the little man. No doubt about it, she felt something. Maybe it was the three gimlets she'd had while being put into her gown. Maybe the wine with dinner. But she was being turned on by Larson Wyllit, who barely made it to her chin. She was pitching.

Pitching was a good sign, a healthy sign, a sign Terry had been anxiously waiting for. She would have welcomed it joyously . . . with anyone but this boy disaster.

Larson Wyllit knew what Mona was doing, caught her pitch instantly. He said, 'Perhaps not *that* code, Mona. But there are others. Codes to suit all occasions.'

Mona said, 'Sommy dear, please move over and let Mr. Wyllit tell me about his codes.'

Sommy hesitated a moment before shifting to Stad's chair. Lars stepped between them and sat down. And became the pitifully fragile and shabby thing again . . . or so it seemed to Terry. Mona saw something else. Mona reacted to something being sent in her own code. As for Sommy, his opinion of Lars

198

had changed. He now viewed him as an annoyance rather than an entertainment. Which made Terry, who hadn't particularly liked him before, actively dislike him. And fear for Lars. And at the same time hope he got his lumps.

Crashing their group and putting down Sommy and coming on this way with Mona Dearn! Who did he think he was?

She picked up her fresh drink, served while she'd been dancing, and looked for Stad. He and the blonde were in front of the shell, frugging away. The blonde wore skin-tight white stretch pants. Stad's gaze was right on target. Terry felt deserted. She sipped and murmured, 'Rye and water suddenly seems out of style.'

Lars had moved his chair close to Mona and was speaking softly. He glanced across the table. 'I drink champagne too, on occasion.' He turned back to Mona. Sommy leaned in on him, frowning. 'I can't quite make you out.'

Lars said, 'I hope not,' and continued his *sotto voce* conversation. Mona giggled and ruffled his hair, which made little difference to its studied disarray. Sommy said, 'Dance, Mona?' Mona said, 'No, not right now. I want to—' Lars put his lips to her ear. She listened and laughed and her arm dropped around his shoulders. Then she pulled back in mock insult. 'You stop that! Some code!'

Sommy stood up. 'You heard the lady.'

Mona stared at him. 'What's the matter with you?'

'I think you've overstayed your welcome, lad.'

Lars raised his head slowly – reluctantly, Terry felt. 'If Miss Dearn says so.'

'I *don't* say so,' Mona said.

'She doesn't want trouble,' Sommy said, 'but your conversation—'

'Is a private conversation,' Lars said, voice still mild. He seemed to realize how foolish it would be to try to fight the massive Englishman.

'And this is a private party,' Sommy said, grabbing Lars by the neck of his sweatshirt with both hands. He lifted him up and out of his chair in one quick movement, actually holding him suspended in air. Lars looked down and, unexpectedly, laughed. Terry said, 'Lars is leaving now, Sommy. Put him down.' Almost at the same instant, Mona said, 'You mother! Let him alone!' Sommy blinked at the combined verbal attack, confused and unhappy, and muttered, 'I wasn't going to *hit* him.' Terry believed him, there being considerable dishonor

199

in striking so small a man; and it looked as if this was one time Lars would help a situation by not playing the maniac.

But looks were always deceiving when it came to Larson W. Wyllit.

Still held by the sweatshirt, several inches of flat white stomach exposed by the bunched-up cloth, toes scraping the floor, Lars place-kicked Sommy in the groin. The Englishman screamed and bent double. Lars stooped to look into his face and had to dodge an outflung fist. He then began throwing punches at Sommy's head. Sommy took time out from his agony to swing once again, hitting Lars in the shoulder and knocking him to the side. Lars came back with judo chops at Sommy's neck. Sommy staggered and threw his right hand in a half-punch, half-push that couldn't miss. It sent Lars sprawling against a neighboring table. He slipped getting up and grinned at a girl's suggestion that he 'run like hell', and during those four or five seconds Sommy's condition visibly improved.

Lars saw it as he came shuffling to the attack. His grin remained, but turned rueful.

It had all happened so quickly people were only now becoming aware of it. Mona had just risen to get away from the melee. Terry still sat at her place, telling herself to watch carefully because this was Larson Wyllit's moment of truth, his comeuppance, his just desserts. Stad was nowhere in sight.

Lars stopped. Still grinning, he murmured, 'Say uncle, Mr. Publius?' Sommy wasn't bent over quite as severely now. His face was up, pale and set, and he watched Lars. Lars said, 'Well, if you can't continue—' Sommy took a long step forward, groaning at what must have been considerable pain, and used that half-punch, half-push again. Lars went backward and down. Sommy went after him. Lars rolled to get away.

Mona said, 'Stop it, stop it, both of you!' but this was one time the fabulous Dearn couldn't control her men. Sommy clutched for any part of Lars and got his heavy blond hair. He hauled up as someone shouted, 'It's Mona Dearn's table!' He held Lars at arm's length. Lars kicked but couldn't reach him. Sommy drew back his big left fist and Terry prayed he wouldn't kill Lars with that blow because there was no way in the world to stop it. Or so it seemed.

Lars grabbed Sommy's right forearm with both hands and used his fingers and Sommy let go as if he'd been burned. Terry heard Stad's voice: 'Let's stop this exhibition! Sommy, your contract states—'

Much as Sommy might care for contracts and careers, he didn't stop. He'd been kicked in the groin, and Lars was a flailing fury, and words were useless. Sommy had his fists up and Lars was swinging and Sommy's head jerked and blood showed at his mouth. Someone whooped and shouted, 'It's Supermouse!' Sommy backed a half-step. Lars drew a quick breath and flung himself forward again, seeming no higher than Sommy's cummerbund. Sommy paid him the compliment of flailing away with both fists as hard as he could. Lars was in close, landing three times to Sommy's once. But that once was a short, crunching blow to the chest. Lars sat down on the floor, sagging forward, mouth open. Sommy was about to go after him when Stad grabbed him around the waist from behind. Stad talked fast and low, and Sommy said, 'Yes, small, but what he did—' Stad said, 'Mona, Terry,' and pulled Sommy toward the door. Terry turned from the small man gasping like a netted fish. 'Mona we have to go.' Mona went to Lars, knelt to him. 'He's hurt!'

'He wanted to be hurt.'

'He needs help!'

'Yes,' Terry said, but to herself. She came around the table, trying not to see Lars.

A boy in a blue blazer came over. 'Let me, Miss Dearn.' He rubbed the back of Lars's neck and looked down Mona's cleavage. 'This always helps.'

Mona said, 'That damned Limey square, picking on a guy half his size!'

'This one isn't half anyone's size,' Terry said, pulling Mona to her feet.

Lars raised his head then. His mouth was twisted, but he made it into something approximating a smile.

A crowd had formed, hemming them in. The door guard was pushing through, calling, 'What's the trouble?'

'This was only round one,' Lars said, speaking as if each word were an egg he was afraid of dropping. Mona knelt again and whispered something. She rose and got her mink, draping it over an arm. The bouncer-guard came over. Mona said, 'That poor man on the floor wasn't to blame. Not at all.'

'You want me to find the other one, Miss Dearn?'

She shook her head. Terry said, 'It was all a mistake.' They went past him and began pushing through staring people. Mona gasped and looked at a sleek, aging type turning away with a too-bland expression. 'Celebrity feeler?' Terry asked. Mona

201

said, 'A *gooser*, the mother!' Terry said, 'Such is the price of fame and going unescorted into crowds.' They reached the door and had to fight their way out against a tide of below-age supplicants for go-go pleasure who, in the absence of the guard, were fighting their way in.

Stad was at the corner and waved them over, 'I sent Sommy to the parking lot. He's still hurting.'

They began to walk up the side street.

'Wyllit's a nut,' Stad said. 'It's proverbial, the small man being on the prod, but Wyllit has fights like I have cigarettes. And I smoke too much.'

Mona put on her coat. 'Chilly. I want to go home,'

'The party,' Stad reminded.

Mona's face grew sullen. 'Take the big hero.'

'Oops. Sommy didn't tell me how it started. Was he—'

Terry stopped. 'We forgot the bill.'

Stad said he would handle it. Terry shook her head. 'See Mona to the car, in case anyone follows. I'll only be a minute.'

She returned to the club. Their waitress was outside, looking around and forming unladylike words with her lips. The lip-act changed to a relieved smile when she saw Terry. They walked inside together and the music was rocking and the dancers dancing. Everything was normally à go-go. Terry paid at the bar and turned to leave, then took a quick look at the area of combat. Lars was still there, though no longer on the floor. He sat at the table, a drink in his hand. With him was a skinny man with heavy moustache and soiled striped shirt who waved his arms as he talked.

Terry's professional radar system indicated an enemy in operation and she made her way to the table. The man looked up and said, 'I told you they'd be worried.'

Lars also looked up. 'You know what this gentleman tells me? We can make a bundle, he and I, by threatening to sue. And I've been trying to tell him I'm independently rich, but he doesn't believe me. He's just dying to be my witness.'

The man stood up. 'Don't blow it,' he said, and ambled away.

'I once wanted to live on the beach,' Lars said. 'I wanted to read a while and write a while and not struggle for money. That was when I was almost convinced it was impossible for me to make money. I wanted to lie there with all the other non-entities and laugh at the society that had licked me and make believe I'd rejected it. Then I met a few of the citizens. Oh,

202

heavens. Maybe I was unlucky. Maybe I missed the big daddys and hit all the finks. But they cured me. And so did that first solid TV sale.'

He raised his glass and took an ice cube into his mouth. His hand shook. His pallor was extreme. There was an opaque look to his eyes. They turned everything back, like a dead man's. She said, 'Can I help you home?'

'Yours?'

'We can take a cab—'

'My car's down the street. In a little while I'll get in it.'

She stood undecided. He raised his head again. The opaque eyes cleared. 'Don't play Florence Nightingale. It's Mamie Stover I want.'

She turned and walked out.

When she got to the parking lot, Mona was behind the wheel of Stad's studio Lincoln. Sommy had walked off in grand dudgeon and Stad had to make sure the new investment got home all right.

Mona drove carefully and well. She asked if Lars was a boyfriend. Terry said no and Mona said he was an interesting man and Terry said, 'Only if you're interested in disasters.'

'He's got guts.'

'Psychosis is often confused with courage.'

Mona asked for a cigarette and they dropped the subject.

LARS WYLLIT

After Terry left, Lars had two more drinks and then a cute, lanky girl all legs and arms and wide smile came over and said, 'Hey there,' He said hey and she pulled out a chair and sat down facing him. She wore a *yé-yé* skirt almost to her pants sitting and she crossed her legs besides. He said, 'Thank you so much for the transfusion.' She said, 'That was SWV you tangled with, you know that?'

He nodded.

'You see many foreign films? English?'

'Some.'

'*Man on Bottom* was his big one.'

'Missed it.'

'Did he hit hard?'

He lifted his eyes from her legs.

203

'Sometimes actors are such phonies. You know, stuntmen to ride and fall and fight for them. Even the big, strong ones. Was this the real thing?'

'Want to touch the bruise?'

'May I?'

He laughed and said, 'I'm expecting someone, so you'll have to excuse me.' She reached out and touched the purple bruise on his cheek. He didn't bother correcting her, but repeated, 'I'm expecting someone,' without laughter this time.

'You must think me positively gruesome. But I'm *so* hipped on celebrities. Especially SWV.'

He sipped his drink. The Five Alive had taken a break. The crowd danced to recorded music. The two girls in the elevated glass cages jerked away.

'I'm a fan of his. We've got a club at Hollywood High. I mean we had, before I graduated. I'm over eighteen now, of course.'

'A girl is joining me—'

She crossed her legs the other way. She wore white pants. 'You know any more movie stars?'

'Not to fight with. Now you'll have really to forgive me, but if my date sees such an attractive chick she'll raise hell.'

'Mona Dearn a friend of yours?'

He looked her right in the eye. 'We fuck occasionally.'

She never even blinked. 'Then it's not true what they say about sex queens being frigid. They say Marilyn Monroe was frigid and that's why she couldn't stay married. You work in movies, don't you?'

He sighed and lit a cigarette. 'I'm tired now, honey.'

'I'd like to hear about directors and actors and all. The inside story. You know about television too? About The Monkees? You have an apartment?'

'Yes, but the bouncer at the door asks for ID cards.'

She smiled. 'No sweat. I really got one. Okay?'

'No thank you.'

Her smile faded.

He finished his drink and looked out at the dance floor, thinking it had finally come, the time when he turned down an attactive lay, when he actually found himself disliking a good-looking girl.

She uncrossed her legs, making a production of it, but he didn't bite. She stood up, very close to him. 'What's the hang-up?'

204

'Must there be one?'

'It's like money, man. No one turns it down.'

'Someone just did.'

She frowned. She stroked her straight brown hair. She nibbled her finger. 'Being a queer midget must be interesting, but kicks come hard, huh, baby?'

He stood up. She was two or three inches taller than he was in her flats. He tucked his cigarettes into his pocket. She said, 'Seriously, you're an old-looking preteen, aren't you?'

He walked slowly away. There were times he longed for New Jersey and the simple, uncomplicated days of sexual starvation.

No he didn't. Not even as a joke. He hated Jersey and memories of what he had been in Jersey. That time in the movie, sitting scrunched up between two big boys who spent a pleasant hour elbowing him, kicking him, threatening to get him outside and beat his brains out, giggling at his proffered gifts of candy and roaring when he suddenly burst from his seat, hurdled into the next row and ran from the theater. Laughing without knowing the terror in little Lars Wyllit, the self-contempt and anguish in little Lars Wyllit.

Little Lars Wyllit. Even at home, three brothers occasionally forgot brotherly love and settled differences of opinion with fist and foot.

And then the thrill of first year high school. Turk Barnessy the basketball hero slapping Lars in the lunchroom for not *immediately* walking away from his girl Melinda when the great man arrived. Lars had registered at the *dojo* over the Japanese restaurant that very same day for the beginner's course in judo; and he had also begun talking to himself a few minutes before bed each night. The talk consisted of calling himself every rotten name other kids had called him: shrimp and peanut and sis and midge and shorty and dwarfy. And names he knew applied as well – coward, yellow-belly, chicken, lily-liver. Three and a half years of judo and self-administered tongue-lashing brought him to graduation day and a confrontation with Turk. He knocked the mortarboard from Turk's head, slapped the smile from his lips. Then, with parents and teachers and fellow students trying to stop it, he kicked and chopped Turk into bloody, sniveling defeat. There were threats of arrest and suit by the Barnessy family, but Lars wasn't worried. He knew now how to make the world give up its sweetness. He also knew Turk would rather die than further advertise his shame.

Lars dated Melinda. Within a month he lost his virginity – she had lost hers sometime before – and embarked on his career as a boy maniac. In college, and then Manhattan, he continued his training in and application of judo, karate and general mayhem, all of which stood him in good stead in Hollywood where he had more than held his own in nearly a hundred fights.

He hadn't quite held his own tonight, he thought, double-clutching the TR4 and feeling the pain in his chest and upper stomach. But tonight hadn't been a critical situation, an important contest for Lars Wyllit, no matter how it had looked to others. Naturally, he had fought as hard as he could, but the driving need to win had been supplanted by a weaker motive – the simple need to survive. Lars would always go after big men – normally big men, that is. Sommy, however, was a step over the line, beyond the Wyllit pale, just too big, too strong to offer any possible area of dishonor.

He roared away from the traffic light, heading east on Sunset. A Jaguar XKE appeared beside him, and the hirsute sport behind the wheel looked at him inquiringly. He didn't floor the pedal when the Jag began to move ahead. He wouldn't drag tonight. He was still a pretty sick boy and should be heading home instead of to Mona Dearn's pad. He'd had a bad moment back at the Go-Go when his heart had done some frightening tricks, skipping beats. He'd wanted to cry out for help, which was when he had told Mona it was only Round One. But it was just talk, just cover. He didn't have it in for the big Englishman.

The heart. The damned heart. If it wasn't for the heart he could have everything under control.

He went along with that notion for a block or two, but it didn't hold up. He had absolutely nothing under control. Not the writing, which came in frenzied spurts, more and more frenzied lately, and made him fear Chuck Halpert. Not the loving, which was kicks, sure, but which he felt could be so much more. And once you started feeling *that* you were looking for Miss Special, and once you started looking for her the act became an uphill thing. Not the economics, because he was a lousy gambler and it was going to catch up with him someday. Not the fighting, because of the carefully buried reality: he was terrified of being afraid and certain that the moment of truth would come – during the most critical brawl, with all the wrong people watching – when he would turn chicken.

No, 'chicken' was a gag word. When the whimpering, cowardly child inside him would emerge and he would be damned forever as a man.

Another few blocks and he exchanged suppressed reality for day-by-day reality. Most of the time he was a sure and skillful writer, a solid money-maker, a certain, erotic lover, a tough, fearless fighter. Screw the heart, it would keep pumping forever. Screw Dr. Feidler and his sad eyes and fearful warnings. Screw *all* the sad, fearful people for they shall inherit sadness and fear. Besides, he was going to write the greatest movie of all time. Halpert too, of course, but who knew how long such a rank amateur would last?

If he wanted to, he could see to it Halpert *didn't* last. He could drop in every week. He could give him 'suggestions'. He could knife him . . .

He didn't pursue that thought, but it was there. He turned to another reality – a triumph in the making. Mona Dearn had whispered, 'I want to see you tonight – my place,' and pain or no pain, you didn't turn down Mona Dearn. To do that would be sacrilege. Pass up an opportunity with the object of a million wet dreams?

Terry Hanford opened the door to the pink hacienda, which made him sad and glad in equal proportions. He didn't want her to see him pitch another woman, yet he wanted her to know he could handle any of them, even Mona Dearn. 'Back from the dead,' he said. She stared at him. 'By invitation,' he added.

Mona came up behind her. 'Hi! You kept us waiting.'

'Not me,' Terry murmured. 'I just wondered why we had to play gin rummy in our evening gowns.'

Lars walked past her and into the house. 'Had to glue myself together.' He smiled at them both and made a decision. It was Mona who wanted him here, so he turned the smile on Mona. 'I think I got all the pieces, but you can check me later.'

She giggled. 'Whoever checks Sommy might find an important piece missing.' She took his arm, and even though she'd changed into flats she was at least four inches taller than he. More than height, she was a broad broad, a big woman, and he had never shown to best advantage, or been entirely comfortable, with big women. But he had pursued some, to prove the point. Adding Mona to his list would be a real coup, a score of epic proportions.

They walked toward a huge living room, Terry coming up

behind them. They sat on the couch, Mona slouching low so that her head came level with his. He smiled at her, ignoring Terry who remained standing. 'You shouldn't have stayed dressed for me,' he said.

'What would you have thought if I greeted you in a messy old nightgown?'

'I'd have thought, let's get Mona Dearn out of that messy old nightgown.'

'Good night,' Terry said. 'I've got a messy old nightgown of my own.'

'Groovy,' Lars said, without removing his gaze from Mona. 'I didn't dare hope you would join us.'

Mona laughed. Terry said, 'You think he's kidding, don't you?'

Lars said, 'Who's kidding?'

Mona's eyes flickered brightly behind her laughter. She hesitated, then said, 'It's all right with me if it's all right with you, Terry.'

'Again, good night,' Terry said, and walked away.

'Good night,' Mona said, locking eyes with Lars.

'Sleep tight,' Lars said. 'Don't let the bedbugs bite.'

Terry was gone. Mona murmured, 'Bedbugs. It's been a long time since I even heard the word. You ever see bedbugs?'

Lars put his hand behind her head and drew her toward him. They touched lips. He thought of Terry and how ridiculous it was to prefer anyone to this gorgeous acre of femininity. 'No,' he said. 'You got any to show me?'

She laughed. 'You break me up.' She pressed her lips to his. 'You tough little bastard.'

It didn't bother him. It was a kick for her and a kick for him. The mismatch of the century. He took her in his arms, bending over her as she stuck her legs straight out and slouched lower. He kissed her hard, slid his lips down her neck to her breasts. She wiggled her legs and said 'Ummm, baby.' He found a zipper near her armpit and worked it. The dress loosened, and he drew it down from her shoulders. He found the hook in back. 'Introducing,' he murmured, and took off her brassiere. Big, all right. A feast, and not only for the eyes. He feasted.

After a while she led him to her bedroom and stripped, turning and posing for his pleasure. She stopped him from undressing. She wanted to do it herself. She undressed him as if he were a baby, cooing over him and doing everything but carry him to the bed. She even tried that, but couldn't make it.

208

He laughed and it was still a kick and he was ready. But she wasn't. She kept stalling, kept playing. An hour passed, a full hour, and he grew tired and testy. 'Be a big girl,' he said, and pushed her down and pulled at her legs. She rolled over onto her stomach, but her backward glance was melting. He realized this was what she wanted. She wouldn't ask for it because asking adulterated true toughness, but she wanted a hard man, a mean man, the man who had kicked Sommy in the nuts. He smacked her big rear end. She said, 'No, I won't!' He smacked it again, the sound ringing out in the silent house. He thought of Terry. Was she next door, listening to them, jealous and sexually excited?

He smacked Mona's rear five times, his hand stinging from the force of the blows, the sound loud enough to waken anyone in the house. Mona whimpered and rolled onto her side. 'You hurt me.' Her eyes blinked back tears. He grabbed her shoulders and shoved her flat on her back. She tried to draw up her legs. He slapped her face. She said, 'Not that.' He slapped her again and jammed his knee between her thighs. 'Not that,' he mocked. 'You want me to pat the famous fanny all night. Not that. You want Lars to perform by the script.'

She wept, pressing her legs together. 'I've changed my mind. Go away. You're not—'

He grabbed a breast. 'If you don't open—'

She cried out. Her legs opened. He stroked her face and kissed her. He told her how beautiful, how desirable she was, and she wept softly and called him a rat and rapist and hugged him and bit his shoulder.

It went very well. As soon as it ended her eyes closed and she began to doze, mumbling that she hadn't slept well all week and please phone her soon.

He washed and dressed and when he left she was deep asleep. He made his way along the foyer, passing two open doors and two closed doors. He wondered which closed door hid Terry, and entered the living room, and stopped dead. Terry was seated in an armchair, wearing a long, quilted housecoat, reading a book. She looked up, startled, then flushed. That flush made him sweat, but he grinned and said, 'Insomnia?' She dropped her eyes back to the book. 'Yes.' He told himself a man who had just laid Mona Dearn had no reason to worry about the opinions of an ordinary woman, a woman moreover who didn't give a damn about him, but he persisted with, 'And in such a quiet part of town too.' She snapped the book shut, rose and walked toward an archway. Anyone else would have called it a night, but he was Lars Wyllit. He followed quickly, saying, 'Could you spare a glass of something wet?' They entered a bright white kitchen. She pointed at the sink, her back to him. He said, 'Cat got your tongue?' She didn't answer, didn't turn. He said, 'Silence is golden. Speak no evil. Seen and not heard. Loose tongue—'

Still not looking at him, she said, 'What is it you want of me, applause or condemnation?'

'You've got me there. But it's obvious I want *something*.'

'I'd have thought you'd be free of wanting for the night.'

'There's wanting and wanting. If I could interest you in a bit of the other variety—'

'Go home,' she said wearily.

'Say good night and I will.'

'Good night.'

'Looking at me.'

She turned, her face as weary as her voice. 'Good night.'

He longed to say something that would make her understand more than she did about him, make her care a little. He went to the sink and took a glass from the drainboard, and spat in the eye of his longing. 'Thirsty work,' he said. There was a slamming sound, followed by her slippered footsteps stamping out of the room.

He went out to his car. His chest ached. He sat still. The ache became pain, piercing pain, then quickly subsided.

Two attacks within a month meant something was happening, something was wrong. Momma's fears were coming true. 'Rheumatic fever at ten means no excitement ever again.' Time to forget the lousy meter and pay heed to the vital message. If it wasn't already too late.

And become what?

He revved up the Triumph and jockeyed it around and roared down the driveway. He hit seventy before the corner and went down through Hollywood Hills as if it were Le Mans. On Wilshire he saw a rod with sixteen-inch smooth-cap racing tires. He knew he could never take a heap like that on a straight run, but he bet the hoody kid behind the wheel five bucks to one he could beat him around the block.

What with parked cars and the kid's fouling on the last two corners, he ended up with a hundred dollars' worth of scraped body and crumpled rear fender. But he collected his dollar, going to the heap and leaning in and holding out his hand and

210

making the kid see he would have to fight for his life as well as the buck.

Then he went home. It all boiled down to one thing: if you have to stop living to avoid dying, you may as well be dead.

CHERYL CARNY

Mr. Collus came to the door of the breakfast room in his red plaid shorts, a smooth-skinned, hairless man who tried to hold in his stomach whenever he spoke to her. At the pool his wife turned and nodded, to show Cheryl she approved of his mission. 'Two solid hours,' he said. 'I think that earns you all a swim.' The twins slammed shut their books and ran for the water, shouting. Mr. Collus said, 'You too, Cheryl,' but she shook her head and said she'd have a cold drink and make a call, if he didn't mind. '*Mind?* When're you gonna stop that! You make yourself at home—' His daughters called him and he turned, grinning.

Cheryl walked to the kitchen. She sat at the counter near the wall phone and poured a diet cola and wanted to call Charles Halpert, and called home. Jim took a long time answering and he was drunk. She asked how he was getting along. 'Why, fine, fine, I'm just sittin' and sippin' and watching exhibition football. How you getting along?' She said fine and was there anything she could bring him when she came home. 'You mean you're coming home?' She said not to be silly. He said, 'Oh, I won't be silly. I'll just get my trusty old *pistola* and come a-lookin'.' He gave a congested little laugh. She asked again if there was anything she could bring him. 'Liquor. Get a few quarts of vodka at Thrifty. The cheapest.' She said all right and did he want anything special for dinner. He said, 'Anything. I don't care. Just make sure you bring the vodka. And cigarettes. I don't want to run out while you're tutoring.' He laughed. 'You think I believe that, don't you? Why won't you give me the telephone number if you're tutoring?' She said she didn't want any calls and he always called.

'I'm going to surprise you one of these days,' he said. 'I'm going to show up when you least expect me. Then we'll finish everything in style.'

'Good-bye, Jim.'

'Bring home a newspaper.'

'All right.'

'I saw a movie on television. *A Face in the Crowd,* remember? You liked it when we first saw it. Andy Griffith. A long time ago.'

He wanted to talk. Beneath the drunken fear and hatred and anguish was the same need to talk that she had. 'Yes,' she said. 'We'll talk when I get home. They're waiting for me.'

'Yeah. He's waiting for you. He's got a nice healthy body, and you don't have to wheel him to bed.'

She hung up and dialed Charles Halpert's number. It rang twice and a woman said, 'Bali-Ho Apartments.' Cheryl had the choice of hanging up, chickening out as she had twice before, or finally asking for him. She asked for him. There was a series of clicks and a minute passed and his voice said, 'Hello?' What could she say? 'Hello?' he said again. 'Anyone there?'

'It's Cheryl Carny. I read about the meeting Friday night. I wondered whether you'd gone to Sequoia afterward.'

'No, I didn't.'

'I'm sorry.' She felt as if she were turning to stone – brain and tongue and all. 'What went wrong?'

'Nothing went wrong. Everything went right.' He sounded excited and happy. 'I'm working on a treatment.'

'*The Eternal Joneses?* You mean—'

He laughed. 'Isn't that something!'

'Yes, it is. Congratulations.'

'Thank you. Now all I have to do is a dramatic summation of two hundred years of American history.' He laughed again. 'Is there anything—'

She said, 'Yes, there *is* something you can do. You can invite me to your place tonight.' She went on before he could answer. 'I don't know exactly what time I'll be there. Between eight and eleven. Might even be later.'

He didn't hesitate. 'Fine. Great.'

She said good-bye. She finished her drink and told herself they would talk and have coffee and laugh it up. Maybe he would kiss her good night.

Cheryl left the Colluses at four. Jim ate a little of the Chinese dinner she brought home and drank half a fifth of vodka. Along with what he had drunk during the day, it made for an early bedtime. But he lasted long enough to twist his hands in her hair and whisper his vengeful obscenities and attain his raging release. She didn't mind as much as usual. She felt she owed him something extra tonight.

He had passed out before she finished tucking the covers around him. She showered and dressed in her last remaining set of black-lace undies and her best blouse and her pale blue suit. She wore heels and black stockings and used her Arpège and brushed her pale brown hair until the blonde highlights shone. She wrote a note in case Jim awakened and put it on his night table: 'Went out for some air. Be back soon.' She said, 'Jim,' once, sharply. He never stirred. She left the apartment, blocking thoughts of broken gas lines and earthquakes and fires. She wouldn't be that lucky. Or unlucky. She didn't hope for such things because she knew what the guilt would do to her.

Charles Halpert opened the door and she walked in and made the usual complimentary remarks about his apartment. He poured drinks and they sat down on his sleeper couch and lit cigarettes. She laughed at his jokes about cooking and cleaning and kept her eyes on her glass and felt he was waiting for an explanation, or at least an opening gambit. And there were no explanations or gambits in her. She was here looking for succor. She was a supplicant, not a swinging married woman with a swinging married man. But how could he know that? How could he have expected anything here that would help her? A church ... a psychiatrist's office ... a bar. But not Charles Halpert's apartment!

He took her hand, and she actually jumped. He looked at her, and she dropped her eyes to her glass. 'Would you like another?' he asked. She said yes, just to get him away. He went into the kitchen unit and poured two drinks and came back. She kept both hands on her glass, as if warming the whiskey, leaving no hand for him to take. She sat hunched and frozen and wondered if she was losing her mind. What did she expect this man to do after inviting herself to his home?

He said, 'It's strange, your calling this afternoon. I was thinking of you. I wanted to tell you the good news. Did a little voice whisper, Call-Charley-Halpert?'

'I thought it was Chuck.'

'Charley to people who count.'

She was going to smile, then realized he meant it. She put down the glass.

He took her hand again, and this time she didn't jump. Their fingers twined. He leaned back and she leaned with him. 'What happened to Jim?'

She began at the beginning and told him everything, includ-

213

ing what had gone on inside her. He maintained silence until she finished, then said, 'My God! What can happen to people.' She began to cry. He pulled her head to his shoulder and pressed it there. 'Just hold on. Time is the only answer.'

She cried wildly, shaking and sobbing, mourning the Cupid Carnys. She had never cried that way before. Not as a child. Not the day of the accident. Not the day they told her Jim was paraplegic. Not the day she realized he wasn't even going to make a try at being human.

Finally she quieted, blew her nose and said, 'What if time gives no answer? What if it goes on exactly this way?'

'Nothing goes on exactly as it is. Everything changes.'

'For the worse, sometimes.'

'What can be worse?'

She smiled a little at that, feeling better after her cry, feeling at ease with him.

'Even if it is worse, from an outside point of view, it won't be worse for you. For example, if he drinks so much he endangers his life. Or if his mental state becomes such that it's no longer safe for either of you. Then you'll be forced to act and he'll be forced to improve.'

'Or go mad.'

'Is that a possibility?'

She shrugged.

'Well, there's hope,' he said. 'There's always hope.'

'Always?'

'Always. Ever read any of the writings of the Jews in the Warsaw ghetto and the Nazi extermination camps? Nothing could be more hopeless than their situation, yet they hoped.'

'They had God. I'm no longer sure I have God. And you, do you have Him?'

'I never had God. My father was a rabbinical student, a *Yeshiva bocha* in Russia, but once here he bought a candy-stand on New York's Lower East Side and educated himself through second year high school and went into a bigger business, a luncheonette, and met my mother and married her and went broke and became a salesman for a credit clothing chain and ended up a tired little man with a wife who despised him and a daughter who despised him and a son who wasn't sure whether or not to despise him. He spent his evenings and weekends in libraries, and when the weather was nice he went to concerts, free ones in the parks, and he was too busy escaping and dreaming to have God. And too bitter.'

214

She was quiet a moment, digesting. 'Your father must have been more than that.'

He smiled. 'He had a Puerto Rican girlfriend. I found out after he died. A round little woman, young, who was deserted by her husband, a seaman. I met her when I tried to take over my father's sales route. I was in my senior year of college, summer vacation, and thought maybe I could become a successful salesman. It lasted two weeks and depressed me into becoming what I didn't want to become, an English teacher. But Irene was cute, and she knew my father in a way the family didn't know him. To my mother he was a *deliberate* failure, someone too lazy to make the money that would give her pride and status in the only world that counted for her – the Prokash family, *her* family. To my uncle, my father's younger brother, he was the *chuchim*, the brain, a dominant force that fell apart and gave him the opportunity to achieve that dream of younger brothers everywhere – lick big brother. To my sister he was something to be ashamed of, someone to be blamed for not getting the boys she wanted. To me he was a mystery, an interesting mystery, but everyone had a bad word for him and how can a kid go against the tide? Later, I began to love him. The last two years of his life–' He shook his head. 'Too late then.'

He was looking somewhere beyond her, into a world that belonged solely to him.

'One thing though, he *was* a failure, and he tried to make a virtue of it. He talked of money-grubbers and thieves. He said my uncles, my cousins, were small minds concentrating on dollars instead of universals. And later, when those arguments failed – when they no longer convinced even him – he tried to explain failure another way. In the blood, he said. In the genes. His father had been a dreamer and a *nebuch,* he said. He was a dreamer and too weak to succeed in this harsh world. And he would look at me and blink his eyes and furrow his forehead. I knew then *I* was doomed to failure. I believed him implicitly.' He paused. 'I guess I still do. Him, or my wife.'

He turned to her. 'You didn't stick your finger in the dike, lady. The flood waters broke through.' He put his lips to her cheek and his hand to her breast. Simply. So very simply. But her reaction wasn't simple. It was chaos, and she fought to sit there and smile and act civilized.

Their mouths met. He pulled back and looked at her, as if

215

startled at what he'd felt, what he'd sensed. She leaned forward, and they kissed again, and this time the kiss was a deep thing that opened up and shook them both. After a while he moved his lips to her ear and whispered, 'What is it that makes one woman better for one man than other women?'

She said, 'Charley,' as if crying, and stood up and unbuttoned her suit jacket. She didn't know what he would think of her for doing this but she couldn't help it. She undressed to her black-lace undies and took off the brassiere and said, voice choked, 'A lot for the money.' He said, 'I could pray to *that*.' She stepped out of the panties, trembling. He half-rose and took her hands and drew her to him. He sat and she stood and he put his arms around her hips and his hands on her bottom and his lips on her belly. She sighed. 'Charley, if I fall in love with you, don't get frightened.'

He pulled her down on his lap and kissed first one breast, then the other. She stroked his neck, his hair. She felt the wildness in him, in herself, felt them both holding back. 'I want to dream,' she said, 'but I don't expect dreams to come true. I half-love you already, Charley. Don't feel you have to say you love me. What you said about one woman being better for one man than other women is enough.'

He began to murmur over her body, describing the bigness of her, her breasts and rear and belly. Then he got up and pulled the spread from the couch-bed. Standing close to her, he took off his clothes, reaching out to touch her every few seconds. Naked, he too was big. Not tight-muscled as Jim was, but hairy and big-armed and big-thighed. Strong-looking in his own way. Terribly exciting!

She couldn't wait any longer. She came up against him, writhed against him, gasped his name into his mouth. They fell to the bed.

It wasn't a gentle thing. Toward the end his face twisted savagely and he pulled at her buttocks as if to tear them apart. She screamed a little and bit a little and had her climax a second before he had his.

She dressed, and he watched her from the bed. He said, 'I once went without it eight months, a bad period with my wife, and I didn't miss it. I doubt I could go that long with *you* in the house.'

She hooked up her stockings, sitting at the edge of the bed, and leaned over to kiss his lips. 'With me in the house you couldn't go without it one day.'

216

'How often are you going to come here?'

'As often as I can manage. Twice a week, with luck. Think you can handle that?'

He said yes, laughing, and she kissed him again and stroked his face. 'Good night, Charley. Think of me. I love you – but as I said, don't let it worry you.' She went to the door, turned off the light and reached for the knob.

'I love you too,' he said.

She turned, annoyed. 'I told you—'

'In my own way,' he said, sitting up and looking across the darkened room at her, 'according to my own capacity. I mean I care what happens to you. I wish you well.'

She went back to the bed, and they kissed. *He cared what happened to her*. She cared what happened to him and decided to tell him something she hadn't thought she would. 'Are you off *Terror Town*?'

'Yes, it's suspended until after *Joneses* is shot.' He smiled. 'We didn't even discuss the big news.'

'*We're* the big news,' she said.

He gave a quick breakdown of the meeting. She said, 'Wonderful!' and then, 'I read your treatment last Friday. I went into your office and took it.'

'I've done considerable polishing since—'

'Let me say it, Charley. You couldn't polish away what I saw. You didn't have a horror film. You had the story of four young people who, by their actions, actions that take up three quarters of the feature, end up in a ghost town where a madman and his sister destroy two of them. You have a series of character studies, and clever ones, in which what these young people *are* determines whether they live or die. But it won't make a Carl Baiglen movie, Charley. And what was your assignment.'

He smiled unconvincingly. 'Makes little difference now.'

'But it *does*, Charley. I'm not just saying this to be critical. You can't think that after—' She faltered at his expression, then pushed on. 'I'm glad you're off *Terror Town*. I think you'll do a lot better on something major, something good. As they say, you were too big for the job.'

His smile wasn't any more convincing, and she was suddenly frightened. *Why had she started this? She couldn't even be sure that she was right, so why had she taken the chance of hurting him?*

She knew why. She wanted to help Charley Halpert, wanted

to pass on an insight she had gained about this business and so help him survive and so have him remain in Hollywood, with her.

Now she had to finish the job.

'What I mean, Charley, is that Carl asked you for one thing and really wanted another. Sure, he hoped for a little class, but not the art-film approach you gave him. If he was blinded enough by his ambition to accept it, Markal would have laughed in his face.'

'That might be,' Charley muttered, and didn't look at her.

'Do you see what I mean, Charley? You *must*. Even on *Joneses* you'll have to watch out for that sort of thing. All that message Markal is talking—'

He lay back and cut her off with a wave of the hand. 'Thank you. I appreciate your concern.'

Well, that was it. Too cold to buck. She forced a laugh. 'As a critic I'm a good secretary.'

'Not at all. You express yourself a hell of a lot better than your boss.'

She felt his withdrawal then and tried to say something else. something light to bring him back to her. He stopped her with a shake of the head, smiling.

'Let's drop it. Let's quarrel about more important things than a lousy horror movie. A canceled one at that.'

She suddenly understood. He was frightened. It wasn't a lousy horror movie for him, canceled or not. His father had been a failure and he felt like a failure and he was using this first job, this lousy horror movie, as a weathervane, as proof of whether or not he could survive in Hollywood. And she had told him he couldn't!

She bent quickly and kissed him and said, 'I'm a nut,' and kissed him again and said, 'Don't pay any attention to what I say,' and kissed him a third time. She felt his chill fear and withdrawal and tried to smile and said, 'Good night, Charley. Please . . . I only meant—'

She had run over Jim and she had trampled over Charley. She had the evil eye, the evil mouth. She was hexed. She didn't want to hurt her men, she wanted to help them. But she hurt them anyway.

She drove home. Jim was still sleeping. She got carefully into bed and looked at him and touched his face as she had Charley's. She moved over and kissed him and he stirred. She remembered the warmth with Charley that was like the earlier, stronger warmth with Jim, and she kissed his lips. He shook his head, coughed, rolled over with his back to her. 'Jim,' she said. 'Listen, I love you.'

She loved Jim and she hated Jim and she loved Charley and Charley didn't love her, not even a little, not after that destructive nonsense about his writing.

Good-bye Charley Halpert. She would be left with Jim whom she loved and whom she hated and no Charley Halpert whom she loved.

Did she love Charley Halpert?

She had even felt something for Devon at one point in their office party. She knew he felt something for her, because he had all the actresses and all the would-be actresses and yet he kept asking her out, kept pleading with her to see him.

If she saw him he would give her a part. What would it be like to act again? Could she handle it? If she was nice to him he would do anything for her. With Devon she could drive hard bargains. But not with Charley Halpert. With Charley Halpert she was vulnerable. As she had been with Jim.

Had she ever loved Jim?

Half-asleep, she remembered classes together and rides together and long walks holding hands and that first time standing up in Theo's apartment, pressed to the wall, saying no Jim please and the way he had nodded and drawn back and then she was pulling him to her saying do whatever you want and she helped him and he took her and it was like it never was with anyone else. And now it was over, true love was over, youth was over, and Charley Halpert would leave her and even half a love would be over and she and Jim would writhe through their half a life and there had to be a way, there just had to be, and in Albuquerque the air was crisp and clean and bubbled in your lungs like champagne and Jim was crippled and she would go to Albuquerque to the Pueblo Indian ruins and down the ladder into the *kiva* where a thousand years ago people put their hands into little prayer holes and touched God and she and Charley would sit there touching hands and smiling into the silence and a thousand years of peace would wash over them and they would touch God, touch joy, and the Lord giveth. There had to be a way . . .

Sunday night, Isa had said, and since Nat Markal couldn't see himself waiting an extra hour, not to say an extra day, Sunday night it was.

It wasn't easy. First he had to explain to Adele, had to lie to her about a special hush-hush meeting on *Joneses*, and this was something he had never done before in any significant situation. Then he had to overcome a whole set of inhibitions that hadn't been involved in Isa's visit to his office, inhibitions against exposing himself to the outside world with attendant risk of being recognized.

He protected himself as best he could: by parking Lainie's Mustang in a dark spot; by waiting until the street was empty before hurrying to the lobby; by wearing a gray straw hat, most uncharacteristic of Nat Markal whose polished dome was as well known as Yul Brynner's. He was unhappy about the hat and didn't quite know why.

Isa had prepared him for the doorman, stationed between entrance and elevators, and he walked by just as she had advised, with a quick nod so the heavyset man wouldn't be tempted to ask whom he was visiting and use the tenant-phone system. The elevator was waiting, empty, and he thanked God for little favors. But it didn't move when he punched the 'Close' button, and he realized it was on a timer.

Voices filled the lobby. The doorman said something and the voices said something and three people entered the elevator. There were two men and a tall, handsome, graying woman. He knew the woman from somewhere.

'Mr. Markal!' she said. 'Good evening!'

He nodded and smiled.

The woman said, 'I didn't know whether you would recognize me.'

He didn't but smiled again and glanced at the two men. One was young, about twenty, with a sour, pockmarked face. The other was older, bigger, far better-looking.

The elevator doors closed; the car moved upward. 'This is my brother, Mark Stangen,' the woman said. 'He's in electronics.' The good-looking man said, 'An honor and a pleasure, Mr. Markal,' and put out his hand. Nat shook it. 'This is my son, Rubin, a law student.' The sour-looking youth nodded briefly. '*The* Nat Markal,' the woman said, her smile nudging

220

the boy to show some enthusiasm. Rubin sighed deeply. 'No use my trying to impress him, Mother. I don't photograph well.' The woman flushed. Her brother's smile was painted. Nat said, 'Better than I do, son.' The woman and her brother broke into appreciative laughter. The boy made no attempt to join in. He was ugly and sensitive and unhappy.

Nat suddenly remembered why he hated the hat he was wearing.

The elevator stopped at twelve, and Nat walked out. The woman called, 'See you at the studio, Mr. Markal.' So she worked at Avalon . . .

But what difference did it make? She couldn't know where he was going, whom he was seeing.

In time she would. He had to get Isa out of here.

He thought he heard voices coming from the elevator shaft. The son catching hell for his surly attitude. But Rubin was right. No use kissing ass. It wouldn't do him any good. Not him. His way would have to be Nat Markal's way. Build your own world, create your own image of success and power that would take the place of looks and personality. Not that Nat Markal had ever been as plain as *that*.

New York and his wide-brimmed hats and thinning hair and paunchy middle. His inept, lower-class Jewish mannerisms. His fear of women and envy of make-out artists.

How incredible that Nathan Jerome Markal should be Emperor Nat! Think of it!

He thought of it and wondered if that anti-Semitic bastard McKee was still with McDevit's Insurance, Ltd., and whether his guts ached thinking of Emperor Nat with his riches and power and women.

McKee had been a great one for women and talking about women. He had liked to torment pudgy *Nat*'n, as he'd called Nat in his insulting caricature of a Yiddish accent, with stories of how he had screwed this Brooklyn girl named Ruth one Saturday night and her mother Naomi the next. Or how this rabbi's daughter had gone down on him in an empty subway car, then thanked him humbly for the privilege. Lies and fantasies, obviously, but then again McKee hadn't meant to be taken literally, just to dig and insult and hurt.

He was at Isa's door, tensed and tight, thinking he could have McKee traced and call Ricci in Las Vegas and without actually saying anything compromising . . . No, that was silly and stupid.

He looked at the door, breathing hard, and wondered at himself. What sort of nonsense was this? These were sick thoughts – thoughts befitting a failure, not Emperor Nat Markal.

Even so, he pictured McKee spying on him now, eating his heart out as he realized Nat Markal was going to make love to a beauty like Isa Yee, raging as he thought of Nat's office and his mansion and his Century Plaza suite and *Joneses,* suffering as he understood the rich, rich life of *Nat'n.*

The door opened, and Isa smiled at him. She was wearing a simple black sheath and looked lovely, but he was disappointed that she hadn't greeted him in a sheer black negligee, or a pajama top and spike heels, or better still absolutely nothing. *That* would have torn the guts out of McKee!

He came inside and tossed his hat on a foyer table and raised his hand to smooth his hair ... and remembered again why he couldn't stand hats, the stupid goddam things. He had worn hats as a young man in New York. His father had worn hats and his friends had worn hats and so he had worn hats, even though he hated the way he looked when he glanced at himself in a shop window, a fat man hurrying down the narrow, gloomy streets to McDevit's Insurance, Ltd. And hated the way he looked when he took off a hat, with his thin hair plastered to his sweaty scalp. Hats and a small, grim life.

He dropped his hand. He had no hair to smooth. He hadn't lost it, he'd shaved it. He had changed his appearance himself, changed his life himself.

'Are you all right, Nat?'

She was looking at him closely, and he turned away, nodding, examining the apartment.

Changes. Doubt and disquiet and changes taking place.

She took his hand and led him toward the living room. 'Our first date,' she said, looking back at him.

He was actually dating a girl – the first time since marrying, the first time since becoming Emperor Nat Markal.

At that, he felt he understood his strange mood – his memories, his anguish at the past. Emperor Nat had succeeded with everything but women, had yet to triumph with women.

He smiled, since the chances of his failing were nil. He took Isa in his arms and ran his hands over her body, just as he wanted to, just as McKee never could.

'Welcome,' she said. 'I didn't think you were with us for a while there.'

222

Bright, perceptive creature. He kissed and caressed her and was impatient to get into bed and taste joy and triumph and dispel the lingering memories of bleakness, of failure. With Isa his life would become a *total* triumph.

She turned and somehow was out of his arms. 'What will you drink?'

'Brandy.'

She shook her head. 'The next time I'll know. I've got vodka, gin, Scotch and bourbon. Some wine too.'

He said bourbon, and he couldn't wait for Isa to return. He paced the living room, examining the wallpaper and the framed Japanese prints. He stopped at a waist-high, six-handed goddess, obviously Indian, at a dozen Chinese figurines, at a painting of a Balinese dancer. The room was a mish-mash of Oriental culture. He wondered what her background really was.

She came in with his drink. He took it, gulped it, handed her the empty glass.

'I'll get you another,' she said.

'Aren't you joining me?'

'I don't need alcohol tonight.' She fixed him with her black eyes.

'Then forget mine too. You haven't shown me the bedroom.'

She led him there. She lay down on the bed and looked at him. She wasn't smiling any more. He couldn't read that look and was suddenly unsure. 'No games,' he said firmly. She continued to look at him. He said, 'You don't want to muss that dress.' She shrugged. 'I don't mind.' He hesitated, then took off his jacket and sat down at the edge of the bed, his back to her. He removed his shoes and stood up and unbuckled his belt. He glanced over his shoulder. She hadn't changed position or expression. 'I'm undressing,' he announced. She nodded. He unzipped his trousers but didn't let them fall. He went to the door, closed it, turned off the light and stripped rapidly, tossing his clothes in the general direction of the chair. He turned to the bed, but couldn't make her out. The blinds were drawn and it was very dark. 'Isa?'

He heard rustling. He climbed onto the bed and felt around it. Empty. There was a shadow-movement across the room, a blur of white. Her naked body coming to him!

The bed creaked and he reached for her and touched cloth. 'A nightgown?' he asked.

'Something special, Nat.' She got under the covers.

He got under with her, pressed against her, tried to free her breasts. The nightgown was unmanageably high and tight in front. He reached down to the hem and couldn't find it and couldn't draw it up. It seemed wrapped around her feet. 'What is this? The damn thing goes on forever!' She laughed softly. 'It *is* a little long. I'll take it off in a minute.'

He pressed up against her, but everything he wanted was under a substantial layer of cloth. He lost his temper finally and tore at it. It came up and apart and his hands gripped her body. She gasped and said, 'You're hurting me.' He muttered apologies and was gentle for a while, and then heaved himself up and on her, straddling her, pressing her down. 'Nat, your weight—'

Again he said he was sorry, but he was at fever pitch and didn't stop. He had her legs apart and was sweating and pushing and still couldn't quite effect entry.

'Let me,' she whispered, and took him in her hand, squeezing. He said, 'No more of that! I'll drop you from *Joneses,* I swear it!' She laughed softly. 'Command me then, master.' He said 'Put it in.' She said, 'Rougher, my Emperor, my Lord.' He said, 'Shove it in, you bitch!' meaning it by now because she kept squeezing it to the lips and he was gasping and trying to kiss her breasts and all his frenzy was being blocked, being thwarted. She moaned and moved violently beneath him, almost throwing him off, and he suddenly found her rear under his genitals. The feeling was fantastic, but he was being cheated and grabbed her shoulders and took them, and as he did her buttocks heaved up and he was being milked into them and he sobbed his disappointment and his ecstasy and rolled to the side.

She cleaned them both and leaned over him, touching his face. 'The best things come hard, Emperor Nat. The best things come after long, long wanting, and sometimes the very best don't come at all.'

'You cheated,' he gasped, almost crying, yet knowing it was a game and that he was taking part in it and that the prize would be increased excitement, increased pleasure, a putting off of the inevitable end of excitement and pleasure. 'I wanted love—'

'You wanted common love, ordinary love, what you can get from anyone, from your own wife.'

He fought off Adele's image.

'But I'm not the common, the ordinary. You can always find that. Pier Andrei's around and you know she'd give you that

224

until you couldn't walk. Almost any starlet on the lot would give you that. If I did too, what would be my worth, my value? Where would I fit in as something special in your life?'

'Something special wasn't in our agreement.'

'Something special is my entire concept of life.'

He closed his eyes. She kissed his eyelids and nipples and navel, and suddenly plunged her hand into his stomach, into the soft flesh. He made a strangling sound, his head and knees jerking up. She smothered his mouth with her own and her hand moved down and tugged at him so viciously he could have screamed. But whatever skill, whatever magic, whatever instincts she had for love were strong, and fifty-year-old Nat Markal was functioning again. She began sliding her lips along his body, keeping her eyes on his as long as she could.

The phone rang. He said, 'Don't answer!' It rang and rang, and she sat up. 'It'll only take a minute.' He stared up at the ceiling, holding to the hot and wonderful sensation. She said, 'Yes?' and then said nothing for what seemed a long time. He finally looked at her. She turned her back to him, hunching over the phone. 'No, I don't think that would be a good idea.' Her voice was very casual. She listened again, and again it was for a long time. She said. 'I don't agree at all,' and he thought he detected rising tension. She started to speak, listened, then said, 'No, sorry, that's ... no, good-bye.' She turned back to him, smiling. 'An old flame,' she said, before he could ask.

'He wanted to see you?'

She nodded and bent to him again.

He tried to stop her, tried to bring her under him in the normal position of love. But she wouldn't have it, and her mouth moved over him, and he began to gasp. Abruptly, she raised her head. 'I want to go out.'

He stared at her.

'To a club, a restaurant. Or just for a ride, a walk. I want you to take me someplace.'

'All right, but ... some other time.'

She seemed frightened, which had to be more of the game. He reached for her. She drew back. He controlled the urge to shout. 'First I have to set it up,' he said. 'My reputation ... you understand. I have to make it look like part of the promotion on *Joneses*.'

She didn't seem any happier.

'We'll go to Chasen's' he said, pleading. 'Other places. The best places.' She crouched there, face somber. 'And you'll

225

move,' he said, offering goodies. 'Wherever you'd like. Century City, maybe, near my hotel, so it'll be easier to meet.'

She took a deep breath and nodded slightly. 'I'd like that. I'd accept that, because it's as much for you as for me.'

He reached again, and this time she came to him, let him take her as he wanted to. This time it was everything he'd hoped it would be – fire and velvet and satisfaction and triumph. Now he was Emperor Nat in *every* way. Now failure was behind him, forever behind him with McKee and McDevit's Insurance, Ltd. Now *Nat*'n was finally laid to rest.

ISA YEE

As soon as Markal left, Isa jumped out of bed. She had feigned sleep in order to get rid of him. She didn't want him around in case Barchester was serious about coming up.

But he couldn't be! As she had told him at the studio and tried to tell him on the phone twenty minutes ago, she *wouldn't* see him! (Wouldn't see any man, for that matter, even the most eligible white, because she already had the one man who could give her the world on a platter.)

She dressed quickly, ran to the door, then stopped. Humphrey Barchester was chasing her from her own home!

She made sure the door was locked and went back to the living room and sat down.

She smoked a cigarette, tensed and tight, thinking several times she heard footsteps in the hall, prepared to let him knock until he went away. But when the soft knock finally came, she walked to the door. 'Yes?'

'Humphrey,' he said.

She stood there, trying to think. She knew what she *should* do, what she had planned to do; and she asked, foolishly, 'What is it?'

He didn't answer. She opened the door a crack just to send him away. He stood there, dressed in a neat gray suit with skinny pants. He said, 'Hi.' She said, 'All right, just a moment,' and opened the door. They walked to the living room, and he sat down on the couch. She hesitated, then sat down beside him. He looked around. 'Crazy,' he said. 'Like Charlie Chan on television.'

'You watch much television?'

226

'No. Short of time.'

'Busy selling black?'

'Yes.'

'What does that mean, selling black?'

'It means making Negroes believe they're human. Making them believe they're men and women.'

'You're in civil rights then. CORE? SNCC?'

'I was in SNCC. I'm in business for myself now.' He didn't smile, so it wasn't a joke.

'Black Panthers? Something like that?'

'Something like that.'

'What's it called? Maybe I heard of it.'

'You didn't hear of it. Not yet. But you will. Now it's real small but someday it'll swallow all the others.'

'Because *you* got the word?' They were sitting and talking and she wasn't worried anymore and began to jab at him. 'Because *you* got the solution no one else has?'

'Because I've got me, Humphrey Barchester. Because Humphrey Barchester has three worlds going for him.'

'What's that supposed to mean?'

'Humphrey has ghetto Watts and middle-class Pacoima and intellectual USC.'

'Super!' she said. And then, 'How'd you get three worlds?'

'I swim.'

She still didn't understand.

'My father was in jail,' he said, 'from eighteen to twenty. Not a long stretch for a Southern Negro, but it was my biggest break. He learned a trade, shoemaking and repairing, and when he came to L.A. and married my mother he worked steady and stayed home. So I had a full-time father as well as mother, which made me something special right off.'

She didn't have to ask what he meant by *that*. There had been no fathers in the Walters family.

'He took me to the YMCA for swimming twice a week and to parks and playgrounds, and he made sure I kept going to school. Then we moved. Pacoima was open and we bought a nice little house. I swam in high school and swam every chance I got and won prizes. I also won a swimming scholarship.'

'Oh . . . that's how you went to college.'

'That's how *every* black man goes to college. Or almost every. We're the last of the gladiators, performing in the arena for the white nobility. We fight with fists, baseballs, basketballs and footballs; in swimming pools, on tennis courts,

227

anywhere they'll let us. Sometimes we win money. Sometimes, if we're very lucky, we win scholarships, win a way out of Watts and Harlem and Hough and Southside. Where did you win out of?'

Without thinking, she said, 'Dovenville.' And then, quickly, 'It's getting late. You'll have to go.'

'Dovenville? That the South?'

'No.' She had to change the subject and she picked something she knew would grab him; 'How does Emma fit into your life?'

His face changed and his voice changed and he looked unhappy. But he didn't duck it. 'My mother's sister. My folks had their problems after moving to Pacoima, though they were together when my father died. I would stay with Emma certain times. I did right up until a few months ago, when my uncle—' He shrugged. 'I've talked enough about me. It's your turn.'

She stood up. 'I've got an early shooting. Good night, Humphrey.'

'Call me Free. It was my baby name and it's even better now.'

She liked it. He stood up and took her by both wrists and drew her slowly toward him. 'Well,' she said, 'A good-night kiss.' And why not? She would never let him touch her again, so what was the harm in it? Why not see what it was like? Just a kiss . .

But she winced as he put his lips to her cheek and stiffened as his arms went around her. Was it disgust? Was it fear?

He gave her a hard look, a harder grin. 'Some kick, huh, baby? A shine lover.'

She jerked her head up to tell him to stop, and he ground his lips down viciously, hurting her, holding the painful kiss as she fought to end it. When he finally let go, she jumped back and rubbed her mouth with the back of her hand.

'You don't mean that,' he said, and made a laughing sound. 'You're thinking of all those dirty stories. You know, how we're a foot long and thick as telephone poles. Better than big dogs. Better than small ponies. Black cock, *um-mmmmmmm*!'

She wanted to hit him. He made the laughing sound again and stepped toward her. She ran to the bedroom and locked the door. She sat down at the edge of the bed, sick and shaken, and began to cry, and hated herself for the gasping sobs.

She heard the doorknob rattle, and grew still. 'I'm sorry,'

he said. 'I had so many nice things to say, so many soft things to say, and then I ... I just said those other things. But you know *why* I said them, don't you?'

She told herself she didn't.

'I'll come back another time,' he said. 'We'll start all over.'

'Never,' she said, but her voice was a whisper and his footsteps were already moving away. Later, she came out of the bedroom and locked the front door and heated up some milk. She sat watching television and sipping, then spoke to the empty room: 'See? Give them an inch and they'll take a mile.'

ALAN DEVON

On his way to the john Monday morning, Devon glanced into Cheryl's office, hoping she'd be alone. She wasn't. She was talking to Halpert, and the way she looked at him ...

Just past the doorway, Devon stopped, searching his pockets as if he'd forgotten something. Cheryl was saying, '—be a forward hussy and ask you to lunch again.'

Devon's hands clenched.

Halpert said, 'I'm sorry, but my agent—'

Devon heard footsteps and went on. He seethed. She was looking at Halpert and smiling at Halpert the way he wanted her to look and smile at him. And was Halpert any special sort of man? Hell no! A goddam writer ... and a lousy one at that. An amateur. Markal had gone overboard for an unknown novelist who talked well at meetings. But talking and writing a movie were two different things ... especially when Alan Devon was one of the judges of that writing! As soon as Halpert put together fifty pages, Devon planned to read them, find the weaknesses he expected, then go to Markal. He'd line up support from Lars Wyllit who had a great deal to gain by Halpert's bombing out.

When he came back from the john, Cheryl was alone. He told himself to keep going. It made sense to wait until he had disposed of Halpert.

Cheryl looked up and smiled, and his heart leaped. He went in, glancing quickly to the right to make sure the Bagel's door was closed. Not that he had anything to worry about. This office was being transformed into headquarters for *Joneses,* and he was producer and therefore operational head on the project. He had business here, from now on. He was boss here, from now on. Or once things settled into a routine.

He said hello and how're things and you're looking lovelier than ever darling. She said thank you and how are things at Devon Productions?

'Drop in once in a while and see.'

'I guess I'll have to, under the new organization.'

'You don't have to wait for business.' He paused. 'You haven't been in since . . . that day.'

'Busy, busy,' she murmured, and opened a letter.

'Too busy for lunch?'

She looked up.

He felt she was about to say no and added, 'The commissary, with everyone and his brother around. And no desks.' He kept it light. 'You'll be safe as a babe. Make that a baby.'

'That's nice of you, Dev—'

'Twelve-thirty then? Pick you up here? Okay?' He began to back away, grinning and trying to get out before she said anything more. He just couldn't wait for Halpert to be gone. He wanted to be with her. God, how he wanted to be with her!

'I don't think so,' Cheryl said before he could get to the door.

He stopped. 'Why, when we ... you know, Cheryl.'

'I can't talk now, Dev.' At least she was soft-spoken. She hadn't been soft-spoken the last few times. At least she felt sorry.

But that was *bad*. Something had happened. He couldn't reach her anymore, and she felt sorry for him.

'You said you wanted to act.' It was his ace card, and he had to play it right now. 'I've got a part for you.'

She stared.

'A good part. Not just a walk-on. Lines and a credit.'

'You're kidding.'

'*Winninger's Winners*.' It was his top series, a situation comedy about a racetrack tout. 'You'll make better than a thousand dollars.'

Her lips parted. He had her hooked. 'I'll give all the details at lunch.'

'What do I play,' she muttered, 'one of the horses?'

'You play a girl,' he said, angry at her for that. 'You play a normal-type girl whose boyfriend gambles away her dowry and Winninger helps her. I'll see you at twelve-thirty.'

'Dev, I haven't acted in four years, really.'

230

'You said you were good. You said you were on television. This could be a new beginning for you. You're mature now. You've suffered. I can judge actors. I wouldn't try to cast you as an Ann-Margret. But a Shelley Winters, a young one . ; . for that you'd be perfect.'

She began to speak. He rushed on, backing again toward the door. 'And I'll decide the non-star casting in *Joneses*, you know. There'll be a *hundred* parts for you there.'

'You can't be serious.'

'Very.' He went out, not wanting to hear anymore. She would end up caring for him, if only a little. That was all he wanted — for her to care a little and let him love her while caring. That was all any man could ask from any woman. Simple enough, and yet without it the whole sex business was sweaty, smelly, like going to the toilet.

Had he felt this way ten years ago, even five years ago? He wasn't sure. He'd had so much steam at one time, twice a day wasn't enough.

But ten years ago meant nothing. The day before yesterday meant nothing. Carla had been everything and Carla had died and Carla was nothing. Today was everything. He returned to his office and called Lars Wyllit.

CHARLEY HALPERT

Charley had come in at eight this morning and, except for a few words with Cheryl, had worked straight through to ten-thirty. He was supposed to be *reading*, not writing, steeping himself in American history and waiting for the experts to start sending in tasty tidbits. But he couldn't wait. He had been thinking all week-end and he had to get something down on paper, convince himself that his ideas were as good as they seemed.

He still wasn't sure, but at least an opening was beginning to develop, a story in which the Jones family was coming alive.

It was important that he fight off his old enemy fear. He couldn't use FDR's challenge, 'We have nothing to fear but fear itself.' He had an enormous task to fear and his inexperience to fear. But it was Markal saying he had bombed on the *Terror Town* treatment, and Cheryl echoing the opinion, and his father's thesis that failure was genetic in all Halperts that was giving him the real twist in the gut.

At ten-thirty work came to an end, and fear was driven, at least temporarily, from his mind. The office boy came in and dropped an envelope on his desk. It was from 'Payroll and Disbursement' and contained $1,800 for the *Terror Town* treatment. It also contained a notice that Avalon 'was not exercising our option' on his further services. Which meant he was now working without a contract and that Ben Kalik should have spoken to Markal first thing this morning and that he should be hearing from the agent.

He turned back to the typewriter, but couldn't concentrate and daydreamed about working straight through on *Joneses* with Lars and whomever else Markal hired; dreamed about getting at least a third of the biggest movie credit in history; dreamed of forever vanquishing fear of failure.

Which reminded him of Celia and that he should send her some money. He fiddled with a pencil and pad and decided he could pay back Kalik's five hundred, keep eight hundred to live on, and send Celia five hundred.

He wished it could be more. She wouldn't be impressed by five hundred. A thousand would be so much more substantial.

He could put off repaying Kalik. The man was going to earn a fat fee for doing nothing.

If the deal went through.

Good God, he must have been insane, telling Kalik to turn down anything under $25,000. Markal would never pay ...

The phone rang. 'Ben Kalik, Chuck. It took some doing, buddy, but we came through. Twenty-five thou, just like you wanted. I used every ploy in the book—'

He went on, and what it amounted to was that he had told Markal Charley's price, take it or leave it, and Markal had taken it.

Charley sank back in the chair and grinned up at the ceiling and listened to Kalik buddy-this and buddy-that and waited for a break in the stream of bullshit. 'When do I get the money?'

'Since it's a big job, you'll get a five-grand advance on signing the contract, ten at the halfway mark and ten on completion. No cutoffs, buddy. As long as you hand in the work, they pay.'

Charley said, 'Great!' and wanted to do something – shout or sing or drink a gallon of wine.

'I think we should talk,' Kalik said. 'Not just about *The*

Eternal Joneses, though of course it's all-important. But we've got to look ahead. It might end with the treatment. I hope not, but it might. Then we'd have to see if we could put you into another feature right away. You'll get some good publicity out of this, Chuck. Should lead to other assignments. We'll work it out at lunch. You need organization. You need planning.'

Charley needed a party. He said see you and jumped up and danced around the office and then stopped and looked at the phone. Twenty-five thousand! Celia couldn't psychologize *that* away with talk of failure! The money was guaranteed him. But had he really made it as a writer? That *Terror Town* treatment ...

But he couldn't kill his joy. Not today. He waltzed around again and thought of telling Cheryl, and there was a knock at the door. He was ready for company. He was ready for conversation. He was ready to laugh and kid around and forget work ... at least until after lunch. He said, 'Come ahead!' In walked Lois and Sugar – probably the only two people in Hollywood he *didn't* want to see just now. Not that they didn't look good. They wore tight bright dresses and their usual subdued make-up. But they wanted him to introduce them to Baiglen, and the thought made him sweat.

Lois dropped onto the couch and her short skirt rode to her panties and she said, 'Man, we're beat.' Sugar came toward him, ready for a kiss. He said, 'The door,' and went quickly past her and closed it. She kissed him lightly, murmuring, 'Gotta look fresh on the lot.' She smelled particularly good, and almost by reflex he stroked her behind. She snuggled and giggled and said, 'The man's ready, day and night.' Lois said, 'These hip New Yorkers,' but without her usual élan. 'We got home five o'clock. Today, daddy, *today*.' She rubbed her eyes, a sleepy little girl. 'And that big deal who invited us, *wowee*! I mean, how low can a guy get?'

He wanted them out of here. Though Sugar was right – he was ready. She patted his cheek and said, 'Tonight, kicky-poppa.' He said, 'I won't be in tonight,' and was proud of himself.

'Can you imagine?' Lois said, and yawned. 'He had seven guys and no girls. Eight counting him. A little freak show, the bastard. Pardon, but can you imagine?'

Sugar joined her on the couch. 'Fun's fun,' she said, 'but like I told Lois, no sir. I wanted to cut out right then, but Lois has a head on her.'

233

'What I did was pick the two oldest and talk to them private and sure enough they had plenty bread.'

'Though we still don't know for sure if they're in show biz like they say.'

'We went to Vegas. We had a ball and I bet those others were really steamed.'

Sugar giggled. 'Maybe they helped each other.'

'I wouldn't put it past the bastard. He had that look, didn't he?'

'Man, you better know it. Imagine thinking we'd go for anything like that. All we got's our reputation.'

'And cheap is cheap, anyplace you go.'

'Nothing kills your chances faster than to be counted cheap.'

'You better know it,' Lois sighed and, leaned back and closed her eyes. 'I just wish we'd got a little more sleep.' She suddenly looked at Charley. 'You think he might give us a reading or something today?'

'Who?' Charley said weakly.

'Baiglen,' Lois said frowning. 'Get with it, Chucky-babe.'

Chucky-babe grew desperate. 'I'm afraid that's impossible. He isn't seeing actors. *Terror Town* is suspended. I'm off it.'

Sugar said, 'Well sure, man, we got the poop. It's all over the place. There's this *Joneses* thing. You're writing that now. Baiglen's not the producer, but he can still help us, can't he?'

'I doubt it.'

Lois stood up, her expression thoughtful. 'Now stop me if I'm wrong, Sugar, but you think we're being brushed?'

Sugar also stood up. 'Nooo, not kicky-poppa. We were nice to him, and he was nice to us. He's no bastard like the bastard.'

'You putting us on, Chuck?'

He muttered that he was terribly sorry and quite willing to help out if they needed money and as soon as he heard of anything ...

Sugar came forward. 'You just *gotta* do it, Chuck. We're fighting for our *careers*.'

Charley waved his hands helplessly. Lois looked at Sugar. Sugar went to the couch and lay down. She pulled her dress above her waist and her pants below her knees. 'Oh, God,' she whimpered. 'Oh God he made me do it. He made me—' Lois went to the door, voice rising. 'What sort of place is this where a kid, a real kid ... I walk in and my sister ... only seventeen—'

The door was half-open before he unfroze. He lunged for-

234

ward and shoved it shut and said, 'Okay,' Sugar turned her head and grinned at him. 'With guts you can do anything.' He was shocked more deeply than he wanted them to know. Lois got her bag from the couch. 'Mr. Blessington,' she mused, 'said we was devils and he hated us.' Charley looked at Sugar, and she sat up very slowly and said, 'Kicky-poppa don't hate us at-all at-all.' She was right. He couldn't help looking at her and wanting her and he despised himself for the feeling.

'How'd you two get this way?'

'What way?' Lois asked, and she wasn't joking.

'So ... capable of using your bodies. Weren't you ever taught—'

'We were taught by the best, baby. Loving Uncle Heston.'

'Really your uncle?'

Sugar adjusted her clothing. 'Pop's brother. First Mom and then Lois and then me. And Pop into him for two thousand and afraid to ask questions. Not that we minded. Like mother like daughters, I guess.'

'Let's not go into *that*,' Lois said, and for once she looked grim and bitter.

They reached into their bags and examined themselves in small mirrors and touched up eyes and lips. Charley watched them, saddened, because whatever they were and whatever they'd done he had thought of it as pure animal, pure young joy-in-the-morning-of-life and therefore basically clean and right. But he'd been fooled and now he would never again see them as frisking young tail in a field of men. They walked to the door and out into the hall and he followed, seeing shadowy doubles walk with them, affecting the way they moved and tainting their pretty faces.

But that didn't change what was going to happen. What could he say to Baiglen to mask the obvious? And Cheryl ...'

He still hadn't thought of anything when he ushered them into the office. He spoke quickly as Cheryl looked up. 'Hi again. These young ladies are interested in meeting Mr. Baiglen. They're actressses, and neighbors of mine.'

Cheryl said Mr. Baiglen had left and wouldn't be back until two, two-thirty. Lois said, 'Oh, that's too bad 'cause Chuck promised we'd get to see him today.' Sugar said, 'Can we come back later?' Lois said, 'That would be all right, wouldn't it, Chuck?'

Charley smiled as hard as he could and said, 'It isn't up to me, kids,' and saw the way Cheryl was looking at them, the

235

flicker in her eyes, the recognition of that hack show-biz situation, the payoff. She said, 'I think it would be all right, Mr. Halpert. Shall we say four o'clock to be safe?' He nodded, and Lois and Sugar looked at him, smiling promises of great-big-juicy-thanks-to-come. Cheryl made a note on her calendar and gave him a neat, secretarial smile. 'You'll be available to introduce the young ladies, won't you, Mr. Halpert?' He wanted to say he had a twenty-five-thousand-dollar treatment to do, but nodded. Lois and Sugar were full of squeals and enthusiasm and said *bye* now to Cheryl and she said *bye* now to them and turned to her typewriter.

He led the sisters out to the hall. They were bubbling about what a doll he was and what they were going to do to show their appreciation, and he was sure the walls had ears and tried to shush them. Desperately, he said he had to work. They decided they would wander around the lot and meet him for lunch at the commissary. He said he was meeting his agent. 'Then we'll find someone else to buy us eats,' Lois said, patting his cheek while Sandy from Devon Productions watched with interest. They went down the stairs, waving and throwing him kisses.

All right. The way to handle it now was to play man-of-the-world and do the leering before Baiglen could. Then if the producer would give them a little encouragement, promise them his good offices in getting a test for *Joneses*, or hold out the hope of a bit in *Terror Town* when it was rescheduled, the payoff would be complete. He didn't think they would pressure him too much once the score was even, to their way of thinking. His problem was to see that it stayed even, that he didn't run up any more debts. He had to keep away from them, starting today.

He went back up the hall and stopped in the doorway. Cheryl turned in her swivel chair. 'Yes?' He came in. 'I wish we could have lunch today. Sunday night was something special. *You're* something special.'

Her face flushed.

He said, 'Those two girls—' and floundered.

She made it easy for him. 'Let's not confess things to each other. Let's keep it simple. You still want to see me?'

'Of course.'

'Even after ... that nonsense about your treatment?'

He shrugged uncomfortably.

'You'll never go back to it, or anything like it. The bigger the job, the more ambitious the producer, the better for you.'

He said, 'Thanks for the vote of confidence,' relieved and pleased.

She hesitated a moment. 'What I said about not taking producers at face value, not giving them what they *say* they want—'

He nodded. 'I'll just have to feel my way with Markal. Well, back to that diamond-studded grindstone.'

He was almost at the door when she spoke. 'Before I come to your apartment. I'll be sure to give you ample warning.'

She was a woman. She had to dig a little in spite of herself. He faced her. 'Cheryl, listen, I want to do all I can for you, for myself. We're both mixed up in other lives and other people and there's no changing it. But we can be good for each other. Is that enough?'

'Yes,' she said.

He felt the words, the words taught by books and movies, the words that came when a woman was good for you. He didn't use them, but his feeling was so strong she just had to understand.

And she did.

'Charley,' she said, voice thick, 'get out of here. Get out before we create a scandal.'

LARS WYLLIT

He had worked all Sunday on *Streets* and three hours this morning and was going to keep up the accelerated pace until he finished the first draft. He would do the same, he vowed, on the second draft. With luck, he could be free for *The Eternal Joneses* by Christmas. Which should be just about the time Halpert was getting his walking papers. If he lasted *that* long.

Lars was no longer worried about competing with the novelist. Not after Alan Devon's call. He didn't know what the producer had against Halpert, but it wasn't anything minor. His animosity showed like a red flag.

It was fatal to have the producer dead-set against you. The executive producer wasn't likely to fight his right-hand man on something as relatively unimportant as the block-out writer. Besides, unless Halpert created a work of art, giving Markal not only what he wanted but also what he hadn't the foresight and imagination to want, anyone could shake the Emperor's confidence in him.

Works of art were rare, especially in Hollywood, so Lars didn't feel he would have to do much knifing to land a lion's share of the *Joneses* assignment. In fact, he'd had to keep the project from intruding on his current work. Hot ideas were already cropping up.

At least Halpert would be paid. Lars hoped he was getting a decent piece of change. His own fee for the treatment, whether or not he reworked Halpert's or another man's material, would be thirty-five to fifty-thousand. Then a big hunk for the first draft – at least seventy-five. Which would make poker less painful for the next year or two. Not that he had money worries. Despite his gambling, he'd put thirty-one grand in savings and loan company accounts.

He got up from the typewriter. He was too rich to work this close to lunchtime. And he was too rich to lunch alone.

He didn't admit to himself where he was going until he was almost at the Publicity Department. And then he hurried on before memories of Saturday night could put the chill on his purpose.

Terry was on the phone when he entered. She looked up, did what amounted to a double-take, then said, 'Get back to me, would you, Clee?' She laughed. 'That's right. Even columnists. It's the truth. I'm fighting off hordes. We're having two-shift tours of the Washington set, and it's not even completed.' She laughed again and said good-bye and hung up. Her laughter faded. 'Hi.'

'The warmth of your greeting overwhelms me.'

She smiled thinly. 'What can I do for you?'

'Eat lunch.'

'I have a date.'

'Tomorrow.'

She looked at him a long moment. 'Mona was very happy this morning.'

'I'd be happy too if I had her bank account ... and her sleep-in friend.'

'She got up for breakfast for the first time in weeks. She insisted on making eggs and toast and coffee herself. She talked about marriage and how it can work for opposites.'

He laughed. 'If you don't want to lunch with me, just say so. Don't rope poor Mona in as the excuse.'

'I'm just saying you've made quite an impression.'

'I always do. Now if you'd sample the product—'

She shook her head.

'Why?' He lowered his guard for a moment, letting her see his hunger. 'Give me one good reason for not dating a man who is so obviously interested.'

'No chemistry, I guess.'

'That's not so.' But he wasn't sure. 'That kiss ... you felt something.'

'I'm a red-blooded American girl. Most men can make me feel *something*. You're a good kisser.'

'For openers.'

She flushed. 'You're also a little too ... precocious for me.'

'Children are precocious. I'm an adult.'

'Now *that's* the question. Are you really?'

He came around the desk and leaned close to her. 'Am I being challenged?'

She rolled her chair back toward the window. 'I meant your pugnacity.'

He followed her, excited now, wanting to touch her, kiss her, take her right here and now in the chair or on the floor. He said, 'I hereby give notice to all and sundry that I accept the lady's challenge.'

She couldn't move back any more, being stopped by the wall. She said, 'I repeat, I never meant—'

'And that at a time and place to be later specified, we will meet upon the field of combat where I will for once and all give proof positive' – he touched her hair with his mouth – 'that I am indeed an adult male in full possession of his faculties, physical and otherwise.'

She was rigid. He drew back. 'With the exception of one faculty, which is slightly impaired. The faculty that maintains a man's objectivity, self-possession, even sanity when dealing with members of the opposite sex. One member of the opposite sex.'

'Mona, I hope,' she said, and stood up and quickly moved away. She looked as if she might actually run from the office.

'Look. Mona is very nice—'

'And she expects to see you again, soon.'

He nodded slowly. 'All right. So she'll see me again, soon. But I'm talking about us, and that's a very different kettle of cuttlefish.'

'No, sorry. I just don't dig brawlers.'

He felt the blood rushing to his face and turned quickly to hide it. 'Brawlers make great bedmates.'

'If that's what you want.'

He strode to the door. 'And you of course are beyond that.'

'I'm beyond *you*.'

He turned then, and she met his look, and he finally believed her. He gave a flip wave of the hand and said, 'Gawd, to think we have to work on the same movie,' and, 'Meet you at Mother Mona's,' and, 'Buy a good pair of earplugs,' and was gratified to see her face blanch. He swaggered out of the office and down the hall, and was stricken deep inside. He felt he had lost something very important and quickly promised himself one hell of a good time with Mona. By God, little Terry would sweat through a few very hot evenings. Little Terry would get proof of Lars Wyllit's adulthood, in spades. He'd make that goddam hacienda rock.

TERRY HANFORD

Terry called Markal. 'I was thinking of returning to my own apartment.'

'Only if Mona says so. Has she?'

'Well, no. But if I leave it up to her—'

'It's not too painful, is it? You get along well, don't you? Besides, I want her to see very clearly why she's going to ... expose so much more of herself in *Joneses* than in her other pictures.'

'Then she *is* going to have nude scenes?'

'For her good as well as the picture's. She's slipping.'

'But the figures released on her last two features—'

'Gross figures. Her net has been in steady decline. We spend more and more to produce and promote a Mona Dearn feature and make less and less on it. She has to reverse the trend.'

'Does she know that?'

'Her agent does. But Jerry is too smart to tell her. And so are you.' He paused. 'Mona's a very sensitive woman. She's had hard times in the past. I know how depressed she can get and I want you around in case she ... misunderstands. What we have to do is keep her happy, keep her thinking positive. You're good for her.'

Terry was silent.

'Once she's before the cameras, she'll be all right.'

'That'll be *months*, Mr. Markal!'

'Yes, and if she wants you during shooting—'

'I think that goes far beyond the call of duty,' Terry muttered. 'I really do.'

'Tell you what. Send me the rent bills on your apartment. The least Avalon can do is pay for what you won't be using. And I think it's time you had another raise. I'll speak to Cole about it. Say two thousand?'

'That's generous of you, Mr. Markal, but I—'

'Fine, fine. Don't hesitate to come to me with any problems, personal or otherwise. Avalon stands behind you, Terry. Don't forget that. You have a future here.' He chuckled. 'Unless some young man is planning to steal you away?'

This wasn't Markal's style. The dour, somewhat ascetic approach was missing. 'If he is, it's kidnapping, not romance.'

'I'm both relieved and sorry to hear it. But even when the day comes, and it has to for so attractive a girl, we'll work something out. I want you with us as long as possible.'

'Thank you. I—'

'Your little sacrifices won't be forgotten.' And the jolly Emperor was gone, his chuckles seeming to echo from the phone.

What in the world was *happening* to everyone around here!

She slumped back in her chair, grimly considering six or more months with Mona. She was still considering when the phone rang and Bertha said, 'Mr. Markal forgot to tell you, Terry. There's an eleven o'clock meeting in his office Thursday. You and Jerry Storm.'

Terry muttered, 'Strategy for stripping Mona, I presume.'

Bertha laughed. 'No. I think it has to do with Isa Yee.'

Terry said she'd be there; and then, 'Does Mr. Markal strike you as ... more cheerful than usual?'

'You've noticed it too? This new project seems to have changed him completely. Humming and ... well, just so different, so happy.'

'I wish *I* could feel the same.'

Bertha commiserated with her on having to board with Mona and congratulated her on the raise. 'Seven thousand a year is pretty good heart-balm, wouldn't you say?'

Terry had to agree. But it didn't make her any happier about the next six months.

241

As soon as she and Devon left the Western Building, Cheryl heard her name called. She didn't believe it and turned. It was Jim. He was wheeling himself from the corner of the building where, she realized, he'd been able to see everyone come out without being seen himself. 'Your husband?' Devon whispered, and she nodded and moved forward.

'Hi,' Jim said and smiled past her at Devon. 'Surprise. Thought I'd join you for lunch.' His eyes were much too bright. He wasn't drunk, but seemed filled with tremendous excitement.

She said she was so pleased and how nice he looked in his gray slacks and sports jacket, and noticed the brown-paper bag wedged between his body and the side of the chair. She reached down for it, saying, 'That must be uncomfortable,' intending to put it in the plastic side-pouch, wanting to fuss over him and gain more time to compose herself. He placed his hand on the bag, blocking hers. 'It's all right.' She straightened, looking from the bag to his face and back at the bag. He said, 'You see, I'm getting better. I called for a cab and the driver helped me and here I am.'

Devon came up, smiling miserably. 'Well, we've heard a lot about Cheryl's husband.' Which was the wrong thing to say. But then again there were no right things to say to Jim Carny. Dev introduced himself, putting down his hand. Jim shook it, smiling, his eyes glinting, left hand resting lightly on the paper bag. 'I was walking over to the commissary with your wife ... lunch ... why don't we all eat together?'

Jim said, 'Thank you, I'd like that,' eyes fixed on Devon's. Devon took out a package of gum and stripped a piece and put it in his mouth, talking all the while about what a nice day it was and how they served stuffed peppers at the commissary on Mondays and that Jim should try it.

'I will,' Jim said, and wheeled between them. They started through the bright sunshine for the commissary. Cheryl looked down and Jim looked up and she wanted to see what was in that bag and was suddenly frightened.

'How did you get in?' she asked. 'No one called to ask me—'

'Did you hear that, Mr. Devon?' Jim said, chuckling. 'You've been in this business a while. You know how I got in.'

Devon said well he wasn't sure but guessed they wouldn't

turn away a man whose wife worked on the lot. Jim chuckled. 'Mr. Devon is reticent about the truth. But he shouldn't be. Not on my account.' He paused as if to give Dev a chance to speak, then said, 'He knows how sensitive motion-picture companies are to the needs of the public. He knows that if a man without the use of his legs comes to the gate and humbly asks if he might look around the studio whose films have made his life a little brighter, everyone brushes away a tear and helps him. And it's only right. Places like this were built on sentiment. Many a cripple tugged at the heartstrings of audiences in the thirties and forties, right, Mr. Devon?'

Devon chewed his gum frantically. 'Well, yes—'

Cheryl knew Jim was giving Dev a bad time, but that paper bag dominated her thoughts. Let him say what he wanted as long as he didn't take something out of that bag – something dangerous.

'Of course,' Jim said, 'we – I mean the cripples of the world – also make excellent villains. The cripple is often an effective heavy. I remember a Humphrey Bogart picture—'

Devon said he never thought of 'the disabled' that way.

'You mustn't think me touchy, Mr. Devon.'

Devon said his friends called him Dev. Jim turned to Cheryl smiling and nodding. 'Dev. Yes. Well, Dev, take the man horribly burned and somewhat embittered by the circumstances of a fire. *Phantom of the Opera* classification. He seeks revenge and becomes a killer. Or the man who loses his legs in a railway accident and decides the railroads must pay more than a few thousand dollars. He becomes a saboteur. Or perhaps a paraplegic, who finds he can no longer give his family, let's say his wife, the support, attention and satisfaction a normal woman requires, and consequently becomes a cuckold. He persecutes the poor woman and tries to destroy her love.'

Devon stared straight ahead. 'That's grim thinking for a young man. You haven't mentioned that the disabled often live full, rich lives. That paraplegics work and play and raise families. That they—'

'But we were speaking of *movies*, Mr. Devon. I mean Dev. We were speaking of fiction. As for myself, I know how rich and full a life the disabled can live. After all, I have Cheryl.'

He looked up at her. She said, 'I'm starved.' Devon said, 'I'll only be able to stay for a quick sandwich and coffee.' Jim said, 'Gee, that's too bad, and they have stuffed peppers today.'

They took one of the large round tables against the left wall.

243

Only after they were seated did Cheryl realize that Charley and a slender, wavy-haired man were just two tables away against the center wall. Something must have shown in her face because Jim said, 'Another friend?' and turned to look. 'Which one?' He asked. The waitress came, and Cheryl engaged her in conversation. The waitress said yes indeed the stuffed peppers were *excellent*. 'You ask Mr. Devon. He never skips 'em. Right Mr. Devon?' Dev said he would have to skip them today, press of urgent business, and ordered a Swiss on toast and coffee. Cheryl ordered the stuffed peppers. Jim turned from Charley's table and said it was a special occasion, his first visit to Avalon, and he would stand cocktails all around. Devon said there was no liquor. The waitress said there was beer. 'Then the stuffed peppers and a beer,' Jim said, and again turned to look at Charley's table. 'Let me guess,' he murmured. 'The thin one? No, too talky. Too involved in himself. The big one?' He faced Cheryl, smiling, 'Right size, anyway. Scholarly-looking. He's a friend.'

Cheryl said it was Charles Halpert, Mr. Baiglen's writer, now working on *The Eternal Joneses*. She made sure not to look at Charley as she launched into a description of how she was helping organize the office for the new operation. 'And she's a tutor,' Jim said, nodding at Devon. 'In addition to her job here and her housewifely duties, she also works week-ends tutoring the twin daughters of a real estate dealer. That's right, isn't it, honey?' Cheryl said yes. Jim said, 'I have a lot to be thankful for, Dev. The accident that deprived me of mobility hasn't been entirely without benefit. I learned just how loving a wife Cheryl is.' He smiled and his hand touched his paper bag, and she froze. 'Yes, loving is the word for Cheryl . . . isn't it, Dev?'

Devon was pale, his smile transparently pained. When the waitress brought their order, he wolfed his sandwich, said, 'Nice meeting you, Jim, this is on me,' and fled. He stopped only long enough to sign for the check at the register.

Jim looked after him. 'Fine fellow. Nicely dressed. A nervous type, but well-spoken. Well-preserved, too.' He turned to her. 'Gets it up when you need it, does he?'

His hand was still on the bag. She leaned forward. 'Why can't we have a pleasant lunch, Jim? Why can't we try—'

'Money too, obviously. Could easily afford twenty-five or thirty a week . . . for a tutor.'

She ate her peppers. He played with his fork and drank

his beer. 'Why the hell don't they serve liquor here anyway?'

'You've got a bottle in the bag,' she said, hoping. 'Pour some.'

'In this bag?' He placed it on the table and smiled. His smile was bad now, violent now. 'There's something far more interesting than alcohol in this bag.' He turned again to look at Charley. 'Now that one seems right for you somehow. I'd like him to come over and say hello. Wave at him.'

She tried to eat, but her throat constricted and she couldn't swallow. 'Have some of the pepper. It's delicious.'

'Get him to come over,' Jim said softly, and opened the mouth of the bag so she could see inside.

She put down her fork. 'It isn't loaded?' She knew it was. It always was.

He turned the bag around and put his hand inside and put it on his lap. 'Call him over.'

'No.'

'If you've nothing to hide—'

She stood up. He said, 'Sit *down*!' She began to walk away. He called, 'Cheryl!' sharply. She kept walking, wondering what it felt like to have metal tear into your back and rip through your heart, lungs or stomach. She bent forward a little in anticipation of agony and hoped he wasn't insane enough to do it.

Outside, she grabbed for the wall and bent her head. Someone asked if she felt all right. She said, 'It's nothing, thank you,' and went across the road to Stage 11, where she waited.

Jim wheeled out a moment later and was helped down the step by two pretty girls in go-go costume – short skirts and high boots. He thanked them and they walked away and he looked after them. Cheryl felt like crying. For the handsome young man nailed to that lousy chair. For the virile young man who liked girls and good times and could have liked his wife if she hadn't destroyed him.

She went across the road. The bag was wedged back in its corner of the chair. She put it in the plastic side-pouch, and he didn't try to stop her. He said, 'Why wouldn't you call him over if there's nothing between you?' She got behind the chair and pushed. He said, 'Let that alone!' and spun it away from her. 'Answer me. Why wouldn't you call him over?'

'Because I won't compound your insanity.'

He wheeled himself off. She walked alongside him. When B-gate came into view, he said, 'I'd like to see more of the lot, long as I'm here.' His voice was low, tired.

'All right. There's the Western town and one of the most complete stages for shooting water sequences and a recreation of Washington—'

She took an hour to show him around, and he looked and listened and said nothing. She led him through C-gate and asked the guard to call a taxi. 'I have to get back now, Jim.' She bent and kissed his cheek. He said, 'It was a very interesting visit. I learned a lot,' trying to give it double meaning. But there was no conviction to his voice, his expression.

She said, 'I'll introduce you to whomever you want the next time you come. If there's no paper bag.'

He raised his head then. 'Devon was not without guilt. Perhaps it was only his thoughts he felt guilty about—'

'Well, if it's *thoughts* you're after, you might as well shoot *me*. Every time I see a certain actor—'

He shook his head, staring out at the street. She said goodbye and went back through the gate.

Devon was watching for her and left his office as she came up the stairs. 'I couldn't stay,' he said, face white. 'I wanted to, but I felt so . . . so—'

'Ashamed?'

'No, not ashamed! I felt afraid. Afraid he'd see through me and hurt you.'

'You should have worried about yourself too.'

'I did, a little.' He looked miserable. 'It's so . . . wrong, so confusing when you see a man like that.'

She started away. He said, 'Can we make it tomorrow?'

'You just said it was wrong.'

'I meant the whole situation. A young man like that crippled. A beautiful woman like you tied to him. Everything about it, wrong.'

'And you're going to make it better?'

'Please don't ask such questions, Cheryl. If I didn't care about anything except . . . *that*, I'd stay away from you now, wouldn't I?'

'I guess so.'

'Tomorrow then? We have to discuss that TV role.'

'When Jim hears about it, he's going to be very suspicious.'

'We'll work it out. I don't want to hurt him, but I have to do what I have to do. Tomorrow?'

She hesitated, thinking of the money and the kick. A new career. A marked-down Shelley Winters. And she also thought of Devon and his hopes and wondered whether he was absolu-

246

tely wrong there. She had given herself to him once. If he persisted ...

She said, 'If you'll still want to, after I tell you he had a gun
in that bag.'

'That paper bag? A gun? You're joking.'

She shook her head. He came closer. 'You'll have to go to
the police! He might hurt you!'

'Worry about yourself.'

He looked at her and moved his lips and finally said, 'All
right. I'll worry. At lunch tomorrow.' He turned back toward
his office.

She threw him a high hard one. 'Worry about this too.
There's someone else. Another man. He means a great deal—'

'Tomorrow,' Devon said firmly, and walked away.

For the first time, she admired him. And later realized that
he had acted very much like a man in love. And Charley had
looked at her like a man in love. And she was going to appear
on television. And, with luck, in *The Eternal Joneses*.

Sitting at her desk, she suddenly laughed and shook her head.
Things were looking up for fat Cheryl. Now if only her husband didn't kill her, or Dev, or Charley, or himself, there might
be a few nice moments.

CHARLEY HALPERT

Charley was so busy listening to Ben Kalik and deciding that
he didn't like him that he never noticed Cheryl until someone
called her name. By then she was walking out, and he realized
that the man in the wheelchair must be her husband. They'd
obviously had some sort of scene.

Kalik was in his late forties, small, dark and intense. He said,
'You understand you're to forget that *Terror Town* contract.
They didn't exercise their option so we're clear. The Bagel
called me about eleven this morning. Imagine, he thinks he
can get you back after *Joneses*!' He laughed.

Cheryl left the commissary. Charley said, 'You mean he
wanted me?'

'*Wanted* you? He practically cried! Said your treatment was
a classic and would make your reputation once it got translated
to the screen. Since I have other clients, all levels, I didn't laugh
in his face. Just said we'd see. But if he thinks—'

247

'Then he *liked* the treatment?'

'Didn't he discuss it with you?'

'I haven't seen him since the meeting.'

Kalik said well forget him and who do you think wants to read one of your novels but Moe Sholub of all people. Said he'd met you and was impressed. Also Aldrich of Palomar-ABC.

Charley watched Jim Carny maneuver his chair away from the table and asked Kalik when all this had happened. 'Phone's been ringing since nine-thirty. Four calls concerned *you*. Now what we're going to do is play it cozy—'

Kalik went on, no longer delivering fact but a sell of himself as Hollywood's smartest agent and one devoted to Charley's interests. Charley stopped listening and watched Jim Carny wheel toward the doors. It gave him a rotten feeling. Not that he thought of what he had done as putting horns on the man, dishonoring him, or any other medieval concept. But it *was* cheating, and if Carny found out it would hurt him.

'Sholub employs Lars Wyllit,' Kalik was saying. 'You've got to watch that little mother. He'll try to carve you up and get the job all for himself.'

Charley said Lars was his friend.

'No one's your friend when a hundred grand worth of assignment is on the line! Don't you realize Markal's going to want *one* of you, not both? It's got to be that way. You're not a team. This has to be your baby, right from the beginning, and you've got to make Markal see that it's *your* work he likes—'

Then again, Charley thought, watching Carny leave the commissary, Cheryl needed him and he needed her. They were crippled too, cheated too – she by Jim Carny's refusal to adjust, he by three thousand miles and wife of little faith.

Kalik continued to talk nonstop and picked up the check at the end of the meal, shaking his head and saying, 'I'm going to make so much money off you, Chuck, I'm almost ashamed of myself. You can write, baby, and that's something so few people out here can do it's pathetic.'

Charley said, *Sure, sure,* to himself, but while walking Kalik to the gate wondered if he hadn't done the man an injustice. After all, it was an agent's business to be aggressive, to be hard with the market . . .

He didn't work too well after lunch and spent most of the time reading a pocket history of the United States. Then the dread hour of four struck, and he went to Baiglen's office. Lois and Sugar were sitting on the couch. They jumped up. Cheryl said, 'Mr. Baiglen's expecting you,' and smiled and turned back to her typewriter. Charley moved on leaden feet. He opened Baiglen's door and ushered the sisters inside. And realized he just didn't have the guts to carry off that man-of-the-world plan.

Baiglen rose from behind his desk. Charley made his little introduction, using phrases like 'friends and neighbors' and 'lovely, talented kids' to help take the curse off.

Baiglen nodded and came around the desk to squeeze first Lois's hand and then Sugar's. They smiled and said they were *so* happy to meet Mr. Baiglen whom they'd heard *so* much about and they were *so* anxious to show what they could do. Charley winced; and was surprised to see the look on Baiglen's face. The man was interested – thoughtful and interested.

'How old are you?' Baiglen asked Sugar, and quickly added, 'The truth now. I don't mind hiring minors, but I have to know.'

Sugar glanced at Lois, and Lois nodded. Sugar said, 'Seventeen last month.'

Baiglen smiled. 'Very mature for your age, my dear.'

Baiglen turned to Lois. 'And you?'

Lois was eighteen and a half.

'You think of yourselves as a team, do you?'

Lois hesitated, and Sugar said, 'Well, we'd *like* to, being we're so close, but of course, in show business—'

Lois said, 'We understand that parts come one at a time.'

Baiglen nodded. 'There's a very big feature in planning right now. You've heard of it perhaps?'

They nodded. '*The Joneses* or something,' Lois said.

'Yes. Later we'll be testing for parts. Featured parts. I can promise you a test.'

Charley was amazed. He stood to the side and watched Baiglen sizing up the two girls and just didn't feel the producer was interested in them personally. And yet, what else could it be?

Baiglen said, 'And there's also television, something to get you started. But let's think of those tests, shall we?'

Lois said, 'Oh gee, *thanks*, Mr. Baiglen!' and looked happy enough to explode. Sugar said, 'Kicky!' and glanced from Baiglen to Charley and back to Baiglen as if wondering where she should start paying off.

That appeared to be decided when Baiglen said, 'Thanks, Chuck. I know you're busy, so you needn't hang around. I'll talk to the girls a while longer.'

Charley muttered, 'Sure,' and headed for the door.

'By the way,' Baiglen said, 'I hope your agent told you how much I thought of the treatment. I finally got the chance to read the carbon last night.' Charley turned. Baiglen said, 'I don't know what Markal or anyone else thinks. I suspect they consider it too . . . too long-hair. At least for *my* operation.'

Charley smiled vaguely. Baiglen sighed. 'Well, another time, Chuck. It could make a hell of a movie.'

Charley said, 'I sincerely believe so, Carl. And thank you.' He left, and the feeling he had was more gratifying in some ways than learning he was getting the twenty-five thousand. Because Cheryl was wrong and he was right. Because someone, finally, had liked something he'd written, not three and five and ten years ago in New York, but last week, here in Hollywood where it counted.

He wished Baiglen joy in Lois and Sugar.

CARL BAIGLEN

Within fifteen minutes the two sisters knew exactly what he wanted. At first they were upset that the payoff wasn't the usual toss in the hay, but a little sweetening of the pot with promises of immediate television work, a little reassurance that there was no way they could get into trouble, and they agreed.

When they left, he got on the phone to Pen Guilfoyle. Avalon's head of casting did some verbal leering, and Carl reminded him of several favors owed. Pen agreed to send Misses Lane and Smart around on TV casting calls, with a strong recommend. 'They can act, can't they?'

'They can shake it. What else do they need for TV walk-ons?' Then he called Dr. Eddering and said he was checking a script and had run into a doubtful situation. 'A photographer and his model plan to blackmail a wealthy man with pornography. The man rejects the model's advances, so the photographer drugs him, puts him in bed with the model, and the model makes love to him for the camera. Is it possible?'

Eddering chuckled. 'You mean you're worried about the *biological* reality? What sort of movies are you filming these days, Carl?'

'This is to settle a bet, Doctor. Is it possible for an unconscious man to have an erection?'

Eddering was silent a moment. 'I'd say yes, it's possible. Manipulating the male organ sets up certain purely physical responses. The erectile tissue operates independently, to some degree, of the consciousness. Men have erections while asleep, and not all are connected with dreams. But I don't know how you can win your bet without an actual demonstration—

Carl said he would call the bet off. Eddering said, 'For the purposes of your movie, Carl, the photographer wouldn't worry about it. Visually, the sex act is among the simplest of human functions to fake. If the victim responded to manipulation and had an erection fine. If not, the pictures could still be taken. Either way, the evidence would be damning.'

Carl thanked him and promised to send over tickets for the next Avalon preview. Dr. Eddering was right. The photographer wouldn't worry about it.

He was feeling better than he had in weeks when he arrived home that night. He kissed Ruth and asked for Andy and nodded when she said the boy was studying with a friend. Then she surprised him. 'Have you been quarreling with Andy?'

'Not any more than usual. Why?'

'Well, I was wondering . . . he's been spending so much time away from home lately.'

He thought it over, and she was right. 'Boys his age like to run in packs.'

'He's not running in a pack. He's with one friend most of the time. That boy in Bel Air.'

'Richard Sewal?'

'Yes. He hasn't a mother, and his father's a gay widower. I don't know if they have proper supervision.'

'Richard seems a nice enough kid, from the few times I've met him. Very quiet.'

'He struck me as sort of . . . listless.'

He looked closely at her. 'If anything's worrying you, tell me. I can ask Andy to bring his friends here for a change.'

She shook her head and said it would only puzzle the boy and she guessed she was being foolish.

'It's girls, isn't it?' Carl asked with a smile. 'You're worried those two are bringing girls into Richard's house.'

She hesitated, then muttered, 'I don't know. He just hasn't been a happy child lately.'

251

He said adolescence wasn't a particularly happy period and Andy seemed fine to him.

'You're probably right. Still, I wish he'd stay home more often.'

'I think the problem is *we* stay home too often. How about a movie?'

'Don't you see enough movies in your line of work?'

He put his arm around her waist and tightened his lips à la Bogart. 'Not with a beautiful broad like you, baby.'

She said, 'You're absolutely right,' and went to get her wrap.

ISA YEE

Shroeder worked the cast hard Monday, and though bad luck and bad actors continued to plague him he managed to put two scenes in the can. Isa didn't get home until after five, and this, coupled with her six a.m. awakening, made her one very tired girl. She showered, got into a comfortable nightgown, and slipped an old bathrobe over it. Then she had a pre-mixed Manhattan on the rocks and a sandwich and decided on another Manhattan to ease those tense nerves and muscles.

She was reading through a script Jerry had sent her as a 'possible' when there was a knock at the door. She walked down the foyer, feeling that second drink in her legs. 'Who is it?'

'I've come to apologize,' Free Barchester's voice said.

She put the chain on the hook and opened the door a little. 'All right, apologize.'

'I'd like to come in.' He wore mod pants and a real cool Carnaby jacket and said, 'See? All for you.'

She smiled, and caught herself at it, and thought she should never drink Manhattans. She still wasn't going to let him in, but she had a joke to make and took the chain off and opened the door wider and pointed at her ankle-length slob outfit. 'See? All for bed. So good-night.' She began to close the door, but he stepped forward. And she let him come in. Maybe if he had tried to touch her then, or tried to walk by her, she'd have thrown him out. But all he did was let the door close and say, 'Yesterday was all wrong, Isa. Yesterday was anger. But only because I . . . think so much of you.'

She shrugged and walked ahead of him to the living room.

'Five minutes,' she said. 'By the clock.' She waited until he was seated on the couch, then took the armchair across the room. 'Are you very angry?' he murmured, face solemn, like a bad little boy's.

She almost laughed. 'Look, can't you understand it makes no difference whether I'm angry or not? Can't you understand nothing's going to make any difference between us?'

'No, I can't understand that,' he said, his voice so low it was almost a whisper. 'I'll never understand that.'

She stood up. 'Then there's no use talking even five minutes. I want you to leave.'

He didn't move.

'I mean it, Free! Right now!'

The phone rang. He sat still. She turned to the bedroom, then thought better of it and went to the kitchen and the wall unit. She stood across from the sink and said, 'Yes?'

'Nat Markal, Isa.'

In the living room, footsteps sounded.

'How are you, Nat?'

'I'd like to come over for a while.'

Free came to the kitchen entrance. *God, if he said anything! If Markal heard another man!* She said, 'Oh, Nat, any other night,' and saw Free smile and was chilled at the thought that he might have guessed whom she was speaking to.

Why had she allowed him in! Why, when she had everything going her way at last and this could ruin it all.

'You're not well?' Markal asked.

Free walked into the kitchen. She shook her head at him. 'Just terribly tired,' she said. 'Shroeder was pushing hard.'

Markal said that was understandable since he was way behind schedule. He went on to discuss Shroeder's failings, and Free came closer. Isa shook her head violently. Free pointed at the sink, made a drinking motion, smiled innocently.

'He seems under pressure,' she said. 'But in all fairness, he has a terrific handicap. Two in fact. His stars—' She went on talking and Free came right up to her and cleared his throat. She slammed her hand over the mouthpiece. Markal said, 'Isa? Hello?' Free said, 'I'll be quiet baby, if you'll be quiet.' She turned her back on him, showing as much contempt as she could. She said, 'Nat? Must have been some trouble on the line.' He said he knew what she meant about Lobo and Nina, but that they were expected to do very well at the box office. He talked on, and she was glad *she* didn't have to do any talking

253

... because Free had one arm around her, reaching for her breasts, and the other hand was lifting her robe and nightgown. Markal paused, and she asked, 'Did you ever meet Nina's mother? A real Hollywood stereotype.' And kicked back hard. She covered the mouthpiece as Markal talked, and Free said, 'Act nice now. Whoever he is, he's not going to like my being here.'

She had no choice. She kept Markal talking and Free drew her clothes up around her waist and she was naked to his touch.

'I really have to hang up now,' she said, careful this time not to use Nat's name since Free hadn't guessed. Free kissed her neck and his hand in front and his hand in back worked on her and his breath was so loud ... or was it *her* breath?

Markal wanted to talk about *Joneses*. She said, 'I'm so sorry, dear. I'm just about falling off my feet.' Free did something to his clothes and rubbed against her and she had to hang up and tell him it was rape and he would rot his life away in jail!

'Well,' Markal said, 'if you're *that* tired.' He sounded annoyed, but she couldn't worry about it because Free's hands and Free's body were at her and in another moment it would be too late and she would begin to scream, scream!

'Yes,' she said, fighting to keep her voice normal. 'Goodnight.' She hung up and twisted around. Free held her close, his face not at all as she'd thought it would be; soft and full of wonder and his voice the same. 'Isa, I knew you were beautiful, but I never knew what it would be like to see you this way, to touch you—'

She was going to scream him out of here. Of course she was. But his lips stopped her and his hands took off her robe and pulled the nightgown away from the top and she stepped out of her clothes and was drawn into him, into his partial nakedness, into the enervating and mind-dulling heat. They kissed. She had the word 'rape' on the tip of her tongue, but he took that tongue and sucked it into his mouth. She shook her head, weakly, weakly. She was afraid of him, more afraid than of any man ever before. Because this feeling was too sweet, too much; this feeling was what they made movies about.

He took her hand and put it on him and she had to laugh, remembering what he had said last night. He understood and murmured, 'I was drummed out of the pony regiment long ago,' and she said, 'Good thing too, the way I'm built.' And told herself to *stop* that talk, to stop the whole thing ... and knew it was beyond stopping.

254

He kissed her again. Dear Lord he was a Negro and it couldn't work even if he wasn't because Nat Markal had to be the only one.

She was being carried. She was blood and she was being carried by her blood lover and it was so sweet not to be a living lie for once.

They were in the bedroom and he was taking her. He was trembling and saying he loved his little yaller, his little Chinese blood, and would never leave her. She was helping him, guiding him. She was loving and being loved. She was free of hate and fear now, free of doubt now.

She told him who she was and it made the act of love the truth. He said he was happy he'd been right because he wanted her to be blood, wanted her to join him in his work ... and there the doubts stirred and tried to return; but while the act of love went on there were no doubts.

He brought her to a mountain and threw her off and she didn't fall, she flew. She spiraled into valleys of pleasure she had never dreamed existed. She didn't want to land on earth again. But she did. And when she did, the doubts were there to greet her.

He was lying beside her, hands behind his head, his body flat and hard and black where Markal's had been all jellied whiteness. He lay there as if he would be lying there forever, and that couldn't be. Her flight was over. He had to go.

She said she had another early call.

He dressed and she watched him and he waved his hand and walked from the room. She called, 'Free!' He came back to the door. 'Is that all?' she asked. He nodded. 'That's all from me. The rest has to be you. You said some loving things a while back, but how you *really* feel—' He shrugged.

'I ... like you very much, Free. I wish—'

He waited. When she didn't finish, he said, 'Wishes won't make it so. You know I'm listed as Morse in Central Casting. I'm in the book as myself. And on Wednesdays and Fridays I'm at a club in Watts called The Blacks. From Genet's play. You ever read it, see it?'

She said no. He said she could find it in the library. It would help her to understand a little more about Humphrey Barchester. 'This year's Humphrey Barchester,' he added, smiling. He turned to leave again. She asked if it was *his* club. He said, 'You want me to undress and get back into bed and talk?'

She shook her head. He said, 'Let me know when you do,'

and left. She listened to his footsteps and wanted to call him back to make her fly again, make her life the truth again.

She didn't. And later, swallowing a pill to end what had become an endless evening, she felt certain she never would. It had been something very special and it was over.

The Blacks weren't for Isa Yee.

BRAD MADISON

After half an hour in the Molina Blanca Brad Madison (John McNaughton was the phony now) knew his information was wrong. No matter what Bill Cromer, his neighbor, had heard, this dull, anonymous little bar was no rendezvous for the gays.

He ordered a second bourbon and water and told himself to examine the other patrons more carefully. And after five minutes of close examination still couldn't spot a prospect.

Not that he was very disappointed. He might even have felt a touch of relief. Because it was one thing to *want* something and another thing to implement that wanting when you were twenty-six years old and had never allowed yourself a single step in that direction. Because the mask was glued on so tight you began to wonder whether you could survive taking it off.

He sighed and sipped and wondered if perhaps there wasn't a woman, an unusual and wonderful woman, who could turn him on, make him happy . . .

Or was it that he wanted only *one* man, *one* boy? Like Andy Baiglen . . .

Wouldn't the Bagel drop dead if he learned his son was gay! But gay he was; this Brad was sure of. A look had passed between them in the Baiglen living room. A look that revealed everything, though the boy had immediately dropped his eyes and assumed his own mask. Besides, how could Baiglen have decided that a six-foot-four ex-cop was gay unless Andy had told him?

No use thinking of Andy. Much too young. A sixteen-year-old under close parental supervision might not even have begun experimenting.

Which only made him more desirable to Brad Madison. Together they could learn. Together they could build a lasting relationship . . .

He shouldn't be thinking that way! You couldn't push a man

256

like Baiglen too far. Never knew when he would break, as he had with his first wife. And Brad Madison had too much to lose now. He had a sweet apartment and a good wardrobe and two thousand dollars to spend. He had his first part in a TV show, a very good part, much better than Baiglen could have anticipated when he set up the meeting with Myles Stone. He was a villainous Don Juan who lasted almost to the end of an hour-long *Winning the West* show. A real break, and if he handled it well it was bound to lead to other parts. And four or five such credits could lead to consideration for something in Markal's big production. A decent part in *that* could make him. He could become a happy man ... if only some love would enter his life. He had lived too long without love.

The bartender came over and Brad was about to ask for the tab when he noticed a newcomer at the curved end of the bar. A lean, clean-looking girl who was just lowering her gaze from *him*. He said, 'The same,' and busied himself with a fresh cigarette and felt her eyes again and looked up. She met his look a brief instant before turning away.

Surprisingly, it didn't bother him, as Margo Cromer's heavy flirtations did.

He smoked and sipped his third drink and the girl was served a martini.

He examined her surreptitiously, wishing she would get up so he could see her whole body. She wore her hair pulled back severely, very little makeup, and had a good hard face with soft hollows in her cheeks. She was small-breasted despite the standard uplift, outthrust bra. When she glanced up from her glass, her eyes were wide-set, level, direct.

She finished her drink and ordered another. He was disappointed that she didn't look at him again and was puzzled at himself. Now what did he want from a woman? There was no one here for him to fool, and he certainly wasn't going to fool Brad Madison. (Could she be that unusual woman? That wonderful woman to turn him on?)

A while later she rose and walked to the ladies' room. He followed her in the back-bar mirror and was pleased with what he saw. Lean hips. Small, tight rear. Rather thick legs in medium-high heels. A simple blue skirt.

He waited for her return, feeling the excitement grow and wondering at it and beginning to visualize what it would be like to hold her. (Why not? The right woman might make a difference.)

257

She came back to the bar. He watched her openly and when she finally looked his way he smiled. She reddened. He got up and walked over. 'Good evening. I'm Brad Madison. May I buy you a drink?'

Her name was Aileen. She was twenty-four and worked for a bank and her family lived in Wyoming. Yes, it *was* lonely for the transplanted, even though she met people at the bank and on the tennis courts. She was a dedicated tennis player, at least three sessions a week, which explained her muscular body.

It wasn't easy. She had to consume quite a bit of liquor before leaving with him, and quite a bit more in his apartment before falling into his bed, and even then she resisted his removing her clothing and pleaded and wept a little. She was, incredibly, a virgin. He swore he wouldn't change that. He got to his feet and stood at attention with his right hand, among things, upraised and thought *talk about camp*! and swore he would not break her hymen. She lay down quietly. 'I trust you, Brad. You're clean-cut.' She allowed him to remove her panties. She may have wondered why he didn't remove her brassiere, but she wasn't the type to say anything or do it herself. He kissed her and played with her powerful legs and hard buttocks, and poured her another drink.

She was pretty high when he turned her on her stomach. A moment later he asked her to get on her knees, explaining that this was the only way he could keep his oath. She mumbled that it was 'shameful' and positioned herself as directed.

She cried out once.

Toward the end he gasped, 'Andy!' And understood that the 'right woman' was only a faint image of the right man. But he was tender with Aileen. She had helped him.

The mask was loosened.

ISA YEE

Again the nightclub scene. Again Lobo Stretch banging away at his guitar and talking through his nose. Again Nina Pearl shaking her big boobs in everyone's face and thinking that was acting. Isa was sick of it. She wanted *Waikiki Nights* to end. And it would, for her, as soon as she completed one last dance number on this overcast Thursday afternoon.

The unusually gray day was reflected in her thoughts. She hadn't heard from Markal since his call Monday night. She hadn't heard from Free either, but that was fine. It showed he meant what he'd said about waiting for her to take the initiative. It would save her the unpleasantness of turning him away.

But knowing it was fine and *feeling* it was fine were two different things. She should never have allowed him into the apartment, not to say her bed. He had scored too well. She had thought of him too often in the past two days.

And Markal . . . what was happening with him? Had he decided she was just a cheap lay? Had he seized on her refusal to see him Monday as a way out?

She had phoned Markal twice Tuesday and twice Wednesday and been told that he couldn't speak to anyone, he was out, he was in conference. That was when thoughts of Louella Walters and Coontown had begun to press back in on her.

Like her mother and grandmother before her, Louella had been used by white and black alike, conned by white and black alike! They'd given her a lot of talk, and she, the smart one, had fallen for it! They were probably laughing at her this very moment. Markal was lining up new bedmates, and Humphrey Barchester was telling his friends at The Blacks what a ball he'd had. All she had to do now was become pregnant and carry on the long line of Walters bastards!

Agitated, she got up off the stool in her shadowy corner. She wanted to run, to go somewhere and do something to shake the growing fear.

Shroeder called for her. She hurried to the set, grateful for the opportunity to work. She listened as Mike Fandem, the choreographer, gave a little pep talk; then she stepped out with the three Hawaiian dancers. This was a small bit, her fadeout, but she was featured and would shine.

It was a hoked-up hula and modern combined. They hadn't given it enough time in the rehearsal hall, and Fandem decided he didn't like the first take. He began making changes, going through the new steps with Isa following behind him. Then he worked with the other three, and Isa waited under the lights.

She was still waiting when the heavy soundproof door far across the cavernous stage opened, and three figures entered, outlined against the brief flash of daylight from the not-yet-shut outer door. Shroeder turned, prepared to express annoyance, but instead hurried forward to join the three. They were Nat Markal, Jerry Storm and Terry Hanford.

Fandem looked for Shroeder to begin the action. Shroeder stood near the door and talked to Markal. Then all four came up behind the camera, and Shroeder said, 'Got Miss Yee's routine settled yet, Mike? Mr. Markal wants to see her work.'

Fandem said all ready. Markal nodded at her. Jerry Storm (who was known to visit only *star* clients) took off his jaunty little Alpine hat and waved it at her.

Isa turned and caught a glimpse of Nina Pearl's face on the sidelines. A study in scarlet; Lobo didn't look particularly happy either. As for the others, they buzzed until Shroeder called, 'Action!'

She began to dance. There was the music and the new routine and no time to look at anyone. But louder than the five-piece combo was the music inside her.

Nat Markal was here. Jerry Storm was here. Mona Dearn's publicist was here.

She danced, her heart pounding with more than the physical activity. She danced and knew that all around the set the thoughts were buzzing, the speculation mounting. She danced and the excitement proved too much and she *muffed*! At the worst possible time, she *muffed*!

Mike Fandem said, 'Oh for the love of Pavlova!' Markal said something to Shroeder, and Shroeder said, voice sharp, 'I agree. Pavlova herself couldn't get through *that* pretzel-bend routine. Straighten it out, Mike.' Fandem looked shocked and muttered, 'Well . . . let's try it this way.' He worked it back to where it had been before. 'With a bop bop bop *bop* and *turn* and once again yes Isa *yes* and the other way, perfect—'

She danced. She did it right this time. But it was no longer important. The gray day was over. The gray life was over. Because she knew, she knew, that the insurance was being drawn up and Century City was here and Coldwater Canyon was almost here and Coontown was long gone.

CHARLEY HALPERT

Charley called home Thursday evening from a phone booth on the lot. He called at five, to make sure Bobby would be up, but he didn't expect to speak to him, and he didn't. Celia said, 'He's in the bath. I'll give him your love.'

He said, 'All right. Something rather wonderful has happened to us, honey. I waited until I signed the contract—'

She said, 'I've seen a lawyer, Charley. I've talked about a divorce.'

It jolted him. They'd had trouble, a lot of it, but a divorce? He had never thought of anything that permanent. He had always thought . . .

What *had* he thought? That it would go on until Celia said, 'You're the greatest, Charley,' and they would live happily ever after? He said, 'What I've got to tell you will change things, I've landed a twenty-five-thousand-dollar assignment.'

'Twenty-five thousand? That's definite?'

'Yes. I haven't done any writing yet, but the way it works is that I'll get paid just as long as I hand in the proper amount of pages. They might not like it, but they have to pay for it. That's the Writers' Guild. Couldn't we use them in publishing!'

To her credit, she said, 'How wonderful! I'm so happy for you, Charley!'

'Happy for *us*. There's no reason to think of divorce now, is there, Celia?'

She didn't answer right away. Then: 'Happy for us. Because the settlement can be reasonable now and protect Bobby.'

He was stunned. 'Then you've made up your mind? You . . . don't care anything for me anymore?'

'I think the question should be, "Then we don't care anything for *each other* anymore?" When you drove away without letting me—'

'I don't want to go into that again,' he said, voice shaking, and was surprised at his sudden pain. He had Cheryl and he could have Lois and Sugar and he could have other women, he was beginning to see that now. He had twenty-five thousand dollars and if he wanted to be tough she wouldn't get much of it. He had a new approach and new confidence and a new life.

Maybe she was right. Maybe she didn't belong in his new life. But if she divorced him and stayed in New York, he wouldn't be able to see his son more than once or twice a year.

He couldn't consider that. He could go without seeing Bobby, without speaking to Bobby, as long as he had to, as long as he knew the time would come when he would see him every day. Anything else was intolerable.

'All right, Charley. We won't go into it again. We won't go into anything again. You'll hear from my lawyer.'

'Celia, I don't know what to say.'

261

Her voice changed, seemed to grow blurry. 'You would if you—' And then it cleared. 'I'd like to hear how you make out; I wish you the best, Charley.'

'Do you think I *can* make out?'

'Well, if you've got a big contract—'

'Then you now see me succeeding as a writer?'

'If what you say is true.'

'Then why the divorce? The last time we talked it was my unwillingness to admit I couldn't succeed as a writer. It was my agony and my wasted life and your suffering with me. So if I succeed—'

'I guess I don't believe you will.'

'That makes no sense, Celia. Let's hold fire on this divorce talk, honey. Let's give it some time.'

'No.'

'But people don't break up a home, a family—'

'You left your home, your family.'

'Come out here tomorrow. Leave the house with an agent and pack a few things and take Bobby and come out. We've got security for a year or more. Put the family together again.'

'I didn't break it up in the first place, Charley. *You* put it together again.'

'Celia, you're being unreasonable! Or you don't *want* to stay married!'

She was quiet a moment. 'Maybe. I haven't thought of it . . . I haven't been honest with myself, or you. So let's say you're right.'

'But there's no other man? No immediate reason for a divorce? Why would you want one then?'

'I . . . don't know.'

'For Christ sake, you *have* to know why you're breaking up a marriage of fourteen years!'

Her voice grew blurry again. 'The last few years . . . how much have they meant to you, Charley? Bobby means everything. I don't want to hurt . . . not you . . . not my baby. But *me?* How much do I . . . nothing, Charley . . . so *you* be honest—' She couldn't go on. She was crying.

He tried to say something, but he was stricken. How much *had* she meant to him in the last few years? His wife, his Celia, his once-great love? Celia of the blue gown at her cousin Arlene's wedding where he had come as a friend of the groom's. Celia of the incisive speech and high principles and declama-

262

tory phrases. Celia of the overwhelming shyness and childishness in matters of love. Celia the dairyman's daughter who was taught and had absorbed to her very bone that man must toil by the sweat of his brow, day by day, in a *job*, and who had grown frightened and later bitter with the husband who couldn't survive that way. Celia, who would throw away abbath and shul, and even bar mitzvah for her son because Charley cared nothing for it, but who held to something more Jewish than all of that, as Jewish as the religion itself – the concept or morality being tied to industry, of *machen a leiben* – making a living – as a Vulgate holy of holies.

Celia, whom he had not looked at and into for years.

'I don't want a divorce,' he said.

The weeping drew away. Sniffling and blowing and finally silence took its place.

'I want to see you, to talk face to face, before making any such decision.'

'Yes, well, I can't think now.'

He knew what he had to say, what a man had to say to a woman to justify staying together for a lifetime. And he couldn't say it, because he no longer knew if it was true. And because he suddenly remembered Cheryl. And because even Lois and Sugar ... and a world of women ... and what was this Love that he had to invoke as a magical power to bring him together with his wife and his son?

He could say it to Bobby. It was simple there. But it had ceased being simple with Celia. It had grown complicated with Celia, and love couldn't be complicated.

'Would you let me speak to Bobby?' he asked.

'I ... no.'

'Do you hate me so much?'

'No.'

'Then why?'

'I—' She struggled, and then, running the words together, 'Best he gets used to it. Good-bye.' The line was dead.

He didn't believe her. She had hidden the truth, whatever it was. 'If it's the only way to bring you home ...' his father-in-law had said.

'How can I go home?' he asked aloud, and the phone rang twice. 'How, with everything *here*?' And did 'everything' include Cheryl Carny who was reaching into his heart as once Celia had? The phone rang again, insistently, and he began to leave the booth. But he remembered he had money now and

263

there was no need to run from the sweet-voiced operators and their extra charges.

He lifted the receiver. He put change into the phone and said, 'You're welcome,' and walked into the somber evening. He met Cheryl on the way up the stairs. She said, 'I'll try to get away tonight. I wasn't going to, but seeing you—'

He worked until seven, worked better than at any time since coming to Hollywood. He sketched broad outlines of his characters. He put them together, men and women, in two's, in three's, in families, in love, in hate. Death he let come when it seemed inevitable, and then he didn't dwell on it, gave it no meaning beyond that door slamming hollowly in the face of the living.

The Eternal Joneses were eternal in their progeny, in their humanity, in their celebration of life. Disease and death came, but the Joneses went on.

Charley Halpert, too, went on ... went on home to assert his humanity. And to celebrate life. And only after Cheryl had left did he ask himself: How much celebrating had he done with Celia?

Book Three

FEBRUARY TO MAY

LARS WYLLIT

Lars went directly from Halpert's office to Devon Productions. He waved at the girl and she started to say something but he went right on by and into Devon's office and sat down on the couch. Alan Devon was behind his desk, picking his teeth. He looked at Lars and then at the doorway where his secretary stood, a sour expression on her young face. 'Close the door, Sandy.' When she had gone, Devon said, 'In deference to my age if not my position—'

Lars said, 'Halpert finished his treatment.'

'He mentioned it to me yesterday. It's a monster, isn't it? The last I saw, it was over two hundred pages. He must think he's writing another novel. How long did it finally run?'

'Three-ten.' Devon began to comment. Lars cut him short. 'You were going to stop him at fifty. Then at a hundred. Then you said you'd wait until it was finished. So it's finished.'

'He has to polish and submit to me formally. Then I have to submit to Markal.'

'And then?'

Devon kept his eyes down. 'First of all, it's too long. And the structure is impossible. Do you know how many major scenes he has in two hundred pages?'

'Dev, let's stop kidding ourselves. He has a fantastic piece of writing there.'

'I disagree. I think he's gone overboard on the hate sequences and lots of other things.'

'Minor things,' Lars said, and took out a cigarette and lit up. 'It's a good treatment. It's better than good. It's ... great.'

'You're a very young man. Fantastic. Good. Great. All very subjective words. I could say bad, terrible, awful, and be as close to the truth as you.'

Lars shook his head. 'Not this time.'

'*All* the time. Writing isn't a science. No one can apply acid to Halpert's treatment and make it prove out gold or dross. *Opinion* is all we can apply to writing. And my opinion is that

267

it's overblown and amateurish and very weak in spots. Yes, there *is* some fine writing, but it doesn't compensate for the technical weaknesses. If it'll make you feel any better, we'll be able to salvage parts of it when you take over.'

Lars had been shaking his head all through this. Devon leaned forward. 'You've finished your script for Sholub, haven't you? Then what's the problem? Do you want that juicy assignment, that fat revision fee? Or have you decided money is no longer important?'

Lars smiled thinly. 'I had my price set months ago. Then I saw his first seventy pages, and my price dropped. In fact, I dropped . . . right out of the treatment, only I didn't admit it until today.' Devon began to speak. Lars said, 'Tell me, why didn't you start your knifing job after the first fifty pages, as per your plan?'

Devon remained calm and sure of himself. 'Knifing job? My dear boy—'

'Why didn't you go to Markal two months ago?'

'I didn't think there was enough evidence.'

'The first fifty pages were great, that's why. And the next fifty were great. Now they're all great.' He put out his cigarette in an end-table ashtray. 'I won't get between Markal and that treatment.'

Devon went through his gum routine: stripping, folding and chewing. 'Then we'll just have to get another writer. And, let me warn you, you still haven't got a contract for any part of *The Eternal Joneses*.'

'Do you think I'm walking away from our little understanding because I *want* to?'

'The suicidal enthusiasms of youth. Just don't say anything until Markal's had a chance to read it and I've had a chance to discuss it with him.'

'Don't you say anything, Dev. You'll end up looking like a fool, or a plotter.'

Devon stiffened. 'That's enough! It's my professional opinion that neither Halpert *nor* you is suited—'

Wyllit smiled. 'Confidentially, what's the beef between you two? What'd he do anyway?'

Devon attacked a second stick of gum, and his anger. He was successful with both. 'Will you promise not to say anything until Markal has a chance to react? For all you know he might hate it.'

Lars shrugged. He walked out and passed Halpert's office.

That damned typewriter was going again. He felt lousy. He felt like a beginner in New York again, hating Chuck Halpert for his novels. He felt there was no way a man could *learn* to write like Halpert, which was from the genitals and the viscera. He had read a carbon last night and into this morning and he had returned it to Halpert and said, 'Tough stuff, man,' and smiled and come directly to Devon. Now he went out C-gate and walked three blocks to Yankee's Bar and had two martinis-on-the-rocks because he needed a fast, hard belt. Keerist! Big brother could still lick him!

But later, with the booze warming his blood, he said to himself, 'How the hell do I know I'm right? It *is* opinion. So I think it swings. So maybe Markal won't. Anyway, Halpert has never written a script. He'll need a professional to guide him. It'll be the easiest bread I ever made, and I'll have my name on a really big show.'

He nibbled a pretzel and thought of Terry. She'd been freezing him. It was time to give her another rough night.

He phoned Mona from a booth. She said, 'Well now, after three weeks I don't know if I should even *talk* to you.' He said, 'Had to work the old tail to the bone.' She was quiet. 'But I've got some left.' She tried to stifle laughter. 'I've missed you, oh queen babe. Please let me prove it.' She said well, and yes I missed you too and how about eight tonight. She wanted spareribs and tall drinks at Trader Vic's. And then? And then they'd see.

He went on home. He read some notes he'd made for *Joneses* and threw them away. He watched television, and kick-in-the-head he came upon an old *Alfred Hitchcock Presents* he'd done his first year out. Another nice little residual, and the story was damned good. Encouraged, he made more notes for *Joneses* – how to sharpen certain scenes of Halpert's, how to eliminate others that weren't altogether necessary. He could earn his way, old Larson W. could. He had finished a big movie and he was going to celebrate at Trader Vic's with the juiciest chick in the world and later he would climb into the juiciest saddle in the world.

Make with joy, Larson! Whoop it up *babeee*!

He said, 'Hey hey hey!' and jumped into the shower and sang and jumped out and called Kip Daily, a TV writer he liked on occasion, and Kip wasn't going too well on the pilot of a situation comedy and said a workout at the club grabbed him just fine.

They killed each other with judo and three rounds of dirty boxing. Then dirty pool and dirty dice-for-drinks, and the day was comfortably shot. He went home to shower again.

Halpert called at six. 'Glad you liked the treatment, Lars. I'm worried about some of the scenes. Especially the contemporary stuff. Does it hang together?'

'Not altogether. There are some problems. Nothing serious. Nothing we can't work out, if and when Markal decides they have to be worked out.'

'I'd appreciate any suggestions.'

'At the right time, Chuck. Which is when I've got my contract and we're off and running. Then we'll research it together.'

'Yes, of course. I just wish we could talk *now*.' He sounded wound-up tight.

'Relax,' Lars said, still flip and oh-so-experienced. 'Walk away from it a while.'

'You're right. But … so damned many characters! And Veronica Jones and the racist group—'

Lars was silent.

Halpert muttered, 'Sorry. I'm pushing, I know.' Lars said he understood. Halpert said he was looking forward to sitting down and getting at those problems together and he hoped Markal would let him work on the script with Lars.

'I think he will,' Lars said, and then, 'Gotta gallop.' He felt a little ashamed. He also felt a lot better. Halpert himself didn't know what he had. Why should Markal?

CHERYL CARNY

Devon suggested they work at his home for a change. Cheryl said the rehearsal hall was just fine and asked how she was coming along on her third television role. He said, 'You've reached an impasse. You're as good as you were in your last part, but no better. And you have to get better. You need more intense training. It's time to forget being a secretary, just as you forgot being a tutor, and concentrated on *acting* as a career.'

It was 6.30. Sandy had left, and Cheryl was sitting in Devon's office. She had already called Jim to explain that she had another rehearsal. He made no complaint, no biting remarks. He had been very subdued lately. He didn't even ask when she'd be home. All he said was, 'Sure,' when she told him to take out the plate of cold cuts from the refrigerator. He had seen her in her first *Winninger's* show last week and it had seemed to stun him. They had been college thespians together and young hopefuls together and now she was being featured on prime-time network television and if she wasn't top-notch she was at least professionally able. 'Not bad,' he had muttered, then drunk himself unconscious.

Devon came to the couch and sat down close beside her. She said, 'Shouldn't we go?' but didn't expect that they would. He put his arms around her, kissed her cheek when she turned her lips aside. His hands went under her sweater; his fingers pushed inside her brassiere. She sighed and gave him her lips ... even though Charley Halpert was in her mind, her heart. Devon never stopped trying, and she was tired, and how many times could she push him away and still accept his help, take the parts he gave her in his television shows?

His hand went under her dress. She broke free and stood up. He stood up too, his veiny, speckled hands trembling. She was upset by that sign of age – of hunger and pain and age.

'If you'd rather skip rehearsal?' she asked.

He said no, she had to rehearse. It was his new show and he couldn't have anyone fouling it up, including the girl he loved. He said it just like that, as an old and established fact: 'The girl I love.'

He turned off the inner office lights. She moved past him into the outer office. He turned those lights off too from the panel on the wall near Sandy's desk ... and suddenly caught her from behind, his breath rushing in her ear. 'Please, please,' he whispered. 'All these months!' He turned her around and took her hand and put it on him. 'For heaven's sake just help me!'

She couldn't say no again. She allowed him to direct her hand inside his trousers. But when he tried to raise her dress she began to withdraw. He stopped. She stroked him. He whispered hoarsely, 'I can't get there that way, darling. If you—' His fingers touched her lips.

She hesitated, then went down on her knees in the darkness and began serving him as she served Jim, expertly, with cool detachment, the difference being that his hands caressed her hair instead of tearing at it. But otherwise it was the same: the gasps and sighs and breath quickening toward a conclusion, the passion somewhere above her and a million miles away. And all the time she held to the image of Charley Halpert and

271

how she was going to see him tonight and how he gave her one thing no one else in all this world could – hope.

The hall door opened. 'Mr. Devon? Are you in there?'

She tried to get up and slipped and fell backward, sitting down on the floor. Devon said, 'I'll be ... in just a moment, Halpert. Your office.'

Charley Halpert stood in the lighted doorway. 'Oh ... yes, sorry ... I just—' He closed the door again.

Devon said, 'Why didn't I lock that door!' and, 'The damned fool never goes home!' He went to the door and locked it and came back to her. 'Just don't leave me this way.'

Dazed, she continued. And it was now exactly the same as with Jim, because an unseen hand was tearing at her, punishing her.

Afterward, she asked if he thought Halpert had been able to see them in the dark office.

'Most likely.' Devon seemed *pleased* at the possibility. 'Let's get to the rehearsal hall.'

She shook her head. 'Are you going to speak to him?'

'No.' He smiled. 'Are you?'

'If he saw me. If he despises me—' She walked away from him. He said, 'He's married and you're married and it can't mean anything anyway.'

She turned in the doorway. 'Whatever you do or don't do for me, you're not to touch me again. Not ever again, Dev!'

She walked out and past Halpert's office. She went down the stairs, afraid he would open his door and see her. Yet she had to go to him tonight. She had to find out if she'd lost him.

Had he seen her? Had he seen what she'd been doing? Could she make him understand it was an act of mercy, of charity?

She laughed sharply and drove the Plymouth off the lot. Dark already. Winter in Los Angeles. Rain sometimes and early sunsets and chill evenings. And last Saturday the temperature had been in the eighties and she and Charley had driven to Santa Monica and looked at Nat Markal's cliff house from the beach and wondered what it would be like to have all that money and power. And walked hand in hand and kissed in the car.

Would he ever want to kiss her again?

272

CHARLEY HALPERT

Charley waited until he was certain Devon wasn't going to come to his office, waited until the footsteps moved past his door and down the stairs. They didn't hurry as Cheryl's had. They strolled. They seemed to draw attention to themselves. Devon was bragging.

Charley felt something. Not anger. No jealousy. Not anything he expected to feel.

He felt pity. For Cheryl. For her confusion, her being thrown into a maelstrom of men and emotion and passion. By a lousy accident. By crippling the man she had loved very much and perhaps still loved.

He puffed a cigarette-size cigar and fingered the thick typescript that was his treatment. Writing it had swallowed his life these past three months. He had seen Cheryl, and he had seen Lois and Sugar twice, when they'd found time to turn on that pornographic spigot of his nature, and he dutifully phoned Celia, though not as often as he had before. Even his hunger for Bobby had dulled while working to bring the Joneses alive.

Now he was finished, no matter what he had told Lars and Devon. Now there was no more polishing to do, nothing that would make any difference at this pre-script stage. Now he didn't want to hand his work to Devon, because he understood that Devon was an enemy. He had suspected before, but now he *knew*.

He finished his cigar and looked at the treatment. Cheryl had typed it and said it was 'unbelievably' good. Lars had liked it, though he seemed to have reservations. As for Devon, it was hard to know what he thought, what he meant when he said he 'couldn't tell' after two hundred pages. And Charley Halpert? He felt he had done a good job, but he couldn't be sure. There were areas in which he felt dishonest – especially the Negro ghetto scenes.

He would have to experience the ghetto for himself, not via the ton of printed material sent him by Markal's research team. He would have to walk its streets, listen to its speech, smell its smells, get into a home or restaurant or club. Otherwise, he would never know whether what he was doing was fact or some white researcher's fantasy.

He smoked another little cigar and decided he would bring the treatment to Markal tomorrow morning. He didn't know whether Devon would consider it an affront to his position. Perhaps *Markal* would. But he was feeling his way through something that menaced his work and he was determined that nothing would prevent its receiving an honest reading and a fighting chance.

He drove to the Bali-Ho and used the lobby phone to call Celia. He asked after her health, Bobby's health, her father's health. The old man was sick with an intestinal virus. She'd had to stay home and take care of him. Charley said, 'Why don't you get a housekeeper for a few weeks?' She said, 'Money isn't that easy to come by.' He said, 'What are you talking about? You've got the ten thousand I sent. *I'm* absorbing all the taxes.'

'That's Bobby's. It'll be part of the divorce settlement. I'm not looking to take you for anything.'

He changed the subject, telling her he had finished his treatment and was now waiting to see if he would be assigned to the script. 'Kalik is going to ask for seventy-five thousand.'

'My God,' she muttered. 'I never realized there was so much money for the writers. The ones that aren't well known, I mean.'

'That's nothing. In a budget of this size, a known writer might get as high as half a million for the complete job. Perhaps a percentage too. It's not unheard of.'

'Your agent actually believes you'll get seventy-five thousand?'

'Depends on how the treatment is received. I'll be happy with fifty.'

She made a sound of wonder. He decided the time had come to ask her to join him, but instead he said, 'Can I speak to Bobby?'

'No.'

Now was the time to ask her to come to him. Now was the time to tell her he would come to her.

He said, 'Then there's nothing more to say.'

'I guess not.' Her voice was tired. Nursing the old man was no fun. And her job . . .

'Give Bobby my love.'

'I always do.'

'What do you tell him, to explain my silence?'

'That you're very busy. That you have to call while he's at school. And I read him parts of your letters.'

'I see.' Then quickly, 'It's surprising, isn't it, Celia? I'm finally beginning to make it. You never thought I would, did you?'

'No.'

'And now?'

'Now I don't know.'

'All that money, Celia. We never made that much,'

'In advertising—'

'Never so much, so fast.'

She was quiet.

He said, 'Well, anyway, we'll see. Hope your father feels better.' (He didn't call him 'Pop'.) 'Let me know how things go.' He hung up before she could.

In his apartment he got a bad feeling, a lowdown feeling, as if he'd kicked her.

That was foolish! *She* was the one who had made the decision to break up. She was the one who had done the kicking, refusing to allow him to speak to his son.

He wondered if Cheryl would come tonight. He wanted her to. He would have phoned if he hadn't feared Jim Carny might answer. He wanted her to know he understood her life, its pressures. If she didn't come . . .

He had worked very hard the past few months. He was out from under tonight and needed to celebrate. If Cheryl didn't come by nine, nine-thirty, he would go somewhere. A topless club. The Whiskey À Go-Go. Or just a movie and a late dinner. A big dinner. He was down to his best weight since 1946. He had earned himself a big, fattening dinner.

His mouth began to water. He changed into trunks and went down to the pool. No one else was there, and he knew why when he took off his robe. It was *cold* tonight. But the pool was heated and he swam fourteen laps and came out tingling all over.

At eight, he was sitting with a drink and wondering whether he should bother waiting for Cheryl. He didn't know exactly what she and Devon had been doing in that dark office, but it certainly wasn't rehearsing for those parts he was feeding her.

He wanted to speak to her. He wanted to tell her she must never fear his opinion. She was a wonderful person. She was carrying the biggest cross in the world without bending, without weeping and wailing. He admired her, maybe even loved her. The way she smiled . . .

Cheryl Carny's smile wasn't very strong, very successful. It started out all right, but rarely finished. At one time, with her

275

handsome Jim, she must have smiled often and all the way. Now the agony of her life aborted it, fractured it.

He wanted to write something for her. A poem.

How long had it been since he had written a poem? One for Bobby, which hadn't turned out well, about three years ago. Before that, several for Celia when she was pregnant with Bobby.

He went to the counter and used pad and pencil to block out his thoughts; then typed them up. He repeated the process, and began to feel he had something, and kept changing and adding and typing.

He didn't leave at nine-thirty. He didn't go out and celebrate. He had a sandwich and worked on the poem. Cheryl knocked at ten-thirty. She stood in the doorway, face pale, eyes fixed somewhere around his knees. 'May I come in?'

He poured her a drink, which for once she really wanted. He talked about the treatment and about delivering it directly to Markal. She murmured, 'Yes, that's smart. Don't rush Dev.' He said he had spoken to his wife and nothing had changed and he didn't know what was going to happen but it looked like there was no way of saving the marriage. She kept her eyes on her glass and asked for a refill. On the way back from the kitchen he stopped at the counter and picked up the poem. He gave her the drink. 'Cheryl, look at me.'

She tried to, but her eyes fell away. 'You saw me and Dev,' she said, voice barely audible.

He held out the sheet of paper.

'What is it?'

'A poem. Good for at least a laugh.'

She put down the glass and took it. 'For me?'

'Yes.'

She hunched forward, staring at it. 'A poem should be read aloud.'

'Whatever you want.'

She read in a very low voice, to herself actually. There was no title.

> Fractured, the smile advances
> And dies aborning.
> Fractured, the smile touches
> a face that refuses it through fear,
> yet is so illuminated by the abortive,
> the fractured,

the shoot that withers,
So illuminated
So touched
So revealed
That I too am revealed.

With someone, the smile was less fractured
Less abortive.
With someone, the smile claimed the face.
With someone, some other time,
Some lost and other time.
the length of the woman.
That fracture runs through her to me.
That fracture, the cancer that corresponds to mine.
Though we be divided by walls on walls on years
on places on things on other loves
Though we make two and three and more with others
And our others be strangers
Though we be strangers multiplied by strangers
And other loves
Still runs the fracture through you to me.

It is not to be revealed, this fracture.
Other loves do not reveal this fracture.
It exists only as we exist, the you and the I
standing together one-flash-of-understanding long.
It exists only as I see you through walls on walls
on years on places on things on other loves.
It dies as die the you and the I.

The smile laughs.
The smile talks, words tumbling on words
to tell the untellable,
To tell the fear and weeping,
The girl torn within the woman's form,
The woman torn within the girl's dream.
The smile hopes, while turning back hopeless,
Fractured, the smile dies aborning,
And no one sees to care
If I'm not there to see.

She looked at him and read the poem again, mumbling the
words under her breath. And yet a third time. Then she folded

the sheet of paper carefully and put it in her purse. 'Thank you.'

He flushed at the tremor in her voice. 'Cassius Clay could do better.'

She ignored that. 'It makes me feel even dirtier about Devon.'

'I wrote it for exactly the opposite reason. To tell you ¿¿¿ well, not to have to tell you anything.'

'I know that. But I want you to understand—'

'Remember what you said after I brought my two little neighbors in to see Carl? Let's not confess things to each other. It's enough that we're able to get together when we can.'

She began to answer. He bent over and kissed her. She said, 'If you were a fastidious man—' He said, 'Shut up!' and shook her and kissed her again, and this kiss carried them past talking.

JIM CARNY

He opened his eyes and cleared his throat and mind. His mind needed less clearing than usual because he had dumped most of what Cheryl had thought he'd been drinking. She had gone to her lover. *And one night soon she would go to hell!*

He reached to the night table and took out the gun. He rubbed its cool length and visualized just how it would be. He would kill her lover in front of her eyes, hurting him while killing him, putting that first bullet into his genitals and savoring his screams. Cheryl he would kill as quickly as possible for auld lang syne. Then he would sit amidst the blood and the death and enjoy it.

He twisted his shoulders and arms until he was able to shove the gun down behind the headboard, jamming it into the tight space between mattress and wall. It lodged there, where Cheryl wasn't likely to find it. He straightened and closed his eyes and visualized the whole thing over again.

Any day now! When he was ready! When enough time had ticked away and the hatred inside him exploded and wiped the slate clean!

He pictured the man as Devon, because all those acting parts and all that money made it almost certain to be Devon. But he would have preferred Halpert or Baiglen. A younger man had so much more to lose.

TERRY HANFORD

It was three in the morning before Lars left Mona's room and walked down the hall. His footsteps paused momentarily outside Terry's closed door, and she sat up, ready to throw her disgust and anger in his face if he dared enter. Then he went on, and she lay down again, curling into a tight knot, tight inside as well as out. The sounds had been going on since he and Mona returned to the pink hacienda at midnight. The sounds had filled the foyer, had carried through walls and doors, and Terry hadn't dared leave her room for fear she would run into him. The sounds of a long, erotic bout of love: blows and small screams and weeping and prolonged gasping laughter as he tickled her in some obscene manner that had her begging for mercy. And when 'mercy' did come, it was more eloquent by its silence than all the noise had been. 'Mercy' had filled the house with an almost palpable tension that had Terry straining to hear against every conscious desire, that had her waiting for the conclusion as if it were her own.

She hated Lars Wyllit! She wanted to gouge his thin, mocking face, his obscene satyr's face, with her nails! He had become her implacable enemy. He *wanted* her to hear everything he did with Mona. She read it in his eyes when he looked at her, his smile when he laughed at her.

She was sitting up again, fists clenched and breath raging. She lit a cigarette and felt anger for Mona too. How could she allow herself to be used that way? How could she make those *sounds* when she knew Terry was two doors down the hall?

She stubbed out her cigarette as if jabbing it into her enemy's face. She got up and wanted a cup of something hot, something soothing, and was afraid Mona might have gone to the kitchen. She paced the room, raging at Nat Markal for having put her in this impossible situation. Then she stopped.

It was too much to take.

She went back to bed, her mind made up. At breakfast she would speak to Mona, tell her she couldn't stay on any longer. Mona wouldn't mind, now that her lover had returned.

Lover! It was ridiculous to use such a delicate term for so vile, filthy . . .

She closed her eyes. It would all end tomorrow, and she would be safe in her own apartment. She thought of home and faithful old Bert. She thought of leaving L.A., of changing her life in some radical fashion, and fell asleep.

In the morning she had breakfast with Mona and talked of everything and everyone – except Lars Wyllit and returning to her own place. She noticed how Mona's crooked smile lingered and how Mona's eyes softened when they met hers and how Mona's robe kept flapping open and how Mona wore nothing underneath.

She didn't eat much. She said she had to get to the studio, the work on *Joneses* was enormous. Mona put an arm around her shoulders and walked her to the door. 'It means so much to have you here, sweetie. You know that, don't you? You know it makes my life complete, don't you?' Mona kissed here – just a touch of the lips on the cheek. It didn't mean anything. Neither did the accompanying hug. Just girl-to-girl affection.

All right, she would go on a little longer. She would serve the client a while longer. Wyllit didn't come around *that* often.

She began to wonder just when he would next visit the pink hacienda, and the wonder was tinged with an element of excitement, and the excitement wasn't altogether unpleasant.

She had to stop thinking of Wyllit and Mona! She had important work to do on an important film!

She drove to the studio and entered her office and checked her calendar and note pad. Markal had asked her to spend more time on Isa Yee. She got out Yee's folder. It was thin, consisting of a biography, six photographs and some notes Terry had made months ago. One of the notes was typed in capital letters:

MARKAL SEES YEE AS STAR POTENTIAL

She began to read the bio with Jerry Storm's letterhead, but her thoughts drifted.

Miss Yee should be made to understand the risks of stardom. Miss Yee should be made to study the case histories of the Monroes and Landises – and the Mona Dearns with their *near* suicides. There was danger in becoming a star. Unknown danger, different for every personality, but as real as machine-gun bullets.

She brought her mind back to the biography. She took a yellow pad and began making notes:

'Change bio. (Galápagos? Not really? More turtles than people there. Too easy to disprove. Check Jerry Storm. Why not States? Enough romance in genetics.) Check her apartment. Opportunity for unusual decor. Check Oriental occasions ... have her involved in Chinese New Year? Visit of Chinese diplomats? Farmer's market – food from both worlds? (Can't see Spanish bit. Get straight info from Storm! Maybe date with new Argentinian tennis doll?) Work up personality. Clothes. (Special style. Yee-Yee dresses instead of Yé-Yé? Mini with slit?) Yee-Yee good gimmick phrase. Interviews. Call Sheilah Graham. Merri owes favor. Skolsky on lot Friday. Tour of Vietnam? American Oriental cheering on American fighting in Orient? (Bad taste?) Exciting dates. Lover types. (Whatever happened to Turhan Bey?)'

She stopped to light a cigarette, then smiled as an idea hit her.

'Screen mag article. Jazzy titles. Yay for Yee.' She hummed 'Tea for Two', then sang, 'Yay for Yee and Yee for you—'

MONA DEARN

Mona soaked luxuriously in the sunken, pink-marble bath. She lay back, eyes half-closed, and let warmth and comfort drift over and through her. Her thoughts stirred lazily, erotically, and she didn't try to stop them when they turned to Terry, when they went beyond any thoughts she'd ever had of herself and a woman. Not that she was certain she would consummate these thoughts.

Slowly, sensually, she soaped her heavy breasts and smiled. Terry had already given her a certain amount of physical satisfaction. Through Lars. Or with Lars. Mona wasn't sure just how it had happened, but last night she had become aware of it and been able to enjoy it.

Lars alone was enough to give her enjoyment. She had begun to care for the tough little man. And somehow, this was tied in with Terry.

Lars and Terry had a thing between them. What it was Mona couldn't tell. It was nothing simple, that was sure. Terry disliked Lars, or seemed to. Lars found Terry a funny square, or seemed to. Before last night, Mona had worried about it occasionally, felt frightened that these two people, so important to her, would find their way to each other and leave her out in the cold.

But last night she had decided it was something else completely, something very promising in terms of bringing Terry to her. And wouldn't *that* be wonderful!

Even now it was wonderful. She would settle for now. She would fight for now if either Terry or Lars tried to leave her. She would walk out on *The Eternal Joneses* and Markal would pressure Terry and Lars and things would go back to now.

She wouldn't worry about afterward, of the day *Joneses* went into the can and there was no more pressure to apply. By then things would have been settled. By then Terry would either be hers, or she would marry Lars.

But no need to think seriously of marriage now. Last night would be repeated again and again, and last night was something *super*. One minute she had been worried about the noise they were making, worried that Terry would hear, as she had all the other times ... the next minute she was making even more noise, *wanting* Terry to hear. One minute she and her lover had been alone in bed – and they weren't kidding when they called them *creative* writers! – and the next minute someone else was in there with them.

Not really, of course. Not so you could touch. But in Mona's mind, Terry had suddenly been with them. In Mona's mind, Terry had been watching Lars doing all those things to her. In Mona's mind, Terry had begun to hunger, and not for Lars, no, because it wasn't Lars but Mona Dearn who was the center of attraction, Mona Dearn who was crying out for Terry to hear.

Knowing Terry heard brought her into it. Bringing her into it made them three instead of two. And the three of them made it love as love could never be with just one, no matter how much you cared for that one.

Lars and Terry, her two dear friends, her lovers. Yes, Terry, too, because she listened at night and in the morning her eyes were different, each time a little different, and that meant she was breaking down, she was coming closer. One night Mona would go to her and Terry would open her arms and it wouldn't be those dirty pictures Peter had kept of his first wife and her girlfriend. It would be two women whose hearts were together, forever. Then she might not need, or want, Lars anymore.

Yes, Terry above all desires, but she would settle for Lars, with Terry as observer. And if Terry broke away completely, then she would have Lars alone.

But one of those three conditions *had* to become permanent. One of those three could make her life right again. No, not *again*. It had never been right before. Not with Peter and not with Carrew and not with Walter, her first husband a million years ago in Queens . . .

She decided she had been in the bath long enough. Once she started thinking of Walter and Queens, she always went on to Angel and how it had all ended. And that could lead to not being able to sleep nights and pills and terrible blues, the way it had happened when she'd thought her heart was stopping, when she'd *wanted* her heart to stop.

She called Lena and the maid dried her and helped her dress. Yes, now that she had her two dear friends, life was fine and dandy. And she was going to be the biggest star *ever* when *The Eternal Joneses* was shot. Terry said so. Markal said so. Jerry said so almost every other day. The nude scenes would be handled *artistically*, with distortion lenses and all that shimmery, cloudy stuff. Hadn't Elizabeth Taylor been shot nude in *Cleopatra*? So Mona Dearn would show a little more. And the fans would line up by the millions. And while Jerry hadn't been able to work a percentage, a cool million wasn't bad, especially with the rider clause assuring her a percentage of her next picture.

She wished the script were completed so she could get to work studying. She *needed* work. It was fine when Terry was home, but the days were lonely.

She decided she would sculpt today.

Yes! For the first time in six months she had the feeling!

She went to the last room down the hall from her bedroom and used the key. She always kept her studio locked. She even dusted and cleaned it herself. She didn't want anyone looking at her work. She wasn't sure enough of it. Which was why few people even knew of it, and she didn't allow Terry or anyone else to make it part of her publicity. Her instructor, Igor Severin, was a big name who had a piece on exhibition at the Whitney in New York, and he said her work had definite depth, definite promise. But instructors were like agents: they had a stake in saying you were good. She had once showed a small clay head, one of her best according to Igor, to an Italian painter and sculptor who was flying back to Rome later that same day. He had tried to act impressed, but she had known he hadn't liked it.

Well, screw 'em all. Someday when the acting was finished and she retired to Malibu or Palm Springs, she would build a house with a special indoor-outdoor courtyard, a gallery of her own, and important people would be invited there. They would marvel that Mona Dearn had produced such important work and word would get around and a piece or two would go to the big museums. Then Terry would see she had depth, had a soul and a brain.

She uncovered the partially completed torso of a gladiator begun during that Roman Legion picture two years ago. She had lost feeling for it after her affair with Gordon Hewlett broke up. Now she decided she would start all over again, but this time the gladiator would be a small, thin, hard-faced man.

After that she would do a woman – a reclining nude. Perhaps she would ask Terry to pose for her. Perhaps after a few more nights of listening, of knowing what was happening to Mona Dearn in her bedroom, Terry would be ready to pose.

NAT MARKAL

He was surprised when Halpert brought the completed treatment to his office Wednesday morning. 'Didn't you know Alan Devon was supposed to get it first?' Halpert nodded. 'He'll get a carbon today.' Nat looked at the writer. 'Problems?' he asked. Halpert said, 'Not that I know of. I'm finished and I want my work to be read by the person whose opinion counts.' Nat began to lecture him on chain of command and delegation of authority ... but after a few words suddenly stopped. 'All right. As long as it's good. Do you think it's good?' Halpert said, 'I want to make a million changes. I have nightmares about dishonesty and historical mistakes and technical mistakes—' He paused. 'Yes, I think it's good. As good as anything I've ever done, anyway.' Nat said, 'Good-bye. Tell my secretary I'm not to be disturbed. I'll get back to you sometime today, or tonight, according to when I finish reading and finish making up my mind.'

When Halpert left, Nat opened the folder and turned the title page – and found he was almost afraid to begin reading. The treatment was the bone structure over which the flesh

284

of dialogue would be laid. The treatment was all-important.

At noon he asked Bertha to have a steak sandwich and coffee delivered to his office. She asked if he wanted a list of the people who had called. He said, 'No,' firmly, and went back to reading.

At three-thirty he knew Charles Halpert had been the right choice. There were scenes he wanted changed, others he wanted eliminated, and the mulatto girl character would be further explored, her importance increased. Some of the hate scenes were too raw, especially the burning alive of three Negroes in nineteenth-century Kansas. Also, the cattle-car shipments of Apaches to Florida smacked a little too strongly of Nazi Germany, and people were sick of that. Perhaps some toning down of *all* the hate stuff.

But it was a masterful job. Perhaps the best Nat Markal had ever read. He finished at four-thirty and immediately phoned Halpert. 'It works,' he said. 'There's plenty that needs fixing, but it works. And we can save the fixing for the first draft. I want you to go ahead immediately. Do you feel you can use help?'

That question must have thrown Halpert. He hadn't expected a choice, and took some time to answer 'I've always worked alone. But this time, because of lack of experience in technique, no other reason, understand . . . If I could have help without interference—'

'Is Lars Wyllit all right?'

'Lars is fine. But won't he—'

'I'll explain what I want. He's to consider himself a technical assistant – a guide more than a collaborator.'

'He won't like that. No writer would.'

'He'll like it, when he hears I'll pay his price.'

'And *my* price?'

Markal smiled to himself, realizing he'd given Halpert a club to bargain with. 'I have a limit. Exceed it and I'll say no.'

'I want seventy-five thousand.'

'It's a lot for anyone with your lack of experience, and even more compared with twenty-five for the treatment. But you've got it. I'll have Bertha contact your agent.'

'Thanks Mr. Markal!'

'Don't be so enthusiastic. How do you know my limit wasn't twice seventy-five?'

'It's not just the money. It's the green light. Maybe later I'll wonder how much I could've gotten. But right now—'

285

'I was thinking in terms of fifty thousand, Charles. I don't really know what my limit was. You'll earn bigger fees in the future, but for now you've done damn well. Your muscle is growing faster than I thought it would.'

'Because of your confidence in me, Mr. Markal.'

'I think it's time we dropped that Mr. Markal. The name's Nat.' And then, 'Keep yourself clear for Saturday night. We've got to have a party. To celebrate the true launching of *The Eternal Joneses.* Bertha will contact you with the details. Then next week we'll fly to New York and a press conference to top all press conferences. You live in New York, don't you? You can see your family, on Avalon.'

Halpert didn't respond as Nat had expected, merely said, 'Yes.'

'Of course, if you feel you shouldn't break the forward movement of your writing, if you're afraid of losing momentum—'

'I am a little afraid of that, Mr. ... Nat. I'd like to see how things go. Is it important that I be with you?'

'No. You're not a name yet, and only names count at press conferences. Actors, mainly. So suit yourself.' As soon as he hung up, he had Bertha get him Alan Devon. Nat wanted to keep Devon from blowing up at Halpert, wanted to keep the producer happy. He wasn't important at this stage of the game, but later, when the enormous spade work began ...

And he wanted to tell him, too, that he'd found a part for Pier Andrei, in spite of both Baiglen and Devon feeling that she would be more trouble than she was worth. Because now, after reading the treatment, he saw there was a part, a small one, just perfect for her: the mulatto girl's drunken employer in modern Los Angeles who epitomized what Halpert called 'the American sickness' – recognition of the basic emptiness of life. Contrasting this with the mulatto's drive and energy, contrasting Pier's ruined beauty with Isa's fresh flowering, would make for an effective bit of drama.

Bertha announced Devon on the phone. Quickly, Nat said he had read Halpert's treatment and it was excellent.

Devon was silent. Nat said, 'I wanted to see it today. I hinted, and he brought it over. I told him you wouldn't be too sensitive about it.' He chuckled. 'Alan, we've *got* something in that man. I want you to bring him along, keep him happy.' Devon still hadn't said a word. 'Your percentage will be worth close to a million, if all goes well. Consider that, Alan. Three years

286

of television and B features—' Devon finally spoke. 'Two,' he said, and they laughed together. Devon said, 'Glad you liked it, Nat. I felt you would, though I have reservations—'

He went on, and Nat leaned back in his chair, smiling. Devon had picked up the ball like the pro he was. Devon would go along with Halpert, no matter what the nature of the clash between them. And with Nat's suggestion that Pier Andrei get the little role. There was his salary and his percentage and his reputation. You could always count on the Alan Devons. Writers and actors were something else again. Directors could be most difficult of all, as Tyrone Chalze occasionally demonstrated. But this project had the smell of money, the feel of success. This project was drawing talent like no other Nat Markal had ever handled. The stars were beating down his door. The agents were begging to make deals and showing willingness to cut prices. It was a mark of honor to be signed for *Joneses*.

Isa had a lot to be grateful for. Isa would be with the biggest names in the industry. And her role, when he finished cueing Halpert, would be among the most important in the picture. It would make her a star overnight.

He went across the room, taking a ring of keys from his pocket. He opened a closet door to the right of the bench and unlocked the metal case on the stand and took out the large black phone, the private phone, the secret phone only Bertha knew about. He'd had it installed by an electronics outfit six years ago, when a fight with New York interests seemed imminent. Dave Sankin had almost sold a crucial block of stock at that time. Olive Dort had almost won the company from him. He had needed an absolutely safe phone, one that couldn't be tapped. This one had a scrambler system, brought up to date periodically, that even the FBI couldn't crack. Not that he needed it now. But he punched the red button after dialing, thinking he might as well get *some* use out of a gadget that cost him along with the monthly de-bugging service of home and office, seventy-five thousand a year.

Isa's Century Towers phone rang five times before the switchboard cut in. He left word for her to call Mr. Markal's Plaza suite after seven p.m., then put the phone away. Fox and Mayer and Skouras hadn't needed such crap. But then again, this was a different day and age.

He had worried that someone with an ax to grind – Olive, for example – might try to gain a hold over him. Isa could be a

287

very definite 'hold' in the wrong hands, which was why he was taking every possible precaution. Moving her to Century City, within walking distance of the Plaza, had worked out well. A huge hotel was like a city, affording excellent opportunity for anonymity. Isa would drop in some evenings for a drink at the bar or dinner in the dining room and then simply leave. That she took an elevator to the twentieth floor wasn't noticed amidst all the other comings and goings, the flow of people to and from rooms and meetings and conventions and parties. Once she was in his suite, he never used room service, never allowed anyone to enter. It was the safest system he could devise, safer than setting her up in a private home, where his arrival could mean only one thing. Safer than using different hotels and motels, which aside from the obvious inconvenience meant false registrations and chance meetings with people they knew.

And still, he worried. Which was why he was paying Brecht-Ryan Associates an additional fee to run spot checks on whether he was being tailed, watched, spied on in any way. Arnold Ryan was handling the details himself, to keep any word from leaking.

He had Bertha get his home and told Adele he would be working late. 'Again?' she muttered. He said he'd received a treatment from the writer and it needed careful going over.

'Then you'll be at the office?'

Was it his imagination, his sharpened instinct for self-preservation, or did she sound ... different? Bitter, perhaps?

'No, not the office. I'll be with the writer and maybe the casting director and maybe Devon. Around. Here and there. Do you want me to call you later?'

She said no, and he said he would try to take the weekend off, and she said, 'All right,' very subdued. He called Bertha in. He dictated a brief invitation to be sent to everyone connected with *Joneses* for a party at his suite Saturday night. He added that each could bring a guest, and listed a few columnists, a few personalities, a few actors who hadn't as yet nibbled and whom he might want. He concluded with, 'Send one to yourself, Bertha.' She flushed happily and he patted her shoulder as he walked to the door. She was a fine woman. She reminded him of Adele, even though they differed physically. Loyal women. Clean, moral and devoted.

He sighed as he walked toward the Imperial. Why couldn't a man find passion and pleasure with the loyal woman in his

288

life, the moral women in his life? It would be so much simpler that way, so much safer.

But driving to the Plaza he thought of last Friday and the game of leapfrog Isa had improvised, and the loyal women, moral women fled his mind. The hunger began to build, and he hoped she wouldn't be too late returning his call, hoped nothing would prevent her from coming to him, felt something very much like panic at the thought that he might not be able to see her tonight. She didn't know it, and he would never tell her, but he needed her even more than she needed him.

ISA YEE

Isa had never been to Watts and Willowbrook, the Negro ghettos that, under the single name Watts, had become nationally known in August of 1965. Now she had a few hours to kill and drove her new Corvair hardtop (four-on-the-floor, full power and air-conditioning, courtesy of Nat Markal's liberal trade-in plan) down Central Avenue and into Clovis Avenue. It wasn't Coontown as she had imagined it would be. It certainly wasn't Chicago's Southside. No narrow, tenement-lined streets here. The California sun played over wide avenues, private homes and two-story, pink-stucco apartment houses. Not much different from other lower-middle class sections of L.A., with black instead of white faces.

But soon she began to see the differences. The boys hanging around the corners – hard, listless, vagrant boys – and that was like Southside. The men walking slowly, aimlessly, and others standing around like the boys, and still others looking out of windows – in the middle of a working day, which meant no work. The children: so many and so poorly dressed, so few accompanied by parents. The litter. The run-down look of people as well as places.

And then she turned onto 103rd Street and came upon a really shocking difference – a difference that applied not only to white areas but to all other Coontowns as well. As far as she could see there was rubble, not buildings but vacant lots covered with the remains of buildings, for block after block on both sides. This was, she remembered, the street reporters had

289

called Charcoal Alley, because it had been almost completely burned out by rioters.

Watts frightened her. She wanted to get out ... But she had come this far to see Humphrey Barchester's club and she might as well go a little farther. She watched the streets and made a right at the metal skeleton of what had been a large building and saw the painted-over storefront, white with black lettering: *The Blacks*. A dingy little shop, closed and dead. Well, what had she expected from Coontown?

She used the freeways to get to Santa Monica Boulevard and a section of Los Angeles that had once been part of the Fox movie studios, a section surrounded by prestige areas – Beverly Hills, the Los Angeles Country Club, Westwood Village, Brentwood, Santa Monica – and itself perhaps the most prestigious of all. 'Step into the 21st Century', an Alcoa Properties booklet stated, and that was exactly what it felt like as she turned onto the Avenue of the Stars.

The contrast of Century City to Watts was like ice water thrown in her face. The tall, white, ultramodern buildings. The open space and grass and trees. The futuristic shopping center. The fountains, putting greens, pool and gardens. The manicured, spotless look. And the only black faces to be seen belonged to plump, middle-aged doormen – one of whom she thanked as he ushered her into the lobby of the Century Towers Apartments. 'That's quite all right, ma'am,' he murmured, smiling and ducking his head. A sudden urge to shout, 'Goddam Tom!' grabbed her by the throat, and she hurried away.

She rode a silent elevator to the ninth floor and entered her four-room apartment, furnished by one of L.A.'s best-known decorators in 'Oriental Modern'. Her eight-hundred-dollar-a-month apartment, with terrace and air-conditioning and maid service and everything else you could think of. Her super-luxurious apartment, courtesy of Nat Markal and his insistence on 'star-potential' surroundings.

She checked the switchboard. Her lord and master wanted her to call the royal suite. In half an hour. So of course she would. And then she would go to him, being careful not to be seen, and slip into her most important role, that of passionate lover to a pile of white flab.

Again she asked herself what was wrong. She had no cause to think of him that way. He was giving her the moon on a silver platter. If she wanted to escape him later, after *Joneses*, she could. No reason to feel anything but affection for him.

She showered and chose white lace underwear and used scent carefully. She wore a blue silk shantung suit because it was attractive without being conspicuous. She swallowed her daily contraceptive pill, returned his call and left for the ten-minute walk to the Century Plaza.

He greeted her with kisses and a gift: a lovely pair of diamond earrings. She liked them. They suited her. But she turned them down. He wanted to know why. She said because they were an out-and-out payment. He flushed and said that was foolish. She knew it was. but she had to play her man carefully. The apartment was partly for his convenience. The car too, since he felt her growing importance required new if not expensive transportation. But the earrings? Just a gift.

He put them away and drew her onto his lap. He said he had another gift for her. He told her about the treatment and explained how important how big, her role was going to be. Equal to any in the film! She wanted to know more. He showed her the manuscript and pointed out things, and took her to bed. She sat astride him and teased and tormented him and, when he was sick with desire, satisfied him. (Afterward, she remembered what it was like with Free – that mountain and flying off it and spiraling through valleys of delight.)

That night she dreamed she was walking down a street in Watts, wondering what she was doing there, afraid of being there. But the hard men and boys barely gave her a glance, and she approached the row of little stores and looked at Free's club. And saw herself reflected in that painted-over window. Like a mirror, it threw back her image, and she touched her face and said, 'No!' She was *black*! She rubbed and rubbed but it wouldn't come off. She was really black! Markal wouldn't want her and no other producer would want her and she was a black woman living in that lousy Coontown. Then Free came out and put his arm around her shoulders. 'Hey,' he said softly, 'let's go home.' They went off together and the fear and despair was mixed with singing, with a happiness so big it almost killed the fear and despair. Almost, but not quite.

CARL BAIGLEN

At three-thirty a messenger brought Carl a mimeographed copy of Charles Halpert's treatment for *The Eternal Joneses*. With it was a note from Markal asking him to begin thinking of the special effects that were indicated and to prepare to discuss ways, means and costs sometime within the month – 'just for the budget'.

Carl didn't begin reading, even though he'd been waiting for something specific to do on this assignment and was interested in seeing just what Halpert had done. He was too tense to read. He was expecting a very important phone call.

Just before noon he had received a mimeoed invitation to a party at Nat Markal's Century Plaza suite this Saturday night. He hadn't called to tell Ruth, even though the invitation stated he could bring a guest. He would explain tonight that he had to take Brad Madison for business purposes.

But he couldn't invite Madison. That would be completely out of character. Madison had to invite himself. So Carl sat and waited, hoping. This was the right time, the natural time, to get Madison off his back.

The ex-cop was doing quite well, from what he and his agent and Pen Guilfoyle said. He was actually in demand and not only at Avalon. He'd been working steadily, but he'd also been pushing Carl steadily. He now drove a Porsche 901, and Carl knew the model because he had paid over five thousand dollars for it. He was also pushing hard to test for a part in *Joneses*, and Carl would have to deliver just as soon as Markal began casting for nonstar roles – unless his plan worked. Madison kept saying the time was getting close when he would no longer need Carl's 'help', but Carl felt that time wouldn't come until Brad Madison was as well established as Cary Grant. And Madison had visited his home again just last week and spoken to Ruth and Andy and left his 'regards' for Carl.

The ax was still sharp and ready to fall on Carl's neck, Madison was saying.

At ten to five Cheryl buzzed. Brad Madison was on the line.

'What is it?' Carl asked, making his voice sharp. Madison said, 'Easy, old man. This is social, not business. A little birdie tells me Nat Markal is giving a party this Saturday night. Principals of *The Eternal Joneses* and guests. I'd like to be your guest.'

'I have a wife, remember?'

'Oh yes, I remember very well. Just *you* remember.'

Carl said nothing.

'If you want to take Ruth, get me in as someone else's guest. I don't care how you do it, but I want to be at that party. I want to be introduced to Markal and Devon. I want to meet all the big names.'

'All right,' Carl muttered. After which Madison said he wouldn't be bothering Carl much longer and things were really swinging and he'd landed a fat TV part and a decent bit in a Jerry Lewis movie. 'By the way, I've decided I need a better address. I found something in West Hollywood, a condominium. The down payment is a little steep, but the rental is only a few dollars more than what you've been paying'

Carl said they would talk about it at the party. Madison said fine.

Carl called the Bali-Ho Apartment Hotel and asked for Miss Lane or Miss Smart. Lois, the dark-haired one, answered. She sounded edgy, and he asked, 'Didn't that *Disaster Squad* part come through?' She said yes, but ; . . . and then, emotionally, 'Just because Sugar's the jail bait and you need her more than me don't mean you should get her all the good parts and me just the walkons! It's not fair, Mr. Baiglen!'

He said this was the first he'd heard of it. 'I can only put in a good word with the directors, the casting people. After that it's up to them.'

'We've had four jobs and that's okay. Mr. Baiglen. I sure thank you. You've been real nice and all. But after the first job, when we both had little parts, she's been getting lines and not me. And this last show. *Disaster Squad*, they gave her a *real* part, big enough for a credit, and all I do is sit at a table.'

He didn't know what to say. He wanted them *both* happy, but he couldn't control their careers. That was show biz.

She said, 'I know what you're thinking, but I'm a lot better actress than she is. I mean, I'm the brains of the team. Back home everyone knew that. Sugar knew it too. Only now she's getting a swelled head—'

There was an angry voice in the background. Lois went on, louder. 'She sings better, but we ain't . . . we had no singing parts, so if it was a fair shake I'd be at least even with her, wouldn't I?'

He murmured it seemed that way to him.

'Would you try to talk to that guy Brennen at *Disaster Squad* and tell him I'm at least as good—'

'When it comes to the tests on *Joneses*, I'll make sure you both have equal opportunity. Same lines, same costumes, same everything.' He paused. 'Mr. Markal is giving a party for those connected with the picture. A lot of very important people will be there.'

'Can we go?'

'I'm going to see that you can.' He gave her the particulars, and as she started thanking him said, 'By the way, our friend will be there.'

'You mean the guy we got to—'

He said yes, and he would introduce them at the party and tell her what to do afterward.

She sighed. 'You sure this won't get us in trouble?'

He said it would be less trouble than their normal relations with men.

'That's not trouble,' she said, perking up. 'That's kicks. You ought to find out for yourself, Mr. Baiglen.'

He said he was very tempted but business before pleasure.

'How we gonna do it at a big party like that?'

'I'll have a room on the same floor. He'll go there with you, I'll take a few pictures, and then you can return to the party and mix with all the important people, all the big stars. It might lead to some valuable contacts.' When she began to ask more questions, he said, 'You and Sugar go out and buy gowns. It's a formal party, and I want you to make a good impression on Nat Markal. Send me the bill. Don't be afraid to spend a few hundred.'

'A few *hundred*? You *mean* that?'

He said yes and not to worry about the TV parts because she would get her chance in *Joneses*, he would see to that personally. She sounded like her old self when she thanked him.

He called Pen Guilfoyle and asked about the sisters. 'The brunette, nothing,' Pen said. 'The blonde is something else again. She's funny. Sexy funny, the way Monroe was in her early stuff. You seen any of her footage?'

'No. Should I?'

'You might want to, for *Joneses*. I've put her down with a few other names for Devon. She's got a sappy grin, and with that body of hers ... you wouldn't believe how she photographs. Busting-out-all-over. *Hot*. If she's not too dumb to learn, she might be a valuable property. A pocket-sized Jayne

294

Mansfield. But different. Really different.'

Carl shook his head. What *couldn't* happen in this town! The strange twists. That little blonde slut . . .

He told Cheryl he was leaving for the day. She was busy typing and filing and answering the special *Joneses* phone. She said, 'All right,' looking harried. He asked if the work was getting heavy. She said, 'If it gets any heavier. *I'll* need a secretary.' He said the way her acting was coming along, she would soon be able to drop the secretarial work. She nodded, but didn't offer any information. He left, wondering if Devon was truly sold on her as an actress, or whether it was something else. But why would he fall for Cheryl Carny? No, it must be that she was really good.

He drove to Sawyer's Devil Bar off the Strip. The place was almost empty. Len Sawyer was in a booth, eating a sandwich and reading the L.A. Times. Carl walked over and sat down opposite him. Sawyer looked up. 'Hey, baby, where you been keeping yourself?'

'Oh, around.' He lit a cigarette and waited for the waitress to take his order. Then he said, 'I need a favor.'

'You know me, Carl. Anything for the man who gave work to the worst actor in Hollywood.'

Carl smiled.

Len waited. Carl smoked and looked at the bar. The girl brought his Scotch and he drank it down fast and said, 'No questions, Len.'

Len's face changed, grew worried.

'Relax, it's not money.'

Len relaxed. 'This place keeps me happy, but my savings don't add up to more than a weekend a year at Vegas.'

'A pill.'

Sawyer stared.

'For a gag. A knockout pill, or knockout drops, or whatever they call it.'

Sawyer laughed. 'Why man, that sort of thing is strictly from movies. Bad ones, like I used to be in.'

'I remember one night you had a mean drunk here. Your bartender couldn't get him out and you didn't want the police and he had one drink on the house and within ten minutes he was sleeping.'

Sawyer muttered, 'Well, tranquilizers work like that, if they're strong enough. Like what they shoot into a lion or tiger if he escapes from his cage.'

'Your bartender, Billy, said you kept it in your safe in back. He said—'

'He had a big mouth. That's why he isn't my bartender anymore.'

'I want what put your drunk to sleep. What you keep in the safe in back.'

Len was quiet. Carl said, 'Anything for the guy who gave you parts – and three thousand for the down payment on the Devil Bar.'

'Yeah,' Len said flatly, and got up and went to the bar. He talked to a man drinking beer and went through the door to the kitchen. Carl waved at the waitress and ordered another Scotch. Len came before she did. 'This stuff works different on different people, Carl. I've even heard of it working *too* good!' He gave Carl a white business-size envelope. Carl put it in his breast pocket. The waitress came and Carl gulped his drink. Len said, 'Remember, it's stronger than legal. Remember, it *could* be dangerous—'

At home, Carl opened the envelope. The tube was about half an inch long, the size of a cigarette filter, of clear plastic with a brown rubber stopper. The liquid was colorless and, after an experimental sniff, almost odorless. In an alcoholic drink, it should also be tasteless.

He joined Ruth at the table and asked for Andy. She said he was having dinner at his friend Richard's house. 'Again?' he muttered. She nodded, and said, 'You really *must* talk to him. Find out why he's avoiding his own home.' He said he would, once he cleared up some pressing business. She said something else, but he wasn't listening.

He was worrying. He was visualizing Brad Madison dying and Lois, Sugar and Len pointing accusing fingers at him.

BRAD MADISON

He had followed Andy Baiglen's Honda six times from Beverly Hills west to the newer, equally posh area of Bel Air. Now he was almost certain Carl's son was an active homosexual. Not that he had actually seen anything, contenting himself with simple stakeouts, but the circumstantial evidence was overwhelming.

Andy had slept over twice, on Friday nights, and he and his

296

friend had been alone until three or four in the morning. On both those occasions the house had darkened within moments of Andy's arrival, except for one corner room in back, which meant they had gone directly to a bedroom and spent hours there.

It was now eight-thirty and very dark. After a clear morning, heavy clouds had formed, and Brad Madison had prepared for rain with a new London Fog coat and hat. In fact, he hoped for it, wanting the cover. He sat in his Porsche across the steeply climbing street from the fieldstone ranch belonging (according to the bell plate) to 'Ennis Sewal, Jr.' Mr. Sewal was either divorced or widowed and spent a good many of his evenings away from home. Except for a maid, who left after dinner, Sewal and his son lived alone. Andy was their most frequent visitor.

Madison was using everything he had learned in the police academy and on the force and for once enjoying it. He didn't know what he was going to do with the information he had gathered, but he wanted to go on until he had proof positive of Andy's sex life.

And then? Then he would file it for future reference, for the time Andy was legally an adult and Brad was no longer squeezing Carl Baiglen.

He stared at the lighted living room window and thought of the delicious boy inside and thought how different it would be with him than with Mickey.

He had removed the mask with Mickey, but only in the rawest physical sense. Mickey was a male prostitute who had picked Brad Madison up on the street outside the Molina Blanca. 'All the shy boys go there,' he had laughed later. 'All the big strong boys who want and can't. Like you, lover.' Mickey was strictly cash – twenty dollars each and every time. Mickey was a bitchy, dangerous queen, volatile and cruel, who took heroin and had a police record and couldn't be trusted with a man's name and address. Brad knew it was insane to mess with Mickey, but he hadn't been able to approach anyone else, anyone on his own level.

Or was it that he didn't want anyone but Andy Baiglen?

Rain began to fall. Brad squirmed into his coat. Andy Baiglen was game, something to kill a few lonely evenings, a game that would end tonight.

He smoked and waited – waited a full half-hour before the door across the street opened. The stocky man hesitated, speaking to someone inside, then ran to the Chevy Impala in the driveway. He backed out, swung around and drove off. Within five minutes the light in the fieldstone ranch house went out – all except that back corner room with one window on the driveway near the garage.

Brad Madison waited another ten minutes to give them time to get past the preliminaries, then turned the Porsche's dome light to 'Off', opened the door and stepped into the rain. Now he would get his proof positive and end the game.

He crossed the street, bending his head and moving quickly and trying not to think of the chance he was taking. The driveway had a tall wall of hedging on the left, but the neighboring house was a two-story affair with windows that easily overlooked it. It didn't stop him. He had his story prepared. He retained his Devereux badge and could flash it should anyone but an officer question him. He was a plainclothesman checking on reports of a prowler in the neighborhood.

It was the window that stopped him. He stood in the rain, staring at it, wondering what to do next. It was completely covered by drawn venetian blinds, which allowed a certain amount of light to seep out but no sight at all to get in. He looked toward the garage and thought he saw some reflection of light there too. He walked another few steps and was at a back yard. There was a gate, unlocked, and a second lighted window.

He was in luck. The blinds were carefully drawn, but not as carefully lowered. By stooping a bit, he could see through an inch-wide gap into a boy's room, complete with model ships and sports pennants.

He moved his eyes from left to right, sweeping the room. On his left was a large blind area, then came a door, closed, and a dresser, and the bed, and a closet. But no boys. He looked to the left again. He shifted as far right as he could, to diminish that blind area – and there they were, up against the wall, embracing! He caught his breath. Andy had his hand inside the stocky boy's fly.

The rain increased, began to lash down in heavy waves, but Brad Madison didn't move. He watched for more than half an hour, and when he left he was gasping as if he had run miles. Andy was the most beautiful being he had ever seen. Andy was a little Greek god.

Mickey was a poor substitute, but all he had. He drove to the downtown Los Angeles rooming house and climbed the flight of

298

stairs and knocked. Mickey's high voice called out, *Entrez*, baby, I'm alone.' Brad went inside. The plump man with bleached blond hair was lying on the couch bed, watching television. He wore pale yellow stretch pants and a loose white shirt. 'In a minute,' Mickey said, and ignored Brad until the next commercial. 'So it's you, my handsome, helpless hunk? How about thirty green ones this time? I've got a wild pink jock—'

Brad Madison stood up, fists clenched. Mickey said, 'Well, cool it, sweetie, I was only testing, one-two-three-four testing.' Brad Madison didn't explain that it wasn't Mickey he was raging at but himself. For being here. For not having the guts to go out and find someone like Andy.

He turned to the door. Mickey jumped off the couch and caught his arm. 'Hey, *toro*, you're something else again tonight. Let Doctor Michael ease your tensions.' His fingers rubbed Brad's stomach, then slid down.

After what he had seen tonight, it was ugly, it was repellent! He flung his arm, out, slamming Mickey back against the wall. The prostitute squealed and spewed obscenities. Brad turned to him, thinking it was too bad Mickey had gotten between Brad Madison and his self-contempt. He swung once, a short right that caught Mickey under the ear. Mickey toppled and lay on his face. He was just beginning to groan when Brad left.

At home he had two stiff drinks, then showered. Nude, he went to the bedroom to get pajamas and saw himself in the dresser mirror. He stepped back for a better view and felt a tingle of narcissistic excitement. If Andy was a little Greek god, Brad Madison was a *big* Greek god. It was all there – the bone structure and muscle and firm flesh. It was all there, and in perfect balance.

He stared at himself. The excitement grew.

He was *beautiful*! He had known it, yet not *felt* it until now. He was beautiful as few people were. He was desirable as few people were. If a man were to see him as he saw himself in that mirror . . .

There would be men he could respect, men he could desire, at Markal's party Saturday night. Some of the biggest names in show business would be there.

He went to bed. He was calm now, happy, now, as he had never been after a session with Mickey. The time had come at last to rid himself of the mask, to throw it away forever.

It had taken a little over five months to kill Patrolman John

McNaughton. Not too bad, when you considered he had dominated Brad Madison for twenty-six years. Not bad at all. He
had been unrealistic to expect an *immediate* change.

The party. The party would be John McNaughton's funeral.

CHARLEY HALPERT

Charley came home early Friday evening. He had left Avalon
at a few minutes after four, drained of energy and will-to-write,
but happy. He had written his opening scene, and it was what
he wanted it to be. More than that, he had suddenly understood he *could* write scripts.

It was that simple. One scene – ten minutes to read and ab-
sorb one scene, and doubt had begun to vanish.

He had just put on his trunks when there was a knock. He
went to the door, opened it a little, stood behind it to look outside. 'Hey,' Lois said, strangely solemn, 'just like the first time,
remember, with you standing behind the door?' She put her
hand inside and touched him, as she had the first time, but
briefly. He opened the door and she came inside and he kissed
her, not so briefly. He said, 'Well now, it's been quite a while.'
She was passive in his arms. 'Yeah,' she said. 'You know how it
is. We been working some and dating some and besides, you
got that fat secretary.' He let her go. She walked to the couch
and sat down. He studied the lean brunette a moment. 'You
aren't sick, are you?' he asked.

'You better know it, daddy. Sick to death of that sister of
mine. You know what she said to me this morning? We got up
together to go to the studio where we got lunch dates with these
two guys from a production company and she says' – she pursed
her lips and made her face silly and raised her voice to a
squeak – "Now you let me handle the important one 'cause
he's got it bad for me and we want to get started in features." '
She looked at Charley. 'You ever hear such shit? Pardon, but
you ever *hear* shit like that? She can't say two words without
me helping her and she wants to handle the producer and I
should get the assistant. Just because Lou Grayson shoved his
hand up her twat last week and I wasn't about to let him treat
me like that and he saw it and went to her. I mean, everyone
knows Grayson. He'd screw a cow if she'd let him. That's right,
isn't it?'

'So they say,' Charley murmured, and went to the couch and sat down beside her. He took her and and patted it. 'Sugar's a baby. You're the big sister. You'll have to be understanding.'

'Understanding? Why man, I've been so goddam understanding it's coming out my ears. And anway, it's not that she's acting like a baby. More like a *bitch*!'

Charley wanted to turn her off, change the subject. He said he felt funny sitting in just trunks and would slip on a robe. She said, 'You shouldn't oughta, Chuckey. You've been looking good lately.'

He said sure and he'd start going to the studio in his BVDs soon. She smiled a little, but then said, 'And at lunch she hogged the conversation and kept getting them to talk to her and freezing me out. Not that I couldn't stop her dead if I'd wanted to, but in front of those guys—' She plunged her face into Charley's bare chest and wept. 'I don't know what's wrong. I swear to God I don't!'

She was lying. She knew what was wrong. So did Charley. He had heard talk about Sugar Smart on the lot. Cheryl said she was getting bids from several big agents. Moe Sholub had asked Charley questions, having heard Sugar was his neighbor, and indicated he was thinking of casting her as a teen-aged prostitute in *Streets*. And there was a photograph of her floating around – Sugar as a topless-bottomless dancer. Word was the photographer had placed similar shots in half a dozen men's magazines and was hopeful about a spread in *Playboy*.

Lois had been photographed too, but no pictures of *her* were causing comment. Lois had been with Sugar on every TV assignment they'd had, but Moe Sholub wasn't asking about *her*, no one was talking about *her*.

He stroked her head and said she had to be patient and that little sisters often got headstrong. 'After all, what difference does it make *who* had the good fortune? It's share and share alike, isn't it?'

She calmed down. She put her head on his chest. 'I guess it'll work out,' she muttered. 'It's just that I got to get a real *acting* part.' She paused, and he knew what was coming. 'Is there anyone you can talk to, Chuck? Anyone you can get to give me a chance, a *real* chance, to show my talent?'

He said he would speak to Alan Devon, but not to count on anything.

She turned her lips to his flesh. She stroked his arm and murmured, 'You always been *right* with us. Chuck. You gave

301

us our start when you drove us on the lot that time.' She paused. 'You're doing pretty good now, aren't you?'

He said yes, ready to agree to lend her money. But she said, 'Someday, after *Joneses* is out and I've shown what I can do, someday you and me we'll get together. I mean we'll spend some time talking and having kicks, just you and me alone.'

He said, 'I'm flattered.'

'We'll both be big time,' she murmured, eyes closed. 'We'll both be loaded and famous and if we want to, well, we could make it permanent.' She opened her eyes. 'You're not too old, Chuckey. And you're ditching that wife of yours, right?'

He laughed a little and sat her up straight and said she was getting ahead of the game. Her face changed. 'The brush', she muttered grimly. 'That's all I been getting lately, the brush. Even an old guy—'

He said it wasn't the brush and took her in his arms and tried to kiss her. She stood up. 'You just wait till *Joneses* is shot! You just wait! Carl's not a make-out producer and he's giving us both the same chance and I'm going to show what I can do. I'm going to *act* and she can't beat me when it comes to acting. And then *you'll* come begging—'

There was a knock at the door. She said, 'Guess who?' and sat down again and took his arm. He said, 'Come in,' and it was Sugar. She smiled at them. 'Hey, a kicky little scene. I'm not interrupting any action, am I?' Lois said, coldly, 'Yes, you are.' Sugar came to the couch and sat down on Charley's other side and took his other arm. 'Well, the way it looks it's either finished or not started yet, so I'll stay.' Lois jumped up. 'Then I'll leave.'

Charley pulled her down again and talked quickly and told them they had to get along better than this because after all who did they have but each other? 'Everyone else is out for something,' he said. 'Everyone else is looking to use you' – he paused – 'as much as you're looking to use them. So Lois and Sugar must remember they're in this thing together, make it or not. Lois and Sugar' – and here he turned to Sugar – 'have to carry each other, help each other, no matter who has the good month, the good year. Lois and Sugar are sisters, and that's more important than casting directors and producers.'

They were quiet; then Lois muttered, 'Well, sure, *I* know that,' and Sugar shrugged and said. '*Everyone* knows that, and Charley said they'd drink to it. He went to the kitchen to pour three bourbons over ice and the girls talked to each other, cautiously, and Sugar said she'd come to find Lois because the woman at the dress shop had called to say their alterations would be completed tomorrow noon. Charley brought the drinks and Sugar said it was the first time he'd offered them whiskey and he replied he was forgetting she was underage in honor of the peace treaty.

'You forgot it other times too,' she said, rubbing his knee as he sat down. 'A different kind of *piece* treaty.'

He raised his glass and they drank, Lois taking it down like a trouper and Sugar sipping and clearing her throat and sipping again. The girls kissed him and Sugar said remember-the-first-time-in-your-shorts and he had another drink and Lois said let's-do-it-just-like-that-first-time and he wanted them and was happy and had a third drink and was sad because Sugar was the one he wanted most and that was the way it would be, Sugar the one everyone would want most. They got into bed and he concentrated on Lois and was sadder still because she used it, drew attention to it, and it meant nothing to Sugar who was the one everyone would want and kept smiling and kept looking at her sister with eyes that didn't smile.

He had two more drinks after they left and was high when he ate a sandwich and then had another two drinks, getting higher still, and this was in celebration of that first *Joneses* scene and in memoriam of Lois Lane who was going to die a lot of little deaths in the near future. And had a final drink to bury his relationship with the sisters, which he had ended in his mind as soon as they'd left, ended as it had begun – 'in his shorts' and with both of them talking away – only this time the talk had been a cover for something sad, for change and growth and little deaths.

BERTHA KRAUS

Bertha had always admired Cary Grant and tingled to Marlon Brando, and while she'd met both in the course of her secretarial duties this was the first time she'd ever had a drink with Grant and been offered a canapé by Brando. Neither had signed for *Joneses*, and neither was likely to, not only because of the enormous price each commanded but also because Markal didn't want Avalon's Gordon Hewlett overshadowed.

There were many other big names present. Markal was seen

303

talking very seriously to Audrey Hepburn and Marlene Diet-
rich. But here there was no possible conflict with Mona
Dearn, since the three were stars of totally different casting
caliber. Markal also talked to Lorne Greene of *Bonanza*, Bill
Cosby of *I Spy*, and several other television personalities.

The four-room suite filled up as the evening progressed,
until by ten it had wall-to-wall people. Bertha eventually found
herself near her employer. After complimenting her on her
evening gown, he said, 'I expected a few crashers, a few extra
guests on some invitations, but I think we've got a third more
than we invited. A mark of success, I guess.' Then he was drawn
into a four-way conversation with two agents and a publicist.
Mrs. Markal hadn't put in an appearance, which was unusual.

Cheryl Carny in cocktail gown was standing with Charles
Halpert in business suit, and both nodded at her.

Lars Wyllit was wearing what looked like green corduroy
coveralls with buckskin game-warden boots – a standout in the
crowd. Mona Dearn came over to him, as Bertha squeezed by,
and ruffled his hair. There was much talk about those two.

Isa Yee was chatting with a very tall, very good-looking
man, who waved as Carl Baiglen entered the main room. Baiglen pushed over to him, and the good-looking man excused
himself and moved away with the producer.

Terry Hanford, Pen Guilfoyle and Tyrone Chalze were off
in a corner together.

Alan Devon was talking with Sol Soloway and Ron Besser,
but the situation was saved from being an eyebrow-raiser by the
presence of Lou Grayson and his blonde, pretty, sad-faced wife.
Grayson would be on reasonably good behavior tonight, though
his eyes flickered constantly, casing the females in the room.

Nat Markal now dominated a group including Rock Hudson, Paul Newman, a top man at William Morris and Freda
Breghoff, a free-lance critic appearing in egghead magazines.
Bertha again felt pride in working for him and, yes, affection
for the man himself, the fine and wonderful man himself. Nat
Markal was unique in Hollywood. Nat Markal was someone to
respect on every level.

She smiled at people and moved on. Olive Dort stood near
the bar table, talking to several columnists, including Sidney
Skolsky – doing *Joneses* little good, Bertha supposed, but
Markal couldn't be worried about her because she'd been invited this time.

Bertha met George Doherty of UP. They were old friends

and talked about two subjects dear to both their hearts: the L.A. Rams and the Ecumenical Council. George had been widowed six months ago and was only now coming out of mourning. After a pause in the conversation he asked her to lunch. She said, 'When you're feeling more like it, George,' and he nodded and they went back to the Rams. He was a sweet man – a face like a basketball and a body like a fireplug, but a genuine human being. Later, after bringing her a plate of cold lobster and tossed salad, he again asked her to lunch, saying he was 'lonely for some good talk'. She looked at him closely. 'Are you trying for inside information on *Joneses*, George?' He flushed. 'You know better than that, Bertha.' She said, 'Well, I *thought* I did, but all this insistence on lunch when we never before—' He flushed again, deeply, and she suddenly felt herself fishing too.

George Doherty? Good old George Doherty? At this late stage of their lives? No. It was ridiculous.

He didn't get the chance to mention lunch again because Nat Markal found her and asked her to find Charles Halpert. 'Bring him to me. I want him to meet people. The way he talks about *Joneses*, he's better than the whole publicity department – especially with a highbrow like Freda Breghoff who won't even tour our Washington set.'

Bertha found Halpert with Lars Wyllit and Isa Yee. She brought him to Markal and began looking for George, thinking he'd been lonely . . . but that was when Pier Andrei started shouting at the top of her lungs at a young blonde about being jostled and insulted. She was really plastered and tried to claw the blonde, but the blonde and another girl, a brunette, grabbed her arms in a very professional manner and quieted her down. Markal talked to Pier a while and she cried and left, staggering and looking like the end of the world. Bertha felt sick, really sick, when she remembered how Pier had looked the first time she saw her. Pier Andrei had been almost *too* beautiful.

As she began looking for George again, one of her favorite crooners stood up on a chair and announced a parody of *The Jones Boy*.

> The whole town's talking about the Joneses,
> The Joneses,
> The Joneses,
> The whole town's talking about the *Jooneses*
> That Metro's making to Nat Markal.

The second verse got naughty and the third, fourth and fifth naughtier still. Some of it couldn't have been much fun for Mona Dearn and Gordon Hewlett, but they smiled and took it in good spirits. And so did Bertha, though her face got red. Then a rock 'n' roller got up and sang three more verses, really rough ones, and Bertha had a second drink and found herself laughing much too loud. But everyone else was doing the same and she didn't care, she was that relaxed and happy. She could see Nat Markal standing beside the Eurasian actress, Isa Yee, and Bertha caught his eye and they exchanged a glance and he shook his head, laughing. It was just the most *wonderful* party!

ISA YEE

Someone took Nat Markal away to introduce him to someone else, and Isa found herself with Charles Halpert and Lars Wyllit. The first time Halpert mentioned Watts, Isa merely nodded, agreeing with him as anyone would that it would be helpful to see the place before writing about it. Then he and Lars Wyllit got into a discussion of the Negro as he would appear in *Joneses*. Wyllit said there should be fewer scenes but a sharper definition of his changing status. Halpert said maybe, but how much had his status *really* changed? A close reading of history, he said, would show the Negro had always been in revolt against white society, from the first plantation insurrections to the burning of Watts. Wyllit said that was broad-scale sociology when what was needed was close-up drama. Halpert said broad-scale or close-up, nice houses or ghetto rooms, high income or low, the Negro was still in revolt because the Negro was still looked at as a Negro. And not as a *man*.

Isa remembered what Free had said that first time in her apartment, explaining that 'selling black' meant making Negroes believe they were men and women.

Wyllit made an impatient gesture. 'You're intellectualizing. The reality of the situation is that most Americans feel the *Negro* has to carry the ball. If he says, Learn Baby Learn, we're his friends. If he says, Burn Baby Burn, we're his enemies. In self-defense, we're his enemies.'

'In self-defense,' Halpert murmured, 'be his friend.'

'I hope you don't put too much of that into *Joneses*, Chuck. It'll antagonize the audience, including the majority of Negroes.'

Halpert smiled and said he wondered about that majority. 'It's one of the reasons I want to visit Watts. Do you know anyone who lives there?'

Wyllit said his cleaning lady, but she hadn't been handing out invitations. That was when Isa said, 'Emma, a makeup assistant at Avalon, lives in Watts. She's a friendly sort. Want me to speak to her?'

Halpert said *wonderful* and he hoped Lars would come along. Wyllit said sure and called to Terry Hanford, who was nearby with Jerry Storm. She came over and Wyllit said Terry should be in on it too, as publicist for *Joneses*. She said all right, though without much enthusiasm. Wyllit said, 'It's settled then, Chuck. You and Isa, me and Terry,' and took Terry's arm. Isa was sure Terry stiffened and in order to stop anything unpleasant from developing she took Halpert's arm and vamped it up. Later, Halpert asked, 'When can you arrange it?' She said she would prefer to wait until she was finished with an assignment. He nodded. 'The Watts sequences aren't until the last part of the script.'

A month or so, they decided. She would let them know. And then they separated.

Later, she was upset with herself. Why had she opened her mouth? Why did she want to go back to that lousy Coontown?

She gave herself an answer. It wasn't the truth, but it made sense. Helping Halpert was helping *Joneses,* the movie that would make her a star. So helping Halpert was helping herself.

She had a drink. She ate lobster salad. She talked to lots of good-looking men. But she couldn't lose the feeling of discomfort, the vague premonition of something going wrong.

CARL BAIGLEN

While the parodies were being sung, Carl managed to take Lois and Sugar aside. Smiling in case anyone looked his way, he whispered to the blonde, 'Of all the times to cause a disturbance!' She whispered right back, 'I didn't cause anything! The guy she was with started talking to me, and she blew sky high.

307

She's got the sign of the sauce – a real lush!' He said, 'All right,' checking his watch. It was eleven o'clock, time to make a move. 'Just be sure you can see me from now on.' They nodded, and he left to find Madison.

It was Madison who found him. 'Carl.' He turned at the tap on his shoulder. 'I haven't met Markal yet.'

'He's got a million people—'

'I want to meet him now,' Madison said peremptorily and finished what looked like a martini. Carl said, 'After I have a Scotch,' and began to move off. Madison moved with him. As they came in sight of the bar table, Carl saw Alan Devon. The producer was just turning away from a stout couple when Carl said, 'Alan, here's someone you should meet.' He introduced them and quickly asked, 'What're you two drinking?' Devon said Scotch, Madison said an extra dry martini, Carl said, 'Back in a minute.' He went to the bar, reaching into his pocket and touching the tiny plastic tube, his head pounding with more than the noise of the party. He ordered three drinks, downed his while standing at the table, lit a cigarette and looked around. Madison and Devon were talking. Carl took the tube from his pocket, holding it in his right hand, and with his left flicked ashes from his cigarette. He smoked a while, then ground the cigarette into an ashtray and at the same time pried the rubber stopper from the tube with his thumb. He raised the martini, put his right hand over it as if to switch hands, and poured the mickey. Then he put down the glass, felt around in his pocket as if looking for something, and rid himself of tube and cork.

As he carried the drinks away from the table, he saw Lois and Sugar talking to four young men. Sugar was really pouring on the charm, but Lois glanced his way and he knew she would see to it that the deal went through – for that equal chance at a dramatic role in *Joneses*.

All right. The first part of his plan was in operation. He wouldn't think of what remained. So much was up to chance: how soon the drug acted. How strongly it acted. Whether anyone would interfere by trying to help Madison. Whether he could get Madison down the hall to the room he'd rented earlier in the day. And that one terrifying possibility – that the drug would kill the ex-cop.

He reached the two men and handed them their drinks and began talking about Halpert's treatment. Madison took a long sip and looked at his glass. Carl went rigid. Madison sipped

308

again, pursing his lips. 'When do you think you'll be testing for supporting roles, Mr. Devon?'

Devon said it all depended on when the writers completed a first draft.

Carl said he didn't think it would take long, the treatment was that complete. Devon said, 'Maybe *too* complete, Carl. I know I'm in the minority, but there are things about Halpert's approach that worry me.' Madison drank and lit a cigarette. Carl asked him for one, but Madison didn't seem to hear. He was rubbing at his eyes. 'Getting stuffy, isn't it?' Devon nodded, and asked Carl if he'd done any thinking about the special effects. Carl said yes, a little. Devon said the disaster scenes in Halpert's treatment would cost five million alone – not counting that enormous Washington set. Carl said not with the proper effects, and he would work to keep costs down. Madison swayed, muttered, 'I'm not feeling—' and dropped both glass and cigarette. Devon jumped back, his trousers splattered. Carl grabbed Madison around the waist, said, 'Let's get some fresh air,' and moved him away. He looked back at Devon, who was staring after them, and mouthed, '*Lush.*' Then he concentrated on reaching the hall door.

It wasn't easy. Madison was a heavy load to support and with every step more of that load was sagging against Carl. 'Sick,' he mumbled. 'My head . . . sick—'

They kept bumping into people, and Carl kept saying, 'Pardon,' and smiling knowingly. About ten feet from the door Madison began to crumple. Carl took a tighter hold, but had to come to a stop. He didn't know how he was going to continue and was just beginning to feel panic when the girls arrived. Lois took Madison around the waist from the other side and said, 'Sugar, walk in front.' Madison's head fell all the way forward. They began moving again. Madison made a whistling exhalation that sounded just like a death rattle in a Carl Baiglen production, and Carl's mouth went bone dry.

Somehow, they reached the hall. Madison's feet were dragging. He was dead weight between Carl and Lois, and the girl gasped, 'You sure he's *alive* to take pictures?'

Carl said, 'Just drank too much,' and pushed on, struggling to keep Madison from falling and himself from panicking. They reached the door to his room, but he couldn't let go to open it. He told Sugar the key was in the left pocket of his jacket and prayed no one would come along. After an interminable period of fumbling she got it and opened the door. She couldn't find

309

the light switch, but Carl didn't wait. He lunged forward and the doorway was too small and Lois let go. Madison began falling and Carl made a supreme effort and practically threw him inside. Sugar found the light. 'Close the door!' Carl snapped. Then they all looked at Madison, who lay on his back, absolutely still. Carl bent quickly and put his ear to Madison's chest. The heartbeat was loud and clear. He straightened, trembling with relief. 'Okay, let's get his clothes off.'

Fifteen minutes later Brad Madison was on the bed, flat on his back, arms outstretched, breathing heavily through his open mouth. He was naked except for black socks and garters, which Carl felt was the proper adult costume for Impairing the Morals of a Minor, Statutory Rape, and Unnatural Acts.

He had set up his cameras – a Rollei on a tripod and a hand-held thirty-millimeter Nikon, both with strobe flash units – which he'd brought to the room before the party. Sugar was removing her gown and Carl asked her to hurry up. She said, 'It took half an hour to get into these kicky threads, and I'm not ruining it for *anything*. I'm meeting Mr. Markal, remember?' Finally, she was down to skin – and very delicious skin it was, Carl admitted. He told her to get on the bed and embrace Madison, to fondle and kiss him, to place his hands in strategic locations. She did, and he used the Rollei. Then he moved around the bed with the Nikon, giving instructions and taking close-ups. After a while he went back to the Rollei. And after that he said, 'It's not absolutely necessary, but I'd like to get a proper response from him. A doctor assured me we could.'

The blonde looked Madison over and said, 'I hope he's right. But out cold like this? You sure?'

Lois said, 'He's something else again, Carl. Real tough. What'd he do that you have to squash him?'

Carl said never mind, just work on him. Sugar worked and Lois joined her and the two did just about everything Carl had ever heard of and seemed to enjoy it. He took pictures and knew he had more than enough and was about to call a halt when Madison stirred and sighed. A moment later Sugar raised her head. 'He's getting there?' Madison's eyes flickered. Sugar went back to work. Madison groaned. Lois said, 'Even when they're half-dead!'

Carl gave new instructions. Sugar got on Madison. Carl worked quickly, reloading on the move, anticipating an end to the situation. But he was able to total a hundred shots with the Nikon and thirty-six with the Rollei and Madison's condition still hadn't changed. Carl sank into an armchair, sweating. Sugar looked at him. 'You finished?'

He nodded.

'Mind if *I* finish?'

He laughed. 'Be my guest.'

She didn't have to worry about camera angles now. 'You know,' she panted, 'it's kinda kicky this way, him out and being watched and pictures and all.' Lois came over to Carl and they both watched and Lois cleared her throat. 'I know you don't cheat on your wife, but after all *this*—' She sat on the arm of the chair and stroked his neck.

Madison moaned and rolled his head. Sugar kissed him and whispered sweet obscenities. Carl hesitated then said, 'Not that I wouldn't enjoy it—' Sugar suddenly stopped and looked down. Her obscenities ceased being sweet. Lois laughed. 'He's beddybye again.' Sugar left the bed and looked at Carl. Lois said, 'Uh-uh. The man won't play.' Sugar sighed and began dressing. Lois said, 'Don't forget now, Carl. We helped you, and you're going to help us.'

He said he had and would continue to. Lois kissed his cheek. 'When I get married I want someone like you. I mean, a *saint* would've cracked after all this!' Sugar was fixing her makeup and said, 'For me, get a guy like the one on the bed. You see the *size* of him? I don't mean his height either, baby!'

They both laughed and started for the door, then looked back at Carl. He said, 'I'll be along in a while to introduce you to Nat Markal.' Lois said, 'Groovy!' and they left. He went to the bed and covered Madison's nakedness with the bedspread. 'Brad, wake up!' Madison stirred. Carl slapped his face, six times, as hard as he could. Madison mumbled and moved his head, but didn't awaken. Carl raised his fist. 'You bastard! I've got you now, you faggot bastard!' He turned away without throwing the punch. Everything had gone beautifully, and he would have the pleasure of showing Madison those photographs and telling him to go to hell. That was enough.

He gathered his equipment and put it in his gray suitcase. He took the suitcase to the basement garage and locked it in the trunk of his car. Then he returned to the party.

He introduced the girls to Nat Markal, and Markal said something that made Sugar glow and Lois look grim as death. 'Yes, Miss Smart, I've heard all sorts of good things about you. A fine prospect for *Joneses,* I'm told,' Carl quickly said

Miss Lane was also a fine prospect, as a screen test would prove, and Markal nodded and turned back to Charles Halpert and two men Carl didn't know.

The crowd thinned out at one, and some of the younger people began dancing to rock 'n' roll from a hi-fi. Carl saw Sugar with Bobby Chankery, one of the fastest-moving actors' representatives in the business. Bobby moved fast with Sugar too. When they left shortly afterward, Chankery's hand was resting in casual proprietorship on her rear.

Lois wasn't doing so well. She continued dancing with a young assistant director who had come as Devon's guest, and assistant anythings were a dime a dozen.

Carl said good night to Markal and Halpert, congratulating both on the treatment. Then he went down the hall to his room. Madison had turned on his side and seemed to be sleeping normally. Carl shook him. Madison's eyes flickered and he mumbled, 'What is it?' but he didn't awaken.

Carl went home. It was after three when he got into bed, but he kissed Ruth until she opened her eyes. 'That must've been *some* party,' she said, and came into his arms.

NAT MARKAL

He told Isa to leave with the last of the guests, then to return. It was after five when she really left, and it was after six when he reached home and walked down the main foyer past Adele's room. The house was dark, asleep, and he would be able to claim a much earlier return . . .

'Nat?'

He froze. 'Yes, dear, it's me, go back to sleep.'

'I wasn't asleep.'

She didn't sound angry. He walked to the doorway. She was sitting up, the pillow propped against the headboard – sitting in the darkness. 'I woke at four. You weren't here, and I couldn't get back to sleep. Tell me about the party.'

'At breakfast. I'm exhausted.' He came to the bed. She offered her cheek for his kiss. 'Sleep here tonight,' she murmured.

He hesitated. Isa had given him everything. Isa had thrilled and satisfied him and emptied him of desire. The thought of touching Adele actually repelled him at the moment.

312

'If you don't want to—' She slid down, pulling the pillow with her.

'Of course I want to. But I have to shower first. It'll be half an hour—'

'And you're exhausted. I know. Good night.'

He laughed. 'Don't tell me you're jealous of your fifty-year-old husband?'

'I'm fifty-one.'

And she looked it. Every year of it and more. The face was puffy, the neck sagging, the breasts flaccid. She was an aging woman, and he had the most beautiful girl in Hollywood for his own.

But she was also his wife, his friend and partner in the long years of struggle. If youth and beauty were the only qualifications for a lasting marriage, half the country would be divorced tomorrow.

He bent and kissed her. She put her arms around him – but no matter what he *wanted* to feel, he couldn't make her any younger or more desirable.

He couldn't think now, couldn't handle his feelings now. He straightened. 'I'll be back in a while.' He went to his room and undressed. Isa's scent was on his chest and shoulders and probably elsewhere.

He tingled. He wanted to be with her. She had been particularly avid and creative tonight. That was after he had told her she was getting a lead role, a tour-de-force role on *The Glenmore Theatre,* Avalon's most prestigious television show. He had offered Clete a special budget and suggested he sign a top male lead to play opposite her in the adaptation of a Prix Goncourt novel. He'd explained it as part of the continuing buildup of *Joneses* actors.

He showered and got into pajamas and then decided to shave. It was almost seven and growing light when he moved barefoot through the short connecting foyer to Adele's door. He listened a moment, then opened it slowly. She was lying on her side, breathing softly, evenly. He made a little throat-clearing sound, waited a moment, then backed gratefully out of the room. Just before he closed the door, he thought he heard her move. But when he stopped to listen he heard nothing. He went back to his room and fell into immediate, heavy slumber.

He woke at one, Sunday afternoon, and Adele was gone, along with Lainie. 'Her mother's,' Tess said, serving him a fluffy omelet, toast, sausage and coffee. He shook his head at the

313

omelet and toast, and nibbled a sausage and drank his coffee black. Tess muttered to herself as she cleared the table. He said, 'Now don't get sensitive. You know I'm dieting.'

'And the missus not eating 'cause she has headaches and Lainie not eating 'cause she's busy asking the missus what's wrong and the only one eats anything around here is me 'cause it's a sin to let such food go to waste.'

'Headaches? When did this start?'

She muttered it wasn't her place to tell a husband his wife's troubles, and he said he'd been unusually busy lately, and she said, 'That's why the headaches. If you was *my* mister—'

Angrily, he said, 'That's enough!' and went into the study to phone Century Towers. Isa answered, her voice sleepy. He said he found himself free. She said she had planned to 'just laze around the apartment.'

'Laze around the suite instead.'

'The way *we* laze, I can barely walk afterward.'

He laughed, inflamed on the instant, and murmured. 'Please.'

'All right. Give me an hour.'

He dressed in one of his new, leaner-cut suits and went to the garage. He decided on the Ferrari Berlinetta. He hadn't used it a dozen times this year. It was a young man's car, a lucky man's car – and he was beginning to feel very young and very lucky.

Perhaps later he would take Isa for a ride. Perhaps later they would go up the coast toward Oxnard and stop some place where Nat Markal wasn't known and have a seafood dinner. She had been very good about not going out together, but every so often she let him know she wanted to. So did he, for that matter. He was proud of Isa. He wanted other men to see her and to envy him for being with her. It was, as she would say, part of his kick.

Yes, after it got dark.

Or better still, In New York next week.

But Adele would expect to go along.

He would find some way to discourage Adele. A two-day trip, he would say (and then stretch it into four or five). A mad, mad rush centered around a press conference with no opportunity for relaxation or pleasure.

He went down the steep driveway and put on the FM radio and drove to the Pacific Coast Highway. He refused to worry about Adele and her decision to spend all day and perhaps the night away from him. Tomorrow night or the night after he would reassure her, would give proof of his love.

It was a bright day – sun above and sea off to his right and young people stopping to stare at the Berlinetta and the whole world glistening like new. A gray Ford sedan swung into his rear-view mirror, and he glanced at it and hummed along with the music. He had no reason to suspect the Ford was following him, and if he had, would have assumed it was one of Arnold Ryan's personal spot checks – the random-interval followings by car to make sure no other car was following him.

Except that the man behind the wheel looked nothing like Ryan.

CHARLEY HALPERT

Wednesday morning Charley picked up his mail before leaving for the studio. There were two ads, a registered letter from Ben Kalik, an airmail letter from Collin Warner. He got into his car and opened Collin's first.

> Dear Charley:
> I'm looking forward to seeing you late this week. The papers say Nat Markal and many of those associated with *The Eternal Joneses* will be flying into New York. Let's get together for lunch at the Gold Coin. If you bring Celia, I'll bring old Judy, even though her belly's rather unwieldy now that it's seven months' big. I'll call Celia to find out just when you're arriving . . .

Charley put the letter aside without finishing it. Why the hell couldn't Collin mind his own business!

He tore open Kalik's letter so roughly he almost tore the checks inside. One for nine thousand dollars – ten thousand minus the agent's ten percent – in final payment for the treatment. And another for twenty-two thousand five hundred – twenty-five thousand minus the ten percent – as advance payment on the script.

He sat there holding thirty-one thousand five hundred dollars and tried to *feel* it. He had never had that much money at one time in all his life. It meant security for at least two years, and there was more to come.

Somehow, he couldn't grasp it. Great. Yeah. But he had that enormous script to write – which was why he wasn't flying to

New York. Just too much work to do. Just too dangerous to break the forward movement . . .

All right! He didn't *want* to go home! It would rip open all the old wounds and accomplish nothing.

And he was really moving now. Lars was helping by setting up a sort of technical chart for the various scenes in the treatment, by changing an occasional bit of dialogue or camera direction, but mainly by staying out of the way. Devon had asked to see his daily output and he'd said it was impossible – he wouldn't show *anyone* less than fifty pages. He knew by the way Devon stalked out he would complain to Markal and later in the day had received the expected call from Emperor Nat. Before he could attempt to explain, Markal said, 'I told Alan he was to let you work your own way. I told him I'd check you myself, after a reasonable interval.' He paused. '*You* can set that interval.'

He returned to Collin's letter and read about friends who were selling books and friends who had given up trying to sell books, then heard his name and looked up. A white Falcon convertible had pulled alongside him. Sugar was behind the wheel, laughing and waving.

'Now don't tell me you've given up hitchhiking?'

'I signed with Bob Chankery! He gave me an advance! He figures out how much a client's going to make, *minimum*, and he carries them along! He said I needed a car, so we went together and *look*! The *kickiest*, isn't it!'

Lois sat beside her, slouched low and casual. She gave Charley a little nod. Sugar seemed to remember her and quickly added, 'Bob's going to keep his eye on Lois. He says maybe in a few months—'

Lois said, 'I got my own agent lined up.'

Sugar looked at her. 'Who?'

'Never you mind. Meanwhile Central Casting and my own contracts are good enough. When I sign it'll be with someone big, like Jerry Storm.'

Sugar laughed. Lois sat up, face paling. 'Now listen—'

Charley said, 'You going to the studio?'

Sugar nodded excitedly. 'I'm speaking lines today! *Disaster Squad!* And if I told you who I was having lunch with you'd die!' She sang a few words in imitation of a famous rock 'n' roller. 'He starts shooting in two weeks. He's going to give me a script and if—'

Lois said, 'He's going to give you what they all give you.'

316

Sugar looked in the mirror, patting her heavy blonde hair. 'Well now, we never ran away from it, long as it made some sort of sense. Only in your case it isn't making much sense or much difference.'

Lois slammed out of the car. Sugar said, 'You'll never get a cab in time. You want Mr. Brennen to drop you? C'mon, get back in.'

'Only if you don't talk to me,' Lois said, voice trembling. 'Just don't talk to me!'

Sugar smiled and made a turning-the-lock gesture at her lips. Lois got back in. Sugar waved at Charley and rocketed out of the lot in a cloud of burning gas and rubber. Charley hoped she lived long enough to enjoy her new car and new agent.

He put the letters in the glove compartment and the checks in his wallet and started the Rambler. His life was here, not in New York. When he did go back, it wouldn't be for a two-day visit but to get his family.

Later, depositing the checks in the Bank of America, he realized he was no longer certain he would *ever* go back to New York and wondered whether he was beginning to accept certain changes, certain separations, as permanent.

NAT MARKAL

In New York, the Avalon group numbered twenty-three, and Nat had them all put up at the Americana. (He also had a room under an alias at a small, downtown hotel so he and Isa could get together.) They had arrived at Kennedy Airport at noon and were settled in their rooms at one-thirty. With the conference scheduled to start at ten P.M. (the earliest the management of The Forum of the Twelve Caesars would close their doors to the general public), everyone had a chance to relax and see Manhattan.

Nat had his usual suite – the Presidential. Mona, Jean, Gordon, Frank, Jack, Tony and Dick had suites befitting their star status. They were the seven he had already signed, and he would announce it at the press conference and discuss bids made to three other top names. Lou Grayson also had a suite, because he was a star in his own right if not in *Joneses*. Nat had picked a role for him – a strong role, though it ended in the

317

first quarter of the film. He had already told Grayson about it, and the comic had seemed pleased, saying it was just what he'd asked for. Then there were suites for Devon and Chalze, and everyone else had nice rooms. Nat would have given Isa a suite, but that would have created talk. 'After *Joneses*,' he said. She kissed him and said he was sweet and thoughtful. With all he had to look forward to, it was that little downtown hotel that gripped his mind.

He placed a call to Adele to let her know he had arrived safely and to stress that this was a hectic, unpleasant business. She wasn't home. Lainie said she'd left about nine and would be gone three days: a trip down the coast to Baja California with Lurelle Wanfred, wife of the network executive, on Wanfred's yacht. Nat was surprised. Adele wasn't the yacht type, which was the main reason they didn't own one. And she had always waited at home when he flew, waited for his safe arrival.

He showered and called Dave Sankin. They talked and Sankin said what with the Washington set and other *Joneses* costs he might have to negotiate a five-hundred-dollar loan at the Morris Plan. They laughed, and Nat asked, 'Want to sell a few shares?' Sankin said, 'You offering points, Nat?' Nat laughed again, alone this time. 'Why should I? I know where your stock stands. And you know where mine stands. Together, Dave, together.' Dave said he'd see Nat at The Forum.

Nat was in the bedroom, lying down and thinking of calling Isa, when the phone rang. It was Pier Andrei, whom he'd included in the trip when she begged him early on the evening of the Century Plaza party.

'This room, Nat, it's terrible! I can't turn around, it's so small! And drafty—'

He said there wasn't a room at the Americana *that* small, not to say the first-class rooms he'd rented, and that drafts were impossible because of the sealed air-conditioning-heating system. She asked if he couldn't see his way clear to getting her a suite – 'Just a *small* one.' He already regretted taking her along, having seen how much liquor she'd consumed on the plane, and how edgy she was with the stars. He said, sharply, that he was very busy.

She was polluted, in a sadly grand mood. 'That is not kind, Nat. Do you remember the suite I had at the Pierre? And when we announced *Lost Desire,* almost an entire floor at the Astor?'

'Yes, and do you remember how we bombed with *Lost Desire?*'

318

'I was miscast. And the bad press—'

Impatient to be rid of her, he interrupted. 'I suppose your drinking and screwing around had nothing to do with it?'

'That was very unkind, old friend.'

'I guess I'm not really kind, or your old friend. I'm a business-man, and you're not very good business anymore.'

She began to weep. He said, 'Either stop drinking and pull yourself together, or forget *Joneses*. I mean that, Pier.'

The weeping lessened.

'You have a chance tonight to get back in the columns and back into pictures.' He hung up, then called the switchboard to say he wasn't to be disturbed.

He was at The Forum with Bertha at nine-thirty, sitting at the bar and talking over the arrangements with the captain. The 'Silver Wagon' would provide the entrées, a selection of six meat and fowl dishes, plus three of Nat's favorites – the Sir-loin in Red Wine, Marrow and Onions, the Wild Fowl of Samos, and the Roast Saddle of Venison. There would be three seafood appetizers and three sumptuous desserts. Also, the choice of the bar and all five of The Forum's great coffees. 'No limit on the wine,' Nat said, 'but the champagne stops at twelve cases.' The captain nodded and smiled. 'For newspapermen, this is indeed a Lucullan feast.'

Nat made a mental note to look up 'Lucullan'. Something to do with Romans and eating – he knew that much. He also made a note to give the captain a smaller tip than he'd originally planned. He didn't like anyone talking above his head.

But he liked everything else, from the inverted centurion helmets (solid antique silver) used to chill wine, to the flaming café Diabolus (three-fifty for two and worth it in pyrotechnic display alone) – liked all of New York tonight and all the people in it! He was exhilarated by what he was going to tell the world and by the crisp winter weather and by the knowledge that Isa would be in his arms tonight. It was a dream, this life of his! It was a triumph and a glory!

He insisted Bertha have a champagne cup with him. She said, 'It'll turn my head,' and he came back with, 'If only *I* could,' and squeezed her arm. She turned pink, and he laughed and looked around. The last few diners were finishing up. Soon, Nat Markal's guests would begin to arrive.

ISA YEE

There were four or five Negroes in the crowd. One woman Isa
recognized from network television: a reporter who specialized
in entertainment news. Another was a tall, light-skinned man,
an ex-sports figure who came over and chatted with Mona and
then with Isa. He was with one of the press services. As for the
others, they blended in very well with the crowd, light-skinned
and dark, because they had the easy manners, the smiles and
smooth talk of the white world.

Isa wondered how Free would blend in here. He *could*, if he
wanted to. But he would not want to.

Markal announced the signing of his seven stars and explained that this was most unusual because only the treatment
had been completed. Stars of 'such magnitude' ordinarily
wouldn't even consider signing until they had read a script and
'made sure it fulfilled their every desire'. He also announced
that Lou Grayson would do a character part, and Pier Andrei
a vignette.

At this, Pier rose from her table and waved broadly and began to speak. She was terribly stoned, and Markal drowned
her out with, 'Thank you, Pier. We'll answer questions from
the press in a little while.' She fell rather than sat down, tugged
by someone at her table, and raised her voice angrily. Isa was
afraid she would blow up the way she had at the party the
week before, but whoever was sitting with her did some fast
talking, and Markal was able to go on. He said that three more
big names were close to signing and that announcements would
be made from Hollywood when they did. He described the
Washington set, 'for the few who haven't yet seen it'. He spoke
of the writers, Charles Halpert and Lars Wyllit, pointing at
Wyllit, and said that one was a brilliant novelist and the other
a top-flight scripter. He then went into a description of *Joneses*
and talked of its budget, its length, its importance in terms of
Hollywood regaining pre-eminence as the place where great
movies were made. Isa was completely unprepared for what
he said next.

'We're going to have dinner, and then a question-and-answer
period, and then just enjoy ourselves until The Forum throws
us out.' Laughter. He raised a hand. 'But first, I want to say that
Joneses, as we call it around the studio, is going to bring several
exciting new personalities before the public as well as its un-

320

paralleled lineup of stars. Prime among these is an actress who has already made a reputation for herself in Hollywood both in features and TV. If Miss Isa Yee will stand up, you'll understand why.'

She rose, smiling at him. There was a round of applause started by Terry Hanford and a few other studio people, then she heard Pier Andrei's shrill laughter and blurry speech: '—used to play servants and chop suey waitresses, now he gives them—' Markal's eyes snapped to Andrei and his face hardened. He quickly covered with a smile and said, 'For those of you who have never eaten at The Forum, my advice is, have at least one of everything.'

People came to Isa's table during dinner and afterward — columnists, feature writers and assorted legmen who wanted interviews with the new actress Emperor Nat Markal had singled out for special attention. She tried to keep her appointments logical, and chronological, but played safe by asking them to double-check tomorrow with Terry Hanford. Then she got to Terry, who said she would set up an interview session in one of the meeting rooms Mr. Markal had reserved at the Americana. As for individual interviews with the more important writers, they could be held at breakfast, lunch and dinner in the next day or two. If more time was needed, Isa could stay over as long as necessary. 'It's going beautifully,' Terry said. 'Even *Harper's* and *The Atlantic* are represented. They'll make fun of Markal, as will *Esquire* and some others, but that will only spread the word to the intelligentsia about *The Eternal Joneses*. Circulate around a bit, will you, Isa?'

Isa circulated, enjoying the attention coming her way — more attention than she had ever received before.

The photographers had set up a little shooting area near the hatcheck room, and the stars were moving in and out of there. Isa turned back, thinking it best not to push too hard; then Markal was beside her, hand on her elbow. He said there had been requests for her from several photographers and as they moved through the crowd he whispered, 'That drunken tramp is finished. For what she said about you. Finished!' She murmured that Andrei hadn't bothered her, and then they were taking pictures and she took several with Gordon Hewlett and one with Mona Dearn and one with Markal.

She ran into Lars Wyllit, who looked worn and tired. She said, 'No speciality acts tonight, please?' and smiled to show she was kidding. 'Not me,' he said. 'Not here. But I'd like to blow this imperial hole and see if the New York I knew is still there. Want to come along?'

It was *just* what she would have liked to do. But she had to stay available for Nat Markal.

The waiters wheeled out several carts with silver bowls of café Diabolus. They set the blend of coffee, spices and liquor aflame over blazing Sterno units and ladled it high and fancy from silver dipper into silver bowl and then into narrow little cups. Every so often a dramatic puff of fire rose into the air. Isa said, 'Can't miss tasting that wonderful-looking stuff.' Lars shrugged. 'If you've tasted one cup of flaming piss you've tasted them all. And get too close to one of those volcanoes and you'll never taste anything again.' She said, 'You *are* happy tonight and he said, 'That's because I'm wet-nursing the man who's writing the greatest motion picture of all time.' She looked closely at him. 'Maybe you'd better blow this imperial hole after all, with or without company. It wouldn't do to upset the Emperor in his forum.' He nodded and disappeared. Only then did it strike her that a Lars Wyllit speciality act might have been useful to Isa Yee. Anything that hit the front part of the newspapers and made the radio and television newscasts would have the effect of spreading whatever had happened at The Forum to people more quickly. And what had happened at The Forum was very important to Isa Yee.

She moved restlessly through the crowd until she saw Pier Andrei. Andrei was seated with a shabby, middle-aged man who wore a small camera and flashbulb unit around his neck. The Italian rocked in her chair and whispered in the man's ear. He nodded without seeming to listen and ate from a tall glass of whip-creamy dessert. Isa smiled to herself and turned toward them.

A waiter came pushing a cart of café Diabolus and fruit tarts. Isa sat down beside the photographer at Andrei's table and sighed wearily. 'Mind if I have my coffee here?' Andrei focused on her with difficulty. The photographer came alive, half-rising. 'Not at all, Miss Yee. Ida, is it?'

'Isa.' She nodded as the waiter stopped. 'I'll have a Diabolus.'

The photographer said he would too, and Andrei said, 'As I was saying, Mr. Yaleman—'

The photographer said he'd like to get a few candid shots and Isa said of course and Pier Andrei asked the photographer for a cigarette. He put the pack on the table and rose. Andrei gave him an outraged look. He stepped back and raised his camera.

'Just talk to Miss Andrei and forget I'm here. Have your coffee.'

Isa smiled at Andrei. Her voice low, she said, 'I hear you play my mistress, a drunken whore.'

Andrei's left eye twitched. She lit a cigarette and said, thickly, 'You play a nigger maid. You *are* a nigger maid. Now get away from my table.'

Isa kept smiling. The waiter began his lighting and ladling routine. He stood at a safe distance between Isa and Pier and the orange flame belched up from the Sterno unit and the blue-flame liquid trickled from ladle to basin and Isa murmured, 'I know you've been rehearsing that drunken whore role for years, but you can stop now. Mr. Markal said he was dropping you.'

The photographer said, 'Miss Yee, if you'd stand as if looking for someone?'

Andrei twisted in her seat. 'I do not wish to be photographed! Please leave!' People nearby began to look at her.

The photographer muttered that he would respect Pier's wishes and continued shooting Isa, who rose as he directed. Pier also rose, lurching into the table and knocking over a glass. *Papa-razzi!* Always with the filthy cameras!' Her voice was a blurry shout, and half the room now turned their way. 'Always prying into the lives of the stars!' She turned on Isa. 'You would not know what that means, you – you—'

Isa said to the photographer, 'I'm sorry, some other time.' When Pier didn't continue her tirade, she added, 'She's not quite sane, you know,' and walked away.

Andrei screamed something in Italian. Isa glanced back. Andrei was launching herself around the table, hands extended. What happened next took only a few seconds, but each event was so clearly etched, so distinct in Isa's mind, that it seemed to be running in slow motion.

The waiter was between Isa and Andrei, just now ladling flaming coffee into two cups. He managed to say, 'Watch—' when Pier Andrei ran full tilt into him and his serving table. The ladle flew out of his hands, the Sterno unit overturned, flames belched and splattered – mainly in Pier's direction.

The waiter cried out. Pier Andrei grabbed her face. Isa Yee suddenly realized she was going to have a much bigger story than she'd counted on.

Pier Andrei was still screaming, but with pain now. The waiter was grimacing, dabbing at his hands with a towel. Andrei continued to hold her face, but it was her hair that

323

gripped Isa's interest. That overdyed, overdried, red cotton-candy hair was smoking – then flaming!

'Burn, baby, burn!' Isa murmured to herself, laughter rising hysterically. Andrei's dress began to smolder. Isa ran to the table and ripped the heavy white cloth off in a crash of glassware. By the time she reached Andrei, the Italian was fully ablaze, her screams drowned out by shouts and screams from around the room. Isa threw the tablecloth over Andrei's head, getting one clear look at a scalp bubbling like ribs on a barbecue, and bore the Italian down beneath her. Other hands took over then, lifting her up and pouring pitchers of water onto the cloth.

Isa moved back. The photographer was right in front, taking pictures like crazy. 'Full color!' he muttered feverishly. 'Jesus Christ, full color!'

Markal found her, pressed a key into her hand and told her to get to the downtown hotel. He would join her as soon as he could.

Two men were bending over Pier Andrei, removing the wet tablecloth. Isa waited until she got one clear look, then pushed through the milling crowd. Pier Andrei's head, face and upper body were black, as black as . . .

At the small hotel, she lay in bed and smoked and listened to the radio, and heard the two-o'clock news. Pier Andrei had been taken to the hospital with 'first- and second-degree burns over sixty percent of her body. The once-famous film actress has been placed on the critical list.'

Isa took a hot shower and tried to feel sorry for Andrei and couldn't. She could only think of Andrei's voice saying, 'You play a nigger maid. You *are* a nigger maid.'

She must have fallen asleep because the next thing she knew Markal was in bed with her, apologizing for being so late. It was four o'clock. He'd had to stay at the hospital with Pier Andrei.

'How is she?'

'Dead,' Markal muttered. 'Heart gave out.'

Isa lay there a moment, testing herself – and felt nothing. She turned to Markal and, voice trembling, said how sorry she was and how she felt it was partly her fault for sitting down at Andrei's table and angering her.

'Don't you *ever* feel that way,' Markal said. 'Last week it was that little blonde, Sugar Smart. Tonight it was you. Next week it would've been someone else. It would've *always* been

324

someone – someone young and attractive. She couldn't stand pretty women, knowing what she'd become. She was cracking—' Then he took Isa in his arms.

She lay quietly, passively. He stopped and murmured in her ear. She said, 'I'm sorry, Nat. All this . . . her dying . . . I just can't—' She had always been good at crying.

He said he understood, but she could feel his need, his disappointment. She snuggled her nude body against him, saying she felt like a lost child, and while snuggling aroused him even more. She made believe she'd fallen asleep. He held her and his breath stayed fast and ragged. She moved, as if in sleep, and her thigh rubbed his organ. He said, 'Christ!' under his breath and took her hand and put it on him. She maintained the even tenor of her breathing, stayed determinedly 'asleep', while he used her hand and grunted and muttered.

He couldn't make it. She smiled to herself. *Burn, baby, burn!*

BRAD MADISON

So Baiglen had gotten off the book. At first it had frightened Brad Madison. At first he had panicked inside, wondering if he could really make it alone. But he hadn't revealed any of this when he'd sat in Baiglen's office Monday morning and looked at those vile photographs and read that lying deposition by his seventeen-year-old 'victim'. Instead, he had laughed. 'Better get a check ready for my condominium apartment.' Baiglen hadn't answered. Brad had stood up, face hard, and said he was going to teach Bagel a lesson for poisoning him Saturday night. Baiglen had been prepared all the way; he'd drawn a gun from his desk. Brad had shrugged and left, but he'd returned Tuesday with the mortgage papers. 'The down payment, or I'll send Myra's letter to Devereux. I mean it. I'm well on my way. I can afford to lose you if I have to.' Baiglen had said, 'You have lost me, faggot,' and rung for his secretary.

Brad had held one more card and played it that night by going to Baiglen's home. Baiglen had told him to get out, right in front of his shocked wife. Brad had stepped close and murmured, 'This is my last word,' and Baiglen had replied, 'Mine too. I'm *sure* of a conviction. Are you?' That's when Brad had known it was over – not because of what Baiglen actually had, but because he was ready to stand by it. That's when he shrugged and said, 'Just don't try to hurt me professionally, Carl.' Baiglen had walked him to the door, smiling. 'You and your profession can go straight to hell. Just don't come near me or my home.' Without warning he'd shoved Brad hard, sent him stumbling down the three front steps, and slammed the door.

Brad had gone home and told himself to forget it. Let Baiglen enjoy his little triumph. He had earned it by six months of paying bills and opening doors. Besides, on Thursday a new assignment came through and it was the best one yet – a strong featured role in a Four Star television special that would give him the chance to sing as well as act. He was going to be very busy during the next month – studying, taking voice lessons, shooting two Avalon assignments, working three or four days in the Jerry Lewis pic. Much too busy to think of revenge, which was pointless anyway. (He would *not* think of Andy Baiglen because it was dangerous. Besides, he had made his first meaningful contact and didn't need Andy anymore.)

But later that day, the first of several side effects of Baiglen's drug bit became clear – far more serious side effects than awakening in that hotel room with his guts crawling and his head splitting. He met Alan Devon near Stage 4 and stopped to chat with the man who was his best hope for a *Joneses* screen test now that Baiglen was lost to him. Brad asked if he would like to see clips of one of his television roles. Devon nodded, but without enthusiasm, and Brad suddenly remembered that it was Devon he'd been talking to when whatever Baiglen had put in his drink had taken hold. He said, 'About that business at the party—' Devon shrugged and said, 'We all drink too much at times.' When Brad tried to explain that it hadn't been drink but sudden sickness, Devon said, 'Have to lush,' then reddened and muttered. '*rush!*' and waved and was gone.

Anger flared. But he got it under control, telling himself there was no particular hurry when it came to *Joneses*. They wouldn't be testing for months yet, and by then he would have several more TV roles to his credit. Even if Baiglen was able to queer it with Devon, Lee could get to Markal, and Emperor Nat judged on talent alone. He would get a part in *Joneses* — which would be a sweet way of striking back at the Bagel.

He was at his agent's office at six that evening to sign the Four Star contracts. Lee offered him a drink. Brad refused, and said, 'I suppose you heard about Markal's party.' Lee said, 'Yes, and

326

with everything opening up so strong for you, kiddo, we don't want the slightest cloud on our horizon. Understand?' Brad said yes, he understood, and explained carefully that he was *not* a drinker. Lee said, 'That's good news,' and put away the whiskey decanter.

Anger came again. Slow, long-lasting anger this time. Anger that was still with him Friday evening when he went to the phone for the call he'd been thinking of all week. Whatever else had happened at Markal's party, he had finally made contact: a young director whom he had watched, then followed into one of Markal's two bathrooms, saying, 'It's so damned crowded—' Lyle was small, slim, dark – and very nervous when Brad had locked the door. 'Go ahead,' Brad murmured, hiding his own nervousness. Lyle had gone ahead, and their eyes had finally met, and Brad had seen the change taking place. But when he stepped forward, Lyle twisted away, fixing his clothes and whispering, 'Insane! Just being in here together—' He pushed past Brad and out the door. A little later, Lyle called him over to where he was standing with his arm around a thin, intense-looking girl. 'Want you to meet Rena Broon. Rena—' Brad quickly supplied his name and they chatted and Lyle said, 'About that heavy bit in the Chandler script, give me a week to clear things up, then call. Better take the number.' He gave name as well as number – and one very quick look from deep-set brown eyes that told Brad all he wanted to know.

But when he phoned Friday evening, Lyle was a different man. He 'didn't recall' asking Brad to phone. He 'didn't *quite* recall' Brad himself. When Brad got specific, mentioning the bathroom, Lyle murmured, 'Oh yes, and after the bathroom you faw down, go boom.' The line clicked.

That did it. The anger became something else – determination to strike back at Baiglen. And there was only one way he could do that – through Andy. Two birds with one stone. And one of the birds was the marvelous child, that queen in embryo, that longed-for lover . . .

He read of the press conference in Saturday's papers. Because of Pier Andrei, it had hit page one of the L.A. *Times,* with a more complete description of the affair on a back-page continuation. Carl Baiglen wasn't mentioned, but Brad knew he'd been invited. In fact, Brad had been thinking of getting Carl to take him along – but that was before Markal's party.

He phoned the Baiglen home Saturday at six P.M. The maid answered and said Mr. Baiglen wasn't in. He asked for Ruth.

327

'She's with Mr. Baiglen in New York.' He smiled and asked to speak to Andy.

The first thing the boy said was, 'I don't know when my parents will be home, Mr. Madison.'

'Then you remember me?'

'Well, sure.'

'Saturday night's the big night for young people. Dates and all. You going out tonight?'

Andy didn't answer right away, then, 'Mom says I'm too young to date.'

'Ah, yes, wise.' He fought uncertainty, telling himself he could easily handle this child. 'Girls can be ... troublesome to a growing boy.'

Andy Baiglen laughed. 'That's not how the guys look at it.'

'How *do* they look at it?'

'Well, *you* know. As an actor and all – a good-looking guy like you.'

It was beginning. The queen was swishing her skirts. Brad said, 'If you mean all the tail available in show biz, I'm not very receptive '

Andy laughed again, a little too hearty and masculine. 'Hey, that sounds like trouble, Mr. Madison.'

'Brad.'

'I've got to get ready for my date, Brad. I'll tell my father you called.'

'I thought you said your mother didn't allow you to date.'

'I don't mean I'm dating a girl. I'm going to a friend's house.'

'Oh,' Brad said softly. 'Date with a boy?'

'Well, yeah, studying and bulling and all.'

'Friend of yours in Bel Air?'

'How did—' Andy fell silent.

This was the critical point. 'Why don't I pick you up and we'll discuss it?'

'Discuss what?' Fear and antagonism entered Andy's voice. 'I don't see what we have to discuss.'

'Your relationship with the Sewal boy.'

'You . . . you know my friend, Richie?'

'Let's say I've seen you and Richie. I'll pick you up in about half an hour. Does that give you enough time?'

'I *can't*! My folks—'

'Your folks would be very interested in you and Richie Sewal.'

328

'What're you talking about, Mr. Madison?' He was really frightened now, and that made Brad feel good, give him command of the situation.

'Please call me Brad. If we're going to be friends – I'll pick you up in half an hour – half an hour, Andy.'

'No, Mr. Madison! I'm going to hang up now!'

'I wouldn't do that.' He was sweating. The boy was fighting too hard. Brad had expected a quick capitulation once Andy realized his secret was out. 'I'd have to tell them.'

'You're crazy, Mr. Madison! I don't know what you're talking about!'

'Tell them what an expert little cock-sucker you are.'

There was a long silence. When Andy finally spoke, his voice was different. 'You talk dirty, Brad. My father wouldn't like it if he knew you talked that way to me.'

Brad's voice also changed, became a murmur. 'He'd like it even less if he knew what his son did with Richie Sewal, standing up against the wall of Richie's bedroom, then on Richie's bed.'

'You lousy fink,' Andy said, but the words were delivered playfully. 'You followed and peeked.'

'Half an hour, Andy.'

'You want to blackmail me? You want my bank account? I've got sixty dollars. Is that what you want, Brad?'

'Naturally.'

'Or is it something else? Did watching us give you ideas? Did the handsome actor decide he'd find out what it's all about?'

'I knew what it was all about long before—'

'You're a beginner. You're nowhere. And if I decide not to meet you, you won't do a thing.'

'An anonymous note to your father—'

Andy laughed. 'Then how would you get at me? No, you won't send any notes. And I'm not meeting you.'

Brad Madison tried to think of something to say, some way to pressure the boy. And ended up whispering brokenly, '*Please*, Andy. I've thought of you so many times.'

'Sorry. Not tonight. Maybe tomorrow.'

'All right,' Brad said, jumping at the opening. 'Tomorrow.'

'Call me.'

'But if your parents—'

'They won't be back until Monday. Call me at six. Be very convincing. Tell me why I should prefer you to Richie. Tell me what's so special about a six-three baby boy.'

'Six-four.'

'Well, well. I might have to take vitamins.' Still laughing, he hung up.

Brad Madison sat beside the phone, trembling. Andy was so right. He was a beginner. He was nowhere.

And if he let Andy call the tune, he would *remain* nowhere. Those goddam Baiglens, pushing him around!

He grabbed his jacket and left the apartment. He reached the Beverly Hills house at six-twenty-five and parked near the corner, hoping Andy hadn't already left. Then he waited twenty tense minutes before the boy zoomed out of the garage on his motor-cycle.

He followed, and on a quiet side street with darkness falling fast he came up close and tapped his horn. Andy pulled to the right to allow the Porsche to pass. Brad passed, then cut in toward the curb. Andy was forced to stop. Brad walked back to the boy. Andy sat his cycle quietly.

'Get in the car.'

'My Honda—'

'We'll pick it up on the way back.'

Andy hesitated. Brad grasped his arm. Andy said, 'Take it easy.' He parked his cycle and walked to the Porsche. They drove off, Andy staring straight ahead, Brad glancing at him occasionally. At a red light, Brad tried to draw the boy close. Andy jerked free. 'You ever see two men hugging at a red light? You ever see two men kissing at a drive-in movie. Don't you know *anything* about the way we live!' Brad was ashamed – and worried. The boy had spoken with such contempt, such dislike.

As soon as they entered Brad's apartment, Andy said he had to call his friend. When Brad said that could wait, Andy snapped, 'He's expecting me by now. He'll call my home and Violet'll think I had an accident and start calling the police or my parents in New York. Is that what you want?' Again the contempt, the dislike.

Brad muttered that the phone was in the bedroom. Andy went in, slamming the door behind him. Brad dropped into an armchair. It was all wrong. He should have waited for tomorrow night. He should have played it Andy's way. Now it was spoiled.

He heard the boy speaking, then silence. He waited, but Andy didn't come out. He wondered if it wouldn't be best to

330

take him back to his cycle and hope for a fresh start some other time.

He went to the kitchen and poured two Cokes over ice. He opened a can of peanuts, a bag of potato chips, put everything on a tray and carried it into the living room. The bedroom door remained closed.

'Refreshment time,' he called.

No answer.

He put down the tray and walked to the door. 'May I come in?'

Silence.

Andy was gone. He was suddenly sure of it. They were on the ground floor and it was only a three- or four-foot drop to the street. Andy had gone out the window. He would never see him again.

He opened the door. Darkness. He went to the window. It was down and the blinds were drawn. Now how ...

'Over here.'

He whirled, peering at the bed, then stepped to the switch and threw it. Andy lay curled on his side, naked except for tight pink panties. 'Richie kept begging me, so I finally said I'd wear them.' He uncurled onto his back and stretched slowly, sensually. 'They feel good, even if they're about to pop this way.'

'This way' kept Brad Madison riveted in his tracks. 'This way' sent the blood pounding through his veins.

'Do you like it?' Andy asked.

Brad Madison nodded.

Andy stretched again, smiling. Brad Madison moved toward him. Andy murmured, 'I hope you're as strong as you look.'

Brad Madison made himself laugh, to hide the shameful trembling, the sudden pressure of tears behind his eyes. At last. Dear God, at long last he had someone to love.

DAVE SANKIN

Lou Grayson didn't return to Hollywood with the rest of the group on Monday morning. He had lunch with Dave Sankin at a little Italian restaurant that no one who was anyone patronized. Over espresso, Grayson said he wanted to buy all the shares of Avalon common Sankin would sell. As Sankin smiled and began shaking his head, Grayson named a figure fully twenty percent over market price. Sankin stared at him.

'If I needed the money, Lou—'

'You will, once the take from pre-*Joneses* features dries up. Do you know how much that Washington set will cost when they slap on the last coat of paint? I mean *really* cost, not what Nat tells us. A million and a half. *One set!* And he's going to burn it. Olive is sure of it. So you'll need money, Dave. Everyone will.'

'Then why should *you*—'

'Everyone but me, that is. I'll continue making Lou Grayson pictures whether it's at Avalon or Fox or in my own back yard. And continue making money. I can afford to collect antique cars and jade figurines and Avalon common.'

Sankin said it was an attractive offer, but no thanks. Grayson said, 'No rush, Dave. Anytime you're ready. Just think of it a while.' Sankin said there was nothing to think of and called for the check.

But he *did* think of it. Twenty percent above market value! And market value might never again be this high – would be considerably lower if *The Eternal Joneses* failed to draw like Markal said it would. And that set. Nat had assured him it wouldn't run more than half a million and would be used over and over again to make back its cost. No, Nat would never do anything so wasteful as to *burn* it!

They parted outside the restaurant. Sankin took a cab home and firmly pushed frightened thoughts, thoughts of playing it safe, away. He trusted his old friend Nat Markal.

ISA YEE

Tyrone Chalze was directing the tests, though 'directing' was far too strong a word for the relaxed way he was handling Isa. He sat off to the side, letting his chief cameraman, Bernie Wales, place her and do all the actual work. Toward the end he came forward and motioned her to move more, to be more physical. Isa didn't agree that the scene called for so much activity. Aimelee Jones, as she read Halpert's script, was a quiet, watchful girl who fought her slave status with her beauty, intelligence and inner life of dreams. But you didn't argue with Tyrone Chalze. She obeyed – and was disappointed

332

in him. Then, at the end, he came over and said, 'Your way was right. I had to be sure. Let's shoot it again.'

He took her to lunch in the commissary and said very little while drinking four cups of coffee and eating half a sandwich. His long, gaunt face seemed carved in wood – remote, impressive and mysterious. Then she remembered he had married a sixteen-year-old high school girl last year, and when asked why had answered, 'For the same reason any man marries, to get a good bedmate. Jeanie is the best.' Nothing very remote, impressive and mysterious about *that*.

She lit a cigarette and murmured, 'How's your wife?'

'Pregnant. Baby due in less than two months. The twenty-third of May, to quote the obstetrician. But I told him I always bring my productions in a little late.'

She smiled. 'Imagine, she'll be a seventeen-year-old mother.'

Chalze turned his deep-set eyes on her. 'And she might become an eighteen-year-old divorcée. What difference does her age make?'

She looked away, feeling that the great man was flashing his nonconformity. He said, 'Because the American peasant thinks a certain way, you think I do too? Because the American peasant says love and marriage are heaven blessed and forever, you think it's so?'

'I don't even know who the American peasant is.'

'You'd better find out, if you're going to work on *The Eternal Joneses*.'

She stared at him. 'Farmers?'

'Just about everyone Halpert has written about. The American *people* – with a handful of exceptions.' He smiled a little. 'Like you and me.' She said nothing. 'The people whose depth and taste have made *Bonanza* America's most popular cultural achievement. The peasant stands fast, Dostoyevsky said. He stands fast against change, against innovation, against thought. *The Eternal Joneses* – that brute ninety-nine and nine-tenths percent of America.'

She found she agreed with him, though she had never thought of it in quite that way. 'Halpert must be a cynic,' she said.

'Not at all. He's an enthusiast. A believer in people. But he's also a first-rate mind and when he finishes painting a scene the peasant is there for the cynic to see.'

'Then *you're* the cynic.'

'Since the age of ten. And you?'

333

'Oh, I'm not the type to think of such things.'

His gaze dug deep. 'I don't believe you. Let's talk further about it, tonight.'

She said she was flattered, but Jeanie . . .

'You don't give a goddam about Jeanie. And I don't give a goddam about Jeanie. Or about anyone except Tyrone Chalze. We're exactly alike.'

She laughed, making a joke of it, but was instantly uncomfortable. She lit a cigarette and changed the subject, and he asked if she wanted to watch another test with him.

They went back to Stage 6, and Isa watched him take a more active part in testing a little blonde named Sugar Smart who wore a ripped chemise and cheerfully accepted rape at the hands of a platoon of British during the burning of Washington. The girl seemed woefully inadequate to Isa, but Chalze walked up to her at the end and shook her hand. 'By God, that is *just* how Betsy would take it. You're either one hell of an actress, or lifecast for the part.' Instead of laughing at the great man's joke, the blonde leaned over to adjust something or other, presenting Chalze with a full view, and asked, 'Does it matter, Mr. Chalze?' Surprised, Chalze said no, and the girl said Betsy was a 'kicky' part, and Chalze wandered off with her in the direction of the portable dressing rooms, leaving Bernie Wales to conduct four more tests.

Thursday afternoon Isa sat with Markal, Chalze and Bertha Kraus in the small screening room down the hall from Markal's office. Her test was run first. When it was over, Markal lit a cigar and turned to Chalze. The director spread his hands, and for a moment Isa went cold, thinking he was going to knife her because she'd turned him down in the commissary. But he said, 'No problem. She's fine. She'll always be fine. She's an actress.'

They watched the Sugar Smart test and Isa was amazed at the way the girl photographed. She seemed to fill the screen with unadulterated sexuality. Her close-ups were almost pornographic, yet she drew chuckles from Markal and Chalze with some of her lines. 'Marvelous,' Markal said, and turned to Bertha. 'I want her agent in my office tomorrow. I want her to get as much exposure on television as possible, fast. And maybe a spot in a feature. Anything light being shot?' Bertha said Lou Grayson was going into production in two weeks, and Sy Mandel had a little musical for under a million. That was about all. Markal said Miss Smart would have no problem landing a part with Grayson; he would call Lou later. As for Mandel, have him drop by the office. 'Run it again,' he said, and they watched the sappy little blonde burn up the screen, and Markal and Chalze laughed, and Isa knew Sugar Smart was a natural. Sugar Smart was going to make it young and make it easy – and perhaps on a level with Mona Dearn.

Markal said, 'Her sister shot a test too, didn't she?'

Chalze said yes, and Markal said Baiglen felt she might have something, and Chalze called for the Lois Lane test. It came on. The lean brunette was wooden and pathetic. Markal said, 'Who else?'

More tests were run, and Markal and Chalze talked, arriving at decisions that would make or break half a dozen actors and actresses. Markal asked to have the test on Charyl Carny rerun. 'What do you think?' he asked Chalze.

Chalze shrugged. 'All right, for the limited footage she'll get. Devon seems to feel she's got possibilities, but he hasn't made clear just what *as*. She's too wholesome to be another Mae West and too heavy to be much else. Her face doesn't match her body.'

Markal said he didn't understand why Devon wanted her, but he wouldn't get in the way. 'Listen, let him know I want her to lose some weight.' He relit his cigar. 'Anyone else?'

Chalze said there was a promising romantic type – Brad Madison. They watched the test, and Isa felt he was really beautiful, tall and well put together and not bad as an actor – but somehow soft. Markal said, 'I seem to remember a phone call about this one. Bertha?' Bertha murmured and Isa heard something about a drinking problem. 'A lush?' Markal muttered. 'He doesn't look like a lush. You sure Carl passed that on?' Bertha said she could check Mr. Baiglen again. Markal asked Chalze's opinion, and Chalze said Madison seemed all right. 'The girls will love him, if that's important.' Markal said only as important as money and Madison was in – but he'd be made to understand that any drinking and he was out again.

Isa got home at four and found another message from Halpert, the third in two days. She knew what he wanted and couldn't put off returning the calls any longer. She got him at Avalon and apologized, saying that between a *Winning the West*, her *Joneses* tests and *I Spy*, she'd been frantic the past ten days. 'And I'll be getting a *Glenmore Theatre* script from Clete Brown shortly.'

'That *is* a busy life. I was hoping we could make that Watts trip.'

'Watts trip?' He might drop it if he thought she'd forgotten. And she wanted to forget it, just as she had forgotten Free Barchester.

'At Markal's party, remember? We were talking about Watts and you said you had a friend, a makeup assistant—'

'Oh, Emma. You really want to waste time that way?'

He said yes, firmly. 'And walk around a bit too.' She said, 'I'm almost afraid to do it. I mean, it's not Beverly Hills, you know.'

'Exactly why I want to go there. Besides, anyone who could do what you did in that New York nightclub can't be afraid of much.'

She murmured, 'That was different.' He was referring to the spread of color photographs that had appeared in *Life* magazine a few days after The Forum press conference. They showed her trying to smother the flaming Pier Andrei with a tablecloth. It looked far more dangerous than it actually had been. 'If it's really important,' she said.

'It is.' He went on, explaining how he was setting up the scene in Watts, how important it was to Aimelee, the role Isa played.

'All right,' she said. 'I've got a tough week coming up, so we'd better do it tomorrow. I'll speak to Emma first thing in the morning.'

Halpert said he would phone Wyllit and Terry Hanford. 'But isn't it short notice for Emma?' It was, Isa admitted, but the makeup assistant was an accommodating sort. (What she meant, what she *knew,* was that Emma was plenty Tom and wouldn't be likely to refuse a request from whites, especially those who worked at the studio.) Halpert thanked her and said, 'If you don't hear from me, we're on.'

Markal phoned at four-thirty. She told him about tomorrow and he said be careful and asked her to come to the suite. She pleaded exhaustion and in turn asked when he was going to take her out. 'I'm going stir-crazy, Nat,' He muttered he knew they hadn't gone out enough but they would.

'*Enough*? Except for that ride in the Ferrari so long ago I can't even remember, we haven't gone anywhere *ever*!'

'We could talk about it tonight.'

'I want to talk about it now.' And yet she didn't. Going out with him wasn't that important. But something else was. Making him sweat a little was.

She told herself it was all part of the plan to keep him hot for her until she was on top and could walk away from big-bellied white men forever. She told herself it was logical and useful and had nothing to do with senseless emotions like anger or hate.

'I'm tired of eating TV dinners and sitting around alone.'

'You don't have to eat in,' he said. 'Eat wherever you want. You're making good money, and I'll see you make more if that's what's bothering you.'

'And can I date someone when I'm eating out? Can I talk and laugh and dance with someone when I'm eating out?'

He said they would go out as soon as he could make it look like part of her publicity buildup. She said he had told her the exact same thing months ago. He said maybe the weekend after this.

She heard herself say, 'Friday, Nat. I've been working and working and sneaking up to the suite and I'm young and I've got to have some fun or I'll bust! *Friday!*'

'Be reasonable! I can't set it up in one day!'

'Yes, you can. Tell a few people. Call a columnist or whatever you do when you give an actress an evening on the town.'

'That's just it. I've *never* given an actress an evening on the town. Alone, that is. Lunch, yes – once in a while. But ... I *am* married, you know.'

She made her voice bitter. 'You bet I know!'

He said nothing. She said nothing. Finally he muttered, 'I'll see what sort of arrangements I can make. I'll call back.'

She was surprised. She hadn't expected she could really make him do it.

When he called to say he would pick her up Friday at seven, she had to fight off laughter. 'Formal, Nat?'

'That'll only make us more conspicuous.'

'It'll look as if we're going to a party later and fit in with the publicity story.'

He said anything to make her happy and he hoped she realized what a chance he was taking; then he paused, as if expecting her to relent and say they didn't have to go. She said, 'I've got a new gown. Wait until you see it.'

Emperor Nat Markal was really hooked! The fay bastard was hooked through the heart as well as the balls! She could do whatever she wanted with him from now on! The world's biggest producer – and Isa Yee could do just as she pleased with him!

Which would be everything to advance her career, she told herself. Nothing else, Certainly nothing foolish, nothing dangerous. Why would she want to do *that*?

CHARLEY HALPERT

The white stucco house had heavy rust stains around the outside pipe connections, but other than that it looked neat and substantial as they parked at the curb. Then, as they walked up a concrete path that split a deep lawn, Charley saw signs of decay and neglect. The grass was burned out. The path itself was cracked in half a dozen places. Off to the right a garage was crammed with junk. The porch they approached had a split stair, rickety furniture and was badly in need of paint.

'You can *see* they don't own it,' Lars said.

Isa had filled them in on what she had learned of the makeup assistant as they drove from Avalon to Watts in her Corvair. Emma Dale had a husband, Walter, and three children ranging in age from six to seventeen. The eldest was from Walter's previous marriage.

Isa looked around and murmured, 'You can take the Negro out of the slum, but can you take the slum out of the Negro?'

Terry said, 'This *is* a slum, and for a slum it's rather nice.'

Charley said, 'A lot nicer than a certain tenement in which I spent my first twelve years.'

Lars said, 'They used to say that slum-thing about Jews, Italians and Irish too.'

Isa stopped at the porch steps. 'Let's not forget I'm the one with the dark skin and slanty eyes.' She smiled.

They all spoke at the same time, saying they hadn't meant to jump on her, and she said she hadn't meant to sound like a bigot, and Charley said, 'I think we're all feeling the *strangeness* and it's time to admit it.'

No one argued with him, which meant they had all reacted somewhat the same to their walk through Watts and their meal in the diner on Imperial Highway. There had been very few whites in the shops they'd entered, except for some of the storekeepers. There had been even fewer walking the streets, especially couples. There had been no whites at all in the diner

338

(which had been doing a good business at five P.M.) and a sullen waitress had made it plain that she for one preferred it that way. Wherever they'd gone, they'd been looked at as strangers.

Charley said it was partly in their own minds, because they *were* strangers, and partly because they had no legitimate business in the area. 'We're here to examine them. Two men and two women, not going anywhere in particular, just walking around, gawking.'

Lars muttered, 'I think it's because of the riots.'

'The one here was *years* ago,' Isa said.

'The memory lingers on. And there have been incidents every summer since then. Whites have left this community. The few that lived here moved, and most burned-out white businesses never reopened. It's a total ghetto now.'

'It's different in Pacoima,' Terry said. 'Different in any of the smaller Negro neighborhoods, the better neighborhoods.'

'Not to bring Mr. Marx into it,' Charley murmured, 'that old debbil money makes a lot of difference.'

They paused outside the door. Charley felt like an intruder. As if reading his mind, Isa said, 'I asked if it would be a bother.'

'In a sense you're her employer,' Charley said. 'How could she say no to you?'

The door opened. The lean, smiling woman in the gray print dress said, 'You gonna stand out there till night?'

Isa said, 'Hi, Emma,' and introduced the others. They came inside. The hallway was short and opened into a living room furnished in plastic-covered couch and chairs, bright and cheerful. They sat down, and Emma asked if anyone was hungry. They said they'd just eaten, and Lars named the diner. Emma said, '*That* place!' her attractive face twisting in distaste. 'You shouldn't have. I wouldn't feed my dog there, if I had one!' Charley said the food wasn't bad. Emma said only the 'worst kind' ate there, and then, quickly, 'You couldn't know, of course.' Charley said the people had been fine, 'though one waitress seemed to prefer Jim Crow to us.' He smiled. Emma laughed and shook her head vigorously, her hair flying – her obviously straightened hair. Charley noticed that she wore makeup – some sort of whitish pancake to lighten her skin. She said, 'Some of the people around here, you wouldn't believe it! Like that club, The Blacks. Criminals, Walter calls 'em. We're moving soon as Walter feels our bank account is strong enough. Someplace in the Valley where he's got relatives.'

Charley felt lousy. It was wrong to make a woman perform like this, even if she did it for herself and her family too. He looked at the others. They seemed more at ease now. He wondered if he looked the same.

He asked about Walter. Emma beamed. Walter owned a two-man floor-waxing and polishing business. He worked nights, since that was when buildings and offices were empty. It was a new venture, but it was growing. 'Mr. Bates, the man he used to work for, said Walter was a born go-getter. Walter's out right now seeing about a new account. That's his picture.'

She pointed at a framed photograph on a lamp table. Charley walked over and picked it up. He noticed it left a slight discoloration on the wood top, where it must have stood for some time. There was another discoloration beside it, but no other photograph.

Walter was light-skinned and aging, and wore a serious go-getter expression. Isa said Emma better not let him visit the studio too often — she'd lose him to some starlet. Emma laughed. 'I don't think I got to worry much. How many colored starlets are there anyway?'

Charley asked about her children. She said they were upstairs, 'where they won't bother the grown-ups'. She asked if they would like to see the rest of the house. They followed her. The kitchen was long, narrow and not as cheerful as the living room, due mainly to a very old stove, refrigerator and sink. There were two bedrooms in back. The master had a large double bed and two chests of drawers in dark veneer. Emma said, 'We wanted that Danish modern furniture, but decided we'd save the money and get out of here that much sooner.' They murmured that-made-sense, and Emma led them past a closed door with the offhand statement that it was 'the other bedroom'.

Upstairs were two attic rooms holding three children. 'Not fancy,' Emma said of the pine furniture, 'but all paid for, praise be.'

Emma's seven-year-old son Clyde was wrestling with his six-year-old sister, and she was crying. Emma slapped Clyde's hands, and both children stared up at the guests with streaming eyes. The older girl, Arlene, said hello and looked at her brother and sister with the natural contempt of a teen-ager for infants. All three were pale-skinned like the father; all three were dressed for company. Arlene was a busty knockout.

Looking at her nubile stepdaughter, Emma said, 'Raising

340

children decent is some chore here, the good Lord knows! I can't let them out lessen I know who they're with and I got to tell them to come right in if bad kids come around. As the twig is bent, so grows the tree. We don't want them ending up at hoodlum clubs like The Blacks, now do we!'

Charley wanted to hear more about The Blacks, but Isa began discussing the movie she and Emma had worked on together.

They went downstairs again. They had coffee and talked, and Charley asked for the bathroom. Emma said it was in back.

While he was in the bathroom, the doorknob rattled. He came out, and there was no one in the little hallway; but that door to the second bedroom was now ajar. He walked by. As he entered the kitchen, he glanced back. A very black, very bent old lady came out and disappeared into the hallway. He heard the bathroom door close.

He hesitated. Hiding grandma was a game white people played too; nothing unusual there. But he went swiftly, silently back to the room and looked inside. Old furniture. A torn window shade. A faded bedspread. Again, a game white people played with grandma. But it wasn't the furniture or shabby accessories that grabbed his attention. It was the pictures — framed photographs, a half-dozen or so placed haphazardly on the dresser top and several more on a lamp table and two on a chair. Photographs of men, women and children, most blown up from snapshots, a few studio shots. People in farm clothes or posed stiffly in go-to-meeting best. Photographs from a hard past that Emma had gathered up from around the house and put in this room. Old photographs of black people that Emma had shut away with an old black lady because Isa and her friends were coming to visit.

He returned to the living room. Emma had brought out candy, and Isa was nibbling on a piece and talking about the service at the Century Towers. Emma said, 'You're lucky. From what I know, some of the best places have the worst kind of help. People who just don't care about holding a job. People who don't know how to work, only how to take Welfare!' Lars was smoking and Terry was nodding and everyone looked relaxed and comfortable.

It *was* relaxed and comfortable in this house — because this was the way things had always been, because there was no change in this house from what had been thought and said in the past twenty-thirty years.

341

He liked Emma. He disliked Emma. He disliked himself for making judgments based on a walk and a meal and a half-hour spent in a woman's house – and felt there was no real hope for the Negro in what he had seen in this house. He wanted something else for the Negroes in *Joneses* – whether or not it was relaxed and comfortable.

Emma put on the lights. Charley waited for his chance and brought up the riots of 1965. Emma took a deep breath. 'We didn't dare go out of our house. We kept the door locked and Walter missed three days of work and so did I.' Charley asked if there was any justification for such violence. Emma stared at him. 'You mean if they was *right*? How could gangsters be right? They robbed and burned and beat and even killed. How could that be right?' Charley was tempted to discuss revolutions, but Emma's face was so pained, so worried, that he nodded and said, 'Of course, it couldn't be.' Emma began to quote her husband on the way the police had 'babied those savages', and the doorbell rang. She left the room. They heard subdued voices, and then a male voice sharply raised. Emma returned, hurrying to keep ahead of a tall young man. 'Here's my nephew,' she said, her smile obviously and painfully forced. 'He just happened—'

'I didn't just *happen*,' the young man interrupted brusquely. 'I recognized that new Corvair with the studio sticker and figured a slumming party—'

'Now you stop that! Or get yourself right out of here! I told you when you took up with those crazy fools—'

'My aunt feels that anyone who tries to replace the white power structure in Watts with a *black* power structure—'

'With a *Welfare* power structure, you mean!'

'Ah, Walter's deathless prose.'

'Yes, and if he comes home—' She suddenly stopped and turned to the four in the living room. 'I don't know how to apologize.'

Lars said *she* had nothing to apologize for. He stared at the young man and added, 'If I can help in any way—'

The young man laughed. Lars stood up. Emma said, '*Please*, Mr. Wyllit.' Lars sat down again, slowly. Emma turned to her nephew. 'How can you act this way with Miss Yee here and you knowing her and my job at the studio—' Her voice choked off.

The young man was looking at Isa. Isa was looking at her hands. The young man said, 'And all the pictures put away and all the Negrotude put away—'

342

Emma slapped him. He smiled and walked out. Emma stood there and the four sat there and the silence was thick enough to cut with a knife. Then Emma's teen-aged daughter came running down the stairs. 'Was that Free, Mom? I want to ask him—' Her voice died at Emma's look. Emma said, 'You got homework, haven't you?' The girl nodded. 'Then *do* it!' The girl looked shocked and went back upstairs. The silence deepened. Charley finally said, 'I guess Free belongs to that club you disapprove of?'

Emma nodded, eyes down. 'The Blacks. And with his education, his opportunities and advantages—' She shook her head. 'What you must think of us!' They all murmured disclaimers. 'I don't know what got into him,' Emma said. 'I don't know why he was so – so *nasty*. I mean, he believes those things I know are wrong, but to come to my house this way ... He and Walter had their big fight and he doesn't come around when Walter's here. But I get him acting jobs once in a while and he promised not to talk to Arlene like he used to about race and all and he *never* busted in like this before. I just can't figure it out.'

Isa said it was time to go. Emma said they had to come again when Walter was home. Charley said she and Walter would have to be his guests in the commissary soon. Emma said, 'Oh, Walter's not much for eating out and such.'

In the car, Terry turned in her seat beside Isa. 'Poor Emma! We *would* have to witness a family argument.'

Charley and Lars sat back. Charley said, 'That wasn't a family argument. That was a schism in a race's thinking.' Lars said, 'You push too hard for theme, Chuck baby.' Charley hunched forward. 'You know the man, Isa. What would you say?'

'Me? Know the man? I met him on the set a few times.' She swung onto the freeway. 'He seems like a dangerous kook.'

Charley leaned back. 'I'd like to talk to him. Emma's only one side of the coin.' Lars said, 'She's a little Tommish, true, but I'd say she represents what most colored people think and feel.' Isa laughed. 'You hope.' Terry said, 'Yes, that's it, we hope.'

But Charley *didn't* hope Emma was the majority voice. He for one wanted to hear other voices.

Nat still considered himself a moral man, a family man. He had merely included a beloved mistress in his family. Not unusual for anyone in his position, for a man called *Emperor* Nat Markal, was it?

Adele and Lainie continued to play important roles in his life, and he continued to visit Adele's room, though perhaps not as regularly as before. But that was a matter of physical strength, not affection.

His life had balance and proportion, was nothing like the sexual athletes who prowled Hollywood, was nothing like Pier Andrei's had been. He was a sensible man and very happy at the way things were working out.

Or he *could* be very happy. If only Isa would stop being so — so demanding.

Maybe 'demanding' was the wrong word. She didn't want *things*. She didn't even press for favors careerwise (though here she was getting as much as she could handle). It was a certain tension he sensed in her, a tension that made him feel she was demanding what was beyond his power to give. Like more and more time. Time that belonged to Adele and Lainie.

Yet here he was, driving up to the Century Towers, in the Ferrari Berlinetta no less, and in formal dress. Here he was, calling openly on Isa Yee, taking her to Chasen's for dinner and then to the Coconut Grove.

He had covered as best he could, telling Pen Guilfoyle that he was starting a drive to get Isa Yee into the columns as his personal choice for stardom. 'As Cohn of Columbia pushed Kim Novak, Pen—' He had phoned Sheilah Graham and repeated his story there. 'Isa Yee will emerge as one of Avalon's hottest properties, Sheilah. That's why I'm going to invest some time of my own in promoting her.'

Dangerous. People would talk. Emperor Nat Markal out with a beautiful starlet, and Adele Markal at home.

It was a mild, springlike evening, and they drove with the windows down. At a traffic light, Isa said, 'Look at the people staring, Nat.' He shriveled and muttered, 'It's the car.'

There were only a few names at Chasen's, but it was different at the Coconut Grove where, as luck would have it, Lettie L'Andeaux was being feted after the preview of her new picture. At least a dozen big names came to the table, and he

344

introduced Isa in such a way as to make each actor, producer, director and columnist look at her with more than the ordinary amount of interest. They stayed until twelve, and then Isa asked for a tour of the newer spots. 'Where the kids and the cognoscenti make the scene. Want me to list them?'

She had been fighting him in that tense, subtle way all evening. He hadn't taken her up on it until now, as they were driving out of the parking lot. 'I may not make the scene very often myself,' he said, 'but I know and am known at every one of those places. Moreover, I'm one of very few people who can command a table without a reservation.'

'Gee, dad, that's terrific!' She smiled, not very pleasantly.

He was suddenly enraged, and stamped down on the gas pedal, rocketing the superb Italian machine forward. Her head snapped back. 'Drag it, man!' she said, and laughed with a wildness, an abandon that bothered him. But then again, she'd had several glasses of wine with dinner and two cocktails at the Grove and she wasn't much of a drinker.

They club-hopped along the Strip until two A.M., and it became less and less pleasant for him, though there was still nothing specific to pin down.

They ended up at the Haunted House on Hollywood. He'd had enough and said so. As they were leaving, she took his hand and drew him toward the floor. 'Dance with me, Nat.' He held back. 'You know I don't do those dances.'

'Why not? They're simple. I'll teach you.'

'Stop it!' She was pulling hard and laughing, and Val Bandrin, script consultant on *Winningers Winners*, was watching them from the bar, though he quickly turned away when Nat glanced at him. 'You've had too much to drink!' he snapped.

For a second her face hardened, her lips tightened. He thought she was about to erupt; then she smiled and murmured, 'Lead on, Master.'

He led her to the parking lot, where a cluster of teens and twenties boys were examining the Ferrari. They pushed through and got in. One of the boys said, 'Bet the chick's more expensive than the car. Ask the Nat Markal who owns one.' Nat backed up quickly, scattering the kids, who raised angry voices. He roared forward and out of the lot.

'Where are we going now?' she asked, head back, smiling.

'Home.'

'You sound unhappy.'

'You've made things . . . unpleasant for me.'

'Really?' She kept smiling up at the roof. 'Then you can just drop me at my apartment.'

He said nothing.

'In fact, we needn't continue seeing each other, if it's unpleasant for you.'

'I know it,' he snapped. 'And I'll tell *you* when that time comes.'

'Perhaps I'll tell you first.'

He glanced at her. She still smiled. He drove faster.

'I want to go to The Insomniac,' she said.

'All the way to Hermosa Beach? In time for the place to close?'

'If it closes, we'll have had a nice ride. And a nice ride back.'

'No. We're going to bed.'

'That sounds like a command. I'm a slave only in *Joneses,* Nat. Otherwise, I am a free woman.'

'Are you? Are you really?'

'Drop me and find out.'

'From *Joneses* too?'

'From everything.' She still hadn't looked at him. 'I'm going to be a star with or without you. I don't owe you a thing. I've taken nothing without giving in return. If anything, I've given *more* than I've got, because every acting job you've helped me land will make money for you, including *Joneses.*'

He took a cigar from his leather case and bit off the end. He lit it and turned toward the freeway and Hermosa Beach. 'They're probably closed already,' he muttered.

She let him get to the freeway entrance, then said, 'All right, let's go home.'

He turned back toward Sunset, which he would take to La Cienega and then to Santa Monica Boulevard. He said, 'I know you're a free woman. I know you give as much as you get. I . . . respect you, Isa.'

She didn't answer, but a little while later moved closer. Her hand came to his thigh. He looked at her, and she was turned to him, her face very close. His heart leaped. She was so beautiful. God, so young and so beautiful. And free. She would always be free, unless he married her. And he couldn't do that. He didn't want her to be free for the young men with their hungry eyes and hands, the young men waiting to be turned loose once Emperor Nat Markal was out of the picture. He

346

didn't want her to be free and couldn't marry her and couldn't buy her and was afraid.

'I like the things you like,' she said, voice very quiet, very serious. 'I've tried brandy and it's good and *escargots* and they're good, and all the tricks you like in bed and they're good.' She moved closer, her breast pressing him. 'Sodomy isn't exactly comfortable for the woman – not the way you did it last time, remember?' He nodded, breathing hard, and pulled to the curb and kissed her. One hand wormed into the low-cut back, under the tight cloth to her buttocks. He bit her lip in a frenzy of desire, and she grunted but didn't try to get away. When he finally released her, she said, 'I go along with everything, try and enjoy everything, but it's one-sided, your way alone, nothing of mine. I don't think it can go on like that. I don't think either of us can find joy in it much longer like that.'

'But what do you expect me to do? Dance the jerk, the frug, the bugaloo in front of half of Hollywood? I'm fifty years old, Isa. My position—'

'If your age and position make you too old for me, admit it.'

She was still close, still quiet and serious, but her lips were tightening. He *wasn't* too old for this girl. His heart and body assured him he wasn't. But he wouldn't tell her – wouldn't beg. He was Emperor Nat Markal, and she was pushing him too damned hard!

'You know what that would mean,' he said, keeping his own voice quiet. 'I'd have to step away from your career—'

'We've *been* through that once. I'm not threatening *you*, am I? I'm not spelling out what *you* would lose. Let's just say it's over and we're even and good night.'

He pulled into the circular parking area between the Century Tower's two hi-risers. It was dark and still. The doormen were either inside or off duty. She opened the door. 'Good-bye, Nat.'

He took her arm. 'Isa—' She didn't face him. 'Can I see you upstairs?'

'No.'

'I'll take lessons,' he muttered. 'I'll learn those dances.'

She turned. 'It's not just dances, It's an attitude of *joy* you have to learn.'

He was suddenly very alert, very worried. She knew something about him no one but Nat Markal should know. He had never been young, never had joy – until Isa.

'You don't know how to play, to pleasure yourself.'

'Pleasure myself?'

'An old Eurasian expression,' she said. 'You go at everything, at me, as if you're . . . going into business.'

He flushed. 'You'll teach me to pleasure myself.'

'Then you'll have to work at it. Will you?'

He nodded and reached for her. She let him take her in his arms and returned his kiss and smiled. She said, 'C'mon now,' and got out of the car and he joined her. 'Lesson Number One.' Still smiling, she removed a lipstick from her bag and bent down. Using the lipstick as chalk, she sketched out a hopscotch court. 'Tangerine,' she murmured as she worked. 'Shows up clearly, doesn't it?' She didn't wait for an answer. 'Double boxes one and two,' she said under her breath. 'Single three. Double four and five. Single six. Double seven and eight. And . . . that's . . . it.' She straightened. 'Just a small court. For a small game'

'Hopscotch? *Here?*'

'Then you've played it?'

'I've seen my daughter play it. But not at two-thirty in the morning. Isa, we can't—'

'To pleasure ourselves,' she said, searching her purse. 'For kicks. For fun. What we were talking about. What you promised you would learn.'

He looked around. Both lobbies were about forty feet away. The sky was bright and aided by a pole lamp some fifteen feet away. There was sufficient light for their game, and sufficient light for anyone coming along to see them at their game. And if a tenant were to look out his window . . .

He told her it worried him. She said, 'I don't see any people. And who'd be looking out the window this time of night? And if they did, who would know you from ten or twenty stories up?'

He continued to feel threatened and frightened and vulnerable. And not just because of people. The game. Would he be able to play the game without appearing ridiculous?

'Knew I had some candies,' she said, and took out a cellophane-wrapped Charm. 'The potsie. Want to go first?'

'Ladies first.' He made himself smile and took out his lighter, then decided against using it and merely chewed the cigar. The flame might draw attention to them.

Isa tossed the square of candy into Box 1. She hopped on her left leg into Box 2. 'You never enter the box with the potsie,'

348

she explained, and hopped into Box 3, then jumped and landed spraddle-legged, one foot in Box 4 and one in Box 5. 'You never touch a line of the court.' She hopped into Box 6. She jumped into Boxes 7 and 8, then jumped again, completely around, facing him. She laughed. 'Like dancing.' She made her way back quickly, landing on one foot in Box 2 and, bending gracefully, picked up the potsie and hopped out of the court. 'Your turn.'

'Aren't you supposed to go on until you miss?'

'If you want to play a full game instead of one turn each—'

He muttered no. She handed him the potsie. Grimly, he came up to the line. She said, 'You're playing a game, Nat, not facing a committee.'

He chuckled and threw his cigar away. He considered dropping the potsie out of Box 1, but she wouldn't accept that, would *know* he had deliberately fouled out. He tossed it into Box 1. A car roared by on the Avenue of the Stars. He looked around, took a deep breath, said, 'Here goes.' She nodded and smiled. He hopped into Box 2, then 3, jumped into 4 and 5, hopped into 6, jumped into 7 and 8, jumped around to face front. He was pouring sweat. Nat Markal in formal dress playing hopscotch in a parking area at two-thirty A.M.!

'That's pretty good,' Isa said. Her smile was very wide now, and he wondered if she was laughing at him. 'Just come on back.'

He reversed the process. When he reached 2, he stood on one leg and bent toward the potsie. He felt himself tottering and quickly straightened. His leg ached from supporting all his weight. He paused a moment, panting, and heard the car. A gray Ford sedan drove into the entrance road and up before Isa's building. A man and woman got out and the man began to close the car door – and saw them. Isa said, 'Don't stop now, Nat. If you do, you'll have to take your turn again.' The man said something to the woman and she turned and glanced at them and then tugged the man's arm. They entered the hi-riser.

Nat stood on one leg and choked back a curse. He began bending his knee, trying to lower himself by degrees, and was getting there. He reached out for the potsie and began to lose his balance.

The man came out of the lobby, obviously having seen the woman to an elevator. Nat was looking at him even as he toppled. In order not to land on his face, he tilted back and sat

349

down abruptly. The man paused at his car to stare, then got in and drove past the second hi-riser and into the parking area. Nat was up and had turned his back when the man drove by on his way to the Avenue of the Stars. He heard Isa laughing and looked. She was bent over, shaking in helpless spasms. He chuckled to show he was a good sport. She said, 'Did fine,' voice strangled. He brushed at his seat and chuckled again. 'Sure.' Isa took a deep breath. 'It was fun, wasn't it, Nat?'

He was burning with shame, but told himself she was right. He had to learn to be a good sport. 'By God, it *was* fun, though I could've done better.' She came to him and hugged his arm. 'You will, the next time.' He nodded glumly. She said, 'Now we'll play leapfrog.' He began to shake his head, and she pulled him toward the lobby, murmuring, 'In bed.' She was looking up into his face and whispering to him and what she was saying made him forget caution, forget to keep a businesslike distance from her when the doorman appeared, forget everything but the love and the fire she promised.

It would be all right. Neither the doorman nor the couple in the car knew who he was, and no one else had seen them, and he wouldn't take chances like this again. One time was all right.

CARL BAIGLEN

Ruth called him at the office Monday morning. Her voice tense, she said, 'Carl, a crisis. I don't know how to tell you. Andy—'

Fear swept him in a hot wave. 'He isn't hurt, is he? The Honda—'

'No, nothing like that. He's in school. But . . . I found something in his room. I was looking . . .' She interrupted herself with, 'Carl, please come home,' and hung up.

She was waiting at the door. 'I told Violet to visit her sister. Here, look.'

He took the photographs, but first he looked at her face. She was pale. His own face went pale a moment later.

'They were in the closet,' she said as they walked into the living room and sat down. 'If I hadn't been looking for something secret, something hidden away, I'd never have found them. In an envelope wrapped in an old shirt and stuffed into his fishing-tackle box. As it was, it took me three weeks. I

350

searched that room inch by inch, feeling there had to be *some* sign.'

'You suspected this for three weeks?'

'Longer than that. But I told myself I was imagining things.'

He slumped low in the couch. 'I saw no signs of it. Maybe I haven't really looked at the boy lately.'

'I didn't see it in him either. He's too close to us. I saw it in his friend Richard. And I realized Andy had dropped all his other friends – the ones that used to sneak looks at my legs.' She asked for a cigarette. He lit it for her and mumbled he couldn't believe it and went through the pictures again.

Polaroid black and whites. Richard Sewal nude, with an erection. Richard dressed in a high school baseball uniform, masturbating. Richard soaping himself in the shower. Richard kneeling on the floor with something – a candle perhaps – in his rectum. And then three shots that might have been taken by an automatic timer. Andy and Richard in bed together, doing nauseating things to each other.

He put them down on the table. 'How did it happen? *Why* did it happen?'

She shook her head.

'There are injections for this, aren't there? For boys who aren't masculine enough?'

'If there were, we wouldn't have any homosexuals, and you know how many there are in this town alone.'

'I mean for kids not yet set in their ways, not yet real faggots.'

She glanced at the pictures. 'Wouldn't you call *that* set in his ways?'

He made a helpless gesture.

'If it's hormones you're thinking of, Carl, I don't believe it would work. Analysis is our best bet, but even there—'

'You seem up on it. Been reading?'

She nodded. 'Ever since I first suspected. And I talked to Dr. Eddering, and my sister's psychiatrist, Dr. Sherman.'

He waited.

'The modern view doesn't offer much hope of a cure. What it boils down to, after all the talk of guidance and motivational substitution and father images, is that *we* have to be cured – of the illusion that we can change him. We have to learn to live with him, accept what he is, and let him be. Dr. Sherman said it was too bad Andy had been so precocious, and careless. Many homosexuals manage to reach adulthood without their parents knowing that they belong to, as Sherman put it, the

351

third sex. Then, when they finally do suspect, their boy is on his own, usually in a different city. Homosexuals usually leave their hometowns, he said. They congregate in big cities – true cities and not suburban aggregates like L.A., unless they're connected with TV and the movies.'

'Then I'll lose him,' Carl muttered. 'If we let him go on this way he'll leave us and we'll never see him again and his life will be with those dirty—'

She put her hand on his arm. 'We'll do what we can, but you mustn't think of it as *dirty*, Carl. Don't talk like that. Like a – a religious zealot, a John Bircher, a hater. I'm hurt too. I'm frightened too. But only because I want our son to have the best possible chance at happiness. I think of how good our marriage has been and I want the same for him.' She wiped at her eyes. 'Andy's not filthy. He's ... sexy. His own sex. We've got to help him have a normal life, even if it's a normal homosexual life.'

He jumped up. 'He'll never touch another man if I have to beat him unconscious!'

'That's the most futile thing of all, Carl.'

He knew it. He sat down again. The other things she had said – he knew they were true too. He turned to her. She moved closer, took both his hands. They sat together. 'We have to talk to him,' he said.

'I don't know. We'd have to admit I searched his room. And then, what would we talk about? How he blows his friend?'

His face twisted. 'Don't say such things.'

'But if we talk to him, that's what we'll have to talk *about*. It's in the pictures, Carl. That's what he does with his friend.'

He tried to think. He said, 'An expert will tell us what to do,' and saw in her eyes that she didn't believe it. 'We just can't ... *accept* it!'

She said nothing.

'Can we?'

'We can,' she said. 'I'm going to put those pictures back where I found them. I'm not going to say anything and I pray you won't either. Until we find a way to change him, we'll go on as if we know nothing. We'll go on as we have before, as a family.'

'But letting him—'

'Anything else will break us up. Once he knows we know, he won't be able to live here. We'll have to send him to boarding school, which will give him even *more* freedom for sex and

352

deprive you of your son.' She paused. 'You still want him with you, don't you?'

He nodded miserably. 'Always such a good kid. So honest. So loving. Bright in school.' He was thinking back. 'Maybe Myra's neuroses—'

He stood up and went to the sideboard and looked at the Scotch and decided it was too early to drink. 'We have to do *something*. At least stop him from seeing that boy. Maybe it's Sewal's fault. Maybe he . . . seduced Andy. Maybe away from him Andy will become normal, turn to girls—'

His voice ran out. She didn't have to say it; he knew he was clutching at straws.

'Carl, we can't forbid him to see Richard. We would have to give a reason and there is no reason except the truth. But we could speak to Mr. Sewal. Of course, he might act rashly, and Andy would find out we know. The best thing is to say we want Richie to come here more often, sleep over here instead of Andy sleeping over there. We'll be home and they won't have as much opportunity to be alone.'

'All that'll do is cut *down*, not cut *out*.'

She nodded. 'But it would be the same if he were sleeping with a girl, wouldn't it? We could cut down, perhaps cut that one girl out of his life completely, but there would still be a world of girls. Once a boy becomes a man, that way, he'll always find a girl to sleep with. It isn't too different with Andy.'

He changed his mind about a drink – poured and gulped. 'So young,' he muttered. 'Boys don't start so young with girls.'

'Things have changed, Carl. Kids move very fast nowadays.'

He said he had to get back to the studio – a lunchtime conference with Alan Devon. He asked her to check further, get Eddering or Sherman to recommend a specialist, an expert opinion. She said she would. He left quickly, wanting to flee this house and its problem.

God will punish you, Myra's sister had said.

TERRY HANFORD

Monday night Terry listened. She no longer tried to excuse it as unavoidable. She simply listened, trying to hear everything, trying to visualize everything. Lars was using that tickling routine, but Mona's laughter was blocked, choked, as

353

if she had something in her mouth. Terry visualized that too. There was no longer any anger. Weariness, yes, and a growing impatience, but no anger.

Mona had asked her to pose for a reclining nude. Terry had laughed and shaken her head, but if Mona had persisted a little more, she knew she would have agreed. Mona hadn't persisted. Mona had put an arm around her waist and walked her to the door and kissed her cheek and said, 'Well, some other time. Have a nice day, honey. Remember how much your being here means to me.'

Terry had called Stad Homer. They had gone out together and ended with a nightcap at Stad's apartment. That was three weeks ago. She had planned to go to bed with him and just hadn't been able to. Meaningless. Empty. Two strangers copulating.

She had phoned White Plains and asked her mother to give Bert Colwell her best. It had the expected results. Within a week Bert had written and asked if Terry was coming home to visit or whether she had changed her mind about receiving him as a visitor in Hollywood. Which made her realize she didn't want to see him. Which made her realize he too was a stranger now.

She wouldn't accept strangers anymore.

Mona was no stranger. And neither was Lars, vile little thug though he was. Mona and Lars, the only non-strangers in her life, however it had happened.

She worked very full, very hard days now. The publicity on Mona Dearn, Gordon Hewlett and Isa Yee was in her bailiwick, as well as general publicity on *Joneses*. Markal was giving her more and more responsibility. He had promised her another raise at the end of the project, and she was considered a natural to take over from Cole Staley when the aging head of Publicity finally retired, or was discharged.

She should be very happy. It was why she had left White Plains and come to Hollywood. A career. Success. A busy, exciting life.

She wasn't happy. She was satisfied in some ways, but not happy. She was waiting. She was letting time pass and waiting for love.

She had been thinking of Bennington lately and that boy with the deep, hesitant voice; that boy who had touched her heart, and died. She felt that something had to happen soon – change, conclusion, climax. She had been listening and observ-

354

ing for too long. She had to become a participant soon.

She had already dreamed of Mona coming to her room and her bed, but had awakened before allowing unconscious desire full latitude. She never thought of it directly. It was what saved her from running. It was what kept her ready for the night when it would be too late to run.

Monday night she tried to remember her earlier feelings about Mona Dearn, and couldn't, and listened a little more, and began to doze. She awoke when Lars walked by her room. He never paused anymore. He knew there was no hope. She closed her eyes again, but other footsteps approached. Terry sat up. Mona was there, touching the door, fingers scraping softly as if to reach through. Terry grew absolutely still. 'Are you up?' Mona whispered. 'Terry, do you hear me?' Terry didn't answer. Terry would never answer. Mona would have to open that door without answers and come to her without answers and then perhaps the answers would be waiting.

Mona stood there a moment, and went away. Terry lay down again. Not tonight. But soon.

Sleep wouldn't come. She got up, as she had so many times after Lars left, and took her book to the living room. She sat down in the striped armchair, the lamp with the comforting yellow shade behind her – the lamp that reminded her of fire-light and the tradition of kerosene lamps and candles, of reading and writing by flickering flame. But what she read was far from that romantic tradition; it was a book of prophetic pain and fury – *The Fire Next Time*, by James Baldwin.

She found it hard to concentrate, for her fire-next-time had nothing to do with black ghettos, but with that touching of her door, that whispering of her name.

She read on. She read until her eyes grew leaden and the words blurred and James Baldwin's voice was a lullaby, not an alarm.

CHARLEY HALPERT

Lars spent an hour with Charley Wednesday morning, going over a scene and making recommendations. By the time they finished it was twelve, and Lars said, 'Hey, man, you're beginning to look like an appendage to that typewriter. Let's go have a lunch with booze.'

Charley was pleased. Not that Lars had been unfriendly. He just hadn't been available for lunches. Charley felt he knew why and didn't blame Lars. He said, 'Great, but no alcohol. I slow down too much.'

'To a gallop, poor guy.'

They walked to the commissary, Lars turning to look at a tall platinum blonde busting out of silver tights and halter. 'Not a bad Ophelia,' he said.

Lars seemed to be pushing gags and laughter, pushing them harder than usual. Charley knew better than to ask what was wrong. With Lars, no sympathetic ears need apply.

They'd just been served when Lars murmured, 'Well, well, if it isn't De Lawd.'

Charley glanced up. Emma's nephew Free was coming through the crowded room, coming right at them. He reached the table, and Charley said, 'Hi. You working in a new—'

'I'm not working at all,' Free interrupted. 'I used my old pass to come here yesterday and I used it to come here today. To find *you*. One of you who patronized my aunt.'

Lars put down his fork. 'I know it's unfashionable, but you're one Negro I could easily hate.'

'Unfashionable? Why, man, you're running with the pack.'

'You've braced us twice now,' Lars said, voice getting tight. 'I don't know about anyone else, but that's about my limit.'

Free began to answer. Charley stood up and said, 'Before we kill each other, let's get acquainted. I'm Charles Halpert, and this is Lars Wyllit. We're writers—'

'I know. *The Eternal Joneses*.' He ignored Charley's outstretched hand. 'I put myself to sleep at night reading the trade papers.'

Charley lowered his hand and went on. 'The women with us were Terry Hanford and Isa Yee. I believe you know Isa. We went to Emma's house—'

'Does she call you Charles or Mr. Halpert?'

Charley blinked.

'Then you call her Mrs. Dale.'

Charley sat down. 'Mrs Dale was kind enough to allow us—'

'After you asked if you could see the inside of a Watts house, like looking at monkeys in the zoo. And when did you ever hear of a monkey saying you couldn't come look at him?'

Charley winced. 'I'm sorry if we offended you, Free.'

356

'Mr. Barchester. Humphrey Barchester.'

Charley said he was sorry if they'd offended Mr. Barchester, but Mrs. Dale *hadn't* been offended.

'And that's what's bugging our fiery panther here,' Lars said. 'It's not that we intruded on his aunt, but that he's *ashamed* of her. He doesn't want us judging Negroes by Emma Dale. That's right, isn't it, Mr. Barchester?'

'You think you know something about Negroes, do you, Mr. Wyllit?'

'I know something about people, yes.'

'I said Negroes, not people.'

'Negroes aren't people?'

'They're not *just* people. They're special people. Made special by you.'

Lars picked up his fork. 'Go away. You're spoiling a perfectly good lunch.'

'You must be quite the terror in Beverly Hills,' Free said, lips curling.

Lars stiffened. Charley put out his hand to prevent any sudden moves. 'Mr. Barchester, you *are* pushing hard.'

'That's because I'm a black. A *representative* black. Far more so than my aunt. And you two don't know anything about me. And you have to. Or is it only publicity about *The Eternal Joneses* being largely concerned with Negroes?'

Lars began to say something. Charley said, 'Wait,' and, 'It's true, Mr. Barchester.'

'If you want to know what blacks are *really* like, what they *really* think of this country and of whites, come to my club tonight. I speak on Wednesdays and Fridays. Come on down, all of you who made my aunt perform—'

Lars began to get up. Charley grabbed him and pushed him back down again. Lars's voice shook. 'Don't *do* that, Chuck!' Charley said, 'This is what I need, what I want!' and let him go. Lars's face was white, but he stayed seated. Charley said, 'I'd like that, Mr. Barchester, but tonight is short notice.'

Lars said, 'I've got a date to clean my toenails. I wouldn't break it for anyone like *him*.' Barchester said, 'The tough man. I've heard of you. Come to The Blacks. Come on *our* turf. See how tough you are.'

Charley said, 'Friday then?' Barchester nodded. Lars said, 'So we can be ganged?' Barchester said, 'Yes, by ideas. By a point of view you can't get here, or in Auntie Tom's cabin.' Charley said they would be there. Barchester said, 'Don't forget. I want you all. The four of you. I want you to see the real Watts.' He went back through the tables.

Charley looked at Lars. 'This is a tremendous break! The young revolutionaries. Exactly what I've been wanting!'

'The young pricks,' Lars muttered. 'When I was in Harlem, old Drew and his brother—' He waved his fork. 'Ah, screw it. Let's eat.'

They ate. Lars said, 'A whole club of pricks like that. I don't know how safe it is to take the girls.'

'It's perfectly safe. The man is trying to prove something. We'll be his *guests*. He won't forget it – if *you* won't.'

Lars said, 'Do you think I'm suicidal?' and went back to his salad.

The moment he reached his desk, Charley phoned Terry Hanford. She said it was fine with her. He asked her to make sure Isa Yee came along. 'Barchester was definite about wanting the four of us.' Terry said she would present it as a matter of importance to the *Joneses*.

She called in an hour to say it was all set for Friday. Charley got back to work. Later, he thought of Lars saying, 'Do you think I'm suicidal?' and began to worry.

Lois and Sugar came to Charley's door Thursday evening. He hadn't seen them in weeks and said hi and how's-it-going. Sugar said great and looked it. The blonde was flowering, taking on the glow of success. Lois said, 'Yeah, great,' and primped her hair, and he knew it was bad – the small deaths had commenced for her. 'I'm going home for a visit,' she said. 'I figured what the hell, I'm between engagements and why not?' He said certainly, why not. She moved forward. He said he was sorry he couldn't ask them in, he was expecting someone. Sugar said, 'Have fun, daddy,' and turned away. Lois, however, said, 'C'mon, Chuck. Just a half-hour's bull. I don't want to sit in that apartment with the world's greatest liar.' Sugar whirled around, eyes and face cold. 'She asks me, and I tell her. I tell her I've worked three days in a musical at Paramount. I've got an appointment to see Lou Grayson for a part and to see Mr. Mandel for a part and my agent says I'm in with *Joneses*.'

Lois said, 'Yeah, she's in all right. They bounce her a few times and she believes—'

Sugar said, 'You think she's going home to *visit*, Chuck? She's going home to *stay*. Say good-bye to Lois Lane, girl

358

nothing. No jobs, no auditions, no agent. You knows who's been paying the rent and the bills?' She tapped herself on the chest. 'She barely pays for her *clothes*. So, instead of saying thanks, she knifes me. *Let* her go home!'

Lois seemed out of answers. She forced a smile and shrugged. 'Maybe I *will* stay on the farm. This scene doesn't grab me anymore. I can lose it like *that*.' She snapped her fingers.

Sugar saw the implied surrender and calmed down. 'Well, if you want to come back to baby sister, you better shape up. I mean it, Lois. I got my own way to go and I don't want you or anyone else clawing my back. If you can't be nice, forget it, stay home. I'm paying the fare there too.'

Lois said nothing, smiling that ghastly little smile, then moved forward to enter the apartment. Charley blocked her path. 'As I said, I'm expecting someone.'

'The fat secretary?' Lois asked venomously.

'Good night,' he said.

The brunette must have been desperate for some sort of success. She actually pushed at him, murmuring, 'I've got that feeling tonight, Chuckey. You and me, we'll play bingo till morning. Or at least till the secretary comes. Okay? Just till she comes?'

'I've got work to finish.'

'Aw, listen—'

Sugar came over. 'Will you cool it, Lois! The man wants to work!'

Charley shut the door.

Sugar said, 'Hey, man, don't bleed about it. She's just low.'

Lois said, 'Let him bleed, the old fink.'

Sugar said, 'Chuck, it's not *me* saying those things. I'm with *you*, baby. See you at the studio?'

He said, 'Yes, good night,' and went back to the counter. He'd been trying to write a letter to Celia. He hadn't phoned her in months, hadn't written her more than two brief notes since receiving Collin's letter. She hadn't answered him. She knew he could have come to New York with Markal's group. She probably thought he was copping out on the marriage.

Well, wasn't he?

He tore up the note. He would call Sunday, or early next week. He turned to his script. He began reading what he had done that day.

It was going well and going quickly. He was writing twelve, fifteen pages a day, finished copy, outstripping the best output he'd ever had on a novel. And he was more certain of himself than ever before – especially since Markal had flipped over the first half of the script. Now Lars came in once or twice a week, wise-cracking about being too big an executive to work, and read what he'd written and talked about camera directions or a scene to be revised, slightly. Now Devon didn't come in at all.

The buzzer sounded for a call. It was Cheryl. Jim, it seemed, hadn't drunk much and was unusually talkative. She'd finally run down to the supermarket for some ice cream and was calling from there. 'I'm sorry, honey,' she said. 'I wanted to see you tonight. So much.'

He was sorry too. Now he was left with that unwritten letter to Celia and his unresolved ache for Bobby.

ALAN DEVON

He actually dialed Carny's number, but hung up before the first ring sounded. It would be so easy. Cheryl was at her desk. Carny was alone in his apartment. All Devon had to do was disguise his voice – a handkerchief over the phone would do nicely. All he had to say was, 'Your wife visits Charles Halpert's place at night.'

That would end it. That would finish her seeing Halpert. She hadn't allowed Devon a moment alone with her since the night Halpert walked in on them. He had gotten her a screen test for *Joneses*, then pushed until she was given a part. Any other actress would have kissed his feet; but what had Cheryl done? Said, 'Thank you, Mr. Devon,' and walked away! That's when he swallowed the hard fact that as long as Halpert was in her life Alan Devon was out.

Informing Carny was the only way.

Except that he was afraid. Cheryl said Carny owned a gun, had carried it in that paper bag when he came to the studio last fall.

She might have been lying. Devon himself hadn't seen a gun. She might have been testing him or trying to scare him off.

But what if Carny *did* have a gun? What if he used it? What if he tried to kill Halpert?

All right! The man was playing at love with another man's wife! He had to expect some risks!

What if Carny used his gun on both Halpert *and* Cheryl?

Carny wouldn't do that. He would simply stop Cheryl from seeing Halpert and later she would come around to Alan Devon and it would all work out.

One step at a time. First get rid of Halpert.

He used his handkerchief on face and hands and placed it over the phone. He dialed Carny's number again and hung up again. He was trembling, sweating. He just couldn't do it. Cheryl was too important to him. Too important to let go and too important to place in danger.

There had to be another way.

But hours later, getting an early start on his weekend in Palm Springs, he still hadn't found it.

ISA YEE

Friday at seven they left the lot in Isa's car. She was edgy, nervous, and told herself it had nothing to do with seeing Humphrey Barchester. Near the freeway entrance, she said, 'The more I think of this the less I like it. I mean, we all know what these people can do. They're *dangerous*.'

They sat as they had when they'd visited Emma – Halpert and Wyllit in back, Terry Hanford in front beside Isa. Halpert said, 'It'll be eight before we get there, and we won't stay long.'

Isa accelerated to swing into freeway traffic. 'What good will it do? We'll be more out of place than we were in that diner last week.'

Wyllit leaned forward. He seemed angry. 'Listen, I had *many* Negro friends in New York. I went up to Harlem with old Drew and his brother, and we had some crazy times. Girls and booze and all-night discussions and everything – everything you do with friends. And in the Village, at least a dozen Negro cats, men and women. I *lived* with a colored girl in her pad when I was broke. And old Drew had a white chick. It was give and take. We *knew* each other, for Christ sake! If old Drew was here—' He stopped and thought a moment, then remained silent.

Halpert prodded him. 'Do you think if you met Drew tonight—'

Wyllit muttered, 'He'd probably kick the crap out of me,' and sank back and lit a cigarette.

Isa stayed in the slow lane, the entrance and exit lane, feeling that Wyllit didn't really want to go and that together they might be able to cancel out this trip. She said, 'I'd like to turn back, honest. I'm . . . afraid. How about you, Lars?'

Wyllit said, 'It's too early in the season for race riots.' Terry said they were all being much too serious about a simple sight-seeing trip. Halpert said he was certain Free Barchester would see to it they were treated well.

Isa swung into the fast lane. If everyone thought it was safe, why should *she* worry? If they wanted to sit around and listen to a pack of kooks, why should *she* care? So she'd waste an hour or two. So what? Seeing Free meant nothing to her. Not anymore.

She found a parking spot a little past The Blacks and carefully locked the Corvair. Two teen-aged boys lounging against the wall looked at them and said things to each other with bad smiles on their faces. The taller one wore a 'Saint Malcolm' sweatshirt, the dead leader's bearded face on the front. He held up his hand as they passed, three fingers raised. Isa saw how Lars's mouth tightened and how Halpert looked away and she wondered what that hand-bit meant. And began to worry about Wyllit. She'd forgotten his speciality act. If he tried it here, they could all get killed!

They reached the door, which was painted-over glass, and Halpert put his hand on the knob. She quickly asked about the boy's gesture. 'Burn, baby, burn,' Halpert explained. He smiled thinly. 'Not exactly a sign of love and friendship.' He opened the door and she went in, heart pounding, mouth dry.

It was a shabby store with four rows of folding chairs facing a beat-up old desk. About twenty people, two or three of them women, sat on the chairs, and Free Barchester stood behind the desk, talking to them. There were some posters on the walls and a blackboard on one side of the desk and a flag on the other. The flag hung limp, but she could make out a black animal on a white background – panther, probably. The blackboard had three words chalked on it in huge letters – BLACK BLACK POWER. And that was it.

Free was saying, '—bring everything, I mean *everything*, to a standstill in Watts! *And* in every black community in this country, including Washington, D.C.! Then they'll know they can't run our lives for us!' The crowd began to say, 'Yeah!' and 'Speak it, baby!' and stamped and clapped. Free shouted, 'Then

362

we'll have *black* storekeepers, not Jews robbing us blind! Then we'll have *black* officers, not white cops beating us bloody! Then we'll have *black* teachers and delivery men and garbage men and firemen and politicians and everything else, because no white will be able to stay alive in this community or any other black community—' At that moment he saw Isa and the others, and paused. That's what we mean by Black Power,' he continued more quietly. 'That's freedom. That's what we want, not the cheat, the racket they call integration.'

The applause and shouts took over, and Free looked at Isa and smiled a little. She wanted to ask him what in the world he had to smile about. Twenty nuts and a lousy store? The poorest Southside street church had more going for it. She wanted to laugh in his face. *This* was The Blacks? *This* was his life's work? *This* was what was going to make him known throughout the country?

Big deal! As with everything in Coontown, she should have known they'd be all talk and no performance. Amos 'n' Andy at the Mystic Knights of the Sea Lodge, making like a political party. Amos 'n' Andy, right down to the funny hats – the fezzes and fur things scattered throughout the audience. And that cat in the green poncho! Wow! The Kingfish!

She almost expected him to turn and say, '*Hello* dere, Andy!'

And then he did turn, and she forgot Amos 'n' Andy and funny shines and felt cold inside. He said, 'Hold it. We're invaded by The Man,' and others looked and a few laughed. It wasn't friendly laughter and after a moment it was gone and the room just stared. Isa had to fight to keep from shrinking back. Because it felt like a great big *hate* lamp had been turned on full blast!

Free said, 'My guests are here. Movie people. They've left the land of make-believe for a little of the real thing. They don't know how real things can get down here, do they?' The audience laughed, and the hate seemed to go out of them. Free waved his hand at the front row. 'Four seats of honor, just for you.' Halpert went first and Isa followed him, down the side of the room and around the front. Halpert sat down next to a girl wearing a tight black dress and a cold look on her face. He nodded at her. She turned and looked at Free. Isa sat down beside Halpert, and Terry sat down beside her, and Wyllit took the seat on the aisle.

'My guests are late,' Free said, leaning forward on the desk. 'They've missed a lot. But since we're running this club for ourselves, since we're talking for *black* people, they'll just have to guess.'

The audience roared approval, shocking Isa with the noise they made – the angry, raging noise they made. No, the hate wasn't gone. She looked at the girl near Halpert, and the girl was pounding her hands together and chanting, 'Yeah! Yeah!' Free said, 'But we'll allow them equal rights with blacks tonight. They haven't earned equal rights the way we have, with two hundred years of sweat, of slave and near-slave labor. But we'll let them take part in our question-and-answer period.' He looked at the first row, running his eyes up and down the four from Avalon, and he didn't seem to know Isa was there. 'Because we're *human*,' he said softly. 'Because our hands, our hearts, our history aren't red with blood like theirs.'

This time the murmured approval seemed even louder than the shouts. This time Isa felt everyone's eyes, and for one crazy moment she wanted to say, 'Don't look at *me. I'm* not white.'

Halpert raised his hand. Free nodded. Halpert said, 'Could you give us a brief summation of your philosophy?'

Wyllit's hand went up, and he said, 'I can answer that,' and even though Halpert shook his head Wyllit continued: 'Invite people to your club and then insult them.' His face was tight, and his eyes hot and narrow.

There was an angry muttering, and the girl beside Halpert said, 'Why do we have to have them anyway, Free? Why don't you tell 'em to split right now? You always said this was one black club no white would ever invade. One black club that wouldn't allow—'

Free shook his head, smiling easily. 'Wait a while, Pearl. They'll go soon enough. They won't be able to take the heat. Like Mr. Wyllit can't already.'

Wyllit seemed about to get up and answer, but Free turned to Halpert. 'In a nutshell, our philosophy is a reversal of the old saw: If you're white, all right. If you're brown, stick around. If you're black, stand back.' He made a little circle in the air. 'We start with black and leave the whites out in the cold.'

'Does saying make it so?' Halpert asked.

'Sure. To the black, the ghetto black. If we say it loud enough, often enough, so that he believes it. Believing makes it so.'

'I don't quite see—'

'How did the Irish get political power? By first getting *Irish*

364

power. The same with the Italians and Jews. They used the Democratic Party and organized into streets, neighborhoods, wards. Soon they controlled—'

'*That* baloney again,' Wyllit said, and he didn't bother raising his hand and he looked at Free a certain way that frightened Isa. 'Quarter-truths. And you're not using the Democratic Party because they wouldn't have you. And the Irish and Italians and Jews didn't hate everyone who wasn't Irish or Italian or Jewish—'

'I suppose we invented anti-Semitism?' Free interrupted. He wasn't blowing his cool; he looked amused.

'No, you took that from us. You took the very *worst*—'

It was Terry who stopped him. She put her hand on his arm and said, 'That's an important point, Mr. Barchester. We've heard and read the explanations of black anti-Semitism – slum shopkeepers and all – but it doesn't really explain how Negroes can overlook the enormous help they received from Jews in the early days of the civil rights movement. And recently too. What about the two Jewish boys killed in Mississippi? What about all the Jews, the vast majority who don't own stores in ghetto areas? But above all, how can you use racist arguments—'

Free interrupted, 'It's the one way to go, baby.' The audience chuckled. Someone in back called, 'We learned everything from Mister Charlie.' Someone else said, 'Love ain't worked in two hundred years, so we're trying hate.' The laughter rose, and even though bad things were being said, Isa glanced around and it didn't *feel* bad, didn't *feel* dangerous. Halpert looked upset, but Terry was smiling and even Lars seemed to have calmed down.

Isa allowed herself a small smile. Free looked at her. Their smiles met. He seemed strong and sure, standing there. He was saying things these whites couldn't answer – and she remembered his arms and warmed inside. He said, 'In order to organize the black people, and make them act in concert, together for once in their history, we have to find something they share. *All* of them. Every black mother's son and daughter. *Hate for Whitey.* The one thing that lies in every black heart. So we're going to use hate to make blacks move together, vote together, buy together, refuse to buy together. We're going to use hate as a political power tool to gain true freedom.'

Terry said, 'I . . . just can't believe it will work.' She wet her

365

lips nervously. 'Let's make the question personal and specific. Do you hate *me*?'

Voice calm, manner reasonable, Free answered: 'As you would hate someone who kidnapped your grandparents, raped your mother, whipped and lynched your father, prostituted your sister, castrated your brother and made you ashamed of being a pretty girl with' – he made a show of examining her carefully – 'blue eyes, red hair and pink complexion.'

Terry flushed. Isa thought, *How right! How smart!* Lars raised his voice. 'That was a long time ago. If everyone hated back two hundred years—'

Free interrupted him sharply. 'We hate back to the minute before this one, which is usually when we've had our latest dose of white benevolence.'

Charley raised his hand and spoke at the same time. 'You lump all whites together, just as white bigots lump all Negroes together. You're all on Welfare, the white bigot says—'

'And he's not far from wrong,' Free interrupted. He looked to the back of the room. 'Uhuru, come up here and give these people some statistics.' Isa turned, and it was the kook in the green poncho. Free said, 'Uhuru's name means "Freedom" in Swahili. Uhuru's costume is the *buba*, a native African dress. Why do you wear it, Uhuru?'

The kook reached the desk and stood beside Free. He was tall and his head was shaved and he had long, hollow cheeks and wore heavy wraparound sunglasses. 'I wear it to bug Whitey.' He didn't smile. Isa felt he *never* smiled. He chilled her. 'I wear it to draw hatred. I feed on hatred and return it tenfold.' He moved his head a little, taking in the four from Avalon. 'You want statistics?' He leaned forward, hands on the desk. He spoke to the first row only, spoke with venom. 'Watts. It's young because we don't live too long. Sixty-three percent of Watts is under twenty-five. Compare *that* with the national average. And think of it when people tell you middle-aged blacks won't join the black revolution. Even if it's true, who needs more than sixty-three percent? And it's not true. We've got middle-aged men just aching to do something with their worthless lives. Because thirty percent of adult Watts is un-employed, and sixty percent on some sort of dole.'

Free said, '*Sixty percent* on some sort of dole, Mr. Halpert. So when the white bigot says we're all lazy, shiftless, living on white taxes, he's almost right. And it doesn't bother us. Do you know why?'

366

Halpert surprised Isa by answering. 'Because as a race you've earned it with two hundred years of slave and near-slave labor. I've heard the argument.'

'And you disagree with it?'

'I'm not sure. But I know that it doesn't help Negroes achieve respect—'

'Blacks, Mr. Halpert. *Nothing* will help blacks achieve respect. *Nothing*. No matter what blacks do. It's *your* sickness, daddy, your hang-up, not what *we* do or don't do. That's why this club is the wave of the future. We're not the NAACP. We don't care what whites think of us. We know they think the worst!' His voice was rising steadily. 'We've gone from trying to educate whites about blacks to educating *blacks* about blacks! We've turned from caring about white opinion to caring about *black* opinion!' His hands clenched into fists. 'We don't give a damn what Whitey says or does anymore! He hates us for being what we are – *black* – and we can't change that and we're not going to try!'

The audience was actually *throbbing* with him now, rocking and saying, 'Yeah!' and Isa felt she too was going to throb and rock and say, 'Yeah!'

'They tell us to wait, wait, wait! That soon we'll all be living together as equals. But they're lying! Maybe some of them don't know it, but that doesn't change the lie! There's no hope of living together! We don't want integration! We want our own power structure. They warn us white business isn't coming back to the ghetto. We won't allow it back! We want a string of black communities, owned by blacks and run by blacks, from coast to coast, that can be delivered as a political bloc to the highest bidder – to whoever gives us the most in jobs and other economic opportunities.'

The shouts and applause drowned him out. He wiped his face with a handkerchief.

Halpert didn't bother raising his hand. 'What you're saying is that you intend to use violence, riots—'

'Riots to Whitey,' Free interrupted. '*Revolution* to us. Riots in the white newspapers and on white television, because Whitey has to make dirt out of everything a black man does. Whitey wants us to think white and act white, to iron our hair and powder our faces. He especially wants us to *pray* white, because that'll keep us in line. But we reject it all. The black people reject it *all*!'

After the clapping, cheering, and stamping had died down,

Halpert looked around and said, 'The black people? I see only a handful of blacks here. Why aren't they jammed to the walls? Why don't you rent the Hollywood Bowl if all of Watts agrees—'

Isa saw he was getting to Free. Isa realized this was Free's weak spot. And just then Free interrupted, shouting over Halpert's voice. 'Every revolution is led by a small cadre, a cell, a group of dedicated visionaries! But all of Watts *does* agree with us!'

The girl named Pearl said, 'They just don't know it yet! They're confused by our Toms and the opiate of religion, but they *will* know it! Free and Uhuru and the rest of us'll *make* them know it!'

Halpert turned to Pearl. 'And the white majority? What if they decide not to allow you to burn out white businessmen and take over communities? What if your violence gives our extremists the chance—'

Free banged his fist on the desk. 'Will you allow Uhuru to finish his statistical report?'

Wyllit laughed, very softly. Isa still felt Free had strength, had fire, had an excitement these whites didn't have. But he didn't have all the answers. What *would* happen if whites got mean – meaner than they'd ever been? What if like Hitler and the Jews . . .?

Uhuru was speaking again. There wasn't a single movie theater in Watts or a single accredited hospital. There were far too few cars for a city where you couldn't live and work without a car. The birthrate went up and up and Watts grew more and more a crowded 'concentration camp'. Uhuru raised his voice and his right fist. 'And when it explodes, the pieces are going to blot out Whitey all over this land! When it explodes, we going to find freedom at last – freedom and power!'

He went back to his seat amidst cheers and applause. But Isa was wondering how could black blot out white when, as Halpert had said, white was so much more and stronger?

Free called on Pearl, the girl beside Halpert, for 'the woman's viewpoint'. She glared at the four from Avalon and in a shrill voice said, 'The black will get nothing from the white without exerting power. Women will play an important role in this effort by blacks. Because black women, like Russian and Chinese women, aren't *soft*. They're *tough*. They can work and fight with their men. And that'll help make up the difference between the number of whites and blacks.'

Halpert asked, 'What *sort* of power can you exert?'

'*Fear*. The black doesn't yet have the power of money, of majority of numbers, of balance-of-power voting. But *fear* is power. Making the white man afraid is the *only* power the ghetto has, and it *must* use it.'

'Dreams, dreams, dreams,' Wyllit muttered, but loud enough for Pearl to hear. 'Nazi beer-hall philosophy, with no chance of success. All the other choices for Negroes forgotten.'

'What do you know about choices?' Pearl snapped. 'We've got the same two choices we had during slavery. We can be field niggers or house niggers. Field niggers live in Watts and Harlem and all the other holes. House niggers live closer to the white masters. But they're still niggers. Emancipation will come when it no longer matters what the white man does to the black, but what the black does to *himself*! We've got to burn out every last white in every last black community, that's what we got to do!'

Wylitt stood up. 'Good night,' he said to Free. 'I doubt that even the few people here believe this nonsense. But for those who do, may I say I'm sincerely sorry for you.' He wasn't putting them on. He looked sad, looked sorry, and so did Halpert, and so did Terry. Someone said, 'Sit down!' and someone else said, 'Let 'em go!'

Isa didn't know what she felt, but she knew that Free was burning at Wylitt's ending things the way he had. She saw he was going to say something hard in reply, and she didn't want any more hard talk. She stood up and said, 'Free,' and beckoned. He looked at her, then spoke to the members. 'We'll discuss recruitment in a little while.' He came from behind the desk, still hard and angry. She smiled and held out her hand. He took it and she smiled again and murmured, 'We heard an awful lot of tough talk, isn't that so? I mean, we took it and took it and it wasn't supposed to be that way, was it?'

He shrugged and said, 'The truth is usually tough.' She began to withdraw her hand. He tightened his grip and turned to Halpert. 'Walk around. Look at the walls – at the posters and buttons. We print our own. We've got the standards: *Black Power*. *The Vietcong Never Called Me Nigger*. And so on. Then we've got a few that aren't standard. Take the button for our light-skinned brothers. *I Only* Look *White*.'

Isa froze. Halpert said he would appreciate a tour. Free led them to the side. He still held onto her hand, and Isa saw that

Lars had noticed. She made a face, as if to say, 'What can I do?' Wyllit didn't react, just lit a cigarette.

The members stood around talking, and Wyllit seemed satisfied at having had his way, and everything was cool now, safe now.

There were pictures of Negro leaders and slogans and parts of speeches. There was a big picture of Free and some of his statements. Isa felt they were sharper statements, brighter statements, than all the others. She wondered if maybe he *was* strong enough, smart enough to become a national leader. Her hand felt warm in his and she glanced around and no one seemed to notice and she squeezed his fingers.

Just then, Pearl came up. 'You were going to talk to my friend,' she said, and looked down at their hands. 'We been waiting while you waste time.' She was still full of anger, but it was a different *kind* of anger now.

Free let Isa's hand go. Isa felt anger herself, because she was certain that Pearl had more than *political* steam for her leader!

Free said, 'In a few minutes, Pearl,' and tried to move her away. She flung his hand off her arm. 'You know how hard I worked getting Barbie down here! You know how long I been touting her off poppin' pills and blowin' weed! Now when she's ready to check it out and dig, you're playin' around with Whitey!'

Free took her around the waist and muscled her away. They reached her friend, a small, curvy girl in tight pink pants and a man's white shirt with tails hanging loose. They talked a minute, and the small girl nodded. Free returned to where Isa now stood with the other three. 'An intense type,' he said blandly. 'I'd better walk you people to your car.' He looked at Isa, spoke only to Isa. 'I hope you'll visit us again.'

'Well,' Lars said, and sucked his teeth reflectively. 'So the man hates white, does he?'

Isa said, 'We're *going* now, Lars,' and turned to the door. So did Terry and Halpert, but Lars didn't move.

Free maintained his cool. 'Hating white is the smallest part of it.'

Lars dropped the cigarette and ground it under his heel, keeping Free fixed with his eyes. 'That seems to be a contradiction of everything we've seen and heard. Is it permitted to ask the leader to explain, or is a slogan all the white devils can hope for?'

Free smiled a little. Halpert said, 'Come on now, Lars.'

Free said, 'I'll explain, Whitey, even if you seem underage.'

Terry actually paled. Isa saw it and remembered that it had been some sort of crack reflecting on Wyllit's size that had set off the brawl in the commissary. But Lars merely lit a fresh cigarette and waited.

'The black community is flooded, inundated, *obliterated* by things white. Especially the black intellectual. White books and white plays and white art. Not to say white newspapers, movies and television. An all-white culture surrounds us and makes us despise our natural black looks and natural black ways. So the black revolutionary learns to love black.' He stared at Wyllit. 'Is it clear now, Whitey? I don't hate white nearly as much as I love black.'

'Very clear, Blacky.' Lars turned his eyes and a small, insinuating smile on Isa. 'Like all men on white horses – pardon, *black* horses – you've got holes in your intellectual pants.'

Free said nothing, but Isa could hear him breathing.

Terry said, 'Lars, please—'

Lars raised his voice so that everyone could hear them. 'You say you love black. Only black.' He continued to look at Isa, and she saw it coming and couldn't do a thing. 'Like our little black Yee here?'

Free stood absolutely still. Lars said, 'Speechless for once? Well, once is the best we can hope for.' He started to walk away. Isa murmured good night and followed, Terry and Halpert right behind her. Nothing happened and she let out her breath.

They were almost at the door when Free burst past her, knocking her aside. He swung at Wyllit, hitting the small man on the head, and began to swing again. Wyllit turned, crouching, and Free's punch missed. Wyllit straightened with his right hand held stiff-fingered before him. Isa couldn't see where it went because Free was blocking her view, but Free made a funny sound and bent over. Wyllit chopped him on the back of the neck and Free went to his knees.

Halpert had her arm and Terry's and was pulling them to the door Lars held open. They were out on the street and running. She was scared, terribly scared, because men were piling out of that club shouting filth and murder! And Free wasn't with them. Free was back there on his knees. Back there where he couldn't stop his friends if he'd wanted to and couldn't tell them she was blood and she was going to die in this lousy Coontown. She was going to die because she had let her past touch her and let a black man touch her.

Lars was pulling at the door of the Corvair, except that she had locked all the doors because everyone knew they stole everything that wasn't tied down in a Coontown. She would die because of that too.

Running, she tried to open her purse – to get the keys and throw them to Lars. But footsteps pounded behind her, and she was flung away from Halpert. And Lars was dancing away from the car now, hands up and out in judo fashion. She heard Halpert shout, 'Wait! It was a personal—' and then he grunted. She turned and saw him falling against the building with two men punching at him and he was punching back, his face all twisted. Wyllit came at the two men and they turned to him and then there were four and then there were too many to count and they were all punching and someone hit her in the back and she fell on the hood of the car. She looked up and saw Terry shaking her head and screaming and a man back-handing her yelling, 'Susie-belle-cracker! Susie-belle-cracker!'

There was no one to save them and she screamed along with Terry, letting fear and self-hatred take her completely. Because she was to blame thinking she could love black. She was to blame thinking she could love anything. She was to blame for not knowing she had to hate them all, white and black and brown and yellow, the whole damn human race and their fists and their hates.

LARS WYLLIT

Lars had always known it would come – the comeuppance, the final brawl, the day he got his lumps. But he'd been sure it would be with the Hell's Angels or American Nazis or another brand of fascist bully boy. He wasn't a bleeding heart, but he knew himself as a liberal, a man with a feeling for the pains and woes of other men. Specialty act or not, private madness or not, he'd believed in his heart that all men were brothers.

But now he was getting it from his black brothers, and they weren't his brothers, they were his deadly enemies. He wished he could kill every mothern' black brother here and save himself and the girl he loved. But he caught a fist in the mouth and felt his teeth break, his beautiful teeth. He hit back as hard as he could, going for larynx and balls and solar plexus, and got another shot in the mouth and two in the stomach and then so many he went down sobbing and trying to cover up. So many black brothers, God, and he couldn't take it, wouldn't live to die of his pounding, paining heart.

He heard Terry scream and would have gone to her except he was being stomped and was trying to hold to his consciousness so as to protect his head, protect his brain that was being kicked and scrambled.

He began to lose hold. He shouted and his shout was drowned out in the curses of his black brothers and he cursed them back with everything he had never thought he would say.

The kicking and stomping stopped. He heard someone saying, 'No, not the time ... between me and him ... not the women—' He took his bloody hands from his bloody eyes and saw things at a crazy angle but it was Barchester and he was running around pushing and yelling. Then the one in the green *buba* hit Free a beaut in the face and the great leader staggered back and another hit him another beaut and they said lousy-finking-Tom and house-nigger-go-on-back-to-Pacoima and they both hit him and Free turned, half-falling, and tried to get to the car where Isa was lying face down on the hood. But they chased him and the great leader ran and the ring of black brothers closed in again. Lars picked his head up and shouted, 'You dumb mothers! Pick your enemies more care—' And caught a foot in the head. He begged a little then, because it was a matter of living or dying and he didn't want to die.

Everything stopped. Hands dragged him up and he said, 'No more, please,' and was ashamed but Christ his face and his guts hurt so. 'All right,' the voice said. He opened his eyes. It was a black face and through his busted teeth he said, 'C'mon, man, cool it already.' The black face said, 'It's all right,' and he saw it was a cop. A beautiful Negro cop and he was taken into a car and put in the back. There were other cops and other cars, but it still wasn't all right because he heard shots, two of them, and there were a hundred black brothers on the street looking and moving around and windows crashed somewhere and if the firebombs started and the burning started and the hundred black brothers became a thousand and let their hate and despair break out then it was going to be the beginning of the end and not only for poor Lars, Terry, Isa and Chuck but for his mothern' poor Watts and its mothern' poor people. 'Oh God!' he said, and put his head back and fell out of everything.

TERRY HANFORD

Terry collapsed when the man hit her and screamed and he screamed louder than she did, calling her that hate-name of his, 'Susie-belle-cracker'. He stood over her and kept screaming while she waited for more and wept into the pavement that the violence she'd always despised and the brutality she'd always feared should come to her.

When nothing more happened and she was helped up she was first surprised and then felt dull and uncaring and sat next to Lars without looking at his bloody face and without thinking to fear for his head-back-eyes-closed stillness. She felt packed in tons of cotton. Halpert talked to the officer who drove the car and the officer said, 'Luckiest thing. We were just cruising by, keeping our eye on that place—' Someone shook her arm and said things and she recognized Isa's voice but she couldn't turn. No, better sit just this way and forget things. Just this way . . .

In the doctor's office, she felt the needle bite her skin and looked at the big, grayish-blond man. She said, 'Are they all right?' and before he could answer she began to cry. She cried so hard she fell over on the little table. She cried until suddenly it seemed foolish to cry, then sat up and looked for the doctor. A nurse was there and said he was in the next room with the 'small man'. Halpert and Isa were in the waiting room. She got off the table and the nurse watched her and she went into the waiting room. Halpert had a dark swelling on his cheek and a scrape on his forehead but said he was fine. Isa didn't have a scratch. Halpert said Lars had taken a bad beating. They were waiting to find out exactly how bad.

A policeman came in and told Isa the Corvair would be delivered to her home address later tonight. 'It's already out of the riot zone.' Halpert's face went gray and he said, 'Riot zone?' The officer said a *small* riot contained to an area of three blocks and just about over. He asked questions about pressing charges and identifying assailants and they all shook their heads and said they didn't know who had done what. The officer, a white man, said, 'Yeah, they're all alike, the bastards,' and then left. They sat on soft pastel-colored chairs and looked at pastel-colored walls. 'Well,' Isa murmured, 'he's not far wrong, in my opinion.' Halpert lifted his head, and Terry wanted to say something, but Isa said, 'Spare me the

374

civil rights speeches because I don't give a damn. I just don't give a damn!' She began to cry.

Later, the doctor came out and said he had taken and developed X-rays and Lars had abrasions and contusions and a bruised rib or two but 'miraculously no broken bones and no internal ruptures. His dentist won't be nearly as pleased as I am.' No one said anything, and the doctor looked at them in stern-father fashion. 'Would you people mind telling me why you go to that hell-hole anyway? Can't you get your kicks in *safer* ways?'

Terry would have told him off but this was Markal's doctor, and she remembered now how they had come to him — remembered things heard in the police car.

It was Isa who had insisted they be taken here and not to a hospital; Isa who had told the official that they couldn't afford bad publicity and that Emperor Nat Markal was responsible and that Mr. Markal would be 'very grateful'. The officer had been worried about Lars, but just then Lars had mumbled sure, sure he was okay and give him a cigarette for Christ sake. So they'd come to Dr. Theodore Wallach who was Markal's family physician and would keep things in the family. So they couldn't tell Dr. Theodore Wallach he was a silly ass who should stick to medicine and leave fatherly lectures to their fathers. Terry murmured it was all a ghastly mistake, and just then Lars came in. Talk about ghastly mistakes! Terry's stomach twisted.

Lar's face was a mass of scrapes and swellings and cuts and bruises. He walked bent over with tiny shuffling steps and spoke strangely, thickly through broken teeth and swollen lips. 'Does it hurt? Only when I breathe.'

They called two cabs, one to take Lars right home. He crawled painfully in back, then leaned on the window. 'Tell Mona,' he said to Terry, 'I won't be able to keep our date.' The cab began to move. 'Think of a good excuse,' he said.

Isa laughed. Halpert smiled and shook his head. But Terry couldn't find it in her heart to admire the man. Her heart was a very small and cold thing right now.

The second cab came, and they dropped Isa off at Century City, then went on to Avalon where they had left their cars in the commercial parking lot. Halpert asked if she wanted to drive with him and pick her car up tomorrow. She said no, she was fine, and they went their separate ways.

Incredibly, it was only ten o'clock when she entered the hill-top hacienda. She asked for Mona, and Lena said, 'Don't you remember? She's gone to a preview. She won't be home till late.' And then, 'What's wrong, Miss Hanford? Your lips . . . and you look . . . funny.' Terry felt funny. Lena was black and Lena was someone she saw every day and she was uncomfortable with Lena now. Fighting tears, Terry said, 'Lena, please tell Miss Dearn I'm not feeling well and I've gone to bed,' Lena asked if she'd like some cocoa and Terry said yes, that was just what she needed.

But she needed more. She was alone. She needed a friend. More than a friend. Tonight she needed a closeness that was more than friendship.

She got into her nightgown and came to the kitchen. She took two pills the doctor had given her and drank the cocoa and went to her room. The pills drugged her. The pills put her under. But sometime later she heard her name and pushed open her eyes. Mona was standing there, standing in the darkness near her bed, still dressed in gown and mink and smelling of the crisp evening. 'Lena said you were crying . . . your lips were puffed . . . news reports of a riot in Watts . . . were you—'

She couldn't focus very well on the voice or the woman, but Mona was concerned for her, Mona was sitting at the edge of her bed and stroking her hair and crying for her.

'All right,' she said. 'Just . . . tired.'

Mona went away, and Terry seemed to sleep, but through the sleep she was listening. Not to Lars and Mona tonight. Listening for something else. Sounds made by another two. Terry and Mona.

The night seemed to pass. She drifted just above sleep, drugged, but not as heavily as she told herself she was. Drugged, but still she could get up and go to the door and press the button lock. She had never used it before . . . but tonight she should.

Mona was back, sitting at the edge of her bed. Mona was stroking her hair again. 'If you'd been hurt . . . my heart almost burst . . . care so much . . . Terry, open your eyes . . . tell me—'

Terry lay drugged, telling herself she was deep under, too deep to open her eyes or know or care what was happening. Mona's hand went from her hair to her face, to her neck, to her breast lightly and briefly, to her arm. Both Mona's hands stroked her arms and Mona's breath touched her cheek and Mona's lips whispered, 'Terry, look at me honey. Terry, I love you. Let me—' Terry went under deeper, telling herself she couldn't hear and couldn't react and couldn't move. But her shriveled heart, her cold and frightened heart, beat faster, warmer, swelling as she was told she was needed above everything in the world, as she was touched on the breast again, kissed on the lips and held close.

Drifting, drifting, and how could she know what Mona was doing? Drifting drugged and helpless, and how could she be responsible for what happened?

Mona was lying beside her on the narrow bed. Mona's arms held her and they were mouth to mouth and their breath mixed and their lips touched, but how could she know what Mona was doing and how could she stop what Mona was doing when she was drugged?

Mona's hands rolled up her nightgown and stroked her body and clasped her. Mona was wearing nothing and her heavy breasts pressed Terry's breasts and her knee squirmed between Terry's thighs and her hands moved and her fingers touched and she whispered into Terry's mouth her need, her love, her desire. 'Please, please wake up, Terry, and help me.' But how could Terry hear and know and help when the doctor had given her two pills and she was deep, deep under?

Mona's hands took Terry's hands and placed them on Mona's body. Mona moved those hands around and said, 'Do it yourself, darling, please!' But Terry couldn't because she was deep, deep under.

Mona kissed her again and again, hurting her bruised lips with the force of those kisses. Mona finally said, 'Tomorrow, Terry? Tomorrow when you're well?' Mona got up and stood near the bed. Terry managed to open her eyes a slit. Mona stood in the faint glow from the window, gleaming white and beautiful. Mona said, 'Tomorrow, Terry,' and went out.

Terry slept, but a built-in alarm clock was ticking away. She was up at six, thick-headed, groggy. She washed herself awake and took a few necessities from her dresser and put them in her big handbag. She left the house quietly and drove to her apartment and called airline ticket offices until she got a reservation for that evening – an eight o'clock jet to Kennedy Airport. She had a breakfast of black coffee and stale cookies and felt it was late enough to make her other calls. The first was to Markal's home. She told him she had to get away for two weeks – just had to. He was properly sympathetic. He said thank God she and Isa and Halpert hadn't been hurt and thank God Lars hadn't been hurt *seriously*. He understood her feelings, but this was such a busy time and couldn't she do with just *one* week?

377

She said nothing. He sighed and said, 'All right. But let Cole know.' She phoned Cole Staley. He sounded half-asleep, but came fully awake when she told him. She said Leon Genning would have to cover for her. Cole said, 'Leon? You think he can handle it? Christ, what a time to leave . . . but maybe you'll get back a little early. At least to handle the *Look* group on the Washington set?'

She murmured, 'Maybe,' and didn't tell him as she hadn't told Markal that she might *never* get back. If she could make something out of this trip home; if she could find someone to hold onto this trip home . . .

Otherwise, she would be returning to Mona.

MONA DEARN

It was just one week since Terry had left, a Friday night, and Mona Dearn lay in bed, thinking and worrying about it. So Terry had needed a vacation. But why leave without a word, without a good-bye? Could it have been because of Mona's coming to her bed that night? Could it be that she had misread all the signs?

Every instinct told her that Terry was not only ready but eager for the affair to begin. Which meant Terry was running from it, running from herself. Which meant that nothing would be changed when Terry came back and that Mona had nothing to worry about. *If* Terry came back. But she had to, didn't she?

She continued to worry, and turned to Lars for talk, for amusement, for an end to worry. He lay beside her, flat on his back, dozing. This was the first time they'd gotten together since the Watts business, and only because she had called him twice this afternoon, pleading, saying she expected nothing but his company. Of course, after half an hour together they had gone to the bedroom. But he wasn't his usual self. His face was healing, but was still quite a mess. His dentist had worked overtime, but the caps were temporaries and just didn't look right. And she'd never seen so much black and blue on a human body before!

He had ended by depressing rather than cheering her, but she felt no man could have helped very much. It was Terry she wanted, she now knew. Terry's body and Terry's love. At least to try. At least to end the speculations and fantasies and

378

dreams. At least as *part* of Mona Dearn's love life.

She wasn't ready to give up Lars Wyllit – not by a long shot. She didn't want to give up either of them. Both were her wonderful friends; both could be her wonderful lovers. After all, she was not an ordinary woman, she was Mona Dearn. And she had the right to expect and get more from life.

She shook Lars. He opened his eyes and cleared his throat. 'Hey,' he muttered, and began to stretch and stopped, wincing. He sat up slowly and put his feet over the edge of the bed and went to the chair on which she'd put his clothing. 'Don't go,' she said. 'Stay the night.'

'You can't have me here in the morning when your maid comes.'

'She won't come until eight. It's only twelve. Talk to me. You never talk to me.'

He walked back to the bed. She smiled at him. 'It's funny about men. Big men can be small and small men big. My baby Don Juan.'

He lay down carefully beside her. She raised herself on an elbow, her heavy breast brushing his lips. He kissed it. She shivered and said, 'Where do you come from?'

'New Jersey.'

'What were you like as a kid?'

'Ordinary.' He sighed. 'I really don't feel well enough to stay. *Next* Friday—'

'There's no hurry. Tomorrow's Saturday. You don't have to go to the studio, do you?'

'I'm a writer. I work any day I can, anyplace there's a typewriter. Of course, *this* lousy assignment is more like Welfare than work.'

'I never really knew a writer. I met a lot, but you're the first in bed. Would you believe it?'

He smiled. 'Barely.'

'We were fated. Do you know that? I wanted the lead in the feature you wrote before *Joneses – The Streets at Night*. If I'd got it we'd have met then. But Markal said it wasn't glamorous enough. Now you're writing for me anyway.'

'Not me, baby. Chuck Halpert.'

'I met Ernest Hemingway. That was before I was well-known. Papa, they called him.' She could see how tired he was, could see he wanted to go – and was afraid to have him go, was afraid of being alone tonight. Alone with her thoughts. 'I met Irving Wallace. He won a Nobel Prize.'

379

'No. He wrote a novel about the Nobel Prize.'

'I've been married to an actor and a director. A writer can give so much more to a woman, can't he?'

'You've had samples.'

'He can talk to you. All those words in his mind. He can make life interesting. He can communicate. None of my three husbands could communicate.'

His eyes cleared. 'I never knew there were *three* marriages.'

She'd slipped. And now that she had she was almost relieved. Maybe talking about it would be good. She had never talked about it, except to that psychiatrist, and she hadn't told him everything. 'The first time in Queens, to an accountant. I don't talk about it much.'

'Many stars have marriages like that. Early marriages to cops or butchers. Or accountants.' His eyes lost their look of interest, became tired again. 'Outgrow them. An embarrassment.'

'He died,' she said, her voice tightening. 'It wasn't my fault. A burglary. Nat Markal knows about it.'

He was quiet.

'I knew the boy who did it. The cops killed him in a pawnshop. I shouldn't have talked to him, but I was only seventeen when I got married and except for two days a week in dramatic class I was always in that apartment. Anyway, Walter wasn't my type. I should never have married him. I was immature. He was eleven years older than me. He should have known better.'

He nodded. He put his hands behind his head and closed his eyes.

'You could write a book about it. There was this apartment house, a cooperative. It was new and very nice. I thought it was the most beautiful place in the world. But just downstairs and around the corner was a street, as bad as the one I came from. I came from a slum and my father wasn't very nice and I got married to get away from him and the sort of life I was living. I went to college at night, you know. The two days I had dramatic classes I also went to N.Y.U. and took English and art courses. I wanted to keep going, but then it happened and I got the insurance and I came to Hollywood.'

He nodded a little, eyes still closed.

'Angel, the boy who did it, he was only nineteen. He had a thing for me. I talked to him, but I didn't mean to encourage him. He was a rock, a real delinquent, and what did I need with rocks when I married Walter to get away from a neighborhood full of them?'

'Just downstairs and around the corner,' Lars said, and the way he said it showed he was half-asleep.

'You in dreamland, baby?'

He made himself come awake. 'Has a ring to it. Name the book *Just Downstairs and Around the Corner,* subtitle, *The Early Years of Mona Dearn.*'

'I was only kidding about a book. Just a lousy B-picture.'

He sat up. He was trying to show her he was interested when all he wanted was to go home and sleep. But that was because he hadn't really recovered yet. If they had talked like this when he was well ...

'Tell me,' he said.

'Nothing to tell. A kid gets married for the wrong reasons to a nice, quiet man. The kid is too dumb to know she's well off and that love sometimes comes later and that sometimes it doesn't come at all, not with a hundred men. Anyway, she plays around a little, just flirting, you know, with maybe a kiss in a car, nothing more. But she picks the wrong guy to play with, the kind of guy she grew up with, the kind she hates but at the same time the only kind who can kick her into orbit. You understand?'

He nodded. 'Attracts and repels. Love and hate closer than we think.' He leaned against the headboard and instantly his eyes closed.

'Not love. Just ... well, anyway, he was setting me up and took my house key and I didn't know. I thought I'd lost it. He said he'd meet me at the movies the night Walter went to his Knights of Pythias lodge, but he didn't meet me. He went to the apartment and Walter came home early and Angel knifed him and two weeks later Angel got killed trying to pawn Walter's tape recorder and fighting a cop. He never got the chance to bring me into it and no one knew. So it was over. No book there.'

'Maybe a short story,' Lars mumbled. She laughed, and his eyes flew open. 'What'd I say?'

'Nothing.' But he was right. It wasn't worth more than a short story, a half-hour TV show, if that. Girl plays around and husband gets killed and boyfriend gets killed. The end. Now she could play around and no one got killed. That was the advantage of belonging to the Hollywood elite. People drank themselves to death and pilled themselves to death but no one cared enough for anyone else, love or hate, to kill anyone else. They didn't care enough to even raise a fuss unless their publicity

381

She brought herself up short. It wasn't true in her case. She had her two wonderful friends, two wonderful lovers. She cared about them, and they cared about her.

Lars was falling asleep, leaning back with mouth slightly open. But that was because he was still one sick boy. She said, 'Before you leave, I want to show you something.'

He dressed. She took him down the hall past Terry's room to the locked door and used her key. 'I never show my work to anyone,' she said, and put on the lights.

She made herself look at the sculpture and not his face. She was afraid to look at his face. Yet she had to prove that Mona Dearn was something special.

When she got to the Roman gladiator, she turned to him. For a moment his face was blank; then his lips twitched and he nodded and said, 'I think I know that little bastard,' and he laughed.

He'd recognized himself, that's all his laughter meant. The shock of recognizing himself. She said, 'I was going to ask you to pose, but I remembered so well—'

He nodded, still laughing and said it was a good likeness. 'But forgive me, I never realized how silly I'd look in the kilt and greaves.' She said he didn't look silly! He stopped laughing and put his arm around her. 'I'm an uncultured sort. I peek under fig leaves at museums. Don't expect sensitive reaction or criticism from me.'

She was mollified – a little – but not happy. He hadn't said a word about her other work, and how could she ask? She walked him to the door. He said, 'Next Friday I'll be a lot sharper,' and pinched her breast. She giggled. He stepped outside, and spoke without turning. 'Will Terry be back then?' She said she thought so. He waved and walked away.

As she was turning off the bedroom light, he took off down the driveway in that hellcar of his, exhausts roaring – those buzz-saw exhausts so popular in L.A. Glasspacks, Angel had called them in Queens, a million years ago.

She didn't like the way her thoughts were going. She knew from past experience the blues were on their way.

She went to the living room and made herself a bourbon and water, a stiff one. She drank it and smoked a cigarette and leafed through a magazine. Then she went to bed. And couldn't sleep. She turned on her side, groaning, and the black thoughts descended. She turned on her other side, whispering, 'Hail, Mary, full of grace . . .' and couldn't go on because her mouth

382

was impure and her soul impure and he hadn't been to Confession in years. How could she, with Walter on her conscience?

'Oh God, it wasn't my fault, let me sleep.'

It *wasn't* her fault! The psychiatrist Nat Markal had sent her to said so. Not her fault, he'd said. Unwarranted guilt triggered by distorted memories, he'd said. If she'd been able to go to Confession, the priest might have said the same thing, in the way priests said those things. But she was married three times and divorced twice and all the screwing around and now Terry and going to church only on Easter and Christmas and not always a Catholic church, like last Christmas at the Unitarians and they were so *plain* about God.

She was sorry she hadn't made Lars stay, if only to sleep next to her.

Without Lars and Terry she was alone – and Lars was lost for a week and Terry too. Seven days, and nights, alone.

She would *never* have been alone if Walter had lived and they'd had children and a plain, quiet life together.

When the hell would she fall asleep!

Angel had put his hands on her and made his coarse pitch. She had laughed instead of run – and that laugh had murdered Walter. No matter what psychiatrists or priests or anyone else said, she and God knew her laugh had murdered Walter.

She got up and went into the bathroom and took a pill. She drank a glass of water slowly, talking to herself, working on herself to ease the pain.

Twelve years ago. Two husbands ago. Lars and Terry ago. It no longer bothered her. She had meant Walter no harm. If only he had gone to his lodge meeting that night. She hadn't given Angel more than a kiss or two, a little petting, pulling him off once in his car. She'd only been a kid – a stupid kid. She'd been about to stop seeing him. Anyway, it was so long ago and she had known so many people, so many men since then, and why should it keep coming back to tear at her?

She finished the water and washed her face, looking in the mirror. She wasn't even the same woman anymore. Mona Elgert was as dead as Walter Elgert. Mona Dearn couldn't even remember Walter Elgert's face, not unless she looked at that one remaining snapshot, and even then it was a stranger smiling at her – a square-looking guy, not at all her type.

She returned to bed. The pill and the bourbon got together and began to work. She began to drift away. And laughed at herself for having thought tonight's blues were serious, were

383

anything like that black pit of memory and fear that had almost swallowed her last fall.

So she was going to be lonely for a week. So what was one lousy week? She had Lars and Terry. She just had to keep that in mind. She had Lars and Terry. Either one was enough to make her life complete, and she had both.

She smiled, the blues going, going, gone.

CHARLEY HALPERT

Charley slept late Saturday morning, tired after a week of heavy writing – long hours put in at the studio and three long nights at his typewriter here. And the other two nights hadn't been what he could call restful since Cheryl had come over. But more than the drain of long hours had been the drain of grim thoughts. He had to write the violent aspects of the civil rights movement – The Blacks and their Humphrey Barchester – into *The Eternal Joneses,* and it had not been an easy job to do. He had to make clear the reasons for The Blacks, to justify their existence if not their methods. He had worked hard at it and now it was done. It had slowed him down and robbed him of joy in writing, but it was done. Now it was up to others to decide whether or not he had made his point – that the true path lay with neither Emma Dale nor Humphrey Barchester, but somewhere in between.

He had a breakfast of oatmeal and black coffee and whistled as he changed into bathing trunks and bathrobe. It was a bright, warm April day and he would go down to the pool. He was definitely feeling better today – was coming out from under the pall of last Friday night.

He slipped into his zoris, and there was a knock at the door. He opened it. The mailman held out a thick, much-stamped envelope. 'Certified airmail special, Mr. Halpert. You sure must owe money somewhere.' Charley laughed at the man's joke as he signed the registry card, but the pall had descended again. He knew what was in that envelope with the New York legal firm's return address.

He went to the couch and sat down, hoping against hope that he was wrong – until he held the forms in his hand. One, the *Summons,* was a single sheet, almost square, smaller than typing paper. The other, the *Complaint,* was three pages long

and slightly larger than typing paper. Together they constituted the first forms served in a divorce action originating in
New York State. From Celia to Charles Halpert. She was
charging him with desertion, but that was something the lawyers knew he could fight with a good chance of success, so there
were also charges of adultery and mental cruelty. The letter
from Winston Perrins, Jr., made it plain that the firm hoped
he would go along with their client, that he would in fact *aid*
her and so make an out-of-state action unnecessary.

He was expected to get an attorney of his own and file a
notice of appearance in New York to answer the charges. If he
did nothing, an inquest could be held and 'a default declared'.

He sat there and read the papers again and again. He wasn't
surprised, but he was shocked. He remembered that their fifteenth anniversary was coming up in June, and this added to
the shock. He hadn't spoken to Celia in months, hadn't written
to her in months, was deeply involved with Cheryl Carny – and
yet he was shocked.

He put the papers back in the envelope and the envelope in
his dresser. He wasn't ready to answer Belish, Wallestein,
Perrins & Perrins. He wasn't ready to answer Celia. He wasn't
ready to tell his son he was giving up being his father, because
with Bobby in New York and he here . . .

He wasn't ready to think of any of it. They would have to
wait.

He went down to the pool and saw Lois Lane coming out of
the west wing doorway that led to the lobby. He waved. She
came over, holding two packs of cigarettes in her hand. He
began to say something about her trip home. She cut him short,
smiling thinly. 'Yeah, after five days I was climbing the walls,
so I called Sugar and she wired me some bread and I flew on
back. Walk me to the pad, Chuckey? You never even seen it, far
as I can remember. Unless you and Sugar touched a few bases
while I was away.'

They walked to the back entrance, Charley saying he was
glad Lois had finally come to terms with her sister. 'Me?' she
retorted. 'I'll pay off her bread soon as I land a decent part.'
But the old pizzazz was lacking: Lois was neither convincing
nor convinced. She was back, on Sugar's money and Sugar's
sufferance – which meant she had accepted certain conditions,
whether or not they had been stated. This became painfully
clear when they entered the ground-floor apartment on the
other side of the pool. It was no larger than Charley's, but had

two sleeper couches instead of one, joining as a sectional unit in the corner. Sugar sat sprawled there, reading a script, wearing a shorty nightgown of thin white material. She smiled at Charley and said, 'Hey kicky-poppa, how goes it?' and only then stood up. 'Wasn't expecting man-type company. Guess I better put on pants.' She moved leisurely toward the bathroom. 'Listen, sister, give me some warning next time. Chuck likes black lace.'

Lois muttered she'd thought Sugar would be dressed.

Sugar disappeared into the bathroom. 'You know I got that Lou Grayson part to learn. You know I'm staying in all day today and tomorrow.' She reappeared, black lace showing through the thin nightie. 'That better, Chuck?'

'I'm a man-type man. I liked it better the other way.'

Sugar smiled. 'How'd that old farm-girl thing go, Lois? You know, about *wra*stling?'

Lois shrugged and dropped the cigarettes on the coffee table. 'They were out of king-size. I figured I'd better stick to your brand.'

Sugar said fine and come-on-now. Lois said, 'I can't wrastle but you oughta see me box.'

Sugar laughed. 'Mr. Blessington called it evil. No, *vulgar*. He said it was vulgar and please not to say it. But every time she said it he got that look and his paws started pawing. You see Mr. Blessington while you were home, Lois?'

Lois sat down in the one armchair and opened a pack of cigarettes. 'No.'

'I told you she'd be back, Chuck. No one could make it down there after being in God's country. I mean, like Hollywood is *heaven*! She tell you about what's happened to me?'

Lois said she hadn't gotten the chance. Sugar said, 'The Lou Grayson part came through real fast. And Mr. Mandel's musical – but there I've got a *fat* part! I mean, that could be it! I sing and I get to kiss Rory Rourke and I do a kind of striptease on a night-club table. My agent says he's got parts lined up for a good three years! But we're not signing for more than these two and *Joneses,* because he wants strong featured or even starring from here on. And there's a French producer in town and he's impressed and he might put me in with Jules Farineux. That could be it too! Anyway, my head's busting from all the work and I've got advances like I never dreamed. I mean, *eight grand,* Chuckey!'

He said that was marvelous. Sugar said, 'Lois, let's have some

386

Cokes. I mean, long as you brought Chuck around we might as well relax.'

Chuck said they could see he was dressed for swimming. 'Or balling,' Sugar said, and jumped up and ran to him and gave him a hug that turned on that old pornographic spigot. 'Um*mmm*! When I think how it was you got me started I could just eat you up!' She bit his cheek. He disengaged himself, watching Lois take Cokes from the refrigerator. Sugar drew him to the couch and curled up with her knees in his lap. Lois handed them each a bottle and went back to the armchair. Whatever she felt – and knowing Lois it must have been plenty – she said nothing, didn't even allow her expression to change.

'Lois got a part too. Tell him, Lois.'

Lois shrugged.

Sugar looked at her and waited. Lois said, 'I'm in another *Desert Marauders*. Harem girl again.'

'Only this time she's got lines. Tell Chuck.'

Lois looked at him – a bleak, controlled look. 'I say, "When the moon rises my master will come to me. It is then that the captain can escape." '

'And how'd you get those lines?' Sugar urged, nodding and smiling. 'How come they changed you from a walk-on to lines?'

Lois sipped her Coke and dragged deeply on her cigarette. 'Sugar spoke to her agent, and he's got an in.'

'He said I'd do a part for them next month if I have time.' She grinned. 'They gave her the line because—'

Charley wanted to ask her not to spell it out in block caps, but listened while she did. He said it was time for a few laps in the pool, then back to the old typewriter. Sugar said, 'Sure. It's the only way to make it, right, Chuck? When the time comes, give it all you got. Bobby says – Bobby Chankery, my loverboy agent – he says I'm on the threshold.' She giggled. 'Only he didn't say it that way. Ass on the table, he said. It means something different than it sounds.'

'Moment of truth,' Charley said. 'An old Yiddish expression.' He stood up. 'You want to swim, Lois?'

She began to rise, but Sugar said, 'Maybe later. She's got to hear my lines. I mean, it's her bread and butter too, isn't it, Chuck? Just like you told us. If one's making it and the other isn't—'

Charley waved and ran, feeling the room was full of raw wounds and salt.

Carl looked uncomfortable. Ruth asked him what was the matter. He murmured he'd thought this yacht party was going to have a broader mixture of guests. 'Not quite so many members of the Let's-Kill-Nat-Markal-Society.' She said that just because Olive Dort was there was no reason to assume . . .

'And Sol Soloway and Ron Besser, and all three buzzing around like busy little bees.'

'But this is Lou Grayson's yacht. Grayson owes Markal his career. He wouldn't—'

'Oh, wouldn't he?'

'Has anyone said anything to you yet?'

'No. And I'm beginning to wonder why I'm here.'

'Alan Devon's here. And other pro-Markal or nonpartisan producers.'

'Devon's not so pro-Markal lately. He didn't like Halpert's treatment, and I think Markal rode right over his opinion. Also, he's not getting to see the script as it's written. It goes directly to Markal. I'd be a little sensitive about that if I was the producer of record.'

Ruth accepted another champagne cocktail from a steward wearing a white uniform with the initials LG embossed over breast pocket and on a cap emblem. They were cruising north toward San Francisco, and the night was slightly foggy and turning cool. She asked Carl to get her wrap from the dining salon.

Margaret Sholub came over and said it had been a long time and how was Carl. Ruth said fine and how was Moe. Margaret looked around and lowered her voice. 'Have you heard about Markal? They've kept it out of the columns, but it seems he and a little Eurasian slut are burning up the Century Plaza.'

'Where did you hear *this*?'

'Moe just told me. Ron Besser told him. Oh, it's authentic, all right. The great man and all that crap! I think his wife was having him followed, and the detective leaked the news to Olive.'

Ruth said she was sorry to hear it, if it was true, 'But even so, it wouldn't be the first time a big man played a little.'

'Well, yes, if that big man didn't jump all over everyone *else* for playing a little. I mean, if he's that kind of hypocrite, how can we feel safe having him control our destinies?'

388

'Are you working at Avalon now, Maggie?'

'You know what I mean. Moe has been listening like a good boy to his Emperor and he's shelved everything but *Streets at Night* until after *Joneses* and Lord knows how long *that* will be. Now we find out Markal's balling it up—'

Ruth said she saw Carl and please excuse her. Margaret's face hardened. 'And if it was *your* husband?'

'But it's not. It's my husband's boss.' She walked away and met Carl near the cabin door. 'You were right,' she murmured. 'This *is* a back-stab operation.'

'I know I'm right. Sol Soloway just told me about Markal and Isa Yee.'

'Aren't they being silly? What can Markal's private life have to do with *The Eternal Joneses*? And it's Sankin they have to convince, not anyone here.'

'Yes, but with some of the people here to join them, convincing Sankin might be possible.'

'You really think so?'

'If *I* was Sankin, with every dime tied up in Avalon common and solid Avalon people like Devon, Grayson and Moe Sholub worrying out loud whether Markal was to be trusted with the very life of the studio, *I'd* worry. If they told me that the Washington set cost a million-five and was going to be burned, I'd *sweat*. And if they said, as Soloway said to me, that Markal was using the film as a means to personal aggrandizement – his exact words – and to push the career of his girlfriend and didn't care how much it lost—'

'You wouldn't believe it.'

'I wouldn't have to. Soloway also said I should've been shooting *Terror Town* and getting ready with my next production. He said if it was up to him, solid profit-makers like myself would have long-term contracts at increased budgets.'

'Uh-oh,' she muttered.

'Well, Markal *did* yank me off as if I was some kind of office boy. He didn't bother *asking*, just stole my writer, dumped my feature and put me back on special effects. And his choosing Brad Madison for a featured role in *Joneses* – an unknown with all sorts of personal problems – after I warned him—' He shook his head. 'I don't know what's been happening to him, but maybe playing around *is* taking his mind off business. Maybe he's not the man we should trust with our future. *I* certainly have no reason to support him. What did he ever do for me? I mean, I turned out one money-maker after the other—'

'I've got the message, Carl.'

He reddened. 'Well, dammit, I've got a right to look out for myself, haven't I?'

She was saved from having to answer when Grayson's voice boomed over the ship's loudspeaker system: 'Now hear this! Dancing on the deck to Rico Miranda and his Latin Lunatics. No more shoptalk, kiddies. Let's swing!'

But there was plenty more shoptalk, both that night and the next day. And no one seemed upset at the sly-dog methods Olive and her coterie had employed. In fact, everyone seemed a little pleased that the great man had been shown as human as they were, and might not be a great man for long.

Including, Ruth noted sadly, Mr. Carl Baiglen.

She was out on deck when they came in sight of Santa Monica Sunday afternoon. Olive Dort was standing at the rail between Moe Sholub and Clete Brown. She pointed at Markal's cliff house and said, 'Somehow, I expected it would have slid into the sea last night.' Sholub and Brown both chuckled.

Ruth hoped Dave Sankin was a loyal friend. If he wasn't, Olive might soon be making many more jokes at Nat Markal's expense. If he was, all the joking and gossiping and back-stabbing wouldn't mean a thing.

NAT MARKAL

Arnold Ryan called him Wednesday morning. 'Call me back on the special phone. Nat.' Nat did. Arnold had spotted a tail last night. 'From the studio to the Century Plaza. A gray Ford. Then it went to the Century Towers. It seemed to be on a dark girl walking to the hotel. I wish to hell we had run these checks two and three times a week, Nat. Who knows how long they've been watching you?'

Markal said there was nothing to worry about.

'C'mon now, Nat. We're old business acquaintances.'

'We're better than that. We're friends.'

'I'd hoped so. I think the Ford was taking infra-red photographs. If you've got anything to hide, prepare yourself. It's as good as out.'

'Nothing to hide, Arnie.'

'Whatever you say, Nat. But if it's a shakedown, I want you to let me know. It can be handled, with money or without.'

390

Markal was silent a moment. 'Find out who and why, Arnie.'
'Right.'

Nat Markal locked up the closet phone and returned to his desk. And slumped in his chair and put his hands to his face. The pain came. The shame came. Then he took hold of himself and smoked and paced the office. He hoped it was Adele. He could handle her. But if it was Olive . . .

He began putting things together. Lou Grayson had given a yacht party last weekend. Devon had been there, and Sholub and Baiglen and several others connected with *Joneses*.

He called Devon. 'How was the yacht party, Alan?'

Devon's voice was smooth and cheerful – and somehow different. 'Sort of dull, Nat. With his wife along, Lou wasn't his usual self.' He laughed.

Nat said, 'I heard some rumors about the talk that went on.' He waited. Devon waited. He outwaited Devon. The producer spoke hurriedly, running his words together. 'You know Olive, Nat. She's always clawing a little. No one believed—'

Nat said he was glad to hear that, and Devon asked when could they lunch, and Nat said, 'Today. We're going into immediate production.'

'You mean . . . *Joneses*?'

'That's right. Chalze has gone over the script – the first half – and says it's ready. Halpert is moving quickly on the second half, and it's going well. The Washington set will be completed this week. No reason to wait another day.'

Devon said, 'Don't you think we should discuss—'

Nat said, 'At lunch, Alan.'

It had to be Olive. Arnold Ryan would check, but Nat wasn't waiting for confirmation of what had to be the facts. He was in for it now. No matter what countermeasures he took, the rumors would fly.

There were two things he had to do immediately: start filming and drop Isa. They were necessities. No room for doubt there.

He felt there was something else, something vital.

He paced and smoked and his instincts functioned and a hunch developed.

He called Dave Sankin in New York, not bothering with the special phone. If the story was out, it was out. 'Something's happened to me, Dave. Purely personal. Nothing to do with *Joneses* or business. But since we're so dependent on each other . . . Do you remember Isa Yee?'

It hurt like hell, reducing a lifetime pride this way, stripping himself bare in front of Sankin. But when it was over, he felt it had worked.

'Sorry to hear this,' Sankin murmured. 'Does Adele—'

'I don't think so.'

'I'll keep it in strictest confidence.'

'I'm glad you know. It's a load off my mind.' Which was about the biggest lie he'd ever told!

'What do you intend to do about it, Nat?'

'Stop seeing the girl, of course.'

Sankin sounded pleased. 'Of course.' His voice changed, became chuckly-manly-hearty. 'Everyone's allowed *one* slip. I'm sure it'll all work out.'

Nat went to the washroom and took two aspirin and scrubbed a film of oil and perspiration from his face. He lit a fresh cigar and thought of Isa, thought of not seeing her anymore, made it specific by telling himself she wouldn't be in his arms tonight.

It hurt. It hurt worse than telling Sankin. It hurt worse than thoughts of gossip and confrontations with Adele. It hurt worse each second, and he tried to reason it away – after *Joneses* they could take up again.

After *Joneses*. A year. She would find someone else. He would lose her.

But he phoned the Towers and told her what was happening. He said, 'We can't see each other—' and tried to say, 'anymore,' and couldn't. 'For a while.'

'I'm sorry,' she said, but she didn't sound sorry enough. 'Well, see you at the studio.'

'Will you . . . begin dating again?'

'I think so. Life goes on.'

It was what they said when someone died. Life goes on.

'Isa,' he whispered, voice breaking. 'Isa, don't . . . see other men.' He was ashamed of himself, of his weakness, but the pain was too much, the need for Isa Yee too much. 'It'll only be for a little while. Wait a month. We're beginning *Joneses*. There'll be opportunities . . . while working . . . we can get together.'

'It's all right with me,' she said coolly, 'but don't kid yourself. Once people know, they know. You can never get away with sneaking it again. If you want to see me, make up your mind it's public knowledge.'

'You sound almost . . . happy about it.'

'Of course not. But it's a fact. I'm good at accepting facts. Are you?'

He said he had to think things out. She said, 'Good-bye.' He said, 'Wait. Saying good-bye on the phone this way ... Let's meet once more, at the suite, tonight.'

'All right. But it's stupid.'

She was right. He said, 'Forget it.' Again she said good-bye. Again he said wait. 'Is there any way ... can you think of any way, Isa?'

'Yes. One way. Marriage.'

He laughed – a sound of surprise and shock.

'I don't think you have any problem, Nat. Not as long as you can laugh at me.'

He said he hadn't been laughing at *her*. But the line clicked in his ear.

Well, one of them had to hang up. It was all for the best. He walked around the office and smoked. He thought of the last time and her nails digging into him and her voice thick and sweet in his ear. And afterward, holding her while she slept.

It hurt. God, how it hurt!

ISA YEE

Thursday at six Isa bathed and dressed, smiling to herself as she put on makeup. Markal had called twice while she was out testing at Universal this afternoon. Yesterday he'd said they couldn't see each other, and today he had phoned twice. But she wasn't returning his calls. He would have to come here, on his knees, before she'd give him any hope. He would have to eat that laughter of his for breakfast, dinner and supper before she would give him so much as a smile.

He didn't know Jerry Storm was pushing her for the second lead in *Vietnam Story*. He didn't know Universal was looking forward to stealing her once *Joneses* had made her a star. And if Jerry was right about the contract he could get, she would never need another Nat Markal again.

But that was in the future. Nat Markal was still important to her present.

She stopped and looked at herself in the mirror. Present or future, as *Mrs*. Markal she would be half-owner of an empire.

393

It wasn't altogether impossible. She might be able to work it. If he was hooked hard enough . . .

The phone rang. Probably Markal. Time to give him more cool words. She would let him know she was dating the handsome English star, SWV. He wouldn't have to know Jerry had arranged it. He could sweat tonight, thinking she might open her arms to the Limey.

She said, 'Yes?' very sweetly.

It was Free. 'Hey, you want to come to the club tonight?'

She laughed. 'I wouldn't go back to that freak-out joint if they were giving away solid gold panthers. You must be flipped even to suggest it.'

'It was Whitey got clobbered, not you. A little push—'

'And what about *you*? I seem to remember your catching a few cute ones in the mouth.'

'Nothing,' he muttered. 'Talked to the boys the next day and it was all smoothed out. I'm a full-time resident of Watts now. My going home to Pacoima every so often was a greater irritant to the brothers than I realized. Now they've welcomed me back.'

'As *leader*?'

He hesitated. 'There's no one leader. Denny and Uhuru and I are sharing the speaking chores. But in time—'

She laughed again. 'Well, have to run. The Man is waiting for me. Whitey. Mr. Charlie. The fay. How I suffer.' Her laughter kept coming. She'd shaken loose of Humphrey Barchester. He was ridiculous to her now, just another horny male now. Not that she wouldn't have liked him for an occasional toss in the hay. He was good that way. He turned her on that way. But she suspected that was because he was black and black had become her kick and any young Negro would do.

She would have to check it out. She thought of the big raw-boned kid in the supermarket near Avalon who flashed his eyes and teeth at her every time she came in. Wouldn't he just cream if she took him home with her! To carry a particularly heavy delivery, of course. And then a little teasing. And then . . .

The feeling she got was unmistakable. But it wasn't anything that would get in her way. Nothing like that again.

Free said, 'In time you'll understand the complexities of the revolution. Until then, I'll come to your place. Tomorrow night?'

She laughed and laughed.

'Let me know when you're finished laughing,' he said. 'But don't hurry. I've got plenty of time and plenty of dimes.'

'I'll never finish laughing.'

'I'll be there in an hour.'

'Anytime is fine for standing around outside a door, if that's your kick.'

'Sure, like the last time.'

'No, not at all like the last time. Because I'm laughing now.'

'Listen, Isa—'

'Humphrey Barchester, the great emancipator!' She laughed so hard the tears came to her eyes. And laughing, hung up.

Sommy Virgil arrived and they drove to the party that Joe Levine was hosting at the Beverly Hills Hotel. Gordon Hewlett, alone and a little high, made a strong play for her, and Sommy pressed his own suit. Both danced much too close and kept taking her out on the terrace and Hewlett tried to get her to leave with him. Fun-fun with people looking and whispering, and maybe some of the whispers about Nat Markal, and that was all right too because it was all hot publicity for Isa Yee who was on her way to Coldwater Canyon or maybe that tremendous house atop the Pacific Palisades.

In the car, later, Sommy grew overardent and talked about getting her a featured role in his next picture. They reached the Century Towers and she told him it was the wrong time of the month and after a little wrestling he drove away.

She felt marvelous about the way things were going. She took a leisurely bath to extend this wonderful evening and thought about Free, briefly. Perhaps she shouldn't have put him down so hard, but what did it matter anyway? He couldn't hurt her even if he wanted to, and why would he want to? They'd spent a few great moments together, a few bad moments together, and now it was over.

No one could hurt her. She had it made.

FREE BARCHESTER

'What sort of scoop is it?' Killerboy Collerby asked his old friend. Free had phoned him at the studio about an hour before he was to go on the air. 'I'm a deejay, not a reporter.'

Free said he didn't expect Killerboy to spread the word himself. 'Suggest names of people who might be interested in a movie actress who's hiding her race.'

'If you're going to say Elizabeth Taylor, I'll be forever grateful. *She's* what we need, not Uhuru.'

'Not that well-known. But on her way.'

Killerboy gave him three personal friends on L.A. papers, two more who would take a chance on hot items and one very big New York columnist who was slipping and would print anything sensational. 'You going to let me guess about this, Free?'

'For the moment, yes.'

'Hope she's foxy and frisky.'

'She is.'

'Well, all right then. I always enjoy adding another prime prospect to the race. Except for their strong smell, I kinda like nigger gals.'

Free chuckled. Killerboy was black and tough about it. He was one of the most successful disk jockeys in L.A., and not just among black listeners.

'Can you back this up, Free? Do you know where she was born and the name on the legals? Could you check her birth certificate if you had to?'

'Yes. She told me everything herself.'

'I can imagine when.'

Free wrote several carefully worded letters that night, signing them and giving his Pacoima address. Each had as its central theme the fact that Isa Yee was excited about her role in *The Eternal Joneses* for more than the usual reasons. She had been telling friends, he wrote, that playing a slave and the descendants of that slave was particularly meaningful to her because she was herself part black. Miss Yee's purpose in revealing her true racial origin was a most laudatory one. She wanted to give assistance to her people at a time when they seemed to need it most. She expected to hold a news conference in the near future to announce her full participation in the civil rights movement.

He made five more copies, changing the wording slightly in each, and addressed them to the publicity directors of the major civil rights organizations. Then he put all the letters away in a drawer. If Isa called his Pacoima home, his sister would let her know where he was. Isa could tell him she was sorry. She could tell him she wanted to see him.

He would wait a few days, a week or two. He would give her a chance.

He wrote another letter, to Ollie Smith of a Malcolm X group in Harlem. Ollie might provide The Blacks with its first East Coast branch. He went downstairs and ran into Mrs. Edder waddling across the hall. She was a widow of sixty, enormously fat, who kept a clean, quiet house. A Tom like Aunt Emma, but without an Uncle Walter around to bug him. She saw Ollie's letter in his hands and nodded her approval. 'Always let the folks back home know how you are. Tell them you're in a nice home, Humphrey. Tell them Mrs. Edder don't allow no carrying on.' He said he would and went out. He mailed the letter and got in his car. He drove to downtown L.A. and saw a movie and ate in a good cafeteria. It was such a relief to get out of Watts!

Later that night, he read over the letters on Isa. Down the street one of Watts's hot-pillow motels was rocking. Killer-boy's program was on in at least half the rooms. In the other half they'd lowered the volume, for a while.

He put the letters away, turned off the light and got into bed. Tomorrow he too might avail himself of the motel's advertised special – '$3 for 2 hrs. Free ice.' Pearl was willing. Pearl was eager. And there were other Pearls. Watts was full of them. He could have his pick – including, if Emma only knew, his sweet baby cousin Arlene, just dying to break away from Momma-Tom and cut loose with Black Power.

But he would wait for Isa's call.

If she called.

For one agonized moment he felt he could never mail those letters. He didn't want to hurt her, he wanted to love her – that night in Isa's honey arms . . .

The moment ended. If she didn't call him she was rejecting her race. And her race was his life.

LARS WYLLIT

He had promised to see Mona on Friday, and see her he did. But it wasn't the happiest of dates. The weather had turned damp and unpleasant. His bruises still ached. Her hair looked limp. For the first time they exchanged harsh words – about the restaurant (he was sick of the flashy, overpriced

397

joints she equated with quality) and about what to do after-ward (he wanted to attend a party in a small theater where an experimental film was being shown, and she called it 'hippie crap'). They compromised by eating at a little fish house he liked and going to the Coconut Grove.

The compromise didn't make him any happier. Nothing Mona did would make him happier. And he knew why. He had expec-ted to see Terry at the pink hacienda. He had primed himself for her return and for the long-promised solution of his problem.

But Terry hadn't been there, and Mona hadn't received so much as a postcard in the last two weeks. When Lars asked, 'Why not call White Plains?' the answer was a sharp, 'I did, twice last week. She was out. Now would you mind *terribly* if we stopped talking about Terry and got going?'

Mona was miffed and he was disappointed. Terry had put her mark on this evening.

Not that Lars felt he could go on much longer with the mag-nificent Dearn in any event. She had a good heart, America's Sex Queen did, but her head was sadly deficient. At least in Lars Wyllit's opinion. Their conversations reminded him of dialogue from dumb-blonde movies. And that sculpture ... hooboy! Even the wild body was beginning to pall – like ten chocolate-cream pies for dinner.

Yet sex reared its lovely head on the way home. Mona moved closer and he put an arm around her and they kissed at a traffic light. He drove a little faster. At a Full Stop sign on a dark street she came at him as if she wanted it right there, and she almost got it. Then he really made the Triumph move.

He roared up the driveway – and almost into the back of a car that hadn't been there when they'd left. Terry's Mustang. They went inside and Lena said Miss Hanford had gone to bed and Mona dismissed her. The maid left for the cottage she shared with her husband. Mona took Lars by the hand and straight to the bedroom. It surprised him. She hadn't ever been that direct. Not that he didn't welcome it. The sooner started, the sooner finished.

But he would hold back. He wouldn't spend himself. He would stay ready for Terry.

He thought of this during the undressing and playing. He thought of it when Mona threw her head from side to side and said things he couldn't quite understand. Then it was over and he lay beside her, considering how best to get out of the room. Mona saved him the trouble. She mumbled she was 'beat' and turned her back on him. But he was afraid she would waken if she thought he was leaving the house.

He got up. 'I could eat something. Going to the kitchen.' She didn't answer. 'Mona? You awake?' She breathed evenly. He dressed in the darkness, picked up his shoes and moved silently out of the room. He shut the door, waited, and when nothing happened padded down the hall to Terry's room. He thought how wild this was and turned the doorknob slowly, carefully. The latch clicked open. He stopped. No sound from inside. He opened the door and was able to see by the light of the window behind the bed. Terry lay on her back, eyes closed. He could hear her breathing. Surprisingly heavy breathing for one asleep.

Could she know he was there? Could she be listening, waiting, her excitement mounting?

His own excitement increased. If only she would welcome him. If only she would *give* him her love.

He stepped inside and closed the door. He was as quiet as possible, but the latch snapped into place noisily. He put down his shoes and moved toward her. Her breathing seemed louder – or was it his own?

He was at the bed. He bent toward her. Her eyes opened. Her face froze, then began to change. He lunged forward as she opened her mouth. He clamped his hand over it, dropped his weight on her. She was screaming under his hand, the sound stifled but full of rage – and outrage.

If only she had welcomed him.

But it made no difference. He would have her no matter what the consequences. And there would be no consequences. That much he had thought out in advance. Let her yell cop and she would find herself in a *ménage-à-trois* scandal that would make her back off double-quick!

He kept her pinned beneath him. He said, 'It's no use. I have to.'

Her struggles ceased. Her eyes locked with his. He touched her face with his lips. 'Too many thoughts, Terry. It's my only way out.'

Her eyes spilled tears. It wrenched at him. He had been thinking only of his own need. The barracks-room, back-alley, barnyard boys thought only of their own needs. Their 'cunts' were faceless, soulless. That was what he had tried to make of Terry. But her eyes spilled tears and she sobbed beneath his hand, and he was stricken.

399

He got off her and sat at the edge of the bed, looking down at his stockinged feet. His fantasy of quick release was ended. He waited for whatever she would say, and she said nothing, and he again looked at her. She had her head turned from him, was crying silently. The light from the window showed him how beautiful she was. This square little redhead. This woman who touched him as no woman touched him, and for no particular reason. This refutation of reason. This proof positive of saccharine Hollywood love.

He bent to her again, kissed the wet face. He was prepared for whatever would come – angry words or blows. Anything, and he'd take it, but first . . .

His lips moved over her face. She spoke in a shaky whisper. 'No, get out.'

He would go, but first a touching of lips.

He bent farther, and her lips were salty wet, and he wasn't altogether sure some of that salt wasn't his own. He was breaking inside, not his sick heart but something else, something just as vital. *The tough man, the boy maniac,* he mocked himself. He wanted to beg and he didn't know how and pressed her lips and wondered if she could feel him coming apart.

'Animal!' she said, turning her head away. But her voice was a whisper, and her movement weak and slow. He put his hands on her bare arms and stroked the cool flesh and visualized the freckles. She shook her arms, rejecting him, but again weakly, slowly. 'Can't you find a girl who *wants* you?' she whispered, and shivered. He stared at her. He stroked her arms again, and again she shivered.

He seized her, took her against him all at once. He didn't know what he was saying, but it was what he could never say to Mona Dearn or Lispeth Auron or any of the others.

He undressed and got under the covers. Their bodies touched. Her lips opened beneath his. It was what he had come for, yet it wasn't enough.

'Tell me you want me.'

'Get out!'

'I want no one but you. Tell me you want me – at least among those you *can* want.'

'Get out!'

He began to caress her, to explore her. He ceased being gentle. She buried her head in his chest. 'Get out,' she whispered to his flesh.

'You want me.'

She didn't say it but it was true. She would say it the next time, or the time after that. He wasn't in any hurry. She would have forever to say it, because he would never let her alone! Whatever this surrender meant, it would turn to love. He would train her to love him!

TERRY HANFORD

When Terry heard the soft footsteps in the hall, she closed her eyes and folded her hands. It was why she was here. She had gone home and seen her parents and seen Bert and spent twelve days with them and nothing had happened. It was no longer her life. She had flown back to the pink hacienda and Mona Dearn. Now Mona was coming for her. Now she would wait and Mona would enter and she would open her eyes and hold out her arms. She would try for something important with Mona. If it didn't work, she wouldn't be any worse off than before. She wouldn't even be changed, she insisted . . .

Fear or not, doubt or not, change and abnormality or not, she waited. She was here and she was committed. This emptiness had to pass. This emptiness that had crept up on her as she went about her life. This emptiness worse than fear and doubt and abnormality.

She heard the door open. She heard Mona approach. She wanted to keep her eyes closed, but it was past time for such games and she had to join in, had to give herself. She looked at her lover . . .

It took a few seconds to register. *Lars Wyllit.* It took a few seconds to make sense, and then his being here was a complication, an affront, an obscenity that caused nothing less than a convulsion in her mind.

She could not handle it, and so fury came. And so she screamed – or tried to.

She fought him as if he were death come upon her. But strangely, the fury was short-lived, and she heard what he was saying, and it was an explanation of sorts. He was trying to tell her it wasn't lust but love. As if he with his tickling and his obscenities were capable of love! He was asking her to give herself so he could be free of her, of thoughts of her.

It made sense, in a way. And when she wept he withdrew. He would leave now; she knew it. She had only to gather her coldness, her outrage, and fling it in his face. But she couldn't stop crying. He kissed her again, softly, with an inner pain that reached her. She told him to go. She tried to mean it. She kept telling him to leave her, but knew she wasn't convincing. He kept kissing her, her lips, her arms, and the warmth rose and she told him to leave and he didn't leave. He undressed, telling her how much she meant to him, yet never actually using the word love. He begged her to give him some encouragement, to say she wanted him. She wouldn't. He had come to her room to rape and that was what he would have to do. She wouldn't fight. She was too empty and alone to fight. But she wouldn't help.

He grew rough with her. He grew erotic with his hands.

She said no one last time, meaning it then because it was al-most too late. She tried to push him away, and he pinned back both her hands, holding them by the wrists, and worked his body against hers until she no longer meant the no-no-no.

He made love to her a long time. A very long time. She was ashamed when her arms and legs clamped about him and she said the little love words she had never thought to say to this dirty, violent man.

She thought he would leave then. He didn't. He held her and stroked her, talking about himself as a boy in Somerville and asking questions. It was impossible not to answer. Once he left this bed she would wipe him from her world completely, but now his mouth spoke almost into hers and it was impossible not to answer. He kept asking questions – about her childhood, her parents, the years in Hollywood. After a while she turned from him and said what had happened would be forgotten, but he had to leave.

He touched her again, and she caught fire again. She said, 'I want you to get out!' and he came at her and they made love so violently, so successfully, the concept of Mona as a love-mate was burned from her mind and body. Time after time she had to fight to keep her ecstasy from erupting in cries, in wild moans. She buried her cries and moans in his mouth.

He used the word *love* now, and it was good to hear, helped her achieve the ecstasy.

When it ended, he fell to her side, pressing his lips to her hand. She was so exhausted, so drained, she just had to close her eyes a moment – after which she would make him leave. And never allow him back. Because, she insisted, nothing had changed between them. Lars Wyllit was still the same sordid

402

little man who had tormented her all these months. His words of love were the words all men used in climax, her words the ones all women used. He had come to rape and that was what he had done. If he had helped her in any way, it had been inadvertent. If she had responded, it was not to Lars Wyllit but to a male animal. To her own hunger and needs.

His lips loved her hand. She tugged it, but he held on. She sighed. Another moment.

MONA DERN

Mona lay with fists clenched tight, straining to hear the front door's heavy, closing sound. Lars had left her and it seemed like hours ago, but that front door hadn't yet closed.

What was he doing in the kitchen, cooking and eating a ten-course dinner? Probably just goofing around, planning to come back to her. He hadn't worked as hard as usual tonight.

But she wouldn't allow him to come back. Terry was just down the hall. Terry was waiting for her. As soon as Lars left, she would go to Terry.

Damn it, leave already!

She fought for patience and lost. She got up, walked on tiptoes to the door, stood listening. She opened it, went into the hall and moved toward the kitchen, barefoot and silent.

The kitchen was dark. The entire house was dark. Lars had left. She must have dozed a little and missed hearing the front door close. Or he had left so quietly . . .

What the hell difference did it make when or how he had left! She was alone with Terry! She could go to Terry!

She went through the living room and down the hall. She reached the door and opened it and began to walk inside. And stopped dead.

She saw them. Asleep together. Face to face. The blankets back a little. Their whiteness and nudity. Her Terry and her Lars. So close and tender. As Lars would never sleep with her. As Terry would never sleep with her. Sweet and clean somehow. Lovers.

She turned away, leaving the door open. She went back to her room and lay down. How long had they been lovers? How long, as they served the great whore Mona Dearn, had they cleansed themselves with each other? How long had they played

403

together? What had they said about her? Had they laughed or felt pity?

She shook her head then, the numbness giving way to anguish. He had stopped to say good night, and it had happened. Hot pants incident. Quick kick.

She got up and went back down the hall. She paused at the open door and looked in – as Lars stirred and put his arms around Terry and kissed her head. 'Love you, love you,' he murmured.

Mona ran from it. She made noise and didn't care. They would know she had seen them but she didn't care. And *they* wouldn't care. They had each other. Her friends and lovers weren't her friends and lovers. They cared nothing for her. They cared only for each other.

She was alone.

Sometime later she heard the front door close. Lars was gone. And Terry would also be leaving, now that she'd been caught with Lars. Well, it didn't matter anymore. So she would be alone. She had always been alone.

She went to the bathroom and took a pill and wondered if she should make sure by taking two. But she didn't want to get up with a barbiturate hangover tomorrow. It would lead to drinking and the weekend would be shot and she wanted to be perfectly fresh for her seven A.M. call Monday. She was going before the cameras Monday. They were beginning *The Eternal Joneses* Monday.

She took another pill. And then thought, *Why worry about Monday?* Any whore could fill her role.

She took a third pill and returned to bed. The barbiturates did their job. She heard exhausts roaring and tires screaming. She was in Queens, in the kitchen that had seemed so grand. There were children, many of them, and they were hers and she was happy. Until she looked at the walls and the walls were black, and the children also looked and grew frightened. She wept for them because she was Mona Dearn and had no children and would never allow herself to have children. They went away. They went through the black walls, looking back at her; went to that terribly sad place of the unborn, the unrealized; went accusing her with their eyes, the girls like her and the boys like Walter.

She stood in the black kitchen, clutching her old polka-dot dolly. But even that didn't want to be with her, stirred and moved and left her. She stood alone in the black kitchen. She

404

no longer wept. She was beautifully dressed and applause sounded and she turned and walked proudly, regally, to the strains of 'You're the Top'. But wherever she walked the walls were black, and her clothing fell away, and she was naked and the applause turned to laughter and she finally understood. She didn't deserve bright walls. She didn't deserve children. She didn't deserve Lars or Terry. She deserved only one thing – to be Mona Dearn.

She walked faster. Walked right into Angel. She screamed at him, clawed at him. She told him what he had done to Walter, to the children, to Mona Dearn. 'You've damned Mona Dearn!' she screamed. 'And no God's mercy and no Holy Mother and no Holy Ghost—' His hard face didn't change. His big, lean body slouched loose and casual as always. He sucked on a cigarette and said, 'Blab, blab, blab,' as her father had said to her mother and slammed her in the mouth as her father had slammed her mother and shoved her down and came after her and she thrilled – thrilled with Walter gasping out his life in the foyer and the black walls closing in.

She awoke at five, the light gray, her spirit gray. The dreams were too much.

She went to the living room and the bar and drank vodka – drank quickly, steadily for ten minutes, gulping doubles and triples and wincing and shuddering. She returned to her room, took a pill, lay down and closed her eyes. And saw Lars and Terry. And saw Angel and Walter and her unborn children.

She went to the bathroom and took another pill and then another. She looked at herself in the medicine chest mirror and took more, took all, toasting herself with the water glass, and thought to hell with the hangover and the lost days. To hell with all the lost years!

She sat down on the floor. In a little while she would get up and go to bed. But for the moment she would sit here.

She cradled emptiness in her arms – her polka-dot dolly, her unborn child. She crooned a lullaby, more and more thickly, more and more weakly. She sat on the bathroom floor and rocked the years to sleep.

NAT MARKAL

He lay awake early Wednesday morning, a pad and pencil in his hands. This was the time he had always been able to think best – five to six A.M., the predawn to dawn period, the muted roar of ocean below unspoiled by roar of cars. This was the time Emperor Nat Markal had formulated more ideas for films, for promotions, for distributions than any other.

The pad was blank. *Too many things happening, so terribly fast.*

Mona Dearn. The worst break possible! He hadn't believed it when Terry called him Saturday morning. He hadn't believed it until he'd seen her crumpled on the bathroom floor. And Terry's hysteria, partly dulled by what the ambulance doctor had given her. Her weeping against him. Her confused, not really intelligible words about Lars and Mona, words hooking up with rumors that had been around for quite some time. With Mona dead they couldn't begin shooting *Joneses* Monday. And pausing at this critical time could ruin everything.

Why had Mona killed herself? He'd known she was neurotic about her New York past. But recently she seemed to have shaken it.

He went to his bathroom and washed with cold water. He looked at himself in the mirror. No one shook his past – either far past or recent past. Everything that happened stuck. *Nat'n* still haunted him in dreams. Isa Yee was beginning to haunt him in reality.

He came out and looked across his room at a door that stood slightly ajar; it led to the short connecting foyer that ended in Adele's room. Adele's door had been locked – not just closed but locked – for a week now. And Adele wasn't talking to him – not the old pouts of previous quarrels, but a red-eyed, stony-faced withdrawal that made him feel it was all over between them. It wasn't, of course. He would patch it up once he had solved some of his other problems.

He left the bedroom by the main foyer and went to the kitchen. He put water on to boil, then sat down with his pad, hand poised to list ideas, hunches, solutions.

No solution for Mona Dearn. No solution for death. He would simply have to find someone big enough to take her place. If Monroe were alive ... yet the role wasn't quite right for Monroe. Nor for Kim Novak. Certainly not for any of the big foreigners, like Loren, with their accents.

Would Taylor consider it? She would demand the right to make whatever changes she considered necessary in her part, and he shuddered to think how many and how severe they would be. Also, she would cost a mint. And being as independent as she was . . .

Yet he had to have someone. He had to get *Joneses* before the cameras, fast! Dave Sankin was flying in today. He'd told Dave it wasn't necessary, but Sankin had been frantic. 'Not necessary! When will it ever be *more* necessary? We've lost our biggest property, Nat!'

Nat had tried to remind him of Dearn's failing net value, but Sankin had been beyond reason. He was coming here and he was staying here 'until all the crises are past!'

One blessing. Sankin wouldn't arrive in time for today's inquest. Nat could concentrate on that without Dave looking over his shoulder.

But the rumors! He had told Dave about Isa, but the rumors were so much *stronger* than anything he'd said. The rumors – and the reality.

Arnold Ryan had called him Sunday and they'd met at a restaurant on Wilshire. It was Olive who had hired the tail, an ex-police officer named Joseph Kappy. Arnold had easily persuaded Kappy to cooperate. A few hundred dollars had done it. But it was too late to buy or coerce him into changing sides.

'He'd have come over to us, Nat, if we'd spotted him a little earlier. But he's already handed everything to Olive – including these.'

Arnold had fifteen photographs and an explanation about advanced techniques in infra-red light, lenses and film, an exegesis Nat didn't understand and impatiently ended. The important thing was that Olive had them too. They were photographs of Nat seemingly dancing with Isa at a nightclub, Nat playing hop-scotch (a whole series of these) and four clear shots of Nat and Isa petting in the Ferrari.

'This isn't too bad,' Ryan had murmured. 'So a man plays like a kid. All right. Not a hanging offense. But—' He'd taken out Xerox copies of a detailed time-report. 'Three months' listings of Miss Yee's arrivals and departures to and from your Century Plaza suite, with depositions of five separate witnesses – professionals, of course, but damning enough.

'And some nonprofessionals, Nat. We're never as careful as

407

we think we are. Waiters saw her. Two desk men. The bartender was suspicious. Now, if no one was out to get you, it
wouldn't mean a thing. But Kappy spread a few bucks. Kappy
got them all on paper, and Mrs. Dort has it. Make whatever
deal you can, Nat. There's no other way.'

He had tried. He had phoned Olive four times since Sunday.
She'd been 'out' every time. Yesterday he'd decided it was
time to forget Olive and what she might do to him personally
and line up support for himself as head of Avalon, support for
Joneses. Not that anyone could hurt him unless Sankin helped
them, but with Dave coming here the old hunch mechanism
told him he might need friends.

He'd started with the toughest and worked his way down.
And failed with every one of them.

Sol Soloway had blandly pleaded ignorance. Besser had been
just as unwilling to talk turkey. 'Rumors? I haven't heard them,
Nat. And what have rumors to do with our work at the studio?
Yes, I'd love to lunch – but I'm dieting this week.'

Devon had been refreshingly frank. 'Certain people are going to use Mona's suicide, and all the rumors, to try and
dump *Joneses* – and you. But a few changes and we can stop
them.'

Nat had asked what Devon wanted done.

'Get rid of Halpert. He's an amateur. He can't handle this
big, this important a job. Give it to Lars Wyllit. Better still,
bring in Abby Mann, Dalton Trumbo, anyone of equal stature.
Then I'll be able to believe in *Joneses*. Then you and I will talk
to Sankin together. And I think I can help pull a few other
doubters into line.'

Nat hadn't been able to help it. He'd laughed, saying Halpert's
script was a *masterpiece*. Devon's voice grew chill. 'Well, that's
what makes horse races – and proxy fights.'

Nat had tried Lou Grayson, whose judgment Sankin respected. There'd been no return of his calls, and he'd finally
walked into Grayson's Avalon office. 'Hey,' Grayson had said,
sprawled on a couch with a script. 'Meant to see you, Nat.
Afraid I have to duck out of that part in *Joneses*.' He'd waved
the script. 'Got something here that's perfect for me. Going
into it the day I finish *Baby's Helper*. I know you won't mind.
That friggin five-line part can be filled by Flipper.' Nat had suggested Lou pick another supporting role. Lou grinned. 'I'm
a star, Nat – or haven't you heard?' Nat had refused to take
any more and stalked out.

The kettle whistled. He got up from the table and mixed a cup of instant coffee. He sipped, his face grim. He had coddled Olive too long. She would be barred from the lot. And Soloway was finished. Out! Besser would be allowed to stay, after he had humbled himself properly.

Devon and Grayson brought money into Avalon, so nothing could be done about them. But he would watch their nets like a hawk, and at the first deep dip . . .

He shoved back his chair and stood up, face twisted. What the hell! He was sick of having to depend upon Sankin, upon *anyone* for support! He had enough money, or could raise it by selling certain out-of-industry stock, to buy what would amount to a controlling interest in Avalon. It had to be from Sankin, but that shouldn't be too difficult. If the man was panicky about his investment, a little bonus should separate him from a big chunk of common. All right, it would mean that Nat would have to break one of his cardinal rules – never put all your eggs in one basket, if that basket rises and falls on the exchange. It would mean selling low in certain areas, and draining his cash reserve, but he could do it. That, along with the usual percentage of small-investor proxies that would come his way in any showdown, would maintain him perpetually in office.

He went to his room and got a cigar from the humidor. He returned to the kitchen, made a second cup of coffee, and worked the deal out, in specifics, in *dollars,* on his pad. He would speak to Sankin today and call his broker tomorrow. He would buy half of Sankin's total common holdings.

The decision made, he had a leisurely shower and dressed. He met Lainie in the hall and said, ' 'Morning, honey.' She burst into tears and fled back to her room. He stared after her, then winced. The rumors had reached not only his wife but his daughter. They must be pretty widespread. But at the right moment he would convince Adele that Isa meant nothing and keep her from doing anything foolish.

But could he keep *himself* from doing anything foolish?

Isa wasn't returning his calls. He shouldn't be calling her. It was insanity to think of seeing her at this time, but he had to call her, had to see her. A motel somewhere outside L.A. Just for an hour or two. Just to say good-bye and to plan for an eventual renewal of their relationship. Just to make sure she didn't allow herself a serious relationship with anyone else.

That's what tormented him most of all. That's what got in the way of the other problems. That she might fall in love. That she might be lost to him forever.

He went to his study and closed the door. Insane to call her from home! But he called her. The phone rang twice, and the switchboard cut in. She hadn't been taking her calls. She'd been using the switchboard as a secretary. He said, 'Mr. ... Emperor calling.' The switchboard cut out a moment, then the girl said, 'Sorry Miss Yee doesn't know any Mr. Emperor. He called again. He gave his name. Isa answered. 'You woke me,' she muttered. He asked why she hadn't been answering her phone. 'Because I haven't an unlisted number like you, and I've been getting kooks who talk like a garbage dump.' He said he was sorry. 'If you want to move ... perhaps a little place in Malibu?' She laughed. 'Something closer to your home, your wife?' He was quiet. She said, 'I meant to ask you, or Devon – what's the new schedule for *Joneses*? I'm on Monday's call sheet, along with Hewlett and Dearn. Now what?' He said it wasn't definite, but he hoped they could start in two weeks.

'You have someone to take Dearn's place?'

'Not yet. We can shoot around her. Listen, I want to see you.'

'Don't be a fool.'

The cold words jarred but didn't deter him. 'We'll meet somewhere. Friday night. There's a motel in San Gabriel—'

'No. If you want to see me, you'll have to come here.'

'You're joking.'

'I'll wait for you until eight Friday. Then I'm going out.'

'What sort of nonsense—'

She hung up. He realized he'd shouted and glanced at the door as if expecting Adele to be there. He lit a cigar. He'd be damned if he'd walk into that apartment house for all the world to see! The girl must be losing her mind!

He phoned for the chauffeur. He was picking up Terry Hanford. He wanted one last chat with her. He had spoken to many people about how they would testify at the inquest. He wanted to make sure nothing was said that would damage Mona – and through her, Avalon. With all the news coverage ...

He thought of the columnists and the legmen who would be there, most of whom were bound to have picked up the rumors about him and Isa. He took a deep breath, then went to Adele's room and knocked. After a moment he opened the door. She wasn't there.

He walked through the house, and Lainie was in the kitchen,

410

having coffee with Tess. He asked for Adele. Lainie didn't answer, chewing stolidly at eggs and bacon, her plain face slightly flushed. Tess looked from one to the other and said, 'Went out. That hospital thing. What's going on here anyway?' Lainie's head jerked up. 'That's not for you to ask!' Tess rose and walked away. Nat murmured to be careful, they'd had Tess a long time. Eyes down, voice thick, Lainie said, 'You've had *us* a long time, but it doesn't seem to make any difference.' He froze. She tried to resume eating and began to cry. He went to her, touched her shoulder. She threw his hand away. 'No! It's true! I can tell!' He waited until he was certain he could reply in a steady voice. 'You're not a child, Lainie. You know ... these things happen. It doesn't have to end love between father and daughter.'

'And between father and mother?'

'Not there either.'

She smiled – a ghastly, raging thing. 'You're in for a surprise. You don't know your wife and your daughter.' She ran from the kitchen.

No, he didn't know them. And they didn't know him. Because through all the shame and pain of this scene, he was still thinking of Isa.

LARS WYLLIT

The coroner's inquest produced no surprises for Lars or anyone else, though it did have a few sweaty moments. The cover-up was in operation, and everyone did a little white-lying under oath. The only people in the overcrowded room who *weren't* satisfied were the reporters, poised like vultures over their hot little notebooks. They had already done a pretty good job of indirect smearing, describing Lars as 'Miss Dearn's steady escort' and Terry as her 'confidante and constant companion'. It was intimated that the three had spent much time together, day and night, 'which caused wonder among Mona's older friends, including this reporter'.

In itself, this wouldn't have bothered Lars too much, but it had led to his receiving some very sick phone calls. And Terry was bound to be more sensitive to that sort of thing than he was.

Not that he actually knew what had been happening to her

411

since he'd left the hacienda Friday night, beyond what he'd read in the papers. Her home phone was off the hook. She hadn't showed up at her office. And when he'd approached her as she entered the inquest room, she'd looked right through him, gone right by. She was followed by Markal, who *did* look at him – a look cold enough to freeze the Mojave in July.

Terry was first on the stand. She said she'd gone to bed at eleven-thirty Friday night, but heard Mona and her escort, Lars Wyllit, come in sometime after twelve. Lena, the maid, could give the exact time. After ten or fifteen minutes, Mr. Wyllit had left, Mona had dismissed Lena, and Terry had fallen asleep. The next morning, Terry had finished breakfast at ten, talked for a while with Lena, bathed and dressed, and finally looked into Mona's room to see why she was sleeping so far past her usual hour. She had discovered the body in the bath-room.

The D.A. rose for questioning. 'What was your position in the Dearn household?'

The reporters came awake.

'I was her publicist and a personal friend. She'd asked me to stay as her house guest until her new picture, *The Eternal Joneses*, was filmed. Mr. Markal, the studio head, thought it advisable, so I agreed.'

'Can you think of anyone who might have *forced* Miss Dearn to take those sleeping pills? Was there any chance that while you slept someone entered the house and committed violence?'

Terry said she supposed anything was possible, but all the doors were locked, she'd heard nothing, and there were no signs of violence.

The D.A. nodded and sat down.

Terry returned to her first-row seat beside Markal. Lars tried to catch her eye. She kept her gaze firmly away from him.

Lars was called. He repeated Terry's story, as she would have repeated his had he testified first. He added that Miss Dearn had seemed somewhat depressed while they were at dinner and not her usual self at the Coconut Grove. However, actresses were emotional beings, and he'd thought nothing of it.

The D.A. asked Lars to describe his position in relation to the deceased. 'A writer on the picture in which she was to star. A friend and admirer.'

'Do you know of any reason why she should wish to take her own life?'

412

Lars said he hadn't been close enough to Miss Dearn to be privy to her innermost feelings.

The D.A. dismissed him.

Lena and Buddy Warnt substantiated Terry and Lars. Lars was sure Markal would help them find suitable employment.

Markal provided the motive for suicide, obviously having decided it was best to close this thing out once and for all and end at least one area of speculation. He said he had, with Miss Dearn's permission, received reports from a psychiatrist she had visited. A tragic first marriage had preyed on her mind for years. 'A beloved first husband' had been killed during a robbery, and Miss Dearn had blamed herself, unjustly, for not being with him at the time. In the manner of 'many devoted Catholic wives', she had been unable to forget him or to consider herself really free to love another – which explained the failure of her second and third marriages. 'They foundered on memories of her earlier, simpler life,' Markal said quietly, 'and on her inability to have children.' Despite all that her friends and employers could do, she was 'gradually robbed of joy and purpose in life'. Of course, no one knew how strong 'the desire to rejoin her one and only love' had become, otherwise steps would have been taken to protect her. Finding herself alone on still another weekend, she had 'simply forgotten the injunction against taking one's own life and slipped peacefully away'.

The inquest was, for all practical purposes, over.

The industry had united solidly behind Markal to thwart the press. But no matter what Markal and the industry wanted, innuendo would show up in news reports and there would be talk about Mona, Terry and Lars for quite some time. And there would be those sick telephone calls for quite some time. Lars hoped Terry wasn't letting them get her down.

He couldn't take his eyes off her. He hungered for her voice, for some sign that she was going to make him part of her life. She couldn't go back to ignoring him, not after Friday night.

He wanted to leave, but couldn't. It would be tantamount to walking out on Mona's eulogy. Besides, he wanted to say a word to Terry and Markal, to make the first move toward some sort of accommodation. Let Markal blow off a little steam if he wanted to, just so long as he didn't harbor any strong resentments.

After medical evidence that boiled down to 'heart failure due to narcotic action upon the central nervous system', the

413

jury of four men and three women delivered their verdict at noon: '. . . took her life by her own hand . . .' Terry and Markal came up the aisle toward Lars's fourth-row seat. He quickly slid by people and murmured, 'Terry, Mr. Markal, tragic business.' He began to walk with them. Markal walked faster, staring straight ahead. Terry glanced at Lars and shook her head. Lars stopped, fists clenching, anger pounding up in him. But you didn't hit Nat Markal. You just prayed he didn't hit you.

The reporters mobbed him, flinging their pointed questions at his head. He simply walked away. In the hall, TV floodlights blazed in his eyes, club-like microphones were shoved at his mouth, he was asked to make a statement. He cleared his throat with as phlegmy a sound as he could manage – and went on. He reached the street, followed by a dozen cameramen and reporters. He kept his head down as they ran in front of him, asking their seemingly polite but basically threatening manner for 'just a moment of your time'. He walked and turned into another street and then another and kept walking and soon there were only three reporters and then there were none.

He returned to the parking lot, got his car and drove to Chinatown. He had a lunch of soup and Mandarin duck in a little place that stayed half-empty and drank tea and smoked cigarettes.

He thought of Mona. He didn't really know what he felt about her. She was a stranger despite the jousts in bed. She hadn't been very important to him alive and in all honesty she wasn't very important to him dead. He was sorry for her, sorry if he had given her any pain, but he didn't feel guilty in the slightest. Suicide was a very personal thing. It derived from the mass of what lay within a person, not the minutiae that lay without.

He returned to the studio and called Terry. Her line was busy. He read a carbon of Halpert's last scene – the man allowed nothing to stop his output – and tried Terry again. Still busy. He wondered if she had taken her phone off the hook, as he had yesterday after one too many calls.

Those calls. There was considerable creative talent going to waste in America today. The Rightest nuts, for example. The way they managed to combine politics, religion, anti-Semitism and obscenity was brilliant. One woman had asked if his real name wasn't Isidore Worshofsky. He said no, she had the wrong party. She said, 'I know you, Izzy. I know you and your whole race—' She went on to accuse him of conspiring to take

414

over the government for the Jewish Communist Party, which controlled the movie and television industries as well as the labor unions, the publishing firms and the Los Angeles branch of the telephone company that censored her calls, kept her son's calls from reaching her and continually overcharged her. Mona had been a victim too. 'Mona Dearn, blessed sacred heart of America, was raped and then murdered. A doctor named Cohen lied and made it look like suicide. You and Nat Markal and other members of a Hollywood synagogue, whose names are known to me and the Klan, all took part in this hellish crime.' He had groaned, 'My God, how did you find out?' There had been a few seconds of silence and then an outpouring of obscenity that drew murmured bravos from Lars, who considered himself an authority. When she said she was going to visit him one night and tear off his genitals, he said, 'I'm looking forward to the kick, baby,' and went into a description, firmly voiced over her ranting, of how he would utilize those genitals before she took them away.

There was the soft-spoken man who begged for details of Mona's sex life. And the whisperer, unidentifiable as to sex, who prayed for Lars's soul and used every four-letter word Lars had ever heard interspersed with sections from the Old and New Testaments.

And the gigglers, teen-aged girls who lost their nerve and waited for Mona Dearn's lover to say terrible things. And the breathers who never said a word, just breathed heavily at the other end until he bade them a good night in hell and hung up. He estimated he'd received twenty nut calls before taking his phone off the hook both in the office and at home.

He tried Terry again. This time the phone rang, but no one answered. He called the switchboard to ask if Miss Hanford had checked in for messages today. She had. She was taking a late lunch and would return at about three. He picked up Halpert's screenplay. He wouldn't phone Terry anymore. He would go to see her.

TERRY HANFORD

Terry was shocked by the number of rubbernecks, sensation-seekers, real square types right here at Avalon. The calls, bad as they were, didn't surprise her, but this did. People

415

had come by her door during the few hours she'd put in Monday and Tuesday, and they'd been coming by since she'd returned from the inquest at twelve-thirty today. Some looked straight ahead, but snapped their heads at the last moment to stare at her. Others sauntered by, sometimes in pairs, taking a long, supposedly casual look. Still others, whom she knew personally, came in and looked grim (and excited) and said things like, 'My *God,* I was shocked!' and 'What do you suppose made her do it?' and 'Imagine being there and not being able to help!' Then they waited for revelations.

It was Terry's habit to work with the door open, and she vowed she wouldn't close it for anything, but by two o'clock Wednesday afternoon she was beaten. It was Mathilde Ceste from Wardrobe, a known Lesbian but very cautious on the lot, who did it. She came in and asked about the costumes Mona had kept from her last film . . . and then began probing, like the others, but with a different goal. She didn't want revelations. She wanted Terry. She was sounding her out on those rumors.

Terry got rid of her by picking up the phone, which she'd kept off the hook, and saying she had to speak to Nat Markal. Mathilde said they had to have lunch soon and not in that noisy commissary and strode out with her mannish shoulders squared and her mannish head high. Terry closed the door and sat down, hands over her face. How could she ever have thought to enter such a relationship, such a life!

The rumors about her and Mona had started long before she'd dreamed of such a thing. Lars had mentioned them that night of the fight at the Whiskey A Go-Go. But they wouldn't have bothered her if they hadn't turned out to be almost true. You heard such things about fully half the names in Hollywood and about all the women who were in or past their thirties.

Thank goodness Markal had been frank. He had voiced the rumors and dismissed them. But he hadn't dismissed those about Lars and Mona. He wanted confirmation from Terry, feeling that what she'd said Saturday morning indicated she knew the facts. She'd replied that shock and hysteria had led her to say things easily misunderstood. 'I've never had reason to believe Mr. Wyllit was anything but a casual friend of Mona's, Mr. Markal.' That's where they'd left it – but she knew Markal had spoken to Lena, had spoken to Jerry Storm and others. She knew he had made up his mind Lars had been sleeping with Mona that last night of her life.

Poor Mona . . .

The phone rang. It jolted her because she'd thought it was off the hook. She remembered now, she'd hung it up without thinking after faking the call for Mathilde Ceste.

It rang on and on. She raised it.

'Miss Hanford?' the brisk voice asked. Male, but high-pitched. She didn't answer. The voice said, 'A thousand miles down, the core of the earth is molten metal. In that molten metal float heads. They scream through all eternity. Mona Dearn's head is screaming there now. Yours and Larson Wyllit's will be screaming there soon. Molten metal will fill your mouth, your eyes, your gaping cunt—' She hung up. She told herself to pity the sick fool, but her stomach churned and her head began to spin. She stood up, holding to the edge of the desk, breathing deeply, willing herself not to cry. She would have some lunch now. She would eat and feel better.

She left word with the switchboard and walked down the hall, and every time she passed an open door she felt stared at and talked about. She came out into a close, smoggy afternoon. Back in White Plains it was cool, rainy, with occasional days of crystalline brightness. Back in White Plains it was early spring and beautiful.

She hadn't allowed herself to see that beauty during her two-week stay. She'd been looking for answers in *people*. Now she wouldn't expect answers, just peace – just escape from this town.

People back home would be shocked at Mona Dearn's death, but few would experience the sense of involvement those in Hollywood did. By next week the subject would be dead, and no one except family and a few friends would know that the Hanford girl had been involved. She could answer the phone or take walks or visit relatives and feel perfectly safe, perfectly at ease. Which now seemed the most valuable, the most desirable of all human conditions. She could relax, rest, hibernate . . . and let time pass. Then she could move into the city. Manhattan had millions of people, and millions of jobs. It also had old friends who could lead to new friends . . . to a new life.

The urge to leave was so strong she almost turned then and there to the parking area and her car. But she made herself go on to C-gate. She would do this thing right. She would tie up some loose ends and resign her job and say good-bye to her friends.

LARS WYLLIT

Lars didn't get around to visiting Terry's office until four. His agent had called. Mick Malloy was upset. When he told Lars why, Lars Wyllit was upset. Nat Markal had informed Malloy that Lars wouldn't be expected to show up at Avalon anymore. The contract would be honored, Markal had said, even though it could be broken through the morals clause. Markal was very cold – very cold and very angry. He blamed Lars for something, though he wouldn't say what. 'That Mona Dearn thing, Lars—' Lars said shut up and Mick said sure and Lars said what are you going to do and Mick said he'd look around for a new assignment and Lars said, 'How about the Fox deal you were talking up last month?' Mick said he'd call right away. And then, laughing heartily, falsely, 'Well, at least you won't starve. You're getting your dough for *Joneses*. That should last a while.' Lars said he intended to blow it all on a custom Rolls and a week in Vegas, 'So get busy.'

He sat still a while, telling himself he wasn't afraid. He called Markal all sorts of names, then slammed the desk with his fist and picked up the phone. He asked for Markal's office. Bertha Kraus answered, sounding somewhat less than her usual cool, efficient self. Markal would be back between four and five. He thanked her without giving his name and headed for Terry's office. He kept telling himself it would all work out.

Terry's door was closed. He knocked and walked in. She was cleaning out her desk, and her face went white.

'Don't worry. I only rape on Fridays.'

She didn't smile. Her head went down, and she continued taking things from drawers. He came farther inside and watched a while. 'Going somewhere?'

'Home.'

'You were just there, weren't you?'

'For good.'

He didn't believe it. He *wouldn't* believe it. 'I know things are kind of rough right now, but there's no reason—'

'I don't want to talk about Mona.'

'I wasn't going to talk about Mona. I was going to talk about us.'

She didn't seem to hear him. 'I know I'm as much to blame as you are for what happened, but it's finished and I—'

'That's awfully big of you,' he said, and didn't want to say

418

that kind of thing, and said more. 'I certainly appreciate it. I guess I can stop worrying about the police now, can't I? I mean, not only for murder but for rape. I still bear the marks of that terrific fight you put up. And the way you screamed for help. And my having to beat you into submission the second time around . . . it all weighs heavily on my conscience.'

She took it. He had to give her that much. Her face paled further, but she stood there and took it.

He ran out of words and anger. She said, voice unsteady, 'Did I ever approach you, ever ask you for anything? Did I ever move in your direction? Did I ever extend invitations, explicit or otherwise?'

'No.'

'Then why do you feel—'

'There are obligations in *being* wanted as well as wanting.'

'That's poetic.' She went back to emptying drawers.

It was finally over. He had tried everything. He turned away and in lieu of falling to his knees said, 'You can't be giving up your work in movies?'

'I think my work in movies stinks.'

He went to the door, numb all over. She said, 'You should know that Markal really has it in for you. I'm afraid you're the goat. If you could speak to him, get him to stop feeling you're responsible for Mona's death—'

'If I can't stop *you,* how can I stop him?'

He went to his office, exchanging cracks with several people along the way – people who looked at him with spite or envy, people who would watch with interest or amusement as he was destroyed. Because he was the boy maniac. Because he was the man with the speciality act. Because he was long overdue for his lumps.

He closed the door behind him, the grin still on his lips, and moved to the desk and sank into his chair. The grin began to fade, but he brought it up to full bright and picked up the phone. He leaned back and put his feet on the desk and said, 'Nat Markal's office, you gorgeous telephonic creature you.' The switchboard girl laughed, and then he was speaking to Bertha and no ducking out on the issue. 'Mr. Markal, please. Larson Wyllit calling.' She hesitated for only the briefest instant, but it was enough. He knew what was going to happen. 'I'm sorry, Mr. Wyllit. Mr. Markal left instructions—' She paused, as if hoping he would get her off the hook. He said nothing. 'Have you spoken with your agent today?' He said

419

he had and that was why he wished to speak to Mr. Markal; it was all a silly mistake. She said, 'Yes, well, I'll give him your message.' And that was that.

He smoked a cigarette, trying to think of what to do, and there was nothing, absolutely nothing. He had slept with Mona Dearn and Terry Hanford in the same house on the same night – the last night of Mona Dearn's life – and it had become public suspicion if not public knowledge – a twisted, distorted suspicion but there it was, not much more shocking than the truth. It had also become an affront to Nat Markal and Avalon and a blow to the dignity and prestige of *The Eternal Joneses* – at least in Markal's mind. And every time the Emperor thought of Mona Dearn he would blame his whipping boy, Lars Wyllit, and there was nothing Lars Wyllit could do about it. No way of changing Terry and no way of changing Markal.

He called his agent. He told him to get in touch with Markal and make him understand it was all a pack of lies, rumors, no truth at all in them. Mick Malloy said he would try. Lars mentioned an idea he'd had for an original screenplay. 'I'll work up a page or two outline. Why not try Paramount? They're pretty active right now, aren't they? Maybe Green Rouse. Or Quine. How about Hawks?' He went on a while longer, and Mick had nothing to say. Absolutely nothing. 'You still with me, Mick?' Mick said, 'I've got someone here so I can't talk but let's bite a martini in a week or two.' Lars said, 'Yeah.' He could feel the disengagement starting. If Nat Markal hated someone's guts and that someone was represented by Mick Malloy then Mick Malloy wouldn't be able to sell another writer at Avalon even if that writer's name was Will Shakespeare.

Lars smoked cigarette after cigarette. He walked around his office and looked out the window at Stage 13 and at actors, actresses, grips and technicians breaking for the day. That was where *The Streets at Night* was finishing up this week. The last Sholub-Byrne production until after *Joneses*. The last Lars Wyllit script . . .

Moe Sholub *loved* his work! Moe would certainly use him again once *Joneses* was finished!

He left his office and the lot before he could think that through. He drove to Santa Monica and a pseudo-hippie bar where the action started early. He had a few enchiladas and danced with a worn broad who kept feeling his thigh and saying, 'Youth is all hardness. Want to come to my place and drink

420

hundred-year-old brandy?' He knocked down a big kid at nine-thirty and was thrown out. Starting up the Triumph, his chest began to ache. He belched and told himself it was those lousy enchiladas. He went to Malibu and an expensive fish house and ate a little and drank a lot and took a girl away from a heavyset guy in a yachting cap by talking opportunities in movies. The guy shrugged and walked out. Lars was disappointed. He'd wanted the fight more than the girl. But she was a doll and he took her to his place and they showered together. She really flipped, but that wasn't enough tonight. He took her home and went to the Strip and drove around – and then realized *nothing* was going to be magic tonight.

He went into Dino's and put away as much booze as possible before they closed. He came out, juiced to the ears, and stumbled into a phone booth and dialed Terry. Busy signal.

He drove home and got into bed. He was numb with alcohol. There was no pain in his chest, but the fear of death was on him. Just as in Watts, he felt he was being murdered. He lay curled in a tight knot and shook. He was going to show up at Avalon as if nothing had happened. Markal had acted in the heat of the moment, in the heat of this lousy day. Terry too. She wasn't leaving, and Markal wasn't going to destroy him. Both would change tomorrow.

And even if they didn't change, why lie here shaking? This was a town full of broads. And a town full of studios.

He laughed. Broads weren't Terry. And who in Hollywood wanted to antagonize Nat Markal? And even if you could find one such, why would he want a writer whose personal rep stank to high heaven?

He almost got up again. He almost started for the door and Nat Markal's home and a confrontation that would either see Markal convinced or one of them dead. Terry said the movie business stank and seemed happy to give it up. He knew it was everything good in his life. If he lost it . . .

He reached for the lamp table and his off-the-cradle phone. He depressed the buttons for a dial tone and called Terry again, just to be doing something, just to stop thinking. Busy signal. He hung up, and almost immediately the phone rang. He grabbed it, and the woman's voice said, 'Is this Izzy Worshofsky?' He slammed it back down again and wanted to talk to someone and decided he would call Chuck Halpert and ask how things were going. So it was four A.M. So what? He'd think of excuses once a human voice was in his ear. He raised

421

the phone and there was no dial tone and the woman said, 'Is this—' He cursed and hung up, but as long as *she* didn't hang up, her connection to his phone would remain unbroken. Lousy stupid telephone system!

His brain was full of fireworks and he was almost insane with rage and fear, and to top it all his chest began to ache. 'Bust already!' he shouted.

Surprisingly, it did. It finally did. The pain was unbelievable and he screamed and flailed at the phone and got it and tried to speak and the woman's voice said, 'Is this Izzy Worshofsky?' He made sounds and fell into a red hole that began to blacken toward the bottom. The woman said, 'You're not frightening *me* with those crazy sounds. We're coming to get you—' He couldn't hold onto the phone and the darkness grew thick and cold and he spoke into it, asking his mother to find him and Terry to find him.

In a brief instant of clarity, he said, or thought he said, 'Now why did I let people worry me so?'

NAT MARKAL

On Wednesday, 28th April, one week from the day he'd arrived in Los Angeles, Dave Sankin finally phoned Nat Markal at the office. Markal was speaking to Tim Stern, his stock-broker, who had flown in with every share of Avalon common he'd been able to buy. It wasn't nearly enough for what Markal had in mind, and Stern was saying the obvious – that others were buying firstest with the mostest. 'Only Sankin has enough for a controlling interest, Nat—' And that's when the call came through.

Stern went outside and sat down near Bertha and remarked that the Emperor wasn't looking his old regal self. 'He's had problems,' Bertha muttered. 'Certain people ... you have no idea the lengths to which they'll go. The lies—' She stopped then. She wouldn't be caught dead repeating such things about Mr. Markal. She knew him better than that. He was a moral man, a good man, a man fighting to produce the greatest of all motion pictures while small minds, jealous and vicious minds, thought only of dollars and cents and sought to tear him down. Well, now that Dave Sankin was in touch, they would fail! She was certain Nat could convince his old friend ...

Markal and Sankin went through the amenities.

'I'm fine, David. And you?'

'Fine, fine. Little touch of bursitis, but otherwise fine.' He sounded nervous. 'Meant to return your calls, but Julie was under the weather and then she wanted to see her friends in San Francisco and . . . well, here I am.'

'Let's have lunch today.'

'I, uh, have another appointment.'

The amenities ended. 'What is it, Dave? Why are you avoiding me? I told you about those rumors, didn't I? Is there anything else bothering you?'

'No, of course not, what could be bothering me?'

'Then let's get together. I want to start shooting *Joneses* Monday. I've got someone for Mona's role. Just have to finalize the terms.'

'Better wait,' Sankin muttered.

'Wait? Why should I?'

Sankin didn't answer.

'I'm coming to the hotel, Dave.'

'If you wish. I'd better warn you that Julie found out about the rumors. You know how fond she is of Adele. She's very upset.'

'Then come here.'

Again Sankin was silent.

'I'm going to make you an offer, Dave. You're nervous in the Avalon service. I'm going to take some common off your hands. Give you points. I know how tight things are for you right now. This'll allow you some breathing space.'

'No good, Nat.'

'What?' Suddenly he knew. He'd suspected all week and now he knew. But he told himself it was impossible. Dave wouldn't do such a thing. 'You haven't sold to anyone else? Not without giving me first crack? You wouldn't cut my throat that way?'

'I never wanted this crazy picture!' Sankin shouted. 'From the beginning I begged you. I pleaded. I told you I didn't like it and Julie didn't like it—'

'Keep your wife out of this. Act like a professional for once.'

'I think a good deal of my wife's opinions, whatever you happen to think of yours! And everyone agrees with her! Not just Olive and Sol and Ron, but Devon and Grayson and Moe Sholub and – and everyone! Big people and little people. Baiglen doesn't like it and Charabond doesn't like it and the TV

423

people don't like it. No one likes it! Only you like it and you're not trustworthy anymore, lying about the cost of that overblown set and playing games in the street like a maniac! And even without that, one opinion against all the others—' He was screaming now, having worked himself into a fury to deliver the shameful news, the news he couldn't have delivered in cold blood. 'Have I sold any stock? You bet I have! Half my holdings to Lou Grayson! And Soloway is taking a little more and so is Besser and one day I'll get out of this lousy business! I've had it! I trust a man with my life's blood and he—'

Markal hung up and sat absolutely still, thinking. Then he buzzed for Bertha. The moment she entered she asked, 'What is it, Mr. Markal? Are you ill?'

He shook his head. 'I want you to call a meeting for seven this evening. All those concerned with *Joneses*. Same as the first meeting, but with the addition of Olive Dort and the stars. Get on the phone right away. Reach them. Send telegrams if you have to. Use the word *urgent*. And get my lawyer.'

Bertha rushed out. Nat waited for the buzz, then asked Steve Bliss to come to the office. A proxy fight was in the making. Matter of life and death. Start thinking on the way over.

Bliss asked what was the situation on Dave Sankin. 'Is he sitting this one out?'

'Half his stock is in the enemy camp.'

Bliss sighed.

'Maybe all.'

'Then why should I rush, Nat? We've discussed this possibility before. With Sankin neutral, you might be able to lick Olive in a proxy fight. With Sankin on Olive's side, it's hopeless and there'll be no proxy fight. You'll merely be voted out in an executive meeting. The bylaws plainly state—'

Nat Markal knew the bylaws and knew his position seemed hopeless, but he also knew something Bliss didn't know – he still had a fighting chance. First he had to get them all here in this office, where they could feel the weight of his personality and power (even if it was only a *memory* of power). Then he had to talk. *And talk and talk!* He had to frighten those who held stock and could lose money with poor management; and they included Sankin, who still had half his life's earnings in Avalon common. He had to encourage those who still believed in him and had been stampeded by Olive and Sol; and they he was sure, again included Sankin. Enough forceful and convincing words and he would awaken hidden reserves of goodwill in at least half of those present, split the ranks of those aligned against him, stalemate his enemies long enough to gain a few weeks time.

Even a few *days* would be enough, because he held one more ace. That Washington set. If he could shoot the burning of Washington, Avalon would be committed to the extent of two million dollars! If he could shoot the burning of Washington with a thousand extras as British and a thousand extras as citizens, Avalon would have taken a giant step toward producing *The Eternal Joneses*. Then Olive, Sol and Besser would find themselves alone. Then Sankin, Grayson, Devon and the others would fear changing management in midstream.

He had a lot to do and practically no time to do it in. He phoned Tyrone Chalze's office, his home, and finally got him at his tennis club. He said, 'This is off the record, Ty,' and told him what he wanted. Chalze murmured, 'No stars?' Nat said, 'We'll work them in later. Right now all I want is the burning of Washington, the big scene, with all the extras. Can you have everything ready by tomorrow?' Chalze laughed. Nat said, 'The British did it in twenty-four hours, why can't you?' Chalze said, 'I'm of Austrian stock.' Nat said, 'You told me you'd already mapped out a shooting plan. And I don't expect perfection – just lots of balls.' Chalze was quiet. 'Are you with me, Ty?' Chalze said, 'Always, Nat.' Nat said, 'Good. Then we shoot tomorrow night. Talk to Pen Guilfoyle. Tell him exactly what you'll need. I'll call first, so he won't start screaming.'

He called Guilfoyle. The casting director was shocked. 'But costumes—'

'Pay whatever is necessary. *Do* whatever is necessary. Make deals with every studio in town. Redcoat uniforms are rotting in half a dozen warehouses, not counting the private costumers.'

'But so many extras by tomorrow afternoon! And how to get them fitted and ready—'

'What did the Seabees say during the war, Pen? "The difficult we do immediately. The impossible takes a little longer." So you've got a little longer.' Guilfoyle began another 'but'. Nat said, 'Do it, Pen!' and hung up.

He called Sankin. Julie answered. He asked for Dave. Her voice frigid, she said, 'He's in the shower.'

'Then get him out of the shower.'

Sankin was on a moment later.

'Calmly, Dave, calmly. It's your stock and you have the right

425

to do as you wish with it. But remember that you still have considerable holdings. No use cutting off your nose to spite me. You'll want to protect your investment. I can tell you it's in danger. Mine too. That's why I'm calling a meeting for tonight. Promise you'll come.'

Sankin muttered, 'What's the point?'

'For old time's sake, Dave.'

Sankin sighed. 'Well—'

Nat said, 'Thanks,' and hung up. He lit a cigar and strode to the center of the office and paced the blue tile circle – the Emperor at bay, but strong again, sure again. He'd make it! He'd show them all!

He returned to the desk and called Isa, giving the switchboard his name. She said, 'Bertha already reached me. What's it all about?' He ignored the question. 'I want you to know I've come to a decision about us. We're going to see each other again.'

'Really?' She was very cool. 'After you didn't show up Friday—'

'I couldn't. Things have been happening. I've been working night and day. But now my mind is made up.'

'Glad to hear it. Make up your mind about something else too. I won't sneak around anymore.'

'We'll discuss what you will or won't do after the meeting tonight.'

He left the office. He drove the Imperial to the back of the lot and the Washington set. The workmen were gone; it was completed. Buildings and bridges and wharfs and ships filled every available foot of space. It had cost one million four hundred thousand, but he wouldn't tell them that tonight. No, not until it was burned and all that remained was the film in the cans.

He walked past the President's House, then stopped as he came behind the realistic building and saw the huge stack of pipes and burners. Far too many to be leftovers. Far too many to be anything but those he had ordered installed.

But he'd *seen* them installed! He'd checked only a week ago and every building . . .

He hurried around the front and up the stairs. A harsh voice said, 'Hey! What're you doing there?'

He turned. It was a uniformed guard, but the uniform wasn't the gray of Avalon Security. He said, 'What are *you* doing here?'

The guard came up the stairs, a wide, heavyset man with a pugnacious look on his face. Nat quickly said, 'I'm Mr. Markal. You'd better learn who your superiors are if you want to last here.'

The man stopped. 'Sorry. Go right in, Mr. Markal.' But his expression didn't change much, and he startled Nat with a sudden, shrill whistle.

Nat turned to the door. He heard the man behind him and then another man running toward them. He opened the door and stepped inside. The paneling and drapes and furniture were there. The table set for Dolley Madison's dinner party was there. Everything was there – except the tank in the corner and the pipe and the burners.

'Who ordered the tank—' he began, and saw the second guard, and waited while the shorter, older man came up and handed him a large brown envelope. Inside was a copy of a restraining order enjoining 'Nat Markal, the management of Avalon and their employees from burning or in any other way demolishing, damaging or changing the motion picture set of Washington, D.C., *circa* 1814 . . .' There was more, but he didn't bother reading it. He held out the envelope. 'It's yours,' the second guard said. Nat nodded and waited. The second guard said, 'All right,' to the first and they went out, leaving Nat Markal alone.

He looked at the envelope and his face twisted and he threw it away. He put a fresh cigar in his mouth and chewed it and looked around. *Not so smart after all, Emperor Nat.* Olive had trumped him. Court order and private guards and before he could counter with his own legal maneuvres he'd be out on his can.

He lit the cigar, then looked at the lighter. The flame burned brightly in the dim interior of the President's House. He walked toward a drapery-covered window, the flame in his hand. Thick, rich, realistic draperies, made to burn, as was everything in this house and on this set.

He stopped in front of the drapes. He held out the flame and his breath came quickly and his hand trembled. Then, quite suddenly, he put the lighter away. No actors, no cameras, nothing to be gained. Revenge for its own sake wasn't in Emperor Nat Markal's bag.

Besides, there was still the meeting tonight. He could still win out, still buy himself some time. And with enough time he could lift the restraining order and shoot the burning three days from now, a week from now . . .

BERTHA KRAUS

Bertha had set up the meeting exactly as she had last October —
but how differently it all turned out! At seven-thirty, only four
people had arrived: Isa Yee, Charles Halpert, Pen Guilfyle
and Cole Staley. Even Tyrone Chalze had deserted the sinking
ship. Guilfoyle said the director had called him all right, but not
to talk about extras and costumes. Chalze had said, 'Forget
Markal's instructions and go home to bed. In the morning you'll
have a different boss.' Guilfoyle, smiling, admitted he'd made
another deal months ago, and was only waiting for the right
time to leave Avalon. That constituted *his* loyalty and courage.

As for Staley, he was glum but not really worried. He had
resisted retirement for two years and when dismissal came
would go on half-salary.

Halpert looked stunned.

Isa Yee, who had more to lose than most, was perfectly composed. Bertha watched her chatting quietly with Halpert. The
Eurasian barely glanced at Markal, and he certainly hadn't
paid her any particular attention.

Filthy lies!

She turned her attention to Markal. He was finished. Bertha
knew that now. So did Markal himself. The frenetic energy
that had driven him all day was gone. He slouched in his chair,
chewing his cigar.

Bertha fought back sudden tears. The injustice of it all! A
great man and a great picture going down the drain for no
reason other than maliciousness and power politics. They had
used false rumors to defeat him.

Now she understood what Olive had been doing at the first
meeting. Now she saw how ruthless and clever Odel Dort's
widow was.

They sat around. Markal seemed half-asleep. It was a quarter to eight and no one else was going to come. It was time to
do something, say something. Bertha rose from her chair and
went to the desk. 'Mr. Markal.' He roused himself, looked up
at her. 'I think you'd better . . . reschedule the meeting. Something seems to have prevented the others from coming.'

He smiled faintly.

Poor man! She wanted to reach out and touch him, stroke
away the tired lines, tell him she knew how good he was, how
right he was.

'Thank you, Bertha. You'll come with me, won't you? When I set up shop again?'

'Of course, Mr. Markal!' Her heart raced. 'And you'll do *The Eternal Joneses* someday, wait and see!'

'I doubt it. I doubt if anyone will do it, ever.' He straightened and spoke to the others. 'Thank you for coming. As you see, we're alone.' He paused. 'By tomorrow, everyone will know that *The Eternal Joneses* has been canceled and Nat Markal is no longer associated with Avalon Pictures. You know tonight.' He paused again, as if trying to make this last speech impressive in some way, meaningful in some way ... and there was no way. 'I appreciate ... I'll remember your courtesy in coming here. If at any time in the future I can be of help—' He made a little gesture. 'Good night.'

Bertha hurried out, afraid she would disgrace herself with tears. She sat down at her desk, fumbling with papers, with letters, with business that no longer made sense. She heard Markal speaking softly, and then the Eurasian girl came out, followed by Staley and Guilfoyle. Markal called to her to come back in with her steno book. He was sitting on the bench beside Halpert, and said, 'I want you to make note of the following, Bertha. I'm asking Mr. Halpert to complete *The Eternal Joneses* and I'm contracting to purchase it as a private individual, unconnected with Avalon Pictures. If they want to hold onto the script—' He smiled at Halpert. 'But they won't. They have to begin production within a year of submission. I wrote that into the contract to protect myself against stalling tactics. Otherwise, rights revert to you, Charles. And knowing Olive, she'll jump at the chance to put that seventy-five thousand back in the hopper and wipe out the last remaining memory of my project. Either way, I want that script – now or in a year. How soon can you finish it?'

Halpert still seemed in a state of shock. 'A month. Three weeks if I—'

'Get it to me at my home in three weeks and there'll be a ten-thousand-dollar bonus.'

'Are you going to produce it yourself?'

Markal shook his head. 'No one man, no matter how wealthy he *thinks* he is, can do *Joneses*. It could wipe me out, and I'm not about to be wiped out.'

'Then why?'

'In the next few months you're going to hear that *Joneses* was a terrible mistake. You're going to read things about bad script and poor casting and Markal's loss of managerial magic. They've got a studio now and they'll plant what they want all over the place.' He stood up. 'But we're going to murder them. We're going to give the trade and the critics and everybody with access to the public the chance to judge for themselves.' He smiled at their blank looks. 'A postmortem attack. A dead man striking back. I'm going to publish your script, Charles. I'm going to give the copies away. A few thousand, in just the right places.'

Halpert said, 'Are you sure that's wise? Maybe it's not as good—'

'Don't doubt yourself,' Markal snapped. 'It's the best!' They shook hands and Halpert left and Markal looked around. 'Well, that's it. Get hold of Cherrins, the decorator who worked on this office. I'll want everything taken out—'

He went on, giving Bertha final instructions, then walked to the door. 'If you really decide to stay with me—'

'I've already decided, Mr. Markal.'

'I don't know exactly what I'm going to do, but I'll certainly need a secretary. Stay on here until I contact you. If they let you go, don't worry. You'll be on my payroll.' He waved and was gone.

Bertha went to the outer office and began transcribing the shorthand notes. She felt better now. She would remain with Nat Markal. A smaller, more intimate operation. He would show them what he could do, and she would help him. Together, they would make Avalon sorry . . .

The phone rang. It was Adele Markal. 'He left just a moment ago, Mrs. Markal. Is it important?'

There was a pause, then, 'Yes.'

Bertha said to hold on, she would see if she could catch him in the parking lot. Adele began to say that was too much, but Bertha was already on her way. Nothing was too much for Nat Markal.

It was dim and silent in the hall, all the offices closed for the night. She came out into a soft evening and hurried across footstep-deadening blacktop. A car was just leaving the parking area, its headlights slicing toward C-gate, but the studio Imperial was still in its reserved spot. She began to run, then slowed, realizing that he hadn't started the engine. She came up on the passenger's side, beginning to smile, about to give him her message. And stopped.

She didn't know where the light was coming from – the sky

or the lamp post near the South Building or the dashboard –
but it was enough. She saw them, Nat Markal and Isa Yee.
Nat Markal was kissing the Eurasian, and one hand was under
her dress. Nat Markal was oblivious to everything, and she
heard his raspy breath through the open window.

She walked away. She reached the office and heard herself
weeping.

It was true. All the filth was true.

She felt cheated. She had believed he was different, better, a
great and good man. He had cheated her.

She regained control and went to the phone. 'He's already
left, Mrs. Markal.'

Adele said, 'Oh. Was he . . . alone?'

Bertha spoke brightly, cheerfully. 'No. I believe he was with
Miss Yee.'

Adele said, 'Thank you,' and the line clicked.

Bertha sat still a while. She had work to do. She didn't do it.
Let someone else do it. She was through being Nat Markal's
secretary. She would go home.

But she didn't move. Mother was home. Complaining age
and approaching death was home. Television and canasta and
hot cocoa was home.

She didn't know where to go. There was no place for her to
go. Markal had cheated her of everything! Markal had cheated
her of her last remaining dream!

She opened her bottom drawer and reached for her bag. She
saw the pink message slip. George Doherty had called while
she'd been out to lunch. She hadn't had a chance to call him
back. George was a plain and unexciting man. George had
seemed pitiful and a little ridiculous and she'd been too busy
for him.

Too busy doing what? Dreaming of a man who didn't know
she was alive? A man who classified her with his desk and
telephone?

George would be home by now. She checked her personal
directory and dialed. George answered, his voice dull and quiet.
She said, 'This is Bertha.' His voice changed. 'That was some
season we Ram fans endured, wasn't it?' He talked and talked.
He no longer seemed pitiful and a little ridiculous. He seemed
warm and pleasant. Then he cleared his throat and became a
mumbler again. 'Guess it's too late for a bite to eat, isn't it?'
She said, 'Not for we movie people. I'm still at the office.' He
was silent a moment. 'Could I pick you up?' She said, 'Sure,'

and he said, 'Fifteen minutes!' and hung up as if afraid she would change her mind.

She used her mirror and makeup and was glad she'd worn her good green suit. She tidied the desk, went to the door of Markal's office and looked around, her long face solemn. Then she flicked the switch, sending the paneled walls and antique chairs and ancient tiles into darkness, turned her back on it and walked out to wait for George Doherty.

CHARLEY HALPERT

Charley got to work as soon as he entered his apartment. It wasn't the ten-thousand-dollar bonus; with what his taxes would be this year, he wouldn't realize very much from *that*. It was wanting to finish. It was also wanting to avoid thoughts of his father and the concept of failure being a Halpert tradition. How could he consider himself a failure with all the money he'd made and Markal so certain people would flip over the script?

But nothing produced. Nothing on the screen. Nothing but finger exercises for a few people. All rehearsal and never a performance.

The phone interrupted him twice within fifteen minutes. First it was Ben Kalik. Ben had heard the news. He wasn't particularly concerned. Tough and all that . . . but two people were interested in Charley's apartment-house novel, *Five Doors*. A name Charley didn't recognize at Twentieth Century-Fox, and Moe Sholub at Avalon. 'It'll go to whoever closes first at seventy-five gees for the book and one hundred for you to script it.' Charley had given up questioning the astronomical figures. He neither believed nor disbelieved. It had happened with *Joneses*; it could happen with *Five Doors*. He just couldn't get involved in speculation right now. He said great and he'd be ready in about a month. 'A month? Why not tomorrow?' He explained about Markal wanting the script completed. Kalik made a sound of derision. 'He'll never do it. Oh, he's good for the dough and you go ahead and make him happy because he'll be around this business one way or another for some time yet. But publish a script and send it out? Malarky. He'll forget all that once he stops burning. He'll tuck it away among the other unfilmed scripts every producer gathers. Now

432

about *Five Doors*—' He wanted to talk further about Fox and Sholub and how he wouldn't go under a hundred-fifty 'gees' for the package, But Charley was edgy and said so and Kalik said sure, he understood, and get ready for some real action soon.

Charley had barely sat down at the typewriter when he was summoned back to the hall phone. It was Cheryl. Jim had drunk a lot tonight, and she could come over. Without hesitating, he said, 'I'm sorry, honey. Not tonight and not for a while.' He explained about *Joneses* and that he wanted to work and work and work. She was silent. He said, 'Don't get sensitive. I'm going to do this thing in two or three weeks. I'm going to finish it in one headlong rush. I feel I have to, or I might not finish it at all. Then we'll sneak you away from your job and spend a day in the mountains, jumping in and out of bed.' She said all right, subdued, and he said he was sorry but that devil Failure was riding his back again. She said she couldn't see where any failure on his part was involved. He said, 'Well, let me work it out.'

And he did. He worked until his shoulders tightened and his eyes blurred and no amount of coffee helped. He wanted to talk to someone about the Vietnam scenes and went to the hall and called Lars Wyllit's number for the third or fourth time that week. Still no answer. He wondered if it was true that Markal had bounced Wyllit off the picture.

Not that it made any difference now. *Joneses* was dead. And why bother with the corpse?

He got back to the typewriter and worked three more hours and then fell into bed, pulling off his shoes and pants and shirt.

This was what his life would be for the next two or three weeks. He would finish *The Eternal Joneses* as he had finished his first and best novel, slaving away day and night and living the action and forgetting everything else.

He tried to get up and change from sweat-soaked underwear into fresh pajamas, but exhaustion gripped him and he fell back and slept.

NAT MARKAL

Nat Markal took Isa to a motel in San Gabriel. They stayed until three A.M., and while he wasn't satisfied with her attitude, her responses, he felt she would change once she understood just how deeply he felt, just how sincere he was in his decision to continue seeing her in spite of everything. She wanted to talk about *Joneses*, about his plans for future operations, but he put her off and took her home and went home himself.

It was after four when he entered the kitchen, thinking of a cold beer – and Adele was sitting there, fully dressed, reading a magazine. Startled, he stopped in the doorway, then began to say something about a late meeting. 'Yes,' she said, 'with Isa Yee. I'm leaving you, Nat. Lainie, Mother and I are going to New York tomorrow. I'll file for divorce through Roger Chennen. You can talk to him if you wish. I expect half of everything in your ... *our* estate. That's California's community property law, you know. The Napoleonic Code. If you try to fight me, I have a full set of those infra-red pictures, and Olive assures me I can call on her for other evidence.' She rose, a cold, hard stranger. 'Good-bye, Nat.'

He wasn't unprepared for this moment. He had planned for it, had things to say, arguments that would sway her, tactics that would delay her.

He was prepared with speeches touching on the differences between love and lust. Pleas for understanding of a man's weakness. Reminders of their years together, their travails and triumphs. And finally his need for her, and their common desire not to hurt Lainie.

He said nothing. He let her walk out of the room, and out of his life, without trying to stop her. It shocked him. It must also have shocked her, because she came back to strike at him.

'One thing,' she said, face set. 'One thing you'll find out very soon. You've thrown away everything you worked for, everything you dreamed of. *Respect*, Nat. That's what you wanted more than money. Respect, admiration, reputation. That's gone. And soon you'll be alone. All alone. Those women ... they'll use you and forget you. And someday you'll grow old and sick and crawl into a corner to die like an animal.'

He laughed. What she was saying frightened him and so he stopped her with laughter. 'The industry could have used you in the old days, Adele. When Odel was making those East Lynne medodramas. Next you'll have me stumbling down Skid Row—'

She left again, for good this time. He had his beer. He was still frightened. But he thought of Isa, and the fear went away. Old things were coming to an end. New things were beginning.

He went to the garage and got the Ferrari. Let them follow

434

him now. Let them take pictures and make notes. He was going to spend the night with Isa, at her apartment. He was going to spend *all* his nights with Isa!

She let him in, confused and sleepy, wearing rumpled pajamas. 'What is it?' she mumbled. He apologized for the hour, then told her to wash her face and sit down with him. They had to talk.

Her eyes cleared. 'I don't have to wash my face. I'm awake. What is it?'

He drew her down on the couch. He smiled at her. 'You once said there was only one way for us to continue seeing each other. Do you remember?'

She frowned. He said, 'Marriage. That's what you said. I laughed. You were angry with me. Rightly so. But at the time ... well, everything's changed. I'm getting a divorce. I can ask you—'

She stood up. She went to a telephone table and got something and came back. It was a sheet of paper with a notation scribbled on it in Isa's spidery hand. He had trouble making it out. He muttered, 'Universal ready ... something, something, contract.'

'Universal ready to talk big contract,' she said. 'Jerry Storm and I had lunch on Monday. With Mona gone, I'm very important to him. He said I should write this down and think of it. He felt you were going to make me some sort of offer and he didn't want me to take it. He's been working hard, trying to get a commitment from Universal. He knew you were finished at Avalon, though he didn't know just when it would become official. He wants me to get away from you and Avalon. He feels—'

Nat stood up. 'What difference does it make *what* he feels and what he wants and what he knows! He couldn't possibly guess at the offer I'm making you now! A share in my life, Isa! To become Mrs. Nat Markal! What has that got to do with Jerry Storm? He gets no commission on your marriage.'

She smiled. 'True. And it would hurt. He could retire on his percentage of all your millions.'

He stared at her.

She tilted her head to one side. 'You're not going to act shocked, are you, Nat? It wouldn't suit you. If I married you, could you convince yourself it was for *love*?' She looked him in the eye, and his stare wavered and fell away. 'I never talked *love,* Nat. I talked career and serving your needs as you served

435

mine. I couldn't do a complete about-face and spout romance. I'm not a good enough actress for *that*. Marriage would have to be on the old basis – serving each other's needs.'

He sat down again. He didn't look at her. She left the room and when she came back she was wearing a bathrobe and carrying a glass. She gave him the glass, and he sipped it. Brandy. He drank it the way good brandy should never be drunk, at a gulp. He reached for cigars and had none. He nodded. 'All right. Love can come later.'

Her smile was broader this time, closer to laughter this time. He managed a quick smile of his own. 'Hack line. I know. But . . . it *can* happen.'

'Then you're asking me to marry you without love? You understand I'll be half-owner of whatever Nat Markal has, and if we break up later I'll expect that half to go with me? You're willing to risk millions—'

'Can't you stop talking about *money*!'

She laughed. She covered her mouth with her hand and tried to stop and couldn't. She turned her back and bent and laughed, kept laughing until he stood up and spun her around and shook her and shouted, 'Shut up! I'm asking you to marry me and I'll take whatever chances I have to take! Is that clear? Is that enough? Can we make plans now?'

Her laughter was gone. She turned her head first to one side, then the other, looking at her shoulders, where his hands were gripping her. She said, '*Don't . . . do . . . that.*' She said it so intensely he actually jumped back. Her eyes seemed to bulge. Her ivory face was deeply tinged with red. He began to say he was sorry, but she cut him short. 'Don't ever put your hands on me again. Don't ever come near me again.'

He could understand sudden anger. He had shaken her in sudden anger himself. But not what she was saying. 'Our marriage—'

'Marriage? Not for ten million! Not for a hundred million! Not for *anything* on earth! Spend every day and every night with a fat old—'

'That's enough,' he whispered, frightened.

But it wasn't enough. Her lips were flecked with spittle and her mouth twisted and her neck corded. He began to turn away, to run from her.

'Fat white bastard! Jelly-belly! Disgusting old fay! Smelly tub of lard!'

He got the door open. She said, 'If you ever get in my way,

436

ever do the slightest thing to hurt me, I'll smear your name like no name has ever been smeared before. I'll let the whole world know the sickening old fool you really are. Emperor Nat Markal in national magazines and newspapers—'

He closed the door and walked to the elevators, legs trembling. He punched the 'Down' button repeatedly and would have taken the staircase if he had seen it. He was in a panic to get away from here – from a specter closing in on him. The specter of fat old jelly-belly *Nat*'n.

OLIVE DORT

On Friday, 30th April, an announcement was made to the trade and press by David Sankin, 'acting president of Avalon Pictures Corporation', that Nat Markal had resigned 'due to reasons of health and personal necessity'. As for *The Eternal Joneses*, Sankin said, 'The project will be carefully reviewed in light of sound business practices and interests of the stockholders.'

At six-thirty that evening, Sol Soloway drove his Continental to Olive Dort's Brentwood estate and strode up the flagstone walk. He was admitted by Olive herself. She didn't ask him to sit down or have a drink, didn't even invite him in from the mirror-lined hallway.

'You're angry, Sol. You've learned David will remain president after the stockholders' meeting.'

'Angry? Confused is more like it! We planned and worked and when we finally got Markal out—'

'*I* planned and *I* worked and *I* finally got Markal out.'

Soloway tried to master his anger. He came closer, put his hand on her arm. 'What happened, Olive? What made you change?'

'Estelle's chicken soup.'

He shook his head. 'I don't understand.'

'You're too fond of it, Sol. Estelle means too much to you.'

He laughed and drew her into his arms. She didn't resist, but turned her head aside when he tried to kiss her. 'You can stay on in your present position, Sol, or you can leave. It's up to you.'

He let her go. 'If it's proof of affection you want, just name it. We haven't been seeing much of each other, I'll admit, but

437

that was the press of business. I . . . love you, Olive. I wouldn't be much use to you or Avalon if Estelle found out about us and created a scandal, but anything short of that—'

'I don't want your love, Sol. I don't want you. Good night.'

He reddened. He opened his mouth. She said, 'Think before you burn your bridges. Grayson, Sankin and I are now very much in agreement, and firmly in control.'

Soloway's mouth closed. He muttered, 'I wasn't about to burn any bridges . . . just wanted to say I'll be there if you ever need me.'

'Thank you. Now if you don't mind, I'm about to have dinner.'

He nodded. He made himself smile. 'I'm lonely already, Olive. I know you will be too, once you've had a chance to think things through.'

After he left, Olive locked the door and went through the big house to the bedroom in back. It was hung with cream satin drapes, and speakers piped in soft music. There was an oval bed and behind it a lighted color photograph of Olive in a huge gilt frame. The photograph was actually a slide projected from a special unit within the wall. The frame held the screen and a lever mechanism in the base. Press a button and a new photograph appeared, one of eighty different poses. Normally, a gowned and bejeweled Olive was on view – a scene from her next-to-last film. But the man operating the lever was examining a carefully lighted shot of Olive wearing a quarter of a million dollars worth of diamonds, black net stockings, silver high-heels and nothing else. She said, 'I shouldn't have told you how that works.'

He turned, his smile nervous. 'How long ago . . . I mean, you're a very beautiful woman.'

'Only last August. A woman photographer who does all my work.'

He glanced from her to the photograph, nodding a little too quickly.

She said, 'I think you need proof.'

'I didn't intend to cast doubt—'

She threw two switches in the panel near the door. Everything darkened but the photograph. She threw another switch, and soft blue light bathed the oval bed from above. She began to undress, dropping her clothing where she stood. Now she was the one who was nervous.

She was nude when he reached her. She put out her arm,

stopping him, and walked to the bed. She lay down carefully, one knee rising, giving herself to the blue light. 'Now, David, when was that picture taken?'

Dave Sankin came to the bed and whispered. 'It doesn't ..., it's not good enough.'

She held out her arms. He bent to her, hesitantly, a man who didn't know how to play, who had yet to experience the young whores who called themselves starlets. She helped him forget his nervousness – and his wife. He was still capable, still strong, and she dreamed her dream of youth and passion under the kindly blue light that hid her varicose veins and his protruding stomach. He cried out his delight toward the end, and for that she promised him unending support in whatever he wanted as president of Avalon.

ISA YEE

Monday morning Isa got another hate call. But with a difference. It had nothing to do with Nat Markal and a life of sin and eternal damnation. 'Black bitch,' the woman's voice whispered. 'Nigger tramp. *Help* your race? You'll be burned alive *with* them when America awakens.' Isa said, 'You must have the wrong party, Mrs. Cracker,' and hung up. The phone rang again as she was preparing to leave for Avalon and her fifth day of work on *The Glenmore Theatre*, a juicy residual from Nat Markal. She hesitated, then picked it up. A man this time, claiming to be a reporter. 'Miss Yee, could you tell me the exact date of your press conference? The announcement was vague as to time and place.' She said her agent would handle the matter and please excuse her as she was late for a shooting.

She drove to the Century City shopping center and bought three papers and sat in her car looking for the answer. She found it on page four of the first paper, a marvelous spot for publicity of the right kind. But this! This had her starting up the car to speed back to the apartment and hide. This was the realization of her worst fears, her most persistent nightmares.

It was a two-column article that included a letter and a picture of her taken at the New York press conference on *Joneses*. The letter was from 'civil rights leader Humphrey Barchester, personal friend and political mentor of rising young actress

439

Isa Yee, soon to be starred as a Negro slave and the descendants of that slave in the Avalon super-epic, *The Eternal Joneses*'. It stated that the role of slave had inspired Miss Yee to reveal her Negro blood in order to give aid and comfort to her race 'at this critical time in its history. While Miss Yee is not in the camp of the Black Nationalist and Black Power groups, she refuses to turn her back on anyone legitimately striving to bring political and economic freedom to her people.'

She cut the engine and read on. Letters had gone out to the NAACP and other 'established Negro organizations informing them of her availability in fund-raising drives, speaking engagements and any other activity in which she might be useful'. This caused the author of the article to comment that 'Miss Yee is showing the same brand of courage that made her risk her life last February in an attempt to save onetime star Pier Andrei'.

The article concluded with: 'There is now some doubt whether *The Eternal Joneses* will go into production on schedule, but this doesn't change the marvelous *heart* shown by Miss Yee in taking what many would consider an enormous professional risk in the interests of others.'

'Enormous professional risk,' hell! Free had murdered her! The bastard had finished her! Courageous Isa Yee was a courageous coon, and after a decent interval of time, after she'd completed the last TV role for which she had a contract, the parts would dry up and Jerry Storm would drop her and she'd wait for the 'courageous Negro' parts that came up once or twice a year. They wouldn't bring in enough money to keep her in Century Towers for three months.

She looked through the other papers. Both had the story. She sat in the pretty little Corvair Nat Markal had brought for her, amidst the futuristic buildings of Century City, and shook in fear.

And then she thought of Markal and the way she'd thrown him out and she bent her head and bit her lip and said, 'Stupid, stupid, stupid!'

She drove onto Santa Monica Boulevard and toward Avalon. She had to fulfill her contract. It meant eight thousand dollars. Eight thousand hadn't seemed too important last night, but this morning it was the Federal mint. She would have to live on that eight thousand a long time.

No one said anything when she arrived on Stage 9. Clete Brown got right to work and they shot four hours of interiors and she didn't have time to wonder who knew and who didn't.

She worked until she could barely stand and began to suspect that Brown was going to rush this thing through with an eye toward dropping it if the sponsor made waves.

They broke for lunch at one, and Brown came over and said, 'Marvelous, Isa. Get a bite to eat, and we'll keep going. You seem to have Anita so right today I don't want to miss a moment of it.'

Which was nice, if true. And which didn't mean a thing because there were some terrific Negro actresses starving in this town.

No one asked her to lunch. Of course, she knew only a few people on the set and had never encouraged familiarity and most were grabbing sandwiches ... but it dug at her and she went off the lot and walked to a luncheonette far enough from Avalon so that the chances of meeting anyone she knew were slight. And who should walk in but one of the supporting players. He hesitated, then came over and sat down with her and they chatted about this and that. Halfway through the meal he suddenly said, 'Saw that article about you only an hour ago. While waiting for my scene. I think—' He waved his hand. 'Wish I had the right words.' She didn't know what those right words would be, but said thanks and changed the subject and began pitching him a little. She was sure that had she given him the same opening Friday he'd have been all over her. Now his eyes seemed to slip away and he smiled too much and he didn't bite. On the walk back she brushed him a few times with shoulder and hip. Still nothing.

He might be married. He might be in love. But she just couldn't believe it was anything but those articles.

What did she expect? Maybe later she would get the invitations. Maybe later the hungry boys would figure she was a good bet for a quick lay. But not yet. Not while her 'courage' was plastered all over the papers.

Near the lot he put his arm around her shoulders, murmured, 'Best of luck, baby,' and ran across the street to a group standing near the lunch wagon. She walked on toward the gate. She didn't look their way but was sure they were watching her, talking about her.

Best of luck, baby.

Brown worked them hard without a break. He came to Isa at five-thirty and talked over a line that needed changing and then said, 'The way we're going, we'll be on location Wednesday, and all through by Thursday.'

441

She went home. All through by Thursday. Exactly.

She called Jerry Storm. The secretary said, 'Mr. Storm is out of the office, Miss Yee. He said to inform his clients he is involved in contract negotiations and might not be available for a few days.'

Isa thanked her and made dinner. *Was Jerry avoiding her?*

What of it? The brush had to start sooner or later. So it was starting sooner. She had always known what would happen if they found out she was Negro. It was happening. Should she jump out the window?

It was a thought . . . but it didn't stick.

She didn't know what she would do. A numbness was setting in – an inability to think things through. Which was good.

She had a few drinks and watched TV. She should get to bed early. Brown would work them as hard tomorrow as he had today. But she couldn't sit still, couldn't face bed, alone.

She remembered last Wednesday with Nat Markal at the motel in San Gabriel. A colored boy had shown them to their room. A stocky kid with eyes like smoldering coal. She had caught those eyes once. She had thought of him while serving the Emperor.

She packed an overnight bag and drove to San Gabriel and the motel. She made sure the boy was there by looking in the office window. Then she asked for a room, and the boy carried her bag. He opened the door, put on the lights, set her bag on the folding stand. She closed the door. He turned at the sound. 'That all, ma'am?' She shook her head. 'Ice water? Cigarettes?' She shook her head. He stood there, puzzled and worried. 'Your tip,' she said, and came toward him. She came right up against him, stood pressing him with her body, and still his arms hung at his sides.

She wanted to get into bed with this boy and forget everything. She wanted to do it now. She didn't want to waste a moment. Games were fun, but some other time, not this bitter night. She put her hand on his fly. His face twisted. 'Why you doin' that?' She kissed him and opened the zipper. He stepped back. 'I'm no stud for *anyone*!' He was just as angry as he was desirous.

She sank down at the edge of the bed. 'This goddam country,' she muttered. 'This lousy fay scene. It spoils everything.'

He was quiet a moment, then: 'You not white?' She said no,

but what if she was? She was here because of him. She had seen him and wanted him and come to him. Why the hell was he wasting time.

His eyes remained suspicious. She got her bag and started for the door. He caught her from behind. He held her a moment, enjoying her with his hands, then pulled her to the bed and took her in her clothes. He said he had to get back to the office but would be off duty at midnight. Could he come back?

She said he damned well better. He smiled, touching her face.

Later, he lay beside her, a beautiful boy with soft lips and hard body. He was eighteen, a high school dropout, and wanted to talk about his ambition to complete his education and work in an airplane plant. She kept him too busy to talk. She didn't give a damn about his ambitions – about anyone's ambitions. She wanted action. And when he had no more action to give, she sent him away.

The next day's shooting went well, and they had a six A.M. transportation-to-location call for Wednesday. She would have liked to have gone to San Gabriel, but couldn't. She went home. She got four calls. Three were filth, and one was a Negro musician she'd met briefly at a party two years ago. He had to reconstruct the entire evening before she remembered him. He felt they should 'get together'.

Anger flared. If she wanted to go out hunting pleasure that was one thing, but *them* asking *her*? She said she was engaged and hung up. Later, in bed, she was sorry she hadn't asked him over. Just for tonight. Just to fill the emptiness that would otherwise be filled by nightmares.

The phone rang at eleven-thirty, at twelve-thirty, at one. She answered the last call, and it was filth. She took the phone off the hook. She lay down again and couldn't sleep. She had to sleep. She had to give Clete Brown a great performance at Big Sur tomorrow.

Why? she asked herself. Why, when he'll never use you again?

Because she was the best. Because she would always be the best. And they had to know it even if they let her rot away and die!

She gave in to the tears that had been building up for two days. She wept and cursed Free Barchester for what he had done to her, and Nat Markal for what she had done to him. She cursed Jerry Storm for beginning to dump her. She cursed

443

Whitey and Blacky, and herself most of all for not being fully of either world.

Then she slept.

LARS WYLLIT

Lars got out of bed and, nodding briefly at the elderly man who shared the semiprivate hospital room, walked slowly into the hall and toward the glassed-in porch. He'd started these walks only yesterday, after two weeks flat on his back. He was supposed to walk a little each day, but that wasn't why he was walking now. It was seven o'clock, and visiting hour was about to begin. Lars didn't like being audience to other people's joys and sorrows. And he didn't like them looking his way and wondering why he had no visitors of his own.

He reached the porch and drew his robe closer about his neck. It was always a few degrees cooler out here. He took a wicker chair near an ashtray and lit up a cigarette and inhaled deeply. He wasn't supposed to smoke. Dr. Feidler was against coronary cases smoking so soon after an attack. But Lars Wyllit didn't care very much what Dr. Feidler was for or against. He didn't really care very much what Lars Wyllit was for or against. He just refused to deprive himself of one of life's few remaining pleasures.

Not that he wanted to die. He had found out in that blinding moment of pain and fear how very much he wanted to live. He had been lucky, and thankful for his luck, but that was two weeks ago and the blinding moment was gone if not forgotten and he was still Lars Wyllit and still faced with a choice of how to live.

Except that the choice was far sharper, far easier to see now. Because he was much closer to death now.

He heard voices, an increase in the ordinary sounds of the small private hospital – the visitors arriving. He dragged on his cigarette, thinking he had a better story than most patients to tell of escape from death.

As Feidler explained it, the usual complication of certain cases of rheumatic fever is an auricular flutter, or heart murmur. Lars had suffered from this since childhood. '—which in turn can lead to stroke if a thrombosis forms in one of the heart's chambers. The thrombosis, or blood clot, tears loose

444

under conditions of strain – and wham! you're either dead or close to it. That was what your doctor at home explained to your mother, which was why she tried to keep you more or less dormant. Which in turn was why I also hoped to keep you from living like a human hurricane—'

So he had suffered a coronary thrombosis during the early morning of Wednesday, 21st April. And since he was alone, and a madwoman had been tying up his telephone, and he'd lost consciousness, he should be neatly buried in Forest Lawn along with Mona Dearn. But that wasn't the way things happened to Lars Wyllit. Nothing neat. Nothing normal.

Mrs. Viola Wanego had come to the hospital a few days ago to explain the miracle of his salvation. It was simple enough, as miracles go. She was the daughter of the madwoman who called him Izzy Worshofsky.

'She's been ... not quite right since my brother died in Korea. She's joined various organizations, the extremist kind, and no matter how my husband and I try to watch her she manages to make those calls. That night the baby had cramps and woke me and I heard her out in the hall. She was on the phone and she was frightened. She began to hang up when she saw me, then handed me the phone and went to her room. I listened. I heard what sounded like someone drowning – choking sounds. Then a moan. I ran to my mother and asked what it meant. She said one of her enemies was making believe he was sick. Just to frighten her, she said. I got your name – your real name – and number from her and called the operator.'

The police had brought him here because he was dying and the private hospital was two streets from his home. The doctors had saved him and Feidler had come and joined in caring for him. In a week or two he would go home. Unless he had another coronary and died. Which was common enough, said Feidler, '—unless you learn to live with it. At first it's like walking on eggshells. Do *nothing* to exert yourself. Later, you can resume a more or less normal life. By that I mean a life in which you eat, drink a little, work at your trade, and exercise in moderation.' Lars had asked, 'What about love?' Feidler had smiled and said he classified that as exercise. Lars had shaken his head and commiserated with Feidler's 'teammates'.

He rose from the chair and walked to the glass wall and looked out from four stories and a hill-high vantage point to Hollywood at night. Off to his right he could see the glow of the Strip. Snaking from Sunset and past the hospital was La Cienega. The action would be hot. The clubs would be rocking, the girls swinging, the boys making out. And it was all lost to him . . . for one hell of a long time.

The speciality act was lost to him forever. If a big guy stepped on his toes, he would have to smile graciously. If the beach bully kicked sand in his face, he couldn't turn to Charles Atlas to build up his muscles. If a live-wire eyed his chick, he would have to look in the other direction and hope she didn't trade a live one for a dead one.

Better dead?

He didn't know. Mind told him better alive in any condition than dead. Gut told him he would never be able to live according to mind.

He walked away from the Turned-on City and its Turned-on People. He walked to the end of the porch and back to the wicker chair and then to the other end of the porch. He wanted to return to his room and his bed. He wanted to read and then go to sleep. Read and sleep and eat. Eat and sleep and read. That was what made the world go 'round for Lars Wyllit right now. Not people, which had always made it go 'round before.

He was tired. He sank into the wicker chair, reached for another cigarette and changed his mind. And then realized he'd changed his mind because he was thinking of Feidler and of death. And took the cigarette and lit it and didn't want it.

He needed help. And not Feidler.

Another voice to clarify the many in his mind. A voice he could accept without reservation because it belonged to the one person . . .

No good. She wasn't in the Turned-on City anymore. She didn't know about him. No one knew, except Mick Malloy. He'd had to tell Mick because he had to maintain himself in the marketplace. Mick had come to see him, once, which was par for a Hollywood agent. Mick had been more cheerful than when Lars had been healthy. Because Nat Markal was out and his power gone and forgotten. Because Moe Sholub had been on the horn about a new picture. Because Lars would be up and around in time if he'd be up and around in early June when *Corinth by Neon* would receive a budget. *Corinth* was an artsy-craftsy novel about Greenwich Village – a natural for the Wyllit touch. Malloy had given him a copy and he'd read it and seen what he would have to throw away and what he would be able to retain. He could do the treatment tomorrow. As for the script ... well, that thing in his chest would have to heal a bit more since scripting was never easy.

He checked his watch. Visiting time was only half over. God, how this hour dragged!

Not that he couldn't have had all the visitors he wanted. Malloy had been ready to spread the word, but Lars had stopped him with the one argument that made sense to a Hollywood agent – his ten percent. Lars had said Sholub might be leery of a post-coronary writer. Others might feel the same. His price might drop if they felt *he* could, and in mid-script. Mick had quickly agreed it was best Lars not be bothered in this critical recuperative period. Ah, the soul of the man!

He stubbed out the cigarette.

'I didn't know you were allowed to smoke.'

Terry came from behind him and drew up another wicker chair and sat down. 'The nurse said you were out here.'

'Nurses have big mouths. So do agents.'

'Don't blame Mr. Malloy. I said it was business. A tip on a big project, for your ears only.'

'That *would* sway Mick. How come you're still in Los Angeles?'

'You don't wrap up almost six years in a day, or even a week. I'm flying out tomorrow evening.'

'All wrapped up *now*, huh?'

She nodded. 'I felt I had to see you once more. I felt I had to say ... I hadn't been fair. I thought you were hiding out because of Markal. Then, when Markal lost his position at Avalon and you still didn't show up, I began to wonder. So I called your agent.'

'Why did you feel you had to see me? What wasn't fair?'

She crossed her legs. She wore a short, chic suit of ice-cream yellow and those legs were bare and sleek and still turned him on. Her hair was crisp and tight around her face and gleamed like good copperware. She looked at her hands.

'Never mind,' he said quickly. 'It makes no difference. Nice of you to come.' He felt small and shabby in his hospital pajamas and robe. He wanted to stand up and move around, wanted to do things to be bigger, stronger in her eyes. 'Drawn-out good-byes bug me. So good-bye.'

She raised her eyes briefly and looked down at her hands again. 'Let me say it. I was unfair to you. You ... helped me. I won't say how, but. if you hadn't come to my room that night—'

447

'Past history. You're safe from me now.' He made a sound of laughter. 'For a while. A good long while.'

'Mr. Malloy said it was a coronary. Very serious. You ... almost died. I'm so glad you didn't die.'

He had to get rid of this chick because she was pulling at his insides and flying away tomorrow. He was going to tell her to flake off because he needed his rest.

She kept her head down. 'Thinking back, I felt there was no one, really, to say good-bye to but you. However it happened, with Mona dead there was no one in this whole town who meant anything – in human terms, I mean – but you. If I didn't see you, if I wasn't honest, if I didn't tell you how I felt—' She rubbed at her face, her eyes, a gesture of frustration. 'Do you understand?'

'No, I don't.' But he was soft-spoken, hoping to understand, not being caustic or clever – not being the boy maniac, the boy wise guy.

She finally looked at him. A little mascara had smudged, but it didn't help him lose the picture of a redheaded angel. 'I care something for you, Lars. You mean something to me. I want you to know that.'

He almost put his hand to his chest. Something jumped there, and he was afraid. He spoke brusquely. 'But you're flying home tomorrow.'

She nodded. 'It's not as if we were ... vital to each other. you do care something for me, but the basis is physical, a certain animal attraction—'

'You make it sound so zoologic.'

She took cigarettes from her bag and looked at them and put them away. She sighed. 'We were never any good at talking, were we?'

'I tried,' he said, seeing the end coming once again. How many endings had he had with this girl? Too many. It should have ended once, finally, and allowed him time to forget. 'I tried like hell.'

She stood up. 'I guess I didn't. Until now. And I didn't do a good job now.' She rubbed the palm of one hand with the fingers of the other. 'I just wanted to tell you ... a proper good-bye.'

He stood up too. She said, 'No, please don't.' She held out her hand. He took it, wanted to bend his lips to it, let it go instead. He said, 'It was a very proper good-bye, Terry. Thank you.' He nodded and smiled, trying to show her he was pleased, trying to get her to leave while he could still show her he was pleased.

Too many endings with this girl!

She said, 'This is the first time we've ever parted the right way.'

He nodded and smiled, wanting to say that *no* parting from her was the right way.

She went to the glass doors and looked back. He nodded and smiled. She went out into the hall and looked back again. He nodded and smiled. He would nod and smile until she was gone no matter what it cost him. He would *not* say he was going to die without her. He would *not* try to coerce her anymore. He would nod and smile so she would be able to leave without pain, without guilt, without any cloud on her departure.

She turned back to him. *Not another ending?* She came up to him and stood looking into his face, straight into his eyes because they were the same height. He nodded and smiled. She put her bag on the chair and cupped his face in her hands. He asked, 'Why?' She said, 'You're crying. Don't you know you're crying? I never thought of you crying.' He said, 'The hell I am.' She kissed him, gingerly, as if afraid he might break. He said he would *not* coerce her, and she said, 'You love me.' He asked what was the big surprise – he had told her that before, hadn't he? 'But not so I could believe it. Not like this.' He asked what difference did it make since it didn't change the way *she* felt, and she said, imitating him, 'The hell it doesn't.' He told her it was impossible because he was sick and she'd be more nurse than lover. She said, 'You're human. You're thinking of someone besides yourself. At last you're human.' He said a remark like that proved it couldn't possibly work. She said, 'Anyway, I can't go home because I hate the winters.' He argued with her and she said, 'You'd die without me. You know that, don't you?' He sneered. He said he was more likely to die *with* her. But he had a good thing going in those tears. They took the curse off Lars Wyllit, made everything he said right with her. Besides, he didn't know how to stop the damned things.

CARL BAIGLEN

'I don't want to rush you,' Carl said, smiling to cover his anxiety, 'but if you've read it—'

'I've read it,' Dave Sankin said, and his tone of voice wasn't

449

encouraging. He sat behind his desk in the temporary office they'd given him down the hall from Markal's, where workmen were removing furniture and antique tile. On the wall hung one of this old Hollywood gag signs that only a newcomer like Sankin would think clever: 'It is not enough to be Hungarian. You must also have talent.'

'I consider it the best treatment I've ever had,' Carl said, putting himself squarely on the line. 'I consider it an opportunity to produce a major feature in the genre of *Psycho* and *Diabolique*. And though I doubt that I can get Halpert to do the script, *any* good writer can follow his guidelines.'

'I've read it,' Sankin repeated, as if Carl hadn't spoken, 'and I'm disturbed.' He picked up the blue-covered Xerox copy, then dropped it. The sound was a flat slap in the silence. What followed amounted to another slap, across Carl Baiglen's face. 'It doesn't strike me as a Carl Baiglen production. Too high tone.'

Carl tried to fight back. 'Would *Psycho* and—'

'Big-budget films, Carl. Forget them. You have your own work, your own style. That's why you were brought into Avalon. Don't forget, I was part of the team that brought you here.'

Sankin had changed. Sankin was harder and colder. Carl could see he wasn't going to be easy to live with, now that he had power and position. But that didn't change the fact that promises had been made to Carl Baiglen.

'All right, I'll admit Halpert wrote it a little ... loose. It should be tightened a bit, perhaps the pace increased. But otherwise he did a wonderful job.'

'That's a matter of some contention. I asked Alan Devon his opinion. He said he found it as disorganized as Halpert's work on *Joneses*.'

Carl muttered that he thought everyone was agreed Halpert's work on *Joneses* had been excellent.

'Then why aren't we producing it, Carl?'

A dishonest question – one for which Carl had some honest answers. *Joneses* wasn't being produced because Olive Dort and company didn't want it produced, and their reasons had nothing to do with the writing. *Joneses* wasn't being produced because Sankin had made a deal with Olive and Lou Grayson to sell them enough stock to dump Markal. The clincher had been their offering him the one thing Markal couldn't – the presidency of Avalon. Almost everyone on the lot knew this,

450

but Carl couldn't say so, unless he was ready to walk away from Avalon.

Sankin looked at the treatment and shook his head. 'I'm not alone in my feelings about this, Carl. Olive read it and said it's much too subtle for a teen-aged audience.'

Carl flushed. However Markal had squeezed him on budget, he had never come right out and classified a Baiglen production as *juvenile*! 'I don't produce pictures for teen-agers, Dave. Olive hasn't been in on things for quite some time.'

'She will, from now on.'

'Fine. But my pictures draw a fully adult—'

Sankin sighed. 'Even if I gave my okay, you could never produce it within budget.'

'That's something else we have to talk about. I was made to understand my budget would be increased.'

'Over a hundred-fifty, two hundred thousand?'

Carl stiffened. 'Over five hundred thousand. Medium budget, Dave. At Lou Grayson's yacht party—'

'Anything on paper, Carl?' Sankin's face was bland.

The accountant in charge, Carl thought. *The goddam adding machine without scruples.*

'No. But even so—' He faltered under Sankin's cool gaze. 'Listen, Dave, eight months ago Nat Markal told me I was getting a quarter of a million for *Terror Town*. And since then—'

'On paper, Carl?'

Carl saw that Sankin didn't care whether he walked out. Carl saw that Sankin was prepared to drop Carl Baiglen right here and now. And Carl Baiglen had no place to go. He lit a cigarette. He shook his head.

'Then I'm afraid I have to insist you stay under two hundred thousand.'

Two-Cent Bagel.

He kept his voice steady. 'Be reasonable, Dave. What can I make for two hundred thousand these days?'

'Just what you've been making before. We're satisfied with your product, Carl. It's solid and it's dependable. Change the structure, and it won't pay.'

'You can't be sure of that.'

Sankin made an impatient gesture. 'All this talk ... I'm only stating what your six-picture deal calls for ... on paper. That clause about increased budget plainly reads, "at the discretion of the management". I'm the management. And pictures with a

451

ceiling of two hundred thousand are all I'll allow you.' He leaned forward. 'Do you understand, Carl? We want six cheapie-creepies. Nothing else.'

Carl didn't trust himself to speak. Sankin let the shaft sink in, then threw the poor mutt a bone. 'Of course, if you hit lucky, there might be some change. Work hard within your budget. Look for bright young people—'

He went on with a lecture so minimal in terms of industry reality it was a worse insult than anything he'd said before.

Carl kept his eyes on his cigarette. Sankin rose. 'Forget big budget. Forget medium budget too . . . at least until lightning strikes. You're making a good buck. Enjoy it. Be satisfied with what you're doing.'

Carl managed a nod. He rose, and Sankin put out his hand. 'Just had to set the record straight, Carl. Just had to spell it out so we both knew where we stood. Now there'll be less chance of friction.'

Carl walked to the door.

'If at any time, however, you feel you can't operate under these conditions—'

Carl didn't turn. 'Right, Dave.'

Bertha Kraus was in the outer office. He wanted to say she'd been crazy not to go with Markal. He wished to hell *he* had been able to . . .

He stopped a moment, then hurried to his office.

Markal was very quiet on the phone and very vague about his plans. 'Doubt if I'll be doing anything like that, Carl.' Carl allowed some of his bitterness to show, saying that Sankin wasn't being fair to him. What Markal then said only added to the bitterness. 'Better stick with him, Carl. I no longer have anything to gain or lose in your affairs, so my advice can be honest. Your pictures are basic, and quite a few television people would be glad to take them over. I know for a fact that Alan Devon is prepared to add them to his schedule if you leave. He'll farm out production and direction and take a small profit. This isn't speculation, Carl. He made me the offer when you were pressing a little too hard for bigger budget.'

Carl said thanks and Markal said best of luck. Carl told Cheryl he was leaving for the day and didn't bother explaining. He drove home and went directly to the living room and the bar. He was pouring his second drink when Ruth joined him. 'I thought it was a burglar, the way you slipped in. Trying to avoid that kiss at the door?'

452

He pecked her cheek and gulped the Scotch. 'Rough day?' she asked.

'Look, can't I have a drink in peace? Must I explain every damned thing I do? Can't you leave me *be*, for the love of God!'

'Yes, a rough day,' she muttered, and turned to go.

He said he was sorry but he had a terrific headache. 'Where's Andy?'

'School, of course.'

'With him, who can be sure? He might be shacked up with his gym teacher.'

Ruth shook her head and left the room. He considered a third drink and decided to shower instead. A hot shower would loosen him up, help him forget the day's humiliations.

Two-cent Bagel. Cheapie-Creepie Bagel.

He showered and tried not to think of Dave Sankin. The bastard! And tried not to think of what Markal had said. And knew he had no choice but to take it, to live with it, to settle for it.

It wasn't as if he were settling for peanuts. After all, how many men had made a hundred twenty-six thousand last year? So he was stuck in his job. So at a hundred grand . . .

But it wasn't the money. It was the dream that had been crushed under Sankin's heavy foot.

He was being punished. Everything had gone wrong since Madison had arrived with Myra's note.

He toweled and dressed and went down the hall toward the living room. He would have another drink, maybe two, and then a good lunch. He would forget this nonsense.

He was passing Andy's room and suddenly turned and went inside. He closed the door and looked around. Model racing cars on the dresser that he had helped his son build. A photograph of the 1965 World Champion L. A. Dodgers; an autographed picture of Sandy Koufax. The small gilt statuette, already tarnished, that Andy had won for placing third in grammar-school track competition. The color photograph of Carl and Ruth. On the wall a framed enlargement of Myra.

He looked at his dead wife. Her thin smile and glittering eyes seemed turned on him. He looked away, then forced his gaze back again, testing himself. He had nothing to fear from Myra. She was dead. Her own sick hatred had killed her. Her own insanity had killed her. But he was afraid to look at her, and so he *kept* looking at her . . . and then gasped as some minor

453

optical illusion made her mouth appear to move. He laughed aloud and walked to the door.

The irrational fear passed. He stopped and looked around again. This was his son's room. No sign of the homosexual here. This was his son's private place, and there was no way of telling what he had become.

How could it be?

He glanced at Myra. That smile. Those eyes. *She* had done it. *She* had left her poison in Andy.

He went to the closet and found the fishing-tackle box in back and inside the box the envelope of Polaroid snapshots. Just as Andy kept them. Just as Ruth had replaced them that last Monday in March, and Carl a week later. And they'd lived with Andy as if they'd never seen the filth. Except that he didn't see Richard Sewal anymore. Carl had taken a chance Ruth hadn't approved of and gone to Mr. Sewal. He had listened, stunned, as Carl told him what the doctors and analysts advised and promised not to throw the facts in his son's face. But he'd shipped Richie off to boarding school in Sacramento all the same.

Carl flipped through the photographs, barely looking at them. Andy's memory lane. Andy's sex goodies. He was about to put them away when something stopped him. The stack seemed thicker than he remembered it. He went on turning the snapshots, then froze with a low, grunting sound, staring at a picture, one that hadn't been there the last time. He turned that one, and there was another, and another. Six new ones in all. Six shots of a man Carl had photographed before, and in much the same way. Except that now Brad Madison had *Andy* with him. Now, instead of Sugar Smart, *Andy* was performing the obscenities. The final shot was of Madison alone, lounging in a chair, smiling.

It was the smile that did it. The thin, mocking smile. Carl tore the picture in half and said, 'Enough.' He said it calmly. He was stating a fact. He'd had enough.

He looked at Myra and she smiled the same smile and he went to her picture. He pulled it off the wall and threw it away from him and didn't hear the crash as it hit Andy's mirror. He walked out and Ruth was there and she said something. He said, 'Enough,' and went to his room and got his revolver. He put it in his jacket pocket and it bulged but he didn't care. It didn't matter if Madison saw it. He wasn't going to play any more games. No more smiling and taking it. No more Two-

Cent Bagel. They had pushed him too far. 'Enough,' he said, and headed for the door.

Ruth was in the foyer. She looked at his pocket and said things and he shook his head. He would explain later, he said.

'There won't *be* any later!' she shouted.

He heard that. And since she kept getting in front of him, he had to stop.

'What are you doing, Carl? What are you thinking of? *Tell* me!'

He told her about Brad Madison. He told her to go to Andy's room and see for herself. Then he tried to walk by her. She threw herself in his way. She gripped him by the arms. He was calm and told her to be calm too.

'Calm! You're thinking of killing him! You're thinking of killing us all!'

He said no, only Madison, and couldn't she understand that he'd had enough? She kept holding him and shouting. She said, 'My God, you're ending everything, you're—' She was crying now and talking at the same time, and he couldn't understand a word she was saying. But he had never been more calm in his life. Except perhaps for the time he had gone from the bathroom to the bedroom and waited for Myra to come toward the staircase. He had been very calm that time too. He'd had enough that time too.

The analogy of his two calmest moments struck him, and he said, 'Then I *did* murder her.'

Ruth grew quiet. He said, 'I'll tell you and you'll see there's nothing to lose and you'll walk away and I'll do what I have to do.'

She said, 'Tell me sitting down. Take off your jacket—'

But he was already telling her. He kept his jacket on and the gun in the pocket and his hand on the gun and told her how he had murdered Myra. He finished and she still stood in front of him. He wanted her to understand fully, so he explained about Madison and how Myra's sister had said, *God Will punish you.* He told her how they called him Two-Cent Bagel and how Sankin had humiliated him and how Markal had confirmed that he was a nothing. He told her how Myra had poisoned Andy and how Madison was the instrument of her continuing vengeance, how he was making their son his whore. 'Enough,' he said. 'I've had enough. I have nothing left, nothing that I value anymore. Now do you understand?'

She nodded. He asked her to step out of his way. She did. He

455

walked by, and with each step his calmness deepened. She said, 'You have nothing left. Nothing that you value anymore. That means I am nothing.'

He couldn't leave her thinking that. He might not be able to come back, might not get a chance to talk to her again. 'You're my wife. My love. You know that.'

'How can that be, Carl?' Her voice shook but she was no longer shouting, no longer crying. 'You're going to kill someone, knowing it will end everything between us. How much can I mean to you if you're able to do that?'

'One thing has nothing to do with the other.' But he knew that wasn't quite right and the calmness weakened and he began to get upset, began to grow angry. 'Can't you see a man can have a wife and a good one and one he loves, but still have nothing? As a man, that is? As a man among men and with his son and with himself?'

'No, I can't see it. As a woman I have you and so I have everything. Did you ever know me to want another man, Carl? Sure Andy hurts, but I have you and that makes it easier to accept. If you were to earn half of what you earn, or a quarter, or less, I'd be sorry but I'd still have everything I need. We don't have children of our own, Carl. I miss that terribly. But I have you and I still have everything I need.'

He wet his lips. 'It's different with a man,' he muttered.

'I don't believe that. I believe you're sick now. Maybe you were sick that moment with Myra too. Not that I believe you murdered her.' She shook her head. 'But even if you did it deliberately, even if you frightened her down those stairs on purpose, I don't care. Not enough to stop loving you. It's more than ten years over and done with and here we are now and you're sick again.'

'Sick? If a man . . . his pride and honor . . . sick?'

'Pride and honor are fine. Go hit him with your fists if you must. Go hit Andy. But not the gun. Not ending everything. *That's* sickness. That's telling me you have nothing to live for and that I am nothing.'

His head hurt. The calmness was fast disappearing. He had to get out this minute or he wouldn't get out at all. She said, 'Let me ask you a question. Please.'

He paused.

'Name one man who has more than you. Just one.'

Was she serious? 'Nat Markal—'

'Has an empty house. His wife and daughter left him. Every-

456

one knows that. And even when he had them, and was president of Avalon, he had to go to another woman for whatever it was he lacked. Do you have to go to another woman, Carl?'

She knew he didn't.

'Name another man who has more than you. Lou Grayson? He has nothing. He has a big emptiness he has to fill time and time again. If you get empty you come to me. If I get empty I come to you. No running in circles. No lies and deceit. We fulfill each other. What can be more important than that?'

He was getting tired now. He went to the living room. She followed, still talking. 'Alan Devon? He's a widower. He gives parts to Cheryl Carny, but she's not his. I'm yours, Carl. And Charles Halpert. Living alone for eight months. Something wrong between him and his wife or she'd be here by now. What has *he* got, Carl? And Moe Sholub, married three times. And Tyrone Chalze, marrying a sixteen-year-old high school girl and playing around anyway. Is it *fun* for them, Carl? Do you think it's fun to do such things? Living alone or sneaking out with women or marrying like some people date. Look at Dave Sankin. I don't know him, but I do know Olive. If she helped him, she'll bed him. Would you like that, Carl? And finally Brad Madison, your enemy, who you say laughs at you and makes a whore of your son. The star-to-be. The man who isn't a man. Who'll have to hide what he is all his life. Our son is that way, and we weep for him. Why shouldn't we weep for Madison too, Carl? He's just as pitiful.'

He sat down. His head ached. He didn't know what was right anymore.

She went on. She talked of others. She challenged him to name anyone with as good a marriage as his. He couldn't.

She came to the couch. 'You have *more* than any man you know, because you have me. I have more than any woman I know, because I have you. We were lucky, Carl. We fell into each other by luck. Deep into each other. We're special, Carl. If you throw us away, you're—' Quite suddenly she stopped. She had run out of words and out of strength.

He said his head hurt. She asked him to lie down. He went with her to their room and she helped him off with the jacket and lay down beside him. She took him in her arms. After a while her words and strength returned. She spoke of the dangers of not really knowing each other. She would tell him things she'd kept secret, and he would do the same. They would use their closeness as protection against moments like this – moments, she said, that came to all men and women. She felt she had made mistakes, the worst in not insisting they adopt a child. They would do it now. Tomorrow they would fill out papers and make the first move toward a child of their own. *Terror Town* could wait a day. It could wait forever, if he so decided. He could go back to special effects. He could go back to a photography studio and commercials. He could sell groceries if he wished to and they would get by. 'Just remember,' she whispered, 'we're the greatest success story on earth.'

He closed his eyes. Her love was more than he deserved. Her love had washed the guilt of Myra's death from his soul.

He nestled in her arms. His head stopped hurting. Everything stopped hurting.

ISA YEE

By Saturday night Isa was talking to herself, but she'd be damned if she would go out to be stared at, or put the phone on the hook for more of those insane hate-calls. This country was even worse than she'd thought it was! This country deserved fire and slaughter! She only wished she could help give it what it deserved. And that included Free Barchester and his black nuts too!

She hated all of them. She hated everything. If she used a black man for bed, it was like using a stick to scratch her back. She would throw it away and get a new stick every time!

She watched television. She'd been watching television since returning from location Thursday afternoon. She had a book Jerry Storm had given her at lunch last week, *Vietnam Story*, the novel bought by Universal for major production. Jerry had hoped she would be signed for the female lead. But that was when he and the rest of this town thought she was Eurasian. No point in reading it now. Nothing would happen.

She made herself a TV dinner and fiddled with it and lit a cigarette. She had no appetite. With *The Glenmore Theatre* finished, she was between assignments. Clete Brown had shaken her hand (not kissed her, as she felt he otherwise would have) and said her work had been 'beautiful' and wished her luck. Everyone kept wishing her luck. Because everyone knew she would need it!

The doorbell sounded. She actually jumped, then sat still,

458

afraid to answer. Jerry Storm's voice called to her and she went to the door and let him in.

'What the hell *is* this!' he said, and ripped off his little Alpine hat and threw it down on the couch. 'Clete told me you were finished Thursday, and I've been calling every hour on the hour since.' He strode to the marble table and slammed the phone back on the hook. 'If you want to stay in this business you can't allow yourself the luxury of three days' uninterrupted rest! We're not quite *that* big, Miss Yee.'

The phone rang. She said, 'You answer it.' He raised the handset and listened. He said. 'The same to you, Mr. Hitler,' and hung up. His eyes fell away. 'Why didn't you use your switchboard?'

'They were giving names of studio people. Besides, I didn't think anything important—'

The phone rang again. He picked it up. His face tightened, and he placed the handset down on the table, just as she'd had it. 'We'll have to get you an unlisted number.'

'Why bother? All this business will be forgotten as soon as I am.'

'You mean you're willing to receive these calls until you're ninety? Because that's how long it's going to take before you're forgotten. *If* you do as your brilliant agent tells you. First thing, we have to hold that press conference.'

'What press conference?'

'The one at which your friend Barchester said you would announce participation in the civil rights movement.'

'Screw the civil rights movement,' she whispered. 'Screw Barchester and Watts and the whole—'

'It's all right with me,' Storm interrupted. 'I don't care how you feel about it, as long as you don't let anyone else know. I figured Barchester didn't have your blessing sending out those letters. Blew the whistle on you for revenge, did he?'

She was staring at him. 'You mean you actually want me to go through with it? You think it will *help*?'

He took a thick envelope from his breast pocket and dropped it on the table in front of her. 'I don't think, baby. I *know*. Didn't my secretary tell you I've been busy on contract negotiations? *Your* contracts. With Universal. They've signed for *Vietnam Story* and two as-yet-unspecifieds. You just have to fulfill one condition. Conduct that press conference as promised. Naturally, you'll mention that *Joneses* is dead and that you've signed to do a new and equally rewarding picture—'

She took a contract from the envelope. She read a little and stepped to the couch and sank down. She turned to the last page and saw the signatures. 'Give me a pen,' she said, her voice husky. 'Quick!'

He gave her his pen. She signed all the copies and put her hands to her mouth and laughed a wild little laugh. 'My God!' she said. She looked at him. 'How come?'

He wasn't smiling. He put the contracts back in his pocket and got his hat. 'What's the matter with you? Did you really think this town, this country is like those nut calls?'

She was back on top again, had to be careful again. 'Barchester obviously did,' she murmured.

'If he's black, he at least has some reason for feeling that way. But you! When did you last look in the mirror? It's all very well to talk of Negro blood, but you're whiter than I am!' He slammed out the door.

He was back in a minute. 'Forgot. You've got a party tonight. I'll escort you myself, about ten o'clock. Several Mr. Bigs and selected press will be there, so look gorgeous. You don't have to look courageous. Everyone in town's talking about your guts and saying they should have figured you for something like this after that Pier Andrei thing.'

Isa waited until he left, then laughed again. This time there was no element of wildness or hysteria – just good old rib-bruising, eye-streaming belly-laughs. She laughed until she was lying face down on the couch, gasping for breath. Then she rose to get dressed for the party.

BRAD MADISON

Acapulco. Sea and beach and hotels and too many tourists and high-priced call girls and girls available without a price. A swinging hunk of the Great Society in Old Mexico.

They were on location for *With the Jet Set*, his first supporting role in a big-budget picture. It was going well. His entire career was going well. So well that Fen Denkerson had come along to see if Brad's part couldn't be upgraded a bit. And it had been. And a song had been thrown in. So life was beautiful.

Except that now it was Saturday night and there would be no shooting until Monday morning. The cast and crew were in the hotel bar mixing it up in good old heterosexual fashion, and

Brad had pleaded a return of Mexican diarrhea to escape the festivities. But there was no way of escaping Saturday night in Acapulco. Music and laughter floated up from the hotel along the jungle-like slope of hill to his cabin. Another kudo, that cabin. Everyone but the director, the three stars and himself had rooms in the hotel.

The hill was dark and silent, the cabins deserted, everyone in the bar or out on private pleasure jaunts. The tropical night belonged to Brad Madison, just as so many Devereux nights had belonged to John McNaughton.

A fine phrase meaning loneliness.

His lights were out. He paced back and forth in the darkness, unable even to hope that the boy would come. He'd had to be so careful, so subtle, there wasn't much chance he'd been understood.

Pablo they called him. He brought drinks out to the pool. He had also been lent by the hotel to serve lunch on location. About fifteen, good-sized for a Mexican, with muscular arms and a broad, flashing smile – a smile that seemed to go in the direction of the men, not the ladies. Brad had chatted with him, tried to sound him out and felt that Pablo was sending signals. But since the others had been around them this afternoon, and Pablo spoke minimal English, Brad's invitation had been limited to a See-John-Run discourse on topography: 'Do you ever walk up the hill? It is nice there. My cabin is there – Number Thirty. At night I look out at the ocean. They say it will be clear tonight.'

He should have gotten the boy alone somehow. He needed him. He'd been eight days without Andy.

Not that Andy was what he had thought he would be. A shallow kid. A demanding kid. Given to strange fits of temper and eyeing other men . . .

He heard something – a rustling outside. He went to the door and listened. The rustling stopped. He opened the door. Pablo stood there in his white pants and red jacket. *'Buenas noches, señor.'* Brad put out his hand. Pablo took it and came inside.

Later, Brad dressed and walked down the path past the hotel to the beach. A fire was going a hundred feet or so to his left. He strolled along the sand and saw the group of three boys and three girls, Americans, singing to a guitar and laughing and horsing around. He went by, aware of his stance, his posture, his walk. He had become more and more aware of such things

461

lately. With good reason. Since Andy, he'd felt a softening of his nature, a feminizing of his character.

He had taken off the mask and given in to his true self. And his true self had many nonmale characteristics.

But they couldn't be allowed to show. He was a big, muscular man, slated for action and romantic parts – an Errol Flynn type, as Fen put it. Any gay gestures and he'd be dead.

He walked on, smoking and looking out at the sea. He was relaxed now, free of tension and desire now, but it wouldn't last. In a few hours the need would return. Tomorrow he would be looking at the beautiful boys again.

The world was full of beautiful boys, he now realized, but they had to be searched out, had to be found. His life would be spent finding them. A marvelous prospect, but not without its risks, its thorns. He had to be on his guard, always, before cameras and people. He had to mask the softening . . .

He stopped. He understood what he was thinking. He must *mask* the softening. He would never be rid of the mask. He had taken it off, but only for a few brief days. Now it had to go back on again, firmer than before. Because he had more to lose now.

He snapped his cigarette into the sea and turned back. He no longer strolled free and natural. He strode by the fire and grinned at one of the girls and saw her pleased smile and saw her escort's sudden frown.

He swaggered up the path to the hotel and went inside. He joined the party at the bar and pitched Flora Dagart and some-time later Mike Vale tried to fight him. He shoved the aging toughguy back into his chair and shrugged at Flora and said good night. His out, thank goodness.

He went up the path to his cabin, the swagger disappearing as he found himself alone. Flora was camouflage, the same as the dates in Devereux. He had hated it then, and he hated it now.

He undressed and got into bed. He wondered where Pablo was and listened to the sounds of Acapulco on Saturday night.

Music somewhere. Bursts of laughter. A woman singing. A man close by talking softly, intensely, persistently: 'Baby . . . no one . . . please.'

He wished Pablo was with him now. To ease a certain fear. To erase a certain bitter taste.

A cabin door slammed. A woman's laughter rose behind it, throatily.

Damn them! They had it so *easy*!

462

CHARLEY HALPERT

A quietness surrounded Charley. He sat at the counter, the typewriter put away for the first time in almost three weeks. He sipped coffee and nibbled a cracker. He had to go shopping. There was practically nothing left to eat in the apartment. But he didn't feel any pressure about it. He didn't feel any pressure about anything. That was the quiet. An interior quiet. After eight months of tension and struggle, eight months of pressure, he sat still and was quiet inside.

He left the dishes on the counter and went to the armchair and looked at the thick, carbon-copy manuscript lying where he'd tossed it yesterday afternoon. He'd had to check the calendar to find out what day it was and whether he'd made Markal's bonus deadline. It had been Monday, 17th May, and he'd gone to the post office and mailed the completed script of *The Eternal Joneses* to Markal's home. Then he'd come back here and gone to bed while it was still light and slept until ten this morning. Now it was eleven-ten. Now he had to pick up the threads of his life. Such as returning Ben Kalik's calls, and responding to the warning letter from Celia's lawyers, and making a decision about Cheryl.

Cheryl was most pressing. Cheryl loved him, and he felt he loved her. But he wasn't sure. You were only sure about love when you were young. He was no longer young.

But he did want to see her. Very much. He went into the hall, thinking it was time he got a private phone, and called her at Avalon. 'It's Charley, got a minute?'

'Charley who? I used to know Charley Halpert, but he dropped off the face of the earth a month ago.'

'A little more than two weeks. Can you come over tonight?'

'Don't you think we should be re-introduced? I feel sort of shy with you.'

He smiled. 'If you'd like to go to dinner—'

'And waste all that time? I'll let you know if and when I can make it.' Her voice dropped. 'I missed you so much. So very much. Did you miss me?'

'Yes.' But he hadn't. He missed her now, but he hadn't been able to miss anything during the insanity of writing. He had been seven different people named Jones the past two and a half weeks. He had been God directing lives and God didn't

463

have time to miss anyone. 'Make it early. Wear the black lacey things.'

'I'll try. You sound different. Quiet.'

'I'm still a little tired.' Which wasn't true. What *was* true lay beyond his consciousness, beyond his understanding. Tired was as close as he could get to it at the moment. 'I think I've gained ten pounds. All flab.'

'I'm glad. I'll feel more at home. You *do* want to see me?'

'Of course. I was working, Cheryl, working my tail off, just as I said. Now I'm finished, and we can begin again.'

'I know. Its just that not hearing from you—' She laughed. 'I feel happy, Charley. It's strange feeling happy.'

It hurt him. He said good-bye, and wanted to move, to breathe deeply and make his blood race. He changed into trunks and went down to the pool. It was a gray day, mild and hazy. The smog that seemed to bother so many people but never bothered him hung low over the hills. He dived into the water and was winded after five laps, a disappointing performance.

He floated a while, then swam again and made another three laps. As he toweled dry, he realized he was starving. He would have a great big lunch. He would drive to La Cienega and Restaurant Row and *gorge* himself!

He went toward the back entrance – and didn't want to eat alone. He wanted someone to share his feast with him. Cheryl . . . but he'd have to rush her out of Avalon and rush her back and he couldn't rush today.

He turned right instead of left. He went to the west building, to Lois and Sugar's apartment. Lois opened the door, wearing a rather somber gray pants suit and an even more somber expression. She said long-time-no-see and who-kidnapped-you and he explained about working and asked if she would like to go out for lunch. Her face lit up. 'Boy, would I ever! I mean, I got the life-sentence blues! Stir-crazy, man! This pad feels like the funny farm. Rubber walls and neck-to-knee girdles. I'm ready to bust out!' She glanced back. 'But I don't know. Sugar's at Desilu on a job, and I'm supposed to nurse the phone.'

They had a private phone now, sitting in pink grandeur on a small table. He wondered aloud about Sugar getting business calls here instead of at her agent's office. 'Oh, Chankery gets the calls for TV and movie jobs. But there's *other* business like producers and directors making dates and sometimes an important actor and that kind of business leads to jobs too.' He

464

said he understood perfectly and perhaps some other time and began to turn away.

'Gee ... wait. Can't you shoot the breeze a while? I been sitting here talking to myself—'

He took a chance and asked how *her* career was coming along. She shrugged and muttered, 'I been in a few things, but now we're going to move and I'm stuck with handling it and all those calls—' She shrugged again. 'I hardly get time.'

He nodded. She said, 'Come in, Chuck, huh?' He said he was a little stir-crazy himself and felt he had to get out. She looked back at the pink phone again. 'That mother!' she said, and he wondered just what, or who, she was talking about. He said so-long. She said, 'Give me fifteen minutes! No one'll call. She'll never know anyway—'

They drove to a place Lois described as 'real class'. They started with cocktails and ate their way through a huge prime-rib lunch. Lois talked continuously, with brief flashes of her old spirit, her old fight and vinegar. But most of the time she rationalized Sugar's dominance, revealing thinly disguised resignation. 'It'll change. She's up now, and I'm down. But once we get settled, and I find a good agent—'

He asked where they were moving. She named a plush hi-riser off the Sunset Strip. 'Three bedrooms and the biggest living room you ever saw. And a fag decorator. I got a nice enough room, and Sugar—' She shrugged. 'Well, it's her bread. And there's only one master bedroom in any apartment. I guess I'd do the same. Anyway, I'll have my own pad in a few months.'

They were moving at the end of May. 'You'll come to see me, won't you, Chuck? I know a lot of guys, sure—' She stared into her chocolate sundae. 'Lately, I don't seem to dig any of 'em. Just low, I guess.' She raised her eyes. 'But you and me, we go back a ways. I got mad at you a few times, but we're old friends, right?'

He said right and they finished and went out to the car. She sat quietly as he drove from the parking lot, then: 'I don't want to go back there. Take me someplace. Palm Springs or Vegas or Mexico. Anyplace.'

He acted as if she was joking. She cut him short. 'It's no put-on, Chuck. Whatever you say'll be all right.'

He chuckled. He said she'd get plenty of takers for that sort of proposition. 'Sure, weekend takers. I don't want a weekend, Chuck. I want to cut out for good. I know you're married.

But you're here all this time and you're not going back. You know you're not.' She grasped his arm. 'So I've got no pride like Sugar says. Let's go somewhere. Let's stay together. I'll work when I can and pay my own way when I can. Honest. I'll fix up a place, and it won't cost you much. We'll have some laughs, Chuck. I'll keep you happy.'

He shook his head. 'That fat secretary?' she asked. He nodded. She sighed: 'How about a movie?' He said sure and they drove to Hollywood Boulevard and the grotesquerie called Grauman's Chinese Theatre. He held her hand throughout the picture. It lay still and dead in his. On the way back to the Bali-Ho he tried to break her silence. 'We'll do this again next week.' She nodded. 'We'll do it *every* week – make a habit of it.' She nodded again. He had nothing more to offer.

He walked her to her door. She said, 'Gee, it's almost six,' and seemed afraid to go in. He said he would explain to Sugar that he'd insisted. She said, 'Well, yeah, but I was supposed—' She opened the door. Sugar called from the bathroom, 'That you, Lois?'

'Yeah. Chuck came and he wanted—'

Sugar walked out of the bathroom, a glittering production in tight black cocktail gown and diamond earrings, her heavy blonde hair falling to her shoulders. She seemed to grow more beautiful, more sexual, every time he saw her. She nodded to him, and spoke to Lois. 'You shouldn't have, but there's no time to talk about it now. You know my date tonight with Bernie Wales?' Lois looked blank. Sugar said impatiently, 'Tyrone Chalze's chief cameraman. He's going to be shooting *Even Steven* in July. I'm working in that. *Now* do you remember?' Lois said yes and Sugar turned her back and said, 'Hook me up. Bernie's waiting out at a beach bungalow. The address is on the table. Shower and get dressed nice and take a cab. Nine o'clock sharp.'

'Me? I don't know—'

Sugar turned. 'I *know* you don't know,' she said, as if to an idiot child. 'That's why I'm telling you. Bernie's important to me. The chief cameraman can make or break an actress. Especially on close-ups. But someone else called.' She touched her diamond earrings and smiled to herself. 'The kickiest,' she murmured. 'The most.'

Lois chewed her lip. 'But me going on *your* date, cold—'

Sugar's voice hardened. 'He's a hip guy. You'll like him. And he's old, so you won't have to stay long.' She glanced at

Charley as if to say, 'Are you still here?' He muttered his good nights and went toward the door. Sugar said, 'Just remember. He's *important* to me. Say I got a headache or something and you're a friend and I'll be in touch as soon—' Charley glanced back before closing the door. Lois was nodding, her face wiped clean of all emotion.

He walked away. There were no fates worse than death in Hollywood. But that of Lois Lane, servant and occasional whore in the employ of her kid-sister-the-movie-star, came pretty close.

He called Ben Kalik at his home. Kalik said it was about time and he'd made a deal. 'A surprise, Chuck. At Paramount, for your air-war book, *Flight of the Drones*. I couldn't get the right price for *Five Doors*, which is a better movie property. So is *The Vital Strangers*. But they'll sell next.' Charley asked how much, prepared for a disappointment. Kalik said, 'Fifty for the book, fifty for the script and no cutoffs. Not what I'd have gotten for *Five Doors*, but do *Drones* right and we'll be in terrific shape. Besides, it'll give you a chance to show your stuff to Joe Levine—'

Charley listened. Kalik was actually apologetic. Charley marveled that he was going to earn ninety thousand dollars, after Kalik's ten percent, for a book that had originally earned a grand total of fifty-three hundred, hard- and soft-covers. News like this deserved hurrahs, not apologies, but after a while Kalik's apologies made sense and he understood he was going to earn a great deal of money because of the enormous publicity on a dead feature – *The Eternal Joneses*. He also understood that Kalik was worried about their relationship, worried that other agents might try to woo him away.

'—Collin sending you out to me and bad communications on both sides at the beginning, Chuck, but now we're beginning to work together. I want to set up a once-a-week luncheon. We have to talk about finding you a decent place to live. And that wagon of yours . . . bad for the image. Do you like sports cars?'

Charley said he liked everything, and Kalik laughed as if it were the funniest gag in the world. Charley said, 'We're doing fine, Ben. Let me rest up and get back to you.' Kalik said rest was just the ticket – try Palm Springs.

Charley went to his apartment and lay down on the couch and said, 'I'm a success. I'm a great big roaring success.'

He wondered why he didn't believe it.

467

For the past two or three weeks it had been almost like the old days. Not that he had been easy on Cheryl, but she had stayed home evenings and talked to him and hadn't tried to duck out no matter how rough he got. She had taken it, and after the first week he had begun to feel she was finished with her lover. He didn't know whether he was relieved or disappointed. For months now, he had been trying to build his courage – and fury – to the point where he could carry out his plan.

But on Tuesday night he noticed a change. She was tense again, leading him to drink again. He obliged her, or seemed to. He filled his glass a dozen or more times with cheap gin from Thrifty's and drank when she looked at him and dumped it in the sink or snake plant or toilet when she wasn't looking at him. He had done this before and not carried out his plan. But if she sneaked away tonight . . .

He faked an early pass-out. She put him to bed in his underwear, took things from the closet and the drawers, left the room. He heard the shower going, and then she was back, dressed and smelling of her good perfume. 'Jim, wake up.' He didn't move. She shook him a little. 'Jim, I have to go out.' He lay still. She wrote on the pad by the bed, and he knew what it would say. She always tore it up and flushed it down the toilet when she came home, but he had read it more than once and it was always the same. A cover, in case he awakened. 'Went out for some air. Be back soon. Cheryl.'

She walked out. He heard the front door open and close softly. His eyes grew heavy. He fought it. He knew what it meant.

The gun was jammed behind the headboard, fully loaded and ready to end this bitter bedroom farce. His plan was all worked out. But his eyes closed and sleep filled his mind and soon he would be unable to act – soon another opportunity would have passed. Because he was afraid. Not of what he had to do. Not of killing them and himself. Of what he had to see.

Cheryl and her lover.

He thought of that – of Cheryl in the arms of another man. Devon, probably. She had taken things from the bottom drawer of the dresser. She kept her good underwear there. That black lace pair she tucked carefully away and never seemed to wear. Cheryl in her black lace underwear. Cheryl moaning in Devon's arms. Cheryl saying things to Devon she had once said to Jim Carny.

His eyes opened. If she had worn the black lace . . .

He rolled to the edge of the bed and put down his hands and then was on the floor. He pulled his dead body to the dresser and opened the bottom drawer and searched.

He couldn't find the black lace. He began to make excuses. It was in the laundry. She had put it someplace else. It had worn out and she'd thrown it away . . .

Suddenly he saw himself, lying on the floor, a stinking dead thing that refused to die. A stinking dead thing made dead by Cheryl. And she was in someone else's arms wearing the black lace.

He pulled himself back across the floor, his decision made. This was the part he had to do for himself. This was the tough part.

He pulled his upper body onto the bed and reached behind the headboard and panicked as he couldn't find the gun. And found it. He fell back to the floor and pulled himself to the chair and his clothing. He put the gun down and dragged his trousers off the chair and began the long struggle to get them on.

He sweated and strained. He cursed and beat the floor with his fists. He got them on.

The tough part was half over. He was trembling with exhaustion. 'A little more,' he whispered. 'Just to the wheelchair, Jim-boy. Get going now. It's a small apartment. Just the bedroom and the foyer and the living room. It's simple, Jim-boy.' He kept it up, driving himself as when he'd run the marathon in college. He repeated the litany first instilled in him by his father as they'd run together when he was in high school and wanted to be a track star. His legs had grown strong; his wind had grown long; he had covered five miles a day without effort. Now he trembled and gasped and almost wept over some thirty-five feet.

But he reached the wheelchair where it stood in its place against the wall near the kitchen. He got into it, and the tough part was over.

He wanted to rest, but was afraid that too much time had passed. She might leave her lover before he could catch her. He wheeled to the phone table and called a cab company, and then to the door and opened the snap lock, and then returned to the bedroom. He got his shirt on and a tweed jacket from the closet and put his revolver in the right-hand pocket. He went to the dresser and the little red-leather box where Cheryl kept their day-to-day cash. There were usually twenty to thirty dollars in it. Tonight there were twelve. But he'd prepared an extra supply of cash as part of his plan. Every so often he'd taken out a dollar and tucked it away under an edge of carpet in the living room.

Back to the living room and sixteen more dollars, and the slip of paper on which he'd written three addresses: Alan Devon's, Charles Halpert's, Carl Baiglen's. Then to the dresser mirror where he examined himself, made himself as neat as possible. His feet were bare, but that was where the cabby would have to help. He got cigarettes from the night table and smoked and wanted a drink and didn't take a drink. His mind had to be clear for what he was going to do.

He waited. It seemed hours before the bell rang and the stocky, red-faced man entered. A Southerner, and very kind and helpful. The socks and slipper shoes were on in a minute, the tip refused with a strong shake of the head. 'You just say where-all you want to go and leave the rest to Dan Bates.'

He gave Devon's address in Playa del Rey and sat in the back of the cab, his chair folded beside him, and looked out at the blur of cars and lights that was Los Angeles. The Golden City. The place that had drawn him from staid Omaha. The place that had delighted him with its warmth and freedom from convention, its geography and opportunity. The place where he had met beautiful Cheryl Blaine and married and lived a brief idyll. And died.

They were in the Marina district. The driver muttered about fouled-up streets, and they pulled to a stop before a fieldstone ranch house. There was only one step at the end of the long concrete path and the driver helped him up it and thanked him for the big tip and returned to the cab to wait until, as Jim had put it, 'I stick my head out the window and say I'm staying.'

He pressed the doorbell. A Japanese houseboy answered. Jim asked for Alan Devon. The houseboy didn't tell him to wait. No one told a man in a wheelchair to wait. He was ushered into a neat living room, where he strained to hear voices. He heard none, until Devon walked in and said, 'Mr. Carny, what—' Jim took the gun from his pocket. 'Where's Cheryl?' Devon tried to speak and had to start all over again. 'Not here, I assure you. What makes you think—' Jim shook his head impatiently. Devon said, 'You can look if you want.'

470

Jim said he would. He put the gun back in his pocket and wheeled slowly after the producer.

They went through every room in the house. 'She left,' Jim said, when they were again in the living room. He put his hand in his pocket. 'I know you two—'

'Not we two,' Devon said, and sat down and stripped a piece of gum with shaky fingers. 'You're right about her having an affair. But not with me. Charles Halpert.' He put the gum in his mouth and chewed furiously. 'That's the truth. If she's gone to anyone, it's to him. I can get you his address—'

Jim said that wasn't necessary. He looked at Devon a moment. Devon chewed and muttered that he didn't blame Jim but not to do anything he would regret. Like hurting his wife. Jim said, 'I won't. Not a thing I'll regret.' He wheeled toward the foyer. 'The door, please?' Devon came up behind him and opened it. Jim turned his head. 'You'll call Halpert now. You'll warn them. I can't allow that.'

'I won't. Why should I get between a man and his rightful—' He faltered under Jim's thin smile. 'As God is my witness, I won't.'

Jim nodded slowly. 'You won't because you know I don't care anymore, because I'll kill you if you get in my way.'

Devon went dead white.

'You'll come along,' Jim said. 'I'll let you off near Halpert's place and you'll take the cab back here – without speaking to anyone.'

Devon said, 'Yes,' voice weak.

'Don't make me kill you,' Jim said, meaning it.

He kept his hand on the gun as the driver put him in back beside Devon. They drove to North Hollywood and Halpert's place. Jim said they would all go inside together. Devon and the driver helped him into the east-building lobby, where they read the tenant listing and saw Halpert was on the second floor. A complication, but not a serious one. Dan Bates was a most willing helper. He held Jim upright while Devon carried the chair to the second-floor landing. Jim waited, hanging limp and helpless in Bates's arms. But he was facing forward, facing the steps, and Devon looked back at him and nodded placatingly. Devon was cowed. Devon wasn't going to do anything. Jim had only one fear now – that Cheryl would come down those steps and see him; that she would understand and run back; that she and Halpert would escape.

They mustn't escape!

471

'You all right?' Bates asked. Jim nodded. Devon came down, and he and Bates carried Jim up the stairs between them and deposited him in the chair. An elderly couple walked by, the woman's face softening as she glanced at Jim.

Poor man, her eyes said. *Poor cripple*. But this poor man, this poor cripple, would assert his manhood tonight!

He wheeled back a little. 'Thank you, Alan. Thank you, Dan.' He took out his money, and Devon said he would pay, and Jim insisted. The driver said it was too much, and Jim said, 'I'm rich.' They walked down the stairs, Devon glancing back, his face so white Jim wondered that the driver didn't notice it. Then the lobby doors swung shut behind them and he was alone. But they opened again almost immediately and a tall woman came in carrying an armload of packages. This was an apartment house. People would be walking in and out all the time. He couldn't wait to be alone. He had to ignore everything but his vengeance and move fast. Devon might be talking to the driver right now.

He turned the chair and wheeled forward, then came to a sudden stop. Halpert's door was the second from the landing. They had been practically in front of it! Halpert could have heard their voices, if he'd been listening!

But he wouldn't be listening. He would be too busy for that. Too busy with Cheryl Carny of the Cupid Carnys.

He faced the door. He came up against it with his knees. He leaned forward, reaching for the knob. It was probably locked. A man locked the door when laying another man's wife. But even so, Halpert would open it a crack, just to tell whoever it was to go away, and the gun would make him open up and there would be Cheryl . . .

Dear Jesus, please let her not be there.

It was a strange prayer for one anxious to end things. It was a prayer that had nothing to do with the desire to live, or to escape the truth. It was a prayer for Cheryl Carny, once of the Cupid Carnys.

He grasped the knob, and heard something. Television? Voices? He also heard people enter the lobby and couldn't stop to worry about them. He put his ear against the door. He heard Halpert and Cheryl. He took the gun from his pocket. '—better not to examine what we feel,' Halpert was saying. Slowly, slowly, he turned the knob. It was locked. Cheryl said, 'I know what I feel. Love. I love you.' He grinned a terrible grin. He had come at the right time. Love. She felt love. And soon she would feel death She said something else, but the people coming up the stairs drowned it out.

He couldn't take his ear from that door. He had to hear every word. His luck had finally turned. His luck was fantastic. He had chosen the perfect moment. God was showing him. It was a miracle to help him kill them both.

The people were almost behind him when they suddenly fell silent. Soon someone might ask what he was doing, might try to stop him. But no one could stop him now. First Halpert, painfully. Then Cheryl, quickly. And when the police came for him, the end.

Ear to the door, he raised his hand to knock. And heard Cheryl say so clearly, so very clearly he felt she was speaking not to Halpert but to him, '—different kinds of love. I can never love anyone the way I loved Jim. I could try. I *am* trying. But that sort of thing is magic. Like magic, it's not to be believed once it's gone. To hear Jim now, you'd never know—'

He smashed his fist on the door, then leveled the gun and fired twice under the knob. Wood splintered and metal rang and there were screams behind him and the door sagged open. He wheeled into the apartment. It was little more than a room. On the bed was Cheryl. Cheryl naked and Halpert naked, still holding each other.

Behind him someone shouted at him to stop and the screaming went on and now Cheryl was screaming and shaking her head, her hair flying and her naked body cowering. Halpert was still holding her – holding her close and staring with glazed eyes.

His hand seemed as dead as his legs. He made the gun rise, but he didn't feel it. Cheryl naked and Halpert naked. It hurt to see them. He almost closed his eyes it hurt so much. Cheryl talking of love. Cheryl remembering love. Cheryl unable to believe he could remember love.

He wanted to say something, some last thing to show her he remembered – that it was all he remembered. But it hurt so much to see them and the gun kept rising and it came to his head and that was the only way to show her he remembered. He squeezed the trigger. The scene was gone and the agony was gone and he was gone.

CHARLEY HALPERT

He left for Sequoia National Park on Thursday morning, remembering how he had planned to go seven months ago. That was before *The Eternal Joneses* and before Cheryl's first visit. That was a lifetime ago.

Sequoia was what the guidebooks said it would be. Beautiful. Inspiring. But there was a bloody memory in the way, and though he stayed three full days and took several tours through the giant redwood country he felt he hadn't seen very much. He would return some other time, when his mind was clear to appreciate trees and mountains and valleys.

He entered his apartment at eight Sunday night. The door had been replaced and the bullet hole in the wall plastered over. But the big dark stain was still on the carpet, and no one seemed to have noticed the faint circular splattering on the wall above the plastered hole.

That splattering made him drop his head and fight nausea, made him see and feel the whole thing over again. The door shattering in a blast of sound. Jim Carny wheeling in, four or five people in the hall behind him. The woman beginning to scream and Cheryl beginning to scream. Shame compounded by their nakedness. The numbness of shock and fear. Carny putting the gun to his head. The spraying of pink fragments against the wall. Carny's brains splattering against the wall . . .

Charley went to the kitchen and poured a stiff bourbon. The numbness had protected him during questioning by police and the brief official investigation the next day. The numbness had stopped him from thinking of Cheryl, who had been taken home by patrolmen after a doctor had given her 'Something to make you rest'. And then he had gone to Sequoia and the numbness had gone with him.

Now it was wearing off. He had a second drink and noticed the envelope propped on the counter. It was addressed to 'Halpert' in script type. He opened it. 'Please come to the office. Your apartment is required. A refund will be made on your May rental. Mr. Terrence.'

He felt anger. It died quickly. He couldn't live here anyway. He finished his drink and went downstairs and drove to the supermarket. He bought a newspaper and stood near the doors, scanning the pages. Nothing about Carny. And there had been nothing in the L.A. papers he had bought at Sequoia.

474

On Wednesday, there *had* been an item, one far less explicit than he had a right to hope for, stating that 'James Carny, a paraplegic, shot himself to death in the North Hollywood apartment of Charles Halpert, with Halpert and Mrs. Carny as horrified witnesses. While Carny left no note, it is believed he suspected his wife of seeing Halpert, and when he found them together ended his life. Halpert is the screenwriter who was completing *The Eternal Joneses* when Mona Dearn committed suicide and started a chain of events that led to the resignation of Nat Markal and the cancellation of the super-epic.' The article went on, but not about Carny. It called *Joneses* a 'jinxed venture', recapped the Mona Dearn suicide and ended with her biography.

Mona Dearn was world-famous and still good copy. Jim Carny was a nobody, neither his life nor his death of import to the general public. Which was a good thing for Charles Halpert, though it didn't make him feel any better.

He returned to the Bali-Ho and tried to sit down to dinner and couldn't. He went to the manager's office. Mrs. Terrence was at her switchboard, the TV blasting away. She didn't respond to his 'good evening', just turned her head, shouting, 'Halpert's here!' Abner Terrence came through a doorway. He looked at Charley – a rather pleased look, though it purported to be disapproving. His voice stern, he said, 'You saw my note?' Charley didn't answer him. Charley suddenly felt he would punch that red, freckled face if he looked at it one second longer. He spoke to Mrs. Terrence. Did I get any calls in the last three days?' She looked at her husband, and Terrence said, 'That's not why—' Charley said, 'My *calls*, please.' Mrs. Terrence went through a stack of pink slips and handed him four. All from Cheryl. All asking him to 'please call'. He said, 'Thanks,' and opened the door. Abner Terrence said, 'You can't stay here. We won't have—' Charley turned. Charley looked at him and Terrence saw what was in Charley's mind. Charley said, 'I'll leave, shortly,' and went out. He heard Mrs. Terrence screeching through the door. 'What sort of man are you anyway? You throw that tramp out or I'll—'

Charley went to the lobby phones. He called Cheryl. Her voice sounded strange – very soft and not at all like her normal voice. 'I've been reading your poem,' she said. 'Why didn't you answer my calls?'

He told her he'd gone to Sequoia. 'You should get away too.'

'Maybe later. Will you come over here tonight?' He said no

475

without having to think about it. She asked when then. He didn't answer. She said, still in that strangely soft voice, 'You're not going to see me anymore, are you?' He said, 'I don't think I can.' She didn't ask for explanations. The explanation was in their memory of Jim Carny's brains flying against the wall. She said, 'Well, he was wrong about us. He thought we were in love.' Charley said, 'We were discussing that when ... it happened.' She said, 'Yes. You were hedging even then.' She made a laughing sound. 'Oh well, he wanted to die anyway. I'm lucky he didn't take me with him. "Be thankful for small favors", my mother always said. "The Lord protects His own", my mother always said.' The line clicked.

He drove to an Italian restaurant on Magnolia. He had spaghetti and meatballs and a split of Chianti and another bottle of Chianti for dessert. He went to a movie and came back to the apartment and slept fitfully.

Before seven he was up, washed and dressed. He went down, and the streets were gray and almost deserted. He drove to Avalon. He still had his pass and he had no place else to go. The guard nodded, and he drove in and parked. He walked to the Washington set. He lost himself among the buildings among thoughts of *The Eternal Joneses* and how it might have been.

CHERYL CARNY

She was up at seven and ready to leave for work by seven-forty-five. A half-hour earlier than usual. Because there was no Jim to care for.

She had coffee and a big slice of apple pie. And then a cheese pastry. And she still had time. She put the dishes in the sink. She began to wash them, then went to the cabinet under the sink and opened it. Jim's supply of gin. She'd prepared well. Five quarts.

She took one out and poured a small drink. She sipped and shuddered. Awful! She gulped it all down, and it was better that way. She poured another, a bigger one, and gulped that too. Now she felt warm inside. She poured a third drink and carried it to the table and felt she had time to eat something substantial. Eggs and bacon and toast. Why not? So she would gain a pound. Who was there to care?

At ten o'clock the phone rang. She carried her drink with

476

her and answered it. Carl Baiglen wanted to know if she was all right.

'Not too well, Carl. Guess I was rushing it a bit, trying to work today.'

He sympathized. He said, as he had when they'd spoken Saturday after the funeral, 'Better take a week or two.' She said he was right, she could see that now.

She went back to the kitchen. A week or two or three or four. What difference did it make? Jim's mother had said, 'You killed him, you dirty whoring murderess.' It hadn't hurt her. She hadn't believed it. Not until Charley's call last night. *Then* it had hurt her and she had believed it because Charley believed it.

She kept drinking, but it wasn't a bad thing, not at all like Jim's drinking, since she was eating right along with the gin. If you ate it wasn't boozing. That's what people said. So she ate. She had a bottomless pit for a stomach. She ate and drank. And why not? She had plenty of money from those acting jobs of Devon's. Plenty. Almost six thousand in the bank. She could call the Quality Deli and they would deliver anything from Pablum to Scotch. She had her checkbook and her phone and here she would stay just as long as she felt like it. She could always get a job. If she felt like it. 'What's on television?' she asked, and went to find out.

It was getting dark when she stumbled into the bedroom. She saw the sheet of white paper, Charley's poem, lying on the pillow beside her own. Jim's pillow. She picked it up and went to the window and tried to read it. But light was dim and her eyes were blurry and she said, 'Oh hell!' and tore it into little pieces and flung them into the air and watched them settle to the floor.

CHARLEY HALPERT

He had lunch at the commissary and saw Alan Devon and began to nod. The man actually paled before turning away. Moe Sholub came over and shook hands and said he'd heard about the Paramount deal and that he was still interested in *Five Doors*. 'For next summer, if your price is sensible'. Charley asked about Lars. Sholub said he was away on vacation and would be doing a picture in a month or two. Charley left the commissary and walked toward the parking lot. He wondered if Markal had liked his ending on *Joneses*. He could call. There was a phone booth up ahead.

He went into the booth, but didn't call Markal. He called Peekskill. He took a deep breath as the ring sounded. Would Celia be home? Would she even talk to him after the long months of silence? Would her father talk to him? Would they at least tell him how Bobby was?

'Hello,' the thin voice said.

He didn't believe it. 'Bobby?'

'Yes. Who's calling?'

So here it was and there was no time to gather his thoughts and plan a constructive, helpful conversation. 'It's Daddy. How are you?'

'Fine. Grandpa's in the bathroom. Should I get him?'

He almost said yes. It would've been so much easier that way. After eight months of longing he was speaking to his son and he didn't know what to say. 'In a little while. How's Mommy?'

'She's mad at you. She cried when I asked her last week. She went to the bedroom but I heard her crying.'

'Asked her what?'

'If I was going to be like Steve Borden. He lives with his mother and grandma, and his father's in the city. They're divorced. His father comes to see him, and they go someplace. Will it be like that?'

'I . . . don't think so.'

'How could you visit me anyway? California's far away, isn't it?'

'Yes. Are you doing well in school?'

'Well.' It was a sigh. 'Mommy had to see Mrs. Frieden. I'm doing better now.'

'I know you are. You'll get a good report card at the end of the year. You remember what I told you about study habits? It's important to start right so when you're in high school—' He stopped. He said, 'I miss you very much, Bobby. You know that, don't you?'

'Yes. Mommy told me. She said you ask for me every week but you have to call when I'm at school. And she reads the parts of the letters where you write to me.'

He hadn't called or written in four months. 'I think of you all the time,' he said. 'I never stop thinking of you. Remember that.'

'Okay. I'm going to Cub Scout meeting. Mrs. Wagner's picking me up.'

'That's right. It's Monday. Got your uniform on?'

'Not yet. I'm going to now. When Grandpa comes out to help with the neckerchief.'

'Mommy's at work?'

'Sure. Till five-thirty. How can you take me out on Sunday like Steve's daddy if you live in California? Can I come to see you?'

'Would you like to?' And why had he asked that? What did he want from the kid, blood?

'I don't know. Could I? If Mommy would let me—'

'We'll work something out.' His voice was hoarse. What could he say to his son? 'You better get ready for Cubs now.'

'All right. When are you going to call me again when I'm home from school?'

'Soon.'

'My friend Chris says you're never coming home. He says his mother said you're going to stay there forever.'

'I *am* coming home.'

'When? Real soon? Tomorrow or Wednesday?' For the first time his voice lifted above a grave conversational tone. For the first time Charley heard the joy of weekends, of summer vacations, of holidays in his son's voice. 'Tell me and make a promise, Daddy!'

'Next week.'

'Make a promise!'

'I promise.'

'I'll tell Chris!'

'Tell your mother too.'

'I'll tell her! I won't forget!'

'Give me a kiss.'

The popping sound came, and he said good-bye and left the booth. He walked to the parking lot and drove to North Hollywood and the Bali-Ho. He began packing immediately. There was little joy in him. There was much fear. He feared Celia. He feared her reaction to him, and his reaction to her.

He loaded the Rambler, then went back to the lobby and called Ben Kalik. Kalik was surprised and dismayed. Charley promised he would return no later than 1st July. 'I've got a house to sell, Ben. A family to relocate.' Kalik said all right and that's what would go on the contract, 1st July. 'I'm glad about the family, Chuck. That business with the paraplegic—'

479

Charley drove to a drugstore and bought a picture postcard and wrote:

Dear Cheryl:
There's so much to say it's better we say nothing. Find happiness.

Charley

On the freeway, he began to feel a lessening of fear, a growth of joy. He was going home.

He didn't kid himself. He couldn't say he loved Celia, or that he had in years. Not Celia alone. But Celia and Bobby *together*, that was something else again. Celia and Bobby together made up so deep a part of his life that not to love them would be suicidal!

There was more he was beginning to feel, more he was beginning to understand. He *was* a success – because people were willing to pay him. That was all it took. But the half of his life represented by Celia and Bobby didn't know this. Until they did, he wouldn't fully know it himself.

What if Celia refused—

But he wouldn't be weak. He would persist. He was afraid of coming back here alone. He was afraid of another Bali-Ho and another Cheryl and other Loises and Sugars.

He drove seven hundred miles before falling into exhausted slumber at the side of the road.

SUMMER came early and hot to Los Angeles. The sun burned its way across a sky clear except for the rich mixture of fog and exhaust fumes. Rain was something only tourists remembered. Brushfires began, threatening the quarter-of-a-million-dollar-and-up homes in Coldwater and other luxury canyons. In the Valley, only children braved the sweltering heat; their elders sat either in air-conditioned homes or in air-conditioned offices.

Watts had few air-conditioned homes and fewer offices. Rumblings of unrest came and went, with a big blowup always imminent. The police remembered 1965 and checked their tactical units and special weapons. The Blacks also remembered and checked *their* tactical units and weapons. The informed word was, 'Not a cool scene, baby.'

Hollywood was sweating too, despite air-conditioning every square foot of the way. This was the time of furious activity in the television industry – the time to count shows 'in the can' for autumn premieres. New movies were also in the works, more and more of them moving to foreign locales where labor costs were low and tax dodges possible. TV producers eyed the practice longingly, and a few took tentative steps in the direction of non-union Spain and Portugal. 'Runaway productions!' the guilds screamed, but the writers kept grinding out their stuff and the actors kept working and almost everyone had a piece of the action.

Alan Devon was a very busy man. He had lost a show, his long-run *Winninger's Winners,* and was replacing it with an apartment-house series, *Hi-Rise City.* He had two big-budget features scheduled. He didn't have time to think of anything except his work.

But he thought of Cheryl Carny. He spoke to Carl Baiglen about her. 'Never came back,' the Bagel said, 'and I wasn't able to contact her. That business of her husband's suicide—'

Devon tried calling her a dozen times. The phone at the other end rang on and on.

The second week in July he drove to the two-story apartment building near Avalon. He knocked at the door to the ground-floor apartment and heard music and voices, but she didn't answer. He went to the super. The man shrugged. 'No one sees her anymore, but the people upstairs sure hear her. She plays the television real loud. And she's always getting deliveries of food and booze.' He was sorry but he couldn't open her door with the master key even if Devon was a relative. It was illegal. Devon offered him ten dollars. The super said it might be a good idea to check if Mrs. Carny was all right.

Devon walked in and closed the door in the man's face. And groaned. Cheryl was sitting in an armchair watching television, the remains of half a dozen meals on a card table before her. She was eating a thick hero sandwich and paused to wash down a mouthful with clear liquid from a water glass. He doubted it was water. There was a bottle of gin on the table and empty bottles all over the place.

There were empty *everythings* all over the place. It looked like a garbage dump and smelled like one too. Bags and cartons and cans and plates and pots and containers and scraps of food and bones and paper and ashes and cigarette butts and wadded tissues and more he couldn't identify – every kind of dirt, everywhere.

But Cheryl Carny was what made him groan, made him want to run from her.

She finally turned her head. She peered at him and cleared her throat and mumbled, 'Long time no see,' and turned back to the television.

She was bloated almost beyond recognition, sodden with food and drink, her face a greasy white basketball framed by wild hair. She wore a terrycloth robe that had once been white and was now a grimy, splotchy mess, bulging at the waist as if she were in the last days of pregnancy.

He said, 'Cheryl,' his voice sick.

He wanted to believe it was none of his business. He wanted to ask if she needed anything and then leave. This was not the girl he had cared for. This was not a girl at all anymore. This was a hog wallowing in filth!

He walked up to her. 'Cheryl, you're coming home with me.' He tried to hold his breath while she tilted her head back to look at him. She stank of gin and sweat and urine. She stank of not washing in weeks. 'What?' she mumbled. Her eyes were filmy, glassy, red. 'Go with you?'

He said yes, but first she had to wash. He helped her up. The stench of her was unbearable.

But he bore it. He led her to the bathroom and took off the robe and washed her. He fought nausea and finished the job and took her to the bedroom. He found a man's topcoat and slippers and that was how he dressed her. He walked her to the door, and she stopped and said, 'No, not out there.'

He said she was going to live with him. He was going to take care of her.

Her huge face swung toward him. Her glassy eyes tried to focus on him. 'Why?'

He said because she needed help, but that wasn't why. 'Guilt makes the world go 'round,' a psychiatrist friend of his had once said. Devon hadn't believed it, then.

In the car she sagged against his shoulder. 'I took care of Jim,' she mumbled. 'You take care of me. History repeats itself.' And she giggled.

He had a moment of pure terror. But he pushed it away. She was going to stop the compulsive eating and drinking. She was going to shape up. Then he would have his reward.

* * *

The Eternal Joneses was published in mid-July. *The New York Times* called it 'a classic case of Hollywood's failure to recognize and implement excellence'. *Time* magazine devoted a column in its book-review section to discussing its worth as history and found it 'lacking in objectivity but with an admirable appreciation of the position of the Negro, which alone would justify its production'. *The Hollywood Reporter* discussed Markal's reasons for the publication and said, '*Joneses* holds the attention every inch of its hundred miles. Cut to normal length, it would make a great pic.' *Variety* felt it was 'impossible to produce with today's high costs, but a beaut of a script none the less'. It got brief mention on Huntley-Brinkley when David closed out the show with, 'It appears all the good movies are being published, and all the bad ones filmed.' Columnists who had disliked Emperor Nat for real or imagined slights dismissed the publication with 'sour grapes', but others said it proved he was a producer of vision and 'we are all the poorer for his leaving the major studio scene'. Markal's publishers felt the reviews were good enough to justify putting *Joneses* on sale in bookstores. It died rather more quickly than any of Charley's novels had.

At lunch with his cousin, Ben Kalik bewailed Halpert's stupidity. 'If he'd only told me Markal was *serious* about publishing that piece of shit, I'd have held off on the Paramount contract. He cost me ten grand! I mean it, Marv. I could've gotten twice as much! You don't know how lucky you are to handle actors. Writers are the biggest schmucks on earth!' Marv said he'd heard this Halpert was pretty good. Kalik snorted. 'What has good or bad got to do with it? If it wasn't for me, Halpert would still be hacking out cheapie-creepies and living away from his family. I put the poor bastard on his feet—'

Lena and Buddy Warnt now worked for Nat Markal. Lena visited Mona Dearn's grave regularly. Sometimes she picked a few flowers from Mr. Markal's garden and took them along. She knew Buddy didn't like it. She knew he had no feeling for Miss Dearn. He said he worked for 'these people' and gave them his best and earned his way and more, but he'd be damned if he had to *like* them. He saved his liking for his wife and for his brother and his family in Macon. He never used the word, but Lena knew he felt she was Tommish.

He was wrong. She bowed her head to no one. She just felt sorry for Miss Dearn. And there was no one else who came to visit the simple gravestone in Forest Lawn-Glendale. Sure, there'd been plenty the first week or two after the funeral – ghouls who stood around talking and smiling and even taking pictures in front of the grave, which was against the rules. But now, no one. No family and no friends.

Forest Lawn was a beautiful place. Lena always visited one of the 'points of outstanding interest'. Her favorite was the Wee Kirk o' the Heather – the prettiest church she'd ever seen. They held weddings there as well as funerals, and she'd stood in back and watched one and wished Miss Dearn had come here sometimes and prayed because then things might have been different.

Today was very hot. She went to the Court of David with its big statue and the voice telling about his life and Goliath and the Twenty-third Psalm. She rested on one of the stone benches, then went to Mona's grave. Before she came down the hill she saw them – the tall Englishman and the other two. She knew the Englishman. He had a long, crazy name, and they called him Sommy. He was an actor Mona had gone out with once and said bad things about. And she knew one of the other two, a publicity man Miss Hanford had dated – Stad Homer. The third man had a leather bag slung over his shoulder.

484

She came up slowly and stood a good distance away. Stad Homer looked at her and said something to the other two and then said hello. She nodded. He came over and said Mr. Sommerset Walpole Virgil had been visiting Mona's grave almost every day, brokenhearted, and this time they'd followed him and that's why they were here. He looked at Sommy and sighed. 'None of us knew how close they really were. I thought they didn't hit it off. I'll bet you did too.' She said nothing. 'But all the time . . . well, I think they'd have gotten married if—' He sighed again and said nice to see you and went back to the others.

He was a liar. Lena had never seen Sommy here. And Miss Dearn never dated him after that first time. She hated his guts. If she'd have married any man, it was the little one. So his was wrong and dirty. Publicity. Like that black kitchen and all those phony dates.

She watched. Sommy looked at her and said something to the others. Stad Homer waved his arms. Sommy knelt in front of the grave and bowed his head. The man with the leather bag had a camera in his hand. He began moving around, taking pictures.

Against the rules. And a sin. Because they were using Miss Dearn.

She went back up the hill. She heard Stad Homer call her name but she kept going. She went to her car and drove home.

A week later she saw it in the papers. Pictures of the English actor and a story about how he'd been the secret romance in Miss Dearn's life. 'His love has never died,' it said. 'His life and work are dedicated to her memory.' And another picture of him shaking his fist at the camera and the words saying he had been caught by surprise and didn't want his secret known.

Lena thought of going to Mr. Markal. But she didn't. He didn't care about anything but girls. Girls coming here all the time. Lena wasn't a prude, not by a long shot, but there had to be a limit, or it got sick.

She stopped visiting Forest Lawn. She prayed for Miss Dearn and kept her picture in a drawer where Buddy wouldn't see it, but she didn't go to the grave.

What was the use? Everything was mixed up here. Not like back home where crying meant pain and laughing meant joy. Where girls and boys meant love, or at least fun. Here it was all mixed up. Movies and real life, all mixed up.

485

Edward Reiser was thirty-six years old. He had published a novel and a collection of short stories, both well-received by the critics. *The Saturday Review* had compared him to Bernard Malamud, but he hadn't sold like Malamud. He'd taught high school English in Detroit and hidden his despair and begun a second novel. But Margaret had become pregnant again and the pressures had mounted and he'd found he had nothing to say beyond, 'Help!'

Someone must have heard that cry. Carl Baiglen had written and offered him five thousand dollars plus agent's fees. To do a movie. Not the kind of movie Bernard Malamud would consider, but Ed didn't kid himself about that comparison anymore. He'd taken a year's sabbatical. He was here and he was going to do everything short of murder to *stay* here!

Baiglen talked about his previous movies as they walked between two warehouses toward the back of the lot and the set Ed had heard so much about. He fought off the excitement gripping him from their tour of the great movie studio. He had to concentrate every ounce of attention on what this man was saying. He had to do exactly what this man wanted him to do if he was to be saved from endless days in a classroom.

'As a writer, Ed, I'm only a craftsman. You can tell that from my story, *Terror Town*.'

Ed made vaguely negative sounds, but having read that cliché-ridden nonsense he felt 'craftsman' was puffery of the most blatant sort.

'Now I need more than craftsmanship. Now I need true creative talent.'

They came toward the end of the studio proper, toward an end of streets, stages, office and technical buildings.

'Your novel, those short stories – brilliant! And not just in characterization, but in pure plot. You're a terrific storyteller, Ed. You're quality, and quality is what I want.'

Ed muttered that Baiglen was being too kind. The producer waved his hand impatiently. 'My story is the bare bones. It's what you do with those bones that counts.' His voice grew intense. 'It's how you spark, what chemistry takes place, that'll determine whether my ten pages become an acceptable movie, a good movie or a major motion picture.'

Ed nodded, beginning to sweat a bit as he thought of those ten pages. 'I'm eager to begin, Carl.'

They came out from between the buildings into a city. That was the only way Ed could describe it. Dated, but a city. And a waterfront. And two ships. And bridges. And more.

Washington. Some twenty key buildings of the old capital. And the President's House directly in front of them down a rutted Pennsylvania Avenue that Jefferson would have found familiar to his feet. 'It must have cost *millions!*' he said.

'A *half* million was Markal's quote,' Baiglen said. 'A million-four or -five was the actual cost.' He paused as they approached the President's House. 'And that's a problem for us, Ed. Management has just decided to make use of this monster. I don't know how you're going to do it, but this set has to be part of our feature.'

Ed looked at him. 'Washington before 1812?'

'Before 1814,' Baiglen corrected crisply. 'The British burned it in July, 1814, trying to influence the peace negotiations.' He smiled. 'Every producer at Avalon is now a *mayvin* on the War of 1812. You'd be surprised at the movies this thing will show up in. When Olive Dort decides to erase a debit—'

'But we need a ghost town,' Ed interrupted.

'Before the ghost town. Where the two boys rob the bank. Where they kidnap the girl.'

Ed looked around, trying to see it. He didn't, but knew he *had* to. 'Well, we'll have to avoid certain easily identifiable buildings.' He pointed. 'I guess to the right there, that narrow street and the brown building, that could be the bank.'

'Sure. And there . . . we can put up a few signs, and it can be a sleepy little Midwest town. The right camera angles – you leave that to me. But maybe you'd better get in a line about Dalesville being patterned after the old capitol. Say the founder was a nut about frontier America—'

There was a creaking sound, and something fell as they turned. A curved section of White House pillar had come loose, exposing raw woodwork within. Baiglen chuckled. 'Maybe part of that million and a half went into Markal's pocket.'

They walked around, talking. Ed looked more closely and saw that paint was peeling, boards pulling away from studs, a considerable amount of deterioration taking place. The image of a city dissolved. 'How old *is* this set?'

'Some of it about a year, like the President's House. Some of it only five or six months. But management was sensitive about the *Joneses* project for a while, so no one came near it. Now they're being realistic.'

As they left Washington, Ed looked back. 'Don't worry

487

about it,' Baiglen said. 'A few nails, a little paint, and we'll have Dalesville.'

They shook hands outside Baiglen's office. Ed started down the hall to the sign reading, 'Charles Halpert.' His own name would go up soon, Baiglen had assured him. His name would *stay* up, if he satisfied Avalon with what Baiglen called 'this pilot project'. His name could command as much respect and money as Halpert's someday.

Baiglen called, 'Good luck.'

Ed turned. He smiled and nodded. 'Thank you. I—' There was too much in his heart – too much hope and too much fear. He nodded again and went into his office.

Sugar Smart was interviewed in the second-floor waiting room of the Los Angeles Airport by local newspapers and television. She was leaving for Cinecittà to star in *Romulus and the Wanton Witch,* and the newsmen had hoped Nat Markal would be with her. He wasn't, but Sugar was doing a fine job of holding center stage all by herself. She wore a broad-striped mod outfit featuring an extreme miniskirt, and was sipping chocolate milk as befitted a growing girl. (Her growth in one area had led to her being named Miss California Dairy Products the previous month.) She was asked how she felt about being considered 'another Mona Dearn'.

Sugar crossed her legs, put back her golden head and laughed throatily. The cameras zoomed for close-ups of thigh, chest and piquant face. 'I'd be very happy if it was true, but I'm content—' A jet drowned her out, and she looked back at her agent, also come to see her off, and began to say something about a 'kicky scene'. Bob Chankery shook his head. He had carefully coached Sugar on this interview. She was being upgraded, and 'kicky' was no longer in her bag.

The jet passed. Sugar continued. 'I'm content to take it one picture at a time. I'm signed for a musical after *Romulus*. After *that,* well, it's not quite finalized, *but*—' A little coaxing and she revealed she had 'been approached' to sign a contract with Avalon. She was asked about her 'romance' with Boyle Hagart. 'Oh, Boyle's a dear friend, but we're both career-minded.' She was asked about her 'personal relationship' with Nat Markal. She grew very serious. 'Mr. Markal is my *dear* friend, the man who gave me my start. I feel toward him as I would toward' – she searched for words – 'toward the President of the United States.'

Chankery winced and wished there were some way to make Sugar mute those times she wasn't parroting his words. He was wrong to feel that way. Her remark did cause considerable laughter, speculation on the extent of Sugar's patriotism and discussion of how *Mrs.* President of the United States might react. But it also made news media coast to coast where the interview itself wouldn't have.

Throughout the entire affair, as Sugar glowed and posed for the cameras, a dark girl stood at the side, holding Sugar's toy poodle, a gift from Tyrone Chalze. When asked who she was Sugar waved her hand and changed the subject. Someone (Chankery perhaps) later suggested she was Sugar's personal maid, and when Sugar seem to nod it was so recorded:

'Walking toward the jet that will carry her to Rome, her personal maid following with Miss Poo, Sugar Smart today served notice that she is the leading contender for the crown left vacant by the death of Mona Dearn . . .'

Buddy drove him to the airport, and they killed time in the parking lot, leaving for the jet with only a few minutes to spare. In that way Nat Markal managed to avoid the newsmen, though he was spotted as he walked down the ramp. One reporter tried to follow and was stopped at the ticket stand.

Not that Nat had anything to hide. Not anymore. That 're-spect, admiration, reputation' Adele had told him he'd lost, the pride she insisted was more important to him than money, had nothing more than a vestigial hold. It was his *privacy* he valued.

He took the outside seat and nodded at the stewardess's ministrations and her murmured assurance that he would be able to retain the empty window seat. She lingered a bit, asking if he wanted this and that, and he noticed that she was good-looking in a big, bucolic way. He finally said, 'You're taking such good care of me. I'll have to return the favor someday.' Her I-know-you're-joking-Mr.-Markal-but-I-wish-you-weren't made him jot down her name and L.A. number.

Poor Adele. She couldn't know how wrong she'd been.

'You've thrown away everything you worked for,' she'd said. 'Everything you dreamed of.'

After Isa's explosion, he had believed it. He had run to the Riviera so as not to think of it. But a week later he'd returned and taken up his life and known himself.

489

What *had* he worked for? What *was* his dream?

Not the surface dream. There Adele was right – power and prestige. But the deep-down dream. The denied dream. The buried and forgotten dream that had burst free with Isa.

To be loved by women.

That old adolescent fantasy of his. That shameful fantasy he had driven from his mind, erased with bankbooks and stocks and real estate. To be a janitor in a whorehouse, paid not in money but in trade. To have his arms full of flesh night and day, his senses sated always.

The other dreams weren't true dreams but *plans* – and he had accomplished them. So Adele would take half his fortune. So he would have to make do with twenty-five instead of fifty million. He cared nothing for Avalon now. With *Joneses* shelved it was a film factory, and he'd have been a wage slave. He wouldn't have stayed anyway.

The news reports of Isa explained her venom. Not that he believed she had broken the story herself. But however it had happened, it explained that otherwise inexplicable scene. *White bastard. Old fay.* The sickness of race. Yes, he understood it now ... but it was still too fresh in his memory, still hurt like hell.

He turned from the hurt, looked back and caught Sugar's eye and nodded. She rose from beside her sister and walked to him. He pointed at the window seat. She slid by him, making a production of it, and sat down with signs and smiles. He asked a few questions and got her talking and kept her going with nods and yesses.

She was a whore – part of his true dream. All Hollywood was a whorehouse – and Rome and Paris and anywhere they made movies. And he was a privileged partner in that world-wide whorehouse. He could pick and choose almost at will.

Sugar was saying something about the stewardess. '—making a fool of herself, and I could tell you were laughing.'

She irritated him, but he had always been a gentleman. Or was that part of the plan for respect, admiration, reputation? The discarded plan?

'Be quiet!' he said. Her voice died. 'She can give me as much as you can. She can perform in bed, and that's all I ask, all I want.'

She stared at him, frightened. 'You shouldn't oughta—'

'I told you to be quiet. If you have any regrets, take a return flight from Rome. A close reading of your contract will show

490

I can drop you at any time for any reason.'

'But – but why are you angry at me, Nat? You know I'd do anything for you.'

He took out a cigar and bit off the end. 'All right. Be quiet for me.'

'—*someday you'll grow old and sick and crawl into a corner and die like an animal.*'

In that one thing Adele was right. But didn't everyone die like an animal? Didn't everyone die alone? You couldn't take wife and child on *that* cold journey.

Jet engines accelerated, shaking the plane. He tightened his seat belt. They moved onto the runway, paused, surged forward, were airborne.

You were so wrong about me, Adele. So wrong.

Yet he missed her. He missed Lainie. The three of them had belonged to each other for a lifetime. That was as much a reality as the whorehouse.

The stewardess came by and saw Sugar and didn't stop. He stopped her. He said, 'I'd like that martini now,' and gave her his warmest smile. She hurried up front. Soon Cinecittà and that noisy, overrated city and those pasta-fed whores. He drank his martini and asked for another. He sipped the fresh drink, tasting the bitter-sweet freedom of his new life. Sugar Smart touched his arm, cleared her throat, murmured timidly, 'Nat?' He turned, patting her hand. 'Yes,' he said. 'Yes, darling.'

The world's greatest novelists now available in Panther Books

Eric van Lustbader

The Ninja	£2.50	☐
Sirens	£2.50	☐
Beneath An Opal Moon	£1.95	☐
Black Heart	£2.95	☐

Nelson de Mille

By the Rivers of Babylon	£1.95	☐
Cathedral	£1.95	☐

Justin Scott

The Shipkiller	£1.95	☐
The Man Who Loved the Normandie	£2.50	☐
A Pride of Kings	£2.50	☐

Leslie Waller

Trocadero	£2.50	☐
The Swiss Account	£1.95	☐
A Change in the Wind	40p	☐
The American	75p	☐
The Family	£1.95	☐
The Banker	£2.50	☐
The Brave and the Free	£1.95	☐
Blood and Dreams	£1.50	☐
Gameplan	£1.95	☐

Peter Lear

Spider Girl	£1.50	☐
Golden Girl	£1.50	☐

Calder Willingham

The Big Nickel	£1.25	☐
Providence Island	£1.50	☐

David Charney

Sensei	£1.95	☐

To order direct from the publisher just tick the titles you want and fill in the order form.

The world's greatest thriller writers now available in Panther Books

Robert Ludlum

The Chancellor Manuscript	£2.50	☐
The Gemini Contenders	£1.95	☐
The Rhinemann Exchange	£2.50	☐
The Matlock Paper	£1.95	☐
The Osterman Weekend	£1.95	☐
The Scarlatti Inheritance	£1.95	☐
The Holcroft Covenant	£2.50	☐
The Matarese Circle	£2.50	☐
The Bourne Identity	£2.50	☐
The Road to Gandolfo	£1.95	☐
The Parsifal Mosaic	£2.50	☐

Lawrence Sanders

The Third Deadly Sin	£1.95	☐
The Tenth Commandment	£1.95	☐
The Second Deadly Sin	£1.25	☐
The Sixth Commandment	£1.95	☐
The Anderson Tapes	£1.50	☐
The Tomorrow File	£2.50	☐
The Pleasures of Helen	£1.95	☐

To order direct from the publisher just tick the titles you want and fill in the order form.

Bestsellers available in Panther Books

Emmanuelle Arsan

Emmanuelle	£1.95	☐
Emmanuelle 2	£1.95	☐
Laure	£1.95	☐
Nea	£1.95	☐
Vanna	£1.95	☐
The Secrets of Emmanuelle (non-fiction)	95p	☐

Jonathan Black

Ride the Golden Tiger	£1.95	☐
Oil	£1.95	☐
The World Rapers	£1.95	☐
The House on the Hill	£1.95	☐
Megacorp	£2.50	☐
The Plunderers	£2.50	☐

Herbert Kastle

Cross-Country	£2.50	☐
Little Love	£1.95	☐
Millionaires	£1.95	☐
Miami Golden Boy	£1.95	☐
The Movie Maker	£2.50	☐
The Gang	£1.95	☐
Hit Squad	£1.95	☐
Dirty Movies	£1.95	☐
Hot Prowl	£1.50	☐
Sunset People	£1.95	☐
David's War	£1.95	☐

To order direct from the publisher just tick the titles you want
and fill in the order form.

All these books are available at your local bookshop or newsagent, or can be ordered direct from the publisher.,

_____

To order direct from the publisher just tick the titles you want and fill in the form below.

Name_____

Address _____

_____

Send to:
Panther Cash Sales
PO Box 11, Falmouth, Cornwall TR10 9EN.

Please enclose remittance to the value of the cover price plus:

UK 45p for the first book, 20p for the second book plus 14p per copy for each additional book ordered to a maximum charge of £1.63.

BFPO and Eire 45p for the first book, 20p for the second book plus 14p per copy for the next 7 books, thereafter 8p per book.

Overseas 75p for the first book and 21p for each additional book.

_____

Panther Books reserve the right to show new retail prices on covers, which may differ from those previously advertised in the text or elsewhere.